Sophie's Choice

"SPLENDIDLY WRITTEN, THRILLING . . . A PASSIONATE NOVEL."

—*The New York Times Book Review*

"A PASSIONATE NOVEL . . . *Sophie's Choice* is a courageous book that treats two doomed lovers . . . It is a thriller of the highest order, all the more thrilling for the fact that the dark, gloomy secrets we are unearthing one by one . . . may be authentic secrets of history and our own human nature."

—John Gardner, front page,
The New York Times Book Review

"A STUNNING WORK . . . A TRIUMPH . . . A compelling drama of our age's central horrors . . . A dazzling, gripping book of the highest intelligence, heart and style. It is literature of the highest order."

—Stephen Becker, *Chicago Sun Times*

"STYRON'S MOST IMPRESSIVE PERFORMANCE . . . It belongs on that small shelf reserved for American masterpieces. *Sophie's Choice* is in the main stream of the American novel. Like *A Portrait of a Lady* or *The Great Gatsby*, it is . . . wonderfully human . . . It offers splendid comedy, too."

—Paul Fussell, *Washington Post Book World*

SOPHIE'S CHOICE

"A MONUMENTAL WORK OF FICTION . . . *Sophie's Choice* is a novel of and for our time . . . It is a novel of great architectural authority and scope . . . It's a work stamped with intelligence, humanity, and, above all, courage."

—Alexandra Johnson, *Christian Science Monitor*

"AN EXTRAORDINARY ACHIEVEMENT . . . Anyone who reads *Sophie's Choice* must be affected deeply and I will venture to say that those whose powers of empathy are strong will find it truly wounding."

—Ralph B. Sipper, *San Francisco Chronicle*

"EERILY MASTERFUL . . . If you read one new novel this summer, it had better be this one. It is a beautiful and audacious work by one of our best living writers."

—Gail Godwin, *Chicago Tribune Book World*

PRE-EMINENTLY GRAND . . . It has a look of permanence about it . . . Sophie is as complex and as plausible a heroine as any in recent fiction."

—Peter S. Prescott, *Newsweek*

SOPHIE'S CHOICE

"BEAUTIFUL AND HORRIFYING . . . A love affair as star-crossed as any in contemporary literature. *Sophie's Choice* is positively staggering."

—Jonathan Yardley, *Washington Star*

"MAGNIFICENT . . . Perhaps the highest compliment one can pay a book that cannot be praised too much is that it fulfills the aspirations of a novelist who has set out to be great."

—Howard Kissel, *Women's Wear Daily*

"SUPERB . . . By far the best book Styron has written in his distinguished literary career. It also may be the best novel so far this year."

—Judson Hand, *New York Daily News*

"BRILLIANTLY SUCCESSFUL . . . Every character and situation he touches springs instantly and memorably to life . . . A triumph on every level."

—Richard Freedman, *Newsday*

William Styron

Sophie's Choice

BANTAM BOOKS
TORONTO • NEW YORK • LONDON • SYDNEY • AUCKLAND

This low-priced Bantam Book has been completely reset in a type face designed for easy reading, and was printed from new plates. It contains the complete text of the original hard-cover edition.
NOT ONE WORD HAS BEEN OMITTED.

SOPHIE'S CHOICE
A Bantam Book / published by arrangement with Random House, Inc.

PRINTING HISTORY
Random House edition published April 1979
1st printing . . . . June 1979
7 printings through October 1979
Book-of-the-Month Club edition July 1979
6 printings through December 1979
Serialized in ESQUIRE MAGAZINE
Bantam edition / July 1980
18 printings through October 1983

Grateful acknowledgment is made to the following for permission to reprint previously published material:

Editions Gallimard, Paris Excerpt from Lazare *by André Malraux.*

W. W. Norton & Company, Inc.: The lines from "The Fourth Duino Elegy" are reprinted from Duino Elegies *by Rainer Maria Rilke, translated by J. B. Leishman and Stephen Spender, with the permission of W. W. Norton & Company, Inc. Copyright 1939 by W. W. Norton & Company, Inc. Copyright Renewed © 1967 by Stephen Spender and J. B. Leishman. Originally published by Insel Verlag, Frankfurt am Main.*

George Weidenfeld and Nicholson Ltd., London: Excerpts from Commandant of Auschwitz *by Rudolf Hoess, translated by Constantine FitzGibbon. English translation copyright © 1959 by George Weidenfeld and Nicholson Ltd. Copyright 1951 by Wydawnictwo Prawnicze, Warsaw. Published in the United States by The World Publishing Company.*

Portions of this book previously appeared in Esquire.

For information address: Random House, Inc., 201 East 50th Street, New York, New York 10022.

ISBN 0-553-24159-1

Published simultaneously in the United States and Canada

Bantam Books are published by Bantam Books, Inc. Its trademark, consisting of the words "Bantam Books" and the portrayal of a rooster, is Registered in U.S. Patent and Trademark Office and in other countries. Marca Registrada. Bantam Books, Inc., 666 Fifth Avenue, New York, New York 10103.

PRINTED IN THE UNITED STATES OF AMERICA

H 27 26 25 24 23 22 21

To the Memory
of
My Father
(1889–1978)

Wer zeigt ein Kind, so wie es steht? Wer stellt es ins Gestirn und gibt das Maß des Abstands ihm in die Hand? Wer macht den Kindertod aus grauem Brot, das hart wird,—oder läßt ihn drin im runden Mund so wie den Gröps von einem schönen Apfel? . . . Mörder sind leicht einzusehen. Aber dies: den Tod, den ganzen Tod, noch vor dem Leben so sanft zu enthalten und nicht bös zu sein, ist unbeschreiblich.

Von der vierten Duineser Elegie
—Rainer Maria Rilke

. . . je cherche la région cruciale de l'âme,
où le Mal absolu s'oppose à la fraternité.

—André Malraux, *Lazare,* 1974

Who'll show a child just as it is? Who'll place it within its constellation, with the measure of distance in its hand? Who'll make its death from grey bread, that grows hard,—or leave it there, within the round mouth, like the choking core of a sweet apple? . . . Minds of murderers are easily divined. But this, though: death, the whole of death,—even before life's begun, to hold it all so gently, and be good: this is beyond description!

From the fourth *Duino Elegy*
—translated by J. B. Leishman
and Stephen Spender

. . . I seek that essential region of the soul where absolute evil confronts brotherhood.

Sophie's Choice

One

In those days cheap apartments were almost impossible to find in Manhattan, so I had to move to Brooklyn. This was in 1947, and one of the pleasant features of that summer which I so vividly remember was the weather, which was sunny and mild, flower-fragrant, almost as if the days had been arrested in a seemingly perpetual springtime. I was grateful for that if for nothing else, since my youth, I felt, was at its lowest ebb. At twenty-two, struggling to become some kind of writer, I found that the creative heat which at eighteen had nearly consumed me with its gorgeous, relentless flame had flickered out to a dim pilot light registering little more than a token glow in my breast, or wherever my hungriest aspirations once resided. It was not that I no longer wanted to write, I still yearned passionately to produce the novel which had been for so long captive in my brain. It was only that, having written down the first few fine paragraphs, I could not produce any others, or—to approximate Gertrude Stein's remark about a lesser writer of the Lost Generation—I had the syrup but it wouldn't pour. To make matters worse, I was out of a job and had very little money and was self-exiled to Flatbush—like others of my countrymen, another lean and lonesome young Southerner wandering amid the Kingdom of the Jews.

Call me Stingo, which was the nickname I was known by in those days, if I was called anything at all. The name derives from my prep-school days down in my native state of Virginia. This school was a pleasant institution to which I was sent at fourteen by my distraught father, who found me difficult to handle after my mother died. Among my other disheveled qualities was apparently an inattention to personal hygiene, hence I soon became known as Stinky. But the years passed. The abrasive labor of time, together with a radical change of habits (I was in fact shamed into becoming almost obsessively clean), gradually wore down the harsh syllabic brusqueness of the name, slurring off into the more attractive, or less unattractive, certainly sportier Stingo. Sometime during my thirties the nickname and I mysteriously parted company, Stingo merely evaporating like a wan ghost out of my existence, leaving me indifferent to the loss. But Stingo I still was during this time about which I write. If, however, it is perplexing that the name is absent from the earlier part of this narrative, it may be understood that I am describing a morbid and solitary period in my life when, like the crazy hermit in the cave on the hill, I was rarely called by any name at all.

I was glad to be shut of my job—the first and only salaried position, excluding the military, of my life—even though its loss seriously undermined my already modest solvency. Also, I now think it was constructive to learn so early in life that I would never fit in as an office worker, anytime, anywhere. In fact, considering how I had so coveted the job in the first place, I was rather surprised at the relief, indeed the alacrity, with which I accepted my dismissal only five months later. In 1947 jobs were scarce, especially jobs in publishing, but a stroke of luck had landed me employment with one of the largest publishers of books, where I was made "junior editor"—a euphemism for manuscript reader. That the employer called the tune, in those days when the dollar was much more valuable tender than it is now, may be seen in the stark terms of my salary—forty dollars a week. After withholding taxes this meant that the anemic blue check placed on my desk each Friday by the hunchbacked little woman who managed the payroll represented emolument in the nature of a little over ninety cents an hour. But I had not been in the least dismayed by the fact that these coolie wages were dispensed by one of the most powerful and wealthy publishers in the world; young and resilient, I approached my job—at least at the very beginning—with a sense of lofty purpose; and besides, in compensation, the work bore intimations of glamour: lunch at "21," dinner with John O'Hara, poised and brilliant but carnal-minded lady writers melting at my editorial acumen, and so on.

It soon appeared that none of this was to come about. For one thing, although the publishing house—which had prospered largely through text-books and industrial manuals and dozens of technical journals in fields as varied and as arcane as pig husbandry and mortuary science and extruded plastics—did publish novels and nonfiction as a sideline, thereby requiring the labor of junior aestheticians like myself, its list of authors would scarcely capture the attention of anyone seriously concerned with literature. At the time I arrived, for example, the two most prominent writers being promoted were a retired World War II fleet admiral and an exceptionally flyblown ex-Communist stool pigeon whose ghostwritten *mea culpa* was doing middling well on the best-seller lists. Of an author of the stature of John O'Hara (although I had far more illustrious literary idols, O'Hara represented for me the kind of writer a young editor might go out and get drunk with) there was no trace. Furthermore, there was the depressing matter of the work to which I had been assigned. At that time McGraw-Hill & Company (for such was my employer's name) lacked any literary éclat, having for so long and successfully purveyed its hulking works of technology that the small trade-book house in which I labored, and which aspired to the excellence of Scribner or Knopf, was considered something of a joke in the business. It was a little as if a vast huckstering organization like Montgomery Ward or Masters had had the effrontery to set up an intimate salon dealing in mink and chinchilla that everyone in the trade knew were dyed beaver from Japan.

So in my capacity as the lowest drudge in the office hierarchy I not only was denied the opportunity to read manuscripts even of passing merit, but was forced to plow my way daily through fiction and nonfiction of the humblest possible quality—coffee-stained and thumb-smeared stacks of Hammermill Bond whose used, ravaged appearance proclaimed at once their author's (or agent's) terrible desperation and McGraw-Hill's function as publisher of last resort. But at my age, with a snootful of English Lit. that made me as savagely demanding as Matthew Arnold in my insistence that the written word exemplify only the highest seriousness and truth, I treated these forlorn offspring of a thousand strangers' lonely and fragile desire with the magisterial, abstract loathing of an ape plucking vermin from his pelt. I was adamant, cutting, remorseless, insufferable. High in my glassed-in cubbyhole on the twentieth floor of the McGraw-Hill Building—an architecturally impressive but spiritually enervating green tower on West Forty-second Street—I leveled the scorn that could only be mustered by one who had just finished reading *Seven Types of Ambiguity* upon these sad outpourings piled high on my desk, all of them so freighted with hope and clubfooted syntax. I was required to write a reasonably full description of each submission, no matter how bad the book. At first it was a lark and I honestly enjoyed the bitchery and vengeance I was able to wreak upon these manuscripts. But after a time their unrelenting mediocrity palled, and I became weary of the sameness of the job, weary too of chain-smoking and the smog-shrouded view of Manhattan, and of pecking out such callous reader's reports as the following, which I have salvaged intact from that dry and dispiriting time. I quote them verbatim, without gloss.

> Tall Grows the Eelgrass, by Edmonia Kraus Biersticker. Fiction.
>
> Love and death amid the sand dunes and cranberry bogs of southern New Jersey. The young hero, Willard Strathaway, heir to a large cranberry-packing fortune and a recent graduate of Princeton University, falls wildly in love with Ramona Blaine, daughter of Ezra Blaine, an old-time leftist and leader of a strike among the cranberry harvesters. The plot is cute and complex, having largely to do with an alleged conspiracy on the part of Brandon Strathaway—Willard's tycoon father—to dispose of old Ezra, whose hideously mutilated corpse is indeed found one morning in the entrails of a mechanical cranberry picker. This leads to nearly terminal recriminations between Willard—described as having "a marvelous Princetonian tilt to his head, besides a considerable

feline grace"—and the bereaved Ramona, "her slender lissomeness barely concealing the full voluptuous surge which lurked beneath."

Utterly aghast even as I write, I can only say that this may be the worst novel ever penned by woman or beast. Decline with all possible speed.

Oh, clever, supercilious young man! How I gloated and chuckled as I eviscerated these helpless, underprivileged, subliterary lambkins. Nor was I fearful of giving a gentle dig in the ribs at McGraw-Hill and its penchant for publishing trashy "fun" books which could be excerpted in places like *Reader's Digest* for a hefty advance (though my japery may have contributed to my downfall).

The Plumber's Wench, by Audrey Wainwright Smilie. Non-fiction.

The only thing going for this book is its title, which is catchy and vulgar enough to be right down McGraw-Hill's alley. The author is an actual woman, married —as the title coyly indicates—to a plumber living in a suburb of Worcester, Mass. Hopelessly unfunny, though straining for laughs on every page, these illiterate daydreams are an attempt to romanticize what must be a ghastly existence, the author eagerly equating the comic vicissitudes of her domestic life with those in the household of a brain surgeon. Like a physician, she points out, a plumber is on call day and night; like that of a physician the work of a plumber is quite intricate and involves exposure to germs; and both often come home smelling badly. The chapter headings best demonstrate the quality of the humor, which is too feeble even to be described properly as scatological: "Rub-a-Dub-Dub, the Blonde in the Tub." "A Drain on the Nerves." (Drain. Get it?) "Flush Times." "Study in Brown." Etc. This manuscript arrived especially tacky and dogeared, having been submitted—according to the author in a letter—to Harper, Simon & Schuster, Knopf, Random House, Morrow, Holt, Messner, William Sloane, Rinehart, and eight others. In the same letter the author mentions her desperation over this MS—around which her entire life now revolves—and (I'm not kidding) adds a veiled threat of suicide. I should hate to be responsible for anyone's death but it is absolutely imperative that this book never be published. Decline! (Why do I have to keep reading such shit?)

I would never have been able to make remarks like the last, nor allude in such a roguish fashion to the house of McGraw-Hill, had it not been for the fact that the senior editor above me who read all my reports was a man sharing my disillusionment with our employer and all that the vast and soulless empire stood for. A sleepy-eyed, intelligent, defeated but basically good-humored Irishman named Farrell, he had worked for years on such McGraw-Hill publications as *Foam Rubber Monthly, World of Prosthetics, Pesticide News* and *American Strip Miner* until, at fifty-five or so, he had been pastured out to the gentler, less hectically industrial surroundings of the trade-book branch, where he marked time in his office sucking on a pipe, reading Yeats and Gerard Manley Hopkins, skimming my reports with a tolerant glance and, I think, avidly contemplating early retirement to Ozone Park. Far from offending him, my jibes at McGraw-Hill usually amused him, as did the general tone of my reports. Farrell had long before fallen victim to the ambitionless, dronelike quietude into which, as if some mammoth beehive, the company eventually numbed its employees, even the ambitious ones; and since he knew that the chances were less than one in ten thousand that I would find a publishable manuscript, I think he felt that there was no harm in my having a little fun. One of my longer (if not the longest) reports I especially treasure still, largely because it may have been the only one I wrote containing anything resembling compassion.

Harald Haarfager, a Saga, by Gundar Firkin. Poetry.

Gundar Firkin is not a pseudonym but a real name. The names of so many bad writers sound odd or made-up, until you discover that they are real. Could this have any significance? The MS of Harald Haarfager, a Saga came neither unsolicited through the mail nor from an agent but was delivered into my hands by the author himself. Firkin arrived in the anteroom about a week ago, carrying a manuscript box and two suitcases. Miss Meyers said he wanted to see an editor. Guy of about 60 I should say, somewhat stooped but strong, middle-sized; weathered lined outdoor face with bushy gray brows, gentle mouth and a couple of the saddest old wistful eyes I've ever seen. Wore a farmer's black leather cap, the kind with snapped-up flaps that come down over the ears, and a thick windbreaker with a woolen collar. He had tremendous hands with great raw red knuckles. His nose leaked a little. Said he wanted to leave a MS. Looked pretty tired and when I asked him where he had come from he said he had just that hour arrived in N. Y. after riding on the bus three days and four nights from a place called Turtle Lake, North Dakota. Just to deliver the MS? I asked, to which he replied Yes.

He then volunteered the information that McGraw-Hill was the first publisher he had visited. This quite amazed me, inasmuch as this firm is seldom the publisher of first preference, even among writers as relatively unknowledgeable as Gundar Firkin. When I inquired as to how he had come to this extraordinary choice he replied that it had really been a matter of luck. He had not intended for McGraw-Hill to be first on his list. He told me that when the bus laid over for several hours in Minneapolis he went around to the telephone company, where he had learned they had copies of the Manhattan Yellow Pages. Not wanting to do anything so crude as to tear off a page, he spent an hour or so copying out with a pencil the names and addresses of all the scores of book publishers in New York City. It had been his plan to start alphabetically—beginning, I believe, with Appleton—and to go right down the list to Ziff-Davis. But when, just that morning after his trip, he emerged from the Port Authority bus station only one block eastward, he looked up and there in the sky he saw Old Man McGraw's emerald monolith with its intimidating sign: McGRAW-HILL. So he came right up here.

The old fellow seemed so exhausted and bewildered—he later said he had never before been east of Minneapolis—that I decided that the least I could do was to take him downstairs for coffee in the cafeteria. While we sat there he told me about himself. He was a son of Norwegian immigrants—the original name had been "Firking" but somehow the "g" got lopped off—and all of his life he had been a wheat farmer near this town of Turtle Lake. Twenty years ago, when he was about 40, a mining company discovered huge coal deposits beneath his land and, although they didn't dig, they negotiated a long-term lease on the property which would take care of any money problems for the rest of his life. He was a bachelor and too set in his ways to cease farming, but now he would also have the leisure to start a project which he had always cherished. That is, he would begin writing an epic poem based on one of his Norwegian ancestors, Harald Haarfager, who was a 13th-century earl, or prince, or something. Needless to say, my heart simultaneously sank and broke at this awful news. But I sat there with a straight face as he kept patting the manuscript box, saying: "Yes sir. Twenty years work. It's right there. It's right there."

And then I had a change of mood. In spite of his hick appearance, he was intelligent and very articulate. Seemed to have read a great deal—mainly Norse mythology—although his favorite novelists were people like Sigrid Undset, Knut Hamsun and those four-square Midwesterners, Hamlin Garland and Willa Cather. Nonetheless, suppose I were to discover some sort of rough-hewn genius? After all, even a great poet like Whitman came on like a clumsy oddball, peddling his oafish script everywhere. Anyway, after a long talk (I'd begun to call him Gundar) I said I'd be glad to read his work, even though I had to caution him that McGraw-Hill was not particularly "strong" in the field of poetry, and we took the elevator back upstairs. Then a terrible thing happened. As I was saying goodby, telling him that I understood how pressed he might feel for a response after twenty years work, and that I would try to read his manuscript carefully and have an answer within a few days, I noticed that he was preparing to leave with only one of the two suitcases. When I mentioned this, he smiled and turned those grave, wistful, haunted, hinterland eyes on me and said: "Oh, I thought you could tell—the other suitcase has the rest of my saga."

I'm serious, it must be the longest literary work ever set down by human hand. I took it over to the mail room and had the boy there weigh it—35 pounds, seven Hammermill Bond boxes of five pounds each, a total of 3,850 typewritten pages. The saga itself is in a species of English, one would think it was written by Dryden in mock imitation of Spenser if one did not know the awful truth: those nights and days and twenty years on the frigid Dakota steppe, dreaming of ancient Norway, scratching away while the wild wind out of Saskatchewan howls through the bending wheat:

"Oh thou great leader, HARALD, how great is thy grief!
Where be the nosegays that she dight for thee?"

The aging bachelor edging up on Stanza 4,000 as the electric fan stirs the stifling prairie heat:

"Sing now, ye trolls and Nibelungs, sing no more
The tunes that HARALD made in her praise,
But into mourning turn your former lays:
O blackest curse!
Now is the time to die, Nay, time was long ago:
O mournful verse!"

My lips tremble, my sight blurs, I can go on no longer. Gundar Firkin is at the Hotel Algonquin (where he took a room at my heartless suggestion) awaiting a telephone call I am too cowardly to make. Decision is to decline with regret, even with a kind of grief.

It may have been that my standards were so high or the quality of the books so dreadful, but in either case I do not remember recommending a single submitted work during my five months at McGraw-Hill. But truly there is some irony in the fact that the one book that I rejected and—at least to my knowledge—also later found a publisher was a work which did not languish unknown and unread. Since those days I've often fantasized the reaction of Farrell or one of the other higher-ups when this book came out under the imprint of a Chicago publisher, a year or so after I had long vacated McGraw-Hill's oppressive pile. For surely my report must have registered in the memory of someone of the senior echelon, and just as surely this old-timer must have returned to the files, and with God knows what cruel mixed sensations of dismay and loss, reread my cool dismissal with its cocksure, priggish and disastrous cadences.

> ... so it is of some relief after these bitter months to discover a manuscript containing a prose style that does not cause fever, headache or retching, and as such the work deserves qualified praise. The idea of men adrift on a raft does have a certain appeal. But for the most part this is a long, solemn and tedious Pacific voyage best suited, I would think, to some kind of drastic abridgement in a journal like the National Geographic. Maybe a university press would buy it, it's definitely not for us.

This was the way I dealt with that great classic of modern adventure, *Kon-Tiki*. Months later, watching this book remain first on the best-seller list for unbelievable week after week, I was able to rationalize my blindness by saying to myself that if McGraw-Hill had paid me more than ninety cents an hour I might have been more sensitive to the nexus between good books and filthy lucre.

Home for me at this time was a cramped cubicle, eight by fifteen feet, in a building on West Eleventh Street in the Village called the University Residence Club. I had been lured to this place, on my arrival in New York, not alone by its name—which conjured up an image of Ivy League camaraderie, baize-covered lounge tables littered with copies of the *New Republic* and *Partisan Review*, and elderly retainers in frock coats fretting over messages and catering to one's needs—but by its modest rates: ten dollars a week. The Ivy League business was, of course, an imbecilic illusion. The University Residence Club was only one small cut above a flophouse, differing from Bowery accommodations to the extent of nominal privacy in the form of a locked door. Nearly all else, including the tariff, fell short of resemblance to a flophouse only by the most delicate of degrees. Paradoxically, the location was admirable, almost chic. From the single grime-encrusted window in my rear fourth-floor cubicle I could stare down into the ravishing garden of a house on West Twelfth Street, and occasionally I glimpsed what I took to be the owners of the garden—a youngish tweedy man whom I fantasized as a rising star at *The New Yorker* or *Harper's*, and his lively and astonishingly well-proportioned blond wife who bounced around the garden in slacks or in a bathing suit, disporting herself from time to time with a ridiculous, overgroomed Afghan hound, or lying asprawl on an Abercrombie & Fitch hammock, where I fucked her to a frazzle with stiff, soundless, slow, precise shafts of desire.

For then sex, or rather its absence, and this insolent and gorgeous little garden—together with the people who inhabited it—all seemed to merge symbolically to make ever more unbearable the degenerate character of the University Residence Club and to aggravate my poverty and my lonely and outcast state. The all-male clientele, mostly middle-aged or older, Village drifters and losers whose next step downward was skid row, emitted a sour smell of wine and despair as we edged past each other in the cramped, peeling hallways. No doting old concierge but a series of reptilian desk clerks, each with the verdigris hue of creatures deprived of daylight, mounted guard over the lobby where one small lightbulb pulsed dimly overhead; they also operated the single creaking elevator, and they coughed a lot and scratched in hemorrhoidal misery during the interminable ascent to the fourth floor and the cubbyhole where, night after night that spring, I immured myself like a half-mad anchorite. Necessity had forced me to this, not only because I had no extra money for entertainment but because, as a newcomer to the metropolis, less shy than simply proudly withdrawn, I lacked both the opportunity and the initiative to make friends. For the first time in my life, which had for years been sometimes witlessly gregarious, I discovered the pain of unwanted solitude. Like a felon suddenly thrown into solitary confinement, I found myself feeding off the unburned fat of inward resources I barely knew I possessed. In the University Residence Club at twilight in May, watching the biggest cockroach I had ever seen browse across my copy of *The Complete Poetry and Prose of John Donne,* I suddenly encountered the face of loneliness, and decided that it was a merciless and ugly face indeed.

So during those months my evening schedule rarely varied. Leaving the McGraw-Hill Building at five, I would take the Eighth Avenue subway train (a nickel) to Village Square, where, after debarking, I made straight for a corner delicatessen and bought the three cans of Rheingold my severe and budgetary conscience permitted me. Thence to my roomlet, where I would stretch out on the corrugated mattress with its Clorox-fragrant sheets laundered to transparency and read until the last of my beers grew warm—a matter of an hour and a half or so. Mercifully, I was at that age when reading was still a passion and thus, save for a happy marriage, the best state possible in which to keep absolute loneliness at bay. I could not have made it through those evenings otherwise. But I was an abandoned reader and, besides, outlandishly eclectic, with an affinity for the written word—almost any written word—that was so excitable that it verged on the erotic. I mean this literally, and were it not for the fact that I have compared notes with a few others who have confessed to sharing with me in their youth this peculiar sensibility, I know I would now be risking scorn or incredulity by stating that I can recall the time when the prospect of half an hour's dalliance with a Classified Telephone Directory caused me a slight but nonetheless noticeable tumescence.

In any case, I would read—*Under the Volcano* was just one of the books which I remember held me captive that season—and at eight or nine o'clock would go out for dinner. What dinners! How vividly there still lingers on my palate the suety aftertaste of the Salisbury steak at Bickford's, or Riker's western omelette, in which one night, nearly swooning, I found a greenish, almost incorporeal feather and a tiny embryonic beak. Or the gristle embedded like an impacted tumor in the lamb chops at the Athens Chop House, the chops themselves tasting of old sheep, the mashed potatoes glutinous, rancid, plainly reconstituted with Greek cunning from dehydrated government surplus filched from some warehouse. But I was as innocent of New York gastronomy as I was of a lot of other things, and it would be a long time before I would learn that the best meal for less than a dollar in the city was a couple of hamburgers and a slice of pie at a White Tower.

Back in my cubicle, I would savagely seize a book and plunge once more into make-believe, reading into the early hours of the morning. On several occasions, however, I was forced to do what I had come distastefully to regard as my "homework," that is, composing jacket blurbs for forthcoming McGraw-Hill books. As a matter of fact, I recall that I had been hired in the first place largely on the basis of a trial blurb I had written for an already published McGraw-Hill tome, *The Story of the Chrysler Building*. My lyrical yet muscular copy had so impressed Farrell that it not only was an important factor in my getting the job but obviously made him feel that I could produce similar wonders for books about to be published. I think it was one of his major disappointments in me that I couldn't repeat myself, not a single time; for unbeknownst to Farrell, and only partly apparent to me, the McGraw-Hill syndrome of despair and attrition had set in. Without being willing quite fully to admit it, I had begun to detest my charade of a job. I was not an editor, but a *writer*—a writer with the same ardor and the soaring wings of the

Melville or the Flaubert or the Tolstoy or the Fitzgerald who had the power to rip my heart out and keep a part of it and who each night, separately and together, were summoning me to their incomparable vocation. My attempts at jacket copy filled me with a sense of degradation, especially since the books I had been assigned to magnify represented not literature but its antipodean opposite, commerce. Here is a fragment of one of the blurbs I was unable to finish.

> As the romance of paper is central to the story of the American dream, so is the name Kimberly-Clark central to the story of paper. Beginning as a humble "one-horse" operation in the sleepy Wisconsin lakeside town of Neenah, the Kimberly-Clark Corporation is now one of the authentic giants of the world paper industry, with factories in 13 states and 8 foreign countries. Serving a host of human needs, many of its products—the most famous of which is undoubtedly Kleenex—have become so familiar that their very names have passed into the language . . .

A paragraph like this would require hours. Should I say "undoubtedly Kleenex" or "indubitably"? "Host" of human needs or "horde"? "Mass"? "Mess"? During its composition I would pace my cell distractedly, uttering soft meaningless vocables to the air as I struggled with the prose rhythms, and fighting back the desolate urge to masturbate that for some reason always accompanied this task. Finally, overtaken by rage, I would find myself saying "No! No!" in a loud voice to the beaverboard walls, and then hurl myself on the typewriter where, cackling wickedly, I would tap out a swift, sophomoric but blessedly purgative variation.

> Kimberly-Clark statistics are staggering to contemplate:
>
> —It is estimated that, during one winter month alone, if all the snot blown into Kleenex tissues in the United States and Canada were spread over the playing surface of the Yale Bowl, it would reach a depth of one-and-a-half feet . . .

—It has been calculated that if the number of the vaginas employing Kotex during a single four day period in the U.S.A. were lined up orifice to orifice, there would be a snatch long enough to extend from Boston to White River Junction, Vt. . . .

The next day Farrell, ever amiable and tolerant, would muse wryly on such offerings, chewing at his Yello-Bole, and after observing that "this isn't quite what I think we had in mind," would grin understandingly and ask me to please try again. And because I was not yet completely lost, perhaps because the Presbyterian ethic still exercised some vestigial hold on me, I would try again that night—would try with all my passion and might, to no avail. After sweaty hours, I would give up and return to "The Bear" or *Notes from the Underground* or *Billy Budd,* or often simply loiter yearningly by the window, gazing down into the enchanted garden. There in the golden spring dusk of Manhattan, in an ambience of culture and unassertive affluence from which I knew I would forever be excluded, a soirée would be commencing at the Winston Hunnicutts', for that was the swank name with which I had christened them. Alone for an instant, blond Mavis Hunnicutt would appear in the garden, dressed in a blouse and tight flowered slacks; after pausing for a peek up at the opalescent evening sky, she would give an odd and bewitching toss to her lovely hair and then bend down to pluck tulips from the flowerbed. In this adorable stance, she could not know what she did to the loneliest junior editor in New York. My lust was incredible—something prehensile, a groping snout of desire, slithering down the begrimed walls of the wretched old building, uncoiling itself across a fence, moving with haste serpentine and indecent to a point just short of her upturned rump, where in silent metamorphosis it blazingly flowered into the embodiment of myself, priapic, ravenous, yet under hair-trigger control. Gently my arms surrounded Mavis, and I cupped my hands under her full, free-floating, honeydew breasts. "Is that you, Winston?" she whispered. "No, it's I," said I, her lover, in response, "let me take you doggie fashion." To which she invariably replied, "Oh, darling, yes—later."

In these demented fantasies I was prevented from immediate copulation on the Abercrombie & Fitch hammock only by the sudden arrival in the garden of Thornton Wilder. Or e. e. cummings. Or Katherine Anne Porter. Or John Hersey. Or Malcolm Cowley. Or John P. Marquand. At which point—brought back to my senses with a punctured libido—I would find myself at the window once more, savoring with longing heart the festivities below. For it seemed perfectly logical to me that the Winston Hunnicutts, this vivid and gregarious young couple (whose garden-level living room, incidentally, afforded me a jealous glimpse of Danish-modern shelves jammed with books), had the enormous good fortune to inhabit a world populated by writers and poets and critics and other literary types; and thus on these evenings as the twilight softly fell and the terrace began to fill with chattering, beautifully dressed sophisticates, I discerned in the shadows the faces of all the impossible heroes and heroines I had ever dreamed of since that moment when my hapless spirit had become entrapped by the magic of the printed word. I had yet to meet a single author of a published book—unless one excepts the seedy old ex-Communist I have mentioned, who once accidentally blundered into my office at McGraw-Hill, smelling of garlic and the stale sweat of ancient apprehensions—and so that spring the Hunnicutt parties, which were frequent and of long duration, gave my imagination opportunity for the craziest flights of fancy that ever afflicted the brain of a lovelorn idolater. There was Wallace Stevens! And Robert Lowell! That mustached gentleman looking rather furtively from the door. Could that really be *Faulkner?* He was rumored to be in New York. The woman with the buxom frame, the hair in a bun, the interminable grin. Surely that was Mary McCarthy. The shortish man with the wry ruddy sardonic face could only be John Cheever. Once in the twilight a woman's shrill voice called "Irwin!" and as the name floated up to my grimy voyeur's perch I felt my pulse skip a beat. It was really too dark to tell, and his back was to me, but could the man who wrote "The Girls in Their Summer Dresses" be that broad burly wrestler hemmed in by two girls, their adoring faces upturned like flowers?

All of these evening sojourners at the Hunnicutts', I now realize, must have been in the ad game or Wall Street or some other hollow profession, but then I remained unshaken in my delusion. One night, however, just before my expulsion from the McGraw-Hill empire, I experienced a violent reversal of emotions which caused me never to gaze down into the garden again. That time I had taken my accustomed post at the window and had my eyes fixed on Mavis Hunnicutt's familiar posterior as she made the little motions which had so endeared her to me—hitching at her blouse and tossing a blond lock back with a finger while chatting with Carson McCullers and a pale, lofty English-looking person who possessed a myopic blink and was obviously Aldous Huxley. What in God's name were they talking about? Sartre? Joyce? Vintage wines? Summer places in the south of Spain? The Bhagavad-Gita? No, plainly they were speaking of the environment—*this* environment—for Mavis's face wore a look of pleasure and animation as she gestured about, pointing to the ivy-covered walls of the garden, the miniature greensward, the bubbling fountain, the miraculous tulip bed set down in bright Flemish hues here amid these somber urban bowels. "If only . . ." she seemed to say, her expression growing strained with annoyance. "If only . . ." And then she whirled in a swift half-circle, thrusting out at the University Residence Club a furious little fist, a darling angry fist so prominent, so bloodlessly agitated that it seemed impossible that she was not brandishing it a scant inch from my nose. I felt illumined as if by a spotlight, and in my pounding chagrin I was certain that I could read her lips: "If only that goddamned *eyesore* weren't there, with all those *creeps* peering out at us!"

But my torment on Eleventh Street was not fated to be prolonged. It would have been satisfying to think that my employment was terminated because of the *Kon-Tiki* episode. But the decline of my fortunes at McGraw-Hill began with the arrival of a new editor in chief, whom I secretly called the Weasel—a near-anagram of his actual surname. The Weasel had been brought in to give to the place some much-needed tone. At that time he was chiefly known in the publishing business for his association with Thomas Wolfe, having become Wolfe's editor after he left

Scribner and Maxwell Perkins, and following the writer's death, having helped assemble into some sort of sequential and literary order the colossal body of work which remained unpublished. Although the Weasel and I were both from the South—a connection which in the alien surroundings of New York more often than not tends initially to cement the relationship of Southerners—we took an immediate dislike to each other. The Weasel was a balding, unprepossessing little man in his late forties. I don't know exactly what he thought of me—doubtless the snotty, free-wheeling style of my manuscript reports had something to do with his negative reaction—but I thought him cold, remote, humorless, with the swollen ego and unapproachable manner of a man who has fatuously overvalued his own accomplishments. In the staff editorial conferences he was fond of uttering such locutions as "Wolfe used to say to me . . ." Or, "As Tom wrote to me so eloquently just before his death . . ."

His identification with Wolfe was so complete that it was as if he were the writer's alter ego—and this was excruciating to me, since like countless young men of my generation I had gone through the throes of Wolfe-worship, and I would have given all I had to spend a chummy, relaxed evening with a man like the Weasel, pumping him for fresh new anecdotes about the master, voicing phrases like "God, sir, that's priceless!" at some marvelous yarn about the adored giant and his quirks and escapades and his three-ton manuscript. But the Weasel and I utterly failed to make contact. Among other things, he was rigorously conventional and had quickly accommodated himself to McGraw-Hill's tidy, colorless and arch-conservative mold. By contrast, I was still very much feeling my oats, in every sense of that expression, and had to bring a facetious attitude not only to the whole idea of the editorial side of book publishing, which my fatigued eyes now saw plainly as lusterless drudgery, but to the style, customs and artifacts of the business world itself. For McGraw-Hill was, after all, in spite of its earnest literary veneer, a monstrous paradigm of American business. And so with a cold company man like the Weasel at the helm, I knew that it was not long before trouble must set in and that my days were numbered.

One day, soon after he assumed command, the Weasel called me into his office. He had an oval, well-larded face and tiny, unfriendly, somewhat weasel-like eyes which it seemed impossible to me had gained the confidence of anyone so responsive to the nuances of physical presence as Thomas Wolfe. He beckoned me to sit down, and after uttering a few strained civilities came directly to the point, namely, my clear failure within his perspective to conform to certain aspects of the McGraw-Hill "profile." It was the first time I had ever heard that word used other than as a description of the side view of a person's face, and as the Weasel spoke, moving up to specifics, I grew increasingly puzzled over where I might have failed, since I was certain that good old Farrell had not spoken ill of me or my work. But it turned out that my errors were both sartorial and, tangentially at least, political.

"I notice that you don't wear a hat," the Weasel said.

"A hat?" I replied. "Why, no." I had always been lukewarm about headgear, feeling only that hats had their place. Certainly, since leaving the Marine Corps two years before, I had never thought of hat-wearing as a compulsory matter. It was my democratic right to choose, and I had given the idea no further thought until this moment.

"Everyone at McGraw-Hill wears a hat," the Weasel said.

"Everyone?" I replied.

"Everyone," he said flatly.

And of course as I reflected on what he was saying, I realized that it was true: everyone *did* wear a hat. In the morning, in the evening and at lunchtime the elevators and hallways were bobbing seas of straws and felts, all perched on the uniformly sheared, closely cropped scalps of McGraw-Hill's thousand regimented minions. This was at least true for men; for the women—mainly secretaries—it seemed to be optional. The Weasel's assertion was, then, indisputably correct. What I had up until then failed to perceive, and was only at this moment perceiving, was that the wearing of hats was no mere fashion but, indeed, obligatory, as much a part of the McGraw-Hill costume as the button-down Arrow shirts and amply tailored Weber & Heilbroner flannel suits worn by everyone in the green tower, from the textbook salesmen to the anxiety-ridden editors of *Solid Wastes Management*. In my innocence I had not realized that I had been continually out of uniform, but even as I now grasped this fact I stirred with mingled resentment and hilarity, and did not know how to respond to the Weasel's solemn insinuation. Quickly I found myself inquiring of the Weasel in tones as grim as his own, "May I ask in what other way I haven't fitted the profile?"

"I cannot dictate your newspaper-reading habits, nor do I want to," he said, "but it is not wise for a McGraw-Hill employee to be seen with a copy of the New York *Post*." He paused. "This is simply advice for your own good. Needless to say, you can read anything you care to, on your own time and in privacy. It just does not look . . . *seemly* for McGraw-Hill editors to be reading radical publications at the office."

"What should I be reading then?" It had been my lunchtime custom to go down to Forty-second Street and pick up the early afternoon edition of the *Post* along with a sandwich, both of which I would consume in my office during the hour allotted me. It was my only newspaper reading of the day. At the time I was not so much politically innocent as a political neuter, a *castrato,* and I read the *Post* not for its liberal editorials or for Max Lerner's columns—all of which bored me—but for its breezy big-city journalistic style and its alluring reports on the *haut monde,* notably those of Leonard Lyons. Yet as I replied to the Weasel, I knew that I was not about to give that paper up, any more than I intended to stop by Wanamaker's and get myself fitted for a porkpie hat. "I like the *Post,*" I went on with a touch of exasperation. "What do you think I should read instead?"

"The *Herald Tribune* might be more appropriate," he said in his Tennessee drawl so strangely devoid of warmth. "Or the *News,* even."

"But they're published in the morning."

"Then you might try the *World-Telegram.* Or the *Journal-American.* Sensationalism is preferable to radicalism."

Even I knew that the *Post* was hardly radical and I was on the verge of saying so, but held my tongue. Poor Weasel. Cold a fish as he was, I suddenly felt a little sorry for him, realizing as I did that the snaffle he was trying to curb me with was not of his making, for something in his manner (could it have been the faintest note of apology, one Southerner reaching out to another in faltering, belated sympathy?) told me that he had no real stomach for these foolish and sordid restrictions. I also saw that at his age and position he was the true prisoner of McGraw-Hill, irrevocably committed to its pettifoggery and its mean-spirited style and its single-minded concern for pelf—a man who could never again turn back—while I, at least, had the freedom of the world spread out before me. I recall that as he pronounced that forlorn edict "Sensationalism is preferable to radicalism," I murmured beneath my breath an almost exultant adieu: "Goodby, Weasel. Farewell, McGraw-Hill."

I still mourn the fact that I lacked the courage to quit on the spot. Instead, I went on a sort of slow-down strike—work-stoppage would be a more accurate term. For the next few days, although I appeared on time in the morning and left precisely at the stroke of five, the manuscripts became piled high on my desk, unread. At noontime I no longer browsed in the *Post*, but walked over to a newspaper stand near Times Square and bought a copy of the *Daily Worker*, which without ostentation—indeed, with grave casualness—I read, or tried to read, at my desk in my habitual way as I chewed at a kosher pickle and a pastrami sandwich, relishing each instant I was able to play, in this fortress of white Anglo-Saxon power, the dual role of imaginary Communist and fictive Jew. I suspect I had gone a little crazy by then, for on the last day of my employment I showed up for work wearing my old faded green Marine "pisscutter" (the kind of cap John Wayne wore in *Sands of Iwo Jima*) as companion headdress to my seersucker suit; and I made sure that the Weasel caught a glimpse of me in this absurd rig, just as I'm certain I contrived that same afternoon that he would catch me out in my final gesture of defection . . .

One of the few tolerable features of life at McGraw-Hill had been my view from the twentieth floor—a majestic prospect of Manhattan, of monolith and minaret and spire, that never failed to revive my drugged senses with all those platitudinous yet genuine spasms of exhilaration and sweet promise that have traditionally overcome provincial American youths. Wild breezes whooshed around the McGraw-Hill parapets, and one of my favorite pastimes had been to drop a sheet of paper from the window and to watch its ecstatic tumbling flight as it sped across the rooftops, often disappearing far off into the canyons around Times Square, still tumbling and soaring. That noon, along with my *Daily Worker*, I had been inspired to buy a tube of plastic bubble material—the kind commonly used by children now, although then a novelty on the market—and once back in my office, I had blown up half a dozen of these fragile, lovely, iridescent globes, all the while anticipating their adventure upon the wind with the greedy suspense of one at the brink of some long-denied sexual blessing. Released one by one into the smoggy abyss, they were more than I had hoped for, fulfilling every buried, infantile desire to float balloons to the uttermost boundaries of the earth. They glowed in the afternoon sunlight like the satellites of Jupiter, and were as big as basketballs. A quirky updraft sent them hurtling high over Eighth Avenue; there they remained suspended for what seemed interminable moments, and I sighed with delight. Then I heard squeals and girlish laughter and saw that a gaggle of McGraw-Hill secretaries, attracted by the show, were hanging out the windows of adjoining offices. It must have been their commotion which called the Weasel's attention to my aerial display, for I heard his voice behind me just as the girls gave a final cheer and the balloons fled frantically eastward down the garish arroyo of Forty-second Street.

I thought the Weasel controlled his rage very well. "You're dismissed as of this day," he said in a strained voice. "You may pick up your final paycheck at five o'clock."

"Up yours, Weasel, you're firing a man who's going to be as famous as Thomas Wolfe." I did not say this, I'm sure, but the words trembled so palpably on my tongue that to this day I've retained the impression that they were spoken. I think I merely said nothing, only watched the small man wheel about on his small feet and saunter off out of my existence. Then there was an odd sense of release that flooded through me, a physical sensation almost like comfort, as if I had removed warm stifling layers of clothes. Or to be more exact, as if I had remained immersed too long in murky depths and had struggled to surface gulping blissful drafts of fresh air.

"A narrow escape," said Farrell later, reinforcing my metaphor with unconscious precision. "People have been known to drown in this place. And they never even find their bodies."

It was long past five o'clock. I had remained late that afternoon to pack my effects, such as they were, to say goodby to one or two of the editors with whom I had struck up a mildly amiable acquaintance, to collect my last $36.50 and, finally, to bid what turned out to be a surprisingly painful and sad farewell to Farrell, who, among other things, revealed what I might have suspected all along had I really cared or had I been more observant —that he was a solitary and despondent drinker. He came into my office, wobbling a little, just as I was stuffing into my briefcase carbon copies of some of my more thoughtful manuscript reports. I had removed them from the files, feeling a rather wistful affection for my piece on Gundar Firkin, and coveting especially my musings on *Kon-Tiki,* about which I had the odd suspicion that they might comprise someday an interesting sheaf of literary marginalia.

"They never even find their bodies," Farrell repeated. "Have a little snort." He extended toward me a glass and a pint bottle of Old Overholt rye, half full. The rye was heavily aromatic on Farrell's breath, indeed he smelled a bit like a loaf of pumpernickel. I declined the snort, not out of any real reticence but because in those days I imbibed only cheap American beer.

"Well, you weren't cut out for this place anyway," he said, tossing down a gulp of the Overholt. "This wasn't the place for you."

"I had begun to realize that," I agreed.

"In five years you'd have been a company man. In ten years you'd have been a fossil. A fossilized old fart in his thirties. That's what McGraw-Hill would have turned you into."

"Yeah, I'm kind of glad to be going," I said. "I'm going to miss the money, though. Even though it was hardly what you might call a bonanza."

Farrell chuckled and made a modest little burp. His face was such a long upper-lipped Irish prototype that it verged on a joke, and he exuded sadness—something intangibly rumpled, exhausted and resigned that caused me to reflect with a twinge of pain on these lonesome office drinking bouts, the twilight sessions with Yeats and Hopkins, the bleak subway commute to Ozone Park. I suddenly knew I would never see him again.

"So you're going to write," he said, "so you're going to be a writer. A fine ambition, one that I once shared myself. I hope and pray that you become one, and that you send me a copy of your first book. Where are you going when you start writing?"

"I don't know," I said. "I know I can't stay in the dump I live in any longer. I've got to get out of there."

"Ah, how I wanted to write," he mused. "I mean, to write poetry. Essays. A fine novel. Not a *great* novel, mind you—I knew I lacked the genius and the ambition for that—but a fine novel, one with a certain real elegance and style. A novel as good as, say, *The Bridge of San Luis Rey* or *Death Comes for the Archbishop*—something unpretentious but with a certain quality of near-perfection." He paused, then said, "Oh, but somehow I got sidetracked. I think it was the long years of editorial work, especially of a rather technical nature. I got sidetracked into dealing with other people's ideas and words rather than my own, and that's hardly conducive to creative effort. In the long run." Again he paused, regarding the amber dregs in his glass. "Or maybe it was *this* that sidetracked me," he said ruefully. "The sauce. This one-hundred-proof goblet of dreams. Anyway, I did not become a writer. I did *not* become a novelist or a poet, and as for essays, I wrote only one essay in my entire life. Know what it was?"

"No, what was it?"

"It was for *The Saturday Evening Post*. A little anecdote I sent in regarding a vacation that my wife and I took in Quebec. Not worth describing. But I got two hundred dollars for it, and for several days I was the happiest writer in America. Ah, well . . ." A great melancholy appeared to overtake him, and his voice trailed off. "I got sidetracked," he murmured.

I did not know quite how to respond to his mood, which seemed perilously near grief, and could only say, as I continued to stuff things into my briefcase, "Well, I hope we can somehow keep in touch." I knew, however, that we would not keep in touch.

"I do too," Farrell said. "I wish we had gotten to know each other better." Gazing down into his glass, he fell into a silence which became so prolonged that it began to make me nervous. "I wish we had gotten to know each other better," he repeated slowly at last. "I had often thought to ask you to come to my home out in Queens for dinner, but I always put it off. Sidetracked again. You remind me very much of my son, you know."

"I didn't know you had a son," I said with some surprise. I had heard Farrell once allude casually and wryly to his "childless state" and had simply assumed that he had not, as the phrase goes, been blessed with issue. But my curiosity had ceased there. In the McGraw-Hill atmosphere of gelid impersonality it was considered an effrontery, if not downright dirty, to express even mild interest in the private lives of others. "I thought you—" I began.

"Oh, I *had* a son all right!" His voice was suddenly a cry, startling me with its mingled tone of rage and lament. The Overholt had unloosed in him all the Celtic furies with which he had consorted daily in the desolate time after five in the afternoon. He rose to his feet and wandered to the window, gazing through the twilight at the incomprehensible mirage of Manhattan, set afire by the descending sun. "Oh, I *had* a son!" he said again. "Edward Christian Farrell. He was just your age, he was just twenty-two, and he wanted to be a writer. He was . . . he was a *prince* with language, my son was. He had a gift that would have charmed the devil himself, and some of the letters he wrote—some of those long, knowing, funny, intelligent letters—were the loveliest that ever were written. Oh, he was a *prince* with the language, that boy!"

Tears came to his eyes. For me it was a paralyzingly awkward moment, one that appears now and then throughout life, though with merciful infrequency. In grieving tones a near-stranger speaks of some beloved person in the past tense, throwing his listener into a quandary. Certainly he means the departed is dead. But hold! Mightn't he simply have run off, victim of amnesia, or become a fleeing culprit? Or was now pathetically languishing in a lunatic asylum, so that use of the past tense is merely sorrowfully euphemistic? When Farrell resumed talking, still offering me no clue to his son's fate, I turned away in embarrassment and continued to sort out my belongings.

"Maybe I could have taken it better if he hadn't been my only kid. But Mary and I could have no more children after Eddie was born." He stopped suddenly. "Ah, you don't want to hear . . ."

I turned back to him. "No, go ahead," I said, "please." He seemed to be suffering from an urgent need to talk, and since he was a kindly man whom I liked and, furthermore, one who in some fashion had indeed identified me with his son, I felt it would have been indecent for me not to encourage him to unburden himself. "Please go ahead," I said again.

Farrell poured himself another huge shot of rye. He had become quite drunk and his speech was a little slurred, the freckled indoor face sad and haggard in the waning light. "Oh, it's true that a man can live out his own aspirations through the life of his child. Eddie went to Columbia, and one of the things that thrilled me was the way he took to books, his gift for words. At nineteen—*nineteen,* mind you—he had had a sketch published in *The New Yorker,* and Whit Burnett had taken a story for *Story*. One of the youngest contributors, I believe, in the history of the magazine. It was his eye, you see, his *eye*." Farrell jabbed his forefinger at his eye. "He *saw* things, you understand, saw things that the rest of us don't see and made them fresh and alive. Mark Van Doren wrote me a lovely note—the loveliest note, really—saying that Eddie had one of the greatest natural writing gifts of any student he'd ever had. Mark Van Doren, imagine! Quite a tribute, wouldn't you say?" He eyed me as if in search for some corroboration.

"Quite a tribute," I agreed.

"And then—and then in 1943 he joined the Marine Corps. Said he'd rather join up than be drafted. He honestly loved the glamour of the marines, although basically he was too sensitive to have any illusions about war. *War!*" He spoke the word with revulsion, like a seldom-used obscenity, and paused for an instant to shut his eyes and to nod in pain. Then he looked at me and said, "The war took him to the Pacific and he was in some of the worst of the fighting. You should read his letters, marvelous, jolly, eloquent letters, without a trace of self-pity. He never once doubted that he'd come home and go back to Columbia and finish up and then become the writer he was meant to be. And then two years ago he was on Okinawa and got hit by a sniper. In the head. It was July and they were mopping up. I think he must have been one of the last marines to die in the war. He'd made corporal. He won the Bronze Star. I don't know why it happened. *God,* I don't know *why* it happened! God, *why?*"

Farrell was weeping, not obtrusively but with the sparkling, honest tears welling up at the edge of his eyelids, and I turned away with such a feeling of shame and humiliation that years later I am able to recapture the slightly fevered, faintly nauseous sensation that swept over me. This may now be difficult to explain, for the passage of thirty years and the fatigue and cynicism engendered by several barbaric American wars might make my reaction appear to be hopelessly old-fashioned and romantic. But the fact remains that I, too, had been a marine like Eddie Farrell, had, like Eddie, burned to be a writer and had sent letters home from the Pacific that were inscribed in my heart's blood, written with the same weird amalgam of passion, humor, despair and exquisite hope that can only be set down by very young men haunted by the imminent appearance of death. Even more wrenching to recount, I, too, had come to Okinawa only days after Eddie had perished (who knows, I have often wondered, perhaps scant hours after he took his mortal wound), to encounter no enemy, no fear, no danger at all, but, through the grace of history, a wrecked yet peaceful Oriental landscape across which I would wander unscathed and unthreatened during the last few weeks before Hiroshima. I had, in bitter truth, heard not a shot fired in anger, and although in terms of my hide, at least, I was fortune's darling if there ever was one, I could never get over the feeling that

I had been deprived of something terrible and magnificent. Certainly in regard to this experience—or my lack of it—nothing ever pierced me so deeply as Farrell's brief, desolating story of his son Eddie, who seemed to me immolated on the earth of Okinawa that I might live—and write. As Farrell sat weeping in the twilight, I felt foreshortened, shriveled, and could say nothing.

Farrell rose, dabbing at his eyes, and stood by the window gazing out at the sun-encrimsoned Hudson, where the dingy outlines of two great ships moved sluggishly seaward toward the Narrows. The spring wind whistled with the noise of demons around McGraw-Hill's green indifferent eaves. When he spoke, Farrell's voice came from a distance, breathing a despair past telling:

"Everything that man esteems
Endures a moment or a day . . .
The herald's cry, the soldier's tread
Exhaust his glory and his might:
Whatever flames upon the night
Man's own resinous heart has fed."

Then he turned to me and said, "Son, *write your guts out.*" And, weaving down the hallway, he was gone out of my life forever.

I lingered there for a long time, pondering the future, which now seemed as misty and as obscure as those smog-bound horizons that stretched beyond the meadows of New Jersey. I was too young to be really afraid of much but not so young that I remained unshaken by certain apprehensions. Those ludicrous manuscripts I had read were somehow cautionary, showing me how sad was all ambition—especially when it came to literature. I wanted beyond hope or dreaming to be a writer, but for some reason Farrell's story had struck so deeply at my heart that for the first time in my life I was aware of the large hollowness I carried within me. It was true that I had traveled great distances for one so young, but my spirit had remained landlocked, unacquainted with love and all but a stranger to death. I could not realize then how soon I would encounter both of these things, embodied in the human passion and human flesh from which I had absented myself in my smug and airless self-deprivation. Nor did I then realize that my voyage of discovery would also be a journey to a place as strange as Brooklyn. Meanwhile, I only knew that I would go down for the last time from the twentieth floor, riding the aseptic green elevator to the chaotic Manhattan streets, and there celebrate my deliverance with expensive Canadian ale and the first sirloin steak I had eaten since coming to New York.

Two

After my solitary banquet that evening at the Longchamps restaurant on lower Fifth Avenue, I counted my money and reckoned my total worth at something less than fifty dollars. Although, as I said, I was without real fear in my plight, I could not help feeling a trifle insecure, especially since the prospects of getting another job were next to zero. Yet I need not have worried at all, for in a couple of days I was to receive a windfall which would rescue me—for the immediate future, at least. It was a bizarre and phenomenal stroke of luck, my receipt of this gift, and like another instance of great good fortune much later in my life, it had its origins in the institution of American Negro slavery. Although it bears only indirectly upon the new life I would take up in Brooklyn, the story of this gift is so unusual as to be worth recounting.

It has chiefly to do with my paternal grandmother, who was a shrunken little doll of an old lady approaching ninety when she told me about her slaves. I have often found it a little difficult to believe that I have been linked so closely in time to the Old South, that it was not an earlier generation of my ancestors who owned black people, but there it is: born in 1848, my *own* grandmother at the age of thirteen possessed two small Negro handmaidens only a little younger than herself, regarding them as beloved chattel all through the years of the Civil War, despite Abraham Lincoln and the articles of emancipation. I say "beloved" with no irony because I'm certain that she did very much love them, and when she recollected Drusilla and Lucinda (for those were their incomparable names) her ancient trembling voice cracked with emotion, and she told me "how dear, how dear" the little girls were to her, and how in the chill depths of the war she had to search high and low for woolen yarn in order to knit them stockings. This was in Beaufort County, North Carolina, where she had spent all of her life, and it is there that I remember her. Every Easter and Thanksgiving during the thirties we traveled down from our home in Virginia to see her, my father and I, driving across the swampland and the flat, changeless fields of peanuts and tobacco and cotton, the forlorn nigger cabins decrepit and unchanging too. Arriving in the somnolent little town on the Pamlico River, we greeted my grandmother with soft words and exceptional tenderness, for she had been nearly totally paralyzed from a stroke for many years. Thus it was at her bedside when I was twelve or thirteen that I heard first-hand about Drusilla and Lucinda, and camp meetings, and turkey shoots, and sewing bees, and river-boat excursions down the Pamlico, and other ante-bellum joys, the sweet chirpy old voice feeble yet unflagging, until at last it gave out and the gentle lady went to sleep.

It is important, though, to note that my grandmother never told me or my father about another slave child—he bore the jaunty name of Artiste—who, like Drusilla and Lucinda, had been "given" to her by her father and then soon after had been sold by him. As I will shortly demonstrate through two related letters, the reason that she never mentioned the boy doubtless has to do with the extraordinary story of his ultimate fate. In any case, it is interesting that my grandmother's father, after consummating the sale, converted the proceeds into Federal gold dollars of various denominations, no doubt in shrewd foreknowledge of the disastrous war to come, and placed the coins in a clay jug which he buried beneath an azalea at the back of the garden. This was, of course, to prevent their discovery by the Yankees, who in the last months of the war did arrive with a clatter of hoofs and scintillant sabers, dismantled the interior of the house before my grandmother's frightened girlish eyes, ransacked the garden, but found no gold. I am able, incidentally, to recall my grandmother's description of the Union troops with absolute clarity: "Dashing handsome men really, they were only doing their duty when they tore up our house, but naturally they had no culture or breeding. I'm certain they were from Ohio. They even threw the hams out of the window." Arriving back himself from the awful war with one eye missing and with a shattered kneecap—both wounds received at Chancellorsville—my great-grandfather unearthed the gold, and after the house once again became habitable, stashed it away in an ingeniously concealed compartment in the cellar.

There the treasure might have remained until kingdom come, for unlike those mysterious hoards one sometimes reads about in the news—packets of greenbacks or Spanish doubloons and such uncovered by the shovels of workmen—the gold would have seemed destined to be hidden in perpetuity. When my great-grandfather died in a hunting accident around the end of the century, his will made no mention of the coins—presumably for the very good reason that he had passed the money along to his daughter. When in turn she died forty years later, she did refer to the gold in *her* will, specifying that it should be divided among her many grandchildren; but in the fuzzy-mindedness of great age she had forgotten to state where the treasure was hidden, somehow confusing the cellar compartment with her safe deposit box in the local bank, which of course yielded up nothing in the way of this peculiar legacy. And for seven more years no one knew of its whereabouts. But it was my father, last surviving son of my grandmother's six children, who rescued the trove from its musty oblivion amid the termites and the spiders and the mice. Throughout his long life his concern for the past, for his family and its lineage, had been both reverent and inspired—a man quite as blissfully content to browse through the correspondence and memorabilia of some long-defunct, dull and distant cousin as is a spellbound Victorian scholar who has stumbled on a drawer full of heretofore unknown obscene love letters of Robert and Elizabeth Browning. Imagine his joy, then, when going through fading packets of his mother's letters he should discover one written to her from my great-grandfather describing not only the exact location of the cellar cache but also the details of the sale of the young slave Artiste. And so now two letters intertwine. The following communication from my father in Virginia, which I received just as I was packing up to leave the University Residence Club, tells much not only about several Southern generations but about the great events that were close on the modern horizon.

June 4, 1947

My dearest son,

I have at hand your letter of the 26th inst., telling of the termination of your employment. On the one hand, Stingo, I am sorry about this since it puts you in financial straits and I am in no position to be of much help, beset as I am already by the seemingly endless troubles and debts of your two aunts down in N.C. who I fear are prematurely senile and in a pathetic way. I hope to be better situated fiscally in some months, however, and would like to think I might then be able to contribute in a modest way to your ambitions to become a writer. On the other hand, I think you may be well shut of your employment at McGraw-Hill, which by your own account sounded fairly grim, the firm anyway being notoriously little else but the mouthpiece and the propaganda outlet for the commercial robber barons who have preyed on the American people for a hundred years and more. Ever since your great-grandfather came back half-blind and mutilated from the Civil War and together with my father tried to set up a humble trade manufacturing snuff and chewing tobacco down in Beaufort County—only to have their dreams shattered when they were forced out of business by those piratical devils, Washington Duke and his son, "Buck" Duke—ever since my knowledge of that tragedy I have had an undying hatred for the vicious monopoly capitalism that tramples the little man. (I deem it an irony that your education should have been received at an institution founded upon the ill-gotten lucre of the Dukes, though that's hardly a fault of yours.)

You doubtless remember Frank Hobbs, with whom I have driven to work at the shipyard for so many years. He is a good solid man in many ways, born in a peanut patch over in Southampton County, but as you may recall a man of such simon-pure reactionary beliefs that he often sounds rabid even by Virginia standards. Therefore we do not often talk ideology or politics. After the recent revelation of the horrors of Nazi Germany he is still an anti-semite and insists that it is the international jewish financiers who have a stranglehold on the wealth. Which of course would send me into hoots of laughter were it not so benighted a viewpoint, so that even though I concede to Hobbs that Rothschild and Warburg are certainly Hebraic names I attempt to tell him that greed is not a racial but a human predeliction and then I proceed to tick off such names as Carnegie, Rockefeller, Frick, Mellon, Harriman, Huntington, Whitney, Duke, ad infinitum, ad nauseam. This scarcely makes a dent on Hobbs, who in any event is able to direct his bile upon a much easier and more ubiquitous target, especially in this part of Va., i.e., and I do not have to tell you—the negro. This we simply do not talk about much or often, for at aet. 59 I am too old to engage in a fist fight. Son, the handwriting is on the wall. If the negro is as he is so often said to be "inferior," whatever that means, it is plainly because he has been so disadvantaged and deprived by us the master race that the only face he can present to the world is the hangdog face of inferiority. But the negro cannot stay down forever. No force on earth is going to keep a people of whatever color in the squalor and the poverty I see hereabouts, city and countryside. I do not know if the negro will ever begin to be re-enfranchised in my lifetime, I am not that optimistic, but he certainly will be in yours, and I would give almost anything I own to be alive when that day comes, as it surely will, when Harry Byrd sees negro men and women sitting not at the back of the bus but riding free and equal through all the streets of Virginia. For that I would willingly be called that hateful epithet "nigger lover," which I am sure I am called already in private by many, including Frank Hobbs.

Which brings me in a roundabout way to the main point of this letter. Stingo, you may recall a number of years ago when your grandmother's will was probated we were all baffled by her reference to a certain sum in gold coins which she bequeathed to her grandchildren but which we could never find. That mystery has now been resolved. I am as you know historian of the local chapter of the Sons of the Confederacy and while in the process of writing a fairly lengthy essay on your great-grandfather I examined in detail his truly voluminous correspondence to his family, which includes many letters to your grandmother. In one letter, written in 1886 from Norfolk (he was traveling on business for his tobacco firm, this being just before the villainous "Buck" Duke destroyed him), he disclosed the true whereabouts of the gold—placed not in the safe deposit box (your grandmother obviously became confused about this later) but in a bricked-up cubbyhole in the basement of the house in N.C. I am having a photostatic copy of this letter sent to you later on, as I know of your interest in slavery and should you ever want to write about that institution this tragic epistle might provide you with fascinating insights. The money it turns out was the proceeds of the sale of a 16-year-old negro boy named Artiste, who was the older brother of your grandmother's maidservants, Lucinda and Drusilla. The three children had been orphans when your great-grandfather had bought them together at the Petersburg, Va., auction block in the late 1850s. All three young negroes were deeded over into your grandmother's name and the two girls worked around the house and lived there, as did Artiste who, however, was mainly hired out around the town to do chores for other families.

Then something ugly happened which your great-grandfather speaks very delicately about in his letter to my mother. Apparently Artiste, who was in the first lusty flush of adolescence, made what your great-grandfather calls an "improper advance" toward one of the young white belles of the town. This of course caused a tremor of threat and violence to run immediately through the community and your great-grandfather took what anyone of that time would have considered the appropriate course. He spirited Artiste out of town to New Bern, where he knew there was a trader trading in young negroes for the turpentine forests down around Brunswick, Georgia. He sold Artiste to this trader for $800. This is the money which ended up in the basement of the old house.

But the story doesn't quite end there, son. What is so heartrending about the letter is your great-grandfather's account of the aftermath of this episode, and the ensuing grief and guilt which so often, I have noticed, attends stories about slavery. Perhaps you have already anticipated the rest. It develops that Artiste had made no such "advance" toward the young white girl. The lass was an hysteric who soon accused another negro boy of the same offense, only to have her story proved to be a falsehood—after which she broke down and confessed that her accusation against Artiste had also been mendacious. You may imagine your great-grandfather's anguish. In this letter to my mother he describes the ordeal of his guilt. Not only had he committed one of the truly unpardonable acts of a slave-owner—broken up a family—but had sold off an innocent boy of 16 into the grinding hell of the Georgia turpentine forests. He tells how he sent desperate inquiries by mail and private courier to Brunswick, offering at any price to buy the boy back, but at that time of course communication was both slow and unsure, and in many cases impossible, and Artiste was never found.

I discovered the $800 in precisely the place in the cellar he had described to your grandmother with such care. Often as a boy I stacked cordwood and stored apples and potatoes not six inches away from that cubbyhole. The coins over the years have, as you might imagine, appreciated in value enormously. Some of them turned out to be quite rare. I had occasion to take them up to Richmond to a coin appraiser, a numismatist I believe he is called, and he offered me something in excess of $5,500, which I accepted since this means a 700 percent return on the sale of poor Artiste. This would be a considerable sum of money in itself but as you know the terms of your grandmother's testament state that the amount shall be divided equally among all of her grandchildren. So it might have been better for you. Unlike myself who was prudent enough in this overpopulous age to sire one son, your aunts—my incredibly philo-progenitive sisters—have brought into the world a total of 11 offspring, all healthy and hungry, all poor. Thus your share of Artiste's sale will come to a few dollars less than $500, which I shall remit to you by certified check this week I hope, or at least as soon as this transaction is completed . . .

Your devoted father

Years later I thought that if I had tithed a good part of my proceeds of Artiste's sale to the N.A.A.C.P. instead of keeping it, I might have shriven myself of my own guilt, besides being able to offer evidence that even as a young man I had enough concern for the plight of the Negro as to make a sacrifice. But in the end I'm rather glad I kept it. For these many years afterward, as accusations from black people became more cranky and insistent that as a writer —a lying writer at that—I had turned to my own profit and advantage the miseries of slavery, I succumbed to a kind of masochistic resignation, and thinking of Artiste, said to myself: What the hell, once a racist exploiter always a racist exploiter. Besides, in 1947 I needed $485 as badly as any black man, or Negro, as we said in those days.

I stayed long enough at the University Residence Club to receive the check from my father. Given proper management, the money should last me through the summer, which was just beginning, and maybe even into the fall. But where to live? The University Residence Club was no longer for me a possibility, spiritual or physical. The place had reduced me to such a shambles of absolute impotence that I found that I could not even indulge myself in my occasional autoerotic diversions, and was reduced to performing furtive pocket jobs during midnight strolls through Washington Square. My sense of solitariness was verging, I knew, on the pathological, so intensely painful was the isolation I felt, and I suspected that I would be even more lost if I abandoned Manhattan, where at least there were familiar landmarks and amiable Village byways as points of reference to make me feel at home. But I simply could no longer afford either the Manhattan prices or the rent—even single rooms were becoming beyond my means—and so I had to search the classified ads for accommodations in Brooklyn. And that is how, one fine day in June, I got out of the Church Avenue station of the BMT with my Marine Corps seabag and suitcase, took several intoxicating breaths of the pickle-fragrant air of Flatbush, and walked down blocks of gently greening sycamores to the rooming house of Mrs. Yetta Zimmerman.

Yetta Zimmerman's house may have been the most open-heartedly monochromatic structure in Brooklyn, if not in all of New York. A large rambling wood and stucco house of the nondescript variety erected, I should imagine, sometime before or just after the First World War, it would have faded into the homely homogeneity of other large nondescript dwellings that bordered on Prospect Park had it not been for its striking—its overwhelming—pinkness. From its second-floor dormers and cupolas to the frames of its basement-level windows the house was unrelievedly pink. When I first saw the place I was instantly reminded of the façade of some back-lot castle left over from the MGM movie version of *The Wizard of Oz*. The interior also was pink. The floors, walls, ceilings and even most of the furniture of each hallway and room varied slightly in hue—due to an uneven paint job—from the tender *rosé* of fresh lox to a more aggressive bubble-gum coral, but everywhere there was pink, pink admitting rivalry from no other color, so that after only a few minutes contemplating my prospective room under the proud eye of Mrs. Zimmerman, I felt at first amused—it was a cupid's bower in which one could only barely restrain raucous laughter—and then really grimly trapped, as if I were in a Barricini candy store or the infants' department at Gimbels. "I know, you're thinking about the pink," Mrs. Zimmerman had said, "everybody does. But then it gets you. It wears on you—nice, really nice that is, I mean. Pretty soon, most people they don't want no other color." Without my questioning, she added that her husband, Sol—her late husband—had lucked into a fantastic bargain in the form of several hundred gallons of Navy surplus paint, used for that—*"you know"*—and halted, finger quizzically laid aside her porous spatulate nose. "Camouflage?" I ventured. To which she replied, "Yeah, that's it. I guess they didn't have much use for pink on those boats." She said that Sol had painted the house himself. Yetta was squat and expansive, sixty or thereabouts, with a slightly mongoloid cast to her cheerful features that gave her the look of a beaming Buddha.

That day I had been persuaded almost at once. First, it was cheap. Then, pink or not, the room she showed me on the ground floor was agreeably spacious, airy, sun-filled, and clean as a Dutch parlor. Furthermore, it possessed the luxury of a kitchenette and a small private bathroom in which the toilet and tub appeared almost jarringly white against the prevailing peppermint. I found the privacy itself seduction enough, but there was also a bidet, which lent a risqué note and, electrically, unconscionably stirred my expectations. I also was greatly taken by Mrs. Zimmerman's overview of her establishment, which she expounded as she led me around the premises. "I call this place Yetta's Liberty Hall," she said, every now and then giving me a nudge. "What I like to see is my tenants enjoy life. They're usually young people, my tenants, and I like to see them enjoy life. Not that I don't gotta have rules." She lifted the pudgy nub of a forefinger and began to tick them off. "Rule number one: no playing the radio after eleven o'clock. Rule number two: you gotta turn off all lights when you leave the room, I got no need to pay extra to Con Edison. Rule three: positively no smoking in bed, you get caught smoking in bed—*out*. My late husband, Sol, had a cousin burned himself up that way, plus a whole house. Rule number four: full week's payment due every Friday. End of the rules! Everything else is Yetta's Liberty Hall. Like what I mean is, this place is for grownups. Understand, I'm running no brothel, but you wanta have a girl in your room once in a while, have a girl in your room. You be a gentleman and quiet and have her out of there at a reasonable hour, you'll have no quarrel with Yetta about a girl in your room. And the same thing goes for the young ladies in my house, if they want to entertain a boyfriend now and then. What's good for the gander is good for the goose, I say, and if there's one thing I hate, it's hypocrisy."

This extraordinary broad-mindedness—deriving from what I could only assume was an Old World appreciation of *volupté*—put the final seal on my decision to move to Yetta Zimmerman's, despite the all too problematical nature of the free hand I had been given. Where would I get a girl? I wondered. Then I was suddenly furious at myself for my lack of enterprise. Certainly the license that Yetta (we were soon on a first-name basis) had given me meant that this important problem would soon take care of itself. The salmon-hued walls seemed to acquire a wanton glow, and I vibrated with inward pleasure. And a few days later I took up residence there, warmly anticipating a summer of carnal fulfillment, philosophical ripening and steady achievement in the creative task I had cut out for myself.

My first morning—a Saturday—I rose late and strolled over to a stationery store on Flatbush Avenue and bought two dozen Number 2 Venus Velvet pencils, ten lined yellow legal pads and a "Boston" pencil sharpener, which I got permission from Yetta to screw to the frame of my bathroom door. Then I sat down in a pink straight-backed wicker chair at an oaken desk, also painted pink, whose coarse-grained and sturdy construction reminded me of the desks used by schoolmarms in the grammar-school classrooms of my childhood, and with a pencil between thumb and forefinger confronted the first page of the yellow legal pad, its barrenness baneful to my eye. How simultaneously enfeebling and insulting is an empty page! Devoid of inspiration, I found that nothing would come, and although I sat there for half an hour while my mind fiddled with half-jelled ideas and nebulous conceits, I refused to let myself panic at my stagnation; after all, I reasoned, I had barely settled into these strange surroundings. The previous February, during my first few days at the University Residence Club, before starting work at

McGraw-Hill, I had written a dozen pages of what I planned to be the prologue of the novel—a description of a ride on a railroad train to the small Virginia city which was to provide the book's locale. Heavily indebted in tone to the opening passages of *All the King's Men,* using similar rhythms and even the same second-person singular to achieve the effect of the author grabbing the reader by the lapels, the passage was, I knew, to say the least, derivative, yet I also knew that there was much in it that was powerful and fresh. I was proud of it, it was a good beginning, and now I took it out of its manila folder and reread it for perhaps the ninetieth time. It still pleased me and I would not have wanted to change a line. Move over, Warren, this is Stingo arriving, I said to myself. I put it back in its folder.

The yellow page remained empty. I felt restless, a little goatish, and in order to keep the curtain drawn down over my brain's ever-handy peep show of lewd apparitions—harmless, but in relation to work distracting—I got up and paced the room, which the summer sun bathed in a lurid flamingo light. I heard voices, footsteps in the room above—the walls I realized were paper thin—and I looked up and glared at the pink ceiling. I began to detest the omnipresent pink and doubted gravely that it would "wear" on me, as Yetta had said. Because of the problems of weight and volume involved, I had brought only what I considered essential books with me; few in number, they included *The American College Dictionary,* Roget's *Thesaurus,* my collection of John Donne, Oates and O'Neill's *Complete Greek Drama,* the *Merck Manual of Diagnosis and Therapy* (essential to my hypochondria), the *Oxford Book of English Verse* and the Holy Bible. I knew I could eventually build up my library piecemeal. Meanwhile, now to help summon my own muse, I tried to read Marlowe, but for some reason that lilting music failed to stir me as it usually did.

I put the book aside and moseyed into the tiny bathroom, where I began to take inventory of the articles I had placed in the medicine chest. (Years later I would be fascinated to discover a hero of J.D. Salinger duplicating my ceremony, but I claim priority.) This was a ritual, deeply rooted in the soil of inexplicable neurosis and materialistic urgency, which I have gone through many times since when vision and invention have flagged to the point of inertia, and both writing and reading have become burdensome to the spirit. It is a mysterious need to restore a tactile relationship with mere things. One by one with my fingertips I examined them where I had placed them the night before, there on the shelves of the wall cabinet which like everything else had fallen prey to Sol Zimmerman's loony incarnadine paint brush: a jar of Barbasol shaving cream, a bottle of Alka-Seltzer, a Schick injector razor, two tubes of Pepsodent toothpaste, a Dr. West's toothbrush with medium bristles, a bottle of Royall Lyme after-shave lotion, a Kent comb, an "injecto-pack" of Schick injector blades, an unopened cellophane-wrapped box of three dozen rolled and lubricated Trojan condoms with "receptacle tips," a jar of Breck's anti-dandruff shampoo, a tube of Rexall nylon dental floss, a jar of Squibb multivitamins, a bottle of Astring-o-sol mouthwash. I touched them all gently, examined the labels, and even unscrewed the cap of the Royall Lyme shaving lotion and inhaled the fruity citrus aroma, receiving considerable satisfaction from the total medicine-chest experience, which took about a minute and a half. Then I closed the door of the cabinet and returned to my writing table.

Sitting down, I lifted my gaze and looked out the window and was suddenly made aware of another element which must have worked on my subconscious and caused me to be drawn to this place. It was such a placid and agreeable view I had of the park, this corner known as the Parade Grounds. Old sycamore trees and maples shaded the sidewalks at the edge of the park, and the dappled sunlight aglow on the gently sloping meadow of the Parade Grounds gave the setting a serene, almost pastoral quality. It presented a striking contrast to remoter parts of the neighborhood. Only short blocks away traffic flowed turbulently on Flatbush Avenue, a place intensely urban, cacophonous, cluttered, swarming with jangled souls and nerves; but here the arboreal green and the pollen-hazy light, the infrequent trucks and cars, the casual pace of the few strollers at the park's border all created the effect of an outlying area in a modest Southern city—Richmond perhaps, or Chattanooga or Columbia. I felt a sharp pang of homesickness, and abruptly wondered what in God's name was I doing here in the unimaginable reaches of Brooklyn, an ineffective and horny Calvinist among all these Jews?

Apropos of which, I took a scrap of paper from my pocket. On it I had scribbled the names of the six other tenants in the house. Each name had been affixed on small cards by the orderly Yetta and attached to the respective doors, and with motive no more suspect than my usual rapacious curiosity I had late the night before, tiptoed about the floors and copied the names down. Five of the occupants were on the floor above, the other in the room opposite me, across the hallway. Nathan Landau, Lillian Grossman, Morris Fink, Sophie Zawistowska, Astrid Weinstein, Moishe Muskatblit. I loved these names for nothing other than their marvelous variety, after the Cunninghams and Bradshaws I had been brought up with. Muskatblit I fancied for a certain Byzantine flavor. I wondered when I would get to know Landau and Fink. The three female names had stirred my intense interest, especially Astrid Weinstein, who was in fascinating proximity across the hall. I was mulling all this over when I was made suddenly aware—in the room directly over my head—of a commotion so immediately and laceratingly identifiable, so instantly, to my tormented ears, apparent in its nature that I will avoid what in a more circumlocutory time might have required obliqueness of suggestion, and take the liberty of saying that it was the sound, the uproar, the frenzy of two people fucking like crazed wild animals.

I looked up at the ceiling in alarm. The lamp fixture jerked and wobbled like a puppet on a string. Roseate dust sifted down from the plaster, and I half expected the four feet of the bed to come plunging through. It was terrifying —no mere copulatory rite but a tournament, a rumpus, a free-for-all, a Rose Bowl, a jamboree. The diction was in some form of English, garbled and exotically accented, but I had no need to know the words. What resulted was impressionistic. Male and female, the two voices comprised a cheering section, calling out such exhortations as I had never heard. Nor had I ever listened to such goads to better effort—to slacken off, to push on, to go harder, faster, deeper—nor such huzzahs over gained first downs, such groans of despair over lost yardage, such shrill advice as to where to put the ball. And I could not have heard it more clearly had I been wearing special earphones. Clear it was, and of heroic length. Unending minutes the struggle seemed to last, and I sat there sighing to myself until it was suddenly over and the participants had gone, literally, to the showers. The noise of splashing water and giggles drifted down through the flimsy ceiling, then there were padding footsteps, more giggles, the sharp smack of what sounded like a playful paw upon a bare bottom and finally, incongruously, the ravishing sweet heartbeat of the slow movement of Beethoven's Fourth Symphony from a phonograph. Distraught, I went to the medicine chest and took an Alka-Seltzer.

Shortly after I returned to my table I realized that now in the same room above a spirited argument was in progress. It had come with phenomenal speed, this dark and stormy mood. I couldn't hear the words, due to some acoustical quirk. As with the marathon venery just completed, I could hear the action in almost baroque detail but the speech stayed muffled and indistinct, so I got the impression of shuffling angry feet, chairs wrenched around impatiently, banged doors, and voices rising in rage uttering words I was only partly able to comprehend. The male's voice was dominant—a husky and furious baritone that all but drowned out the limpid Beethoven. By contrast the voice of the female seemed plaintive, defensive, growing shrill at moments as if in fright but generally submissive with an undertone of pleading. Suddenly a glass or china object—an ashtray, a tumbler, I knew not what—crashed and shattered against a wall, and I could hear the heavy male feet stamping toward the door, which flew open in the upstairs hallway. Then the door went shut with a tremendous clatter, and I heard the man's footsteps tramping off into one of the other second-floor rooms. Finally the room was left—after these last twenty minutes of delirious activity—in what might be termed provisional silence, amid the depths of which I could hear only the soft heartsick adagio scratching on the phonograph, and the woman's broken sobs on the bed above me.

I have always been a discriminating but light eater, and never sit down to breakfast. Being also by habit a late riser, I await the joys of "brunch." After the noise subsided above, I saw that it was past noon and at the same time realized that both the fornication and the fracas had in some urgent, vicarious way made me incredibly hungry, as if I had actually partaken in whatever had taken place up there. I was so hungry that I had begun to salivate, and felt a touch of vertigo. Except for Nescafé and beer, I had not yet stocked either my cupboard or my minuscule refrigerator, so I decided to go out to lunch. During an earlier stroll through the neighborhood there had been a kosher restaurant, Herzl's, on Church Avenue which had caught my eye. I wanted to go there because I had never before tried authentic, that is to say *echt*, Jewish cuisine and also because—well, When in Flatbush . . . I said to myself. I shouldn't have bothered, for of course, this being the Sabbath, the place was closed, and I settled on another, presumably non-Orthodox restaurant further down the avenue named Sammy's, where I ordered chicken soup with matzoh balls, gefilte fish and chopped liver—these familiar to me as an offshoot of wide reading in Jewish lore—from a waiter so monumentally insolent that I thought he was putting on an act. (I hadn't then known that surliness among Jewish waiters was almost a definitive trait.) I was not particularly bothered, however. The place was crowded with people, most of them elderly, spooning their borscht and munching at potato pirogen; and a great noise of Yiddish—a venerable roar—filled the dank and redolent air with unfathomable gutturals, as of many wattled old throats gargling on chicken fat.

I felt curiously happy, very much in my element. Enjoy, enjoy, Stingo, I said to myself. Like numerous Southerners of a certain background, learning and sensibility, I have from the very beginning responded warmly to Jews, my first love having been Miriam Bookbinder, the daughter of a local ship chandler, who even at the age of six wore in her lovely hooded eyes the vaguely disconsolate, largely inscrutable mystery of her race; and then later I experienced a grander empathy with Jewish folk which, I am persuaded, is chiefly available to those Southerners shattered for years and years by rock-hard encounter with the anguish of Abraham and Moses' stupendous quest and the Psalmist's troubled hosannas and the abyssal vision of Daniel and all the other revelations, bittersweet confections, tall tales and beguiling horrors of the Protestant/Jewish Bible. In addition, it is a platitude by now that the Jew has found considerable fellowship among white Southerners because Southerners have possessed another, darker sacrificial lamb. In any case, sitting there that lunchtime at Sammy's I positively glowed in my new environment, as it dawned on me with no surprise at all that an unconscious urge to be among Jews was at least part of the reason for my migration to Brooklyn. Certainly I could not be more deep in the heart of Jewry had I just been set down in Tel Aviv. And leaving the restaurant, I even confessed to myself a liking for Manischewitz, which in fact was lousy as an accompaniment to gefilte fish but bore a syrupy resemblance to the sweet scuppernong wine I had known as a boy in Virginia.

As I wandered back to Yetta's house I was a bit upset once more by the happening in the room above me. My concern was largely selfish, for I knew that if such a thing went on too often, I would get little sleep or peace. Another part that bothered me, though, was the strange quality of the event—the jolly athletic amour so obviously and exquisitely enjoyed, yet followed by the precipitous slide into rage, weeping and discontent. Then, too, what further got my goat was the matter of who was doing it to whom. I was irked that I should be thrust into this position of lubricious curiosity, that my introduction to any of my fellow tenants should not be anything so ordinary as a "Hi" and a straightforward handshake but an episode of pornographic eavesdropping upon two strangers whose faces I had never even seen. Despite the fantasy life I have described myself as having led so far during the course of my stay in the metropolis, I am not by nature a snoop; but the very proximity of the two lovers—after all, they had nearly come down on my head—made it impossible for me to avoid trying to discover their identity, and at the earliest feasible moment.

My problem was almost immediately solved when I met my first of Yetta's tenants, who was standing in the downstairs hallway, going through the mail which the postman had left on a table near the entrance. He was an amorphously fleshed, slope-shouldered, rather ovoid-looking young man of about twenty-eight, with kinky brick-colored hair and that sullen brusqueness of manner of the New York indigene. During my first days in the city I thought it a manner so needlessly hostile that I was driven several times to acts of near-violence, until I came to realize that it was only one aspect of that tough carapace that urban beings draw about themselves, like an armadillo's hide. I introduced myself politely—"Stingo's the name"—while my fellow roomer thumbed through the mail, and for my pains, got the sound of steady adenoidal breathing. I felt a hot flash at the back of my neck, went numb around the lips, and wheeled about toward my room.

Then I heard him say, "This yours?" And as I turned he was holding up a letter. I could tell from the handwriting that it was from my father.

"Thanks," I murmured in rage, grabbing the letter.

"You mind savin' me the stamp?" he said. "I collect commemoratives." He essayed something in the nature of a grin, not expansive but recognizably human. I made a humming noise and gave him a vaguely positive look.

"I'm Fink," he said, "Morris Fink. I more or less take care of this place, especially when Yetta's away, like she is this weekend. She went to visit her daughter in Canarsie." He nodded in the direction of my door. "I see you got to live in the crater."

"The crater?" I said.

"I lived there up until a week ago. When I moved out that's how you got to move in. I called it the crater because it was like livin' in a bomb crater with all that humpin' they were doin' in that room up above."

There had been suddenly established a bond between Morris and me, and I relaxed, filled with inquisitive zeal. "How did you put up with it, for God's sake? And tell me—who the hell *are* they?"

"It's not so bad if you get them to move the bed. They do that—move it over toward the wall—and you can barely hear them humpin'. Then it's over the bathroom. I got them to do that. Or *him*, that is. I got him to move it even though it's her room. I *insisted.* I said Yetta would throw them both out if he didn't, so he finally agreed. Now I guess he's moved it back toward the window. He said something about it bein' cooler there." He paused to accept one of the cigarettes I had offered him. "What you should do is ask him to move the bed back toward the wall again."

"I *can't* do that," I put in, "I just can't go up to some guy, some *stranger,* and say—well, you know what I'd have to say to him. It would be terribly embarrassing. I just couldn't. And which ones are they, anyway?"

"I'll tell him if you'd like," said Morris, with an air of assurance that I found appealing. "I'll *make* him do it. Yetta can't stand it around here if people annoy each other. That Landau is a weird one, all right, and he might give me some trouble, but he'll move the bed, don't you worry. He doesn't want to get thrown out on his ass."

So it was Nathan Landau, the first name on my list, who I realized was the master of this setup; then who was his partner in all that din, sin and confusion? "And the gal?" I inquired. "Miss Grossman?"

"No. Grossman's a pig. It's the Polish broad, Sophie. Sophie Z., I call her. Her last name, it's impossible to pronounce. But she's some dish, that Sophie."

I was aware once more of the silence of the house, the eerie impression I was to get from time to time that summer of a dwelling far removed from the city streets, of a place remote, isolated, almost bucolic. Children called from the park across the way and I heard a single car pass by slowly, its sound unhurried, inoffensive. I simply could not believe I was living in Brooklyn. "Where is everybody?" I asked.

"Well, let me tell you something," said Morris. "Except maybe for Nathan, nobody in this joint has enough money to really *do* anything. Like go to New York and dance at the Rainbow Room or anything fancy like that. But on Saturday afternoon they all clear out of here. They all go *somewhere.* For instance, the Grossman pig—boy, is she some fuckin' *yenta*—Grossman goes to visit her mother out in Islip. Ditto Astrid. That's Astrid Weinstein, lives right there across the hall from you. She's a nurse at Kings County Hospital like Grossman, only she's no pig. A nice kid, but I would say not exactly a knockout. Plain. A dog, really. But not a pig."

My heart sank. "And she goes to see her mother, too?" I said with scant interest.

"Yeah, she goes to see her mother, only in New York. I can somehow tell you're not Jewish, so let me tell you something about Jewish people. They very often have to go see their mothers. It's a trait."

"I see," I said. "And the others? Where have they gone?"

"Muskatblit—you'll see him, he's big and fat and a rabbinical student—Moishe goes to see his mother *and* his father, somewhere in Jersey. Only he can't travel on the Sabbath, so he leaves here Friday night. He's a big movie fiend, so Sunday he spends all day in New York goin' to four or five movies. Then he gets back here late Sunday night half blind from goin' to all those movies."

"And, ah—Sophie and Nathan? Where do they go? And what do they do, by the way, aside from—" I was on the verge of an obvious jest but held my tongue, a point lost in any case, since Morris, so garrulous, so fluently and freely informative, had anticipated what I had been wondering and was rapidly filling me in.

"Nathan's got an education, he's a biologist. He works in a laboratory near Borough Hall where they make medicine and drugs and things like that. Sophie Z., I don't know what she does exactly. I heard she's some kind of receptionist for a Polish doctor who's got a whole lot of Polish clients. Naturally, she speaks Polish like a native. Anyway, Nathan and Sophie are beach nuts. When the weather's good, like now, they go to Coney Island—sometimes Jones Beach. Then they come back here." He paused and made what seemed to approximate a leer. "They come back here and hump and fight. Boy, do they fight! Then they go out to dinner. They're very big on good eating. That Nathan, he makes good money, but he's a weird one, all right. Weird. Real weird. Like, I think he needs psychiatric consultation."

A phone rang, and Morris let it ring. It was a pay phone attached to the wall, and its ring seemed exceptionally loud, until I realized that it must have been adjusted in such a way as to be heard all over the house. "I don't answer it when nobody's here," Morris said. "I can't stand that miserable fuckin' phone, all those messages. 'Is Lillian there? This is her mother. Tell her she forgot the precious gift her Uncle Bennie brought her.' Yatata yatata. The pig. Or, 'This is the father of Moishe Muskatblit. He's not in? Tell him his cousin Max got run down by a truck in Hackensack.' Yatata yatata all day long. I can't stand that telephone."

I told Morris that I would see him again, and after a few more pleasantries, retired to my room's nursery-pink and the disquietude that it had begun to cause me. I sat down at my table. The first page of the legal pad, its blankness still intimidating, yawned in front of me like a yellowish glimpse of eternity. How in God's name would I ever be able to write a novel? I mused, chewing on a Venus Velvet. I opened the letter from my father. I always looked forward to these letters, feeling fortunate to have this Southern Lord Chesterfield as an advisor, who so delighted me with his old-fashioned disquisitions upon pride and avarice and ambition, bigotry, political skulduggery, venereal excess and other mortal sins and dangers. Sententious he might occasionally be, but never pompous, never preacherish in tone, and I relished both the letters' complexity of thought and feeling and their simple eloquence; whenever I finished one I was usually close to tears, or doubled over with laughter, and they almost always set me immediately to rereading passages in the Bible, from which my father had derived many of his prose cadences and much of his wisdom. Today, though, my attention was first caught by a newspaper clipping which fluttered out from the folds of the letter. The headline of the clipping, which was from the local gazette in Virginia, so stunned and horrified me that I momentarily lost my breath and saw tiny pinpoints of light before my eyes.

It announced the death by suicide, at the age of twenty-two, of a beautiful girl with whom I had been hopelessly in love during several of the rocky years of my early adolescence. Her name was Maria (rhyming in the Southern fashion with "pariah") Hunt, and at fifteen I had been so feverish in my infatuation for her that it seems in retrospect a small-scale madness. Talk about your lovesick fool, how I exemplified such a wretch! Maria Hunt! For if in the 1940s, long before the dawn of our liberation, the ancient chivalry still prevailed and the plastic June Allysons of a boy's dreams were demigoddesses with whom one might at most, to use the sociologists' odious idiom, "pet to climax," I carried self-abnegation to its mad limit and with my beloved Maria did not even try to cop a feel, as they used to say in those days. Indeed, I did not do so much as place a kiss upon her heartlessly appetizing lips. This is not on the other hand to define our relationship as Platonic, for in my understanding of that word there is an element of the cerebral, and Maria was not at all bright. To which it must be added that in those days of the forty-eight states, when in terms of the quality of public education Harry Byrd's Virginia was generally listed forty-ninth—after Arkansas, Mississippi and even Puerto Rico—the intellectual tang of the colloquy of two fifteen-year-olds is perhaps best left to the imagination. Never was ordinary conversation cleft by such hiatuses, such prolonged and unembarrassed moments of ruminant non-speech. Nonetheless, I had passionately but chastely adored her, adored her for such a simple-minded reason as that she was beautiful enough to wreck the heart, and now I discovered that she was dead. Maria Hunt was *dead!*

The advent of the Second World War and my involvement in it had caused Maria to fade out of my life, but she had been many times since in my wistful thoughts. She had killed herself by leaping from the window of a building, and I found to my astonishment that this had occurred only a few weeks before, in Manhattan. I later learned that she had lived around the corner from me, on Sixth Avenue. It was a sign of the city's inhuman vastness that we had both dwelt for months in an area as compact as Greenwich Village without ever having encountered each other. With a wrench of pain so intense that it was almost like remorse, I pondered whether I might not have been able to save her, to prevent her from taking such a terrible course, had I only known of her existence in the city, and her whereabouts. Reading the article over and over again, I verged very close to a state of real upheaval, and found myself moaning aloud at this senseless story of young despair and loss. *Why* did she do it? One of the most poignant aspects of the account was that her body had for complicated and obscure reasons gone unidentified, had been buried in a pauper's grave, and only after a matter of weeks had been disinterred and sent back for final burial in Virginia. I was sickened, nearly broken up by the awful tale—so much so that I abandoned for the rest of the day any idea of work, and recklessly sought a kind of solace in the beer I had stored in the refrigerator. Later I read this passage from my father's letter:

> In re the enclosed item, son, I naturally thought you would be more than interested, inasmuch as I remember how so terribly "keen" you were on young Maria Hunt six or seven years ago. I used to recall with great amusement how you would blush like a tomato at the mere mention of her name, now I can only reflect on that time with the greatest sorrow. We question the good Lord's way in such a matter but always to no avail. As you certainly know, Maria Hunt came from a tragic household, Martin Hunt a near-alcoholic and always at loose ends, while Beatrice I'm afraid was pretty unremitting and cruel in her moral demands upon people, especially I am told Maria. One thing seems certain, and that is that there was a great deal of unresolved guilt and hatred pervading that sad home. I know you will be affected by this news. Maria was, I remember, a truly lustrous young beauty, which makes it all the worse. Take some comfort from the fact that such beauty was with us for a time . . .

I brooded over Maria all afternoon, until the shadows lengthened beneath the trees around the park and the children fled homeward, leaving the paths that crisscrossed the Parade Grounds deserted and still. Finally I felt woozy from the beer, my mouth was raw and dry from too many cigarettes, and I lay down on my bed. I soon fell into a heavy sleep that was more than ordinarily invaded by dreams. One of the dreams besieged me, nearly ruined me. Following several pointless little extravaganzas, a ghastly but brief nightmare, and an expertly constructed one-act play, I was overtaken by the most ferociously erotic hallucination I had ever experienced. For now in some sunlit and serene pasture of the Tidewater, a secluded place hemmed around by undulant oak trees, my departed Maria was standing before me, with the abandon of a strumpet stripping down to the flesh—she who had never removed in my presence so much as her bobbysocks. Naked, peach-ripe, chestnut hair flowing across her creamy breasts, desirable beyond utterance, she approached me where I lay stiff as a dagger, importuning me with words delectably raunchy and lewd. "Stingo," she murmured. "Oh, Stingo, fuck me." A faint mist of perspiration clung to her skin like aphrodisia, little blisters of sweat adorned the dark hair of her mound. She wiggled toward me, a wanton nymph with moist and parted mouth, and now bending down over my bare belly, crooning her glorious obscenities, prepared to take between those lips unkissed by my own the bone-rigid stalk of my passion. Then the film jammed in the projector. I woke up in dire distress, staring at a pink ceiling stained with the shadows of the oncoming night, and let out a primeval groan—more nearly a howl—wrenched from the nethermost dungeons of my soul.

But then I felt another nail amplify my crucifixion: they were going at it again upstairs on the accursed mattress. "Stop it!" I roared at the ceiling, and with my forefingers plugged up my ears. *Sophie and Nathan!* I thought. Fucking Jewish rabbits! Although they might have let up for a brief time, when I listened once more they were still in action—no riotous sport this go-round, however, and no cries or arias, only the bedsprings making a decorous rhythmical twanging—laconic, measured, almost elderly. I did not care that they had slowed down their pace. I hurried—truly raced—outside into the dusk and walked distractedly around the perimeter of the park. Then I began to stroll more slowly along, growing reflective. Walking underneath the trees, I began seriously to wonder if I had not made a grave mistake in coming to Brooklyn. It really was not my element, after all. There was something subtly and inexplicably wrong, and had I been able to use a turn of phrase current some years later, I might have said that Yetta's house gave off bad vibrations. I was still shaken by that unmerciful, lascivious dream. By their very nature dreams are, of course, difficult of access through memory, but a few are forever imprinted on the brain.

With me the most memorable of dreams, the ones that have achieved that haunting reality so intense as to be seemingly bound up in the metaphysical, have dealt with either sex or death. Thus Maria Hunt. No dream had produced in me that lasting reverberation since the morning nearly eight years before, soon after my mother's burial, when, struggling up from the seaweed-depths of a nightmare, I dreamed I peered out the window of the room at home in which I was still sleeping and caught sight of the open coffin down in the windswept, drenched garden, then saw my mother's shrunken, cancer-ravaged face twist toward me in the satin vault and gaze at me beseechingly through eyes filmed over with indescribable torture.

I turned back toward the house. I thought I would go and sit down and reply to my father's letter. I wanted to ask him to tell me in greater detail the circumstances of Maria's death—probably not knowing at the time, however, that my subconscious was already beginning to grapple with that death as the germinal idea for the novel so lamentably hanging fire on my writing table. But I did not write any such letter that evening. Because when I returned to the house I encountered Sophie in the flesh for the first time and fell, if not instantaneously, then swiftly and fathomlessly in love with her. It was a love which, as time wore on that summer, I realized had many reasons for laying claim to my existence. But I must confess that at first, certainly one of them was her distant but real resemblance to Maria Hunt. And what is still ineffaceable about my first glimpse of her is not simply the lovely simulacrum she seemed to me of the dead girl but the despair on her face worn as Maria surely must have worn it, along with the premonitory, grieving shadows of someone hurtling headlong toward death.

At the house Sophie and Nathan were embroiled in combat just outside the door of my room. I heard their voices clear on the summer night, and saw them battling in the hallway as I walked up the front steps.

"Don't give me any of *that,* you hear," I heard him yell.

"You're a liar! You're a miserable lying cunt, do you hear me? A *cunt!*"

"You're a cunt too," I heard her throw back at him. "Yes, you're a cunt, I think." Her tone lacked aggressiveness.

"I am *not* a cunt," he roared. "I *can't* be a cunt, you dumb fucking Polack. When are you going to learn to *speak* the *language?* A *prick* I might be, but not a *cunt,* you moron. Don't you ever call me that again, you hear? Not that you'll ever get a chance."

"You called *me* that!"

"But that's what you *are,* you moron—a two-timing, double-crossing cunt! Spreading that twat of yours for a cheap, chiseling quack doctor. Oh *God!*" he howled, and his voice rose in wild uncontained rage. "Let me out of here before I *murder* you—you *whore!* You were *born* a whore and you'll *die* a whore!"

"Nathan, *listen* . . ." I heard her plead. And now as I approached closer to the front door I saw the two of them pressed together, defined in obscure relief against the pink hallway where a dangling forty-watt lightbulb, nearly engulfed by a cloud of fluttering moths, cast its palsied chiaroscuro. Dominating the scene by his height and force was Nathan: broad-shouldered, powerful-looking, crowned with a shock of hair swarthy as a Sioux's, he resembled a more attenuated and frenetic John Garfield, with Garfield's handsome, crookedly agreeable face—theoretically agreeable, I should say, for now the face was murky with passion and rage, was quite emphatically anything but agreeable, suffused as it was with such an obvious eagerness for violence. He wore a light sweater and slacks and appeared to be in his late twenties. He held Sophie's arm tight in his grasp, and she flinched before his onslaught like a rosebud quivering in a windstorm. Sophie I could barely see in the dismal light. I was able to discern only her disheveled mane of straw-colored hair and, behind Nathan's shoulder, about a third of her face. This included a frightened eyebrow, a small mole, a hazel eye, and a broad, lovely swerve of Slavic cheekbone across which a single tear rolled like a drop of quicksilver. She had begun to sob like a bereft child. "Nathan, you must listen, *please,"* she was saying between sobs. "Nathan! Nathan! Nathan! I'm sorry I called you that."

He thrust her arm down abruptly and drew back from her. "You fill me with *in*-fin-ite revulsion," he shouted. "Pure un-a-*dul*-ter-a-ted loathing. I'm getting out of here before I murder you!" He wheeled away from her.

"Nathan, don't go!" she implored him desperately and reached out to him with both hands. "I need you, Nathan. You need *me*." There was something plaintive, childlike in her voice, which was light in timbre, almost fragile, breaking a little in the upper register and of a faint huskiness lower down. The Polish accent overlaying it all made it charming or, I thought, would have made it so under less horrible circumstances. "Please don't go, Nathan," she cried. "We need each *other. Don't go!"*

"Need?" he retorted, turning back toward her. *"Me* need *you?* Let me tell you something"—and here he began to shake his entire outstretched hand at her, as his voice grew more outraged and unstrung—"I need you like any goddamned insufferable *disease* I can name. I need you like a case of *anthrax,* hear me. Like trichinosis! I need you like a biliary calculus. Pellagra! Encephalitis! *Bright's disease,* for Christ's sake! *Carcinoma of the fucking brain,* you fucking miserable whore! *Aaaahooooo-o-o!"* This last was a rising, wavering wail—a spine-chilling sound that mingled fury with lamentation in a way that seemed almost liturgical, like the keening of a maddened rabbi. "I need you like *death,"* he bellowed in a choked voice. *"Death!"*

Once more he turned away, and again she said, weeping, *"Please* don't go, Nathan!" Then, "Nathan, where are you going?"

He was near the door now, barely two feet away from me where I stood at the threshold, irresolute, not knowing whether to forge on toward my room or to turn and flee. *"Going?"* he shouted. "I'll tell you where I'm going—I'm going to get on the first subway train and go to Forest Hills! I'm going to borrow my brother's car and come back here and load up my things in the car. Then I'm going to clear out of this place." All of a sudden his voice diminished in volume, his manner became somewhat more collected, even casual, but his tone was dramatically, slyly threatening. "After that, maybe tomorrow, I'll tell you what I'm going to do. I'm going to sit down and write a registered letter to the Immigration Service. I'm going to tell them that *you've* got the wrong visa. I'm going to tell them that they should issue you a *whore's* visa, if they've got one. If they don't, I'm going to tell them they'd better ship you back to Poland for peddling your ass to any doctor in Brooklyn that wants a quick lay. Back to Cracow, baby!" He gave a satisfied chuckle. "Oh, baby, back to Cracow!"

He turned and plunged out the door. As he did so he brushed against me, and this caused him to whirl about again and draw up short. I could not tell whether he thought I had overheard him or not. Clearly winded, he was panting heavily and he eyed me up and down for a moment. Then I felt that he thought I had overheard, but it didn't matter. Considering his emotional state, I was surprised at his way with me, which if not exactly gracious seemed at least momentarily civil, as if I had been magnanimously excluded from the territory of his rage.

"You the new roomer Fink told me about?" he managed between breaths.

I answered in the feeblest, briefest affirmative.

"You're from the South," he said. "Morris told me you were from the South. Said your name's Stingo. Yetta needs a Southerner in her house to fit in with all the other funnies." He sent a dark glance back toward Sophie, then looked at me and said, "Too bad I won't be around for a lively conversation, but I'm getting out of here. It would have been nice to talk with you." And here his tone became faintly ominous, the forced civility tapering off into the baldest sarcasm I had heard in a long time. "We'd have had great fun, shootin' the shit, you and I. We could have talked about sports. I mean *Southern* sports. Like lynching niggers—or *coons,* I think you call them down there. Or *culture*. We could have talked about Southern culture, and maybe could have sat around here at old Yetta's listening to hillbilly records. You know, Gene Autry, Roy Acuff and all those other standard bearers of classical Southern culture." He had been scowling as he spoke, but now a smile parted his dark, troubled face and before I knew it he had reached out and clasped my unwilling hand in a firm handshake. "Ah well, that's what could have been. Too bad. Old Nathan's got to hit the road. Maybe in another life, Cracker, we'll get together. So long, Cracker! See you in another life."

And then, before my lips could part to utter protest or counter with an outraged sally or insult, Nathan had turned and pounded down the steps to the sidewalk, where his hard leather heels made a demonic *clack-clack-clack* as the sound receded, then faded out beneath the darkening trees, in the direction of the subway.

It is a commonplace that small cataclysms—an automobile accident, a stalled elevator, a violent assault witnessed by others—bring out an unnatural communicativeness among total strangers. After Nathan had disappeared into the night, I approached Sophie without hesitation. I had no idea what I was about to say—doubtless some gauche words of comfort—but it was she who spoke first, behind hands clenched to a tear-stained face. "It is so *unfair* of him," she sobbed. "Oh, I love him so!"

I did the clumsy thing they often do in movies at such a point, when dialogue is a problem. I pulled a handkerchief from my pocket and silently gave it to her. She took it readily and began to mop at her eyes. "Oh, I love him so much!" she exclaimed. "So much! So much! I'll *die* without him."

"There, there," I said, or something equally awful.

Her eyes implored me—I whom she had never before laid eyes on—with the despairing plea of an innocent prisoner protesting her virtue before the bar. *I'm no whore, your honor,* she seemed to be trying to say. I was flabbergasted both by her candor and her passion. "It is so unfair of him," she said again. "To say *that!* He is the only man I have ever made love to, except my husband. And my husband's dead!" And she was shaken by more sobs, and more tears poured forth, turning my handkerchief into a wet little monogrammed sponge. Her nose was swollen with grief and the pink tear stains marred her extraordinary beauty, but not so much that the beauty itself (including the mole, felicitously placed near the left eye, like a tiny satellite) failed to melt me on the spot—a distinct feeling of liquefaction emanating not from the heart's region but, amazingly, from that of the stomach, which began to churn as if in revolt from a prolonged fast. I hungered so deeply to put my arms around her, to soothe her, that it became pure discomfort, but a cluster of oddly assorted inhibitions caused me to hold back. Also, I would be a liar if I did not confess that through all this there rapidly expanded in my mind a strictly self-serving scheme, which was that somehow, God granting me the luck and strength, I would take over this flaxen Polish treasure where Nathan, the thankless swine, had left off.

Then a tingling sensation in the small of my back made me realize that Nathan was behind us again, standing on the front steps. I wheeled about. He had managed to return in phantasmal silence and now glared at the two of us with a malevolent gleam, leaning forward with one arm outstretched against the frame of the door. "And one last thing," he said to Sophie in a flat hard voice. "One other last thing, whore. The *records.* The record albums. The Beethoven. The Handel. The Mozart. *All* of them. I don't want to have to lay eyes on you again. So take the records—take the records out of *your* room and put them in *my* room, on the chair by the door. The Brahms you can keep only because Blackstock gave it to you. Keep it, see? The rest of them I want, so make sure you put them where I tell you. If you *don't,* when I come back here to pack up I'll break your arms, both of them." After a pause, he inhaled deeply and whispered, "So help me God, I'll *break your fucking arms!*"

Then this time he was gone for good, moving in loose-limbed strides back to the sidewalk and quickly losing himself in the darkness.

Having no more tears to shed for the moment, Sophie slowly composed herself. "Thank you, you were kind," she said to me softly, in the stuffed-head-cold tones of one who has wept copiously and long. She stretched out her hand and pressed into my own the handkerchief, a soggy wad. As she did so I saw for the first time the number tattooed on the suntanned, lightly freckled skin of her forearm—a purple number of at least five digits, too small to read in this light but graven, I could tell, with exactitude and craft. To the melting love in my stomach was added a sudden ache, and with an involuntary motion that was quite inexplicable (for one brought up to mind where he put his hands) I gently grasped her wrist, looking more closely at the tattoo. Even at that instant I knew my curiosity might be offensive, but I couldn't help myself.

"Where were you?" I said.

She spoke a fibrous name in Polish, which I understood, barely, to be "Oświęcim." Then she said, "I was there for a long time. *Longtemps.*" She paused. *"Vous voyez . . ."* Another pause. "Do you speak French?" she said. "My English is very bad."

"Un peu," I replied, grossly exaggerating my facility. "It's a little rusty." Which meant that I had next to none.

"Rusty? What is rusty?"

"Sale," I tried recklessly.

"Dirty French?" she said, with the faintest whisper of a smile. After a moment she asked, *"Sprechen Sie Deutsch?"* Which did not even draw from me a *"Nein."*

"Oh, forget it," I said. "You speak good English." Then after a moment's silence I said, "That Nathan! I've never seen anything like him in my life. I know it's not my business, but—but he must be *nuts!* How can he talk like that to *anyone?* If you ask me, you're well rid of him."

She shut her eyes tightly and pursed her lips in pain, as if in recollection of all that had just transpired. "Oh, he's right about so much," she whispered. "Not about I wasn't faithful. I don't mean that. I have been faithful to him always. But other things. When he said I didn't dress right. Or when he said I was a sloppy Pole and didn't clean up. Then he called me a dirty Polack, and I knew that I . . . yes, deserved it. Or when he took me to these nice restaurants and I always keeped . . ." She questioned me with her gaze.

"Kept," I said. Without overdoing it, I will from time to time have to try to duplicate the delicious inaccuracies of Sophie's English. Her command was certainly more than adequate and—for me, anyway—actually enhanced by her small stumbles in the thickets of syntax, especially upon the snags of our grisly irregular verbs. "Kept what?" I asked.

"Kept the *carte,* the menu I mean. I so often would keep the menu, put it in my bag for a souvenir. He said a menu cost money, that I was stealing. He was right about that, you know."

"Taking a menu doesn't exactly seem like grand larceny to me, for Christ's sake," I said. "Look, again I know it's none of my business, but—"

Clearly determined to resist my attempts to help restore her self-esteem, she interrupted me, saying, "No, I know it was wrong. What he said was true, I done so many things that were wrong. I deserved it, that he leave me. But I was *never* unfaithful to him. Never! Oh, I'll just die now, without him! What am I going to do? What am I going to do?"

For a moment I was afraid that she might soar off on another little mad fugue of grief, but she gave only a single hoarse gulping sob, like some final punctuation mark, then turned away from me. "You've been kind," she said. "Now I must go up to my room."

As she went slowly up the stairs I took a good look at her body in its clinging silk summer dress. While it was a beautiful body, with all the right prominences, curves, continuities and symmetries, there was something a little strange about it—nothing visibly missing and not so much deficient as reassembled. And that was precisely *it,* I could see. The odd quality proclaimed itself through the skin. It possessed the sickish plasticity (at the back of her arms it was especially noticeable) of one who has suffered severe emaciation and whose flesh is even now in the last stages of being restored. Also, I felt that underneath that healthy suntan there lingered the sallowness of a body not wholly rescued from a terrible crisis. But none of these at all diminished a kind of wonderfully negligent sexuality having to do at that moment, at least, with the casual but forthright way her pelvis moved and with her truly sumptuous rear end. Despite past famine, her behind was as perfectly formed as some fantastic prize-winning pear; it vibrated with magical eloquence, and from this angle it so stirred my depths that I mentally pledged to the Presbyterian orphanages of Virginia a quarter of my future earnings as a writer in exchange for that bare ass's brief lodging—thirty seconds would do—within the compass of my cupped, supplicant palms. Old Stingo, I mused as she climbed upward, there must be some perversity in this dorsal fixation. Then as she reached the top of the stairs she turned, looking down, and smiled the saddest smile imaginable. "I hope I haven't annoyed you with my problems," she said. "I am so sorry." And she moved toward her room and said, "Good night."

So then, from the only comfortable chair in my room, where I sat reading Aristophanes that night, I was able to see a section of the upstairs hallway through my partly open door. Once around midevening I saw Sophie take to his room the record albums which Nathan had commanded her to return to him. On her way back I could see that again she was crying. How could she go on so? Where did those tears come from? Later she played over and over on the phonograph the final movement of that First Symphony of Brahms which he so big-heartedly had allowed her to keep. It must have been her only album now. All evening that music filtered down through the paper-thin ceiling, the lordly and tragic French horn mingling in my head with the flute's antiphonal, piercing birdcall to fill my spirit with a sadness and nostalgia almost more intense than any I had ever felt before. I thought of the moment of that music's creation. It was music that, among other things, spoke of a Europe of a halcyon time, bathed in the soft umber glow of serene twilights—of children in pigtails and pinafores bobbing along in dogcarts, of excursions in the glades of the Wiener Wald and strong Bavarian beer, of ladies from Grenoble with parasols strolling the glittering rims of glaciers in the high Alps, and balloon voyages, of gaiety, of vertiginous waltzes, of Moselle wine, of Johannes Brahms himself, with beard and black cigar, contemplating his titanic chords beneath the leafless, autumnal beech trees of the Hofgarten. It was a Europe of almost inconceivable sweetness—a Europe that Sophie, drowning in her sorrow above me, could never have known.

When I went to bed the music was still playing. And when each of the scratchy shellac records reached its end, allowing me in the interval before the next to hear Sophie's inconsolable weeping, I tossed and turned and wondered again how one mortal human being could be the vessel to contain such grief. It seemed nearly impossible that Nathan could inspire this raw, devastating woe. But clearly he had done so, and this posed for me a problem. For if, as I have said, I felt myself slipping already into that sick and unfortified situation known as love, wasn't it foolish of me to expect to win the affection, much less to share the bed, of one so dislodgeably attached to the memory of her lover? There was something actually indecent about the idea, like laying siege to a recently bereaved widow. To be sure, Nathan was out of the way, but wasn't it vain of me to expect to fill the vacuum? For one thing, I remembered I had so little money. Even if I broke through the barrier of her grief, how could I expect to woo this ex-starveling with her taste for fancy restaurants and expensive phonograph records?

Finally the music stopped and she stopped weeping too, while the restless creak of springs told me she had gone to bed. I lay there for a long time awake, listening to the soft night-sounds of Brooklyn—a far-off howling dog, a passing car, a burst of gentle laughter from a woman and a man at the edge of the park. I thought of Virginia, of home. I drifted off to sleep, but slept uneasily, indeed chaotically, once waking in the unfamiliar darkness to find myself very close to some droll phallic penetration—through folds, or a hem, or a damp wrinkle—of my displaced pillow. Then again I fell asleep, only to wake with a start just before dawn, in the dead silence of the hour, with pounding heart and an icy chill staring straight up at my ceiling above which Sophie slept, understanding with a dreamer's fierce clarity that she was doomed.

Three

"Stingo! Oh, Stingo!" Late that same morning—a sunny June Sunday—I heard their voices on the other side of the door, rousing me from sleep. Nathan's voice, then Sophie's: "Stingo, wake up. Wake up, Stingo!" The door itself, while not locked, was secured by a night chain, and from where I lay against the pillow I could see Nathan's beaming face as he peered at me through the wide crack in the door. "Rise and shine," said the voice. "Hit the deck, kid. Up and at 'em, boy. We're going to Coney Island!" And behind him I heard Sophie, in clear piping echo of Nathan: "Rise and shine! Up and at 'em!" Her command was followed by a silvery little giggle, and now Nathan began to rattle the door and the chain. "Come on, Cracker, hit the deck! You can't lie there all day snoozin' like some ole hound dog down South." His voice took on the syrupy synthetic tones of deepest Dixieland—an accent, though, to my sleep-drugged but responsive ears, that was the product of remarkably deft mimicry. "Stir them lazy bones, honeychile," he drawled in the munchiest cornpone. "Put on yo' bathin' *costume*. We gonna hab old Pompey hitch up the old coach-an'-foah and hab us a little picnic outin' down by the seashoah!"

I was—to put it in restrained terms—somewhat less than exhilarated by all this. His snarling insult of the night before, and his general mistreatment of Sophie, had trespassed on my dreams all night in various allusive masks and guises, and now to awake to behold the same midcentury urban face intoning these hokey ante-bellum lyrics was simply more than I could tolerate. I leaped straight out of the bedclothes and hurled myself at the door. "Get out of here!" I yelled. "Leave me alone!"

I tried to slam the door in Nathan's face, but he had one foot firmly entrenched in the crack. "Get out!" I shouted again. "You have your goddamned nerve, doing this. Get your goddamned foot out of that door and leave me the fuck alone!"

"Stingo, *Stingo*," the voice went on in lulling cadences, having reverted to the Brooklyn style. "Stingo, take it easy. No offense meant, kid. Come on, open up. Let's have a coffee together and make up and be pals."

"I don't *want* to be pals with you!" I howled at Nathan. I burst into a fit of coughing. Half strangling on the goo and crud of threescore daily Camels, I was surprised that I was coherent at all. As I hacked away, oddly embarrassed at the croupy noise I was making, I began to suffer further slow surprise—and not a little distress—over the fact that the atrocious Nathan had materialized like some wicked genie at Sophie's side, and seemed once more to be in possession and command. For at least a minute, perhaps longer, I shuddered and heaved in the throes of a pulmonary spasm, having had in the meantime to endure the humiliation of submitting to Nathan in the role of medical savant: "You've got a regular smoker's cough there, Cracker. You also have the haggard, drawn face of a person hooked on nicotine. Look at me for a second, Cracker, look me straight in the eye."

I glared at him through leisurely narrowing pupils fogged over with rage and loathing. "Don't call me—" I began, but the words were cut off by another racking cough.

"Haggard, that's the word," Nathan went on. "Too bad, for such a nice-looking guy. The haggard look comes from being slowly deprived of oxygen. You should cut out smoking, Cracker. It causes cancer of the lung. Also lousy on the heart." (In 1947, it may be remembered, the truly pernicious effect of cigarette smoking on the health was barely surmised even by medical men, and word of its potential erosive damage, when uttered at all, was greeted by sophisticates with amused skepticism. It was an old wives' tale of the same category as that in which it was imputed to masturbation such scourges as acne, or warts, or madness. Therefore, although Nathan's remark was doubly infuriating at the time, piling, as I thought, imbecility on plain viciousness, I realize now how weirdly prescient it really was, how typical it was of that erratic, daft, tormented, but keenly honed and magisterial intelligence I was to get to know and find myself too often pitted against. Fifteen years later, while in the toils of a successful battle with my addiction to cigarettes, I would recall Nathan's admonition—for some reason especially that word *haggard*—like a voice from the grave.) Now, however, his words were an invitation to manslaughter.

"Don't call me Cracker!" I cried, recovering my voice. "I'm a Phi Beta Kappa from Duke University. I don't have to take your rotten insults. Now you get your foot out of that door and leave me alone!" I struggled vainly to dislodge his shoe from the crack. "And I don't need any cheap advice about cigarettes," I rasped through the clogged and inflamed flues of my larynx.

Then Nathan underwent a remarkable transformation. His manner suddenly became apologetic, civilized, almost contrite. "All right, Stingo, I'm sorry," he said. "I'm sorry, I really am. I didn't meant to hurt your feelings. Forgive me, will you? I won't use that word again. Sophie and I just wanted to extend a little friendly welcome on a beautiful summer day." It was positively breath-taking, this swift change in him, and I might have felt that he was simply indulging in another form of leaden sarcasm had my instincts not told me that he was sincere. In fact, I sensed he was suffering a rather painful overreaction, as people sometimes do when after thoughtlessly teasing a child they realize they have caused real anguish. But I was not to be moved.

"Scram," I said flatly and firmly. "I want to be alone."

"I'm *sorry,* old pal, I really am. I was just kidding a little with that Cracker bit. I really didn't mean to offend you."

"No, Nathan really didn't mean to offend you," Sophie chimed in. She moved from behind Nathan to a spot where I could see her clearly. And something about her once more tugged away at my heart. Unlike the portrait of misery she had presented the night before, she was now plainly flushed with high spirits and joy at Nathan's miraculous return. It was possible almost to feel the force of her happiness; it flowed from her body in visible little glints and tremors—in the sparkle of her eyes, and in her animated lips, and in the pink exultant glow that colored her cheeks like rouge. This happiness, together with the look of appeal on that radiant face, was something that even in my disheveled morning state I found altogether seductive—no, irresistible. "Please, Stingo," she pleaded, "Nathan didn't mean to offend you, to hurt your feelings. We just wanted to make friends and take you out on a beautiful summer day. Please. *Please* come with us!"

Nathan relaxed—I felt his foot move away from the crack—and I relaxed, not without a severe pang, however, at the sight of him as he suddenly grabbed Sophie around the waist and commenced to nuzzle her cheek. With the lazy appetite of a calf mooning over a salt lick, he smeared his sizable nose against her face, which caused her to emit a gay burbling laugh, like the fragment of a carol, and when he flicked at her earlobe with the pink tip of his tongue she gave the most faithful imitation of a cat's electric purr I had ever seen or heard. It was a dumfounding tableau. Only brief hours before, he was ready to slice her throat.

Sophie pulled the trick. I was helpless in the face of her plea, and mumbled a grudging "Well, okay." Then just as I was at the point of unfastening the chain and letting them in, I changed my mind. "Screw off," I said to Nathan, "you owe me an apology."

"I *apologized,*" he replied. His voice was deferential. "I *said* I wouldn't call you Cracker any more."

"Not just that," I retorted. "The bit about lynching and all that crap. About the South. It's an *insult.* Suppose I told you that somebody with a name like Landau couldn't be anything but a fat, hook-nosed, miserly pawnbroker out to cheat trusting Gentiles. It'd make *you* mad. It works both ways, these slurs. You owe me another apology." I realized I had become a little pompous, but I was adamant.

"Okay, I'm sorry for that *too,*" he said expansively,

warmly. "I know I was off base there. Let's forget it, okay? I beg your pardon, honestly. But we're serious about taking you on a little outing today. Look, why don't we leave it like this? It's early yet. Why don't you take your time and get dressed and then come upstairs to Sophie's room. We'll all have a beer or coffee or something. Then we'll go to Coney Island. We'll have lunch in a great seafood restaurant I know down there, and then we'll go to the beach. I've got a good friend who makes extra money Sundays working as a lifeguard. He lets us lie on a special restricted part of the beach where there aren't any people to kick sand in your face. So come on."

Sulking rather obviously, I said, "I'll think about it."

"Ah, be a sport, come on!"

"All right," I said, "I'll come." To which I added a tepid "Thanks."

While I shaved and slicked myself up, I reflected with puzzlement on this odd turn of events. What devious motive, I wondered, caused such a good-will gesture? Could it be that Sophie had urged Nathan toward this cordial move, perhaps to get him to make up for his nastiness of the night before? Or was he simply out to obtain something else? I knew the ways of New York well enough by now to at least give passing credence to the idea that Nathan might just be some sort of con man, out to hustle up something as commonplace and as obvious as money. (This prompted me to check the condition of the slightly more than four hundred dollars I had secreted at the back of the medicine chest, in a box meant for Johnson & Johnson gauze bandages. The loot, in tens and twenties, was intact, causing me as usual to whisper a loving little threnody to my spectral patron Artiste, moldering to dust these many years in Georgia.) But that seemed an unlikely suspicion, after Morris Fink's observation about Nathan's singular affluence. Nonetheless, all these possibilities floated about in my head as I prepared with some misgivings to join Sophie and Nathan. I really felt I ought to stay and try to work, try to set some words down on the yawning yellow page, even if they be inane and random jottings. But Sophie and Nathan had quite simply laid siege to my imagination. What I really wondered about was the smoochy détente between the two of them, reestablished short hours after the most harrowing scene of lovers' strife I could imagine this side of a low-grade Italian opera. Then I considered the fact that they both simply might be crazy, or outcast like Paolo and Francesca, caught up in some weird, shared perdition.

Morris Fink was informative as usual, if not particularly illuminating, when I ran into him in the hallway just as I was leaving my room. While we were exchanging banalities I became for the first time aware of a church bell chiming, far-off but distinct, in the direction of Flatbush Avenue. At once poignant and reminiscent of Southern Sundays, it also unnerved me a little, since I had the firm impression that synagogues did not come equipped with belfries. Very briefly I closed my eyes as the chimes descended on the stillness, thinking of a homely brick church in a Tidewater town, piety and Sabbath hush, the dewy little Christian lambs with flower-stalk legs trouping to the Presbyterian tabernacle with their Hebrew history books and Judaical catechisms. When I opened my eyes Morris was explaining, "No, that's no synagogue. That's the Dutch Reformed church up at Church Avenue and Flatbush. They only ring it on Sundays. I go by there sometime when they got a service going. Or Sunday School. They sing their fuckin' heads off. 'Jesus Loves Me.' Shit like that. Those Dutch Reformed broads are something. A lot of them look like they need a blood transfusion . . . Or a hot meat injection." He gave a lewd snort. "The cemetery's nice, though. In the summer it's cool in there. Some of these wild Jewish kids go in there at night and get laid."

"Well, Brooklyn's got a little bit of everything, hasn't it?" I said.

"Yeah. All religions. Jewish, Irish, Italian, Dutch Reformed, boogies, everything. Lots of boogies comin' in now, since the war. Williamsburg. Brownsville. Bedford-Stuyvesant, that's where they're movin' into. Fuckin' apes, I call 'em. Boy, do I hate those boogies. Apes! Aaaa-gh!" He gave a shudder, and baring his teeth, made what I took to be a simian grimace. Just as he did so, the regal, celebrant strains of Handel's *Water Music* shimmered down the stairs from Sophie's room. And very faintly from above I heard Nathan's laughter.

"I guess you got to meet Sophie and Nathan," Morris said.

I allowed that I had, in a manner of speaking, met them.

"What do you think of that Nathan? Don't he break your balls?" A sudden light glowed in the lusterless eyes, his voice became conspiratorial. "You know what I think he is? A golem, that's what. Some kind of a golem."

"Golem?" I said. "What on earth's a golem?"

"Well, I can't explain exactly. It's a Jewish . . . what do you call it?—not exactly religious, but some kind of *monster*. He's been invented, that's what, like Frankenstein, see, only he's been invented by a rabbi. He's made out of clay or some kind of shit like that, only he looks like a human. Anyway, you can't control him. I mean, sometimes he acts normal, just like a normal human. But deep down he's a runaway fuckin' *monster*. That's a golem. That's what I mean about Nathan. He acts like a fuckin' golem."

With a vague stir of recognition, I asked Morris to elaborate on his theory.

"Well, this morning early, see, I guess you were asleep, I see Sophie go into Nathan's room. My room is right across the hall and I can see everything. It's about seven-thirty or eight. I heard them fightin' last night, so I know that Nathan's gone. Now guess what I see next? This is what I see. Sophie's cryin', softly, but still cryin' her head off. When she goes into Nathan's room she leaves the door open and lays down. But guess where she lays down? On the bed? No! On the fuckin' *floor!* She lays down on the *floor* in her nightgown, all curled up like a baby. I watch her for a while, maybe ten, fifteen minutes—you know, thinkin' it's crazy for her to be in Nathan's room layin' on the *floor* like that—and then all of a sudden down below on the street I hear a car drive up and I look out the window and there's Nathan. Did you hear him when he came in? He made a hell of a lot of noise, stampin' and bangin' and mutterin' to himself."

"No, I was sound asleep," I replied. "My noise problem there—in the crater, as you call it—seems to be mainly vertical. Directly overhead. The rest of the house I can't hear, thank heaven."

"Anyway, Nathan comes upstairs and goes to his room. He goes through the door and there's Sophie all curled up and layin' on the floor. He walks over to her and stands there—she's awake—and this is what he says. He says, 'Get out of here, you whore!' Sophie doesn't say anything, just lays there cryin', I guess, and Nathan says, 'Get your ass out of here, whore, I'm leavin'.' Still Sophie doesn't say anything and I begin to hear her cry and cry, and then Nathan says, 'I'm goin' to count to three, whore, and if you're not up and out of here and out of my sight I'm goin' to kick your ass into the middle of next year.' And then he counts to three and she doesn't move and then he gets down on his knees and begins to slap the livin' shit out of her."

"While she's *lying* there?" I put in. I had begun to wish that Morris had not felt the need to tell me this story. My stomach stirred with queasy sickishness; though a man of nonviolence, I was nearly overwhelmed by the impulse to rush upstairs, where, accompanied by the *Water Music*'s sprightly bourrée, I would somehow exorcise the golem by battering its brains out with a chair. "You mean he actually *hit* that girl while she was lying there like that?"

"Yeah, he kept slappin' her. *Hard,* too. Right in the fuckin' chops he kept slappin' her."

"Why didn't you *do* something?" I demanded.

He hesitated, cleared his throat, then said, "Well, if you want to know, I'm a physical coward. I'm five foot five and that Nathan—he's a big motherfucker. But I'll tell you one thing. I *did* think about callin' the police. Sophie was beginnin' to groan, those clouts in the face must have hurt like a bastard. So I decided to come down here and call the police on the phone. I didn't have anything on, I don't wear anything sleepin'. So I went to my closet and put on a bathrobe and slippers—tryin' to move fast, see? Who knows, I thought he might *kill* her. I guess I was gone about a minute, at first I couldn't find my fuckin' slippers. Then when I got back to the door . . . Guess what?"

"I can't imagine."

"This time it's the other way around. Like it's opposite, see? This time Sophie's sittin' up on the floor with her legs crossed, and Nathan's sort of crouched down and he's got his head buried right in her crotch. I don't mean he's *eatin'* her. He's *cryin'!* He's got his face right down in there and he's cryin' away like a baby. And all this time Sophie's strokin' that black hair of his and whisperin', 'That's all right, that's all right.' And I hear Nathan say, 'Oh God, how could I do it to you? How could I hurt you?' Things like that. Then, 'I love you, Sophie, I love you.' And she just sayin', 'That's all right,' and makin' little cluckin' noises, and him with his nose in her crotch, cryin' and sayin' over and over again, 'Oh, Sophie, I love you so.' *Ach,* I almost heaved up my breakfast."

"And what then?"

"I couldn't take any more of it. When they finished all this crap and got up off the floor, I went out and got a Sunday paper and walked over to the park and read for an hour. I didn't want to have anything more to do with either of them. But see what I mean? I mean . . ." He paused and his eyes morosely probed me for some interpretation of this evil masque. I had none. Then Morris said decisively, "A golem, if you ask me. A fuckin' golem."

I made my way upstairs in a black squall of gusty, shifting emotion. I kept saying to myself that I couldn't get involved with these sick characters. Despite the grip that Sophie had laid upon my imagination, and despite my loneliness, I was certain that it would be foolhardy to seek their friendship. I felt this not only because I was afraid of getting sucked toward the epicenter of such a volatile, destructive relationship, but because I had to confront the hard fact that I, Stingo, had other fish to fry. I had come to Brooklyn ostensibly "to write my guts out," as dear old Farrell had put it, not to play the hapless supernumerary in some tortured melodrama. I resolved to tell them that I would not go with them to Coney Island, after all; that done, I would politely but decisively nudge them out of my life, making it plain that I was a solitary spirit who was not to be disturbed, ever.

I knocked and entered as the last record ceased playing, and the great barge with its jubilant trumpets vanished around a turning on the Thames. Sophie's room smote me instantly with delight. Though I know an eyesore when I see one, I have had very little sense of "taste," of décor;

yet I could tell that Sophie had achieved a kind of triumph over the inexhaustible pink. Rather than let the pink bully her, she had fought back, splashing the room with complementary hues of orange and green and red—a bright carnation bookcase here, an apricot bedspread there—and thus had vanquished the omnipresent and puerile stain. I wanted to burst out laughing at the way she had imbued that dumb Navy camouflage paint with such joy and warmth. And there were flowers. Flowers were everywhere—daffodils, tulips, gladioli; they sprouted from small table vases and from sconces on the wall. The place was fragrant with fresh flowers, and although they were abundant, there was no feeling of the sickroom amid all these blooms; they seemed instead simply festive, perfectly consonant with the gay flavor of the rest of the room.

Then I suddenly realized that Sophie and Nathan were nowhere in sight. Just as I was puzzling this out, I heard a giggle and saw a Japanese screen in one of the far corners give a little vibration. And from behind the screen, hand in hand, flashing uniform vaudevillian smiles, came Sophie and Nathan dancing a little two-step and wearing some of the most bewitchingly tailored clothes I had ever seen. More nearly costumes really, they were decidedly out of fashion—his being a white chalk-stripe gray flannel double-breasted suit of the kind made modish more than fifteen years before by the Prince of Wales; hers a pleated plum-colored satin skirt of the same period, a white flannel yachting jacket, and a burgundy beret tilted over her brow. Yet there was nothing hand-me-down about these two relics, they were clearly expensive and too well-fitting to be anything but custom-made. I felt desolate in my white Arrow shirt and its rolled-up sleeves and with my nondescript baggy slacks.

"Don't worry," Nathan said a few moments later, while he was fetching a quart bottle of beer from the refrigerator and Sophie was setting out cheese and crackers. "Don't worry about your clothes. Just because we dress up like this is no reason for you to feel uncomfortable. It's just a little fad of ours." I had slumped pleasurably in a chair, utterly shorn of my resolve to terminate our brief acquaintance. What caused this turnabout is almost impossible to explain. I suspect it was a combination of things.

The delightful room, the unexpected and farcical costumery, the beer, Nathan's demonstrative warmth and eagerness to make amends, Sophie's calamitous effect on my heart—all these had wiped out my will power. Thus I was once again their pawn. "It's just a little hobby of ours," he went on to explain over, or through, limpid Vivaldi as Sophie bustled about in the kitchenette. "Today we're wearing early thirties. But we've got clothes from the twenties, World War One period, Gay Nineties, even earlier than that. Naturally, we only dress up like this on a Sunday or a holiday when we're together."

"Don't people stare?" I asked. "And isn't it kind of expensive?"

"Sure they stare," he said. "That's part of the fun. Sometimes—like with our Gay Nineties outfit—we cause a hell of a commotion. As for expense, it's not much more expensive than regular clothes. There's this tailor on Fulton Street will make up anything I want so long as I bring him the right patterns."

I nodded agreeably. Although perhaps a touch exhibitionistic, it seemed a fairly harmless diversion. Certainly with their splendid good looks, emphasized even more by the contrast between his smoky Levantine features and her pale radiance, Sophie and Nathan would be an eyeful sauntering along together in almost anything. "It was Sophie's idea," Nathan explained further, "and she's right. People look drab on the street. They all look alike, walking around in uniform. Clothes like these have individuality. Style. That's why it's fun when people stare at us." He paused to fill my glass with beer. "Dress is important. It's part of being human. It might as well be a thing of beauty, something you take real pleasure in doing. And maybe in the process, give other people pleasure. Though that's secondary."

Well, it takes all kinds, as I had been accustomed to hear from childhood. Dress. Beauty. Being human. What talk from a man who only shortly before had been mouthing savage words and, if Morris could be trusted, had been inflicting outrageous pain on this gentle creature now flitting about with plates and ashtrays and cheese, dressed like Ginger Rogers in an old movie. Now he could not have been more amiable and engaging. And as I relaxed fully, feeling the beer begin to softly effervesce throughout my limbs, I conceded to myself that what he was saying had merit. After the hideous uniformity in dress of the postwar scene, especially in a man-trap like McGraw-Hill, what really was more refreshing to the eye than a little quaintness, a bit of eccentricity? Once again (I speak now from the vantage point of hindsight) Nathan was dealing in small auguries of the world to come.

"Look at her," he said, "isn't she something? Did you ever see such a dollbaby? Hey, dollbaby, come over here."

"I'm *busy*, can't you see?" Sophie said as she bustled about. "Fixing the *fromage.*"

"Hey!" He gave an earsplitting whistle. "Hey, come over here!" He winked at me. "I can't keep my hands off her."

Sophie came over and plopped down in his lap. "Give me a kiss," he said.

"One kiss, that's all," she replied, and smacked him lightly at the side of his mouth. "There! One kiss is all you deserve."

As she squirmed on his lap he nibbled at her ear and squeezed her waist, causing her adoring face to glow so visibly that I could have sworn he had twisted some kind of knob. "I can't keep my hands off you-*u-u,*" he hummed. Like others, I am embarrassed by unprivate displays of affection—or of hostility, for that matter—especially when I am the solitary onlooker. I took a large swallow of beer and averted my eyes; they of course lit upon the outsized bed with its coverlet of luscious apricot where my new friends had transacted most of these goings-on, and which had been the monstrous engine of so much of my recent discomfort. Maybe my renewed outbreak of coughing betrayed me, or I suspect Sophie sensed my embarrassment; at any rate, she leaped up from Nathan's lap, saying, "Enough! Enough for you, Nathan Landau. No more kisses."

"Come on," he complained, "one more."

"No more," she said sweetly but firmly. "We're going to have the beer and a little *fromage* and then we're all going to get on the subway train and go have lunch at Coney Island."

"You're a cheater," he said in a kidding voice. "You're a *tease*. You're worse than any little *yenta* that ever came out of Brooklyn." He turned and regarded me with mock gravity. "What do you think of that, Stingo? Here I am pushing thirty years old. I fall crazy in love with a Polish *shiksa* and she keeps her sweet treasure all locked up as tightly as little Shirley Mirmelstein I tried to make out with for five whole years. What do you think of that?" Again the sly wink.

"Bad news," I improvised in a jocular tone. "It's a form of sadism." Although I'm certain I kept my composure, I was really vastly surprised at this revelation: Sophie was not Jewish! I could not really have cared less one way or another, but I was still surprised, and there was something vaguely negative and self-preoccupied in my reaction. Like Gulliver among the Hounyhnhnms, I had rather thought myself a unique figure in this huge Semitic arrondissement and was simply taken aback that Yetta's house should shelter another Gentile. So Sophie was a *shiksa*. Well, hush my mouth, I thought in mild wonder.

Sophie set before us a plate containing squares of toast upon which she had melted little sunbursts of golden Cheddar-like cheese. With the beer, they tasted particularly delicious. I began to warm to the convivial, gently alcoholic mood of our tiny gathering as does a hound dog who slinks out from chill, comfortless shadows into the heat of the midday sun.

"When I first met this one here," Nathan said as she sat down on the rug beside his chair and contentedly leaned against his leg, "she was a rag and a bone and a hank of hair. And that was a whole year and a half after the Russians liberated that camp she was in. How much was it you weighed, sweetie?"

"Thirty-eight. Thirty-eight kilos."

"Yeah, about eighty-five pounds. Can you imagine? She was a *wraith*."

"How much do you weigh now, Sophie?" I asked.

"Just fifty."

"One hundred and ten pounds," Nathan translated, "which still isn't enough for her frame and height. She should weigh about one-seventeen, but she's getting there —she's getting there. We'll make a nice big milk-fed

American girl out of her in no time." Idly, affectionately he fingered the butter-yellow strands of hair that curled out from beneath the rim of her beret. "But, boy, was she a *wreck* when I first got hold of her. Here, drink some beer, sweetie. It'll help make you fat."

"I was a real wreck," Sophie put in, her tone affectingly light-hearted. "I looked like an old witch—I mean, you know, the thing that chases birds away. The scarecrow? I didn't have hardly any hair and my legs ached. I had the *scorbut*—"

"The scurvy," Nathan interjected, "she means she'd had the scurvy, which was cured as soon as the Russians took over—"

"*Le scorbut*—scurvy I mean—I had. I lose my *teeth!* And typhus. And scarlet fever. And anemia. *All* of them. I was a real *wreck.*" She uttered the litany of diseases with no self-pity yet with a certain childish earnestness, as if she were reciting the names of some pet animals. "But then I met Nathan and he taked care of me."

"Theoretically she was saved as soon as the camp was liberated," he explained. "That is, she wasn't going to die. But then she was in a displaced persons' camp for a long time. And there were thousands of people there, tens of thousands, and they just didn't have the medical facilities to take care of all the damage that the Nazis had done to so many bodies. So then last year, when she arrived over here in America, she still had a quite serious, I mean a really serious, case of anemia. I could tell."

"How could you tell?" I asked, with honest interest in his expertise.

Nathan explained, briefly, articulately, and with a straightforward modesty that I found winning. Not that he was a physician, he said. He was, rather, a graduate in science from Harvard, with a master's degree in cellular and developmental biology. It had been his achievement in this field of study which had led him to be hired as a researcher at Pfizer, a Brooklyn-based firm and one of the largest pharmaceutical houses in the nation. So much, then, for the background. He claimed no intricate or extensive medical knowledge, and had no use for the lay habit of venturing amateur diagnoses of illness; his training had, however, made him more than ordinarily enlightened about the chemical vagaries and ailments of the human body, and so the moment he first laid eyes on Sophie ("this sweetie," he murmured with enormous concern and gentleness, twisting the lock of her hair) he guessed, with dead accuracy as it turned out, that her ravaged appearance was the result of a deficiency anemia.

"I took her to a doctor, a friend of my brother's, who teaches at Columbia Presbyterian. He does work in nutrition diseases." A proud note, not at all unattractive in the sense it conveyed of quiet authority, stole into Nathan's voice. "He said I was right on target. A critical deficiency of iron. We put the little sweetie here on massive doses of ferrous sulfate and she began to bloom like a rose." He paused and looked down at her. "A rose. A rose. A beautiful fucking rose." He lightly ran his fingers over his lips and transferred his fingertips to her brow, anointing it with his kiss. *"God,* you're something," he whispered, "you're the *greatest."*

She gazed up at him. She looked incredibly beautiful but somehow tired and drawn. I thought of the previous night's orgy of sorrow. She lightly stroked the blue-veined surface of his wrist. "Thank you, Monsieur Senior Researcher at Charles Pfizer Company," she said. For some reason, I could not help but think: Jesus Christ, Sophie honey, we've got to find you a dialogue coach. "And thank you for making me to bloom like a rose," she added after a moment.

All at once I became aware of the way in which Sophie echoed so much of Nathan's diction. Indeed, he *was* her dialogue coach, a fact which became more directly evident now as I heard him begin to correct her in detail, like an exceedingly meticulous, very patient instructor at a Berlitz school. "Not '*to* bloom,'" he explained, "just 'bloom.' You're so good, it's about time you were *perfect*. You must begin to learn just when and where to add the preposition 'to' to the infinitive verb, and when to leave it out. And it's tough, you see, because in English there's no hard, fast rule. You have to use your instinct."

"Instinct?" she said.

"You have to use your *ear,* so that it finally becomes instinct. Let me give you an example. You could say '*causing* me to bloom like a rose' but not '*making* me to bloom.' There's no rule about this, understand. It's just one of those odd little tricks of the language which you'll pick up in time." He stroked her earlobe. "With that pretty ear of yours."

"Such a language!" she groaned, and in mock pain clutched her brow. "Too many words. I mean just the words for *vélocité*. I mean 'fast.' 'Rapid.' 'Quick.' All the same thing! A scandal!"

" 'Swift,' " I added.

"How about 'speedy'?" Nathan said.

" 'Hasty,' " I went on.

"And 'fleet,' " Nathan said, "though that's a bit fancy."

" 'Snappy'!" I said.

"Stop it!" Sophie said, laughing. "Too much! Too many words, this English. In French it is so simple, you just say *'vite.'* "

"How about some more beer?" Nathan asked me. "We'll finish off this other quart and then go down to Coney Island and hit the beach."

I noticed that Nathan drank next to nothing himself, but was almost embarrassingly generous with the Budweiser, keeping my glass topped off with unceasing attention. As for myself, in that brief time I had begun to achieve a benign, tingling high so surprisingly intense that I became a little uneasy trying to manage my own euphoria. It was an exaltation really, lofty as the summer sun; I felt buoyed up by fraternal arms holding me in a snug, loving, compassionate embrace. Part of what worked on me was, to be sure, only the coarse clutch of alcohol. The rest stemmed from all of those mingled elements comprising what, in that era so heavily burdened by the idiom of psychoanalysis, I had come to recognize as the gestalt: the blissful temper of the sunny June day, the ecstatic pomp of Mr. Handel's riverborne jam session, and this festive little room whose open windows admitted a fragrance of spring blossoms which pierced me with that sense of ineffable promise and certitude I don't recall having felt more than once or twice after the age of twenty-two—or let us say twenty-five—when the ambitious career I had cut out for myself seemed so often to be the consequence of pitiable lunacy.

Above all, however, my joy flowed out from some source I had not known since I had come to New York months before, and thought I had abandoned forever—fellowship, familiarity, sweet times among friends. The brittle aloofness with which I had so willfully armored myself I felt crumbling away utterly. How wonderful it was, I thought, to happen upon Sophie and Nathan—these warm and bright and lively new companions—and the urge I had to reach out and hug both of them close to me was (for the moment at least, despite my desperate crush on Sophie) freighted with the mellowest brotherhood, cleanly, practically devoid of carnal accents. Old Stingo, I murmured, grinning foolishly at Sophie but toasting myself with the foaming Bud, you've come back to the land of the living. "*Salut,* Stingo!" said Sophie, tipping in return the glass of beer which Nathan had pressed on her, and the grave and delectable smile she bestowed on me, bright teeth shining amid a scrubbed happy face still bruised with the shadows of deprivation, touched me so deeply that I made an involuntary, choking sound of contentment. I felt close to total salvation.

Yet beneath my grand mood I was able to sense that there was something wrong. The terrible scene between Sophie and Nathan the night before should have been warning enough to me that our chummy little get-together, with its laughter and its ease and its gentle intimacy, was scarcely true of the status quo as it existed between them. But I am a person who is too often weakly misguided by the external masquerade, quick to trust in such notions as that the ghastly blow-up I had witnessed was a lamentable but rare aberration in a lovers' connection whose prevailing tone was really hearts and flowers. I suppose the fact of the matter is that deep down I so hungered for friendship—was so infatuated with Sophie, and attracted with such perverse fascination to this dynamic, vaguely outlandish, wickedly compelling young man who was her inamorato—that I dared not regard their relationship in anything but the rosiest light. Even so, as I say, I could feel something distinctly out of joint. Beneath all the jollity, the tenderness, the solicitude, I sensed a disturbing tension in the room. I don't mean that the tension at that moment directly involved the two lovers. But there was tension, an unnerving strain, and most of it seemed to emanate from Nathan. He had become distracted, restless, and he got up and fiddled with the phonograph records, replaced the Handel with Vivaldi again, in obvious turmoil gulped a glass of water, sat down and drummed his fingers against his pants leg in rhythm to the celebrant horns.

Then swiftly he turned to me, peering at me searchingly with his troubled and gloomy eyes, and said, "Just an old briar-hopper, ain't you?" After a pause and with a touch of the bogus drawl he had baited me with before, he added, "You know, you Confederate types interest me. You-all" —and here he bore down on the "all"—"you-*all* interest me very, very much."

I began to do, or undergo, or experience what I believe is known as a slow burn. This Nathan was incredible! How could he be so clumsy, so unfeeling—such a *creep?* My euphoric haze evaporated like thousands of tiny soap bubbles all at once. This swine! I thought. He had actually trapped me! How otherwise to explain this sly change in mood, unless it was to try to edge me into a corner? It was either clumsiness or craft: there was no other way to fathom such words, after I had so emphatically and so recently made it a condition of our amity—if such it might be called—that he would lay off his heavy business about the South. Once more indignation rose like a regurgitated bone in my gorge, though I made a last attempt to be patient. I turned up the butane under my Tidewater accent and said, "Why, Nathan ole hoss, you Brooklyn folks interest us boys down home, too."

This had a distinctly adverse effect on Nathan. He was not only unamused, his eyes flashed warfare; he glowered at me with implacable mistrust, and for an instant I could have sworn I saw in those shining pupils the freak, the redneck, the alien he knew me to be.

"Oh, fuck it," I said, starting to rise to my feet. "I'll just be going—"

But before I could set down my glass and get up he had clutched me by the wrist. It was not a rough or painful grasp, but he bore down strongly nonetheless, and insistently, and his grip held me fast in the chair. There was something desperately importunate in that grip which chilled me.

"It's hardly a joking matter," he said. His voice, though restrained, was, I felt, charged with turbulent emotion. Then his next words, spoken with deliberate, almost comical slowness, were like an incantation. "Bobby . . . Weed . . . *Bobby Weed!* Do you think Bobby Weed is worthy of nothing more than your attempt . . . at . . . humor?"

"It wasn't *I* who started that cotton-picking accent," I retorted. And I thought: *Bobby Weed!* Oh shit! Now he's going to get on Bobby Weed. Let me out of here.

Then at this moment Sophie, as if sensing the perhaps sinister shift in Nathan's mood, hurried to his side and touched his shoulder with a fluttery, nervously placating hand. "Nathan," she said, "no more about Bobby Weed. Please, Nathan! It will just disturb you when we were having such a lovely time." She cast me a look of distress. "All week he's been talking about Bobby Weed. I can't get him to stop." To Nathan again she begged, "Please, darling, we were having such a lovely time!"

But Nathan was not to be deflected. "What about Bobby Weed?" he demanded of me.

"Well, what *about* him, for Christ's sake?" I groaned, and pulled myself upward out of his grasp. I had begun to eye the door and the intervening furniture, and quickly schemed out the best way of immediate exit. "Thanks for the beer," I muttered.

"I'll tell you what about Bobby Weed," Nathan persisted. He was not about to allow me off the hook, and dumped more foaming beer into the glass which he pressed into my hand. His expression still seemed calm enough but was betrayed by inner excitement in the form of a waggling, hairy, didactic forefinger which he thrust into my face. "I'll tell you something about Bobby Weed, Stingo my friend. And that is *this!* You Southern white people have a lot to answer for when it comes to such bestiality. You deny that? Then listen. I say this as one whose people have suffered the death camps. I say this as a man who is deeply in love with one who survived them." He reached up and surrounded Sophie's wrist with his hand while the forefinger of his other hand still made its vermiform scrawl in the air above my cheekbone. "But mainly I say this as Nathan Landau, common citizen, research biologist, human being, witness to man's inhu-

manity to man. I say that the fate of Bobby Weed at the hands of white Southern Americans is as bottomlessly barbaric as any act performed by the Nazis during the rule of Adolf Hitler! Do you agree with me?"

I bit the inside of my mouth in an effort to keep my composure. "What happened to Bobby Weed, Nathan," I replied, "was horrible. Unspeakable! But I don't see any point in trying to equate one evil with another, or to assign some stupid scale of values. They're *both* awful! Would you mind taking your finger out of my face?" I felt my brow growing moist and feverish. "And I damn well question this big net you're trying to throw out to catch all of what you call *you Southern white people*. Goddamnit, I'm not going to swallow that line! I'm *Southern* and I'm *proud* of it, but I'm not one of those pigs—those *troglodytes* who did what they did to Bobby Weed! I was born in Tidewater Virginia, and if you'll pardon the expression, I regard myself as a gentleman! Also, if you'll pardon me, this simplistic nonsense of yours, this *ignorance* coming from somebody so obviously intelligent as yourself truly *nauseates* me!" I heard my voice climb, quavering, cracked and no longer under control, and I feared another disastrous coughing fit as I watched Nathan calmly rising to his full height, so that in effect we were confronting each other. Despite the now rather threatful forward-thrusting nature of his stance and the fact that he outmanned me in bulk and stature, I had the powerful urge to punch him in the jaw. "Nathan, let me tell *you* something. You are now dealing in the cheapest kind of New York-liberal, hypocritical horseshit! What gives you the right to pass judgment on millions of people, most of whom would die before they'd harm a Negro!"

"Ha!" he replied. "See, it's even in your speech pattern. *Nig*-ro! I find that *so* offensive."

"It's the way we *say* it down there. It's not *meant* to offend. All right—*Knee-grow*. Anyway," I went on impatiently, "what gives you the right to pass judgment? *I* find *that* so offensive."

"As a Jew, I regard myself as an authority on anguish and suffering." He paused and as he gazed at me now I thought I saw for the first time contempt in his look, and mounting disgust. "As for this 'New York-liberal' evasion, this 'hypocritical horseshit'—I consider that a laughably feeble, insubstantial comeback to an honest accusation. Aren't you able to perceive the simple truth? Aren't you able to discern the truth in its awful outlines? And that is that your refusal to admit responsibility in the death of Bobby Weed is the same as that of those Germans who disavowed the Nazi party even as they watched blandly and unprotestingly as the thugs vandalized the synagogues and perpetrated the *Kristallnacht*. Can't you see the truth about yourself? About the South? After all, it wasn't the citizens of New York State who destroyed Bobby Weed."

Most of what he was saying—especially about *my* "responsibility"—was lopsided, irrational, smug and horrendously wrong, yet to my nearly total chagrin at that point, I found that I could not answer. I was momentarily demoralized. I made an odd chirping sound in the back of my throat and moved in a sort of weak-kneed graceless lurch toward the window. Feeble, impotent though inwardly raging, I struggled for words that would not come. I swilled at a gulp the larger part of a glass of beer, looking through eyes bleared with frustration down at the sunny pastoral lawns of Flatbush, the rustling sycamores and maples, decorous streets all gently astir with Sunday-morning motion: shirt-sleeved ball-throwers, churning bicycles, sun-dappled strollers on the walks. The scent of new-mown grass was rank, sweet, warmly green to the nostrils, reminding me of countryside prospects and distances—fields and lanes perhaps not too different from those once meandered upon by the young Bobby Weed, whom Nathan had implanted like a pulsing lesion in my brain. And as I thought of Bobby Weed, I was overtaken by bitter, disabling despair. How could this infernal Nathan summon up the shade of Bobby Weed on such a ravishing day?

I listened to Nathan's voice behind me, high now, hectoring, reminiscent of that of a squat, half-hysteric Communist youth organizer with a mouth like a torn pocket I had once heard screaming up at the empty empyrean over Union Square. "The South today has abdicated any right to connection with the human race," Nathan harangued me. "Each white Southerner is accountable for the tragedy of Bobby Weed. No Southerner escapes responsibility!"

I shivered violently, my hand jerked, and I watched my beer slosh greasily in its glass. Nineteen forty-seven. One, nine, four, seven. In that summer, twenty years almost to the month before the city of Newark burned down, and Negro blood flowed incarnadine in the gutters of Detroit, it was possible—if one was Dixie-born and sensitive and enlightened and aware of one's fearsome and ungodly history—to smart beneath such a tongue-lashing, even when one knew that it partook heavily of renascent abolitionist self-righteousness, ascribing to itself moral superiority so hygienic as to provoke tolerant though mirthless amusement. In less violent form, in subtle digs and supercilious little drawing-room slanders, Southerners who had ventured north were to endure such exploitative assaults upon their indwelling guilt during an era of unalleviated discomfort which ended officially on a morning in August, 1963, when on North Water Street in Edgartown, Massachusetts, the youngish, straw-haired, dimple-kneed wife of the yacht-club commodore, a prominent Brahmin investment banker, was seen brandishing a copy of James Baldwin's *The Fire Next Time* as she uttered to a friend, in tones of clamp-jawed desolation, these words: "My dear, it's going to happen to *all* of us!"

This understatement could not have seemed quite so ominiscient to me back then in 1947. At that time the drowsing black behemoth, although beginning to stir, was still not regarded as much of a Northern problem. Perhaps for this very reason—although I might honestly have bridled at the intolerant Yankee slurs that had sometimes come my way (even good old Farrell had gotten in a few mildly caustic licks)—I *did* feel at my heart's core a truly burdensome shame over the kinship I was forced to acknowledge with those solidly Anglo-Saxon subhumans who were the torturers of Bobby Weed. These Georgia backwoodsmen—denizens, as it so happened, of that same piney coast near Brunswick where my savior Artiste had toiled and suffered and died—had made sixteen-year-old Bobby Weed one of the last and certainly one of the most memorably wiped-out victims of lynch justice the South was to witness. His reputed crime, very much resembling that of Artiste, had been so classic as to take on the outlines of a grotesque cliché: he had ogled, or molested, or otherwise interfered with (actual offense never made clear, though falling short of rape) the simpleton daughter, named Lula—another cliché! but true: Lula's woebegone and rabbity face had sulked from the pages of six metropolitan newspapers—of a crossroads storekeeper, who had instigated immediate action by an outraged daddy's appeal to the local rabble.

I had read of the peasantry's medieval vengeance only a week before, while standing on an uptown Lexington Avenue local, squashed between an enormously fat woman with an S. Klein shopping bag and a small Popsicle-licking Puerto Rican in a busboy's jacket whose gardenia-ripe brilliantine floated sweetishly up to my nose as he mooned over my *Mirror*, sharing with me its devil's photographs. While he was still alive Bobby Weed's cock and balls had been hacked off and thrust into his mouth (this feature not displayed), and when near death, though reportedly aware of all, had by a flaming blowtorch received the brand on his chest of a serpentine "L"—representing what? "Lynch?" "Lula?" "Law and Order?" "Love?" Even as Nathan raved at me, I recalled having semi-staggered out of the train and up into the bright summer light of Eighty-sixth Street, amid the scent of wienerwurst and Orange Julius and scorched metal from the subway gratings, moving blindly past the Rossellini movie I had traveled that far to see. I did not go to the theatre that afternoon. Instead, I found myself at Gracie Square on the promenade by the river, gazing as if in a trance at the municipal hideousness of the river islands, unable to efface the mangled image of Bobby Weed from my mind even as I kept murmuring—endlessly it seemed—lines from Revelation I had memorized as a boy: *And God shall wipe away all tears from their eyes. And there shall be no more death, neither sorrow nor crying, neither shall there be any more pain* . . . Perhaps it had been an overreaction, but—ah God, even so, *I* could not weep.

Nathan's voice, still badgering me, swam back into hearing. "Look, in the *concentration camps* the brutes in charge would not have stooped to *that* bestiality!"

Would they? Would they *not?* It seemed hardly to matter, and I was sick of the argument, sick of the fanaticism I was unable to counter or find shelter from, sick with the vision of Bobby Weed and—despite feeling no complicity whatever in the Georgia abomination—suddenly sick with a past and a place and a heritage I could neither believe in nor fathom. I had the idle urge now—at risk of a broken nose—to heave the rest of my beer in Nathan's face. Restraining myself, I tensed my shoulders and said in tones of frosty contempt, "As a member of a race which has been unjustly persecuted for centuries for having allegedly crucified Christ, *you*—yes, *you,* goddamnit!—should be aware of how inexcusable it is to condemn any single *people* for *anything!*" And then I found myself so enraged that I blurted out something which to Jews, in that tormented bygone year scant months removed from the crematoriums, was freighted with enough incendiary offensiveness to make me regret the words as soon as they escaped my lips. But I didn't take them back. "And that goes for *any* people," I said, "by God, even the Germans!"

Nathan flinched, then reddened even more deeply, and I thought that the showdown had finally arrived. Just then, however, Sophie miraculously salvaged the entire cheerless situation by swooping down in her campus-cutup costume and inserting herself between the two of us.

"Stop this talk *right now,*" she demanded. "Stop it! It is too *serious* for Sunday." There was playfulness in her manner but I could tell she meant business. "Forget Bobby Weed. We must talk about *happy* things. We must go to Coney Island and swim and eat and have a lovely time!" She whirled on the glowering golem and I was surprised and considerably relieved to see how readily she was able to discard her wounded, submissive role and actually stand up to Nathan in a frisky way, beginning to manipulate him out of sheer charm, beauty and *brio.* "What do you know about concentration camps, Nathan Landau? Nothing at all. Quit talking about such places. And quit shouting at Stingo. Quit shouting at Stingo about Bobby Weed. Enough! Stingo didn't have anything to do with Bobby Weed. Stingo's *sweet.* And *you're* sweet, Nathan Landau, and *vraiment, je t'adore.*"

I noticed that summer that under certain circumstances having to do with the mysterious vicissitudes of his mind and mood, Sophie was able to work upon Nathan such tricks of alchemy that he was almost instantaneously transformed—the ranting ogre become Prince Charming. European women often boss their men too, but with a beguiling subtlety unknown to most American females. Now she pecked him lightly on the cheek, and holding his outstretched hands by her fingertips, stared at him appraisingly as the beet-hued, choleric passion he had vented on me began to recede from his face.

"Vraiment, je t'adore, chéri," she said softly and then, tugging at his wrists, sang out in the most cheery voice of the day, "To the beach! To the beach! We'll build *sand castles."*

And the tempest was over, the thunderclouds had rolled away, and the sunniest good humor flooded into the color-splashed room, where the curtains made a tap-tapping sound upon a sudden gusty breeze from the park. As we moved toward the door, the three of us, Nathan—looking a bit like a fashionable gambler now in his suit out of an old *Vanity Fair*—looped his long arm around my shoulder and offered me an apology so straightforward and honorable that I could not help but forgive him his dark insults, his bigoted and wrong-headed slurs and his other transgressions. "Old Stingo, I'm just an ass, an *ass!"* he roared in my ear, uncomfortably loud. "I don't *mean* to be a *shmuck,* it's a bad habit I've got, saying things to people without any regard for their feelings. I know it's not *all* bad down South. Hey, I'll make you a promise. I promise never to jump on you about the South again! Okay? Sophie, you're the witness!" Squeezing me, tousling my hair with fingers that moved across my scalp as if they were kneading dough and like some overgrown and ludicrously affectionate schnauzer poking his noble scimitar of a nose into the coral recesses of my ear, he fell into what I began to identify as his comic mode.

We walked in the gayest of spirits toward the subway station—Sophie between us now, her arms linked in ours—and he returned to that grits-and-molasses accent he rendered with such fantastic precision; there was no sarcasm this time, no intent to needle me, and his intonation, accurate enough to fool a native of Memphis or Mobile, caused me to nearly choke with laughter. But his gift was not mimicry alone; what emanated from him so drolly was the product of dazzling invention. With the loutish, swollen, barely comprehensible diction I had heard bubble up out of the tonsils of all sorts of down-home rustics, he embarked on an improvisation so crazily funny and so deadly precise and obscene that in my own hilarity I quite forgot that it all involved those people whom he had been flaying only moments before with unpitying and humorless rage. I'm sure Sophie missed many of the nuances of his act, but affected by the general contagion, joined me in filling Flatbush Avenue with noisy runaway laughter. And all of it, I dimly began to realize, was blessedly purgative of the mean and threatful emotions which had churned up like an evil storm in Sophie's room.

Along a block and a half of the city's crowded, easygoing Sunday street, he created an entire southern Appalachian scenario, a kind of darkling, concupiscent Dogpatch in which Pappy Yokum was transformed into an incestuous old farmer consecrated to romps with a daughter that Nathan—ever medically aware—had christened Pink Eye. "Ever git yore dick sucked by a harelip?" Nathan cackled, too loud, startling a pair of window-shopping Hadassah matrons, who drifted past us with expressions of agony as Nathan sailed blissfully on, doing a job on Mammy. "You done knocked up mah precious baby again!" he boohooed in female plaint, his voice a heavenly facsimile—down to the perfect shading of falsetto—of that of some weak-witted and godforsaken wife and victim, blighted by wedlock, history and retrograde genes. As impossible to reproduce as the exact quality of a passage of music, Nathan's rollicking, dirty performance—and its power, which I can only barely suggest—had its origins in some transcendent desperation, although I was only beginning to be aware of that. What I *was* aware of, as my wild laughter sprang forth, was that it was a species of genius—and this was something I would wait another twenty years to witness, in the incandescent figuration of Lenny Bruce.

Because it was well past noon, Nathan and Sophie and I decided to postpone our "gourmet" seafood meal until the evening. To fill the gap we bought beautiful long kosher frankfurters with sauerkraut and Coca-Colas at a little stand and took them with us to the subway. On the train, which was thronged with beach-famished New Yorkers carrying huge bloated inner tubes and squalling infants, we managed to find a seat where we could loll three abreast and munch at our humble but agreeable fare. Sophie fell to eating her hot dog with truly serious absorption while Nathan unwound from his flight and began to get better acquainted with me over the clamor of the train. He was ingratiating now, inquisitive without being nosy, and I responded easily to the questions. What brought me to Brooklyn? What did I do? What did I live on? He seemed tickled and impressed to learn that I was a writer, and as for my means of support, I was about to lapse into my silkiest plantation brogue and say something on the order of "Well, you see, there was this nigger—*Knee*-grow—slave I owned, that was sold . . ." But I thought this might provoke Nathan into thinking I was pulling his leg; he might then embark again upon his monologue, which was becoming a trifle exhausting, so I merely smiled thinly, wrapping myself in an enigma, and replied, "I have a private source of income."

"You're a writer?" he said again, earnestly and with obvious enthusiasm. Shaking his head back and forth as if with the minor marvel of it all, he leaned across Sophie's lap and gripped my arm at the elbow. And I did not feel it at all awkward or emotional when his black, brooding eyes pierced into mine and he told me in a shout, "You know, I think we're going to become great friends!"

"Oh, we're *all* going to become great friends!" Sophie echoed him suddenly. A lovely phosphorescence enveloped her face as the train plunged toward sunlight, out of the claustrophobic tunnel and into the marshy maritime reaches of south Brooklyn. Her cheek was very close to my own, flushed with contentment, and when once again she linked her arms in mine and Nathan's, I felt on cozy enough terms to remove, between my delicate thumb and forefinger, a tiny thread of sauerkraut clinging to the corner of her lip. "Oh, we're going to be the *best* of friends!" she trilled over the train's rackety noise, and she gave my arm a tight squeeze that was certainly not flirtatious but contained something in it more than—well, casual. Call it the reassuring squeeze of one who, secure in her love for another, wished to admit a new-found companion into the privileges of her trust and affection.

This was one hell of a compromise, I thought, pondering the harsh inequity of Nathan's custodianship of such an exquisite prize, but better even this savory little crust than no loaf at all. I returned Sophie's squeeze with the clumsy pressure of unrequited love, and realized as I did so that I was so horny my balls had begun to ache. Earlier, Nathan had mentioned getting me a girl at Coney Island, a "hot dish" he knew named Leslie; it was a consolation to be looked forward to, I supposed in the stoic mood of the perpetual runner-up, decorously concealing by means of a languidly arranged hand the gabardine bulge in my lap. Despite all this frustration, I began to try to convince myself, with partial success, that I was happy; certainly I was happier than I had been in as long as I could remember. Thus I was ready to bide my time and discover what might felicitously happen, see what Sundays like this—entwined amid the other promising days of the onrushing summer—would bring. I drowsed a little. I was set softly aflame by Sophie's nearness, by her bare arm moist against mine, and by some scent she wore—an earthy, disturbing perfume vaguely herbal, like thyme. Doubtless some obscure Polish weed. Floating on an absolute tidal wave of desire, I fell into a daydream through which there rushed back sharp flickering impressions of my hapless eavesdrop of the day before. Sophie and Nathan, asprawl on the apricot bedspread. I could not get that image out of my mind. And their words, their raging lovewords showering down!

Then the erotic glow that bathed my daydream faded, vanished, and other words echoed in my ears and caused me to sit up with a start. For at some point yesterday in that pandemonium of frenzied advice and deafening demand, amid the shouts and muffled murmurs and randy exhortations, had I *really* heard from Nathan the words I now so chillingly recalled? No, it was later, I realized, during one moment of what seemed now their unending conflict, that his voice had come down through the ceiling, booming, with the ponderous, measured cadence of booted footfalls, and cried out in a tone that might have been deemed a parody of existential anguish had it not possessed the resonances of complete, unfeigned terror: "Don't ... you ... see ... Sophie ... we ... are ... dying! *Dying!*"

I shivered violently, as if someone had thrown open at my back in the dead of winter a portal on the Arctic wastes. It was nothing so grand as what might be called a premonition—this clammy feeling which overtook me, in which the day darkened swiftly, along with my contentment—but I was suddenly ill-at-ease enough to long desperately to escape, to rush from the train. If, in my anxiety, I had done so, hopping off at the next stop and hurrying back to Yetta Zimmerman's to pack my bags and flee, this would be another story, or rather, there would be no story at all to tell. But I allowed myself to plunge on toward Coney Island, thus making sure to help fulfill Sophie's prophecy about the three of us: that we would become "the best of friends."

Four

"In Cracow, when I was a little girl," Sophie told me, "we lived in a very old house on an old winding street not far from the university. It was a very ancient house, I'm sure some of it must have been built centuries ago. Strange, you know, that house and Yetta Zimmerman's house are the only houses I ever lived in—real *houses,* I mean—in my life. Because, you see, I was born there and spend all my childhood there and then when I was married I lived there still, before the Germans came and I had to go live for a while in Warsaw. I adored that house, it was quiet and full of shadows high up on the fourth floor when I was very little, and I had my own room. Across the street there was another old house, with these crooked chimneys, and the storks had builded their nests on top of these. Storks, isn't that it? Funny, I used to get that word mixed up with 'stilts' in English. Anyway, I remember the storks on the chimney across the street and how they looked just like the storks in my book of fairy tales by the Brothers Grimm that I read in German. I remember that so very, very plainly, those books, and the color of the outside and the pictures of the animals and birds and people on the cover. I could read German before I read Polish, and do you know, I even spoke German before I spoke Polish, so that when I first went to the convent school I would get teased for my German accent.

"You know, Cracow is a very ancient city, and our house was not far from the central square, where in the middle is this beautiful building that was made in medieval times—the *Sukiennice* it is called in Polish, which I believe translated in English means the cloth-hall, where they would have a market in all types of cloths and fabrics. Then there is a clock tower there on the church of St. Mary's, very high, and instead of bells they have actual live men who come out on a kind of balustrade, these men who come out and blow trumpets to announce the hour. It makes a very beautiful sound in the night. Kind of distant and sad, you know, like the trumpets in one of the suites for orchestra of Bach, that make me think always of very ancient times, and how mysterious is this thing of time. When I was a little girl I would lie in the dark of my room and listen to the sound of the horses' feet on the street below—they did not have too many motorcars in Poland then—and when I would go off to sleep I would hear the men blow the trumpets on the clock tower, very sad and distant, and I would wonder about time—this mystery, you know. Or I would lie there and think about clocks. In the hallway there was a very old clock on a kind of stand that had belonged to my grandparents, and once I opened the back of it and looked into it while it was running and saw a whole lot of levers and wheels and jewels—I think they were mostly rubies—shining in the reflection from the sun. So at night lying there I would think of myself *inside* the clock—imagine anything so crazy from a child!—where I would just float around on a spring and watch the levers moving and the various wheels turning and see the rubies, red and bright and as big as my head. And I would go to sleep finally with this clock in my dreams.

"Oh, there are so many memories of Cracow, so many, I can't begin to describe them! They were wonderful times, those years between those wars, even for Poland, which is a poor country and suffer from, you know, an inferiority complex. Nathan thinks I'm exaggerating about the good times we had—he makes so many jokes about Poland—but I tell him about my family and how we lived in a wonderful civilized way, the *best* kind of life you can imagine, really. 'What did you do for fun on Sunday?' he says to me. 'Throw rotten potatoes at Jews?' You see, all he can think of about Poland is how anti-Semitic it is being and make those jokes about it, which cause me to feel so bad. Because it is true, I mean it is famous that

Poland has this strong anti-Semitism and that make me so terribly ashamed in many ways, like you, Stingo, when you have this *misère* over the colored people down in the South. But I told Nathan that yes, it is true, quite true about this bad history in Poland, but he must understood —*vraiment,* he must comprehend that not all Polish people was like that, there are good decent people like my family who . . . Oh, it is such an ugly thing to talk about. It makes me think sadly about Nathan, he is . . . obsessed, so I think I must change the subject . . .

"Yes, my family. My mother and father was both professors at the university, which is why almost all my memories have this connection with the university. It is one of the oldest universities in Europe, it was started far back in the fourteenth century. I didn't know no other kind of life except being the daughter of teachers, and maybe that is why my memories of all those times are so gentle and civilized. Stingo, someday you must go to Poland and see it and write about it. It is so beautiful. And so sad. Imagine, those twenty years when I was growing up there was the only twenty years that Poland was ever free. I mean after *centuries!* I suppose that is why I used to hear my father say so often, 'These are sunny times for Poland.' Because everything was free for the first time, you see, in the universities and schools—you could study anything which you wished to study. And I suppose that is one of the reasons why people was able to enjoy life so much, studying and learning, and listening to music, and going away to the country on Sundays in the spring and summer. Sometime I have thought that I love music almost as much as life, really. We were at concerts always. When I was a little girl in this house, this ancient house, I would lie awake at night in my bed and listen to my mother play downstairs on the piano—Schumann or Chopin she would play, or Beethoven or Scarlatti or Bach, she was a wonderful pianist—I would lie awake and hear the music faint and beautiful rising up through the house and I would feel so warm and comfortable and secure. I would think that no one had a more wonderful mother and father or a better life than me. And I would think of growing up and what I would become when I was not a child any more, perhaps become married and become a teacher of music like my mother. This would be such a fine life to live, I thought, to be able to play beautiful music, and teach and be married to a fine professor like my father.

"Neither of my parents come from Cracow in the beginning. My mother was from Lodz and my father was from Lublin. They met in Vienna when they were students. My father was studying the law at the Austrian Academy of Sciences and my mother was studying music in the city. They were both very religious Catholics, so I was brought up very devout and went to Mass always and church school, but I don't mean I was, you know, fanatic, nut. I believed very much in God, but my mother and father they were not, you know, I don't know what the exact word is in English, like *dur*—yes, hard, *harsh*. They were not like that. They were very liberal—even, you could say, almost socialist—and always voted with labor or the democrats. My father hated Pilsudski. He said he was a worse terror for Poland than Hitler, and drunk a whole lot of schnapps to celebrate the night Pilsudski died. He was a pacifist, my father, and even though he would talk about these sunny times for Poland, I knew that *au fond* he was gloomy and worried. Once I heard him talking to my mother—it must have been around 1932—and I heard him say in this gloomy voice, 'This cannot truly last. There will be a war. Fate has never allowed Poland to be happy for very long.' This he spoke in German, I remember. In our house we spoke in German more often than we spoke in Polish. *Français* I learned to speak almost perfect in school but I spoke German even more easier than French. It was the influence of Vienna, you see, where my father and mother had spend so much time, and then my father was a professor of law and German was so much the language of scholars in those days. My mother was a wonderful cook in the Viennese style. Oh, there were a few good Polish things she cooked, but Polish cooking is not exactly *haute cuisine,* and so I remember the food she cooked in this big kitchen we had in Cracow—*Wiener Gulash Suppe* and *Schnitzel,* and oh! especially I remember this wonderful dessert she made called Metternich pudding that was all filled with chestnuts and butter and orange skin.

"I know maybe it sound tiresome to say so all the time,

but my mother and father was wonderful people. Nathan, you know, is okay now, he is calm, he is in one of his good times—periods, you say? But when he is in one of the bad times like the time when you first saw him—when he is in one of his *tempêtes,* I call them, he start to scream at me and always then call me an anti-Semitic Polish pig. Oh, his language, and what he calls me, words I've never heard before, in English, then Yiddish, everything! But always like 'You filthy Polish pig, crummy *nafka, kurveh,* you're killing me, you're killing me like you filthy Polish pigs have always killed the Jews!' And I try to talk to him, but he won't listen, he just stays crazy with this rage, and I have always knew it was no good at such a time to tell him about the good Poles like my father. Papa was born in Lublin when it belonged to the Russians and there were many, many Jews there who suffered from those terrible pogroms against them. Once my mother told me—because my father would never talk about such a thing—that when he was a young man he and his brother, who was a priest, risked their lives by hiding three Jewish families from the pogrom, from the Cossack soldiers. But I know that if I tried to tell this to Nathan during one of these *tempêtes,* he would only yell at me some more and call me a dirty pig Polack liar. Oh, I have to be so *patient* with Nathan then—I know then that he is becoming very sick, that he is not all right—and just turn away and keep silent and think of other things, waiting for the *tempête* to go away, when he will be kind and so sweet to me again, so full of *tendresse* and loving.

"It must be about ten years ago, a year or two before the war began, that I first heard my father say *Massenmord.* It was after the stories in the newspapers about the terrible destruction the Nazis had done in Germany on the synagogues and the Jewish stores. I remember my father first said something about Lublin and the pogroms he seen there, and then he said, 'First from the east, now from the west. This time it will be *ein Massenmord.*' I didn't realize completely what he mean then by what he said, I suppose a little bit because in Cracow there was a ghetto but not so many Jews as other places, and anyway, I didn't think about them being truly different or being victims or being persecuted. I suppose I was ignorant, Stingo. I was married then to Casimir—you know, I was married very, very young and I suppose I was still in this state of being a little girl and thinking that this wonderful life so comfortable and safe and secure would continue forever. Mama and Papa and Casimir and Zosia—Zosia, that is the, you know, nickname for Sophie—all living so happy in the big house, eating *Wiener Gulash Suppe* and studying and learning and listening to Bach—oh, forever. I don't understood how I might be so stupid. Casimir was an instructor in mathematics that I met when my mother and father had a party for some of the young teachers at the university. When Casimir and I were married we had these plans to go to Vienna like my mother and father did. It was going to be very much like the way *they* done their study. Casimir would get this *supérieur* degree in mathematics at the Austrian Academy and I would study music. I had been playing the piano myself ever since I was eight or nine years old and I was going to study under this very famous teacher, Frau Theimann, who had teached my mother and was still teaching although she was quite old. But that year there came the Anschluss and the Germans went into Vienna. It begun to be very frightening and my father said we were certain to go to war.

"I remember so well that last year when we were all together in Cracow. Somehow I still could not believe that this life we all have together would ever be changed. I was so happy with Casimir—Kazik—and loved him so very much. He was so generous and loving, and so intelligent—you see, Stingo, how I am attracted only to intelligent men. I cannot say whether I loved Kazik more than Nathan—I love Nathan so much that it hurts my heart—and maybe we should not do such a thing as compare one love with another. Well, I loved Kazik deeply, deeply, and I could not bear to think of the war coming so near and this possibility of Kazik being a soldier. So we put it out of our heads and that year we listened to concerts and read many books and went to the theatre and took long walks in the city, and on these walks I begin to learn to speak Russian. Kazik was in the beginning from Brest-Litovsk, which was for so long Russian, and he spoke that language as good as Polish and taught me it pretty good. Not like my father, who had also lived beneath the Russians but hated them so much that he refused to speak that language unless he was compelled to. Anyway, during this time I refused to think of this life ending. Well, I knew there would be some changes, but natural changes, you know, like moving out of the house of my parents and having our own house and family. But this I thought would come after the war, if there was one, because surely the war would be very short and the Germans would be defeated and then soon Kazik and I would go to Vienna and study like we had always planned to.

"I was so stupid to think of such a thing, Stingo. It was like my Uncle Stanislaw, who was my father's brother and was a colonel in the Polish horse troops. He was my favorite uncle, so full of life and this big laugh and this kind of wonderful, innocent feeling about the greatness of Poland—*la gloire, tu comprends, la patrie,* et cetera, as if Poland had never been under the Prussians and the Austrians and the Russians all these many years but had this *continuité* like France or England or some places like those. He would visit us in Cracow in his uniform with his saber and this mustache of a hussar and would talk very loud and laugh a lot and say that the Germans would be teach a lesson if they tried to fight Poland. I think my father would continue to be nice to my uncle—you know, try to humor him—but Kazik had this very direct, logical mentality and would argue with Uncle Stanislaw in a friendly way and ask him how these horse troops would have effect when the Germans came with their Panzer troops and tanks. And my uncle would say that all that was important was the terrain and that the Polish cavalry knew how to maneuver in the familiar terrain and the Germans would get total lost in the strange terrain, and that is how the Polish troops would turn the Germans back. And you know what happened when there was this confrontation—*une catastrophe totale,* in less than three days. Oh, it was all so foolish and gallant and futile. All those men and horses! And so sad, Stingo, sad . . .

"When the German soldiers came into Cracow—this was in September of 1939—we were all shocked and scared and of course we hate this thing that was happening to us but we stayed calm and hoped for the best things. Truly that part was not so bad, Stingo, I mean in the beginning, because we had faith that the Germans would treat us decent. They had not bombed the city like Warsaw, and so we feel a little special and protected, spared. The German soldiers they had very good behavior and I remember that my father said that this proved what he had believed for so long. And that was that the German soldier was in this tradition of ancient Prussia which had the code of honor and decency and so they would never harm civilians or be cruel to them. Also, it make us to feel calm to hear of these thousands of soldiers speaking German, which to our family was almost like the native tongue. So we had this panic at the very beginning but then it seemed not so bad. My father suffered terribly over the news about what happened in Warsaw but he said we must continue with our lives in the old way. He said that he had no illusions about what Hitler think of the intellectuals but he said that in other places like Vienna and Prague many teachers in the universities was permitted to continue their work, and he thought that he and Casimir would too. But after weeks and weeks passed and anything didn't happen, we saw that this time in Cracow was going to be okay, tolerable I mean.

"One morning that November I went to Mass in St. Mary's church, that is the church that has the trumpets, you know. In Cracow I went to Mass quite often and went many times after the Germans came, to pray that the war be over. Maybe it sound selfish and horrible to you, Stingo, but I think mainly I wished the war to be over so I could go to Vienna with Kazik and study. Oh, naturally there were a million other reasons to pray, but people are selfish, you know, and I felt very lucky that my family had been spared and was safe, so I just wished for the war to be over so that life could be as it was in the old days. But when I prayed at Mass this morning I had a . . . *a prémonition*—yes, the same, a premonition, and was filled with this slowly mounting frightful sensation. I didn't know what the fright was about, but in a sudden the prayer stop in my mouth and I could feel the wind blowing in the church around me, very wet and cold. And then I remembered what caused the fright, something that just came over me like a bright flash. Because I remembered that this same morning the new Nazi Governor General of Cracow district, this man named Frank, had make the faculty of the university to assemble in the *cour de maison,* you know, courtyard of the university, where they were to be told the new rules for the faculty under the occupation. It was nothing. It was to be a simple assembly. They were supposed to be there that morning. My father and Kazik heard about this only the day before and it appeared, you know, perfectly reasonable and no one thought about it very much. But now in this bright flash I felt something very, very wrong and I run from the church into the street.

"And oh, Stingo! now I tell you: I never saw my father or Kazik, ever again. I run, it was not far, and when I got to the university there was a vast crowd of people near the main gate in front of the courtyard. The street was closed to the traffic, and there were these huge German vans and hundreds and hundreds of German soldiers with rifles and machine guns. There was a *barrière* and these German soldiers wouldn't let me pass and just then I saw this older woman I knew well, Mrs. Professor Wochna, whose husband was teaching *la chimie,* you know, chemistry. She became hysterical and crying and she fell into my arms, saying, 'Oh, they are all gone, they have been taken away! All of them!' And I couldn't believe it, I couldn't believe it, but another wife of the faculty came near and she was crying too and she said, 'Yes, it's true. They have been taken away, they took my husband too, Professor Smolen.' And then I begun to believe it little by little, and I saw these closed vans going down the street toward the west, and then I believed it and cried and came into hysteria also. And run home and told my mother and we fell crying into each other's arms. My mother said, 'Zosia, Zosia, where did they go? Where did they take them?' And I said I didn't know, but only in a month we learned. My father and Kazik were taken to the concentration camp of Sachsenhausen and we learned that they were both shot to death on New Year's Day. Murdered only because they were Polish, and professors. There were many other teachers, one hundred eighty total I believe, and many of them didn't come back neither. It was not long after this that we went to Warsaw—it was necessary that I find work . . .

"These long years after, in 1945, when the war was over and I was in this center for displaced persons in Sweden, I would think back to that time when my father and Kazik were murdered and think of all the tears I cried, and wonder why after all that had happened to me I couldn't cry no longer. And this was true, Stingo, I had no more emotions. I was beyond feeling, like there was no more tears in me to pour on the earth. At this place in Sweden, I became friends with a Jewish woman from Amsterdam who was very kind to me, especially after I tried to kill myself. I suppose I didn't try very hard, cut my wrist with a piece of glass, and it didn't bleed much, but this older Jewish woman become very friendly to me and that summer we talked a lot together. She had been at the concentration camp where I was, and lost two sisters. I don't understood how she survived, there were so many Jews murdered there, you know, millions and millions of Jews, but somehow she survived as I did, just a very few of us. She spoke very good English, besides German, and that is how I begun to learn English, since I knew I would probably come to America.

"She was very religious, this woman, and always go to pray at the synagogue they had there. She told me that she still very much believed in God and once she asked me if I did not believe in Him too—the Christian God—just as she believed in her God, the God of Abraham. She said that what happened to her made more strong her belief of Him, even though she knew Jews who felt now God was gone from the world. And I said to her yes, I once believed in Christ and His Holy Mother too, but now after these years I was like those Jews who think God was gone forever. I said that I knew that Christ had turned His face away from me and I could no longer pray to Him as I did once in Cracow. I couldn't any longer pray to Him or could I any more cry. And when she asked how I know that Christ have turned His face away from me, I said I just knew, I just knew that only a God, only a Jesus who had no pity and who no longer care for me could permit the people I loved to be killed and let me live with such guilt. It was terrible enough they died like they done, but this guilt was more than I could bear. *On peut souffrir,* but you can suffer only so much . . .

"You can perhaps think it is a little thing, Stingo, but it is to permit someone to die without a farewell, an *adieu,* a single word of comfort or understanding that is so terrible to bear. I wrote to my father and Kazik in Sachsenhausen many letters but they always came back marked 'Unknown.' I only wanted to tell them how very much I loved them, especially Kazik, not because I loved him any more than Papa but because our very last time together we had a big fight and that was terrible. We almost never had fights, but we were married above three years and I suppose it was natural to quarrel sometime. Anyway, the night before this terrible day we had a big fight, I don't longer remember what it was even about, really, and I told him '*Spadaj!*'—which in Polish is like saying 'Drop dead'—and he rushed away and that night we didn't sleep in the same room. And I never seen him even once after that. So that is what I found it so difficult to bear, that we don't have even a gentle parting, a kiss, an embrace, nothing. Oh, I know Kazik knew I loved him still and I knew he loved me, but somehow it is all the worse that he must have suffered too, from not reaching me to say it, to communicate we love each other.

"So, Stingo, I have lived long with this very, very strong guilt which I can't lose, even though I know it has no reason, like that Jewish woman in Sweden said, when she try to make me see that the love we had was the most important thing, not the silly fight. But I still have this strong guilt. Funny, Stingo, you know I have learned to cry again, and I think perhaps that means I am a human being again. Perhaps that at least. A piece of a human being, but yes, a human being. Often I cry alone when I listen to music, which remind me of Cracow and those years past. And you know, there is one piece of music that I cannot listen to, it makes me cry so much my nose stops up, I cannot breathe, my eyes run like streams. It is in these Handel records I got for Christmas, 'I know that my Redeemer liveth,' that make me cry because of all my guilt, and also because I know that my Redeemer don't live and my body will be destroyed by worms and my eyes will never, never again see God . . ."

At the time of which I write, that hectic summer of 1947, when she told me so many things about her past and when I was fated to get ensnared, like some hapless June bug, in the incredible spider's nest of emotions that made up the relation between Sophie and Nathan, she was working in an out-of-the-way corner of Flatbush as a part-time receptionist in the office of Dr. Hyman Blackstock (*né* Bialystok). At this point Sophie had been in America a little less than a year and a half. Dr. Blackstock was a chiropractor and a long-ago immigrant from Poland. His patients included many old-time immigrants or more recent Jewish refugees. Sophie had obtained her job with the doctor not long after her arrival in New York in the early months of the previous year, when she had been brought to America under the auspices of an international relief organization. At first Blackstock (who spoke fluent Polish aside from his *mamaloshen* Yiddish) was rather distressed that the agency had sent him a young woman who was a *goy* and who had only a smattering of Yiddish learned in a prison camp. But, a warm-hearted man who was doubtless impressed by her beauty, by her plight and by the fact that she spoke flawless German, he hired her for this job which she sorely needed, possessing as she did little more than the flimsy clothes that had been given to her at the D.P. center in Sweden. Blackstock need not have worried; within days Sophie was chattering with the patients in Yiddish as if she had sprung from the ghetto. She rented the cheap room at Yetta Zimmerman's—her first true home in seven years—at about the same time she took the job. Working only three days a week allowed Sophie to keep body and soul together, in a manner of speaking, while also granting her extra days to improve her English at a free class at Brooklyn College and in general to become assimilated into the life of that vivid, vast and bustling borough.

She told me that she had never been bored. She was determined to put behind her the madness of the past—or as much as a vulnerable and memory-racked mind permitted—and so for her the huge city became the New World in spirit as well as fact. Physically she sensed that she was still badly run-down, but this did not prevent her from partaking of the pleasures around her like a child turned loose in an ice cream parlor. *Music,* for one thing; just the availability of music alone, she said, filled her insides with a sense of delectation, as one feels just before what one knows will be a sumptuous meal. Until she met Nathan she could not afford a phonograph, but no matter; on the inexpensive little portable radio she bought there was splendid music emanating from these stations with weird initials she could never get straight—WQXR, WNYC, WEVD—and men with silken voices announcing the enchanted names of all the musical potentates and princes whose harmonies she had been deprived of so long; even a shopworn composition like Schubert's Unfinished or *Eine kleine Nachtmusik* touched her with fresh rapture. And of course there were the concerts too, at the Academy of Music and, in the summer, at Lewisohn Stadium in Manhattan, gorgeous music so cheap as to be virtually free, music like Beethoven's Violin Concerto played one night at the stadium by Yehudi Menuhin with such wild, voracious passion and tenderness that as she sat there alone high on the rim of the amphitheatre, shivering a little beneath the blazing stars, she felt a serenity, a sense of inner solace that amazed her, along with the awareness that there were things to live for, and that she might actually be able to reclaim the scattered pieces of her life and compose of them a new self, given half a chance.

Those first months Sophie was alone a great deal of the time. Her difficulty with the language (soon overcome) made her shy, but even so she was content to be alone a lot, indeed luxuriated in solitude, since privacy had been something she had greatly lacked in recent years. These same years she had been deprived of books, of printed matter of almost any kind, and she began to read greedily, subscribing to a Polish-American newspaper and frequenting a Polish bookstore off Fulton Street that had a large lending library. Her taste ran mainly to translations of American writers, and the first book she finished, she recalled, was Dos Passos' *Manhattan Transfer.* This was followed by *A Farewell to Arms, An American Tragedy* and Wolfe's *Of Time and the River,* the last translated so wretchedly into Polish that she was forced to break the vow she had made, in the prison camp, to forswear for the rest of her life anything written in German, and read a German version that she was able to obtain from a branch of the public library. Possibly because this translation was felicitous and rich, or because Wolfe's lyrical, tragic though optimistic and sweeping vision of America was what Sophie's soul demanded at that moment—she being a newcomer to these shores, with only a rudimentary knowledge of the country's landscape and its gargantuan extravagance—it was *Of Time and the River* that excited her the most of all the books she read that winter and spring. In fact, Wolfe so captured her imagination that she decided to have a go at *Look Homeward, Angel* in English, but quickly gave up that chore, which she found excruciatingly difficult. For the initiate ours is a cruel language, its freaky orthography and idiosyncrasies never so absurdly apparent as on the printed page, and Sophie's skill at reading and writing always lagged behind her—to me—fetchingly erratic speech.

Her whole experience of America was New York—mostly Brooklyn—and eventually she came to love the city and to be terrified by it in almost equal measure. In her entire life she had known just two urban places—tiny Cracow in its Gothic repose and later the shapeless rubble heap of Warsaw after the *Blitzkrieg.* Her sweeter memories—that is, the ones she cared to dwell upon—were rooted in the town of her birth, immemorially suspended in a frieze of ancient rooftops and crooked streets and lanes. The intervening years between Cracow and Brooklyn had forced her—almost as a means of retaining sanity—to try to obliterate that time from recollection. Thus she said that those first mornings at Yetta's rooming house, waking in a strange bed surrounded by strange pink walls as she drowsily listened to the faint far-off rumble of traffic on Church Avenue, she would for long seconds be so unable to name or recognize either herself or her surroundings that she felt herself to be in a somnolent trance, like the enchanted maiden in one of those Grimm fairy tales of her childhood, transported after a nocturnal spell to a new and unknown kingdom. Then, blinking awake with a feeling in which sorrow and cheer were curiously commingled, she would say to herself: You are not in Cracow, Zosia, you are in America. And then rise to face the pandemonium of the subway and the chiropractic patients of Dr. Blackstock. And Brooklyn's greenly beautiful, homely, teeming, begrimed and incomprehensible vastness.

With the coming of spring Prospect Park, so close at hand, became Sophie's favorite refuge—wonderful to recall, a safe place in those days for a solitary and lovely blonde to wander. In the pollen-hazy light, dappled in shades of gold-flecked green, the great towering locusts and elms that loomed over meadow and rolling grass seemed prepared to shelter a *fête champêtre* in a scene by Watteau or Fragonard, and it was beneath one of these majestic trees that Sophie, on her free days or on weekends, would deposit herself, along with a marvelous luncheon picnic. She later confessed to me, with just the vaguest touch of shame, that she became quite possessed, truly unhinged by food as soon as she arrived in the city. She knew she had to exercise caution in eating. At the D.P. center the doctor from the Swedish Red Cross who took care of her had said that her malnutrition was so severe that it had probably caused some more or less permanent and damaging metabolic changes; he cautioned her that she must guard against quick overconsumption of food, especially of fats, no matter how strong the temptation. But this made it all the more fun for her, a pleasant game, when at lunchtime she entered one of the glorious delicatessens of Flatbush and shopped for her Prospect Park spread. The privilege of choice gave her a feeling achingly sensual. There was so much to eat, such variety and abundance, that each time her breath stopped, her eyes actually filmed over with emotion, and with slow and elaborate gravity she would choose from this sourly fragrant, opulent, heroic squander of food: a pickled egg here, there a slice of salami, half a loaf of pumpernickel, lusciously glazed and black. Bratwurst. Braunschweiger. Some sardines. Hot pastrami. Lox. A bagel, please. Clutching the brown paper bag, the warning like a litany in her mind—"Remember what Dr. Bergström said, don't *gorge* yourself"—she would make her methodical way into one of the farthest recesses of the park, or near a backwater of the huge lake, and there—munching with great restraint, taste buds enthralled in rediscovery—would turn to page 350 of *Studs Lonigan.*

She was feeling her way. In every sense of the word having experienced *rebirth,* she possessed some of the lassitude and, as a matter of fact, a great deal of the helplessness of a newborn child. Her clumsiness was like that of a paraplegic regaining the use of her limbs. Small things, preposterous tiny things, still confounded her. She had forgotten how to connect the two sides of the zipper on a jacket she had been given. Her maladroit fumblings appalled her, and once she burst into tears when, trying to squeeze out some cosmetic lotion from an ordinary plastic tube, she applied such careless force that the stuff gushed out all over her and ruined a new dress. But she was coming along. Occasionally she ached in her bones, her shins and ankles mainly, and her walk still had a hesitancy which seemed connected with the spiritlessness and fatigue that often overtook her and which she desperately hoped would go away. Yet if she did not quite exist in the full flood of sunlight, which is the hackneyed metaphor for good health, she was comfortably and safely far away from that abyssal darkness down into which she had nearly strayed. Specifically, this had been not much more than a year ago, when, at the just-liberated camp in the terminal hours of that existence she no longer allowed herself to remember, the Russian voice—a bass-baritone but harsh, corrosive as lye—pierced her delirium, penetrated the sweat and the fever and the kennel filth of the hard straw-strewn wooden shelf where she lay, to mutter over her in an impassive tone, "I think this one is finished too." For even then she knew that somehow she was not finished—a truth now borne out, she was relieved to say (while sprawled on the lakeside grass), by the timid yet voluptuous gurgles of hunger that attended the exalted instant, just before biting down, when her nostrils breathed in the briny smell of pickles, and mustard, and the caraway-tinged scent of Levy's Jewish rye.

But one late afternoon in June nearly brought a disastrous ending to the precarious equilibrium she had devised for herself. An aspect of the city's life which had to be entered negatively into her ledger of impressions was the subway. She detested New York subway trains for their grime and their noise, but even more for the claustrophobic nearness of so many human bodies, the rush-hour jam and jostle of flesh which seemed to neutralize, if not to cancel out, the privacy she had sought for so long. She was aware that it was a contradiction that someone who had been through all that she had should be so fastidious, should shrink so from strange epidermises, from alien touch. But there it was, she could not get rid of the feeling; it was a part of her new and transformed identity. A last resolve she had made at the swarming refugee center in Sweden was to spend the rest of her life avoiding people en masse; the rackety BMT mocked such an absurd idea. Returning home one early evening from Dr. Blackstock's office, she climbed into a car that was even more than normally congested, the hot and humid cage packed not only with the usual mob of sweating, shirt-sleeved and bare-necked Brooklynites of every shade and of every aspect of docile misery but soon with a crowd of screaming high school boys with baseball trappings who flooded aboard the train at a downtown stop, thrusting their way in all directions with such rowdy and brutish force that the sense of pressure became nearly unbearable. Pushed remorselessly toward the end of the aisle in a crush of rubbery torsos and slick perspiring arms, she found herself tripping and side-stepping into the dank dim platform that connected cars, firmly sandwiched between two human shapes whose identity, in an abstracted way, she was trying to discern just as the train screeched to a slow and shuddering halt and the lights went out. She was seized by a queasy fear. An audible feel of chagrin in the car, making itself known by soft moans and sighs, was drowned out by the boys' raucous cheers, at first so deafening and then so continuous that Sophie, rigidly immobilized in the blackest dark, knew in a flash that no cry or protest would avail her when she felt, now, from behind her the hand slither up between her thighs underneath her skirt.

If any small consolation was needed, she later reasoned, it was that she was spared the panic which otherwise surely would have overtaken her in such a tumult, in the oppressive heat and on a stopped and darkened train. She might even have groaned like the others. But the hand with its rigid central finger—working with surgical skill and haste, unbelievably assertive as it probed and burrowed—took care of that, causing simple panic to be superseded in her mind by the shocked and horrified disbelief of anyone experiencing sudden digital rape. For such it was, no random and clumsy grope but a swift all-out onslaught on, to put it simply, her vagina, which the disembodied finger sought like some evil, wiggling little rodent, quickly circumvented the silk, then entered at full length, causing her pain, but less pain than a kind of hypnotic astonishment. Dimly she was conscious of fingernails, and heard herself gasp "Please," certain of the banality, the stupidity of the word even as she uttered it. The whole event could not have been of more than thirty seconds' duration when finally the loathsome paw withdrew and she stood trembling in a suffocating darkness which it seemed would never know light again. She had no idea how long it was before the lights came on—five minutes, perhaps ten—but when they did, and the train began to move with a shuffling around of bodies, she realized that she had not the slightest way of knowing her attacker, submerged somewhere amid the half-dozen male backs and shoulders and protruding paunches surrounding her. Somehow she managed to flee the train at the next stop.

A straightforward, conventional rape would have done less violation to her spirit and identity, she thought later, would have filled her with less horror and revulsion. Any atrocity she had witnessed in the past five years, any outrage she herself had suffered—and she had known both past all recounting—had not numbed her to this gross insult. A classical face-to-face rape, however repellent, would at least permit the small gratification of knowing your assailant's features, of making him know that you knew, quite aside from the chance it presented, through a grimace or a hot level stare or even tears, of registering *something*: hatred, fright, malediction, disgust, possibly just derision. But this anonymous stroke in the dark, this slimy and bodiless entry from the rear, like a stab in the back from some vile marauder unknown to you forever; no, she would have preferred (she told me many months later when distance from the act allowed her to regard it with a saving hint of humor) a penis. It was bad enough in itself, yet she could have borne the episode with comparative strength at some other time in her life. But now her distress was compounded by the way it upset the fragile balance of her newly renovated psyche, by the manner in which this looting of her soul (for she felt it to be that as much as her body) not only pushed her back toward the *cauchemar,* the nightmare from which she was ever so delicately and slowly trying to retreat, but actually symbolized, in its wanton viciousness, the very nature of that nightmare world.

She who had for so long been off and on literally naked and who, these few months in Brooklyn, had so painstakingly reclothed herself in self-assurance and sanity had again by this act, she knew, been stripped bare. And she felt once more the freezing cold of the spirit. Without giving a specific reason for her request—and telling no one, not even Yetta Zimmerman, what had happened—she asked Dr. Blackstock for a week off from work and went to bed. Day after day in the balmiest part of summer she lay asprawl with the blinds drawn down to admit only thin yellow slivers of light. She kept her radio silent. She ate little, read nothing, and rose only to heat tea on her hot plate. In the deep shadows she listened to the crack of ball against bat and the shouts of boys in the baseball fields of the park, drowsed, and thought of the womblike perfection of that clock into which as a child she had crawled in her fancy, afloat on a steel spring, regarding the levers, the rubies, the wheels. Ever threatening at the margin of her consciousness were the shape and shadow, the apparition of the camp—the very name of which she had all but rejected from her private lexicon, and seldom used or thought of, and which she knew she could allow to trespass upon memory only at the danger of her losing—which is to say taking—her life. If the camp came too close again, as it had before in Sweden, would she have the strength to withstand the temptation, or would she seize the cutting edge once more and this time not botch the job? The question helped her to occupy the hours as she lay there those days, gazing up at the ceiling where flickers of light, seeping in from outside, swam like minnows on the desolating pink.

Providentially, though, it was music that helped save her, as it had in the past. On the fifth or sixth day—she recalled only that it was a Saturday—she awoke after a restless night filled with confused, menacing dreams and as if by old habit stretched out her hand and switched on the tiny Zenith radio which she kept on her bedside table. She had not meant to, it was simple reflex; the reason she had shut music out during these days of malignant depression was that she had found she could not bear the contrast between the abstract yet immeasurable beauty of music and the almost touchable dimensions of her own aching despair. But unknown to herself, she must have been open and receptive to the mysteriously therapeutic powers of W. A. Mozart, M.D., for the very first phrases of the music—the great *Sinfonia Concertante* in E-flat major—caused her to shiver all over with uncomplicated delight. And suddenly she knew why this was so, why this sonorous and noble statement so filled with peculiar, chilling dissonances should flood her spirit with relief and recognition and joy. For aside from its intrinsic loveliness, it was a work whose very identity she had sought for ten years. She had been smitten nearly mad with the piece when an ensemble from Vienna had visited Cracow a year or so before the Anschluss. Sitting in the concert hall, she had listened to the fresh new work as in a trance, and let the casements and doors of her mind swing wide to admit the luxuriant, enlaced and fretted harmonies, and those wild dissonances, inexhaustibly inspired. At a time of her early youth made up of the perpetual discovery of musical treasures, this was a treasure newly minted and supreme. Yet she never heard the piece again, for like everything else, the *Sinfonia Concertante* and Mozart, and the plaintive sweet dialogue between violin and viola, and the flutes, the strings, the dark-throated horns were all blown away on the war's wind in a Poland so barren, so smothered with evil and destruction that the very notion of music was a ludicrous excresence.

So in those years of cacophony in bombed-out Warsaw, and later at the camp, the memory of that work faded, even the title, which she ultimately confused with the titles of other pieces of music she had known and loved in time long past, until all that was left was a blurred but exquisite recollection of a moment of unrecapturable bliss, in Cracow, in another era. But in her room that morning the work, joyously blaring through the plastic larynx of the cheap little radio, brought her abruptly upright with quickened heartbeat and with an unfamiliar sensation around her mouth which she realized was a smile. For minutes she sat there listening, smiling, chilled, ravished while the unrecapturable became captured and slowly began to melt her fierce anguish. Then when the music was finished, and she had carefully written down the name of the work as the announcer described it, she went to the window and raised the blind. Gazing out at the baseball diamond at the edge of the park, she found herself wondering if she would ever have enough money to buy a phonograph and a recording of the *Sinfonia Concertante* and then realized that such a thought in itself meant that she was coming out of the shadows.

But thinking this, she still knew she had a long way to go. The music may have buoyed her spirit but her retreat into darkness had left her body feeling weak and ravaged. Some instinct told her that this was because she had eaten so little that the effect had been almost that of a fast; even so, she could not explain and was frightened by her loss of appetite, the fatigue, the knife-edge pains coursing down along her shins, and especially by the sudden onset of her menstrual period, arriving many days too early and with the blood flowing so copiously it was like a hemorrhage. Could this be, she wondered, an effect of her rape? The next day when she returned to work she resolved to ask Dr. Blackstock to examine her and suggest a course of treatment. She was not medically unsophisticated, so Sophie was aware of the irony involved in her seeking the ministrations of a chiropractor, but such strictures involving her employer she had of necessity abandoned when she took the desperately needed job in the first place. She knew, at least, that whatever he did was legal and that, of the multitude of the afflicted who streamed in and out of his office (including a number of policemen), some at least seemed benefited by his spinal manipulations, his pullings and stretchings and twistings and the other bodily stratagems he employed in the sanctum of his office. But the important thing was that he was one of the few people she knew well enough to turn to for advice of any kind. Thus she had a certain dependence on him, totally aside from her meager pay. And beyond this, she had come to be rather attached to the doctor in an amused and tolerant way.

Blackstock, a robust, handsome, gracefully balding man in his middle fifties, was one of God's blessed whose destiny had led him from the stony poverty of a *shtetl* in Russian Poland to the most sublime satisfactions that American materialistic success could offer. A dandy whose wardrobe ran to embroidered waistcoats, broad foulard ties and carnation boutonnières, a great talker and joke-teller (the stories mainly in Yiddish), he seemed to float in such a luminosity of optimism and good cheer that he actually gave off a kind of candlepower. He was a lubricous charmer, an obsessive bestower of fetching trinkets and favors, and he performed for his patients, for Sophie, for anyone who would watch, clever little magic tricks and feats of sleight of hand. In the pain of her difficult transition Sophie might have been dismayed by such boundless and energetic high spirits, these corny jokes and pranks, but behind it all she saw only such a childlike desire to be loved that she couldn't possibly let it offend her; besides, despite the obvious nature of his humor, he had been the first person in years who had caused her honest laughter.

About his affluence he was breath-takingly direct. Perhaps only a man so indefatigably good-hearted could recite the catalogue of his worldly goods without sounding odious, but he was able to, in a guttural hybrid English whose dominant overtone, Sophie's ear had learned to detect, was Brooklynese: "Forty thousand dollars a year income before taxes; a seventy-five-thousand-dollar home in the most elegant part of St. Albans, Queens, free of mortgage, with wall-to-wall carpeting plus indirect lighting in every room; three cars, including a Cadillac Fleetwood with all accessories, and a thirty-two-foot Chris-Craft sleeps six in comfort. All this plus the most darling and adorable wife God ever gave. And me a hungry Jewish youth, a poor *nebbish* with five dollars landing on Ellis Island not knowing a single individual. Tell me! Tell me why shouldn't I be the happiest man in the world? Why shouldn't I want to make people laugh and be happy like me?" No reason at all, thought Sophie one day that winter as she rode back to the office sitting next to Blackstock in the Cadillac after a trip to his house in St. Albans.

She had gone with him to help him sort out some papers in the auxiliary office he maintained at home, and there for the first time she had met the doctor's wife—a buxom dyed blonde named Sylvia, garishly clad in ballooning silk pants like a Turkish belly dancer, who showed Sophie around the house, the first she had entered in America. This was an eerie organdy and chintz labyrinth glowing at high noon in the empurpled half-light of a mausoleum, where rosy cupids simpered from the walls down upon a grand piano in fire-engine red and overstuffed chairs glistening beneath protective shrouds of transparent plastic, and where the porcelain bathroom fixtures were jet-black. Later, in the Cadillac Fleetwood with its huge monogram on the front doors—HB—Sophie watched in fascination as the doctor made use of his mobile telephone, installed only recently for a few select customers on an experimental basis, and in Blackstock's hands, a surpassing implement of love. Later she recalled the dialogue—his part of it, at any rate—as he made contact with his St. Albans abode. "Sylvia sweetness, this is Hymie. Loud and clear you read me? I love you, darling pet. Kisses, kisses, darling. The Fleetwood's now on Liberty Avenue passing just now Bayside Cemetery. I adore you, darling. Here's a kiss for my darling. (*Smack, smack!*) Back in a few minutes, sweetness." And a short while later: "Sylvia darling, this is Hymie. I adore you, my darling pet. Now the Fleetwood is at the intersection of Linden Boulevard and Utica Avenue. What a fantastic traffic jam! I kiss you, my darling. (*Smack, smack!*) I send you many, many kisses. What? You say you're going shopping in New York? Buy something beautiful to wear for Hymie, my beautiful sweetness. I love you, my darling. Oh, darling, I forgot, take the Chrysler. The Buick's got a busted fuel pump. Over and out, darling pet." And then with a glance at Sophie, stroking the receiver: "What a sensational instrument of communication!" Blackstock was a truly happy man. He adored Sylvia more than life itself. Only the fact that he was childless, he once told Sophie, kept him from being *absolutely* the happiest man on earth . . .

As will be seen in due course (and the fact is important to this narrative), Sophie told me a number of lies that summer. Perhaps I should say she indulged in certain evasions which at the time were necessary in order for her to retain her composure. Or maybe her sanity. I certainly don't accuse her, for from the point of view of hindsight her untruths seem fathomable beyond need of apology. The passage a while back about her early life in Cracow, for example—the soliloquy which I have tried to transcribe as accurately as I have been able to remember it—is, I am now certain, made up mostly of the truth. But it contained one or two significant falsehoods, along with some crucial lacunae, as will eventually be made clear. As a matter of fact, reading back through much of what I have written so far, I note that Sophie told me a lie within moments after we first set eyes on each other. This was when, after the ghastly fight with Nathan, she leveled upon me her look of desperation and declared that Nathan was "the only man I have ever made love to beside my husband." Although unimportant, that statement was not true (much later she admitted it to me, confessing that after her husband was shot by the Nazis—a truth—she had had a lover in Warsaw), and I bring the matter up not out of any priggish insistence on absolute veracity but to indicate Sophie's guarded approach to sex. And thus to suggest at this point the difficulty she had in telling Blackstock about the fearful malaise which had overtaken her, and which she felt must be the result of her rape in the subway.

She squirmed at the idea of revealing her secret—even to Blackstock, a professional man and, moreover, a person in whom she knew she could confide. The loathsomeness of what had happened to her was something that even twenty months at the camp—with its daily, inhuman degradation and nakedness—could not make her feel less befouled. Indeed, she now felt even more helplessly befouled because she had thought of Brooklyn as "safe," and furthermore, her shame was anything but lessened by the fact that she was Catholic and Polish and a child of her time and place—that is to say, a young woman brought up with puritanical repressions and sexual taboos as adamantine as those of any Alabama Baptist maiden. (It would take Nathan, she told me later, Nathan with his liberated and passionate carnality, to unlock the eroticism in her which she never dreamed she possessed.) Add to this indwelling shame of the rape the unconventional, to say the least, the grotesque *way* she had been attacked—and the embarrassment she felt at having to tell Blackstock became nearly insupportable.

But somehow, on another trip to St. Albans in the Cadillac, speaking at first in stiff and formal Polish, she managed to get through to him her concern about her health, her languor and the pains in her legs and her bleeding, and then finally spoke almost in a whisper about the episode in the subway. And as she had supposed, Blackstock did not immediately get the drift of what she was saying. Then with hesitant, choking difficulty, which only much later would in itself acquire a faint touch of the comic, she made him understand that no, the act had not been consummated in the ordinary fashion. However, it was no less revolting and soul-shattering for the uncommon way in which it was carried out. "Doctor, don't you see?" she whispered, now speaking in English. Even *more* revolting because of that—she said, in tears now—if he could possibly bring himself to see what she meant. "You mean," he interrupted, "a *finger* . . . ? He didn't do it with his . . ." And delicately paused, for in regard to sex, Blackstock was not a coarse man. And when Sophie again affirmed all that she had been saying, he looked at her with compassion and murmured, very bitterly for him, *"Oy vey,* what a *farshtinkener* world is this."

The upshot of all this was that Blackstock readily conceded that the violation she had suffered, peculiar as it was, could indeed have caused the symptoms that had begun to plague her, especially the gross bleeding. Specifically, his diagnosis was that her trauma, located as it was in the pelvic region, had induced a minor but not to be ignored displacement of the sacral vertebra, with consequent pressure on either the fifth lumbar or the first sacral nerve, perhaps both of these; in any case, it was certainly enough to provoke the loss of appetite, the fatigue and the aches in her bones she had complained of, while the bleeding itself triumphantly ratified the other symptoms. Clearly, he told Sophie, a course of spinal-column manipulations was needed in order to restore normal nerve function and to bring her back to what the doctor called (picturesquely, even to Sophie's inexpert ear) "the full blush of health." Two weeks of chiropractic treatment, he assured her, and she would be as good as new. She had become like a relative to him, he confided, and he wouldn't charge her a penny. And to further cheer her up, he insisted that she witness his newest act of prestidigitation, in which a bouquet of multicolored silks suddenly vanished from his hands in midair, only to reappear in an instant as miniature flags of the United Nations slowly unspooling on a thread from his mouth. Sophie was able somehow to disgorge an appreciative laugh, but at the moment she felt so despairingly low, so ill, that she thought she might go mad.

Nathan once referred to the way in which he and Sophie met as having been "cinematic." By this he meant that they had met not as most people do, thrown together by the common circumstance of upbringing or school or office or neighborhood, but in the delightful and haphazard way of those romantic strangers of Hollywood daydreams, those lovers-to-be whose destinies became intertwined from the first twinkling of their chance encounter: John Garfield and Lana Turner, for instance, utterly doomed from the instant of their mingled glance in a roadside café, or, more whimsically, William Powell and Carole Lombard on hands and knees at the jeweler's, their skulls colliding as they search for an elusive diamond. On the other hand, Sophie attributed the convergence of their paths simply to the failure of chiropractic medicine. Suppose, she sometimes later mused, that all of Dr. Blackstock's ministrations and those of his young associate, Dr. Seymour Katz (who came in after office hours to help take care of the prodigious overflow of sufferers), had worked; suppose the chain of events that led from the vandalizing finger to the sacral vertebra to the compressed fifth lumbar nerve not only had proved *not* to be a chiropractic chimera but had been terminated in triumph, radiantly, healthfully, as a result of Blackstock's and Katz's fortnight of thumping and stretching and drubbing of her tormented spine.

Cured in this fashion, she never would have met Nathan, no doubt of that. But the trouble was that all the vigorous treatment she submitted to only made her feel worse. It made her feel so horrible that she overcame her unwillingness to hurt Blackstock's sensibilities, telling him that none of her symptoms had subsided and that in fact they had grown more nagging and alarming. "But, my darling girl," Blackstock exclaimed, shaking his head, "you've *gotta* feel better!" Two full weeks had gone by, and when Sophie suggested to the doctor, with great reticence, that perhaps she was in need of an M.D., a real diagnostician, he flew into the closest approximation of a rage she had ever seen in this almost pathologically benign man. "A doctor of *medicine* you want? Some fancy *gozlin* from Park Slope that'll rob you blind! My darling girl, better you should take yourself to a veterinarian!" To her despair, he then proposed to treat her with an Electro-Sensilator, a newly developed and complicated-looking device, shaped rather like a small refrigerator and containing many wires and gauges, which was supposed to rearrange the molecular structure of her spinal bone cells and which he had just acquired ("for a pretty penny," he said, adding to her store of idiomatic English) from world chiropractic headquarters somewhere in Ohio or Iowa—states whose names she always got confused.

The morning of the day that she was scheduled to submit to the Electro-Sensilator's macabre embrace she woke up feeling exceptionally worn-out and sick, far worse than ever before. It was her day off from work and so she drowsed through the forenoon, coming fully awake only around twelve. She recalled clearly of that morning that in her febrile doze—a half-sleep in which the far past of Cracow was curiously, senselessly intermingled with the smiling presence and sculpting hands of Dr. Blackstock—she kept dreaming with mysterious obsessiveness of her father. Humorless, forbidding in his starched wing collar, his oval unrimmed professorial spectacles and black mohair suit odorous of cigar smoke, he lectured her in German with the same ponderous intensity she remembered from her childhood; he seemed to be warning her about something—was he concerned about her sickness?—but when each time she struggled up like a swimmer out of slumber his words bubbled away and fled from her memory, and she was left only with the fading apparition of her father, comfortless and severe, somehow even vaguely threatening. At last—mainly now to throw off this irrepressible image—she forced herself to get out of bed and face the meltingly lush and beautiful summer day. She was quite shaky on her feet and was aware that again she had no appetite at all. She had been conscious for a long time of the paleness of her skin, but on this morning a glance in the bathroom mirror truly horrified her, brought her close to panic: her face was as devoid of any of the animating pink of life as those bleached skulls of ancient monks she recalled from the underground sepulcher of an Italian church.

With a wintry shiver that ran through all her bones, through her fingers—skinny and bloodless, she suddenly perceived—and to the cold bottoms of her feet, she clenched her eyes tightly shut in the smothering and absolute conviction that she was dying. And she knew the name of the malady. I have leukemia, she thought, I am dying of leukemia, like my cousin Tadeusz, and all of Dr. Blackstock's treatment is only a kindly masquerade. He knows I am dying and all his care is simply pretense. A touch of hysteria almost perfectly pitched between grief and hilarity seized her as she pondered the irony of dying of such an insidious and inexplicable disease after all the other sicknesses she had survived and after all, in so many countless ways, she had seen and known and endured. And to this thought she was able to add the perfectly logical notion, however tortured and despairing, that such an end was perhaps only the body's grim way of effecting the self-destruction she had been unable to manage by her own hand.

But somehow she was able to take hold of herself and push the morbid thought back into the far recesses of her mind. Drawing away slightly from the mirror, she caught a narcissistic gleam of her familiar beauty, dwelling persistently beneath the white mask, and this gave her a long moment of comfort. It was the day of her English lesson at Brooklyn College, and in order to become fortified for the dreadful trip by subway and for the session itself, she made herself eat. It was a task accompanied by waves of nausea, but she knew she *had* to force it down: the eggs and the bacon and the whole-wheat bread and the skimmed milk she assembled together listlessly in the gloom of her cramped little kitchenette. And while eating she had an inspiration—at least in part produced by the Mahler symphony playing at the moment on WQXR's midday concert. For no clear reason a series of somber chords, struck in the middle of the symphony's andante movement, reminded her of the remarkable poem which had been read to her at the end of her last English class, a few days before, by the teacher, an ardent, fat, patient and conscientious young graduate student known to the class as Mr. Youngstein. Doubtless because of her proficiency in other tongues, Sophie was far and away the prize student among this motley of striving scholars, a polyglot group but mainly Yiddish-speaking refugees from all the destroyed corners of Europe; her excellence had no doubt attracted Mr. Youngstein to her, although Sophie was hardly so lacking in self-awareness as to be unmindful of the fact that her simple physical presence might have worked upon the young man its plainly troubling effect.

Flustered and bashful, he was obviously smitten by her, but had made no advances other than to suggest awkwardly each day that she remain for a few moments after class so that he might read her what he called some "representative American verse." This he would do in a nervous voice, slowly intoning the lines from Whitman and Poe and Frost and others in hoarse, unmusical but clearly enunciated syllables, while she listened with great care, touched often and deeply by this poetry which from time to time brought exciting new nuances of meaning to the language, and by Mr. Youngstein's clumsy and grasping passion for her, expressed in faun-gazes of yearning from behind his monstrous prismlike spectacles. She found herself both warmed and distressed by this callow, transfixed infatuation and could really respond only to the poetry, for besides being, at twenty or so, at least ten years younger than she was, he was also physically unappealing —that is, enormously overweight aside from his grotesquely disoriented eyes. His feeling for these poets, though, was so profound, so genuine that he could scarcely fail to communicate much of their essence, and Sophie had been captured in particular by the haunted melody of one verse, which began:

Because I could not stop for Death,
He kindly stopped for me;
The carriage held but just ourselves
And Immortality.

She adored hearing Mr. Youngstein read the poem and wanted actually to read it herself in her much improved English, along with the poet's other works, so that she might commit it to memory. But there was a small confusion. She had missed one of the teacher's inflections. Sophie had understood that this brief poem, this enchanted, simply wrought vision with its thronging sound of the eternal, was the handiwork of an American poet whose last name was identical to that of one of the immortal novelists of the world. And so in her room at Yetta's, reminded of the poem again today by those somber chords of Mahler, she decided to go before class began to the Brooklyn College library and browse through the work of this marvelous artificer, whom she also ignorantly conceived to be a man. Such an innocuous misunderstanding, she later observed to me, was actually a crucial piece in the finally assembled little mosaic which resolved itself as the portrait of her meeting with Nathan.

She recalled it all so clearly—emerging from the flatulent warmth of the detested subway and onto the sunny campus with its sprawling rectangles of ripe green grass, its crowd of summer-school students, the trees and flowered walks. She always felt somewhat more at peace here than in other parts of Brooklyn; though this college bore as much resemblance to the venerable Jagiellonian University of her past as does a shiny chronometer to a mossy old sundial, its splendidly casual and carefree mob of students, its hustling between-classes pace, its academic look and feel made Sophie comfortable, relaxed, at home. The gardens were a serene and blossoming oasis amid the swarm of a chaotic Babylon. That day as she traversed the edge of the gardens on her way toward the library she caught a glimpse of something which thereafter dwelled so immovably in her mind that she wondered if it, too, was not at last bound up in a mystical way with Nathan, and the imminence of his appearance in her life. What she saw even by the decorous standards of Brooklyn College and the forties was hardly shocking, and Sophie was not so much shocked as fiercely agitated, as if the swift and desperate sensuality of the little scene had the power to stir up embers of a fire within her which she thought had been almost forever quelled. It was the merest fleeting glance she had, this color snapshot of the two dark and resplendently beautiful young people lolling against a tree trunk: with arms full of schoolbooks yet as abandoned as David and Bathsheba, they stood pressed together kissing with the urgent hunger of animals devouring each other's substance, and their tongues thrust and explored each other gluttonously, the darting flesh visible through the black mantle of the girl's rich cascading hair.

The instant passed. Sophie, feeling as if she had been stabbed in the breast, wrenched her eyes away. She hurried on down the crowded sidewalk, aware that she must be blushing feverishly and that her heart was pounding at a gallop. It was unexplainable and alarming, this incandescent sexual excitement she felt everywhere inside herself. After having felt *nothing* for so long, after having lived for so long with dampened desire! But now the fire was in her fingertips, coursing along the edges of all her extremities, but mainly it blazed at the core of herself, somewhere near the womb, where she had not felt such an insistent craving in months and years beyond counting.

But the incredible emotion evaporated swiftly. It was gone by the time she entered the library, and long before she encountered the librarian behind the desk—a Nazi. No, of course he was not a Nazi, not only because the black-and-white engraved nameplate identified him as Mr. Sholom Weiss but because—well, what would a Nazi be doing apportioning volume after volume of the earth's humane wisdom at the Brooklyn College library? But Sholom Weiss, a pallid dour thirtyish man with aggressive horn-rims and a green eyeshade, was such a startling double of every heavy, unbending, mirthless German bureaucrat and demi-monster she had known in years past that she had the weird sense that she had been thrust back into the Warsaw of the occupation. And it was doubtless this moment of *déjà vu,* this rush of identification, that caused her to become so quickly and helplessly unstrung. Feeling suffocatingly weak and ill again, she asked Sholom Weiss in a diffident voice where the catalogue file would be in which she might find listed the works of the nineteenth-century American poet Emil Dickens.

"In the catalogue room, first door to the left," muttered Weiss, unsmiling, then after a long pause added, "But you won't find any such listing."

"Won't find any such listing?" Sophie echoed him, puzzled. Following a moment's silence, she said, "Could you tell me why?"

"Charles Dickens is an *English* writer. There is *no* American poet by the name of Dickens." The voice was so sharp and hostile as to be like an incision.

Swept with sudden nausea, light-headed and with a perilous tingling moving across her limbs like the faint prickling of a multitude of needles, Sophie watched with dispassionate curiosity as Sholom Weiss's face, sullenly inflexible in its graven unpleasantness, seemed to float away ever so slightly from the neck and the confining collar. I feel so terribly sick, she said to herself as if to some invisible, solicitous doctor, but managed to choke out to the librarian, "I'm *sure* there is an American poet Dickens." Thinking then that those lines, those reverberant lines with their miniature, sorrowing music of mortality and time, would be as familiar to an American librarian as anything, as household objects are, or a patriotic anthem, or one's own flesh, Sophie felt her lips part to say, *Because I could not stop for Death . . .* She was hideously nauseated. And she failed to realize that in the intervening seconds there had registered somewhere in the precincts of Sholom Weiss's unmagnanimous brain her stupid contradiction of him, and its insolence. Before she could utter the line, she heard his voice rise against every library decree of silence and cause a distant, shadowy turning of heads. A hoarse rasping whisper—querulous, poisoned with needless ill will—his retort was freighted with all the churlish indignation of petty power. "Listen, I *told* you," the voice said, "there is no *such a person!* You want me to draw you a *picture!* I am *telling* you, do you *hear* me!"

Sholom Weiss may easily have thought that he had slain her with language. For when Sophie woke up some moments later from the dead faint into which she had slumped to the floor, his words still ricocheted crazily about in her mind and she realized dimly that she had fallen into a swoon just at the instant he had finished yelling at her. But everything now had gone topsy-turvy, disjointed, and she barely knew where she was. The library, yes, certainly, that was where she was, but she seemed to be reclining awkwardly on a sort of couch or window seat not from the desk in front of which she had collapsed, and she was so weak, and a disgusting odor flooded the air around her, a sour smell she could not identify until, slowly, feeling the wet stain down the front of her blouse, she became aware that she had thrown up her last meal. A damp carapace of vomit drenched her breast like foul mud.

But even as she absorbed this knowledge she moved her head listlessly, conscious of something else, a voice, a man's voice, orotund, powerful, raging at the half-cowering and perspiring figure whose back was to her but whom she dimly recognized by the green eyeshade gone askew on his brow as Sholom Weiss. And something stern and commanding and consummately outraged in the voice of the man, whom she could barely see from her vantage point, caused an odd and pleasant chill to course up her back even as she reclined there in her feeble, prostrate helplessness. "I don't know who you are, Weiss, but you've got bad manners. I heard every fucking word you said to her, I was standing right here!" he roared. "And I heard every intolerably rude and ugly thing you said to that girl. Couldn't you tell she was a foreigner, you fucking little *momzer* you, you *shmuck!*" A small crowd had gathered around and Sophie saw the librarian quiver as if he were being buffeted by savage winds. "You're a kike, Weiss, a *kike,* the kind of mean little creep that gives Jews a bad name. That girl, that nice and lovely girl there with a little trouble with the language, asks you a perfectly decent question and you treat her like some piece of shit walked in. I ought to break your fucking skull! You got about as much business around books as a plumber!" Suddenly, to her drowsy astonishment, Sophie saw the man yank Weiss's eyeshade down around his windpipe, where it dangled like a useless celluloid appendage. "You nasty little *putz,*" the voice said, full of contempt and revulsion, "you're enough to make *anyone* puke!"

Sophie must have lost consciousness once more, for the next thing she remembered was Nathan's gentle, strong and marvelously expressive fingers streaked, to her intense discomfort, with slimy smears of her own vomit yet endlessly consoling and reassuring as they lightly applied something wet and cool to her brow. "You're all right, honey," he whispered, "you're going to be *all right.* Just don't worry about anything. Ah-h, you're so *beautiful,* how did you get to be so beautiful? Don't move now, you're all right, you just had a funny little spell. Just lie still, let the doctor take care of everything. *There,* how does that feel? Want a little sip of water? No, no, don't try to say anything, just relax, you're going to be all well in just a minute." On and on the voice went, a gentle monologue, lulling, soothing, murmurously infusing her with a sense of repose; it was a soft refrain so sedative indeed that soon she was no longer even embarrassed that the hands of this stranger were greenly stained with her own sour juices, and somehow she regretted that the one thought she had expressed to him, when she had first opened her eyes, had been the impossibly foolish *Oh, I think I'm going to die.* "No, you're *not going to die,*" he was saying again in that voice filled with its infinite and patient strength, as the fingers brought exquisite coolness to her brow, "you're not going to die, you'll live to be a hundred. What's your name, sweetie? No, don't tell me now, just lie still and look beautiful. Your pulse is fine, steady. There, try this little sip of water . . ."

Five

It must have been a couple of weeks after settling comfortably into my pink lodgings that I received another communication from my father. It was a fascinating letter in itself, although I could hardly realize then what bearing it would ultimately have upon my relationship with Sophie and Nathan and the scrambled events that took place later on in the summer. Like the last of his letters I quoted—the one about Maria Hunt—this message had to do with a death, and like the earlier one concerning Artiste, it brought me news of what might be considered something in the nature of a legacy, or a share in one. I set down most of it here:

> Son, ten days ago my dear friend and political & philosophical antagonist Frank Hobbs dropped dead at his office in the shipyard. It was a swift, I should say almost instantaneous cerebral thrombosis. He was only 60, an age I have begun desperately to perceive as being virtually in life's springtide. His passing was a great shock to me and I feel the loss deeply. His politics of course were deplorable, situating him I should say about 10 miles to the right of Mussolini, but withal he was what we who originated in the country have always termed a "good ole boy" and I shall miss intensely his hulking, generous albeit bigoted presence as we drove to work. He was in many ways a tragic man, lonely, a widower, and still mourning the death of his only child, Frank Jr., who you may remember drowned while still in his twenties

not long ago in a fishing accident down on Albemarle Sound. Frank Sr. left no survivors, and that fact is central to this letter and to the reason I am writing you at some length.

Frank's lawyer called me up several days ago to inform me, to my enormous astonishment, that I am the chief beneficiary of his estate. Frank had little money saved and no investments, having been like myself only a high class wage-earner within or perhaps I should say astride the precarious back of the monstrous leviathan known as American business. Thus I regret I do not bring you tidings of the imminent receipt of a fat check to lighten your worries as you labor in the literary vineyard. For many years, however, Frank had been the owner and absentee landlord of a small peanut farm over in Southampton County, a place that was in the Hobbs family ever since the Civil War. It is this farm that Frank left to me, stating in his will that while I could do with it what I wished it was his earnest hope that I continue to farm the place as he had done, realizing not only the very modest profit that can be gained from 60 acres of peanuts but enjoying the pleasant and verdant countryside in which the farm is situated, along with a lovely little stream swarming with fish. He must have known how much I appreciated the place, which I visited a number of times over the years.

This extraordinary and touching gesture of Frank's has, however, I'm afraid, thrown me into something of a quandary. While I should like to do anything within my power to accede to Frank's desire and not sell the place I don't know if I am any longer temperamentally suited to farming after these many years (although as a boy in N.C. I was well acquainted with the heft of a shovel and hoe), even as an absentee owner as Frank was. It still requires a great deal of work and attention and while Frank doted on it I have my own labor cut out for me here at the shipyard. In many ways of course it is an attractive proposition. There are two very able and reliable negro tenant farmers on the place, and the equipment is in reasonably good condition. The main dwelling itself is in excellent repair and would make a fine weekend retreat particularly considering its proximity to that wonderful fishing stream. Peanuts are now a coming money crop, especially since the late war opened up so many new uses for the legume. Frank, I remember, sold most of his crop to Planters in Suffolk, where it went to help satiate America's ravenous need for "Skippy" peanut butter. There are some hogs, too, which of course make the finest hams in all Christendom. Also there are a few acres planted in soybeans and cotton, both still profitable crops, and so as you can see there are totally mercenary aspects of the situation—aside from the aesthetic and recreative—that tempt me into lending my hand to agrarian pursuits after 40-odd years' absence from the barn and the field. Certainly it would not make me rich, though I suspect I might in some small way augment an income badly depleted by the needs of your poor aunts down in N.C. But I am balked by the aforementioned serious qualms and reservations. And this brings me, Stingo, to your possible or potential role in this so far unresolved dilemma.

What I am proposing is that you come down to the farm and live on it, acting as the proprietor in my absence. I can almost feel your chagrin as you read this, and see that "but I don't know a damn thing about raising peanuts" look in your eye. I am well aware how this may not seem at all suitable to you, especially since you have chosen to cast your lot as a literary man among the Yankees. But I am asking you to consider the proposition, not because I don't honor your need for independence as you sojourn in the (to me) barbaric North but out of honest solicitude for the discontent you express in your recent letters, that sense I get that you are not precisely flourishing, spiritually or (of course) financially. But for one thing your duties would be minimal since Hugo and Lewis, the two negroes who have been on the place for years with their families, have the practical matters of the place well in hand so that you would function as a kind of gentleman farmer whose main work, I'm certain, would be the writing of that novel you tell me you have embarked upon. But you would also pay no rent and I'm sure I could manage a small extra stipend for your few responsibilities. Furthermore (and I was saving this for now) I ask you to consider this final inducement, which is the proximity of the farm to the ancient habitat of "ole prophet Nat," that mysterious negro who so frightened the pants off or (if you will pardon the more accurate expletive) the s—t out of an unhappy slave-holding Virginia so many years ago. No one knows better than I of your fascination with the "ole Prophet" since I cannot forget how even as a high school boy you were busy with your maps and your charts and all the meager information you were able to assemble regarding that extraordinary figure. The Hobbs farm is only a hop, skip and a jump from the ground upon which the Prophet set forth on his terrible mission of bloodshed, and I should think that if you took up residence there you might be richly supplied with all the atmosphere and information you need for that book I'm sure you will eventually write. Please think over carefully this proposition, son. Needless to say I would not nor can I disguise the element of self-interest that prompts the offer. I am very much in need of an overseer for the farm, if I am to keep it at all. But if this is true I cannot disguise, either, the vicarious pleasure I take in thinking that you, growing to be the writer I yearned to be but could not, might have such a splendid chance to live on that land, to feel and see and smell the very earth which gave birth to that dim and prodigious black man . . .

In a way it was all very tempting, and I could not deny it. With his letter my father had enclosed several Kodachrome snapshots of the farm; surrounded and shaded by lofty beech trees, the sprawling old mid-nineteenth-century farmhouse looked as if it needed—aside from a coat of paint—hardly anything to make it the comfortable abode of one who might slide easily into that great Southern tradition of writer-farmers. The sorghum-sweet serenity of the place (geese paddling through the weedy summer grass, a drowsy porch with a swing, old Hugo or Lewis sending a grin full of calcimine teeth and pink gums across the steering wheel of a muddy tractor) skewered me squarely for an instant on a knifeblade of nostalgia for the rural South. The temptation was both poignant and powerful, and it lasted for as long as it took me to read the letter twice more and to brood over the house and its homely lawn again, all of it seemingly suspended in a milky idyllic mist, which may, however, have been the result of the film's overexposure. But though the letter tugged at my heart and at the same time possessed, in practical terms, a compelling logic, I realized that I had to turn my father's invitation down. If the letter had arrived only a few weeks before, at the low ebb of my life after being fired from McGraw-Hill, I might have jumped at the chance. But things were now radically altered and I had happily come to terms with my environment. So I was forced to write back to my father a somewhat regretful No. And as I look back now on that promising time I realize that there were three factors responsible for my surprising newborn contentment. In no particular order of significance, these were: (1) sudden illumination about my novel, its prognosis heretofore opaque and unyielding; (2) my discovery of Sophie and Nathan; and (3) anticipation of guaranteed sexual fulfillment, for the first time in my unfulfilled life.

To begin with, a word about that book I was trying to get started on. In my career as a writer I have always been attracted to morbid themes—suicide, rape, murder, military life, marriage, slavery. Even at that early time I knew my first work would be flavored by a certain morbidity—I had the feeling in my bones, it may possibly be called the "tragic sense"—but to be perfectly honest, I had only the vaguest notion of what I was so feverishly setting off to write about. It is true that I possessed in my brain a most valuable component of a work of fiction: a place. The sights, sounds, smells, the lights and shades and watery deeps and shallows of my native Tidewater coast were urgently pressing me to be given physical reality on paper, and I could scarcely contain my passion—it was almost like a rage—to get them down. But of characters and story, a sensible narrative through which I might be able to thread these vivid images of my recent past, I had none.

At twenty-two I felt myself to be hardly more than a skinny, six-foot-tall, one-hundred-and-fifty-pound exposed nerve with nothing very much to say. My original strategy was pathetically derivative, lacking logic and design and substituting for both an amorphous hunger to do for a small Southern city what James Joyce had done in his miraculous microcosm. For someone of my age it was not a totally worthless ambition, save for the fact that even on the more modest level of attainment I sought, there seemed no way to invent Dixieland replicas of Stephen Dedalus and the imperishable Blooms.

But then—and oh, how true it is that most writers become sooner or later the exploiters of the tragedies of others—came (or went) Maria Hunt. She had died just at that moment when I most needed that wondrous psychic jolt known as inspiration. And so during the next few days after getting news of her death, as the shock wore off and I was able to adopt what might be called a professional view of her grotesque ending, I was overtaken by a fabulous sense of discovery. Again and again I pored over the newspaper clipping my father had sent, becoming warm with excitement as the awareness grew that Maria and her family might serve as the exemplary figures for the novel's cast of characters. The rather desperate wreck of a father, a chronic lush and also something of a womanizer; the mother, slightly unbalanced and a grim pietist, known throughout the upper-middle-class, country-club and high-Episcopal echelons of the city for her long-suffering tolerance of her husband's mistress, herself a social-climbing dimwit from the sticks; and the daughter finally, poor dead Maria, doomed and a victim from the outset through all the tangled misunderstandings, petty hatreds and vindictive hurts that are capable of making bourgeois family life the closest thing to hell on earth—my God, I thought, it was perfectly marvelous, a gift from the sky! And I realized to my delight that, however unwittingly, I had already put together the first part of the frame to surround this tragic landscape: my dog-eared train ride, the passage I had cherished and reread with such daft absorption, would now represent the arrival in the town of our heroine's body, disinterred from the potter's field in New York and shipped in a baggage car for final burial in the city of her birth. It seemed too good to be true. Oh, what ghoulish opportunism are writers prone to!

Even before I put my father's letter down for the last time, I breathed a delicious sigh and felt the next scene hatching, so palpable I could almost reach up and fondle it, like a fat golden egg in my brain. I turned to my yellow legal pads, lifted a pencil. The train would be arriving in the riverside station, a dismal quay filled with heat, commotion, dust. Awaiting the train would be the bereaved father, the importunate mistress, a hearse, an unctuous mortician, perhaps someone else . . . A faithful retainer, a woman. An old Negro? *Scratch scratch* went the virginal Venus Velvet.

I remember those first weeks at Yetta's with remarkable clarity. To begin with, there was that magnificent surge of creative energy, the innocent and youthful abandon with which I was able to set down in so short a time the first fifty or sixty pages of the book. I have never written fast or easily and this was no exception, for even then I was compelled to search, however inadequately, for the right word and suffered over the rhythms and subtleties of our gorgeous but unbenevolent, unyielding tongue; nonetheless, I was seized by a strange, dauntless self-confidence and I scribbled away joyously while the characters I had begun to create seemed to acquire life of their own and the muggy atmosphere of the Tidewater summer took on both an eye-dazzling and almost tactile reality, as if unspooling before my eyes on film, in uncanny three-dimensional color. How I now cherish the image of myself in this earlier time, hunched over the schoolmarm's desk in that radiant pink room, whispering melodiously (as I still do) the invented phrases and sentences, testing them on my lips like some obsessed verse-monger, and all the while remaining supremely content in the knowledge that the fruit of this happy labor, whatever its deficiencies, would be the most awesome and important of man's imaginative endeavors—The Novel. The blessed Novel. The sacred Novel. The Almighty Novel. Oh, Stingo, how I envy you in those faraway afternoons of First Novelhood (so long before middle age and the drowsy slack tides of inanition, gloomy boredom with fiction, and the pooping-out of ego and ambition) when immortal longings impelled your every hyphen and semicolon and you had the faith of a child in the beauty you felt you were destined to bring forth.

Another thing I remember so well about that earliest period at Yetta's was the new-found ease and security I felt—this too, I'm sure, the result of my friendship with Sophie and Nathan. I had sensed a glimmering of this in Sophie's room that Sunday. While I had droned in the hive at McGraw-Hill there had been something sick, self-flagellating in my withdrawal from people into a world of fantasy and loneliness; on my own terms it was unnatural, for I am a companionable person most of the time, impelled genuinely enough toward friendship but equally smitten by the same horror of solitude that causes human beings to get married or join the Rotarians. There in Brooklyn I had come to the point where I sorely needed friends, and I had found them, thus soothing my pent-up anxieties and allowing me to work. Certainly only the most sickly and reclusive person can finish hard labor day after day without contemplating in dread the prospect of a room that is a vessel of silence, rimmed by four empty walls. After setting down my tense, distraught little funeral tableau so permeated by human desolation and bereavement, I felt I had earned the right to a few beers and the fellowship of Sophie and Nathan.

Considerable time had to pass, however—at least several weeks—before I was fated to get involved with my new chums in a fever of the same emotional intensity which threatened to consume us all when I first encountered them. When this storm broke anew it was horrible—far more threatful than the squabbles and black moments I have described—and its explosive return almost totally confounded me. But this was later. Meanwhile, like a floral extension of the pink room I inhabited, a ripe peony sending forth its petals, I blossomed in creative contentment. Another point: I no longer had to worry about the boisterous noise of lovemaking from above. During the year or so that Sophie and Nathan had maintained rooms on the second floor, they had cohabited in a rather casual, flexible way, each keeping separate accommodations but sleeping together in whichever bed at the moment seemed more natural or convenient.

It is perhaps a reflection on the severe morality of that period that despite Yetta's relatively tolerant attitude toward sex, Sophie and Nathan felt constrained to live technically apart—separated by a mere few yards of linoleum-covered hallway—rather than moving in together into either one of their commodious rooms, where they would no longer have to enact their formal charade of devoted companions lacking any carnal interests. But this was still a time of worshipful wedlock and cold, marmoreal legitimacy, and besides, it was Flatbush, a place as disposed to the extremes of propriety and to neighborly snooping as the most arrested small town in the American heartland. Yetta's house would have received a bad name had it gotten around that two "unmarrieds" were living together. So the upstairs hallway was for Sophie and Nathan merely a brief umbilicus between what in effect were separate halves of a large two-room apartment. What made it now more restful and silent for me was that my two friends soon transferred both their sleeping arrangements and their deafening amatory rites to the bed in Nathan's quarters—a room not nearly so cheery as Sophie's but now, with the coming of summer, somewhat cooler, so Nathan said. Thank God, I thought, no more annotated climaxes to intrude on my work and composure.

During those first weeks I managed fairly successfully to bury my infatuation for Sophie. I so carefully banked the fires of my passion for her that I am certain that neither she nor Nathan was able to detect the molten hunger I suffered every moment I was in her presence. For one thing, at that time I was laughably inexperienced and even in the spirit of sexual sport or competition I would never have made a pass at a woman who had so clearly given her heart to another. For another thing, there was the simple matter of what I construed to be Nathan's overwhelming seniority. And this was not a trivial question. In one's twenties a few years' edge counts for much more than it does later on in life; that is, that Nathan was around thirty and I was twenty-two made him substantially the "elder" in a way that those years could not have made in our forties. Also, it must be pointed out now that Sophie, too, was about Nathan's age. Given these considerations, along with the disinterested manner I affected, I am almost sure that it never crossed either Sophie's or Nathan's mind that I might be a serious contender for her affections. A friend, yes. A lover? It would have made them both laugh. It must have been because of all this that Nathan never seemed reluctant to leave me alone with Sophie, and indeed encouraged our companionship whenever he was away. He had every right to be so trusting, at least during those early weeks, since Sophie and I never did more than casually touch fingertips despite all my craving. I became very much a listener, and I'm certain that my archly chaste detachment allowed me eventually to learn as much about Sophie and her past (or more) as Nathan ever learned.

"I admire your courage, kid," Nathan said to me early one morning in my room. "I really admire what you're doing, setting out to write something else about the South."

"What do you mean?" I said with genuine curiosity. "What's so courageous about writing about the South?" I was pouring the two of us coffee on one of those mornings during the week after our outing to Coney Island. Defying habit, I had for several days risen just past dawn, propelled to my table by the electric urgency I have described, and had written steadily for two hours or more. I had completed one of those (for me) fantastic sprints—a thousand words or thereabouts—which was to characterize this stage of the book's creation, I felt a bit winded, and therefore Nathan's knock at my door as he passed on his way to work was a welcome distraction. He had popped in on me like this for several mornings running and I enjoyed the byplay. He was up very early these days, he had explained, leaving for his laboratory at Pfizer because of some very important bacterial cultures that needed his observation. He had attempted to describe his experiment to me in detail—it had to do with amniotic fluid and the fetus of a rabbit, including weird stuff about enzymes and ion transference—but he had given up on me with an understanding laugh when, having taken me beyond my depth, he saw my look of pain and boredom. The failure of any mental connection had been my fault, not Nathan's, for he had been precise and articulate. It was just that I possessed small wit or patience for scientific abstractions, and this was something I think I deplored in myself as much as I envied the capacious and catholic range of Nathan's mind. His ability, for example, to switch from enzymes to Quality Lit., as he did now.

"I don't think it's any big deal for me to be writing about the South," I went on, "it's the place I know the best. Dem ole cotton fields at home."

"I don't mean that," he replied. "It's simply that you're at the end of a tradition. You may think I'm ignorant about the South, the way I jumped you last Sunday so unmercifully and, I might add, so unpardonably about Bobby Weed. But I'm talking about something else now—writing. Southern writing as a force is going to be over within a few years. Another genre is going to have to appear to take its place. That's why I'm saying you've got a lot of guts to be writing in a worn-out tradition."

I was a little irritated, although my irritation lay less in the logic and truth of what he was saying, if indeed logical or true, than in the fact that such an opinionated literary verdict should issue from a research biologist at a pharmaceutical house. It seemed none of his business. But when I uttered, mildly and with some amusement, the standard demurral of the literary aesthete, he outflanked me neatly again.

"Nathan, you're a fucking expert in *cells,*" I said, "what the hell do you know about literary genres and traditions?"

"In *De Rerum Natura,* Lucretius pointed out a very central truth concerning the examined life. That is, that the man of science who concerns himself solely with science, who cannot enjoy and be enriched by art, is a misshapen man. An incomplete man. I believe that, Stingo old pal—which is maybe why I care about you and your writing." He paused and held out an expensive-looking silver lighter, with which he ignited the end of the Camel between my lips. "May I be forgiven for abetting your filthy habit, I carry this to light Bunsen burners," he said playfully, then went on, "As a matter of fact, something I've concealed from you. I wanted to be a writer myself until halfway through Harvard I realized I could never be a Dostoevsky, and so turned my piercing mind toward the seething arcana of human protoplasm."

"So you were really planning to write," I said.

"Not at first. Jewish mothers are very ambitious for their sons and all during my childhood I was supposed to become a great fiddle player—another Heifetz or Menuhin. But frankly, I lacked the touch, the genius, although it left me with a tremendous thing about music. Then I decided to be a writer, and there were a bunch of us at Harvard, a bunch of very dedicated book-crazy sophomores, and we were deep into the literary life for a while. A cute little kindergarten Bloomsbury in Cambridge. I wrote some poetry and a lot of lousy short stories, like all my pals. Each of us thought we were going to outdo Hemingway. But in the end I had enough good sense to realize that as a fiction writer I was better trying to emulate Louis Pasteur. It turned out that my true gifts were in science. So I switched my major from English over to biology. It was a fortunate choice, I'm damned sure of that. I can see now that all I had going for me was the fact that I was Jewish."

"Jewish?" I put in. "What do you mean?"

"Oh, only that I'm quite certain that Jewish writing is going to be the important force in American literature in the coming years."

"Oh, it is, is it?" I said a little defensively. "How do you know? Is that why you said I had courage to write about the South?"

"I didn't say Jewish writing was going to be the *only* force, just the *important* force," he replied pleasantly and evenly, "and I'm not in the slightest trying to suggest that you might not add something significant to your own tradition. It's just that historically and ethnically Jews will be coming into their own in a cultural way in this postwar wave. It's in the cards, that's all. There's one novel already that's set the pace. It's not a major book, it's a small book but with beautiful proportions and it's the work of a young writer of absolutely unquestionable brilliance."

"What's the name of it?" I asked. I think my voice had a sulky note when I added, "And who's the brilliant writer?"

"It's called *Dangling Man,*" he replied, "and it's by Saul Bellow."

"Well, dog my cats," I drawled and took a sip of coffee.

"Have you read it?" he asked.

"Certainly," I said, lying with a bald and open face.

"What did you think of it?"

I stifled a calculated yawn. "I thought it was pretty thin." Actually, I was very much aware of the novel, but the petty spirit which so often afflicts the unpublished writer allowed me to harbor only a grudge for what I suspected was the book's well-deserved critical approval. "It's a very *urban* book," I added, "very *special,* you know, a little too much of the smell of the streets about it." But I had to concede to myself that Nathan's words had disturbed me, as I watched him lolling so easily in the chair opposite me. Suppose, I thought, the clever son of a bitch was right and the ancient and noble literary heritage with which I had cast my lot had indeed petered out, rumbled to a feeble halt with me crushed ignominiously beneath the decrepit cartwheels? Nathan had seemed so certain and knowledgeable about other matters that in this case, too, his augury might be correct, and in a sudden weird vision—all the more demeaning because of its blatant competitiveness—I saw myself running a pale tenth in a literary track race, coughing on the dust of a pounding fast-footed horde of Bellows and Schwartzes and Levys and Mandelbaums.

Nathan was smiling at me. It seemed to be a perfectly amiable smile, with not a trace of the sardonic about it, but for an instant I felt intensely about his presence what I had already felt and what I would feel again—a fleeting moment in which the attractive and compelling in him seemed in absolute equipoise with the subtly and indefinably sinister. Then, as if something formlessly damp had stolen through the room, departing instantly, I was freed of the creepy sensation and I smiled back at him. He wore what I believe was called a Palm Beach suit, tan, smartly tailored and perceivably high-priced, and it helped make him appear not even a distant cousin of that wild apparition I had first set eyes on only days before, disheveled, in baggy slacks, raging at Sophie in the hallway. All of a sudden that fracas, his mad accusation—*Spreading that twat of yours for a cheap, chiseling quack doctor!*—seemed as unreal to me as dialogue spoken by the leading stinker in a long-ago, half-forgotten movie. (What *had* he meant by those balmy words? I wondered if I would ever find out.) As the ambiguous smile lingered on his face, I was aware that this man posed riddles of personality more exasperating and mystifying than any I had ever encountered.

"Well, at least you didn't tell me that the novel's dead," I said at last, just as a phrase of music, celestial and tender, flowed down very softly from the room above and forced a change of subject.

"That's Sophie who put the music on," Nathan said. "I try to get her to sleep late in the morning when she doesn't have to go to work. But she says she can't. Ever since the war she says she could never learn again to sleep late."

"What is that playing?" It was naggingly familiar, something from Bach I should have been able to name as from a child's first music book, but which I had unaccountably forgotten.

"It's from Cantata 147, the one that in English has the title *Jesu, Joy of Man's Desiring.*"

"I envy you that phonograph," I said, "and those records. But they're so goddamned expensive. A Beethoven symphony would cost me a good hunk of what I used to call a week's pay." It then occurred to me that what had further bolstered the kinship I felt for Sophie and Nathan during these nascent few days of our friendship had been our common passion for music. Nathan alone was keen on jazz, but in general I mean music in the grand tradition, nothing remotely popular and very little composed after Franz Schubert, with Brahms being a notable exception. Like Sophie, like Nathan too, I was at that time of life—long before Rock or the resurgence of Folk—when music was more than simple meat and drink, it was an essential opiate and something resembling the divine breath. (I neglected to mention how much of my free time at McGraw-Hill, or time after work, had been spent in record stores, mooching hours of music in the stifling booths they had in those days.) Music for me at this moment was almost so much in itself a reason for being that had I been deprived too long of this or that wrenching harmony, or some miraculously stitched tapestry of the baroque, I would have unhesitatingly committed dangerous crimes. "Those stacks of records of yours make me drool," I said.

"You know, kid, you're welcome to play them anytime." I was aware that in the past few days he had taken to calling me "kid" at times. This secretly pleased me more than he could know. I think that in my growing fondness for him I, an only child, had begun to see in him a little of the older brother I had never had—a brother, furthermore, whose charm and warmth so outweighed the unpredictable and bizarre in him that I was swift to put his eccentricities quite out of my head. "Look," he went on, "just consider my pad and Sophie's pad as a couple of places—"

"Your *what?*" I said.

"Pad."

"What's that?"

"Pad. You know, a room." It was the first time I had ever heard the word used in the argot. *Pad.* I liked the sound.

"Anyway, consider yourself welcome up there anytime you want to play the records during the day when Sophie and I have gone to work. Morris Fink has a passkey. I've told him to let you in anytime you want."

"Oh, that's really too much, Nathan," I blurted, "but God—*thanks.*" I was moved by this generosity—no, nearly overwhelmed. The fragile records of that period had not evolved into our cheap items of conspicuous consumption. People were simply not so free-handed with their records in those days. They were precious, and there had never been made available to me so much music in my life; the prospect which Nathan offered me filled me with cheer that verged close to the voluptuous. Free choice of any of the pink and nubile female flesh I had ever dreamed of could not have so ravishingly whetted my appetite. "I'll certainly take good care of them," I hurried to add.

"I trust you," he said, "though you do have to be careful. Goddamn shellac is still too easily broken. I predict something inevitable in a couple of years—an unbreakable record."

"That would be great," I said.

"Not only that, not only unbreakable but *compressed*—made so that you can play an entire symphony, say, or a whole Bach cantata on one side of a single record. I'm sure it's coming," he said, rising from the chair, adding within the space of a few minutes his prophecy of the long-playing record to that of the Jewish literary renaissance. "The musical millennium is close at hand, Stingo."

"Jesus, I just want to thank you," I said, still genuinely affected.

"Forget it, kid," he replied, and his gaze went upward in the direction of the music. "Don't thank me, thank Sophie. She taught me to care about music as if she had invented it, as if I hadn't cared about it before. Just as she taught me about clothes, about so many things . . ." He paused and his eyes became luminous, distant. "About *everything*. Life! God, isn't she unbelievable?" There was in his voice the slightly overwrought reverence sometimes used about supreme works of art, yet when I agreed, murmuring a thin "I'll say she is," Nathan could not even have been faintly aware of my forlorn and jealous passion.

As I have said, Nathan had encouraged me to keep Sophie company, so I had no compunction—after he had gone off to work—about walking out in the hallway and calling up to her with an invitation. It was Thursday—one of the days off from her job at Dr. Blackstock's, and when her voice floated down over the banister, I asked if she would join me for lunch in the park a little after noon. She called out "Okay, Stingo!" cheerily, and then she fled from my mind. Frankly, my thoughts were of crotch and breast and belly and bellybutton and ass, specifically of those belonging to the wild nymph I had met on the beach the previous Sunday, the "hot dish" Nathan had so happily served me up.

Despite my lust, I returned to my writing desk and tried to scratch away for an hour or so, almost but not quite oblivious of the stirrings, the comings and goings of the other occupants of the house—Morris Fink muttering malevolently to himself as he swept the front porch, Yetta Zimmerman clumping down from her quarters on the third floor to give the place her morning once-over, the whalelike Moishe Muskatblit departing in a ponderous rush for his yeshiva, improbably whistling "The Donkey Serenade" in harmonious bell-like notes. After a bit, while I paused in my labors and stood by the window facing the park, I saw one of the two nurses, Astrid Weinstein, returning wearily from her night-shift job at Kings County Hospital. No sooner had she slammed the door behind her in the room opposite mine than the other nurse, Lillian Grossman, scurried out of the house on her way to work at the same hospital. It was difficult to tell which of them was the less comely—the hulking and rawboned Astrid, with her pinkish, weepy look of distress on a slablike face, or Lillian Grossman, skinny as a starved sparrow and with a mean, pinched expression that surely brought little comfort to the sufferers under her care. Their homeliness was heartrending. It was no longer my rotten luck, I reflected, to be lodged under a roof so frustrating, so bereft of erotic promise. After all, I had *Leslie!* I began to sweat and felt my breath go haywire and something in my chest actually dilate painfully, like a rapidly expanding balloon.

Thus I came to the notion of sexual fulfillment, which is another of those items I mentioned a while back and which I considered to be so richly a part of the fruition of my new life in Brooklyn. In itself this saga, or episode, or fantasia has little direct bearing on Sophie and Nathan, and so I have hesitated to set it down, thinking it perhaps extraneous stuff best suited to another tale and time. But it is so bound up into the fabric and mood of that summer that to deprive this story of its reality would be like divesting a body of some member—not an essential member, but as important, say, as one of one's more consequential fingers. Besides, even as I set these reservations down, I sense an urgency, an elusive meaning in this experience and its desperate eroticism by which at least there may be significant things to be said about that sexually bedeviled era.

At any rate, as I stood there that morning, tumescent amid my interrupted labors, I felt that there was being thrust on me a priceless reward for the vigor and zeal with which I had embraced my Art. Like any writer worth his salt, I was about to receive my just bounty, that necessary adjunct to hard work—necessary as food and drink—

which revived the fatigued wits and sweetened all life. Of course I mean by this that for the first time after these many months in New York, finally and safely beyond peradventure, I was going to get a piece of ass. This time there was no doubt about it. In a matter of *hours,* as certainly as springtime begets the greening leaves or the sun sets at eventide, my prick was going to be firmly implanted within a remarkably beautiful, sexually liberated, twenty-two-year-old Jewish Madonna lily named Leslie Lapidus (rhyming, please, with "Ah, feed us").

At Coney Island that Sunday, Leslie Lapidus had virtually guaranteed me—as I shall shortly demonstrate—possession of her glorious body and we had made a date for the following Thursday night. During the intervening days—looking forward to our second meeting with such unseemly excitement that I felt a little sick and began off and on to run a mild but genuine fever—I had become intoxicated mainly by a single fact: this time I would surely succeed. I had it sewed up. Made! *This* time there would be no impediments; the crazy bliss of fornication with a hot-skinned, eager-bellied Jewish girl with fathomless eyes and magnificent apricot-and-ocher suntanned legs that all but promised to squeeze the life out of me was no dumb fantasy: it was a *fait accompli,* practically consummated save for the terrible wait until Thursday. In my brief but hectic sex life I had never experienced anything like certainty of conquest (rarely had any young man of that time) and the sensation was exquisite. One may speak of flirtation, the thrill of the chase, the delights and challenges of hard-won seduction; each had its peculiar rewards. There is much to be said, however, for the delectable and leisurely anticipation which accompanies the knowledge that it is all ready and waiting and, so to speak, in the bag. Thus during those hours when I had not been immersed in my novel I had thought of Leslie and the approaching tryst, envisioned myself sucking on the nipples of those "melon-heavy" Jewish breasts so dear to Thomas Wolfe, and glowed in my fever like a jack-o'-lantern.

Another thing: I had been almost beside myself with a sense of the *rightness* of this prospect. Every devoted artist, however impecunious, I felt, deserved at least this.

Furthermore, it appeared that in all likelihood if I played my cards right, remained the cool exotic Cavalier squire whom Leslie had found so maddeningly aphrodisiacal at our first encounter, if I committed no hapless blunders, this God- or perhaps Jehovah-bestowed gift would become part of a steady, even daily functioning arrangement. I would have wild morning and afternoon romps in the hay and all of this could only enhance the quality of my literary output, despite the prevailing bleak doctrine concerning sexual "sublimation." All right, so I doubted that the relationship would involve much in the way of high-toned love, for my attraction to Leslie was largely primal in nature, lacking the poetic and idealistic dimension of my buried passion for Sophie. Leslie would allow me for the first time in my life to taste in a calm, exploratory way those varieties of bodily experience which until now had existed in my head like a vast and orgiastic, incessantly thumbed encyclopedia of lust. Through Leslie, I would at last assuage a basic hunger too long ruthlessly thwarted. And as I waited for that fateful Thursday meeting, her remembered image came to represent for me the haunting possibility of a sexual communion which would nullify the farcical manner in which I had transported my mismanaged and ungratified and engorged penis across the frozen sexual moonscape of the 1940s.

I think a brief reflection on this decade might now be in order, to lay the groundwork for and to help explain Leslie's initial, devastating effect on me. A lot in the way of bilious reminiscence has been written about sex by survivors of the *fifties,* much of it a legitimate lament. But the forties were really far worse, a particularly ghastly period for Eros, shakily bridging as they did the time between the puritanism of our forefathers and the arrival of public pornography. Sex itself was coming out of the closet, but there was universal distress over how to deal with it. That the era became epitomized by Little Miss Cock Tease—that pert number who jerked off a whole generation of her squirming young coevals, allowing moist liberties but with steel-trap relentlessness withholding the big prize, sobbing in triumph as she stole back to the dorm (O that intact membrane! O those silvery snail tracks on the silken undies!)—is no one's fault, only that of history, yet is a serious shortcoming of those years. In retrospect one must view the schism as completely awful, and irreconcilably complete. For the first time within reckoning society permitted, indeed encouraged, unhindered propinquity of the flesh but still forbade the flesh's fulfillment. For the first time automobiles had large, upholstered back seats. This created a tension and a frustration without precedent in the relationship between the sexes. It was a cruel period for the aspiring swordsman, especially if he was young and destitute.

One could and did, of course, get a "professional," and most of the youths of my generation had had one—usually only once. What was so wonderful about Leslie, among other things, was her explicit promise, her immediate assurance that through her I would be offered redemption from that single pathetic crumpling together which I had experienced and which by haphazard definition could be called sexual congress but which I knew in my secret heart had not been that at all. This had been an ignominious copulation. And the awful fact of the matter is that although what might in a clinical sense be termed full penetration *had* been achieved, I was utterly denied the terminal ecstasy I had so often rehearsed manually since age fourteen. In brief, I considered myself to be literally a freak: a true *demi-vierge*. Nor was there any pathology here, anything to do with sinister psychic repression which might have driven me to seek medical care. No, the orgasmic blockage was a simple matter of being swindled both by fright and by that suffocating quality of the *Zeitgeist* that made sex in midcentury America such a nightmarish Sargasso Sea of guilts and apprehensions. I was a college boy of seventeen at my debut. The comedy, played out with a tired old whore from the tobacco fields in a two-dollar-a-night walk-up fleabag hotel in Charlotte, North Carolina, came to naught not only because of her sullen taunts, as I pumped away athwart her aging loins, that I was "slower'n a broke-kneed turtle," nor only because I was desensitized by the oceans of beer I had drunk to allay my initial anxiety, but additionally, I confess, because during the befuddled preliminaries a combination of delaying tactics and fear of disease had caused me somehow to don *two* condoms—a fact which I discovered to my dismay when she finally heaved me off her.

Aside from that disaster, on the afternoon when I met Leslie Lapidus my past experience had been typically base and fruitless. Which is to say, typically of the forties. I had done a certain amount of smooching, as it was called then, in the balconies of several movie theatres; another time, stranded in the leafy and secret dark tunnel of the local lovers' lane, I had with madly pounding pulse and furtive fingers succeeded in obtaining a few seconds' worth of what was known as "bare tit"; and once, scenting triumph but nearly fainting with exertion, I managed to wrest off a Maidenform bra only to discover a pair of "falsies" and a boyish chest flat as a ping-pong paddle. The sexual memory in which I was drenched during that season in Brooklyn, whenever I forlornly unloosed the floodgates, was of uneasy darkness, sweat, reproving murmurs, bands and sinews of obdurate elastic, lacerating little hooks and snaps, whispered prohibitions, straining erections, stuck zippers and a warm miasmal odor of the secretions from inflamed and obstructed glands.

My purity was an inwardly abiding Golgotha. As an only child, unlike those who have as a matter of course seen their sisters in the nude, I had yet to witness a woman entirely unclothed—and this includes the old floozy in Charlotte who wore a stained and malodorous shift throughout the whole proceeding. I have forgotten the exact fantasies I entertained about my first paramour. I had not idealized "femininity" in the silly fashion of the time and therefore I am sure I did not foresee bedding down some chaste Sweet Briar maiden only after a trip to the altar. Somewhere in the halcyon future, I think I must have reasoned, I would meet a cuddlesome, jolly girl who would simply gather me into her with frenzied whoopees, unhindered by that embargo placed upon their flesh by the nasty little Protestants who had so tortured me in the back seats of a score of cars. But there was one matter of which I had no inkling. I had not yet considered that my dream girl would also lack any inhibition about *language;* my companions of the past would have been unable to utter the word "breast" without blushing. Indeed, I had been accustomed to wincing when a female said "damn." You can imagine my emotions, then, when Leslie Lapidus, a scant two hours after our first meeting, stretched out her resplendent legs against the sand like a young lioness, and peering into my face with all the unrestrained, almond-eyed, heathen-whore-of-Babylon wantonness I had ever dreamed of, suggested in unbelievably scabrous terms the adventure that awaited me. It would be impossible to exaggerate my shock, in which fright, disbelief and tingling delight were torrentially mingled. Only the fact that I was too young for a coronary occlusion saved my heart, which stopped beating for critical seconds.

But it was not Leslie's stunning candor which alone set fire to my senses. The air above that sequestered little triangle of sand which Nathan's lifeguard friend, Morty Haber, staked out on Sunday afternoons as a private social sanctuary, had been filled with the dirtiest talk I had ever heard in what might be termed mixed company. It was something more serious and complex. It was her sultry glare, which contained both direct challenge and expectancy, a look of naked invitation like a lascivious lariat thrown around my ears. She plainly meant action, and when I recovered my wits I replied, in that laconic, detached, Virginia gentlemanly voice with which I was aware (or was vain enough to conceive) I had taken her captive from the outset, "Well, honeybun, since you put it that way, I do suppose I could give you a right warm snuggle between the sheets." She could not know how my heart was racing, after its dangerous shutdown. Both my dialect and my diction comprised a glib contrivance but they had succeeded in wildly amusing Leslie, and obviously winning her. My studied and exaggerated speech had kept her alternately giggling and fascinated as we lazed on the sand. Just graduated from college, daughter of a manufacturer of molded plastics, restricted by the vicissitudes of life and the recent war to travel no further from Brooklyn than Lake Winnepesaukee, New Hampshire (where, she laughingly told me, she had gone for ten summers to Camp Nehoc—a widespread patronymic spelled backward), she said I was the first person from the South to whom she had ever spoken a word, or vice versa.

The beginning of that Sunday afternoon remains one of

the pleasantest blurs amid a lifetime of blurred recollections. Coney Island. Seventy-nine degrees Fahrenheit, in golden effervescent air. A popcorn, candy apple and sauerkraut fragrance—and Sophie, tugging on my sleeve, then Nathan's, insisting that we take all the wild rides, which we did. Steeplechase Park! We risked our necks not once but twice on the Loop-the-Loop and dizzied ourselves on a fearful contraption called The Snapper, whose iron arm flung the three of us out into space in a gondola, where we spun around in erratic orbits, screaming. The rides sent Sophie into what were clearly transports of something past simple joy. I never saw these diversions draw forth from anyone, even a child, such glee, such rich terror, such uncomplicated visceral bliss. She cried out in ecstasy, with marvelous shrieks, all flowing out of some primitive source of rapture quite beyond normal sensations of sweet peril. She clutched at Nathan, buried her head in the crook of his arm, and laughed and screamed until tears streaked her cheek. As for myself, I was a good sport up to a point but balked at the parachute jump, two hundred feet high, relic of the 1939 World's Fair, which may have been perfectly safe but filled me with heaving vertigo just to look at it. "*Coward,* Stingo!" Sophie cried and yanked at my arm, but even her entreaties failed to budge me. Licking an Eskimo Pie, I watched Sophie and Nathan in their old-fashioned clothes grow smaller and smaller as they were hoisted up the guide wires beneath the billowing canopies; they paused at the peak, arrested for a harrowing and breathless moment as in that endless ticktock of time before the condemned fall through the gallows trap, then plummeted earthward with a whooshing of air. Sophie's cry, borne across the milling hordes on the beach below, could have been heard by ships far out at sea. The jump was for her a final intoxication and she talked about it until she was out of breath, teasing me without mercy for my spinelessness—"Stingo, you don't know what is *fun!*" —as we walked along the boardwalk toward the beach amid a pushing and shoving freak show of angular, corpulent, lovely, mottled and undulant human flesh.

Except for Leslie Lapidus and Morty Haber, the half-dozen young people sprawled on the sand around Morty's lifeguard tower were as new to Nathan and Sophie as they were to me. Morty—aggressively friendly, strapping, hairy, the very figure of a lifeguard—introduced us around to three tanned young men in Lastex swim shorts named Irv and Shelley and Bert and three deliciously rounded, honey-colored girls who became known to me as Sandra, Shirley and—then, *ah!*—Leslie. Morty was more than amiable, but something indefinably stand-offish, even hostile, about the others (as a Southerner I was given to a great deal of spontaneous handshaking, while they obviously were not and accepted my palm as if it were a haddock) made me distinctly ill-at-ease. As I scanned the group I could not help but feel at the same time a slight but real awkwardness over my bony hide and its hereditary paleness. Sharecropper-white, with pink elbows and chafed knees, I felt wan and desiccated amid these bodies so richly and sleekly dark, so Mediterranean, glistening like dolphins beneath their Coppertone. How I envied the pigmentation that could cause one's torso to develop this mellow hue of stained walnut.

Several pairs of horn-rimmed glasses, the general drift of conversation and scattered books (among them *The Function of the Orgasm*) caused me to deduce that I was among scholastic types, and I was right. They were all recent graduates of, or in some way connected with, Brooklyn College. Leslie, however, had attended Sarah Lawrence. She was also an exception to the general coolness I felt. Sumptuous in a (for that time) daring two-piece white nylon bathing suit which revealed, so far as I was able swiftly to reckon, the first grown-up female navel I had ever beheld in the flesh, she alone among the group acknowledged Morty Haber's introduction with anything warmer than a glance of puzzled mistrust. She grinned, appraised me up and down with a gaze that was splendidly direct and then with a pattycake motion of her hand bade me to sit down next to her. She was sweating healthily in the hot sun and emitted a musky womanly odor that held me instantaneously captive like a bumblebee. Tongue-tied, I looked at her with famished senses. Truly she was my childhood love, Miriam Bookbinder, come to fruition with all adult hormones in perfect orchestration. Her breasts were made for a banquet. The cleavage between them, a mythical fissure which I had never seen at such close range, gave forth a faint film of dew. I wanted to bury my nose there in that damp Jewish bosom and make strangled sounds of discovery and joy.

Then as Leslie and I began to chat casually (about literature, I recollect, prompted by Nathan's helpful remark that I was a writer), I was conscious that the principle of the attraction of opposites was very much in effect. Jew and *goy* in magnetic gravitation. There was no mistaking it—the warmth for me that radiated from her almost immediately, a vibration, one of those swift and tangible feelings of rapport that one experiences so seldom in life. But we also had simple things in common. Like me, Leslie had majored in English; she had written a thesis on Hart Crane and was very knowledgeable about poetry. But her attitude was refreshingly unacademic and relaxed. This enabled us both to have a smooth, trouble-free conversational interchange, even though my attention was drawn over and over again to those astounding breasts, then to the navel, a perfect little goblet from which, in a microsecond's fantasy, I lapped lemon Kool-Aid or some other such nectar with my tongue. While talking of another Brooklyn laureate, Walt Whitman, I found it easy not to pay perfect attention to what Leslie was saying. At college and elsewhere I had played out this solemn little cultural charade too many times to be unaware that it was a prelude, a preliminary feeling-out of mutual sensibilities in which the substance of what one said was less important than the putative authority with which one's words were spoken. In reality a ritualized mating dance, it allowed one's mind to wander, not alone as in the present case to Leslie's bountiful flesh but to a perception of what was being uttered in the background. Because I only barely understood the words, I could not believe my ears and thought at first I was overhearing some new verbal game, until I realized that this was no joke, there was somber earnestness inhabiting these conversational fragments, almost every one of which began with "My analyst said . . ."

Halting, truncated, the talk bewildered me and at the same time held me enthralled; in addition, the sexual frankness was so utterly novel that I experienced a phenomenon that I hadn't felt since I was about eight years old: my ears were burning. Altogether the conversation made up a new experience that impressed me with such force that later that night back at my room I scribbled verbatim notes from memory—notes which, now faded and yellowing, I have retrieved from the past along with such mementos as my father's letters. Although I promised myself not to inflict upon the reader too many of the voluminous jottings I made that summer (it is a tiresome and interruptive device, symptomatic of a flagging imagination), I have made an exception in this particular instance, setting my little memorandum down just as I wrote it as unimpeachable testimony of the way some people talked in 1947, that cradle year of psychoanalysis in postwar America:

Girl named Sandra: "My analyst said that my transference problem has passed from the hostile to the affectionate stage. He said that this usually meant that the analysis might go ahead with fewer barriers and repressions."

Long silence. Blinding sunlight, gulls against a cerulean blue sky. Plume of smoke on the horizon. A glorious day, crying out for a hymn to itself, like Schiller's "Ode to Joy." What in God's name is ailing these kids? I never saw such gloom, such despair, such blighted numb solemnity. Finally someone breaks the long silence.

Guy named Irv: "Don't get too affectionate, Sandra. You might get Dr. Bronfman's cock inside you."

No one laughs.

Sandra: "That's not funny, Irving. In fact what you just said is outrageous. A transference problem is no laughing matter."

More long silence. I am thunderstruck. I have never in my life heard those four-letter words spoken in a mixed gathering. Also I have never heard of transference. I feel my Presbyterian scrotum shrink. These characters are really liberated. But if so, why so gloomy?

"My analyst says that any transference problem is serious, whether it's affectionate or hostile. She says it's proof that you haven't gotten over an Oedipal

dependence." This from the girl named Shirley, not as nifty as Leslie but with great boobs. As T. Wolfe pointed out these Jewish girls have marvelous chest development. Except for Leslie, though, they all give the impression that they're at a funeral. I notice Sophie off to the side on the sand, listening to the talk. All the simple happiness she had during those crazy rides is gone. She has a sullen sulky look on her beautiful face and says nothing. She is so beautiful, even when her mood is down. From time to time she looks at Nathan—she seems to seek him, to make sure that he is there—and then she glowers while the people talk.

Some random jabber:

"My analyst said that the reason I find it hard to come is that I'm pre-genitally fixated." (Sandra)

"Nine months of analysis and I discover it's not my mother I want to fuck, it's my Aunt Sadie." (Bert) (Mild laughter)

"Before I went into analysis I was completely frigid, can you imagine? Now all I do is think about fucking. Wilhelm Reich has turned me into a nympho, I mean sex on the brain."

These last words, spoken by Leslie as she flopped over on her belly, had an effect on my libido which forever after would render insipid the word aphrodisiac. I was beyond simple desire, borne away rather in a near-swoon of lust. Couldn't she know what she did to me with this concubine's speech, with those foul, priceless words which assailed like sharp spears the bastion of my own Christian gentility, with its aching repressions and restraints? I was so overcome by excitement that the entire sunny seascape —bathers, white-capped waves, even a droning airplane with its trailing banner THRILLS NIGHTLY AT AQUEDUCT RACETRACK—was suddenly steeped in a pornographic glow, as if seen through a filter of lurid blue. I gazed at Leslie in her new pose—the long tawny legs merging with the firm cushioned bottom, an ample but symmetrical roundness which in turn flowed slightly down then upward into a cuprous, lightly freckled back, sleek as a seal's. She must have anticipated my hunger to stroke that back (if not the sweaty palm with which I had already mentally massaged her darling behind), for she soon twisted her head around and said to me, "Hey, oil me up, will you? I'm getting parboiled." From this moment of slippery intimacy—smearing as I did the lotion across her shoulders and down her back to the beginning cleft of her buttocks, a tiny nook suggestively fair of hue, then with fluttering fingers in the air above the rump and on further to the mysterious regions between her thighs, ashine with sweat—that afternoon remains in memory a gauzy but pleasure-charged extravaganza.

There were cans of beer from a boardwalk bar and of course this helped perpetuate my euphoria; even when Sophie and Nathan told me goodby—Sophie looking wan and unhappy and saying she felt a little sick—and abruptly left, I kept afloat on a high cloud of elation. (I recall, however, that their departure caused, for a moment, an uneasy silence in the group on the sand, a silence broken by someone's remark: "Did you see that number on her arm, that tattoo?") After another half-hour the psychoanalytical talk palled on me desperately, and alcohol and randiness emboldened me to ask Leslie if she'd stroll with me someplace where we could chat and be alone. She agreed, since it had clouded up a little anyway, and we ended up at a boardwalk café where Leslie drank 7-Up and I helped swell the flood of my raging ardor with can after can of Budweiser. But let a few more of my feverish notes continue that afternoon's operetta:

> *Leslie and I are in the bar of a restaurant called Victor's and I am getting a little drunk. I have never felt such sexual electricity in my life. This Jewish dryad has more sensuality in one of her expressive thumbs than all the locked-up virgins I ever knew in Va. & N.C. put together. Also, she is exceedingly bright, reinforcing Henry Miller's observation somewhere that sex is all in the head, i.e., dumb girls, dumb screwing. Our conversation ebbs and flows in majestic waves like the sea—Hart Crane, sex, Thomas Hardy, sex, Flaubert, sex, Schopenhauer and*

Nietzsche, sex, Huckleberry Finn, sex. I have turned on her the pure flame of my intellect. Manifestly if we were not in a public place I would have her right this minute in the sack. Over the table I hold her hand, which is moist, as if with the pure essence of desire. She speaks rather rapidly in what I have learned to detect is a higher-class Brooklyn accent, more like that used in Manhattan. She has charming facial gestures, nicely interrupted by many grins. Adorable! But what really gets me is that within the lazy space of an hour I hear her say at various moments words I have never in my life heard spoken by a female. Nor do they really sound dirty, once I am used to them. These include such words as "prick," "fuck" and "cocksucking." Also, she says during that same time such phrases as "go down on him," "jerking himself off" (something having to do with Thoreau), "gave him a blowjob," "muff-diver," "swallowed his sperm" (Melville) (Melville?) She does most of the talking though I do my part and am able with a kind of studied unconcern to utter "my throbbing cock" once, aware even as I say it, incredibly excited, that it is the first so-called hard-core obscenity I have ever spoken in a woman's presence. When we leave Victor's I am nicely plastered and am reckless enough to let my arm encircle her firm bare waist. In doing so I actually stroke her ass somewhat slightly and the responsive squeeze she gives my hand with her arm, also the glimmer in those dark oriental eyes as she impishly gazes up at me, makes me certain that I have finally, miraculously discovered a woman free of the horrendous conventions and pieties that afflict this hypocritical culture of ours . . .

I am a little mortified to discover that almost none of the above was apparently written with the faintest trace of irony (I actually was capable of "somewhat slightly"!), which may only indicate how truly momentous for me was this encounter with Leslie, or how doltish and complete was my seizure of passion—or simply how my suggestible mind was working at the age of twenty-two. At any rate, when Leslie and I made our way back to the beach the late-afternoon light, still quivering with heat waves, flooded the sand around the lifeguard tower from which the dejected group of analysands had now departed, leaving behind them a half-buried copy of *Partisan Review,* squeezed-out tubes of nose balm and a litter of Coke bottles. So, lingering there together in the heat of our charm-bound affinity, we spent another hour or so tying up the loose ends of our conversation, both of us very much aware that we had taken this afternoon the first step of what had to be a journey together into wild and uncharted territory. We lay side by side, bellies down. As I gently traced oval patterns against her pulsing neck with my fingertips she reached up to stroke my hand, and I heard her say, "My analyst said that mankind will forever be the enemy of itself until it learns that each human being only needs, *enfin,* a fantastic fucking." I heard my own voice, haltingly distant but sincere, reply, "Your analyst must be a very wise person." For a long while she was silent, and then she turned to gaze at me full in the face and uttered finally, with unfeigned desire, that languid yet straightforward invitation which made my heart stop and so unbalanced my mind and senses: *"I'll bet* you *could give a girl a fantastic fucking."* And it was then that we somehow made a date for the following Thursday night.

Thursday morning arrived, as I have said, with its sense of approaching bliss, of almost unendurable promise. Sitting there at my pink writing table, I managed, however, to ignore my sickishness and fever and to master my fantasies long enough to get two or three more hours of serious writing done. A few minutes past noon I was aware of a yawning sensation at the pit of my stomach. I had not heard a sound from Sophie all morning. Doubtless she would have spent most of her time with her nose in a book, assiduously continuing her self-education. Her ability at reading English, while still far from perfect, had improved immeasurably in the year since she had met Nathan; in general she no longer resorted to Polish translations and was now deeply engrossed in Malcolm Cowley's *Portable Faulkner,* which I knew both captured and perplexed her. "Those sentences," she had said, "that go on and on like a crazy snake!" But she was an adept enough reader to marvel at Faulkner's intricacy of narrative and his turbulent power. I had practically memorized that *Portable*, which in college had catapulted me into all of Faulkner's work, and it had been upon my recommendation—on the subway or somewhere else on that memorable Sunday of our first encounter—that Nathan had bought a copy and given it to Sophie early in the week. At our several get-togethers since then it had given me great pleasure to help interpret Faulkner for Sophie, not only by way of explaining parts of the occult Mississippi vernacular but in showing her some of the right pathways as she penetrated the wonderful groves and canebrakes of his rhetoric.

With all the difficulty, she was moved and impressed by the stormy assault that this prose made upon her mind. "He writes like someone, you know, *possessed!*" she said to me, then added, "It's very plain that *he* never was psychoanalyzed." Her nose crinkled up in distaste as she made this observation, obviously alluding to the group of sunbathers who had so offended her the previous Sunday. I hadn't completely realized it at the time, but that same Freudian colloquy which had fascinated and, at the most, amused me had been downright odious to Sophie and had caused her to flee with Nathan from the beach. "Those strange creepy people, all picking at their little . . . scabs," she had complained to me when Nathan was not around. "I *hate* this type of"—and here I thought she used a lovely gem of a phrase—*"unearned unhappiness!"* Although I saw exactly what she meant, I was surprised at the fervor of her hostility and I wondered—even as I climbed the steps to take her out on our picnic—if it might not be due only to some irreconcilable discord left over from that stern religion which I knew she had abandoned.

I had not meant to take Sophie by surprise but the door to the room was partly open, and since I could see that she was clothed—"decent," as girls used to say—I entered without knocking. Dressed in some kind of robe or housecoat, she stood at the far end of the big room combing her hair in front of a mirror. Her back was to me and for a moment I could tell she was unaware of my presence as she stroked the lustrous blond tresses with a sizzling sound, barely audible on the noontime stillness. Supercharged with a prurient residue—overflow, I imagine, of my Leslie daydreams—I had a sudden impulse to creep up behind Sophie and nuzzle her neck while filling my hands with her breasts. But the very thought was unconscionable and I belatedly realized, while I stood there in silence watching, that it was wrong enough of me to have stolen in on her in this way and violated her privacy, so I announced myself with a small cough. She turned from the mirror with a startled gasp and in so doing revealed a face I shall never in my life forget. Dumfounded, I beheld—for a mercifully fleeting instant—an old hag whose entire lower face had crumpled in upon itself, leaving a mouth like a wrinkled gash and an expression of doddering senescence. It was a mask, withered and pitiable.

I was literally on the verge of crying out, but she beat me to it, making a gulping noise as she clapped her hands over her mouth and fled to the bathroom. I stood there in pounding embarrassment for long moments listening to the muffled sounds behind the bathroom door, aware now for the first time of the Scarlatti piano sonata that had been playing softly on the phonograph. Then, "Stingo, when are you going to learn to knock on a lady's door?" I heard her call, more teasing in tone than truly cross. And then—only then—did I realize what I had witnessed. I was grateful that she had displayed no real anger, and was swiftly touched at this generosity of spirit, wondering what my own reaction might have been had *I* been caught without *my* teeth. And at that instant Sophie emerged from the bathroom, a faint flush still on her cheeks, but composed, even radiant, all the lovely components of her face reunited in a merry apotheosis of American dentistry. "Let's go to the park," she said, "I'm *swooning* with hunger. I am . . . the *avatar* of hunger!"

That "avatar," of course, was quintessential Faulkner, and I was so tickled at the way she used the word, and by her restored beauty, that I found myself disgorging loud coarse cackles of laughter.

"Braunschweiger on rye, with mustard," I said.

"Hot pastrami!" she replied.

"Salami and Swiss cheese on pumpernickel," I went on, "with a pickle, half sour."

"Stop it, Stingo, you're killing me!" she cried with a golden laugh. "Let's go!" And off we went to the park, via Himelfarb's Deluxe Delicatessen.

Six

It was through his older brother, Larry Landau, that Nathan had been able to get Sophie such a superb new set of dentures. And although it was Nathan's own keen if nonprofessional diagnosis which so accurately pegged the nature of Sophie's malady very soon after this encounter at the Brooklyn College library, his brother was instrumental in helping to find a cure for that problem too. Larry, whom I was to meet later on in the summer under very strained circumstances, was a urological surgeon with a large and prosperous practice in Forest Hills. A man in his mid-thirties, Nathan's brother possessed a brilliant record in his field, having once been engaged—as a teaching fellow at the College of Physicians and Surgeons at Columbia—in some highly original and valuable research in kidney function which had won him excited attention in professional circles at an early age. Nathan mentioned this to me once in intensely admiring tones, obviously cherishing extravagant pride in his brother. Larry had also served in the war with grand distinction. As a senior lieutenant in the Navy medical corps he had performed brave and extraordinary feats of surgical skill while undergoing kamikaze attacks aboard a doomed flattop off the Philippines; the exploit won him the Navy Cross—a citation not too often achieved by a medical officer (a Jew to boot in an anti-Semitic Navy), and one which in 1947, with its resonant and recent memories of war and glory, was something else for Nathan to gently crow over and be proud about.

Sophie told me that she didn't learn Nathan's name until

many hours after he rescued her at the library. What she most deeply and indelibly remembered about that first day, and the days which followed, was his truly awesome tenderness. At the beginning—perhaps only because she recalled him bending over her, murmuring, "Let the doctor take care of everything"—she could not tell that those words had been spoken facetiously, and so she thought he *was* a doctor even later as with a kind of commanding gentleness he held her against his arm, whispering words of comfort and encouragement while they rode back to Yetta's in a taxi. "We've got to get you fixed up," she remembered him saying, in a kind of half-jocular tone which brought to her lips the first trace of a grin since she had collapsed. "You can't run around Brooklyn fainting in libraries and scaring people half to death."

There was something so supportive, so friendly and benign, so *caring* in his voice, and everything about his presence inspired such immediate trust, that when they got back to her room (hot and stifling in the slant of afternoon sunlight, where she again had a brief fainting spell and slumped against him), she had not the slightest trace of discomfiture in feeling him gently unbutton and remove her soiled dress and then with delicate but firm pressure push her slowly down to her bed, where she lay stretched out clad only in a slip. She felt much better, the nausea had vanished. But as she lay there looking up, trying to return the stranger's quizzical sad smile, she could feel the ponderous drowsiness and lassitude persisting to her bone marrow. "Why am I so tired?" she heard herself ask him in a faint voice. "What's wrong with me?" She still had the notion that he was a physician and regarded his silent, vaguely sorrowing gaze upon her as being diagnostic, professional, until suddenly she realized that his eyes had fixed upon the number graven on her arm. Abruptly (and this was odd, for she had long since abandoned any self-consciousness about the marking) she made a move with her hand as if to cover it up, but before she could do so he had gently grasped her wrist and had begun to monitor her pulse as he had done at the library. He said nothing for a while, and she felt perfectly safe and at ease in his calm grip, drowsing off with his words in her ear, restorative, soothing, with that blessed touch of playfulness: "The doctor thinks you need a big pill to try to bring some color to that beautiful white skin." Again: *the doctor!* Peacefully then she fell into a dreamless doze, but when, only moments after, she awoke and opened her eyes, the doctor was gone.

"Oh, Stingo, I remember so well, it was such a long time since I feel this terrible panic. And it was so *strange,* you know! I did not even know him. I did not even know his *name!* I had been with him an hour, I think even less, and now he was gone and I had this panic, this deep panic and fear that he might never come back, that he was gone forever. It was like losing a person very close to you."

Some romantic whim of mine prompted me irresistibly to ask if she had fallen that swiftly in love. Could this have been the perfect example, I inquired, of that marvelous myth known as love at first sight?

Sophie said, "No, it wasn't exactly like that—not love then, I don't think. But, well, it may have been close to it." She paused. "I just don't know. How *silly* in a way for such a thing to happen. How could it be possible to know a man for forty-five minutes and feel this emptiness when he is gone? *Absolument fou!* Don't you think? I was *crazy* for him to come back."

A moveable picnic, our lunchtime repast took place in all of the sunny and shady corners of Prospect Park. I am no longer able to remember how many picnics Sophie and I shared—certainly half a dozen, perhaps more. Nor are most of the spots where we sprawled on the grass very clear to me—the rocky crannies and glens and secluded byways where we took our greasy brown paper bags and half-pint cartons of Sealtest milk and the Oscar Williams anthology of American verse, much thumb-stained and dog-eared, whereby I attempted to continue Sophie's schooling in poetry that plump Mr. Youngstein had inaugurated months before. One place, however, I vividly recall—a grassy peninsula, usually unpeopled at that hour on weekdays, jutting out into the lake where a sextet of large, rather pugnacious-looking swans coasted like gangsters through the reeds, interrupting their swim long enough to waddle up onto the grass and scrounge competitively, with aggressive hissings from their voiceless throats, for the crusts of our poppyseed rolls or other leftovers.

One of the swans, a small male considerably less agile and scruffier than the others, had also been injured near the eye—doubtless in encounter with some savage Brooklyn biped—and was left with a walleyed appearance that reminded Sophie of her cousin Tadeusz from Lodz, who had died many years before, at thirteen, of leukemia.

I was unable to make the anthropomorphic leap and thus failed to comprehend the resemblance between a swan and any specific human being, but Sophie swore that they were dead look-alikes, began to call him Tadeusz and murmured to him in little glottal clucks and clicks of Polish as she heaved at him the debris from her bag. I rarely ever saw Sophie lose her temper, but the conduct of the other swans, bossy and preemptive, so fatly greedy, infuriated her and she yelled Polish swear words at the big bastards and favored Tadeusz by making sure that he got more than his share of the garbage. Her vehemence startled me. I did not—because I could not at the time—connect this energetic protectorship of the underdog (the underswan?) with anything that had happened in her past, but her campaign for Tadeusz was funny and immensely appealing. Even so, I have another and personal motive for sketching a picture of Sophie among the swans. I realize now, after much racking of my mind, that it was here on this little promontory later in the summer, during one long afternoon session which lasted until the sun began to sink far behind us over Bay Ridge and Bensonhurst, that Sophie told me in a voice alternately desperate and hopeful but largely desperate about part of this last convulsive year with Nathan, whom she adored but whom even then (even then as she spoke to me) she had come to see as her savior, yes, but her destroyer as well . . .

When to her fathomless relief he returned to her room that day, half an hour later, he came to her bed and gazed down at her once more with his gentle eyes and said, "I'm going to take you to see my brother. Okay? I've made a few phone calls."

She was perplexed. He sat down beside her again. "Why are you going to take me to your brother?" she asked.

"My brother's a doctor," he replied, "one of the best doctors going. He can help you."

"But you . . . " she began, then halted. "I thought . . ."

"You thought I was a doctor," he said. "No, I'm a biologist. How do you feel?"

"Better," she said, "much better." And this was true, not the least, she realized, because of his comforting presence.

He had brought with him a grocery bag, which he now opened, extracting the contents rapidly and deftly and laying them out on the large board near the end of her bed which served as a kitchen table. "Vot a *mishegoss,*" she heard him say. She began to giggle, for he had gone into a very low-key comedy routine, his accent all of a sudden profoundly and luxuriously Yiddish as he catalogued the bottles and cans and cardboard cartons pouring forth from the bag, his face furrowed in a perfect replica of some elderly harassed, purblind, nervously parsimonious Flatbush storekeeper. He reminded her of Danny Kaye (so many times she had seen him, one of her few movie obsessions), with this wonderfully rhythmic and absurd inventory, and she was still shaking with silent laughter when he ceased, turned toward her and held up a can with a white label, bedewed with frosty beads. "Consommé madrilène," he said in his normal voice. "I found a grocery where they keep it on ice. I want you to eat it. Then you'll be able to swim five miles, like Esther Williams."

She was aware that her appetite had returned and felt an eager spasm in her empty stomach. When he poured the consommé into one of her cheap plastic bowls she raised herself up on one elbow and ate pleasurably, savoring the soup, cool and gelatinous with a tart aftertaste. Finally she said to him, "Thank you. I feel much better now."

She sensed again such intensity in his gaze as he sat beside her, not speaking for a nearly interminable space, that despite her trust in him, she began to feel a little uneasy. Then at last he said, "I will bet anyone a hundred dollars that you have a severe deficiency anemia. Possibly folic acid or B-twelve. But most probably iron. Baby, have you been eating properly recently?"

She told him that except for the short period a few weeks before, when she had caused herself to suffer a half-voluntary rejection of food, she had for the past six months eaten more healthy and handsomely than at any time in her life. "I have these problems," she explained. "I cannot eat much fat of animals. But all else is okay."

"Then it's bound to be a deficiency of iron," Nathan said. "In what you describe you've been eating you'd have had more than adequate folic acid and B-twelve. All you need is a trace of both. Iron's a great deal trickier, though. You could have fallen behind with iron and never had a chance to catch up." He paused, perhaps aware of the apprehension in her face (for what he had been saying puzzled and troubled her), and gave her a reassuring smile. "It's one of the easiest things in the world to treat, once you've got it nailed down."

"Nail down?"

"Once you understand what the trouble is. It's a very simple thing to cure."

For some reason she was embarrassed to ask his name, although she was dying to know. As he sat there beside her, she stole a glimpse of his face and decided that he was exceedingly agreeable-looking—unmistakably Jewish, with fine symmetrical lines and planes in the midst of which the strong, prominent nose was an adornment, as were his luminously intelligent eyes that could switch from compassion to humor and back again so rapidly and easily and naturally. Once more his very presence made her feel better; she was suffused by a drowsy fatigue but the nausea and deep malaise were gone. Then suddenly, lying there, she had a lazy, bright inspiration. Earlier in the day, after looking at the radio schedule in the *Times,* she had been badly disappointed to learn that on account of her English class she would miss a performance of Beethoven's Pastoral Symphony on the early-afternoon concert over WQXR. It was a little like her rediscovery of the *Sinfonia Concertante,* yet with a difference. She *remembered* the symphony so clearly from her past—again, those concerts in Cracow—but here in Brooklyn, because she had no phonograph and because she always seemed to be in the wrong place at the wrong time, the Pastoral had completely eluded her, forever tantalizingly announcing itself but remaining unheard like some gorgeous but mute bird flitting away as she pursued it through the foliage of a dark forest.

Now she realized that due to today's misadventure she

could at last hear the music; it seemed far more crucial to her existence at the moment than this medical talk, no matter how encouraging its overtones, and so she said, "Do you mind if I turn on the radio?" She had scarcely spoken the words when he reached across her and switched it on just an instant before the Philadelphia Orchestra, with its murmurous strings, hesitant at first then jubilantly swelling, commenced that inebriate psalm to the flowering globe. She experienced a sensation of beauty so intense that it was as if she were dying. She shut her eyes and kept them firmly closed to the very end of the symphony, at which point she opened them again, embarrassed by the tears streaming down her cheeks but unable to do anything about them, or to say anything sensible or coherent to the Samaritan, who was still gazing down at her with grave and patient concern. Lightly he touched the back of her hand with his fingers.

"Are you crying because that music is so beautiful?" he said. "Even on that crummy little radio?"

"I don't know why I am crying," she replied after a long pause during which she collected her senses. "Maybe I'm just crying because I made a mistake."

"How do you mean, mistake?" he asked.

Again she waited for a long time before saying, "Mistake about hearing the music. I thought that the last time I hear that symphony was in Cracow when I was a very young girl. Now just then when I listened I realize that I heard it once after that, in Warsaw. We was forbidden to have radios, but one night I listened to it on this forbidden radio, from London. Now I remember it is the last music I ever hear before going . . ." And she halted. What on earth was she saying to this stranger? What did it matter to him? She pulled a piece of Kleenex from the drawer of her table and dried her eyes. "That is not a good reply."

"You said 'before going . . .' " he went on. "Before going *where?* Do you mean the place where they did this?" He glanced pointedly at the tattoo.

"I can't talk about that," she said suddenly, regretting the way she blurted the words out, which caused him to turn red and to mutter in a flustered voice, "I'm sorry. I'm *sorry!* I'm a terrible intruder . . . I'm just an *ass* sometimes. An *ass!*"

"Please don't say that," she put in quickly, ashamed of the way her tone had confounded him. "I didn't mean to be so . . ." She paused, in sequence groping for then finding the right word in French, Polish, German and Russian but totally at sea in English. So she said only, "I'm sorry."

"I have a knack for poking my big *schnoz* into places where it has no business," he said, as she watched the rosy flush of embarrassment recede from his face. Then abruptly he said, "Look, I've got to go. I've got an appointment. But listen—can I come back tonight? Don't answer that! I'll be back tonight."

She couldn't answer. Having been swept off her feet (no figure of speech but a literal truth, for that is just what he had done two hours before; carrying her crumpled in his arms from the library to the place by the curb where he had hailed the taxi), she could only nod and say yes and smile a smile which still lingered as she heard him clatter down the steps. The time after that dragged badly. She was amazed at the excitement with which she had awaited the sound of his stomping shoes when, at about seven in the evening, he returned, bringing another bulging grocery bag and two dozen of the most bewitchingly lovely long-stemmed yellow roses she had ever seen. She was up and around now, feeling almost fully recovered, but he ordered her to relax, saying, "Please, you just let Nathan take charge." This was the moment when she first heard his name. Nathan. *Nathan!* Nathan, Nathan!

Never, never, she told me, would she ever forget this initial meal they had together, the sensuously concocted dinner which he fashioned from, of all humble things, calf's liver and leeks. "Loaded with iron," he proclaimed, the sweat popping out on his brow as he bent over the sputtering hot plate. "There is nothing better than liver. And leeks—*filled* with iron! Also will improve the timbre of your voice. Did you know that the Emperor Nero had leeks served to him every day to deepen the sonority of his voice? So he could croon while he had Seneca drawn and quartered? Sit down. Quit fussing around!" he commanded. "This is *my* show. What you need is iron. *Iron!* That's why we're also going to have creamed spinach and a plain little salad." She was captivated by the way in which

Nathan, ever intent upon cooking, was still able to intersperse his observations on *gastronomie* with scientific detail, largely nutritional. "Liver with onions is of course standard, but with leeks, sweetiepie, it becomes something special. These leeks are hard to find, I got them in an Italian market. It is as plain as the nose on your pretty but incredibly pale face that you need massive infusions of iron. Therefore the spinach. There was some research not long ago which came up with the interesting discovery that the oxalic acid content of spinach tends to neutralize a lot of the calcium, which you probably need also. Too bad, but it's still so loaded with iron that you'll get a good jolt of *it* anyway. Also the lettuce . . ."

But if the dinner, though excellent in itself, was mainly restorative, the wine was ambrosial. In the household of her early youth, in Cracow, Sophie had grown up with wine, her father having possessed a strain of hedonism which caused him to insist (in a country as barren of vineyards as Montana) that her mother's ample and often elegant Viennese meals be accompanied with some regularity by the fine wines of Austria and the Hungarian plains. But the war, which had swept so much else out of her life, had obliterated such a simple pleasure as wine, and since then she had not bothered to go out of her way to drink any, even if she had been tempted to within the purlieus of Flatbush, its constituency pledged to Mogen David. But she had no notion of *this*—this gods' liquor! The bottle Nathan brought was of such a quality as to make Sophie want to redefine the nature of taste; ignorant of the mystique of French wine, she did not need to be told by Nathan that it was a Château-Margaux, or that it was a 1937—the last of the great prewar vintages—or that it cost the flabbergasting sum of fourteen dollars (roughly half her salary for a week, she noted with incredulity as she caught a glimpse of the price on the sticker), or that it might have gained in bouquet had there been time to decant it first. Nathan went on and on divertingly about such matters. But she only knew that the savor of it gave her an unparalleled sense of delight, a luscious and reckless and great-hearted warmth that spread downward to her toes, validating all quaint and ancient maxims as to the healing properties of wine. Light-headed, woozy, she heard herself say to her provider toward the end of the meal, "You know, when you live a good life like a saint and die, that must be what they make you to drink in paradise." To which Nathan made no direct reply, appearing to be pleasantly mellow himself as he peered at her gravely and thoughtfully through the ruby dregs of his glass. "Not 'to drink,' " he corrected her gently, "just 'make you drink.' " Then he added, "Forgive me. I'm a confirmed and frustrated schoolmaster."

Then after dinner was over and they had washed the dishes together they sat down opposite each other in the two uncomfortable straight-backed chairs with which at that time the room was furnished. Suddenly Nathan's attention was caught by the handful of books in a row on a shelf above Sophie's bed—the Polish translations of Hemingway and Wolfe and Dreiser and Farrell. Rising for a moment, he examined the books curiously. He said some things which made her feel that he was familiar with these writers; he spoke with special enthusiasm of Dreiser, telling her that in college he had read straight through the enormous length of *An American Tragedy* in a single sitting, "nearly putting my eyes out in the process," and then in the midst of a rhapsodic description of *Sister Carrie*, which she had not yet read but which he insisted that she do (assuring her that it was Dreiser's masterpiece), he stopped short in mid-sentence and gazed at her with a pop-eyed clownish look that made her laugh, and said, "You know, I haven't the faintest notion of *who you are*. What *do* you do, Polish baby?"

She paused for a long time before replying, "I work for a doctor, part time. I am his receptionist."

"A doctor?" he said, clearly with great interest. "What kind of a doctor?"

She sensed that she was having enormous difficulty in getting the word out. But finally she said it. "He's a—a chiropractor."

Sophie could almost see the spasm that went through his entire body at the sound of what she had said. "A chiropractor. A *chiropractor!* No wonder you've got troubles!"

She found herself trying to make a foolish and lame

excuse. "He's a very nice man . . ." she began. "He's what you call"—resorting suddenly to Yiddish—"a *mensh.* His name is Dr. Blackstock."

"Mensh, shmensh," he said with a look of deep distaste, "a girl like you, working for some *humbug*—"

"It was the only job I could *get,* when I come here," she put in. "It was all I could do!" Now she felt herself speaking with some irritation and feeling, and either what she said or the sudden brusque way she said it caused him to mutter a quick apology. "I know," he said, "I shouldn't say that. It's none of my business."

"I would like something better, but I have no talents." She spoke more calmly now. "I begun an education, you see, a long time ago, but it never was finished. I am, you see, a very uncomplete person. I wished somehow to teach, to teach music, to become a teacher of music—but this was impossible. So I am a receptionist in this office. It's not so bad, *vraiment*—although I would like to do something better one day."

"I'm so sorry for what I said."

She gazed at him, touched by the discomfort he seemed to suffer over his own maladroitness. In as long as she could remember she had never met anyone to whom she was so immediately drawn. There was something so appealingly intense, energetic and various about Nathan—his quiet but firm domination, his mimicry, his comic bluster about things culinary and medical, which, she felt, was the thinnest disguise for his real concern for her health. And at last this awkward vulnerability and self-reproach, which in some remote and indefinable way reminded her of a small boy. For an instant she wished he would touch her again, then the feeling went away. They were both silent for a long moment as a car slithered by on the street outside where a light rain was falling and the evening chimes from the distant church dropped nine notes on Brooklyn's vast, reverberant midsummer stillness. Far off, thunder rolled faintly over Manhattan. It had become dark and Sophie switched on her solitary table lamp.

Perhaps it was only the seraphic wine or Nathan's calm and uninhibiting presence, but she felt the urge not to halt where she had left off but to continue talking, and as she talked she felt her English moving more or less smoothly and with nearly unhampered authority, as if through remarkably efficient conduits she hardly knew she possessed. "I have nothing left from the past. Nothing at all. So that is one of the reasons why, you see, I feel so uncomplete. Everything you see in this room is American, new—books, my clothes, everything—there is nothing at all that remains from Poland, from the time when I was young. I don't even have a picture from that time. One thing I much regret about losing is that album of photographs I once had. If I only had been able to keep it, I could show you so many interesting things—how it was in Cracow before the war. My father was a professor at the university but he was also a very talented photographer—an amateur, but very good, you know, very sensitive. He had a very expensive fantastic Leica. I remember one of the pictures he take that was in this album, one of his best ones that I so regret to lose, was of me and my mother sitting at the piano. I was about thirteen then. We must have been playing a composition for four hands. We looked so happy, I remember, my mother and me. Now, somehow, just the *memory* of that photograph is a symbol for me, a symbol of what was and could have been and now cannot be." She paused, inwardly proud of her fluidly shifting tenses, and glanced up at Nathan, who had leaned forward slightly, totally absorbed by her sudden outpouring. "You must see clearly, I do not pity myself. There are far worse things than being unable to finish a career, not to become what one had planned to be. If that was *all* I had ever lost, I would be completely content. It would have been wonderful for me to have had the career in music that I thought I would have. But I was prevented. It is seven, eight years since I have read a note of music, and I do not even know if I could read music again. Anyway, that is why I can't any longer choose my job, so I have to work in the way that I do."

After a bit he said, with that disarming directness that she had come to rather enjoy, "You're not Jewish, are you?"

"No," she replied. "Did you think I was?"

"At first I guess I just assumed you were. There are not many blond *goyim* roaming around Brooklyn College. Then I took a closer look at you in the taxi. There I thought you were Danish, or maybe Finnish, eastern Scandinavian. But, well—you have those Slavic cheekbones. Finally, by deduction I pegged you for a Polack, excuse me, divined that you were of Polish extraction. Then when you mentioned Warsaw, I was sure. You are a very beautiful Polack, or Polish lady."

She smiled, aware of the warm blush in her cheeks. *"Pas de flatterie, monsieur."*

"But then," he went on, "all these preposterous contradictions. What in God's name is a darling Polish *shiksa* doing working in the office of a chiropractor named Blackstock, and where on earth did you learn Yiddish? And lastly—and goddamnit, you're going to have to put up with my prying nose again, but I'm *concerned* about your condition, don't you see, and I've got to know these things!—lastly, how did you get that number on your arm? You don't want to talk about it, I know. I *hate* asking, but I think you've got to tell me."

She dropped her head back against the dingy pillow of the pink and creaking chair. Perhaps, she thought with resignation, with mild despair, if she explained the *rudimentary* part of it to him now, patiently and explicitly, she would get it all over with, and if she was lucky, be spared any further inquisitiveness about more somber and complex matters which she could never describe or reveal to anyone. Perhaps, too, it was absurd or offensive of her to be so enigmatic, so ostentatiously secretive about something which, after all, should be common knowledge by now to almost everybody. Even though that was the strange thing: people here in America, despite all of the published facts, the photographs, the newsreels, still did not seem to know what had happened, except in the most empty, superficial way. Buchenwald, Belsen, Dachau, Auschwitz—all stupid catchwords. This inability to comprehend on any real level of awareness was another reason why she so rarely had spoken to anyone about it, totally aside from the lacerating pain it caused her to dwell on that part of the past. As for the pain itself, she knew before speaking that what she was about to say would cause her almost physical anguish—like tearing open a nearly healed sore or trying to hobble on a broken limb incompletely mended; yet Nathan, after all, had by now amply demonstrated that he was only trying to help her; she knew she did in fact need that help—rather desperately so—and thus she owed him at least a sketchy outline of her recent history.

So after a bit she began to speak to him about it, gratified by the emotionless, truly pedestrian tone she was able to sustain. "In April of 1943 I was sent to the concentration camp in the south of Poland called Auschwitz-Birkenau. It was near the town of Oświęcim. I had been living in Warsaw. I had been living there for three years, ever since the beginning of 1940, which is when I had to leave Cracow. Three years is a long time, but there was still two years more before the war was over. I often have thought that I would have lived through those two years safely if I had not made a terrible *méprise*—pardon me, mistake. This mistake was really very foolish, I hate myself when I think about it. I had been so careful, you see. I had been so careful that I am a little ashamed to admit it. I mean, up until then I was, you see, well-off. I was not Jewish, I was not in the ghetto, so I could not get caught for that reason. Also, I did not work for the underground. *Franchement,* it seemed to me to be too dangerous; it was a question of being involved in a situation where—But I don't wish to talk about that. Anyway, since I was not working for the underground, I did not worry about being caught for that reason either. I got caught for a reason which may seem to you very absurd. I got caught smuggling meat into Warsaw from a place that belonged to a friend in the country just outside the city. It was completely forbidden to possess meat, which was all commanded to go to the German army. But I risked this anyway, and tried to smuggle the meat so as to help make well my mother. My mother was very sick with—how do you say it?—*la consomption.*"

"Tuberculosis," Nathan said.

"Yes. She had tuberculosis years before in Cracow, but it went away. Then it come back in Warsaw, you know, with these very cold winters without heat and this terrible thing with almost no food to eat, everything going to the Germans. In fact, she was so sick that everyone thought she was dying. I was not living with her, she lived nearby. I thought if I could get this meat it might improve her condition, so on one Sunday I went out to this village in the country and bought a forbidden ham. Then I come back into the city and I was halted by two police from the Gestapo and they discovered the ham. They make me under arrest and bring me to the Gestapo prison in Warsaw. I was not allowed to go back to the place where I was living, and I never saw my mother again. Much later I learned that she died a few months after that."

Where they sat it had become muggy and close, and while Sophie spoke Nathan had risen to open the window wide, letting a small fresh breeze bend and shake the yellow roses he had brought and filling the room with the sound of splashing rain. The mild drizzle had become a downpour, and a short way across the meadows of the park lightning seemed to rend some oak or elm with an instant's white blaze, almost simultaneous with a crack of thunder. Nathan stood by the window, looking out at the sudden evening tempest, hands clasped behind him. "Go on," he said, "I'm listening."

"I spend a lot of days and nights in the Gestapo prison. Then I was deported by train to Auschwitz. It take two complete days and a night to arrive there, although in normal times the train is only six or seven hours. There were two separate camps at Auschwitz—the place called Auschwitz itself and the camp, a few kilometers away, called Birkenau. There was a difference between the camps that one must understood, since Auschwitz was used for slave labor and Birkenau was used for just one thing, and that was extermination. When I come off the train I was selected not to go to . . . to . . . not to Birkenau and the . . ." To Sophie's chagrin, she felt the thin outer layer of her cool façade begin to shiver and crack, and her composure faltered; she was aware of a quirky quaver in her voice. She was stammering. But she quickly gained control of herself. "Not to go to Birkenau and the gas chambers, but to Auschwitz, for labor. This was because I was of the right age, also good health. I was at Auschwitz for twenty months. When I arrived everyone who was selected to be killed was sent to Birkenau, but very soon later Birkenau become the place where only Jews were killed. It was a place for the mass extermination of the Jews. There was still another place not far away, a vast *usine* where was made artificial—*synthétique*—*caoutchouc*, rubber. The prisoners at the Auschwitz camp worked there too, but mainly there was one purpose for the Auschwitz prisoners, which was to help in the extermination of *les juifs* at Birkenau. So the camp at Auschwitz become mostly composed of what the Germans called the Aryans, who worked to maintain the Birkenau crematoriums. To help murder Jews. But one must see that the Aryan prisoners was also supposed to die, finally. After their bodies and strength and *santé* was gone and they was *inutiles*, they would be made to die too, by shooting or with the gas at Birkenau."

Sophie had not spoken for very long, but her diction was rapidly decomposing into French, she felt unaccountably and deeply fatigued beyond the fatigue of her illness—whatever it was—and decided to make her chronicle even more brief than she had intended. She said, "Only, I did not die. I suppose I had more good fortune than others. For a time I have a more favored position than many of the other prisoners, because of my knowledge of German and Russian, especially German. This give me an advantage, you see, because for this time I eat better and was clothed a little better and I had more strength. It give me this extra strength to survive. But this situation did not last too long, really, and in the end I was like all the rest. I starved and because I starved I had *le scorbut*—scurvy I think it is in English—and then I had typhus and also *la scarlatine*. Scarlet fever, I think. As I say, I was there for twenty months, but I survived. If I had been there twenty months and one day, I know I would be dead." She paused. "Now you say I have anemia, and I think you must be right. Because after I was made free from that place there was a doctor, a Red Cross doctor, who told me to be careful because I might develop such a thing. Anemia, I mean." She sensed her exhausted voice trailing off in a sigh. "But I forgot about that. I had so many other things sick with my body that I just forgot about that."

For a long while they were both silent as they listened to the gusting wind and the throbbing patter of the rain. Washed by the storm, the air poured in cool breaths through the open window, bearing from the park an odor of drenched soil, fresh and clean. The wind diminished and the thunder grumbled off eastward toward the far reaches of Long Island. Soon there was only a fitful dripping sound from the darkness outside, and a gentle breeze, and the distant slick murmur of tires on wet streets. "You need sleep," he said, "and I will go." But she later recalled that he did not go, at least then. The last part of *The Marriage of Figaro* was playing on the radio, and together they listened to it without speaking—Sophie stretched out now on her bed, Nathan sitting on the chair beside her—while summer moths swooped and flickered around the dim lightbulb hovering above them. She closed her eyes and drowsed, passing across the threshold of some outlandish but untroubled dream in which the gay redemptive music mingled in soft confusion with a fragrance of grass and rain. Once she felt against her cheek, with movement as light and delicate as a moth's wing, the touch of his fingertips in a moment's gentle tracery, but it was only for a second or two—and then she felt nothing. And slept.

But now it again becomes necessary to mention that Sophie was not quite straightforward in her recital of past events, even granted that it was her intention to present a very abbreviated account. I would learn this later, when she confessed to me that she left out many crucial facts in the story she told Nathan. She did not actually lie (as she did about one or two important aspects of her life in the account she gave me concerning the early years in Cracow). Nor did she fabricate something or distort anything important; it is easy to substantiate nearly everything she told Nathan that evening. Her brief observation on the function of Auschwitz-Birkenau—while of course greatly oversimplified—is basically an accurate one, and she neither exaggerated nor underestimated the nature of her various diseases. About all the rest, there is no reason to doubt anything: her mother and her mother's illness and death, the sequence about the smuggled meat and her own arrest by the Germans followed by her swift deportation to Auschwitz. Why, then, did she *leave out* certain elements and details that anyone might reasonably have expected her to include? Fatigue and depression that night, certainly. Then in the long run there may have been multiple reasons, but the word "guilt," I discovered that summer, was often dominant in her vocabulary, and it is now clear to me that a hideous sense of guilt always chiefly governed the reassessments she was forced to make of her past. I also came to see that she tended to view her own recent history through a filter of self-loathing—apparently not a rare phenomenon among those who had undergone her particular ordeal. Simone Weil wrote about this kind of suffering: "Affliction stamps the soul to its very depths with the scorn, the disgust and even the self-hatred and sense of guilt that crime logically should produce but actually does not." Thus with Sophie it may have been this complex of emotions that caused her to be silent about certain things—this corrosive guilt together with a simple but passionately motivated reticence. Sophie was in general always secretive about her sojourn in the bowels of hell—secretive to the point of obsession—and if that is the way she wanted it, it was, God knows, a position one had to honor.

It should be made plain now, however—although the fact will surely be revealed as this account goes on—that Sophie was able to divulge things to me which she could never in her life tell Nathan. There was an uncomplicated reason for this. She was so chaotically in love with Nathan that it was like dementia, and it is more often than not the person one loves from whom one withholds the most searing truths about one's self, if only out of the very human motive to spare groundless pain. But at the same time there *were* circumstances and happenings in her past which had to be spoken; I think that quite unbeknownst to herself she was questing for someone to serve in place of those religious confessors she had coldly renounced. I, Stingo, handily filled the bill. In retrospect I can see that it doubtless would have been unbearable to the point of imperiling her mind had she kept certain things bottled up; this was especially true as the summer wore on, with its foul weather of brutal emotions, and as the situation between Sophie and Nathan neared collapse. Then, when she was the most vulnerable, her need to give voice to her agony and guilt was so urgent as to be like the beginning of a scream, and I was always ready and waiting to listen with my canine idolatry and inexhaustible ear. Also, I began to see how if the worst parts of the nightmare she had lived through were at once so incomprehensible and absurd as to tax—but not quite defy—the belief of a persuadable soul like myself, they would have found no acceptance whatever with Nathan. He would either not have believed her or thought her mad. He might even have tried to kill her. How, for example, could she ever have summoned the means and the strength to tell Nathan about the episode in which she was involved with Rudolf Franz Höss, SS Obersturmbannführer, Commandant of Auschwitz?

Let us consider Höss for a moment, before returning to Nathan and Sophie and their first days and months together and other happenings. Höss will figure later on in our narrative, a leading villain from Central Casting, but perhaps it might be appropriate to deal with the background of this modern Gothic freak at the present time. After blotting him out of her memory for a long time, Sophie told me, he had flashed across her consciousness only recently, by happenstance a few days before I arrived to take up residence at what we had all come to call the Pink Palace. Again the horror had taken place on a subway train deep beneath the Brooklyn streets. She had been thumbing through a copy of *Look* magazine several weeks old, when the image of Höss burst out from the page, causing her such shock that the strangled noise which came from her throat made the woman sitting next to her give a quick reflexive shudder. Höss was within seconds of a final reckoning. His face set in an expressionless mask, manacled, gaunt and unshaven as he stood in disheveled prison fatigues, the ex-Commandant was clearly at the edge of embarking upon a momentous journey. Entwined around his neck was a rope, depending from a stark metal gallows tree around which a clutch of Polish soldiers was making last preparations for his passage into the beyond. Gazing past the shabby figure, with its already dead and vacant face like that of an actor playing a zombie at the center of a stage, Sophie's eyes sought, found, then identified the blurred but unspeakably familiar backdrop: the squat begrimed shape of the original crematorium at Auschwitz. She threw the magazine down and got off at the next stop, so disturbed by this obscene encroachment on her memory that she aimlessly paced the sunlit walks around the museum and the botanic gardens for several hours before showing up at the office, where Dr. Blackstock commented on her haggard look: "Some ghost you've seen?" After a day or two, however, she was able to banish the picture from her mind.

Unknown then to Sophie or to the world in general, Rudolf Höss, in the months preceding his trial and execution, had been composing a document which in its relatively brief compass tells as much as any single work about a mind swept away in the rapture of totalitarianism. Years were to pass before its translation into English (done excellently by Constantine FitzGibbon). Now bound into a volume called *KL Auschwitz Seen by the SS*—published by the Polish state museum maintained today at the camp—this anatomy of Höss's psyche is available for examination by all those who might thirst for knowledge about the true nature of evil. Certainly it should be read throughout the world by professors of philosophy, ministers of the Gospel, rabbis, shamans, all historians, writers, politicians and diplomats, liberationists of whatever sex and persuasion, lawyers, judges, penologists, stand-up comedians, film directors, journalists, in short, anyone concerned remotely with affecting the consciousness of his fellow-man—and this would include our own beloved children, those incipient American leaders at the eighth-grade level, who should be required to study it along with *The Catcher in the Rye, The Hobbit* and the Constitution. For within these confessions it will be discovered that we really have no acquaintance with true evil; the evil portrayed in most novels and plays and movies is mediocre if not spurious, a shoddy concoction generally made up of violence, fantasy, neurotic terror and melodrama.

This "imaginary evil"—again to quote Simone Weil—"is romantic and varied, while real evil is gloomy, monotonous, barren, boring." Beyond doubt those words characterize Rudolf Höss and the workings of his mind, an organism so crushingly banal as to be a paradigm of the thesis eloquently stated by Hannah Arendt some years after his hanging. Höss was hardly a sadist, nor was he a violent man or even particularly menacing. He might even be said to have possessed a serviceable decency. Indeed,

Jerzy Rawicz, the Polish editor of Höss's autobiography, himself a survivor of Auschwitz, has the wisdom to rebuke his fellow prisoners for the depositions they had made charging Höss with beatings and torture. "Höss would never stoop to do such things," Rawicz insists. "He had more important duties to perform." The Commandant was a homebody, as we shall observe, but one dedicated blindly to duty and a cause; thus he became a mere servomechanism in which a moral vacuum had been so successfully sucked clean of every molecule of real qualm or scruple that his own descriptions of the unutterable crimes he perpetrated daily seem often to float outside and apart from evil, phantasms of cretinous innocence. Yet even this automaton was made of flesh, as you or I; he was brought up a Christian, nearly became a Catholic priest; twinges of conscience, even of remorse, attack him from time to time like the onset of some bizarre disease, and it is this frailty, the human response that stirs within the implacable and obedient robot, that helps make his memoirs so fascinating, so terrifying and educative.

A word about his early life will suffice. Born in 1900, in the same year and under the same sign as Thomas Wolfe ("Oh lost, and by the wind, grieved, Ghost..."), Höss was the son of a retired colonel in the German army. His father wanted him to be a seminarian, but the First World War broke out and when Höss was but a stripling of sixteen he joined the army. He participated in the fighting in the Near East—Turkey and Palestine—and at seventeen became the youngest noncommissioned officer in the German armed forces. After the war he joined a militant nationalist group and in 1922 met the man who would hold him in thrall for the rest of his life—Adolf Hitler. So instantly smitten was Höss by the ideals of National Socialism and by its leader that he became one of the earliest bona-fide card-carrying members of the Nazi party. It is perhaps not odd that he committed his first murder soon, and was convicted and sent to jail. He early learned that murder was his duty in life. The victim was a teacher named Kadow, head of a liberal political faction which the Nazis considered inimical to their interests. After serving six years of a life sentence, Höss drifted into a career of farming in Mecklenburg, got married, and in time sired five children. The years appear to have hung heavy on Höss's hands there near the stormy Baltic, amid the ripening barley and wheat. His need for a more challenging vocation was fulfilled when in the mid-1930s he met an old friend from the early days in the *Bruderschaft*, Heinrich Himmler, who easily persuaded Höss to abandon the plow and the hoe and to sample those gratifications that the SS might offer. Himmler, whose own biography reveals him to be (whatever else) a superlative judge of assassins, surely divined in Höss a man cut out for the important line of work he had in mind, for the next sixteen years of Höss's life were spent either directly as Commandant of concentration camps or in upper-echelon jobs connected with their administration. Before Auschwitz his most important post was at Dachau.

Höss eventually developed what might be called a fruitful—or at least symbiotic—relationship with the man who was to remain his immediate superior: Adolf Eichmann. Eichmann nurtured Höss's gifts, which led to some of the more distinguished advances in *die Todtentechnologie*. In 1941, for example, Eichmann began to find the Jewish problem a source of intolerable vexation not only because of the obvious immensity of the approaching task but because of the sheer practical difficulties involved in the "final solution." Until that time mass extermination—then conducted by the SS on a relatively modest scale—had been carried out either by shooting, which posed problems having to do with simple bloody mess, unhandiness and inefficiency, or by the introduction of carbon monoxide into an enclosed sealed space, a method which was also inefficient and prohibitively time-consuming. It was Höss who, having observed the effectiveness of a crystallized hydrocyanic compound called Zyklon B when used as a vapor on the rats and the other verminous creatures that infested Auschwitz, suggested this means of liquidation to Eichmann, who, according to Höss, jumped at the idea, though he later denied it. (Why *any* experimenter was so backward is hard to understand. Cyanide gas had been used in certain American execution chambers for over fifteen years.) Turning nine hundred Russian prisoners of war into guinea pigs, Höss found the gas splendidly suited to the quick dispatch of human beings and it was employed thereafter extensively on countless inmates and arrivals of whatever origin, although after early April, 1943, exclusively on Jews and Gypsies. Höss was also an innovator in the use of such techniques as miniature minefields to blow up wayward or escaping prisoners, high-voltage fences to electrocute them and—his capricious pride—a pack of ferocious Alsatians and Doberman pinschers known as the *Hundestaffel* that gave Höss mingled joy and dissatisfaction (in a fussy concern that runs persistently through his memoirs), since the dogs, though hounds of hell in savagery by which they had been trained to chew inmates to shreds, did become torpid and ungovernable at moments and were all too skilled at finding out-of-the-way corners to go to sleep. In a large measure, however, his fertile and inventive ideas were successful enough that it may be said that Höss—in consummate travesty of the way that Koch and Ehrlich and Roentgen and others altered the face of medical science during the great German efflorescence of the last half of the previous century—worked upon the entire concept of mass murder a lasting metamorphosis.

For the sake of its historical and sociological significance it has to be pointed out that of all of Höss's codefendants at the postwar trials in Poland and Germany—those satraps and second-string butchers who made up the SS ranks at Auschwitz and other camps—only a handful had a military background. However, this should not be particularly surprising. Military men are capable of abominable crimes; witness, in our recent time alone, Chile, My Lai, Greece. But it is a "liberal" fallacy that equates the military mind with real evil and makes it the exclusive province of lieutenants or generals; the secondary evil of which the military is frequently capable is aggressive, romantic, melodramatic, thrilling, orgasmic. Real evil, the suffocating evil of Auschwitz—gloomy, monotonous, barren, boring—was perpetrated almost exclusively by civilians. Thus we find that the rolls of the SS at Auschwitz-Birkenau contained almost no professional soldiers but were instead composed of a cross section of German society. They included waiters, bakers, carpenters, restaurant owners, physicians, a bookkeeper, a post office clerk, a waitress, a bank clerk, a nurse, a locksmith, a fireman, a customs officer, a legal advisor, a manufacturer of musical instruments, a specialist in machine construction, a laboratory assistant, the owner of a trucking firm . . . the list goes on and on with these commonplace and familiar citizens' pursuits. There needs only to be added the observation that history's greatest liquidator of Jews, the thick-witted Heinrich Himmler, was a chicken farmer.

No real revelation in all this: in modern times most of the mischief ascribed to the military has been wrought with the advice and consent of civil authority. As for Höss, he seems to be something of an anomaly, inasmuch as his pre-Auschwitz career straddled agriculture and the military. The evidence shows that he had been exceptionally dedicated, and it is precisely that rigorous and unbending attitude of spirit—the concept of duty and obedience above all which dwells unshakably in the mind of every good soldier—that gives his memoirs a desolating convincingness. Reading the sickening chronicle, one becomes persuaded that Höss is sincere when he expresses his misgivings, even his secret revulsion, at this or that gassing or cremation or "selection," and that dark doubts attend the acts he is required to commit. Lurking behind Höss as he writes, one feels, is the spectral presence of the seventeen-year-old boy, the brilliantly promising young Unterfeldwebel of the army of another era, when distinct notions of honor and pride and rectitude were woven into the fabric of the Prussian code, and that the boy is stricken dumb at the unmentionable depravity in which the grown man is mired. But that is of another time and place, another Reich, and the boy is banished into the farthest shadows, the horror receding and fading with him as the doomed ex-Obersturmbannführer scribbles indefatigably away, justifying his bestial deeds in the name of insensate authority, call of duty, blind obedience.

One is somehow convinced by the equanimity of this statement: "I must emphasize that I have never personally hated the Jews. It is true that I looked upon them as the enemies of our people. But just because of this I saw no difference between them and the other prisoners, and I treated them all in the same way. I never drew any distinctions. In any event, the emotion of hatred is foreign to my nature." In the world of the crematoriums hatred is a reckless and incontinent passion, incompatible with the humdrum nature of the quotidian task. Especially if a man has allowed himself to become depleted of all such distracting emotions, the matter of questioning or mistrusting an order becomes academic; he immediately obeys: "When in the summer of 1941 the Reichsführer SS [Himmler] himself gave me the order to prepare installations at Auschwitz where mass exterminations could take place, and personally carry out these exterminations, I did not have the slightest idea of their scale or consequences. It was certainly an extraordinary and monstrous order. Nevertheless, the reasons behind the extermination program seemed to me right. I did not reflect on it at the time: I had been given an order and I had to carry it out. Whether this mass extermination of the Jews was necessary or not was something on which I could not allow myself to form an opinion, for I lacked the necessary breadth of view."

And so the carnage begins, beneath Höss's narrow, watchful and impassive eye: "I had to appear cold and indifferent to events that must have wrung the heart of anyone possessed of human feelings. I might not even look away when afraid lest my natural emotions get the upper hand. I had to watch coldly, while the mothers with laughing or crying children went into the gas chambers. . . .

"On one occasion two small children were so absorbed in some game that they refused to let their mother tear them away from it. Even the Jews of the Special Detachment were reluctant to pick the children up. The imploring look in the eyes of the mother, who certainly knew what was happening, is something I shall never forget. The people were already in the gas chamber and becoming restive, and I had to act. Everyone was looking at me. I nodded to the junior noncommissioned officer on duty and he picked up the screaming, struggling children in his arms and carried them into the gas chamber, accompanied by their mother, who was weeping in the most heartrending fashion. My pity was so great that I longed to vanish from the scene: yet I might not show the slightest trace of emotion. [Arendt writes: "The problem was how to overcome not so much their conscience as the animal pity by which all normal men are affected in the presence of physical suffering. The trick used . . . was very simple and probably very effective; it consisted in turning those instincts around, as it were, in directing them toward the self. So that instead of saying: What horrible things I did to people!, the murderers would be able to say: What horrible things I had to watch in the pursuance of my duties, how heavily the task weighed upon my shoulders!"] I had to see everything. I had to watch hour after hour, by day and by night, the removal and burning of the bodies, the extraction of the teeth, the cutting of the hair, the whole grisly, interminable business. I had to stand for hours on end in the ghastly stench, while the mass graves were being opened and the bodies dragged out and burned.

"I had to look through the peephole of the gas chambers and watch the process of death itself, because the doctors wanted me to see it. . . . The Reichsführer SS sent various high-ranking party leaders and SS officers to Auschwitz so that they might see for themselves the process of extermination of the Jews. . . . I was repeatedly asked by them how I and my men could go on watching these operations and how we were able to stand it. My invariable answer was that the iron determination with which we must carry out Hitler's orders could only be obtained by a stifling of all human emotions."

But granite would be tormented by such scenes. A convulsive despondency, megrims, anxiety, freezing doubt, inward shudders, *Weltschmerz* that passes understanding —all overwhelm Höss as the process of murder achieves its runaway momentum. He is plunged into realms that transcend reason, belief, sanity, Satan. Yet his tone is rueful, elegiac: "I was no longer happy in Auschwitz once the mass exterminations had begun. . . . If I was deeply affected by some incident, I found it impossible to go back to my house and my family. I would mount my horse and ride until I had chased the terrible picture away. Often at night I would walk through the stables and seek relief among my beloved animals. When I saw my children happily playing or observed my wife's delight over our youngest, the thought would often come to me: How long will our happiness last? My wife could never understand these gloomy moods of mine and ascribed them to some annoyance connected with my work. My family, to be sure, were well provided for in Auschwitz. Every wish that my wife or children expressed was granted them. The children could live a free and untrammeled life. My wife's garden was a paradise of flowers. The prisoners never missed an opportunity for doing some little act of kindness to my wife or children, and thus attracting their attention. No former prisoner can ever say that he was in any way or at any time badly treated in our house. My wife's greatest pleasure would have been to give a present to every prisoner who was in any way connected with our household. The children were perpetually begging me for cigarettes for the prisoners. They were particularly fond of the ones who worked in the garden. My whole family displayed an intense love of agriculture and particularly for animals of all sorts. Every Sunday I had to walk them all across the fields and visit the stables, and we must never overlook the kennels where the dogs were kept. Our two horses and the foal were especially beloved. The children always kept animals in the garden, creatures the prisoners were forever bringing them. Tortoises, martens, cats, lizards: there was always something new and interesting to be seen there. In the summer they splashed in the paddling pool in the garden, or in the Sola River. But their greatest joy was when Daddy bathed with them. He had, however, so little time for these childish pleasures. . . ."

It was into this enchanted bower that Sophie was to stray during the early fall of 1943, at a time when by night the billowing flames from the Birkenau crematoriums blazed so intensely that the regional German military command, situated one hundred kilometers away near Cracow, grew apprehensive lest the fires attract enemy air forays, and when by day a bluish veil of burning human flesh beclouded the golden autumnal sunlight, sifting out over garden and paddling pool and orchard and stable and hedgerow its sickish sweet, inescapably pervasive charnel-house mist. I do not recall Sophie's telling me about ever being the recipient of a present from Frau Höss, but it confirms one's belief in the basic truthfulness of Höss's account to know that during Sophie's brief stay under the

Commandant's roof she, like the other prisoners, just as he claimed, was never in any way or at any time badly treated. Although even this in the end, as it turned out, was not so much really to be thankful for.

Seven

"So maybe you can see, Stingo," Sophie told me that first day in the park, "how Nathan saved my life. It was fantastic! Here I was, very ill, fainting, falling down, and along comes—how do you call him?—Prince Charming, and he save my life. And it was so easy, you see, like magic, as if he had a magic wand and he wave it over me, and very soon I am all well."

"How long did it take?" I said. "Between the time . . ."

"You mean after that day when he found me? Oh, hardly any time at all, really. Two weeks, three weeks, something like that. *Allez!* Go away!" She skipped a small stone at the largest and most aggressive swan invading our picnic ground on the lake. "Go away! I *hate* that one, don't you? *Un vrai gonif*. Come here, Tadeusz." She made little clucking sounds at her disheveled favorite, enticing him with the remnants of a bagel. Hesitantly, the outcast waddled forward with blowzy feathers and a forlorn lop-sided glance, pecking at the crumbs as she spoke. I listened intently even though I had other concerns in the offing. Perhaps because my coming assignation with the divine Lapidus had caused me to oscillate between rapture and apprehension, I tried to quell both emotions by drinking several cans of beer—thus violating my self-imposed rule about alcohol during daylight or working hours. But I needed *something* to stifle my monumental anticipation and to slow my galloping pulse.

I consulted my wristwatch, to discover with sickening suspense that only six hours must pass before I would be tapping at Leslie's door. Clouds like creamy blobs, iridescent Disneyesque confections, moved serenely toward the ocean, sending dappled patterns of light and shade across our grassy little promontory where Sophie talked about Nathan, and I listened, and the turmoil of traffic on the distant Brooklyn avenues drummed with an intermittent booming sound, very faint, like some harmless, ceremonial cannonade. "Nathan's brother's name is Larry," she continued. "He's a wonderful person and Nathan adores him. Nathan took me to see Larry the next day, at his office in Forest Hills. He gave me a long examination and all during the examination I remember he kept saying, 'I think Nathan must be right about you—it's just remarkable, this natural instinct he has about medicine.' But Larry wasn't sure. He *thought* Nathan must be right about this deficiency I had. I was so terribly pale then. He thought it couldn't be anything else after I told him all my symptoms. But naturally, he must be sure. So he got me an appointment with a friend of his, a *spécialiste* at the Columbia hospital, the Presbyterian hospital. This is a doctor of deficiency—no—"

"A doctor specializing in dietary deficiencies," I said, hazarding a reasonable guess.

"Yes, exactly. This is a doctor named Warren Hatfield, who study medicine with Larry before the war. Anyway, that same day we ride together, Nathan and I, to New York to see Dr. Hatfield. Nathan borrowed Larry's car and crossed me over the bridge to the Columbia hospital. Oh, Stingo, I remember that so well, that ride with Nathan to the hospital. Larry's car is a *décapotable*—you know, a convertible—and all my life ever since I was growing up in Poland, I wanted to ride in a convertible, like the ones I had seen in pictures and in the movies. Such a silly ambition, yes, to ride in an open car, but here I was on this beautiful summer day riding with Nathan and the sun coming down and the wind blowing through my hair. It was so strange. I was still sick, you see, but I feel *good!* I mean I *knew* somehow I was going to be made well. And all because of Nathan.

"It was early in the afternoon, I remember. I had never been to Manhattan except by the subway train at night, and now from the car for the first time I see the river by daytime and the incredible skyscrapers of the city and the airplanes in the clear sky. It was so majestic and so beautiful and exciting, I was near to crying. And I would look at Nathan from the corner of my eye while he talked very fast about Larry and all of these marvelous things he done as a doctor. And then he would talk about medicine, and about how he would now wager anything on earth that he was right about my condition, and how it could be cured, and et cetera. And I don't know how to describe this feeling I had, looking at Nathan as we drove up Broadway. I suppose you would call it—what?—*awe*, there's a fine English word. Awe that this sweet gentle friendly man would come along and just be so caring and serious to make me well. He was my savior, Stingo, just that, and I never had a savior before . . .

"And of course he *was* right, you see. At Columbia, at the hospital, I stay for three days while Dr. Hatfield makes the tests, and they show that Nathan is right. I am profoundly lacking iron. Oh, I am lacking some other things too, but they are not so important. It is mainly iron. And while I am there for those three days in the hospital Nathan comes to visit me every day."

"How did you feel about all this?" I asked.

"About what?"

"Well, I don't mean to pry," I went on, "but you've been describing one of the wildest, nicest *whirlwind* encounters I've ever heard of. After all, at that point you're still pretty much strangers. You don't really know Nathan, don't know what motivates him, other than that he's obviously very much attracted to you, to say the least." I paused, then said slowly, "Again, Sophie, stop me if I'm getting a little too personal, but I've always wondered what happens in a woman's mind when a terrific, forceful, attractive guy like this comes along and—well, to use that expression again, sweeps you off your feet."

She was silent for a moment, her face pensive and lovely. Then she said, "In truth, I was very confused. It had been so long—oh, so very long—since I had any, how shall I say"—she paused again, mildly at a loss for words —"any *connection* with a man, any man, you know what I mean. I had not cared about it this much, it was a part of my life that was not terribly important, since I was putting so much of the rest of my life together. My health, for the principal thing. At that moment I only knew that Nathan was saving my life, and I did not think much of what would happen later. Oh, I suppose I think from time to time how I am in Nathan's debt for all this, but you know—and it is funny now, Stingo—all of this had to do with *money. That* was the part that most confused me. The money. At night in the hospital I would lie there and stay awake and think over and over again: Look, I am in a private room. And Dr. Hatfield must cost hundreds of dollars. How will I ever pay for this? I had terrible fantasies. The worse one was about going to Dr. Blackstock for a loan and he asking me why, and me having to explain that it was to pay for this treatment, and Dr. Blackstock getting angry with me for becoming cured by a *medical* doctor. I don't know why, I have this great fondness for Dr. Blackstock that Nathan don't understand. Anyway, I did not want to hurt him, and I had such bad dreams over the money part . . .

"Well, there is no need to disguise anything. In the end Nathan pay for it all—*someone* have to—but by the time he pay for it, there was nothing for me to be embarrassed about really, or ashamed. We were in love, that is to make a long story short, and it wasn't that much to pay anyway, since of course Larry would take nothing, then also Dr. Hatfield asked nothing. We were in love and I was getting healthy taking these many iron pills, which was all I needed for making me to bloom like a rose." She halted and a cheerful little giggle escaped her lips. "Stinking infinitive!" she blurted affectionately, mocking Nathan's tutorial manner. "Not *to bloom,* just *bloom!*"

"It's really incredible," I said, "the way he took you in hand. Nathan should have been a doctor."

"He wanted to be," she murmured after a brief silence, "he so very much wanted to be a doctor." She paused, and the light-heartedness of just a moment before faded into melancholy. "But that's another story," she added, and a wan, strained expression flickered across her face.

I sensed an immediate change of mood, as if her happy reminiscence of their first days together had (perhaps by my comment) become adumbrated by the consciousness of something else—something troubling, hurtful, sinister. And at that very instant, with the dramatic convenience which the incipient novelist in me rather appreciated, her suddenly transformed face seemed almost drowned in the blackest shadow, cast there by one of those fat, oddly tinted clouds that briefly obscured the sun and touched us with an autumnal chill. She gave a quick convulsive shiver and rose, then stood with her back to me, clutching at her bare elbows with fierce hunched intensity, as if the gentle little breeze had pierced to her bones. I could not help—by her dark look and by this gesture—being reminded again of the tormented situation in which I had ambushed them only five nights before, and of how much still remained to be understood about this excruciating connection. There were so many imponderable glints and gleams. Morris Fink, for example. What about that gruesome little puppet show which he had witnessed and described to me—that atrocity which he viewed: Nathan hitting her while she lay on the floor? How did that fit in? How did *that* square with the fact that on each of these succeeding days when I had seen Sophie and Nathan together the word "enraptured" would have seemed to be a vapid understatement for the nature of their relationship? And how could this man whose tenderness and loving-kindness Sophie recollected with such emotion that from time to time, when speaking to me, her eyes had brimmed with tears—how could this saintly and compassionate fellow have become the living terror I had beheld on Yetta's doorstep only a short time ago?

I preferred not to dwell upon the matter, which was just as well, for the polychrome cloud went on its way eastward, allowing light to flood around us once again; Sophie smiled, as if the sun's rays had dispersed her moment of gloom, and hurling a final crust at Tadeusz, said that we should be getting back to Yetta's. Nathan, she declared with a touch of excitement, had bought a fabulous bottle of Burgundy for their evening dinner, she had to shop at the A & P on Church Avenue for a fine steak to go with it; that done, she added, she would curl up all afternoon and continue her monumental wrestle with "The Bear." "I would like to meet this Mr. *Weel-yam* Faulkner," she said as we strolled back toward the house, "and tell him that he make it very difficult for Polish people when he don't know how to end a sentence. But oh, Stingo, how that man can write! I feel I'm in Mississippi. Stingo, will you take Nathan and me to the South sometime?"

Sophie's lively presence receded, then disappeared, from mind as I entered my room and once again with heart-stopping distress was smitten by one of those sledgehammer thoughts about Leslie Lapidus. I had been foolish enough to think that on this afternoon, as the fleeting hours ticked away before our rendezvous, my customary discipline and detachment would allow me to continue my usual routine, which is to say, write letters to friends down South or scribble in my notebook or simply loll on my bed and read. I was deep into *Crime and Punishment,* and although my ambitions as a writer had been laid low by the book's stupefying range and complexity, I had, for several afternoons now, been forging ahead with admiring wonder, much of my amazement having to do simply with Raskolnikov, whose bedeviled and seedy career in St. Petersburg seemed (except for a murder) so closely analogous to mine in Brooklyn. Its effect on me had indeed been so powerful that I had actually speculated—not idly either, but with a moment's seriousness, which rather scared me—on the physical and spiritual consequences to myself were I, too, to indulge in a little homicide tinged with metaphysics, plunge a knife, say, into the breast of some innocent old woman like Yetta Zimmerman. The burning vision of the book both repelled me and pulled me back, yet each afternoon its attraction had won out irresistibly. It is all the greater tribute, then, to the way in which Leslie Lapidus had taken possession of my intellect, my very will, that this afternoon the book went unread.

Nor did I write letters or indite in my notebook any of those gnomic lines—ranging from the mordant to the apocalyptic and aping in style the worst of both Cyril Connolly and André Gide—by which I strove to maintain a subsidiary career as diarist. (I long ago destroyed a great deal of these leakages from my youthful psyche, saving only a hundred pages or so with nostalgic value, including the stuff on Leslie and a nine-hundred-word treatise—surprisingly witty for a journal so freighted otherwise with angst and deep thoughts—on the relative merits, apparent friction co-efficients, fragrance and so forth of the various lubricants I had used while practicing the Secret Vice, my hands-down winner being Ivory Flakes well-emulsified in water at body temperature.) No, against all dictates of conscience and the Calvinist work ethic, and despite the fact that I was far from tired, I lay flat on my back in bed, immobilized like one near prostration, bemused in the realization that the fever which I had run for these recent days had caused my muscles to twitch, and that one could actually be taken ill, perhaps seriously so, with venereal ecstasy. I was a recumbent six-foot-long erogenous zone. Each time I thought of Leslie, naked and squirming in my arms as she would be in the coming hours, my heart gave that savage lunge which, as I have said, might be perilous in an older man.

While I lay there in my room's peppermint-candy glow and the afternoon minutes crept by, my sickness joined company with a kind of half-demented disbelief. Remember, my chastity was all but intact. This enhanced my sense of dwelling in a dream. I was not merely on the verge of getting laid; I was embarking on a voyage to Arcady, to Beulah Land, to the velvet black and starry regions beyond Pleiades. I recalled once more (how many times had I summoned their sound?) the pellucid indecencies Leslie had uttered, and as I did so—the viewfinder of my mind reshaping each crevice of her moist and succulent lips, the orthodontically fashioned perfection of the sparkling incisors, even a cunning fleck of foam at the edge of the orifice—it seemed the dizziest pipe dream that this very evening, sometime before the sun should fulfill its oriental circuit and rise again on Sheepshead Bay, that mouth would be—no, I could not let myself think about that slippery-sweet mouth and its impending employments. Just after six o'clock I rolled off the bed and took a shower, then shaved for the third time that day. Finally I dressed in my solitary seersucker suit, extracted a twenty-dollar bill from my Johnson & Johnson treasury, and sallied forth from the room toward my greatest adventure.

Outside in the hallway (in memory, the momentous events of my life have often been accompanied by sharply illuminated little satellite images) Yetta Zimmerman and the poor elephantine Moishe Muskatblit were embroiled in a vigorous argument.

"You call yourself a godly young man, and yet you do

this to me?" Yetta was half shouting in a voice filled more with severe pain than real rage. "You get robbed in the subway? Five weeks I've given you to pay me the rent—five weeks out of the generosity and goodness of my heart—and now you tell me this old wives' tale! You think I'm some kind of innocent sweet little *faygeleh* that I should accept this story? *Hoo-ha!*" The "*Hoo-ha!*" was majestic, conveying such contempt that I saw Moishe—fat and sweating in his black ecclesiastical get-up—actually flinch.

"But it's true!" he insisted. It was the first time I had heard him speak, and his juvenile voice—a falsetto—seemed appropriate to his vast, jellylike physique. "It's true, my pocket *was* picked, in the Bergen Street subway station." He seemed ready to weep. "It was a colored man, a tiny little colored man. Oh, he was so fast! He was gone up the stairs before I could cry out. Oh, Mrs. Zimmerman—"

The "*Hoo-ha!*" again would have shriveled teakwood. "I should believe such a story? I should believe such a story even from an almost rabbi? Last week you told me—last week you swore to me by all that was holy you would have forty-five dollars on Thursday afternoon. Now you give me this about a pickpocket!" Yetta's squat bulk was thrust forward in a warlike stance, but once more I felt there was more bluster in her manner than menace. "Thirty years I run this place without evicting nobody. Pride I've got in never kicking anyone out except for some weird *oysvorf* in 1938 I caught dressed up in girls' panties. Now, after all this, so help me God I've gotta evict an almost rabbi!"

"Please!" Moishe squeaked, with an imploring look.

Feeling myself an interloper, I began to squeeze by, or through, their considerable mass, and excused myself with a murmur just as I heard Yetta say, "Well, *well!* Wherefore art thou going, Romeo?"

I realized it must have been my seersucker suit, freshly laundered and lightly starched, my plastered-down hair and, doubtless above all, my Royall Lyme shaving lotion, which, it suddenly occurred to me, I had slathered on with such abandon that I smelled like a tropical grove. I smiled, said nothing and pressed on, eager to escape both the imbroglio and Yetta's vaguely lewd attention.

"I'll bet some lucky girl's gonna have her dream come true tonight!" she said with a thick chortle.

I flapped an amiable hand in her direction, and with a glance at the cowed and miserable Muskatblit, plunged out into the pleasant June evening. As I hurried down the street toward the subway I could hear above his feeble peeping protests the hoarse gravelly female voice still yakking furiously, yet dying away behind me with an undertone of patient forbearance that told me that Moishe would hardly get thrown out of the Pink Palace. Yetta, I had come to learn, was deep down a good egg, or, in the other idiom, a *balbatisheh* lady.

However, the intense *Jewishness* of the little scene—like a recitatif in some Yiddish comic opera—caused me to grow a bit apprehensive about another aspect of my onrushing encounter with Leslie. Rocking north in a pleasantly vacant car of the BMT, I tried distractedly to read a copy of the Brooklyn *Eagle,* with its parochial concerns, gave up the effort, and as I thought of Leslie it occurred to me that I had never in my life set foot across the doorstep of a Jewish household. What would it be like? I wondered. I suddenly worried whether I was properly clothed, and had a fleeting notion that I should be wearing a hat. No, of course, I assured myself, that was in a synagogue (or was it?), and there quickly flashed across my mind a vision of the homely yellow-brick temple housing the Congregation Rodef Sholem in my hometown in Virginia. Standing diagonally across the street from the Presbyterian church—equally homely in the ghastly mud-colored sandstone-and-slate motif dominating American church architecture of the thirties—where as a child and growing boy I observed my Sunday devotionals, the silent and shuttered synagogue with its frowning cast-iron portals and intaglio Star of David seemed in its intimidating quietude to represent for me all that was isolate, mysterious and even supernatural about Jews and Jewry and their smoky, cabalistic religion.

Strangely perhaps, I was not totally mystified by Jews themselves. Within the outer layers of civil life in that busy Southern town Jews were warmly, thoroughly assimilated and became unexceptional participants: merchants, doctors, lawyers, a spectrum of bourgeois achievement. The deputy ("vice-") mayor was a Jew; the large local high school took exemplary pride in its winning teams and that *rara avis,* a hotshot triple-threat Jewish athletic coach. But I saw how Jews seemed to acquire another self or being. It was out of the glare of daylight and the bustle of business, when Jews disappeared into their domestic quarantine and the seclusion of their sinister and Asiatic worship—with its cloudy suspicion of incense and rams' horns and sacrificial offerings, tambourines and veiled women, lugubrious anthems and keening banshee wails in a dead language—that the trouble began for an eleven-year-old Presbyterian.

I was too young, I suppose, and too ignorant to make the connection between Judaism and Christianity. Likewise, I could not be aware of the grotesque but now obvious paradox: that after Sunday School, as I stood blinking at the somber and ominous tabernacle across the street (my little brain groggy with a stupefyingly boring episode from the Book of Leviticus that had been force-fed me by a maidenly male bank teller named McGehee, whose own ancestors at the time of Moses were worshipping trees on the Isle of Skye and howling at the moon), I had just absorbed a chapter of the ancient, imperishable, ever-unfolding history of the very people whose house of prayer I was gazing upon with deep suspicion, along with a shivery hint of indefinable dread. Dolefully I thought of Abraham and Isaac. God, what unspeakable things went on in that heathen sanctum! On Saturdays, too, when good Gentiles were mowing their lawns or shopping at Sol Nachman's department store. As a junior Bible scholar, I knew both a great deal about the Hebrews and too little, therefore I still could not truly picture what transpired at the Congregation Rodef Sholem. My childish fancy suggested that they blew a shofar, whose rude untamed notes echoed through a place of abiding gloom where there was a rotting old Ark and a pile of scrolls. Bent kosher women, faces covered, wore hair shirts and loudly sobbed. No stirring hymns were sung, only monotonous chants in which there was repeated with harsh insistency a word sounding like "adenoids." Spectral and bony phylacteries flapped through the murk like prehistoric birds, and everywhere were the rabbis in skullcaps moaning in a guttural tongue as they went about their savage rites—

circumcising goats, burning oxen, disemboweling newborn lambs. What else could a little boy think, after Leviticus? I could not understand how my adored Miriam Bookbinder, or Julie Conn, the volatile high school athletic coach whom everyone idolized, could survive such a Sabbath environment.

Now a decade later I was more or less free of such delusions, but not so completely free that I was not a little apprehensive about what I might find *chez* Lapidus in my first encounter with a Jewish home. Just before I got off the train at Brooklyn Heights, I found myself speculating on the physical attributes of the place I was about to visit, and—as with the synagogue—made associations with gloom and darkness. This was not the eccentric fantasia of my childhood. I was scarcely anticipating anything so bleak as the slatternly railroad flats I had read about in certain stories of Jewish city life in the twenties and thirties; I knew that the Lapidus family must be light-years away from the slums as well as from the *shtetl*. Nonetheless, such is the enduring power of prejudice and preconception that I idly foresaw an abode—as I say—of dim, even funereal oppressiveness. I saw shadowy rooms paneled in dark walnut and furnished with cumbersome pieces in mission oak; on one table would be the menorah, its candles in orderly array but unlit, while nearby on another table would be the Torah, or perhaps the Talmud, opened to a page which had just undergone pious scrutiny by the elder Lapidus. Although scrupulously clean, the dwelling would be musty and unventilated, allowing the odor of frying gefilte fish to waft from the kitchen, where a quick glimpse might reveal a kerchiefed old lady—Leslie's grandmother—who would grin toothlessly over her skillet but say nothing, speaking no English. In the living room much of the furniture would be in chrome, resembling that of a nursing home. I expected some difficulty conversing with Leslie's parents—the mother pathetically overweight in the manner of Jewish mothers, bashful, diffident, mostly silent; the father more outgoing and pleasant but able to chat only of his trade—molded plastics—in a voice heavily inflected with the palatal gulps of his mother tongue. We would sip Manischewitz and nibble on halvah, while my becloyed taste buds would desperately yearn for a bottle of

Schlitz. Abruptly then, my primary and nagging concern—*where*, in what precise room, upon what bed or divan in these constrained and puritanical surroundings would Leslie and I fulfill our glorious compact?—was cut off from mind as the train rumbled into the Clark Street-Brooklyn Heights station.

I don't want to overdo my first reactions to the Lapidus house, and what it presented in contrast to this preconclusion. But the fact is (and after these many years the image is as brilliant as a mint copper penny) the home in which Leslie lived was so stunningly swank that I walked past it several times. I could not conceive that the place on Pierrepont Street actually corresponded to the number that she had given me. When I finally identified it with certainty I halted in almost total admiration. A gracefully restored Greek Revival brownstone, the house was set back slightly from the street against a little green lawn through which ran the crescent of a gravel driveway. On the driveway there now rested a spanking clean and polished Cadillac sedan of a deep winy maroon, flawlessly tended; it could have been standing in a showroom.

I paused there on the sidewalk of the tree-lined and civilized thoroughfare, drinking in this truly inspired elegance. In the early-evening shadows lights glowed softly within the house, radiating a harmony that reminded me suddenly of some of the stately dwellings lining Monument Avenue down in Richmond. Then in a vulgar dip of my mind, I thought the scene could have been a glossy magazine advertisement for Fisher Bodies, Scotch whiskey, diamonds, or anything suggesting exquisite and overpriced refinement. But I was chiefly reminded of that stylish and still-beautiful capital of the Confederacy—a cockeyed Southern association perhaps, but one that was underscored in quick succession by the half-crouched cast-iron nigger jockey that grinned pink-mouthed up at me as I approached the portico, and then by the sassy little trick of a maid who let me in. Shiny black, uniformed in ruffles and flounces, she spoke in an accent which my ear—unerringly cued—was able to identify as being native to the region between the Roanoke River and Currituck County in the upper eastern quadrant of North Carolina, just south of the Virginia line. She verified this, when I inquired, by saying that she was indeed from the hamlet of South Mills—"smack dab," as she put it, in the middle of the Dismal Swamp. Giggling at my acumen, she rolled her eyes and said, "Git on!" Then with an effort at decorum she pursed her lips and murmured in a slightly Yankeefied voice, "Miss Law-*pee*dus will be with you direckly." Anticipating expensive foreign beer, I found myself already slightly intoxicated. Next, Minnie (for this, I learned later, was her name) led me into a huge oyster-white living room strewn with voluptuous sofas, portly ottomans and almost sinfully restful-looking chairs. These were ranged about upon deep wall-to-wall carpeting, also white, without a spot or stain. Bookcases everywhere were filled with books—genuine books, new and old, many with a slightly nicked look of having been read. I settled myself deep into a cream-colored buckskin chair planted halfway between an ethereal Bonnard and a Degas study of musicians at rehearsal. The Degas was instantly familiar, but from where precisely I could not tell—until all of a sudden I recalled it from the philatelic period of my late childhood, reproduced on a postage stamp of the Republic of France. *Jesus Christ Almighty* was all I could think.

I had of course been all day in a state of erotic semi-arousal. At the same time I was totally unprepared for such affluence, the likes of which my provincial eyes had glimpsed in the pages of *The New Yorker* and in movies but never actually beheld. This cultural shock—a sudden fusion of the libido with a heady apprehension of filthy but thoughtfully spent lucre—caused me a troubling mixture of sensations as I sat there: accelerated pulse, marked increase in my hectic flush, sudden salivation and, finally, a spontaneous and exorbitant stiffening against my Hanes Jockey shorts which was to last all evening in whatever position I found myself—seated, standing up, or even walking slightly hobbled among the crowded diners at Gage & Tollner's, the restaurant where I took Leslie somewhat later for dinner. My stallionoid condition was of course a phenomenon related to my extreme youth, seldom to reappear (and never at such length after *aet.* thirty). I had experienced this priapism several times before, but scarcely so intensely and certainly never in circumstances not exclusively sexual. (Most notably there had been the occasion when I was about sixteen, at a school dance, when one of those artful little coquettes I have mentioned —of which Leslie was such a cherished antithesis—took me over all possible fraudulent jumps: breathing on my neck, tickling my sweaty palm with her fingertip, and insinuating her satin groin against my own with such resolute albeit counterfeit wantonness that only an almost saintly will power, after hours of this, forced me to break apart from the loathsome little vampire and make my swollen way into the night.) But at the Lapidus house no such bodily aggravation was needed. There was simply combined with the thought of Leslie's imminent appearance a stirring awareness—I confess without shame—of this plentitude of money. I would also be dishonest if I did not admit that to the sweet prospect of copulation there was added the fleeting image of matrimony, should it turn out that way.

I was shortly to learn in a casual manner—from Leslie and from a middle-aged friend of the Lapiduses, a Mr. Ben Field, who arrived with his wife that evening practically on my heels—that the Lapidus fortune derived primarily from a single piece of plastic no bigger than the forefinger of a child or an adult's vermiform appendix, which as a matter of fact it rather resembled. Bernard Lapidus, according to Mr. Field as he fondled his Chivas Regal, had prospered through the Depression years of the thirties manufacturing embossed plastic ashtrays. The ashtrays (Leslie later elaborated) were of the type everyone was familiar with: usually black, circular, and stamped with such inscriptions as STORK CLUB, "21," EL MOROCCO or, in more plebeian settings, BETTY'S PLACE and JOE'S BAR. Many people stole these ashtrays, so there was a never-ending demand. During those years Mr. Lapidus had produced the ashtrays by the hundreds of thousands, his operation from a smallish factory in Long Island City allowing him to live very comfortably with his family in Crown Heights, then one of the tonier sections of Flatbush. It was the recent war which had brought about this transition from mere prosperity to luxury, to the refurbished brownstone on Pierrepont Street and the Bonnard and the Degas (and a Pissarro landscape I was to see soon, a view of a lost country lane in the nineteenth-century wilds outside of Paris so meltingly serene and lovely that it brought a lump to my throat).

Just before Pearl Harbor—Mr. Field went on in his quiet instructive tone—the Federal government opened bidding among fabricators of molded plastic for the manufacture of this dinky object, a bare two inches long, irregular in outline and containing at one end a squiggly bulge which had to fit into a similarly shaped aperture with absolute precision. It cost only a fraction of a penny to make, but since the contract—which Mr. Lapidus won—called for its production by the tens of millions, the midget device gave birth to a Golconda: it was an essential component of the fuse of every seventy-five-millimeter artillery shell fired by the Army and Marine Corps during the entire Second World War. In the palatial bathroom which I later had need to visit, there was a replica of this little piece of polymer resin (for of such, Mr. Field told me, it was made) framed behind glass and hanging on a wall, and I bemusedly gazed at it for long moments, thinking of the unnumbered legions of Japs and Krauts that had been blasted into the sweet by-and-by by grace of its existence, fashioned out of black inchoate gunk in the shadow of the Queensboro Bridge. The replica was in eighteen-carat gold, and its presence struck the only note of bad taste in the house. But this might be excused, that year, with the fresh smell of victory still in the American air. Leslie later referred to it as "the Worm," asking me in addition if it didn't remind me of "some fat species of spermatozoa"—an arresting but chillingly contradictory image, considering the Worm's ultimate function. We talked philosophically at some length about this, but in the end, and in the most inoffensive manner, she maintained a breezy attitude toward the source of the family wealth, observing with a sort of resigned amusement that "the Worm certainly bought some fantastic French Impressionists."

Leslie finally appeared, flushed and beautiful in a bituminous black jersey dress which clung and rippled over her various undulant roundnesses in the most achingly attractive way. She gave me a moist peck on my cheek, exuding a scent of some innocent toilet water that made her smell as fresh as a daffodil, and for some reason twice as exciting as the cock teasers I had known in the Tidewater, those preposterous virgins drenched in their odalisques' reeking musk. This was *class,* I thought, real Jewish class. A girl who felt secure enough to wear Yardley's really knew what sex was about. Soon afterward we were joined by Leslie's parents, a sleek, suntanned and engagingly foxy-looking man in his early fifties and a lovely amber-haired woman so youthful in appearance that she might easily have passed for Leslie's older sister. Because of her looks alone I could scarcely believe it when Leslie later told me that her mother was a graduate of Barnard, Class of 1922.

Mr. and Mrs. Lapidus did not linger long enough for me to form more than a brief impression. But that impression—of a certain amount of learning, of casually expressed good manners, of sophistication—made me cringe at my raw ignorance and the benighted seizure I had had on the subway train, with my simple-minded premonition of squalid gloom and cultural deprivation. How little, after all, did I know about this urban world up beyond the Potomac, with its ethnic conundrums and complexities. Mistakenly, I had expected a stereotyped vulgarity. Anticipating in Lapidus *père* someone like Schlepperman—the comic Jew of Jack Benny's radio program, with his Seventh Avenue accent and hopeless solecisms—I had discovered instead a soft-spoken patrician at ease with his wealth, whose voice was pleasantly edged with the broad vowels and lambent languor of Harvard, from which I discovered he had graduated in chemistry summa cum laude, carrying along with him the expertise to produce the victorious Worm. I sipped at the fine Danish beer I had been served. I was already getting a bit drunk, and felt happy—happy, contented beyond any earlier imagining. Then came another wonderfully pleasant revelation. As the conversation buzzed about in the balmy evening I began to understand that Mr. and Mrs. Field were joining Leslie's parents for a long weekend sojourn at the Lapidus summer home on the Jersey shore. In fact, the group was leaving imminently in the maroon Cadillac. Thus I realized that Leslie and I would be left to frolic in this place, alone. My cup ran over. Oh, my cup turned into a spillway flooding across the spotless carpet, out the door down

Pierrepont Street, across all the twilit carnal reaches of Brooklyn. Leslie. A weekend alone with Leslie . . .

But perhaps half an hour passed before the Lapiduses and the Fields climbed into the Cadillac and headed toward Asbury Park. In the meantime there was small talk. Like his host, Mr. Field was an art collector, and the conversation drifted toward the subject of acquisitions. Mr. Field had his eye on a certain Monet up in Montreal, and he let it be known that he thought he could get hold of it for thirty, with a little luck. For a few seconds my spine turned into a pleasant icicle. I realized that it was the first time I had heard anyone made of flesh and blood (as opposed to some cinematic effigy) say "thirty" as a contraction for "thirty thousand." But there was still another surprise in store. At this point the Pissarro was mentioned, and since I had not seen it, Leslie leaped up from the sofa and said I must come with her right away. Together we went toward the rear of the house to what was plainly the dining room, where the delectable vision—a hushed Sunday afternoon mingling pale green vines and crumbling walls and eternity—caught the last slant of summer light. My reaction was totally spontaneous. "It's so beautiful," I heard myself whisper. "Isn't it *something?*" Leslie replied.

Side by side we gazed at the landscape. In the shadows her face was so close to mine that I could smell the sweet ropy fragrance of the sherry she had been drinking, and then her tongue was in my mouth. In all truth I had not invited this prodigy of a tongue; turning, I had merely wished to look at her face, expecting only that the expression of aesthetic delight I might find there would correspond to what I knew was my own. But I did not even catch a glimpse of her face, so instantaneous and urgent was that tongue. Plunged like some writhing sea-shape into my gaping maw, it all but overpowered my senses as it sought some unreachable terminus near my uvula; it wiggled, it pulsated, and made contortive sweeps of my mouth's vault: I'm certain that at least once it turned upside down. Dolphin-slippery, less wet than rather deliciously mucilaginous and tasting of Amontillado, it had the power in itself to force me, or somehow get me back, against a doorjamb, where I lolled helpless with my eyes clenched shut, in a trance of tongue. How long this went on I do not know, but when at last it occurred to me to reciprocate or try to, and began to unlimber my own tongue with a gargling sound, I felt hers retract like a deflated bladder, and she pulled her mouth away from mine, then pressed her face against my cheek. "We *can't* just now," she said in an agitated tone. I thought I could feel her shudder, but I was certain only that she was breathing heavily, and I held her tightly in my arms. I murmured, "*God,* Leslie . . . *Les*"—it was all I could summon—and then she broke apart from me. The grin she was now grinning seemed a little inappropriate to our turbulent emotion, and her voice took on a soft, lighthearted, even trifling quality, which nonetheless, by force of its meaning, left me close to an insanity of desire. It was the familiar tune but piped this time on an even sweeter reed. "*Fucking,*" she said, her whisper barely audible as she gazed at me, "fantastic . . . fucking." Then she turned and went back toward the living room.

Moments later, having ducked into a Hapsburg bathroom with a cathedral ceiling and rococo gold faucets and fittings, I scrambled through my wallet and got the end of a pre-lubricated Trojan sticking up out of its foil wrapper and placed it in a handy side pocket of my jacket, meanwhile trying to compose myself in front of a full-length mirror crawling at its edge with gilt cherubs. I was able to wipe the lipstick smear away from my face—a face which to my dismay had the cherry-red, boiled appearance of someone suffering from heat stroke. There was nothing at all I could do about that, although I was relieved to see that my out-of-fashion seersucker jacket, a little too long, more or less successfully concealed the fly of my trousers and the intransigent rigidity there.

Should I have suspected something a little bit amiss when a few minutes later, as we were bidding the Lapiduses and Fields farewell on the gravel driveway, I saw Mr. Lapidus kiss Leslie tenderly on the brow and murmur, "Be good, my little princess"? Years were to pass, along with much study in Jewish sociology and the reading of books like *Goodbye, Columbus* and *Marjorie Morningstar,* before I would learn of the existence of the archetypal Jewish princess, her *modus operandi* and her significance in the scheme of things. But at that moment the word "princess" meant nothing more to me than an affectionate pleasantry; I was inwardly smirking at the "Be good" as the Cadillac with its winking red taillights disappeared into the dusk. Even so, once we were alone I sensed something in Leslie's manner—I suppose you could call it a kind of skittishness—that told me that a certain delay was necessary: this despite the enormous head of steam we had built up and her onslaught upon my mouth, which now again suddenly thirsted for more tongue.

I made a direct pass at Leslie as soon as we were back inside the front door, insinuating my arm around her waist, but she managed to slip away with a tinkly little laugh and the observation—too cryptic for me to quite get straight—that "Haste makes waste." Yet I was certainly more than willing for Leslie to assume control of our mutual strategy, to set the timing and the rhythm of our evening and thus to allow events to move in modulated degrees toward the great crescendo; as passionate and yearning as she was, mirror-companion of my own blazing desire, Leslie was, after all, no coarse slut I could merely have for the asking right then and there on the wall-to-wall carpet. Despite her eagerness and all her past abandon—I instinctively divined—she wanted to be cosseted and flattered and seduced and entertained like any woman, and this was fine with me, since Nature had clearly designed such a scheme to enhance man's delight as well. I was therefore more than willing to be patient and bide my time. Thus when I found myself sitting rather primly next to Leslie beneath the Degas, I did not feel at all thwarted by the entrance of Minnie bearing champagne and (another of the several "firsts" I was to experience that evening) fresh beluga caviar. This provoked badinage between Minnie and me, very Southern in flavor, which Leslie obviously found charming.

As I have already pointed out, I had been perplexed to discover during my sojourn in the North that New Yorkers often tended to regard Southerners either with extreme hostility (as Nathan had regarded me initially) or with amused condescension, as if they made up some class of minstrel entertainer. Although I knew Leslie was attracted by my "serious" side, I also fell into the latter category. I had almost overlooked the fact—until Minnie reappeared

—that in Leslie's eyes I was fresh and exotic news, a little like Rhett Butler; my Southernness was my strongest suit and I began to play it then and throughout the evening for all it was worth. The following banter, for instance (an exchange which twenty years later would have been unthinkable), caused Leslie to pat her lovely jersey-clad thighs in merriment.

"Minnie, I'm just *dying* for some down-home food. Real colored folks' food. None of these ole Communist fish eggs."

"Mmmm-huh! *Me* too! Ooh, how I'd love to git me a mess of salt mullet. Salt mullet and grits. Dat's what I call *eatin'!*"

"How 'bout some boiled chitlins, Minnie? Chitlins and collard greens!"

"Git on!" (Wild high giggles) "You talk about *chitlins,* you git me so hongry I think I'll jes *die!*"

Later at Gage & Tollner's, as Leslie and I dined beneath gaslight on littleneck clams and crabmeat imperial, I came as near to experiencing a pure amalgam of sensual and spiritual felicities as I ever would in my life. We sat very close together at a corner table away from the babble of the crowd. We drank some extraordinary white wine that livened my wits and untethered my tongue as I told the true story of my grandfather on my father's side who had lost an eye and a kneecap at Chancellorsville, and the phony story of my great-uncle on my mother's side whose name was Mosby and who was one of the great Confederate guerrilla leaders of the Civil War. I say phony because Mosby, a Virginia colonel, was not related to me in the slightest way; the story, however, was both passably authentic and colorful and I told it with drawling embellishments and winsome sidelights and bravura touches, savoring each dramatic effect and in the end turning on such slick medium-voltage charm that Leslie, eyes ashine, reached up and grasped my hand as she had at Coney Island, and I felt her palm a little moist with desire, or so it seemed. "And then what happened?" I heard her say after I had paused for a significant effect. "Well, my great-uncle—Mosby," I went on, "had finally surrounded that Union brigade in the Valley. It was at night and the Union commander was asleep in his tent. Mosby went into this dark tent and prodded the general in the ribs, waking him up. 'General,' he said, 'git up, I've got news about Mosby!' The general, not knowing the voice but thinking it was one of his own men, leaped up in the dark and said, '*Mosby!* Have you got him?' And Mosby replied, 'No, suh! *He's got you!*' "

Leslie's response to this was gratifying—a throaty, deeply appreciative contralto whoop which caused heads to turn at adjoining tables, along with an admonitory look from an elderly waiter. After her laughter died away, we both fell silent for a moment, gazing down into our after-dinner brandy. Then finally it was she, not I, who broached the subject which I knew had been uppermost in her mind as well as my own. "You know, it's funny about that time," she said thoughtfully. "I mean about the nineteenth century. I mean, one never thinks about them fucking. All those books and stories, and there's not a word about them fucking."

"Victorianism," I said. "Sheer prudery."

"I mean, I don't know much about the Civil War, but whenever I think of that time—I mean, ever since *Gone With the Wind* I've had these fantasies about those generals, those gorgeous young Southern generals with their tawny mustaches and beards, and hair in ringlets, on horseback. And those beautiful girls in crinoline and pantalettes. You would never know that they ever fucked, from all you're able to read." She paused and squeezed my hand. "I mean, doesn't it just do something to you to think of one of those ravishing girls with that crinoline all in a fabulous tangle, and one of those gorgeous young officers —I mean, both of them fucking like *crazy?*"

"Oh yes," I said with a shiver, "oh yes, it does. It enlarges one's sense of history."

It was past ten o'clock and I ordered more brandy. We lingered for another hour, and again, as at Coney Island, Leslie gently but irresistibly seized the conversational helm, steering us into turbid backwaters and eerie lagoons where I, at least, had never ventured with a female. She spoke often of her current analyst, who, she said, had opened up a consciousness of her primal self and, more important, of the sexual energy which had only needed to be tapped and liberated in order to make her the functioning, healthy *brute* (her word) she now felt herself to be. As she spoke, the benign cognac allowed me to run my fingertips very gently over the edges of her expressive mouth, silver-bright with vermilion lipstick.

"I was such a little *creep* before I went into analysis," she said with a sigh, "hyped-up intellectual with no sense at all of my connection with my body, the *wisdom* my body had to give me. No sense of my pussy, no sense of that marvelous little *clit,* no sense of anything. Have you read D. H. Lawrence? *Lady Chatterley's Lover?*" I had to say no. It was a book which I had longed to read but which, incarcerated like a mad strangler behind the wires of the locked shelves of the university library, had been denied me. "Read it," she said, her voice husky and intense now, "get it and read it, for the sake of your salvation. A friend of mine smuggled a copy from France, I'll lend it to you. Lawrence has the answer—oh, he knows so much about fucking. He says that when you fuck you go to the *dark gods.*" Uttering these words, she squeezed my hand, which was now entwined with hers a scant millimeter from the straining tumefaction in my lap, and her eyes gazed into mine with such a galvanized look of passion and certitude that it took all my self-command to avoid, that very instant, some ludicrous, *brutish,* public embrace. "Oh, Stingo," she said again, "I really mean it, to fuck is to go to the dark gods."

"Then let's *go* to the dark gods," I said, practically beyond control now as I urgently signaled for the check.

Some pages back I touched upon André Gide and the Gidean diaries I had been trying to emulate. As a student at Duke, I had read the master laboriously in French. I had admired his journals inordinately, and had considered Gide's probity and relentless self-dissection to be part of one of the truly triumphant feats of the civilized twentieth-century mind. In my own journal, at the beginning of the final part of my chronicle of Leslie Lapidus—a Passion Week, I realized later, which began on that palmy Sunday at Coney Island and ended with my time on the Cross in the small hours of Friday morning back on Pierrepont Street—I brooded at some length on Gide and paraphrased from memory a few of his exemplary thoughts and observations. I won't dwell on this passage here, except to note my admiration therein not only for the terrible humiliations Gide had been able to absorb, but the brave honesty with which he seemed always determined to record them: the more catastrophic the humiliation or the disappointment, I noted, the more cleansing and luminous became Gide's account in his *Journals*—a catharsis in which the reader, too, could participate. Although I can no longer remember for certain, it must have been the same sort of catharsis I was trying to attain in this last section on Leslie—following my meditation on Gide—which I include here. But I have to add that there was something a little freaky about these particular pages. At some point not long after their writing I must have torn them out in despair from the ledger-like book in which I kept my journal, stowing them away in a clumsy wad at the back of the ledger, where I ran across them by luck even as I was re-creating the denouement of this goofy masquerade. What still amazes is the handwriting: not the placid, diligently legible schoolboy script I habitually used, but a savage scurrying scrawl indicating the breakneck speed of distraught emotions. The style, however, as now can be seen, continues to possess an unruffled, wryly sardonic, self-anatomizing quality which Gide might have admired had he ever been able to peruse these humiliated pages:

> *I might be tipped off to what is going on when we get into the taxi after Gage & Tollner's. Naturally by then I am so beside myself with plain old hog lust that I simply wrap Leslie in my arms even before the cab gets moving. Right off it is a repetition of the moment when we went to look at the Pissarro. That foraging tongue of hers is inside me like some shad thrashing upstream for dear life. Never before have I known that kissing can be so* major, *so expansive. Obviously, though, the time has come for me to reciprocate, and so I do. As we ride down Fulton Street I "give tongue" back to her and she clearly loves it, responding with little groans and shudders. By this time I am so hot that I do something I have always wanted to do when kissing a girl but never dared to down in Va.,*

because of its rather blatant suggestiveness. What I do is to slowly and rhythmically move my tongue in and out of her mouth in long copulatory movements, ad libitum. This causes Leslie to groan again and she draws her lips away long enough to whisper, "God! Your guess what in my guess what!" I am not deflected by that odd coyness. I am semi-deranged. It is almost impossible to reproduce my condition at this moment. In a sort of controlled frenzy I decide that now is the time to make the first truly direct move. So very delicately I slip my hand up in a way that will allow it to begin to cup the underpart of her luscious left breast, or right one, I forget which. And at that instant, to my almost total disbelief, with a firmness and a resolve that match my own delicate stealth, she moves her arm protectively into a position which clearly means: "Nothing doing." It is absolutely dumfounding, so completely dumfounding that I think one of us has made a mistake, gotten our signals crossed, that she is joking (a bad joke), something. So, shortly after this, while my tongue is still rammed down her gullet and she continues to make these little moaning sounds, I move toward her other knocker. Wham! The same thing again: the sudden protective movement, the arm flung down like one of those barriers at a railroad crossing. "Do not pass!" It is utterly beyond belief.

(Writing now at 8 P.M. Friday, I consult my "Merck's Manual." From "Merck" I can assume I am suffering from a case of "severe acute glossitis," an inflamed condition of the tongue's surface which is of traumatic origin but doubtless aggravated by bacteria, viruses and all sorts of toxicity resulting from five or six hours of salivary exchange unprecedented in the history of my mouth and I daresay anyone's. "Merck" informs me that this is a transient state, becoming palliated after a number of hours of the tongue's gentle rest, which is a great relief to know, since it is sheer murder to eat anything or to take more than a few sips of beer. It is nearly nightfall, I am writing at Yetta's, alone. I cannot even face Sophie or Nathan. In plain truth I am suffering from a desolation and

letdown such as I have never known, or thought possible.)

Back to Stingo's Progress. Naturally, almost to preserve my reason, I have to think of some rationale to explain her bizarre behavior. Obviously, I think, Les simply and with logic does not wish to have anything of an overt nature take place in a taxicab. Perfectly proper indeed. A lady in a taxi, a whore in bed. With this consideration in mind, I content myself with more labyrinthine tongue-work until the taxi arrives at the brownstone on Pierrepont Street. We disembark and enter the dark house. As Leslie unlocks the front door she remarks that, it being Thursday, it is Minnie's night off, and I construe this to lay emphasis on the privacy we will have. In the soft light of the foyer my membrum, betrousered, is truly rampant. Also a spot of "dogwater" there, pre-coital seepage, as if a puppy had peed in my lap.

(Oh, André Gide, prie pour moi! This telling becomes well-nigh intolerable. How do I make sense of, make credible—much less human—the miseries of the next few hours? Upon whose shoulders rests the blame for this gratuitous torture—mine, Leslie's, the Zeitgeist's? Leslie's analyst's? Certainly someone has a lot to account for in turning poor Les out upon her cold and bleak plateau. For that is exactly what she calls it—a plateau—this forlorn limbo where she wanders solitary and freezing.)

We get started again at about midnight on a couch underneath the Degas. There is a clock somewhere in the house, striking the hour, and at two o'clock I am no further advanced than I was in the taxi. We have fallen into a pretty desperate but generally silent tug of war by now, and I have been working on every tactic in the book—trying to grope tit, thigh, crotch. No go. Except for that gaping oral cavity of hers and that prodigiously active tongue, she might as well be clad in breastplates, full armor. The martial image is apt in another way because soon after I begin making my more aggressive forays there in the semi-dark, fingering the arch of her thigh or trying to get my paw tucked in between her clamped knees, she yanks that flailing tongue out of my mouth and mutters things like: "Whoa there, Colonel Mosby!" Or: "Back up there, Johnny Reb!" All spoken in an attempt to approximate my Confederate accent, and in a light-hearted, giggly but Nonetheless I Mean Business voice that sweeps over me like icewater. Again, throughout this entire charade I really can hardly believe the actuality of what is happening, simply cannot accept the fact that after her absolutely breath-taking overture, all those unequivocal invitations and blazing come-hithers, she is falling back on this outrageous flimflam. Sometime after two o'clock, driven to the brink of madness, I resort to doing something which even while I am in the process of doing it I know will provoke a drastic reaction from Les—though how drastic I can scarcely predict. Still embroiled in our oceanic wrestle, I'm sure she is going to choke both of us on the gagged scream she gives as she realizes what she has got hold of. (This is after I silently unzip my fly and place her hand on my cock.) She sails off the sofa as if someone has lit a fire beneath her and at that moment the evening and all my wretched fantasies and dreams turn to a pile of straw.

(Oh, André Gide, comme toi, je crois que je deviendrai pédéraste!)

Later she bawls like a little baby as she sits beside me, trying to explain herself. For some reason her awful sweetness, her helplessness, her crestfallen and remorseful manner all help me to control my wild rage. Whereas at first I wanted to belt the living shit out of her—take that priceless Degas and ram it down around her neck—now I could almost cry with her, crying out of my own chagrin and frustration but also for Leslie too and for her psychoanalysis, which has so helped create her own gross imposture. I learn about all this as the clock ticks onward toward dawn and after I get my several querulous complaints and objections out of the way. "I don't want to be nasty or unreasonable," I whisper to her in the shadows, holding her hand, "but you led me to believe something else. You said, and I quote you exactly, 'I'll bet you could give a girl a fantastic fucking.' " I pause for a long moment, blowing blue smoke through the gloom. Then I say, "Well, I could. And I wanted to." I halt. "That's all." Then after another long pause and a lot of snuffled sobs, she replies, "I know I said that, and if I led you on I'm sorry, Stingo." Snuffle, snuffle. I give her a Kleenex. "But I didn't say I wanted you to do it." More snuffles. "Also I said 'a girl.' I didn't say me." At this instant the groan I give would stir the souls of the dead. We are both silent for an endlessly long time. At some moment between three and four o'clock I hear a ship's whistle, plaintive and mournful and far off, borne through the night from N.Y. harbor. It reminds me of home and fills me with inexpressible sorrow. For some reason that sound and the sorrow it brings makes it all the more difficult to bear Leslie's overheated and blooming presence, like some jungle flower, now so astonishingly unattainable. Thinking fleetingly of gangrene, I cannot believe that my staff still flaunts itself, lancelike. Could John the Baptist have suffered such deprivation? Tantalus? St. Augustine? Little Nell?

Leslie is—literally and figuratively—totally lingual. Her sex life is wholly centered in her tongue. It is not fortuitous therefore that the inflammatory promise she has been able to extend me through that hyperactive organ of hers finds a correlation in the equally inflammatory but utterly spurious words she loves to speak. While we sit there I recall the name of a ludicrous phenomenon I read about in a Duke Univ. course in abnormal psychology: "coprolalia," the compulsive use of obscene language, often found in young women. When at last I break our silence and banteringly broach the possibility that she may be a victim of this malady, she seems not so much insulted as hurt, and softly begins to sob again. I seem to have opened some painful wound. But no, she insists, it's not that. After a while she stops sobbing. Then she says something which only hours before I would have considered a joke but I now accept placidly and with no surprise as the stark, aching truth. "I'm a virgin," she says in a bleak small voice. After a long silence I reply, "No offense, understand. But I think you're a very sick virgin." As I say this I realize the acerbity of the words but somehow don't regret them. Again a ship's horn groans at the harbor's mouth, touching me with such longing and nostalgia and despair that I think that I too might burst into tears. "I like you a lot, Les," I manage to say, "I just think it was unfair of you to string me along this way. It's tough on a guy. It's terrible. You can't imagine." After saying this I simply cannot tell whether her words make up a non sequitur or not, when she replies in the most desolate voice I've ever heard, "But oh, Stingo, you *can't imagine what it's like to grow up in a Jewish family." She fails immediately to elaborate on this.*

But finally, when dawn breaks and deep fatigue floods through my bones and muscles—including that doughty love-muscle which at last begins to flag and droop after its tenacious vigil—Leslie re-creates for me the dark odyssey of her psychoanalysis. And of course her family. Her horrible family. Her family which, despite the cool and civilized veneer, according to Leslie, is a waxwork gallery of monsters. The ruthless and ambitious father whose religion *is molded plastics and who has spoken a bare twenty words to her since childhood. The creepy younger sister and the stupid older brother. Above all, the ogreish mother who, Barnard enlightenment or no, has dominated Les's life with bitchery and vengeance ever since the moment when she caught Leslie, then three, diddling herself and forced her to wear hand-splints for months as prophylaxis against self-abuse. All this Leslie pours out to me in a terrible rush as if I too were momentarily only another in that ever-changing phalanx of practitioners which has attended her woes and wretchednesses for over four years. It is full sun-up. Leslie is drinking coffee, I am drinking Budweiser, and Tommy Dorsey is playing on the two-thousand-dollar Magnavox phonograph. Exhausted, I hear Leslie's cataract of words as if through muffled layers of wool, trying without much success to piece it all together—this scrambled confessional with its hodgepodge of terms like Reichian and Jungian, Ad-*

lerian, a Disciple of Karen Horney, sublimation, gestalt, fixations, toilet training, and other things I have been aware of but never heard a human being speak of in such tones, which down South are reserved for Thomas Jefferson, Uncle Remus and the blessed Trinity. I am so tired that I am only barely aware of what she is driving at when she speaks of her current analyst, her fourth, a "Reichian," one Dr. Pulvermacher, and then alludes to her "plateau." I make flutters with my eyelids denoting an urgent need for sleep. And she goes on and on, those moist and precious Jewish lips, forever lost to me, driving home the sudden awareness that my poor dear joint for the first time in many hours is as shrunken and as small as that Worm whose replica hangs behind me, there in the papal bathroom. I yawn, ferociously, loud, but Leslie pays this no mind, seemingly intent that I should not go away with ill feelings, that I should somehow try to understand her. But I really don't know if I want to understand. As Leslie continues I can only reflect despairingly on the obvious irony: that if through those frigid little harpies in Virginia I had been betrayed chiefly by Jesus, I have been just as cruelly swindled at Leslie's hands by the egregious Doktor Freud. Two smart Jews, believe me.

"Before I reached this plateau of vocalization," I hear Leslie say, through the surreal delirium of my fatigue, "I could never have said any of those words I've said to you. Now I'm completely able to vocalize. I mean those Anglo-Saxon four-letter words that everyone should be able to say. My analyst—Dr. Pulvermacher—said that the repressiveness of a society in general is directly proportionate to its harsh repression of sexual language." What I say in reply is mingled with a yawn so cavernous and profound that my voice is like a wild beast's roar. "I see, I see," I yawn, roaring, "this word vocalize, you mean you can <u>*say*</u> *fuck but you still can't do it!" Her answer is a blur in my brain of imperfectly registered sounds, many minutes in duration, out of what I am able to salvage only the impression that Leslie, now deep into*

something called orgone therapy, will in the coming days be seated in some sort of box, there to absorb patiently waves of energy from the ether that might allow her passage upward to the next plateau. Close to the brink of sleep, I yawn again and wordlessly wish her well. And then, mirabile ditcu, I drop off into slumberland even as she babbles on about the possibility of someday—someday! I dream a strange confounded dream in which intimations of bliss are transfused with lacerating pain. It could only be a few moments that I drowse. When I wake—blinking at Leslie in the full flight of her soliliquy—I realize I have been sitting ponderously on my hand, which I withdraw from underneath my ass. All five fingers are momentarily deformed and totally without sensation. This helps to explain my ineffably sad dream, where, hotly embracing Leslie once more on the couch, I managed at last to fondle one bare breast, which, however, felt like a soggy ball of dough beneath my hand, itself tightly imprisoned within the rim of a murderous brassiere made of wormwood and wire.

These many years later I am able to see how Leslie's recalcitrance—indeed, her entire unassailable virginity—was a nice counterpoint to the larger narrative I have felt compelled to relate. God knows what might have happened had she really been the wanton and experienced playgirl she had impersonated; she was so ripely desirable that I don't see how I could have failed to become her slave. This would certainly have tended to remove me from the earthy, ramshackle ambience of Yetta Zimmerman's Pink Palace and thus doubtless from the sequence of events that were in the making and compose the main reason for this story. But the disparity between what Leslie had promised and what she delivered was so wounding to my spirit that I became physically ill. It was nothing really serious—nothing more than a severe bout of flu combined with a deep psychic despondency—but as I lay in bed for four or five days (tenderly taken care of by Nathan and Sophie, who brought me tomato soup and magazines) I was able to decide that I had come to a critical extremity in my life. This extremity took the form of the craggy rock of sex, upon which I had obviously though inexplicably foundered.

I knew I was presentable-looking, possessed a spacious and sympathetic intelligence, and had that Southern gift of gab which I was well aware could often cast a sugary (but not saccharine) necromantic charm. That despite all this bright dower and the considerable effort I had put forth in exploiting it, I was still unable to find a girl who would go to the dark gods with me, seemed now—as I lay abed feverish, poring over *Life* and smarting with the image of Leslie Lapidus chattering at me in the dawn's defeated light—a morbid condition which, however painfully, I should regard as a stroke of dirty fate, as people accept any ghastly but finally bearable disability such as an intractable stammer or a harelip. I was simply not old sexy Stingo, and I had to be content with that fact. But in compensation, I reasoned, I had more exalted goals. After all, I was a writer, an artist, and it was a platitude by now that much of the world's greatest art had been achieved by dedicated men who, husbanding their energies, had not allowed some misplaced notion of the primacy of the groin to subvert grander aims of beauty and truth. *So onward,* Stingo, I said to myself, rallying my flayed spirits, onward with your work. Putting lechery behind you, bend your passions to this ravishing vision that is in you, calling to be born. Such monkish exhortations allowed me sometime during the next week to rise from bed, feeling fresh and cleansed and relatively unhorny, and to boldly continue my grapple with the assorted faeries, demons, clods, clowns, sweethearts and tormented mothers and fathers who were beginning to throng the pages of my novel.

I never saw Leslie again. We parted that morning in a spirit of grave though rueful affection and she asked me to call her soon, but I never did. She dwelt often in my erotic fantasies after that, though, and over the years she has occupied my thoughts many times. Despite the torture she inflicted on me, I have wished her only the best of fortune, wherever she went or whatever she ultimately became. I always idly hoped that her time in the orgone box led her to the fulfillment she yearned for, hoisting her to a loftier plateau than mere "vocalization." But should this have failed, like the other forms of treatment she had submitted to, I have never had much doubt that the ensuing decades, with their extraordinary scientific progress in terms of the care and maintenance of the libido, would have brought Leslie an ample measure of fulfillment. I may be wrong, but why is it that some intuition tells me that Leslie ultimately found her full meed of happiness? I don't know, but anyway, that is how I now see her: an adjusted, sleek, elegantly graying and still beautiful woman ungrudgingly accommodating herself to middle age, very sophisticated now in her thrifty use of dirty words, warmly married, philoprogenitive and (I'm almost certain) multiorgasmic.

Eight

The weather was generally fine that summer, but sometimes the evenings got hot and steamy, and when this happened Nathan and Sophie and I often went around the corner on Church Avenue to an air-conditioned "cocktail lounge"—God, what a description!—called the Maple Court. There were relatively few full-fledged bars in that part of Flatbush (a puzzlement to me until Nathan pointed out that serious tippling does not rank high among Jewish pastimes), but this bar of ours did do a moderately brisk business, numbering among its predominately blue-collar clientele Irish doormen, Scandinavian cabdrivers, German building superintendents and WASPs of indeterminate status like myself who had somehow strayed into the faubourg. There was also what appeared to me a small sprinkling of Jews, some looking a little furtive. The Maple Court was large, ill-lit and on the seedy side, with the faint pervasive odor of stagnant water, but the three of us were attracted there on especially sultry summer nights by the refrigerated air and by the fact that we had grown rather to like its down-at-the-heel easygoingness. It was also cheap and beer was still ten cents a glass. I learned that the bar had been built in 1933, to celebrate and capitalize upon the repeal of Prohibition, and its spacious, even somewhat cavernous dimensions were originally meant to encompass a dance floor. Such Corybantic revels as envisioned by the first owners never took place, however, since through some incredible oversight the raunchy entrepreneurs failed to realize that they had located their establishment in a neighborhood substantially as devoted to order and propriety as a community of Hard Shell Baptists or Mennonites. The synagogues said No, also the Dutch Reformed church.

Thus the Maple Court did not obtain a cabaret license, and all the bright angular chrome-and-gilt décor, including sunburst chandeliers meant to revolve above the giddy dancers like glittering confections in a Ruby Keeler movie, fell into disrepair and gathered a patina of grime and smoke. The raised platform which formed the hub of the oval-shaped bar, and which had been designed to enable sleek long-legged stripteasers to wiggle their behinds down upon a circumambience of lounging gawkers, became filled with dusty signs and bloated fake bottles advertising brands of whiskey and beer. And more sadly somehow, the big Art Deco mural against one wall—a fine period piece done by an expert hand, with the skyline of Manhattan and silhouettes of a jazz band and chorus girls kicking up their heels—never once faced out toward a swirl of jubilant dancers but grew cracked and water-blotched and acquired a long horizontal dingy streak where a generation of neighborhood drunks had propped the backs of their heads. It was just beneath a corner of this mural, in a remote part of the ill-starred dance floor, that Nathan and Sophie and I would sit on those muggy evenings in the Maple Court.

"I'm sorry you didn't make out with Leslie, kid," Nathan said to me one night after the debacle on Pierrepont Street. He was clearly both disappointed and a little surprised that his efforts at matchmaking had come to naught. "I thought you two were all locked in, made for each other. At Coney Island that day I thought she was going to eat you up. And now you tell me it all went flooey. What's the matter? I can't believe she wouldn't put out."

"Oh no, it was all right in the sex department," I lied. "I mean, at least I *got in.*" For a variety of vague reasons I couldn't bring myself to tell the truth about our calamitous stand-off, this scratching match between two virgins. It was too disgraceful to dwell upon, both from Leslie's point of view and my own. I plunged into a feeble fabrication, but I could tell that Nathan knew I had begun to improvise—his shoulders were shaking with laughter—and I finished my account with one or two Freudian furbelows, chief among them being one in which Leslie told me that she had been able to reach a climax only with large, muscular, coal-black Negroes with colossal penises. Smiling, Nathan began to regard me with the look of a man who is having his leg pulled in a chummy way, and when I was finished he put his hand on my shoulder and said in those understanding tones of an older brother, "Sorry about you and Leslie, kid, whatever happened. I thought she'd be a dreamboat. Sometimes the chemistry just isn't *right.*"

We forgot about Leslie. I did most of the drinking these evenings, downing my half-dozen glasses of beer or so. Sometimes we went to the bar before dinner, often afterward. In those days it was almost unheard of to order wine in a bar—especially a tacky place like the Maple Court—but Nathan, in the vanguard about so many things, always managed to have served up a bottle of Chablis, which he kept cold in a bucket by the table and which would last him and Sophie the hour and a half we usually spent there. The Chablis never did more than get both of them mildly and pleasantly relaxed, signaled by a fine sheen welling up through his dark face and the tenderest dogwood-blossom flush on hers.

Nathan and Sophie were like an old married couple to me now, we were all inseparable; and I idly wondered if some of the more sophisticated of the Maple Court habitués did not regard us as a *ménage à trois.* Nathan was marvelous, bewitching, so perfectly "normal" and so delightful to be with that were it not for Sophie's wretched little references (sometimes made inadvertently during our Prospect Park picnics) to terrible moments during their past year together, I would utterly have erased from memory that cataclysmic scene when I had first glimpsed them battling, along with other hints I had had of another, blacker side of his being. How could I do otherwise, in the presence of this electrifying, commanding character, part magic entertainer, part big brother, confidant and guru, who had so generously reached out to me in my isolation? Nathan was no cheap charmer. There was the depth of a masterful performer in even the slightest of his jokes, practically all of them Jewish, which he was able so inexhaustibly to disgorge. His major stories were masterpieces. Once as a boy sitting in the Tidewater Theatre with my father as we watched a W. C. Fields movie (I believe it was *My Little Chickadee*) I saw happen what was supposed to happen only as a figure of speech, or in cornball works of fiction: I saw my father caught up in a rapture of such mind-dissolving laughter that he slid completely out of his seat and into the aisle. Laid out, by God, in the aisle! I did nearly the same in the Maple Court bar as Nathan told what I always remember as his Jewish country club joke.

It is like watching not one but two separate performers when Nathan acts out this suburban folk tale. The first performer is Shapiro, who at a banquet is attempting to propose once more his perennially blackballed friend for membership. Nathan's voice grows incomparably oleaginous, gross with fatuity and edged with just the perfect trace of Yiddish as he limns Shapiro's quaveringly hopeful apostrophe to Max Tannenbaum. "To tell what a great human being Max Tannenbaum is I must use the entire English alphabet! From A to Z I will tell you about this beautiful man!" Nathan's voice grows silky, sly. Shapiro knows that among the club members is one—now nodding and dozing—who will try to blackball Tannenbaum. Shapiro trusts that this enemy, Ginsberg, will not wake up. Nathan-Shapiro speaks: "A he is Admirable. B he is Beneficial. C he is Charming. D he is Delightful. E he is Educated. F he is Friendly. G he is Good-hearted. H he is a Helluva nice guy." (Nathan's stately, unctuous intonations are impeccable, the vapid slogans almost unbearably hilarious; the back of my throat aches from laughter, a film blurs my eyes.) "I he is Inna-resting." At this point Ginsberg wakes up, Nathan's forefinger furiously stabs the air, the voice becoming magisterial, arrogant, insufferably but gloriously hostile. Through Nathan, the terrible, the unbudgeable Ginsberg thunders: "J joost a minute! (Majestic pause) K he's a Kike! L he's a Lummox! M he's a Moron! N he's a Nayfish! O he's an Ox! P he's a Prick! Q he's a Queer! R he's a Red! S he's a Shlemiel! T he's a Tochis! U you can have him! V ve don't want him! W X Y Z—I blackball the *shmuck!*"

It was a grand display of wizardry, Nathan's production-inspired mockery of such outrageous, runaway, sublime silliness that I found myself emulating my father, gasping, shorn of strength, collapsing sideways on the greasy banquette. Sophie, half choked on her own mirth, made weak little dabs at her eyes. I sensed the local barflies regarding us glumly, wondering at our delirium. Recovering, I gazed at Nathan with something like awe. To be able to cause such laughter was a god's gift, a benison.

But if Nathan had been merely a clown, had he remained so exhaustingly *"on"* at all times, he would have, of course, with all his winning gifts, become a staggering bore. He was too sensitive to play the perpetual comedian, and his interests were too wide-ranging and serious for him to permit our good times together to remain on the level of tomfoolery, however imaginative. I might add, too, that I always sensed that it was Nathan—perhaps again because of his "seniority," or maybe because of the pure electric force of his presence—who set the tone of our conversation, although his innate tact and sense of proportion prevented him from hogging the stage. I was no slouch at storytelling, either, and he listened. He was, I suppose, what is considered a polymath—one who knows a great deal about almost everything; yet such was his warmth, his wit, and with such a light touch did he display his learning, that I never once felt in his presence that sense of gagging resentment one often feels when listening to a person of loquaciously large knowledge, who is often just an erudite ass. His range was astonishing and I had constantly to remind myself that I was talking to a scientist, a biologist (I kept thinking of a prodigy like Julian Huxley, whose essays I had read in college)—this man who possessed so many literary references and allusions, both classical and modern, and who within the space of an hour could, with no gratuitous strain, weave together Lytton Strachey, *Alice in Wonderland,* Martin Luther's early celibacy, *A Midsummer Night's Dream* and the mating habits of the Sumatran orangutan into a little jewel box of a beguiling lecture which facetiously but with a serious overtone explored the intertwined nature of sexual voyeurism and exhibitionism.

It all sounded very convincing to me. He was as brilliant on Dreiser as he was on Whitehead's philosophy of organism. Or the theme of suicide, about which he seemed to possess a certain preoccupation, and which he touched on more than once, though in a manner which skirted the purely morbid. The novel which he esteemed above all others, he said, was *Madame Bovary,* not alone because of its formal perfection but because of the resolution of the suicide motif; Emma's death by self-poisoning seeming to be so beautifully inevitable as to become one of the supreme emblems, in Western literature, of the human condition. And once in an extravagant piece of waggery, speaking of reincarnation (about which he said he was not so skeptical as to rule it beyond possibility), he claimed to have been in a past life the only Jewish Albigensian monk—a brilliant friar named St. Nathan le Bon who had single-handedly promulgated that crazy sect's obsessive penchant for self-destruction, which was based on the reasoning that if life is evil, it is necessary to hasten life's end. "The only thing I hadn't foreseen," he observed, "is that I'd be brought back to live in the fucked-up twentieth century."

Yet despite the mildly unsettling nature of this concern of his, I never felt during these effervescent evenings the slightest hint of the depression and cloudy despair in him which Sophie had alluded to, the violent seizures whose fury she had experienced firsthand. He was so much the embodiment of everything I deemed attractive and even envied in a human being that I couldn't help but suspect that the somber side of her Polish imagination had dreamed up these intimations of strife and doom. Such, I reasoned, was the stock-in-trade of Polacks.

No, I felt he was essentially too gentle and solicitous to pose any such menace as she had hinted at. (Even though I knew of his ugly moods.) My book, for example, my flowering novel. I shall never forget that priceless, affectionate outpouring. In spite of his earlier remonstrances about Southern literature falling into desuetude, his brotherly concern for my work had been constant and encouraging. Once one morning during our coffee *shmooz* he asked if he might see some of the first pages I had written.

"Why not?" he urged with that swarthily intense and furrowed expression which so often caused his smile to resemble a benign scowl. "We're friends. I won't interfere, I won't comment, I won't even make any suggestions. I'd just love to see it." I was terrified—terrified for the straightforward reason that not a single other soul had laid eyes on my much-thumbed stack of yellow pages with their smudged and rancid margins, and my respect for Nathan's mind was so great that I knew that if he should show displeasure with my effort, however unintentionally, it would severely dampen my enthusiasm and even my further progress. Taking a gamble one night, however, and breaking a romantically noble resolution I had made not to let anyone look at the book until its final sentence, and then only Alfred A. Knopf in person, I gave him ninety pages or so, which he read at the Pink Palace while Sophie sat with me at the Maple Court, reminiscing about her childhood and Cracow. My heart went into a bumping erratic trot when Nathan, after perhaps an hour and a half, hustled in out of the night, brow bedewed with sweat, and sprawled down opposite me next to Sophie. His gaze was level, emotionless; I feared the worst. *Stop!* I was on the verge of pleading. *You said you wouldn't comment!* But his judgment hung in the air like an imminent clap of thunder. "You've read Faulkner," he said slowly, without inflection, "you've read Robert Penn Warren." He paused. "I'm sure you've read Thomas Wolfe, and even Carson McCullers. I'm breaking my promise about no criticism."

And I thought: Oh shit, he's got my number, all right, it really is just a bunch of derivative trash. I wanted to sink through the chocolate-ripple and chrome-splotched tiles of the Maple Court and disappear among the rats into the sewers of Flatbush. I clenched my eyes shut—thinking: I never should have shown it to this con man, who is now going to give me a line about Jewish writing—and at the moment I did so, sweating and a trifle nauseated, I jumped as his big hands grasped my shoulders and his lips smeared my brow with a wet and sloppy kiss. I popped my eyes open, stupefied, almost feeling the warmth of his radiant smile. "Twenty-two years old!" he exclaimed. "And oh my God, you can write! Of course you've read those writers, you wouldn't be able to write a book if you hadn't. But you've absorbed them, kid, *absorbed* them and made them your own. You've got your own *voice*. That's the most exciting hundred pages by an unknown writer anyone's ever read. Give me more!" Sophie, infected by his exuberance, clutched Nathan's arm and glowed like a madonna, gazing at me as if I were the author of *War and Peace*. I choked stupidly on an unshaped little cluster of words, nearly fainting with pleasure, happier, I think—at only small risk of hyperbole—than any single moment I could then remember in a life of memorable fulfillments, however basically undistinguished. And all the rest of the evening he made a glorious fuss over my book, firing me with all the vivid encouragement which, in the deepest part of me, I knew I had desperately needed. How could I have failed to have the most helpless crush on such a generous, mind-and-life-enlarging mentor, pal, savior, sorcerer? Nathan was utterly, fatally glamorous.

July came, bringing varied weather—hot days, then oddly cool, damp days when the wanderers across the park muffled themselves in jackets and sweaters, finally several mornings at a stretch when thunderstorms grumbled and threatened but never broke. I thought that I could live there in Flatbush at Yetta's Pink Palace forever, or certainly for the months and even years it would take to finish my masterpiece. It was hard to hold to my high-minded vows—I still fretted over the lamentably celibate nature of my existence; this aside, I felt that the routine I had established in company with Sophie and Nathan was as contented a daily state as any in which a budding writer could possibly find himself. Buoyed up by Nathan's passionate assurance, I scribbled away like a fiend, constantly lulled by the knowledge that when the fatigue of my labors overtook me I could almost always find Sophie and Nathan, singly or together, somewhere nearby ready to share a confidence, a worry, a joke, a memory, Mozart, a sandwich, coffee, beer. With loneliness in abeyance and with my creative juices in full flow, I could not have been happier . . .

I could not have been happier, that is, until there came a bad sequence of events which intruded themselves on my well-being and made me realize how desperately at odds Sophie and Nathan had been (and still were) with each other, how unsimulated had been that quality in Sophie of foreboding and fright, together with the hints she had let fall of bitter discord. Then there was an even more sinister revelation. For the first time since the night of my arrival at Yetta's house over a month before, I began to see seeping out of Nathan, almost like some visible poisonous exudate, his latent capacity for rage and disorder. And I also began gradually to understand how the turmoil that was grinding them to pieces had double origins, deriving perhaps equally from the black and tormented underside of Nathan's nature and from the unrelinquished reality of Sophie's immediate past, trailing its horrible smoke—as if from the very chimneys of Auschwitz—of anguish, confusion, self-deception and, above all, guilt . . .

I had been sitting one evening at around six o'clock at our usual table at the Maple Court, sipping a beer and reading the New York *Post*. I was awaiting Sophie—due at any moment after her day at Dr. Blackstock's office—and Nathan, who had told me that morning over coffee that he would join us around seven, following what he knew would be an especially long, rugged day at his laboratory. I felt a little starched and formal sitting there, because I had on a clean shirt and tie and was wearing my suit for the first time since my misadventure with the Princess of Pierrepont Street. I was somewhat dismayed to discover a smear of Leslie's lipstick, stale but still flamboyantly vermilion, on the inner edge of the lapel, but I had managed with a lot of spit and a certain readjustment to make the stain practically invisible, or enough so that my father would probably not notice. I was dressed this way because I was due to meet my father at Pennsylvania Station, where he was arriving by train from Virginia later on in the evening. I had received a letter from him only a week or so before in which he said he was planning to pay me a brief visit. His motive was sweet and patently uncomplicated: he said he missed me and since he hadn't seen me in so long (I calculated it had been nine months or more) he wanted to reestablish, face to face, eyeball to eyeball, our mutual love and kinship. It was July, he had vacation time; he was coming up. There was something so infrangibly Southern, so old-fashioned about such a gesture that it was almost paleological, but it warmed my heart deeply, even beyond my very real affection for him.

Also, I knew it cost my father a great deal of emotional capital to venture into the great city, which he loathed utterly. His Southern hatred of New York was not the primitive, weirdly solipsistic hatred of the father of a college friend of mine from one of the more moistly paludal counties of South Carolina: this countryman's refusal to visit New York was based on an apocalyptic and ever-haunting fantasy-scenario in which, seated at a Times Square cafeteria minding his own business, he finds the chair next to him preempted by a large, grinning, malodorous male Negro (politely or rudely preempted, it doesn't matter; propinquity is the sole issue), whereupon he is forced to commit a felony through the necessity of seizing a Heinz Ketchup bottle and bashing it over the black bastard's head. He then gets five years in Sing Sing. My father had less mad strictures about the city, though still intense ones. No such monstrous figment, no werewolf of race stalked the imagination of my father—a gentleman, a libertarian and a Jacksonian Democrat. He detested New York only for what he called its "barbarity," its lack of courtesy, its total bankruptcy in the estimable domain of public manners. The snarling command of the traffic cop, the blaring insult of horns, all the needlessly raised voices of the night-denizens of Manhattan ravaged his nerves, acidified his duodenum, unhelmed his composure and his will. I wanted to see him very much, and was enormously touched that he would make the long trip north, endure the uproar and dare shoulder through the swarming, obstreperous and brutal human tides of the metropolis in order to visit his only offspring.

I waited a little restlessly for Sophie. Then my eyes lit upon something which totally captured my attention. On the third page of the *Post* that evening was an article, accompanied by a most unflattering photograph, concerning the notorious Mississippi race-baiter and demagogue, Senator Theodore Gilmore Bilbo. According to the story, Bilbo—whose face and utterances had saturated the media during the war years and those immediately following—

had been admitted to the Ochsner Clinic in New Orleans to undergo surgery for cancer of the mouth. One of the inferences that could be drawn from the piece was that Bilbo had left to him very little time. In the photograph he looked already a cadaver. Great irony in this, of course: "The Man" who had gained the loathing of "right-thinking" people everywhere, including the South, by his straightforward promiscuous public use of words like "nigger," "coon," "jigaboo," contracting cancer in that symbolic portion of his anatomy. The petty tyrant from the piney woods who had called Mayor La Guardia of New York a "dago" and who had addressed a Jewish congressman as "Dear Kike" suffering a ripe carcinoma which would soon still that scurrilous jaw and evil tongue—it was all too much, and the *Post* laid on the irony with a dumptruck. After I read the piece, I gave a long sigh, thinking that I was awfully glad to see the old devil go. Of all those who had so foully tarnished the image of the modern South he was a leading mischief-maker, not really typical of Southern politicians but because of his blabbermouth and prominence rendering himself, in the eyes of the credulous and even not so credulous, an archetypal image of the Southern statesman and thus polluting the name of whatever was good and decent and even exemplary in the South as surely and as wickedly as those anonymous sub-anthropoids who had recently slaughtered Bobby Weed. I said to myself, again: Glad to see you go, you evil-spirited old sinner.

Yet even as the gentle brew took hold, softly marinating my senses, and I ruminated on Bilbo's fate, I was overtaken by another emotion; I suppose it might be called regret—faint regret perhaps, yet regret. A lousy way to die, I thought. Cancer of that kind must be ghastly, those monstrous metastasizing cells so close to the brain—hideous little microscopic boll weevils invading cheek, sinuses, eye socket, jaw, filling the mouth with its fulminating virulence until the tongue, engulfed, rotted and fell dumb. I shuddered a little. Yet it was not simply this agonizing mortal blow which the senator had suffered that caused me my odd and vagrant pang. It was something else, abstract and remote, intangible yet worrisome to my spirit. I knew something about Bilbo—something more, that is, than was known by the ordinary American citizen with even a marginal concern with politics and doubtless more than the editors of the New York *Post*. Certainly my knowledge was not profound, but even in the superficiality of my understanding I felt there had been revealed to me facets of Bilbo's character that gave the heft of flesh and the stink of real sweat to that shingle-flat cartoon of the daily press. What I knew about Bilbo was not even particularly redeeming—he would remain a first-class scoundrel until the tumor strangled off his breath or its excrescence flooded through the portals of his brain—but it had at least allowed me to perceive human bones and dimensions through the papier-mâché stock villain from Dixie.

In college—where, outside of "creative writing," my only serious academic concern had been the study of the history of the American South—I had hacked out a lengthy term paper on that freakish and aborted political movement known as Populism, paying special attention to the Southern demagogues and rabble-rousers who had so often exemplified its seamier side. It was hardly a truly original paper, I recollect, but I put a great deal of thought and effort into its making, for a lad of twenty or so, and it earned me a glowing "A" at a time when "A's" were hard to get. Drawing heavily on C. Vann Woodward's brilliant study of Tom Watson of Georgia and concentrating on other hagridden folk heroes like "Pitchfork Ben" Tillman and James K. Vardaman and "Cotton Ed" Smith and Huey Long, I demonstrated how democratic idealism and honest concern for the common man were virtues which linked all these men together, at least in their early careers, along with a concomitant and highly vocal opposition to monopoly capitalism, industrial and business fat cats and "big money." I then extrapolated from this proposition an argument to show how these men, basically decent and even visionary to begin with, were brought down by their own fatal weakness in face of the Southern racial tragedy; for each of them in the end, to one degree or another, was forced to play upon and exploit the poor-white rednecks' ancient fear and hatred of the Negro in order to aggrandize what had degenerated into shabby ambition and lust for power.

Although I did not deal with Bilbo at any great length, I learned from my ancillary research (and rather to my surprise, given the truly despicable public image he projected in the 1940s) that he, too, fitted into this classically paradoxical mold; Bilbo in much the same way as the others had commenced with enlightened principles, and indeed like the others, I discovered, had as a public servant produced reforms and contributions that had greatly advanced the common weal. It all may not have been much—measured against his nauseous mouthings which would have caused the most hidebound Virginia reactionary to recoil—but it was something. One of the nastiest abettors of the hateful dogma purveyed below the Mason-Dixon line, he seemed to me also—while I brooded over the haggard figure in a baggy white Palm Beach suit, ravaged like one already seized by death's hand even as he slouched past a frayed palmtree into the New Orleans clinic—one of its chief and most wretched victims, and the faintest breath of regret accompanied my murmured farewell. Suddenly, thinking of the South, thinking of Bilbo and once again of Bobby Weed, I was riven by a sharp blade of despondency. *How long, Lord?* I beseeched the begrimed and motionless chandeliers.

Just then I caught sight of Sophie at the instant she pushed open the grimy glass front door of the bar, where a slant of golden light somehow captured at exactly the right angle the lovely swerve of her cheekbone below the oval eyes with their sleepy-sullen hint of Asia, and the broad harmony of the rest of her face, including—or, I should say, especially—the fine, elongated, slightly uptilted "Polish *schnoz,*" as Nathan lovingly called it, which terminated in a nice little button. There were certain moments when through such a nonchalant gesture—opening a door, brushing her hair, throwing bread to the Prospect Park swans (it had something to do with motion, attitude, the tilt of head, a flow of arms, a swing of hips)—she created a continuum of beauty that was positively breath-taking. The tilt, the flow, the swing together made up an exquisite particularity that was nobody's but Sophie's, and yes, by God, it took the breath away. I mean this literally, for synchronous with the stunning effect she made on my eyes as she stood there arrested in the doorway—blinking at the gloom, her flaxen hair drenched in the evening gold—I listened to myself give a thin but quite audible and breathless half-hiccup. I was still moronically in love with her.

"Stingo, you're all dressed up, where are you going, you're wearing your cocksucker, you look so nice," she said all in a tumbling rush, blushing crimson and correcting herself with a wonderful giggle even as I, too, formed the word *seersucker!* She giggled so much that, sitting down beside me, she buried her face on my shoulder. *"Quelle horreur!"*

"You've been hanging around Nathan too long," I said, joining in her laughter. Her sexual idiom, I knew, was lifted entirely from Nathan. I had realized this since that moment when—describing some puritanical Cracovian town fathers who had endeavored to put a fig leaf on a reproduction of Michelangelo's *David*—she had said they had wanted "to cover up his *schlong*."

"Dirty words in English or Yiddish sound better than they do in Polish," she said after she had recovered. "Do you know what the word for fuck in Polish is? It's *pierdolić*. It just doesn't have the same quality that the English word has. I like fuck much better."

"I like fuck much better too."

The drift of conversation made me both flustered and a little aroused (from Nathan she had also absorbed an innocent candor I was still unable to get used to), and so I managed to change the subject. I pretended nonchalance even though her presence still stirred me to the very pit of my stomach, inflamed me in a way that was all the more distracting because of the perfume she was wearing—the same herbal scent, distinctly unsubtle and loamy and provocative, which had stung my libidinal longings on that first day when we went to Coney Island. Now that perfume seemed to float up from between her breasts, which to my great surprise were most amply on show, appetizingly framed by her low-cut silk blouse. It was a new blouse, I was sure, and not really her style. During the weeks I had known her she had been aggravatingly conservative and low-keyed in her dress (aside from the flair for costumery she shared with Nathan, which was a different matter) and wore clothes clearly not calculated to focus eyes on her body, especially her upper torso; she was excessively demure even at a time in fashion when the womanly figure, badly depreciated, was rather down and out. I had seen her bosom browsing about beneath silk and cashmere and a nylon swimsuit but never with any definition. I could only theorize that this was some psychic extension of the prudish way she doubtless had to cloak herself in the rigid Catholic community of prewar Cracow, a practice she must have found hard to abandon. Also, to a lesser degree, I think she may not have wanted to expose to the world what had been wreaked upon her body by the privation of the past. Her dentures sometimes came loose. Her neck still had unbecoming little wrinkles, slack flesh pulled at the back of her arms.

But by now Nathan's year-long campaign to restore her to health and plumpness had begun to pay off; at least it seemed that Sophie was beginning to think so, for she had liberated her slightly freckled, pretty demiglobes as openly as she could and remain a lady, and I glanced at them with enormous appreciation. All it took for boobs, I thought, was great American nutrition. They caused me slightly to shift my focus of erogenous dreamery away from the few glimpses I had had of her achingly desirable, harmoniously proportioned Elberta peach of a derrière. Now I soon discovered that she had gotten herself rigged out in these sexpot duds because it was to be a very special evening for Nathan. He was going to reveal something wonderful about his work to Sophie and me. It was going to be, said Sophie, quoting Nathan, "a bombshell."

"What do you mean?" I said.

"His work," she replied, "his research. He told me he would say to us tonight about his discovery. They finally make what Nathan calls the breakthrough."

"That's marvelous," I said, genuinely excited. "You mean this stuff he's been so . . . *mysterious* about? He's finally got it licked, is that what you mean?"

"That's what he said, Stingo!" Her eyes were ashine. "He's going to tell us tonight."

"God, that's terrific," I said, feeling a small but vivid interior thrill.

I knew virtually nothing about Nathan's work. Although he had told me in large (though generally impenetrable) detail about the technical nature of his research (enzymes, ion transference, permeable membranes, etc., also the fetus of that miserable rabbit), he had never divulged to me—nor had I out of reticence asked—anything concerning the ultimate justification for this complex and, beyond doubt, profoundly challenging biological enterprise. I knew also, from what she had intimated, that he had kept Sophie in the dark about his project. My earliest conjecture—far-fetched even for a scientific ignoramus like myself (even then I was beginning to rue the lilac *fin de siècle* hours of my college days, with their total immersion in metaphysical poesy and Quality Lit., their yawning disdain of politics and the raw dirty world, their quotidian homage to the *Kenyon Review,* to the New Criticism and the ectoplasmic Mr. Eliot)—was that he was creating life full-blown from a test tube. Maybe Nathan was founding a new race of Homo sapiens, finer, fairer, fleeter than the bedeviled sufferers of the present day. I even envisioned a tiny embryonic Superman whom Nathan might be concocting at Pfizer, an inch-high square-jawed homunculus complete with cape and "S" emblazoned on his breast, ready to leap to his place in the color pages of *Life* as another miraculous artifact of our age. But this was a bootless piece of whimsy and I was really in the dark. Sophie's sudden news that soon we would be enlightened was like receiving an electric jolt. I wanted only to hear more.

"He telephoned me this morning at work," she explained, "at Dr. Blackstock's, and said he wanted to have lunch with me. He wanted to tell me something. His voice sounded so excited, I just couldn't imagine what it was. He was calling from his laboratory, and it was so unusual, you see, Stingo, because we almost never have lunch together. We are working so far away from each other. Besides, Nathan says we see so much of each other that having lunch together is maybe a little . . . *de trop.* Anyway, he called this morning and *insisted* in this very excited voice, and so we met in this Italian restaurant near Lafayette Square, where we had been together last year when we first met. Oh, Nathan was just wild with excitement! I thought he had a fever. And when we ate lunch he started to tell me what had happened. Listen to this, Stingo. He said that this morning he and his team—this research team—have make the final *breakthrough* they were hoping for. He said they were right upon the edge of the final discovery. Oh, Nathan could not eat he was so full of joy! And you know, Stingo, while Nathan was telling me these things I remember that it was right at this same table a year ago that he first told me about his work. He said what he was doing was a secret. What it was *precisely* he could not reveal, even to me. But I remember this—I remember him telling me that if it was successful it would end up being one of the greatest medical advances of all time. Those were his exact words, Stingo. He said that it wasn't his work alone, there were others. But he was very proud of his own contribution. And then he said it again: one of the greatest medical advances of all time! He said it would win the *Nobel Prize!*"

She paused and I saw that her own face was rosy with excitement. "God, Sophie," I said, "that's just wonderful. What do you think it is? Didn't he give you any hint at all?"

"No, he said he would have to wait until tonight. He could not tell me the secret at lunch, just that they had make the breakthrough. There is this great secrecy in the companies that make drugs like Pfizer, that is why Nathan is sometimes so mysterious. But I understand."

"You'd think a few hours wouldn't make any difference," I said. I felt a frustrating impatience.

"Yes, but he said that it does. Anyway, Stingo, we'll know what it is very soon. Isn't it incredible, isn't it *formidable?*" She squeezed my hand until my fingertips went numb.

It's *cancer,* I thought all during Sophie's little soliloquy. I had really begun to burst with happiness and pride, sharing Sophie's own radiant exuberance. It's a cure for *cancer,* I kept thinking; that unbelievable son of a bitch, that scientific genius whom I am privileged to call a friend has discovered a *cure* for *cancer*. I signaled to the bartender for more beer. *A fucking cure for cancer!*

But just at this instant, it seemed to me, Sophie's mood underwent a subtly disturbing change. The excitement, the high spirits fled her and a note of concern—of apprehension—stole into her voice. It was as if she were affixing a gloomy and unpleasant afterthought to a letter which had been all the more factitiously cheerful because of the necessity of the grim postscript itself. (P.S. I want a divorce.) "We left the restaurant then," she continued, "because he said that before we went back to work he wanted to buy me something, to celebrate. To celebrate his discovery. Something I could wear tonight when we celebrate together. Something chic and sexy. So we go to this very fine shop where we have been before and he buy me this blouse and skirt. And shoes. And some hats, and bags. Do you like it, this blouse?"

"It's a knockout," I said, understating my admiration.

"It's very . . . *daring,* I think. Anyway, Stingo, the point is that while we are in this shop and he has paid for the clothes and we are ready to leave, I see something strange about Nathan. I have seen it before but not too often and it always scares me a little. He said suddenly that he had a headache, back here, at the back of his head. Also, he was suddenly very pale and make sweat—perspiring, you know. You see, I think it was as if all the excitement was too much for him and he was having this reaction that made him a little sick. I told him he should go home, back to Yetta's and lie down, take the afternoon off, but no, he said he must go back to the laboratory, there was still much to do. The headache, he said, was terrible. I wanted him so much to go home and rest but he said he must go back to Pfizer. So he took three aspirin from the lady who own the shop, and he is calm now, no longer excited like he was. He is quiet, *mélancholique* even. And then very quietly he kissed me goodby and said he would see me tonight, here—here with you, Stingo. He wants the three of us to go down to Lundy's Restaurant for a wonderful seafood dinner to celebrate. To celebrate winning the Nobel Prize of 1947."

I had to tell her no. I was absolutely crushed at the idea that because of my father's visit I would be unable to join them for the jamboree celebration; what a wicked disappointment! This augury of fabulous news was so itchingly teasing that I simply could not believe that I would be denied participating in the announcement when it came. "I'm just sorry beyond belief, Sophie," I said, "but I've got to meet my father at Penn Station. But look, before I go, maybe Nathan can at least tell me what the discovery is.

Then in a couple of days after my old man's gone we can go out and have another celebration some other night."

She appeared not to be listening any too closely, and I heard her continue in a voice that seemed to me both subdued and invaded by hints of foreboding. "I just hope he is okay. Sometimes when he gets excited so much and gets so happy—then he gets these terrible headaches and sweats so much it go through his clothes, like he's been in the rain. Then the happiness is gone. And oh, Stingo, it don't happen every time. But sometimes it make him so very, very *strange!* It's like he gets so *tellement agité,* so happy and flying that he is like an airplane going up and up into the stratosphere where the air is so thin that he can't fly no more and the only way is down. I mean all the way *down,* Stingo! Oh, I hope Nathan's okay."

"Listen, he's going to be all right," I assured her, a little uneasily. "Anyone with the story Nathan is going to tell has a right to act a little peculiar." Although I could not share what were obviously her deep misgivings, I had to confess to myself that her words put me a bit on edge. Even so, I thrust them out of my mind. I wanted only for Nathan to arrive with news of his triumph and an explanation for this unbearably tantalizing mystery.

The jukebox started to blare. The bar was beginning to fill up with its gray evening habitués—most of them middle-aged and male, porridge-faced even in midsummer, North European Gentiles with flabby paunches and serious thirsts who ran the elevators and unplugged the plumbing of the ten-story Jewish pueblos whose homely beige-brick ranks stretched for block after block in the region behind the park. Aside from Sophie, few females ever ventured into the place. I never saw a single hooker—the conventional neighborhood and the tired and baggy clientele precluded even the idea of any such sport—but there were, this special evening, two smiling nuns who bore down on Sophie and me with some kind of rattling tin-plated chalice and a murmured plea for charity, in the name of the Sisters of St. Joseph. Their English was preposterously broken. They looked Italian and were extremely ugly—one of them in particular, who wore at the corner of her mouth an awesome wen the size, shape and color of one of those University Residence Club cockroaches, out of which hair sprouted like cornsilk. I averted my eyes but scrounged in my pocket and came up with two dimes; Sophie, however, confronted with the jingling cup uttered a "No!" with such vehemence that the nuns drew back with a concerted gasp, then scuttled away, and I turned to her in surprise.

"Bad luck, two nuns," she said morosely, then, after a pause, added, "I *hate* them! Weren't they awful-looking!"

"I thought you were brought up a good sweet Catholic girl," I said in a joshing tone.

"I was," she replied, "but that was long ago. Anyway, I would hate nuns even if I cared about religion. Silly, stupid *virgins!* And so horrible-looking!" A tremor passed through her, she shook her head. "Awful! Oh, how I hate that stupid religion!"

"You know, it's really strange, Sophie," I put in, "I remember a few weeks ago how you were telling me about your devout childhood, and your belief, and all that. What is it that—"

But she shook her head again in a brisk, negative way, and lay her slender fingers on the back of my hand. "Please, Stingo, those nuns make me feel so *pourri*—rotten. Stinking. Those nuns grubbling . . ." She hesitated, looking perplexed.

"I think you mean groveling," I said.

"Yes, groveling in front of a God who must be a *monster,* Stingo, if He exist. A monster!" She paused. "I don't want to talk about religion. I hate religion. It is for, you know, *des analphabètes,* imbecile peoples." She cast a glance at her wristwatch and remarked that it was after seven. Anxiety edged her voice. "Oh, I hope Nathan is okay."

"Don't worry, he's going to be fine," I said again in my most reassuring voice. "Look, Sophie, Nathan's really been under tremendous pressure with this research project, this breakthrough, whatever it is. That strain is bound to make him behave, well, *erratically*—you know what I mean? Don't worry about him. I'd have a headache too if I'd been through his kind of wringer—especially when it's resulted in this incredible achievement." I paused. I seemed constantly compelled to add, "Whatever it is." I patted her hand in return. "Now *please,* just relax. He'll be here in a minute, I'm certain." At this point I made another reference to my father and his arrival in New York (fondly mentioning his generous concern for me, and his moral support, though making no note of the slave Artiste and *his* part in my destiny, rather doubting that Sophie had sufficient comprehension of American history, at least yet, to be able to grasp the complexities of the debt I owed to that black boy), and I continued in a general way to praise the luck of those young men like myself, relatively few in number, who possessed parents of such tolerance and selflessness and the will to have faith, blind faith, in a son reckless enough to seek to pluck a few leaves from the laurel branch of art. I was getting a little bit high. Fathers of this largeness of vision and amplitude of spirit were *scarce,* I averred sentimentally, beginning to feel my lips tingling from the beer.

"Oh, you're so lucky to still *have* a father," said Sophie in a faraway voice. "I miss my father so."

I felt a little ashamed—no, not ashamed, inadequate would be better—thinking suddenly of the story she had told me, some weeks before, about her father herded together with the other Cracow professors like so many pigs, the Nazi machine guns, the stifling vans, Sachsenhausen, then death by firing squad in the cold snows of Germany. *God,* I thought, what Americans had been spared in our era, after all. Oh, we had done our brave and needful part as warriors, but how scant our count of fathers and sons compared to the terrible martyrdom of those unnumbered Europeans. Our glut of good fortune was enough to make us choke.

"It has been long enough now," she went on, "that I no longer *grieve* like I did, but yet I miss him. He was such a *good* man—that is what make it so terrible, Stingo! When you think of all the bad people—Poles, Germans, Russians, French, all nationalities—all these evil people who escaped, people who killed Jews who are still alive right now. In Germany. And places like Argentina. And my father—this good man—who had to *die!* Isn't that enough to make you not believe in this God? Who can believe in God who turn His back on people like that?" This outburst—this little aria—had come so swiftly that it surprised me; her fingers trembled slightly. Then she calmed down. And once again—as if she had forgotten that she had already once told me, or perhaps because the repetition gave her some forlorn comfort—she sketched the portrait she imagined of her father, in Lublin many years before, saving Jews from a Russian pogrom at peril to his life.

"What is the word *l'ironie* in English?"

"Irony?" I said.

"Yes, such an irony that a man like that, a man like my father, risk his life for Jews and die, and the Jew-killers live, so many of them, right now."

"I'd say that's less an irony, Sophie, than the way of the world," I concluded a little sententiously but with seriousness, feeling the need to relieve my bladder.

I got up and made my way to the men's room, weaving slightly, aglow at the edges of my skin with a penumbra of Rheingold, the jolly, astringent beer served at the Maple Court on draft. I richly enjoyed the men's john at the Maple Court, where, cantilevered slightly forward over the urinal, I could brood over the plashing clear stream while Guy Lombardo or Sammy Kaye or Shep Fields or some other glutinously innocuous band rumbled faintly from the jukebox beyond the walls. It was wonderful to be twenty-two and a little drunk, knowing that all went well at the writing desk, shiveringly happy in the clutch of one's own creative ardor and in that "grand certitude" Thomas Wolfe was always hymning—the certitude that the wellsprings of youth would never run dry, and that the wrenching anguish endured in the crucible of art would find its recompense in everlasting fame, and glory, and the love of beautiful women.

As I blissfully pissed I eyed the ubiquitous homosexual graffiti (inscribed there, God knows, not by the Maple Court regulars but by the transient trade which managed to scribble up the walls of any place, no matter how unlikely, where males unlimbered their joints) and with delight gazed once again at the smoke-stained but still vivid caricature on the wall: companion-piece to the mural outside, it was a masterpiece of 1930s innocent ribaldry, displaying Mickey Mouse and Donald Duck in contortionist Peeping Tom postures, gleefully asquint through the interstices of a garden trellis as they observed little Betty

Boop, enchanting and voluptuous of calf and thigh, squatting to take a pee. Suddenly I was stabbed with alarm, sensing an unholy and unnatural presence of flapping vulturous black, until I realized in an instant that the two mendicant nuns had blundered into the wrong facility. They were gone then in a flash, squawking in distressed Italian, and I rather hoped they had gotten a look at my *schlong*. Was it their entry—duplicating the bad omen Sophie had felt only a short while before—that presaged the evil contretemps of the next fifteen minutes or so?

I heard Nathan's voice over Shep Fields' rippling rhythm even as I approached the table. It was a voice not so much loud as incredibly assertive and it cut through the music like a hacksaw. It was filled with trouble, and though I wanted to retreat when I heard it I dared not, feeling something momentous in the air which impelled me on toward the voice and Sophie. And so totally immersed was Nathan in this rancorous message he was imparting to Sophie, so single-minded did he seem at that moment, that I was able to stand waiting by the table long minutes, listening in miserable discomfort while Nathan bullyragged and tore at her, quite oblivious that I was there.

"Haven't I told you that the only single thing I absolutely demand from you is *fidelity?"* he said.

"Yes, but—" She could not get the words in.

"And didn't I tell you that if you were ever with this guy Katz—ever again, outside of work—that if you ever so much as walked ten feet with this cheap *shmatte,* I'd break your ass?"

"Yes, but—"

"And this afternoon he brings you home again in his car! Fink saw you. And not only that, that cheap motherfucker, you take him up to the room. And you're there for an hour with him. Did he lay you a couple of times? Oh, I'll bet you Katz does quite a number with that fast chiropractor's dick of his!"

"Nathan, let me explain!" she implored him. Her composure was fast dissolving, and her voice cracked.

"Shut your fucking yap! There's nothing to explain! You'd have kept it a secret too, if my good old pal Morris hadn't told me he'd seen the two of you go up there together."

"I would *not* have kept it secret," she wailed. "I would have tell you *now!* I did not have a chance yet, darling!"

"Shut up!"

Again the voice was not loud so much as chillingly domineering, scathing, irruptive. I yearned for an exit, but only stood there behind him, hesitant, waiting. My intoxication had bubbled away and I felt the blood pounding against my Adam's apple.

She tried to persist in her plea. "Nathan darling, *listen!* The only reason I took him to the room was because of the phonograph. The changer part has not been working, you know that, and I told him and he said he might be able to fix it. He said he was an expert. And he *did* fix it, darling, that was all! I'll *show* you, we'll go back and play it—"

"Oh, I'll bet old Seymour's an expert," Nathan put in. "Does he do a quick routine on your spinal column when he's humping you? Does he get your vertebrae all in order with those slippery hands? The cheap fraud—"

"Nathan, *please!*" she entreated him. She was leaning forward toward him now. The blood seemed to have drained from her face, which wore an expression of terminal agony.

"Oh, you're some dish, you are," he said softly and slowly, in tones of sarcasm that sounded unbearably heavy, graceless.

He obviously had visited their lodgings at Yetta's after returning from the lab; I inferred this not only because of his reference to Morris Fink's outrageous tattle but because of his dress: he was decked out in his fanciest oyster-white linen suit, and heavy oval gold links sparkled on the cuffs of his custom-made shirt. He smelled pleasantly of a light, jaunty cologne. Plainly he had intended to match Sophie's gala get-up that evening and had gone home to transform himself into the fashion plate I now beheld. There, however, he had been confronted with evidence of Sophie's betrayal—or what he construed as such—and now there seemed no doubt that the celebration had not only become aborted, it was headed for unknown depths of disaster.

Writhing inwardly as I stood there, I held my breath

and listened while Nathan continued. "You're really some Polish dumpling. It was over my dead body that I let you degrade yourself by continuing to work with these charlatans, these horse doctors. Bad enough you accept the money they make stretching the spines of ignorant, gullible old Jews just off the boat from Danzig, with pains that might be rheumatism or might be carcinoma but go undiagnosed because these snake-oil shysters con them into thinking that a simple back massage will return them to glowing health. Bad enough you managed to talk me into continuing this disgraceful collaboration with a couple of medical hoodlums. But it's fucking *unbearable* to think that behind my back you would let either of these mangy characters get into that twat of yours—"

She tried to interrupt. "Nathan!"

"Shut up! I've had just about enough of you and your whorish behavior." He was not talking loudly but there was something mincingly savage in his throttled-back rage that seemed more threatening than if his voice had been a roar; it was a bleak, reedy, thin, almost bureaucratic rage and his choice of phrase—"whorish behavior"—sounded incongruously tight-assed and rabbinical. "I thought somehow you would see the light, that you would abandon your ways after that escapade with *Doctor* Katz"—the accent on *Doctor* was a consummate sneer—"I thought I'd warned you off after that smooching business in his car. But no, I guess those pants you wear get a little too urgently hot in the crotch. And so when I caught you in a bit of hanky-panky with Blackstock, I wasn't *surprised,* given your bizarre predilection for chiropractic penises—I wasn't *surprised,* as I say, but when I blew the horn on you and put an end to it I thought you'd be *chastened* enough to abandon this wretched, *degrading* promiscuity. But no, once again I was wrong. The libidinal sap which courses so frantically in your Polish veins would allow you no ease, and so today once again you choose to fall into the ridiculous embrace—ridiculous, that is, if it weren't really so *vile* and *demeaning*—of Doctor Seymour Katz."

Sophie had begun to sniffle softly into a handkerchief clutched in white-knuckled fingers. "No, no, darling," I heard her say in whispers, "it just *isn't true.*"

Nathan's stilted, didactic enunciation might have been,

under different circumstances, vaguely comical—a burlesque of itself—but now was edged with such real threat, rage and obdurate conviction that I could not help but give a small shiver and feel at my back the approach, like the thudding of gallows-bound footsteps, of some awful and unnamed doom. I heard myself groan, clearly audible above the harangue, and it occurred to me that this dreadful assault on Sophie had weirdly identical resonances to those of the fracas in which I had first glimpsed him acting out his implacable enmity, the scenes distinguished one from the other mainly by the tone of voice—fortissimo that evening weeks ago, now singularly level and restrained but no less sinister. Abruptly I was conscious that Nathan was aware of my presence. His words were flatly uttered and edged with the faintest frost of hostility as he said to me, without looking up, "Why don't you sit down next to the *première putain* of Flatbush Avenue." I sat down but said nothing, my mouth having become parched and speechless.

As I seated myself, Nathan rose to his feet. "It seems to me that a little Chablis is in order now for furtherance of our celebration." I gaped up at him while he spoke in this humorless, declamatory way. Suddenly I got the impression that he was exercising a severe control over himself, as if he were trying to prevent his entire big frame from flying apart or crumpling like a marionette on strings. I saw for the first time that shiny streams of sweat were coursing down his face, though our corner was ventilated by almost frigid breezes; also, there was something funny about his eyes—exactly what, at the moment, I could not tell. Some jittery and feverish nervous activity, I felt, some abnormally frantic interchange of neurons in their chaotic synapses, was taking place under each square millimeter of his skin. He was so emotionally jazzed up that he almost seemed to be electrified, as if he had strayed into a magnetic field. Yet it was all held back under tremendous composure.

"Too bad," he said, again in tones of leaden irony, "too bad, my friends, that our celebration cannot continue in the vein of exalted homage I had intended for this evening. Homage to devoted hours in pursuit of a noble scientific goal which just this day has seen the light of triumph.

Homage to days and years of a team's selfless research terminating in victory over one of the greatest scourges to beset a suffering humanity. Too bad," he said again, after a prolonged pause that was almost unendurable in the burden it imposed on the silently spun-out seconds, "too bad our celebration will be of a more mundane stripe. To wit, the necessary and all-too-healthy severance of my relationship with the sweet siren of Cracow—that inimitable, that incomparable, that tragically faithless daughter of joy, Poland's gem and gift to the concupiscent chiropractors of Flatbush—Sophie Zawistowska! But wait, I must get the Chablis so we can drink a toast to that!"

Like a terrified child clutching at Daddy in the vortex of a mob, Sophie squeezed down on my fingers. We both watched Nathan stiffly shoulder his way to the bar through shoals of shirt-sleeved drinkers. I turned to look at Sophie then. Her eyes were completely out of kilter, unforgettably so in the face of Nathan's threat. I would ever after define the word "distraught" by the raw fear I saw dwelling there. "Oh, Stingo," she moaned, "I knew this was going to happen. I just knew he would accuse me of being unfaithful. He always does when he come into these strange *tempêtes*. Oh, Stingo, I just can't bear it when he become like this. I just know this time he's going to leave me."

I tried to soothe her. "Don't worry," I said, "he'll get over this thing." I had small faith in those words.

"Oh no, Stingo, something terrible will happen, I know it! Always he get this way. First he is so excited, full of joy. Then he comes *down*, and when he comes down, it is always that I have been unfaithful and then he wants to leave me." She squeezed again, so hard I thought that her fingernails might draw blood. "And what I said to him was *true*," she added in a frantic hurry. "I mean about Seymour Katz. It was nothing, Stingo, nothing at all. This Dr. Katz means nothing to me, he is only someone I work for with Dr. Blackstock. And it is true what I said about him fixing the phonograph. That is all he did in the room, fix the phonograph, nothing else, *I swear to you!*"

"Sophie, I *believe* you," I assured her, in a torture of embarrassment over the babbling vehemence with which she was trying to convince me, who was already convinced. "Just *calm down*," I snapped at her futilely.

What happened rapidly thereafter seemed to me unimaginably senseless and horrible. And I realize how faulty were my own perceptions, how clumsily I handled the situation, with what lack of wit and with what ineffectiveness did I deal with Nathan at a moment when supreme delicacy was called for. For if I had only humored Nathan, jollied him along, I just might have watched him expend all of his rage—no matter how unreasonable and intimidating it was—and out of pure exhaustion fall into a state where I might have found him manageable, his fury smothered or at least on a tether. I might have been able to control him. But I also realize that I was at that time in many ways afflicted by a staggeringly puerile inexperience: far from my mind was any idea that Nathan—despite his manic tone of voice, the hectic oratory, the sweat, the walleyed expression, the frazzled tension, the whole portrait he presented of one whose entire nervous system down to its minutest ganglia was in the throes of a fiery convulsion—might be dangerously disturbed. I thought he was merely being a colossal prick. As I say, this was largely due to my age and a real guilelessness. Distracted, violent states in human beings having been alien to my experience—bound up as it had been less with the crazy Gothic side of a Southern upbringing than with the genteel and the well-behaved—I regarded Nathan's outburst as a shocking failure of character, a lapse of decency, rather than the product of some aberration of mind.

This was as true now as it had been on that first night weeks ago in Yetta's hallway when, as he stormed at Sophie and taunted me about lynchings and snarled "Cracker" in my face, I had caught a glimpse in his fathomless eyes of a wild, elusive discord that sent icewater flooding through my veins. And so as I sat there with Sophie, numb with discomfort, grieving at the appalling transformation which had overtaken this man whom I so cared for and admired, yet with indignation scraping me raw over the anguish he was forcing Sophie to endure, I resolved that I would draw the line as to how far Nathan would proceed in his harassment. He would bully Sophie no more, I decided, and he had fucking well better watch his step with me. This might have been a reasonable decision had I been dealing with a beloved friend who had simply let his temper get out of hand, but hardly (and I was not yet beginning to acquire the first flicker of wisdom to realize it) a man in whom paranoia was a sudden rampaging guest.

"Did you notice something very peculiar in his eyes?" I murmured to Sophie. "Do you think he might have taken too much of that aspirin you got for him, or something?" The innocence of such a question was, I now realize, almost inconceivable, given what was eventually to be revealed to me as the cause for those dilated pupils, the size of dimes; but then, I was learning a lot of new things in those days.

Nathan returned with the opened bottle of wine and sat down. A waiter brought glasses and set them before the three of us. I was relieved to see that the expression on Nathan's face had softened somewhat, no longer quite the rancorous mask it had been only moments before. But the fierce strait-jacketed tension remained in the muscles of the cheek and neck and also the sweat poured forth: it stood out on his brow in droplets, matching in appearance —I noted irrelevantly—the mosaic of cool dewdrops on the bottle of Chablis. And then I caught sight for the first time of the great crescents of soaked white fabric underneath his arms. He poured wine in our glasses, and although I shrank from looking at Sophie's face, I saw that her hand, holding the outstretched glass, was quivering. I had committed the major mistake of keeping unfolded on the table beneath my elbow the copy of the *Post,* with its page turned to the photograph of Bilbo. I saw Nathan glance at the picture and make what appeared to be a smirk full of enormous and wicked self-satisfaction.

"I read that article just a while ago on the subway," he said, raising his glass. "I propose a toast to the slow, protracted, agonizing death of the Senator from Mississippi, Mushmouth Bilbo."

I was silent for a moment. Nor did I raise my glass as Sophie did. She lifted hers out of nothing at this point, I was sure, but dumb reflexive obedience. Finally I said as casually as I was able, "Nathan, I want to propose a toast to *your success,* to *your* great discovery, whatever it is. To this wonderful thing you've been working on that Sophie's told me about. Congratulations." I reached forward and lightly, affectionately tapped the back of his arm. "Now let's cut all this ugly shit"—I tried to inject a jovial, conciliatory note—"and let's all relax while you tell us, for Christ's sake, just tell us exactly what the hell it is we're going to celebrate! Man, tonight we want to make all the toasts to *you!*"

A disagreeable chill went through me as I felt the brusque deliberateness with which he pulled his arm away from my hand. "That will be impossible," he said, glaring at me, "my mood of triumph has been seriously compromised if not totally deflated by treachery at the hands of someone I *used to love.*" Still unable to glance at her, I heard Sophie give a single hoarse sob. "There will be no toast this evening to victorious Hygeia." He was holding his glass aloft, elbow propped on the table. "We will toast instead the painful demise of Senator Bilbo."

"*You* will, Nathan," I said, "not I. I'm not going to toast *anyone's* death—painful or not painful—and neither should you. You of all people should know better. Aren't you in the healing business? This is not a very funny joke, you know. It's fucking obscene to toast death." My sudden pontifical tone was something I seemed unable to repress. I raised my own glass. "To life," I proposed, "to your life, *ours*"—I made a gesture which included Sophie—"to *health.* To your great discovery." I sensed a note of pleading in my voice, but Nathan remained immobile and grim-faced, refusing to drink. Stymied, feeling a spasm of desperation, I slowly lowered my glass. I also, for the first time, felt a touch of warm rage churning in the region of my abdomen; it was a slow conglomerate anger, directed in equal parts at Nathan's hateful and dictatorial manner, his foul treatment of Sophie and (I could scarcely believe my own reflex now) his gruesome malediction against Bilbo. When he now failed to respond to my counter-toast, I set my glass down and said with a sigh, "Well, to hell with it, then."

"To the death of Bilbo," Nathan persisted, "to the sounds of the screams of his last agony."

I sensed the blood flashing scarlet somewhere behind my eyes and my heart began a clumsy thumping. It was an effort to control my voice. "Nathan," I said, "not long ago at one point I paid you a slight compliment. I said that despite your profound animosity toward the South, you at least retained a little sense of humor about it, unlike many people. Unlike the standard New York liberal jackass. But now I'm beginning to see that I was wrong. I've got no use for Bilbo and never did, but if you think there's any comedy in this *ham-handed* bit about his death, you're wrong. I refuse to toast the death of *any* man—"

"You would not toast the death of Hitler?" he put in quickly, with a mean glint in his eye.

It brought me up short. "*Of course* I would toast the death of Hitler. But that's a fucking different matter! Bilbo's not Hitler!" Even while I was replying to Nathan I realized with despair how we were duplicating the substance if not the same words of the enraged colloquy in which we had gotten so wildly embroiled that first afternoon in Sophie's room. In the time since that deafening quarrel, which had so nearly become a fight, I mistakenly thought he had relinquished his murky *idée fixe* about the South. At this moment there was in his manner all the identical bottled-up surge of fury and venom which had truly scared me on that radiant Sunday, a day that for so long had seemed comfortably remote. I was scared once more, now to an even greater degree, for I had a grim augury that this time our struggle would not find sweet reconciliation in apologies, jokes and the jolly embrace of friendship. "Bilbo is not Hitler, Nathan," I repeated. I heard my voice trembling. "Let me tell you something. For as long as I have known you—although it is admittedly not long, so I may have gotten the wrong impression—you have honestly impressed me as being one of the most sophisticated, savvy people I've ever known—"

"Don't embarrass me," he broke in. "Flattery will get you nowhere." His voice was rasping, ugly.

"This is not flattery," I went on, "only the truth. But what I'm getting at is this. Your hatred of the South—which often is clearly tantamount to expressing hatred, or at least dislike, for me—is *appalling* in anyone who like yourself is so knowing and judicious in so many other ways. It is downright primitive of you, Nathan, to be so *blind* about the nature of evil . . ."

In debate, especially when the dispute is hot and supercharged and freighted with ill will, I have always been the flabbiest of contenders. My voice breaks, becomes shrill; I sweat. I get a sloppy half-grin on my face. Worse, my mind wanders and then takes flight while the logic I possess in fair measure under more placid circumstances abandons my brain like an ungrateful urchin. (For a time I thought I might be a lawyer. The profession of law, and the courtrooms in which I once briefly entertained fantasies of playing out dramas like Clarence Darrow, lost only an incompetent stick when I turned to the literary trade.) "You seem to have no sense of history at all," I went on rapidly, my voice scaling up an octave, "none at all! Could it be because you Jews, having so recently arrived here and living mostly in big Northern cities, are really *purblind,* and just have no interest in or awareness or any kind of comprehension whatever of the tragic concatenation of events that have produced the racial madness down there? You've read *Faulkner,* Nathan, and you still have this assy and intolerable attitude of superiority toward the place, and are unable to see how Bilbo is less a villain than a wretched offshoot of the whole benighted system?" I paused, drew a breath and said, "I pity you your blindness." And here had I ceased and left it at that, I might have felt that I had registered a series of telling blows, but, as I say, good sense generally has deserted me in the course of such fevered arguments and my own semi-hysteric energy now propelled me into regions of deep asininity. "Besides," I persisted, "you totally fail to realize what a man of real achievement Theodore Bilbo was." Echoes of my college dissertation rattled about in my head with the filing-card rhythm of scholarly blank verse. "When he was governor, Bilbo brought Mississippi a series of important reforms," I intoned, "including the creation of a highway commission and a board of pardons. He established the first tuberculosis sanatorium. He added manual training and farm mechanics to the curriculum of the schools. And finally he introduced a program to combat ticks . . ." My voice trailed off.

"He introduced a program to combat ticks," Nathan said.

Startled, I realized that Nathan's gifted voice was in perfect mockery of my own—pedantic, pompous, insufferable. "There was a widespread outbreak of something called Texas fever among the Mississippi cows," I persisted uncontrollably. "Bilbo was instrumental—"

"You fool," Nathan interrupted, "you silly klutz. Texas fever! You *clown!* You want me to point out that the glory of the Third Reich was a highway system unsurpassed in the world and that Mussolini made the trains run on time?"

He had me cold—I must have known it as soon as I heard myself utter the word "ticks"—and the grin that had appeared briefly on his face, a sardonic flash of teeth and a twinkle that recognized the shambles of my defeat, dissolved even as he now firmly lowered his glass.

"Have you finished your lecture?" he demanded in a voice that was too loud. The menace that darkened his face caused me a prickly fear. Suddenly he raised his glass and downed the wine in a single swallow. "This toast," he announced in a flat tone, "is in honor of my complete dissociation from you two creeps."

A piercing pang of regret went through my breast at these words. I sensed a heavy emotion roiling inside me that was like the onset of mourning. *"Nathan . . ."* I began placatingly, and stretched out my hand. I heard Sophie sob again.

But Nathan ignored my gesture. "Dissociation," he said, with a tip of his glass at Sophie, "from *you,* the Coony Chiropractic Cunt of Kings County." Then to me, "And to you, the Dreary Dregs of Dixie." His eyes were as lifeless as billiard balls, sweat drained from his face in torrents. I was as intensely conscious—on one level—of these eyes and the skin of his face beneath its shimmering transparency of sweat as I was—on a purely auditory level, so rawly sensitive that I thought my eardrums might pop—of the voices of the Andrews Sisters exploding from the jukebox. "Don't Fence Me In!" "Now," he said, "perhaps you will permit *me* to lecture the *two of you.* It might do something for the rottenness dwelling at the *core* of your selves."

I will skim over all but the worst of his tirade. The whole thing could not have taken more than several minutes, but it seemed hours. Sophie suffered the most fearsome part of his onslaught, and it was plainly closer to intolerable to her than it was to me, who only had to hear it and watch her suffer. By contrast I got off with a relatively light tongue-lashing, and it came first. He bore me no real ill feelings, he said, just *contempt*. Even his contempt for me was hardly personal, he went on, since I could not be held responsible for my upbringing or place of birth. (He delivered all this with a mocking half-smile and a controlled, soft voice tinged, off and on, incongruously, with the Negro accent I recalled from that faraway Sunday.) For a long time he had entertained the idea that I was a *good* Southerner, he said, a man emancipated, one who had somehow managed to escape the curse of bigotry which history had bequeathed to the region. He was not so foolishly blind (despite my accusations) as to be unaware that *good* Southerners *did* truly exist. He had thought of me as such until recently. But my refusal now to join in his execration of Bilbo only *validated* what he really had discovered about my "ingrained" and "unregenerate" racism, ever since that night he had read the first part of my book.

My heart fairly shriveled away at these words. "What do you *mean?*" I said, my voice close to a wail. "I thought you *liked*—"

"You have a pretty snappy talent in the traditional Southern mode. But you also have all the old clichés. I guess I didn't want to bruise your feelings. But that old Negro woman in the beginning of the book, the one waiting with the others for the train. She's a *caricature*, right out of *Amos 'n' Andy*. I thought I was reading a novel by someone brought up writing old-time minstrel shows. It would be funny—that travesty of a Negro—if it weren't so *despicable*. You may be writing the first Southern comic book."

God, how vulnerable I was! I was engulfed by swift despair. If anyone but Nathan had said that! But with those words he had totally undermined the buoyant joy and confidence about my work which his earlier encouragement had implanted within me. It was so unutterably crushing, this sudden brutal brush-off, that I began to feel certain crucial underpinnings of my very soul shudder and disintegrate. I gulpingly struggled for a reply, which would not, strive as I might, get past my lips.

"You've been badly infected by that degeneracy," he

continued. "It's something you can't help. It doesn't make you or your book any more attractive but at least it's possible to feel that you're more of a passive vessel for the poison rather than a willing—how would you describe it?—a willing disseminator. Like, say, Bilbo." Now his voice abruptly lost the faint throaty Negroid quality with which it had been touched; in moist metamorphosis the Southern accent faded and died, replaced by thorny Polish diphthongs that were in almost exact mimicry of Sophie's own speech. And it was here, as I say, that his punishing callousness turned into outright persecution. *"Peut-être* after all dese mawnths," he said, leveling his gaze on Sophie, "you kin explain de mystewy of why you are here, you off all people, walking dese stweets, dwenched in enticing perfumery, engaged in suwweptitious venery wiff not wan but *two*—count dem, ladies and gentlemen—*two chiropractors*. In short, making hay while de sun shine, to employ an old bwomide, while at *Auschwitz* de ghosts off de millions off de dead still seek an answer." Suddenly he dropped the parody. "Tell me why it is, oh beauteous Zawistowska, that *you* inhabit the land of the living. Did splendid little tricks and stratagems spring from that lovely head of yours to allow you to breathe the clear Polish air while the multitudes at Auschwitz *choked slowly on the gas?* A reply to this would be most welcome."

A terrible drawn-out groan escaped Sophie then, so loud and tormented that only the frenzied squalling of the Andrews Sisters prevented it from being heard throughout the entire bar. Mary in her anguish on Calvary could not have made a more wretched noise. I turned to look at Sophie. She had thrust her face downward so that it was buried and out of sight, and had clapped her white-knuckled fists futilely over her ears. Her tears were trickling down onto the speckled Formica. I thought I heard her muffled words: "No! No! *Menteur!* Lies!"

"Not so many months ago," he persisted, "in the depths of the war in Poland, several hundred Jews who escaped from one of the death camps sought refuge at the homes of some fine Polish citizens like yourself. These darling people refused them shelter. Not only this. They murdered practically all the rest they could get their hands on. I have brought this to your attention before. So please answer again. Did the same anti-Semitism for which Poland has gained such world-wide renown—did a similar anti-Semitism guide your own destiny, help you along, *protect* you, in a manner of speaking, so that you became one of the minuscule handful of people who lived while *the millions died?*" His voice became harsh, cutting, cruel. "*Explanation, please!*"

"No! No! No! No!" Sophie sobbed.

I heard my own voice now. "Nathan, *for Christ's sake,* lay off her!" I had gotten to my feet.

But he was not to be deterred. "What fine handiwork of subterfuge did you create in order that *your* skin might be saved while the others went up in smoke? Did you cheat, connive, lay your sweet little ass—"

"*No!*" I heard her groan, that sound again wrested from her nethermost depths. "No! No!"

I did an inexplicable and, I'm afraid, craven thing then. Having risen fully upright, I was on the absolute verge (I could feel the impulse in me like a powerful vibration) of leaning forward and grasping Nathan by the collar, pulling him to his feet for an eye-to-eye confrontation, as Bogart had done so many times in Bogart's and my entwined past. I could not suffer what Nathan was doing to her a second more. But having risen, having been galvanized by the impulse, I was with mysterious speed transformed into a triumphant paradigm of chickenshit. I felt a quaking in the knees, my parched mouth gave forth a string of senseless vocables, and then I found myself lurching toward the men's room, blessed sanctuary from a spectacle of hatred and cruelty such as I had never conceived I would witness firsthand. I'll only be here for a minute, I thought, leaning over the urinal. I've got to collect my senses before I go out and deal with Nathan. In a somnambulist's stupor I clutched at the handle of the urinal's valve, an icy dagger in my palm, pumping over and over again sluggish jets of water while the faggot graffiti—*Marvin sucks! . . . Call ULster 1–2316 for dream blowjob*—registered for the hundredth time in my brain like demented cuneiform. Since my mother's death I had not wept, and I knew I would not now, even though the pining lovelorn scrawls against the tiles, blurring into smudge, signaled that I might now come close to weeping. I spent perhaps three or four minutes in this chilly, miserable, indecisive stance. Then I resolved that I would go back out there and somehow cope with the situation, despite the fact that I lacked a strategy and was frightened to the pit of my being. But when I threw open the door again, I saw that Sophie and Nathan were gone.

I was groggy with worry and despair. Nor did I have any idea how to deal with the situation as it now stood, with its overtone of irreconcilable strife. Obviously I had to ponder what to do, had to figure out how to try to set things straight—somehow calm Nathan down and in the process remove Sophie from the target area of his blind and baleful rage—but I was so completely rattled that my brain had become almost amnesic; I was virtually unable to think. In order to collect my senses I decided to stay there at the Maple Court for a while, during which time I hoped to lay out a bright and rational plan of action. I knew that when my father arrived at Penn Station and did not see me, he would go straight to the hotel—the McAlpin on Broadway at Thirty-fourth Street. (In those days everyone from the Tidewater of my father's middle social station stayed either at the McAlpin or the Taft; the very few who were more affluent always frequented the Waldorf-Astoria.) I called the McAlpin and left a message saying I would see him there late in the evening. Then I returned to the table (it was another evil sign, I thought, that in their swift exit either Nathan or Sophie had overturned the bottle of Chablis, which, though unbroken, lay on its side dripping its dregs onto the floor) and sat for two full hours brooding over the way in which I must collect and put back together the shards of our fragmented friendship. I suspected it would be no easy task, given the colossal dimensions of Nathan's fury.

On the other hand, recalling how on that Sunday following a similar "tempest" he had made overtures of friendship so warm and eager as to be almost embarrassing, and had actually apologized to me for his misbehavior, it occurred to me that he might welcome any gestures of pacification I would make. God knows, I thought, it was something I hated to do; scenes such as I had just been a participant in fractured my spirit, exhausted me; all I really wanted to do was to curl up and take a nap. Confronting Nathan again this soon was an idea intimidating and fraught with potential menace; queasy, I felt myself perspiring as Nathan had done. To screw up courage I took my time and drank four or five or, maybe, six medium-sized glasses of Rheingold. Visions of Sophie's pathetic and disheveled agony, her total disarray, kept flashing on and off in my mind, causing my stomach to heave. Finally, though, as dark fell over Flatbush, I wandered a little drunkenly back through the sultry dusk to the Pink Palace, gazing up with tangled apprehension and hope at the soft glow, the color of rosé wine, that blossomed out from beneath Sophie's window blind, indicating that she was there. I heard music; it was either her radio or her phonograph playing. I don't know why I was at the same time so buoyed up and saddened by the lovely and plaintive sound of the Haydn concerto for cello, washing down soft on the summer evening when I approached the house. Children called through the twilight from the Parade Grounds at the park's edge, and their cries, sweet as the piping of birds, mingled with the cello's gentle meditation and pierced me with some profound, aching, all but unrecapturable remembrance.

I caught my breath in anguish at the sight which greeted me on the second floor. Had a typhoon swept through the Pink Palace, there could not have been a more horrendous effect of havoc and shambles. Sophie's room looked as if it had been turned upside down; dresser drawers had been pulled out and emptied, the bed had been stripped, the closet ransacked. A litter of newspapers was strewn on the floor. The shelves had been emptied of books. The phonograph records were gone. Save for the paper debris, nothing was left. There was a single exception to the general look of plunder—the radio-phonograph. Doubtless too large and bulky to have been lugged off, it remained on the table, and the sound of the Haydn emanating from its gorge caused me an eerie chill, as if I were listening to music in a concert hall from which the audience had mysteriously fled. Only steps away, in Nathan's room, the effect was the same: everything had been removed or, if not taken away, had been packed in cardboard boxes that looked ready for immediate transfer. The heat hung close and sticky in the hallway; it was heat unreasonably intense even for the summer evening—adding bafflement to the chagrin with which I was already overwhelmed—and for an instant I thought there must be a conflagration lurking behind the pink walls until I suddenly spied Morris Fink crouched in one corner, laboring over a steaming radiator.

"It must of got turned on by accident," he explained, standing up as I approached. "Nathan must of turned it on by accident a little while ago when he was running around with his suitcase and things. *There,* you cocksucker," he snarled at the radiator, giving it a kick, "that'll fix your guts." The steam expired with a little hiss and Morris Fink regarded me with his lugubrious lackluster eyes. An overbite I had not really noticed before made him look pronouncedly like a rodent. "This place for a while, it was like a cuckoo ranch."

"What happened?" I said, cold with apprehension. "Where's Sophie? Where's Nathan?"

"They're gone, both of them. They finally cut out for good."

"What do you mean, for *good?*"

"Just what I said," he replied. "Finished. For good. Gone for good, and fuckin' good riddance, I say. There was something creepy, I mean sick about this house with that fuckin' golem Nathan. All that fightin' and screamin'. Fuckin' good riddance, if you want to know."

I felt desperation edging my voice as I demanded, "But *where* did they go? Did they tell you *where* they were going?"

"No," he said, "they went in two directions."

"Two directions? Do you mean . . ."

"I seen them come back in the house about two hours ago just when I was walkin' up the street. I'd went out to a movie. Already he was howlin' at her like a gorilla. I said to myself: Oh shit, another fight already, after all these weeks when it was quiet. Now I got to maybe try to save her again from this *meshuggener.* But then when I get to the house here I see that he's makin' her pack up. I mean, he's in his room, see, packin' his own things, and she's in the other room packin' hers. And all the time he's hollerin' at her like a madman—*oy*, what dirty things he calls her!"

"And Sophie . . ."

"And she—she's cryin' her eyes out the whole time, the two of them packin' their things and him screamin' and callin' her a whore and a cunt and Sophie bawlin' like a baby. It made me sick!" He paused, took a swallow of air, then resumed more slowly. "I didn't realize that they were packin' to leave for good. Then he looked down over the railing and seen me and asked where Yetta was. I said she was over in Staten Island visitin' her sister. He threw me down thirty dollars for the rent, Sophie's and his. Then I realized they were gettin' out for good."

"When did they finally go?" I asked. A sense of loss that was as suffocatingly painful as actual bereavement welled up in me; I gagged on a wet heave of nausea. "Didn't they leave an address?"

"I tell you they went in *two different directions,*" he said impatiently. "They get their stuff all packed finally and go downstairs. This was only about twenty minutes ago. Nathan gives me a buck to help bring the baggage down, also to take care of the phonograph. Says he'll come back and get it later, along with some boxes. Then when the baggage is all out on the sidewalk he gets me to go up to the corner and flag down a couple of taxis. When I come back with the taxis he's still hollerin' at her, and I say to myself: Well, at least this time he didn't hit her or nothin'. But he's still hollerin' at her, about Owswitch mainly. Something like Owswitch."

"About . . . what?"

"About Owswitch, that's what he says. Called her a cunt again and asked her this weirdo question over and over. Asked her how come she *lived through Owswitch*. What did he mean by that?"

"Called her . . ." I faltered helplessly, nearly bereft of speech. "Then what . . ."

"Then he gave her fifty bucks—it looked like about that—and told the driver to take her someplace in New York, Manhattan, some hotel I think, I can't remember where. He said somethin' about how happy he'd be never to have to see her again. I've never heard anyone cry like that Sophie was cryin' then. Anyway, after she was gone he put his own things in the other cab and left in the opposite direction, up toward Flatbush Avenue. I think he must of went to his brother's in Queens."

"Gone then," I whispered, evilly stricken now.

"Gone for good," he replied, "and good fuckin' riddance I say. That guy was a *golem!* But Sophie—Sophie I feel sorry for. Sophie was a real nice broad, *you know?*"

For a moment I could say nothing. The gentle Haydn, murmurous with longing, filled the abandoned room nearby with its sweet, symmetrical, pensive cadences, adding to my feeling of some absolute void, and of irretrievable loss.

"Yes," I said finally, "I know."

"What's Owswitch?" said Morris Fink.

Nine

Of the many commentators on the Nazi concentration camps, few have written with greater insight and passion than the critic George Steiner. I came across Steiner's book of essays *Language and Silence* in the year of its publication, 1967—a year which had considerable significance for me, aside from the fairly trivial fact that it marked exactly two decades since that summer of mine in Brooklyn. God, how the time had passed since Sophie, and Nathan, and Leslie Lapidus! The domestic tragedy which I had struggled so to bring to parturition at Yetta Zimmerman's had long before been published (to a general acclaim far beyond my youthful hopes); I had written other works of fiction and a certain vaguely unenthusiastic and uncommitted amount of trendy sixties' journalism. However, my heart was still with the art of the novel—said to be moribund or even, Lord help us, dead as a smelt—and I was pleased that year of 1967 to be able to disprove its demise (to my personal satisfaction at least) by publishing a work which, in addition to fulfilling my own philosophical and aesthetic requirements as a novelist, found hundreds of thousands of readers—not all of them, as it turned out later, completely happy about the event. But this is another matter, and if I may be forgiven the indulgence, I will simply say that that year was, in general, a rewarding one for me.

The small note of qualification arises out of the fact that—as is usual after a number of years spent hard at work on a complex creation—there was a gray spiritless letdown, a doldrum-heavy crisis of the will over what one should do next. Many writers feel this way after completing an ambitious work; it is like a little death, one wants to crawl back into some wet womb and become an egg. But duty called, and again, as I had so many times before, I thought of Sophie. For twenty years Sophie and Sophie's life—past life and of our time together—and Nathan and his and Sophie's appalling troubles and all the interconnected and progressively worsening circumstances which led that poor straw-haired Polish darling headlong into destruction had preyed on my memory like a repetitive and ineradicable tic. The landscape and the living figures of that summer, as in some umber-smeared snapshot found in the brittle black pages of an old album, had become more dusty and indistinct as time for me unspooled with negligent haste into my own middle age, yet that summer's agony still cried out for explanation. Thus in the last months of 1967 I began thinking in earnest about Sophie and Nathan's sorrowful destiny; I knew I would have to deal with it eventually, just as I had dealt those many years before, so successfully and expediently, with another young woman I had loved beyond hope—the doomed Maria Hunt. For various reasons, it turned out that several more years would pass before I began the story of Sophie as it has been set down here. But the preparation I went through at that time required that I torture myself by absorbing as much as I could find of the literature of *l'univers concentrationnaire*. And in reading George Steiner, I experienced the shock of recognition.

"One of the things I cannot grasp, though I have often written about them, trying to get them into some kind of bearable perspective," Steiner writes, "is the time relation." Steiner has just quoted descriptions of the brutal deaths of two Jews at the Treblinka extermination camp. "Precisely at the same hour in which Mehring and Langner were being done to death, the overwhelming plurality of human beings, two miles away on the Polish farms, five thousand miles away in New York, were sleeping or eating or going to a film or making love or worrying about the dentist. This is where my imagination balks. The two orders of simultaneous experience are so different, so irreconcilable to any common norm of human values, their coexistence is so hideous a paradox—Treblinka *is* both because some men have built it and almost all other men let it be—that I puzzle over time. Are there, as science fiction and Gnostic speculation imply, different species of time in the same world, 'good time' and enveloping folds of inhuman time, in which men fall into the slow hands of the living damnation?"

Until I read this passage I had rather simple-mindedly thought that only I had entertained such speculation, that only *I* had become obsessed about the time relation—to the extent, for example, that I had attempted more or less successfully to pinpoint my own activities on the first day of April, 1943, the day when Sophie, entering Auschwitz, fell into the "slow hands of the living damnation." At some point late in 1947—only a relatively brief number of years removed from the beginning of Sophie's ordeal—I rummaged through my memory in an attempt to locate myself in time on the same day that Sophie walked through the gates of hell. The first day of April, 1943—April Fools' Day—had a mnemonic urgency for me, and after going through some of my father's letters to me, which handily corroborated my movements, I was able to come up with the absurd fact that on that afternoon, as Sophie first set foot on the railroad platform in Auschwitz, it was a lovely spring morning in Raleigh, North Carolina, where I was gorging myself on bananas. I was eating myself nearly sick with bananas, the reason being that in the coming hour I was to take a physical examination for entrance into the Marine Corps. At the age of seventeen, already over six feet tall but weighing only 122 pounds, I knew I had to put on three more pounds to satisfy the minimum weight requirement. Stomach grossly bulging like that of a starveling, naked on a set of scales in front of a brawny old recruiting sergeant who stared at my emaciated adolescent beanpole of a frame and uttered a sneering "Je*sus* Christ" (there was also a snotty joke about April Fools' Day), I squeaked past by scant ounces.

On that day I had not heard of Auschwitz, nor of any concentration camp, nor of the mass destruction of the European Jews, nor even much about the Nazis. For me the enemy in that global war was the Japanese, and my ignorance of the anguish hovering like a noxious gray smog over places with names like Auschwitz, Treblinka, Bergen-Belsen was complete. But wasn't this true for most Americans, indeed most human beings who dwelt beyond the perimeter of the Nazi horror? "This notion of different orders of time simultaneous but in no effective analogy or communication," Steiner continues, "may be necessary to the rest of us, who were not there, who lived as if on another planet." Quite so—especially when (and the fact is often forgotten) for millions of Americans the embodiment of evil during that time was not the Nazis, despised and feared as they were, but the legions of Japanese soldiers who swarmed the jungles of the Pacific like astigmatic and rabid little apes and whose threat to the American mainland seemed far more dangerous, not to say more repulsive, given their yellowness and their filthy habits. But even if such narrowly focused animosity against an Oriental foe had not been real, most people could scarcely have known about the Nazi death camps, and this makes Steiner's ruminations all the more instructive. The nexus between these "different orders of time" is, of course—for those of us who were not there—someone who *was* there, and this brings me back to Sophie. To Sophie and, in particular, to Sophie's relation with SS Obersturmbannführer Rudolf Franz Höss.

I have spoken several times about Sophie's reticence concerning Auschwitz, her firm and generally unyielding silence about that fetid sinkhole of her past. Since she herself (as she once admitted to me) had so successfully anesthetized her mind against recurring images of her encampment in the abyss, it is small wonder that neither Nathan nor I ever gained much knowledge of what happened to her on a *day-to-day* basis (especially during the last months) aside from the quite obvious fact that she had come close to death from malnutrition and more than one contagion. Thus the jaded reader surfeited with our century's perdurable feast of atrocities will be spared here a detailed chronicle of the killings, gassings, beatings, tortures, criminal medical experiments, slow deprivations, excremental outrages, screaming madnesses and other entries into the historical account which have already been made by Tadeusz Borowski, Jean-François Steiner, Olga Lengyel, Eugen Kogon, André Schwarz-Bart, Elie Wiesel and Bruno Bettelheim, to name but a few of the most eloquent who have tried to limn the totally infernal in their heart's blood. My vision of Sophie's stay at Auschwitz is necessarily particularized, and perhaps a little distorted, though honestly so. Even if she had decided to reveal either to Nathan or me the gruesome minutiae of her twenty months at Auschwitz, I might be constrained to draw down the veil, for, as George Steiner remarks, it is not clear "that those who were not themselves fully involved should touch upon these agonies unscathed." I have been haunted, I must confess, by an element of presumption in the sense of being an intruder upon the terrain of an experience so bestial, so inexplicable, so undetachably and rightfully the possession alone of those who suffered and died, or survived it. A survivor, Elie Wiesel, has written: "Novelists made free use of [the Holocaust] in their work... In so doing they cheapened [it], drained it of its substance. The Holocaust was now a hot topic, fashionable, guaranteed to gain attention and to achieve instant success..." I do not know how ultimately valid any of this is, but I am aware of the risk.

Yet I cannot accept Steiner's suggestion that *silence* is the answer, that it is best "not to add the trivia of literary, sociological debate to the unspeakable." Nor do I agree with the idea that "in the presence of certain realities art is trivial or impertinent." I find a touch of piety in this, especially inasmuch as Steiner has not remained silent. And surely, almost cosmic in its incomprehensibility as it may appear, the embodiment of evil which Auschwitz has become remains impenetrable only so long as we shrink from trying to penetrate it, however inadequately; and Steiner himself adds immediately that the *next* best is "to try and understand." I have thought that it might be possible to make a stab at understanding Auschwitz by trying to understand Sophie, who to say the least was a cluster of contradictions. Although she was not Jewish, she had suffered as much as any Jew who had survived the same afflictions, and—as I think will be made plain—had in certain profound ways suffered more than most. (It is surpassingly difficult for many Jews to see beyond the consecrated nature of the Nazis' genocidal fury, and thus it seems to me less a flaw than a pardonable void in the moving meditation of Steiner, a Jew, that he makes only fleeting reference to the vast multitudes of non-Jews—the myriad Slavs and the Gypsies—who were swallowed up in the apparatus of the camps, perishing just as surely as the Jews, though sometimes only less methodically.)

If Sophie had been just a victim—helpless as a blown leaf, a human speck, volitionless, like so many multitudes of her fellow damned—she would have seemed merely pathetic, another wretched waif of the storm cast up in Brooklyn with no secrets which had to be unlocked. But the fact of the matter is that at Auschwitz (and this she came gradually to confess to me that summer) she had been a victim, yes, but both victim and accomplice, accessory—however haphazard and ambiguous and uncalculating her design—to the mass slaughter whose sickening vaporous residue spiraled skyward from the chimneys of Birkenau whenever she peered out across the parched autumnal meadows from the windows of the mansard roof of the house of her captor, Rudolf Höss. And therein lay one (although not the only one) of the prime causes of her devastating guilt—the guilt she concealed from Nathan and which, with no inkling of its nature or its actuality, he so often cruelly inflamed. For she could not wriggle out from beneath the suffocating knowledge that there had been this time in her life when she had played out the role, to its limit, of a fellow conspirator in crime. And this was the role of an obsessed and poisonous anti-Semite—a passionate, avid, tediously single-minded hater of Jews.

There were only two major events that took place during her stay at Auschwitz which Sophie ever spoke to me about, and neither of these did she ever mention to Nathan. The first of these—the day of her arrival at the camp—I have already referred to, but she did not speak to me of that until our final hours together. The second event, concerning her very brief relationship with Rudolf

Höss that same year, and the circumstances leading up to it, she described to me during the hours of a rainy August afternoon at the Maple Court. Or, I should say, a rainy afternoon and an evening. For although she blurted out to me the episode with Höss in such feverish yet careful detail that it acquired for me the graphic, cinematic quality of something immediately observed, the memory and the emotional fatigue and strain it caused her made her break off in helpless tears, and I had to piece together the rest of the tale later. The date of that encounter in Höss's joyless attic was—like her April Fools' Day debut—instantly memorable, and remains so still, for it was the birthday of three of my heroes: of my father, of the autumn-haunted Thomas Wolfe, and of wild Nat Turner, that fanatical black demon whose ghost had seared my imagination throughout my boyhood and youth. It was the third of October, and it was embedded in Sophie's own memory by virtue of the fact that it was the anniversary of her marriage to Casimir Zawistowski in Cracow.

And what, I have asked myself (pursuing George Steiner's speculation upon the existence of some sinister metaphysical time warp), were the activities of old Stingo, buck private in the United States Marine Corps, at the moment when the terrible last dust—in a translucent curtain of powdery siftings so thick that, in Sophie's words, "you could taste it on the lips like sand"—of some 2,100 Jews from Athens and the Greek islands billowed across the vista upon which she had earlier fixed her gaze, obscuring the pastoral figures of serenely grazing sheep as completely as if a towering fogbank had swept in from the Vistula marshes? The answer is remarkably simple. I was writing a letter of birthday felicitations—the letter itself easily obtainable not so long ago from a father who has cherished my most vapid jottings (even when I was very young) in the assurance that I was destined for some future literary luminosity. I extract here the central paragraph, which followed an affectionate expression of greetings. I am profoundly appalled now by its collegiate silliness, but I think it worth quoting in order to further emphasize the glaring and even, perhaps, terrifying incongruity. If one is historically minded enough, one can be charitable. Also, I was eighteen years old.

Marine Detachment, U.S. Naval V-12 Training Unit
Duke University, Durham, North Carolina
October 3, 1943

... anyway, Pop, tomorrow Duke is playing Tennessee and the atmosphere is pure (but restrained) hysteria. Obviously we have great hopes and by the time you get this it will be pretty much decided whether Duke will have a chance at the Conference championship and maybe a bowl bid, since if we knock over Tennessee—which is our strongest opponent—it will probably be clear sailing until the end of the season. Of course Georgia looks strong and a lot of people are laying money that they will come out #1 in the country. It's all a horse race, as they say, isn't it? Incidentally, have you heard the rumor that the Rose Bowl may be held again at Duke (whether we take the #1 spot or not) because the gov't. has a ban on big outdoor gatherings in Calif. Afraid of Jap sabotage apparently. Those little monkeys really loused up the works for a lot of Americans didn't they? Anyway it would be great fun if they had the Rose Bowl here, maybe you could come down from Va. for the big show whether Duke plays or not. I'm sure I must have told you that, due purely to an alphabetical coincidence (everything is alphabetical in the service), Pete Strohmyer and Chuckie Stutz are my roommates here. All of us learning to be hotshot Marine officers. Stutz was second team All-American from Auburn last year and I need not tell you who Strohmyer is, I'm sure. This room crawls with reporters and photographers like mice. [Early aptitude for metaphor] Maybe you saw Strohmyer's picture in Time magazine last week along with the article in which he was called easily the most spectacular broken field runner at least since Tom Harman and perhaps Red Grange. He's a hell of a nice guy too, Pop, and I don't guess it would be honest of me if I did not admit that I rather like basking in the reflected glory, especially since the young ladies who flock around Strohmyer are so numerous (and delightful) that there are always some left over for your son,

Stingo, the male wallflower. After the Davidson game last week-end we all had quite a ball . . .

The 2,100 Greek Jews who were being gassed and cremated at the time that these lines were composed did not, Sophie pointed out to me, make up anything like a record for a continuous act of mass extermination at Auschwitz; the slaughter of the Hungarian Jews in the following year—personally supervised by Höss, who returned to the camp after a number of months' absence to coordinate the liquidation, so eagerly awaited by Eichmann, in an operation christened *Aktion Höss*—involved multiple killings of much greater magnitude. But this mass murder was, for its moment in the evolution of Auschwitz-Birkenau, huge, one of the largest yet staged, complicated by logistical problems and considerations of space and disposal not until then encountered at such a complex level. Routinely, it was Höss's practice to report by military air express letters marked *"streng geheim"*—"top secret"—to the Reichsführer SS, Heinrich Himmler, on the general nature, physical condition and statistical composition of the "selections"—an almost daily occurrence (some days there were several) whereby those Jews arriving by train were separated into two categories: the fit, those healthy enough to labor for a while; and the unfit, who were immediately doomed. Because of extreme youth, extreme age, infirmity, the ravages of the journey or the aftereffects of previous sickness, relatively few of the Jews arriving at Auschwitz from any country were deemed able-bodied enough to work; at one point Höss reported to Eichmann that the average of those selected to survive for a time was between twenty-five and thirty percent. But for some reason the Greek Jews fared worse than the Jews from any other national group. Those Jews debarking from trains originating in Athens were found by the SS doctors in charge of the selections to be so debilitated that only a little more than one out of ten were sent to the right-hand side of the station ramp—the side assigned to those who were to live and work.

Höss was puzzled by this phenomenon, deeply puzzled. In a communication addressed to Himmler on that third day of October—a day Sophie remembered as having the first brisk bite of autumn in it, despite the pervasive murky smoke and stench which so blunted one's perception of the change of season—Höss theorized that there was one of four possible reasons, or perhaps a combination of the four, which caused the Greek Jews to be dragged off the cattle cars and boxcars in such a sorry state of deterioration, indeed with so many of the prisoners already dead or near death: bad nutrition at the point of origin; the extreme length of the journey combined with the poor condition of the railroads in Yugoslavia, through which the deportees had to pass; the abrupt change from the dry, hot Mediterranean climate to the damp and swampy atmosphere around the upper Vistula (although Höss added in an aside, uncharacteristic in its informality, that even this was puzzling, since, in terms of heat, at least in the summer, Auschwitz was "hotter than two hells"); and lastly, a trait of character, *Ratlosigkeit,* common to people of southern climes and therefore to those of weak moral fiber, which simply caused them to fail to withstand the shock of being uprooted and the attendant journey to an unknown destination. In their slovenliness they reminded him of the Gypsies, who, however, were conditioned to travel. Dictating his thoughts deliberately and slowly to Sophie in a somewhat harsh, flat, sibilant accent which she had earlier recognized as the voice of a North German from the Baltic region, he paused only to light cigarettes (he was a chain-smoker, and she noticed that the fingers of his right hand, small and even pudgy for such a rather gaunt person, were stained the hue of chestnut) and to brood thoughtfully for many seconds with his hand pressed lightly to his brow. He glanced up to ask politely if he was speaking too fast for her. *"Nein, mein Kommandant."*

The venerable German shorthand method (Gabelsberger) which she had learned at the age of sixteen in Cracow, and had employed so often in the service of her father, had come back to her with remarkable ease after several years' disuse; her speed and skill surprised her, and she breathed a small prayer of thanks to her father, who, though in his grave at Sachsenhausen, had provided for her this measure of salvation. Part of her mind dwelled on her father—"Professor Biegański," as she often thought of him, so formal and distant their relationship had always been—even as Höss, arrested in mid-phrase, sucked on his cigarette, coughed a phlegmy smoker's cough, and stood gazing out over the sere October meadow, his angular, tanned, not unhandsome face wreathed in blue tobacco fumes. The wind at the moment was blowing away from the chimneys of Birkenau, the air was clear. Although the weather outside had a touch of frost in it, here in the attic of the Commandant's house, beneath the sharply slanting roof, it was warm enough to be cozy, the rising heat trapped beneath the eaves and pleasantly augmented by still more heat pouring in from a brilliant early-afternoon sun. Several large bluebottle flies, imprisoned by the windowpanes, made soft gummy buzzings in the stillness or sailed out on tiny forays through the air, returned, buzzed fretfully, then fell still. There were also one or two vagrant, torpid wasps. The room was whitewashed with aseptic brightness, like that of a laboratory; it was dirt-free, spare, austere. It was Höss's private study, his sanctuary and hideaway, also the place where he executed his most personal, confidential and momentous work. Even the adored children, who swarmed at will through the other three floors of the house, were not permitted here. It was the lair of a bureaucrat with priestly sensibilities.

Sparsely furnished, the room contained a plain pinewood table, a steel filing cabinet, four straight-backed chairs, a cot upon which Höss sometimes rested, seeking surcease from the migraine headaches that assailed him from time to time. There was a telephone, but it was usually cut off. On the table was some official stationery in neat stacks, an orderly collection of pens and pencils, a cumbersome black office typewriter with the emblazoned trademark of Adler. For the past week and a half Sophie had been seated for many hours daily, hammering out correspondence either on this typewriter or another, smaller one (kept when not used beneath the table) that had a Polish keyboard. Sometimes, as now, she sat on one of the other chairs and took dictation. Höss's delivery tended to run in quick spurts separated by nearly interminable pauses—pauses in which there was almost audible a thudding tread of thought, the clotted Gothic ratiocination—and during such hiatuses Sophie would stare at the walls, all unadorned save for that work of supremely grandiose *Kitsch* she had seen before, a multi-pasteled Adolf Hitler in heroic profile, clad like a Knight of the Grail in armor of Solingen stainless steel. Adorning this monkish cell, it might have been the portrait of Christ. Höss ruminated, scratching his rather peninsular jaw; Sophie waited. He had removed his officer's jacket, the collar of his shirt was unbuttoned. The silence here, high up, was ethereal, almost unreal. Only two intertwined sounds now intruded, and these faintly—a muffled noise embedded in the very ambience of Auschwitz and as rhythmic as the sea: the chuffing of locomotives and the remote rumble of shunting boxcars.

"Es kann kein Zweifel sein—" he resumed, then stopped abruptly. " 'There can be no question—' no, that's too strong. I should say something less positive?" It was an ambiguous question mark. He spoke now, as he had once or twice before, with an odd inquisitive undertone in his voice, as if he might be wishing to solicit Sophie's opinion without compromising his authority by actually doing so. It was in effect a question addressed to both of them. In conversation Höss was extremely articulate. Yet his epistolary style, Sophie had observed, though workable and certainly not illiterate, fell often into clumsy, semi-opaque labyrinthine periods; it had the prosy, crippled rhythms of a man who was Army-educated, a perennial adjutant. Höss went into one of his protracted pauses.

"Aller Wahrscheinlichkeit nach," Sophie suggested a little hesitantly, though with less hesitation than she might have demonstrated several days before. "That's much less positive."

" 'In all probability,' " Höss repeated. "Yes, that's very good. It allows the Reichsführer more leeway to form his own judgment in the matter. Put that down then, followed by . . ."

Sophie felt a glow of satisfaction, almost pleasure, at this last remark. She sensed a barrier being breached, ever so slightly, between them after so many hours in which his manner had been metallically impersonal, businesslike, the dictation delivered with the gelid unconcern of an automaton. Only once so far—and that briefly the day before—had he let down that barrier. She could not be sure, but she even thought she detected a trace of warmth in his voice now as if he were suddenly speaking to *her*, an identifiable human being, rather than to a slave laborer, *eine schmutzige Polin*, plucked out of the swarm of diseased and dying ants through incredible luck (or by the grace of God, she sometimes devoutly reflected) and by virtue of the fact that she was doubtless one of the very few prisoners, if not the only one, who, bilingual in Polish and German, was also proficient on the typewriter in both languages and knew Gabelsberger shorthand. It was in shorthand now that she completed Höss's penultimate paragraph to Himmler: "In all probability, then, a reassessment must be made of the transport problem of the Greek Jews should any further deportations from Athens be contemplated for the immediate future. The mechanism for Special Action at Birkenau having become severely taxed beyond all expectation, it is respectfully suggested that, in the specific matter of the Greek Jews, alternative destinations in the occupied territories of the East, such as KL Treblinka or KL Sobibór, be considered."

Höss halted then, lighting a fresh cigarette from the butt of the last. He was gazing, with a slight daydream cast, through the partially open casement window. Suddenly he made a little exclamation, loud enough that she thought something might be wrong. But a quick smile spread over his face, and she heard him gasp "*Aaah!*" as he leaned intently forward to peer down into the field adjoining the house. "*Aaah!*" he said again raptly, drawing in his breath, and then half whispered to her, "Quick! Come here!" She rose and stepped to his side, approaching very close to him, so close that she could feel the touch of his uniform, and followed his gaze down into the field. "Harlekin!" he exclaimed. "Isn't he beautiful!"

A splendid chalk-white Arabian stallion was dashing in a long, mad, rapturous oval in the field below, all muscle and speed, grazing the surrounding paddock fence with a white tail held high that flowed behind him like a plume of smoke. He tossed his noble head with arrogant, insouciant pleasure, as if totally possessed by the fluid grace which sculpted and gave motion to his galloping forelegs and hindquarters and by the furiously healthy power energizing his being. Sophie had seen the stallion before, though never in such full poetic flight. It was a Polish horse, one of the prizes of war, and belonged to Höss. "Harlekin!" she heard him exclaim again, entranced by the sight. "Such a marvel!" The stallion galloped alone; there was not a human soul in sight. A few sheep were grazing. Beyond the field, crowding up against the horizon, were the bedraggled and nondescript scrubby woods, already beginning to turn the leaden hue of the Galician autumn. Several forlorn farmhouses dotted the rim of the forest. Bleak and drab as it was, Sophie preferred this view to the one from the other side of the room, which gave onto a busy, overpopulated prospect of the railroad ramp where the selections took place and the grimy dun brick barracks beyond, a scene crowned by the arched metalwork sign which from here read in the obverse: ARBEIT MACHT FREI. Sophie felt a shiver pass through her as, simultaneously, her neck was brushed by a vagrant draft and Höss lightly touched the edge of her shoulder with his fingertips. He had never touched her before; she shivered again, though she felt the touch was impersonal. "Just look at Harlekin," he breathed in a whisper. The majestic animal sped like the wind around the confining rim of the fence, leaving in his wake a small whirling cyclone of ocherous dust. "The greatest horses in the world, these Polish Arabians," Höss said. "Harlekin—a triumph!" The horse passed out of view.

Abruptly, then, he returned to his dictation, motioning to Sophie to take her seat. "Where was I?" he said. She read back the last paragraph. "Ah, now," he resumed, "finish with this: 'But until further information is received, it is hoped that the decision of this command to employ the greater part of the able-bodied Greek Jews in the Special Detachment at Birkenau is approved. Placing those so debilitated in proximity to the Special Action seems warranted by the circumstances, End paragraph. *Heil Hitler!*' Sign as usual and type that at once."

As she quickly obeyed his order, moving behind the typewriter and rolling an original sheet and five copy sheets into the machine, she kept her head bent toward her work, aware now that across from her, he had immediately taken up an official handbook and had begun reading. Her eyes' periphery glimpsed the book. It was not a green SS manual but, rather, a slate-blue Army quartermaster's manual with a title that all but engulfed the paper cover: *Improved Methods of Measuring and Predicting Septic Tank Percolation Under Unfavorable Conditions of Soil and Climate*. How little time Höss ever wasted! she thought. Hardly a second or two had elapsed between his last words and his seizing of the manual, in which he was now totally engrossed. She still felt the phantom impression of his fingers on her shoulder. She lowered her eyes, tapping out the letter, not for a moment fazed by the stark information which she knew lay embalmed beneath Höss's final circumlocutions: "Special Action," "Special Detachment." Few inmates of the camp were unaware of the reality behind these euphemisms or, having access to Höss's communication, would not be able to make this free translation: "The Greek Jews being such a pathetic lot and ready to die anyway, we hope it is all right that they have been assigned to the death commando unit at the crematoriums, where they will handle the corpses and extract the gold from the teeth and feed bodies to the furnaces until they too, exhausted beyond recall, are ready for the gas." Through Sophie's mind ran this adaptation of Höss's prose even as she typed the words, articulating a concept which, a mere six months before, when she first arrived, would have been so monstrous as to have surpassed belief but now registered in her consciousness as a fleeting commonplace in this new universe she inhabited, no more to be remarked upon than (as in the other world she had once known) the fact that one went to the baker's to buy one's bread.

She finished the letter without a mistake, appending an exclamation point to the salute to the Führer with such vigorous precision that it brought forth from the machine a faintly echoing tintinnabulation. Höss looked up from his manual, gestured for the letter and for a fountain pen, which she swiftly handed him. Sophie stood waiting while Höss scribbled an intimate postscript on a slip which she had paper-clipped to the bottom of the original, he muttering aloud in cadence to his written words, as was his habit, "Dear old Heini: Personal regrets at not being able to meet you tomorrow at Posen, where this letter is being routed air courier. Good luck with your speech to the SS

'Old Boys.' Rudi." He gave the letter back to her, saying, "This must go out soon, but do the letter to the priest first."

She returned to the table, straining with the effort as she lowered the leaden German contraption to the floor, replacing it with the Polish model. Manufactured in Czechoslovakia, it was much less heavy than the German typewriter, and of a more recent vintage; it was also speedier and considerably kinder to her fingers. She began to type, translating as she went from the shorthand message Höss had dictated to her the previous afternoon. It concerned a minor but vexing problem, one having to do with community relations. It also had weird echoes of *Les Misérables,* which she recalled . . . oh, so well. Höss had received a letter from a priest in a nearby village—nearby, but beyond the perimeter of the surrounding area, which had been cleared of Polish inhabitants. The priest's complaint was that a small group of drunken camp guards (exact number unknown) had entered the church at night and made off with a pair of priceless silver candlesticks from the altar—irreplaceable objects, really, hand-wrought works of art dating to the seventeenth century. Sophie had translated the letter aloud to Höss from the priest's crucified, splintered Polish. She had sensed the audaciousness, even the brazenness of the letter as she read it; one or the other, or perhaps simple stupidity, had to impel such a communication from an insignificant parish priest to the Commandant of Auschwitz. Yet there was a certain guile; the tone was obsequious to the point of servility ("intrude upon the honored Commandant's valuable time") when it was not delicate to a fault ("and we can understand how the excessive use of alcohol might provoke such an escapade, which was no doubt harmlessly conceived"), but the plain fact was that the poor priest had written in a controlled frenzy of unhappiness, as if he and his flock had been divested of their most revered possession, which they no doubt had been. In reading out loud, Sophie had emphasized the obsequious tone, which somehow underscored the priest's manic desperation, and when she had finished she heard Höss give a groan of discomfort.

"Candlesticks!" he said. "Why must I have problems about candlesticks?"

She looked up to see the wisp of a self-mocking smile on his lips, and she realized—for the first time after these many hours in his mechanically impersonal presence, when any inquiry he might have made of her had strictly to do with stenography and translation—that his mildly facetious, rhetorical question was addressed at least partially to her. She had been so taken off balance that her pencil flew out of her hand. She felt her mouth drop open but she said nothing, and could muster no ability to return his smile.

"The church," he said to her, "we must try to be polite to the local church—even in a country village. It is good policy."

Silently she bent down and retrieved her pencil from the floor.

Then, speaking directly to her, he said, "Of course *you* are Roman Catholic, aren't you?"

She felt no sarcasm in this, but for a long space was unable to reply. When she did, answering in the affirmative, she was embarrassed at finding herself adding a totally spontaneous "Are *you?*" The blood rushed to her face and she realized the extreme idiocy of the words.

But to her surprise and relief, he remained expressionless and his voice was quite impassively matter-of-fact as he said, "I was a Catholic but now I am a *Gottgläubiger*. I believe there is a deity—somewhere. I used to have faith in Christ." He paused. "But I have broken with Christianity."

And that was all. He said it as indifferently as if he were speaking of having disposed of a used piece of clothing. He spoke not another word to her informally, becoming all business again as he instructed her to write out a memorandum to SS Sturmbannführer Fritz Hartjenstein, commanding officer of the SS garrison, directing that a search be made for the candlesticks in the enlisted barracks and that every effort be exerted to apprehend the culprits, who would then be placed in custody of the camp provost marshal for discipline. And so it went—memorandum in quintuplicate, with a copy to be forwarded to SS Oberscharführer Kurt Knittel, manager of Section VI (*Kulturabteilung*) and supervisor of schooling and political education of the garrison; also to SS Sturmbannführer Konrad Morgen, head of the SS special commission for investigating corrupt practices in concentration camps. He then returned to the agony of the parish father, dictating a letter in German which he ordered Sophie to render into the priest's language and which now, this following day, she was transcribing on her machine, rather gratified to feel that she was able to turn the dross of Höss's German prose into finely articulated filaments of golden Polish: Dear Father Chybiński, we are shocked and distressed to hear of the vandalism of your church. Nothing is more grievous to us than the idea of desecration of holy objects and we shall endeavor to take every means at our command to ensure the return of your precious candelabra. While the enlisted men of this garrison have been inculcated with the highest principles of discipline demanded of every SS member—indeed of every German serving in the occupied territories—it is inevitable that lapses will occur, and we can only earnestly hope that you will understand . . . Sophie's typewriter went clickety-clack in the stillness of the attic while Höss brooded over his cesspool diagrams and the flies droned and twitched, and the movement of distant boxcars kept up a blurred incessant rumble like summer thunder.

At the instant she was finished (again tacking on the routine *Heil Hitler!*) her heart once more gave a tumultuous lurch, for he had spoken, and she looked up to see that he was gazing straight into her eyes. Although the clatter of the machine had masked his words, she was almost certain that he had said, "That's a very pretty kerchief." With fluttering fingertips her hand rose automatically, though with a final coquettish flourish, to touch the kerchief at the crown of her head. The scarf, of checkered green and made of cheap prison-stitched muslin, concealed her skull and its ludicrous frizzy locks, growing back in unsightly clumps after having been shorn to the roots exactly six months before. It was also a rare privilege, the kerchief; only those prisoners fortunate enough to work at Haus Höss were ever permitted thus to secrete the degrading baldness which to one degree or another every inmate, male and female, presented to this hermetically sealed world behind the electrified fences. The minuscule degree of dignity it conferred upon Sophie was something for which she felt a meager but real gratitude.

"Danke, mein Kommandant!" She heard her voice fal-

ter. The idea of conversing with Höss, on any level above or removed from her capacity as a part-time amanuensis, soaked her with apprehension, an almost intestinal nervousness. And her nervousness was heightened by the fact that conversation with Höss was, indeed, something she ravenously desired. Her stomach gurgled in fear—fear not of the Commandant himself but of failure of nerve, fear that she would ultimately lack the craft, the power of improvisation, the subtlety of manner, the histrionic gift, at last the beguiling *convincingness* by which she so desperately yearned to maneuver him into a vulnerable position and thus perhaps bend him to serve the modest demands of her will. "*Danke schön!*" she said with clumsy, inexcusable loudness, thinking: You fool, be quiet, he'll think you're an awful little ninny! She expressed her gratitude in a softer voice, and with grave calculation fluttered her eyelids and turned her gaze demurely down. "Lotte gave it to me," she explained. "It was one of two she had been given by Frau Höss and she passed it on to me. It covers my head nicely." Calm down now, she thought. Don't talk too much, don't talk much at all, not yet.

Now he was scanning the letter to the priest, although by his own admission he knew not a word of Polish. Sophie, watching him, heard him say "*. . . diese unerträgliche Sprache*" in a bemused tone, twisting his lips to fit some of the obdurately unpronounceable words of this "impossible language," quickly give up the effort and then rise to his feet. "Good," he said, "I hope we have soothed this unhappy little padre." He strode with the letter to the attic door, threw it open, and vanishing momentarily from Sophie's sight, called down to the landing where his aide, Untersturmführer Scheffler, waited for such peremptorily shouted commands. Sophie listened to Höss's voice, muffled by the walls, directing Scheffler to have the letter delivered immediately by messenger to the church. Faintly from below Scheffler's voice called back, deferential in tone but indistinct. "I'll come up right away, sir!" he seemed to say. "No, I'll come down and show you!" she heard Höss call out impatiently.

There was some misunderstanding which the Commandant now sought to rectify, grumbling to himself as he clumped the few steps downstairs in hard-heeled leather riding boots to confer with the aide, a husky poker-faced young lieutenant from Ulm whom he was just breaking in. Their voices continued from below in opaque colloquy, singsong, a dim babble. Then through or over their words, just for a fleeting instant, Sophie heard something which—insignificant in itself and very brief—later remained one of the most imperishable sensations she retained out of countless fragmented recollections of that place and time. As soon as she heard the music she knew it was coming from the massive electric phonograph that dominated the cluttered, overupholstered, damask-hued parlor four stories below. The machine had played almost constantly during the daytime hours of the week and a half she had spent under Höss's roof—at least whenever she had been within earshot of the loudspeaker, whether in the cramped and dank corner of the cellar where she slept on a straw pallet, or up here now, in the attic, when the intermittently opened door allowed the sound to be wafted to the eaves past her unlistening ears.

Sophie scarcely ever heard the music, indeed blanked most of it out, for it was never anything but noisy German backyard schmaltz, Tyrolean joke songs, yodelers, choirs of glockenspiels and accordions, all infused with recurring strains of treacly *Trauer* and lachrymal outpourings from Berlin cafés and music halls, notably such cries from the heart as "Nur nicht aus Liebe weinen," warbled by Hitler's favorite songbird Zarah Leander and played over and over again with merciless and monotonous obsession by the chatelaine of the manor—Höss's garishly bejeweled and strident wife, Hedwig. Sophie had coveted the phonograph until she could feel it like a wound in her breast, stealing glances at it as she passed to and fro through the living room on those trips it was necessary to make from her basement lodging to the attic. The room was a replica of an illustration she had once seen in a Polish edition of *The Old Curiosity Shop:* festering with French, Italian, Russian and Polish antiques, of all periods and styles, it looked the work of some crazed interior decorator who had dumped out onto the shining parquet floors the sofas, chairs, tables, escritoires, love seats, chaises longues and stuffed ottomans of an embryonic palazzo—shoving into a single large, lofty but finite space the furniture suitable for a dozen rooms. Even in this hideous hodgepodge, though, the phonograph somehow stood out, a fake antique itself in opulent cherrywood. Sophie had never seen a record player that was electrically amplified—those of her experience had been tinny apparatuses, hand-wound—and it filled her with despair that such a marvelous machine should give voice only to *Dreck*. A close passing look had revealed it to be a Stromberg Carlson, which she assumed to be Swedish until Bronek—a simple-seeming but canny fellow Polish prisoner who worked as a handyman in the Commandant's house and was a chief purveyor of gossip and information—told her it was an American machine, captured from some rich man's joint or foreign embassy to the west and transported here to take its place amid the mountainous tonnage of booty assembled with frenzied mania for pelf from all the plundered habitations of Europe. Surrounding the machine were masses of thick record albums in glassed-in cases; on the top of the phonograph itself was perched a fat Bavarian Kewpie doll in pink celluloid, cheeks aburst, blowing on a gold-plated saxophone. Euterpe, Sophie had thought, music's sweet Muse, passing quickly on . . .

> *Die Himmel erzählen die Ehre*
> *Gottes,*
> *und seiner Hände Werk*
> *zeigt an das Firmament!*

The Elysian chorus, thrusting itself up through the muttering chatter of Höss and his aide below, stabbed her with such astonished exaltation that she rose spontaneously from her seat at the typewriter, as if in homage, faintly trembling. What on earth had happened? What fool or freak had put that record on the machine? Or might it have been only Hedwig Höss herself, gone suddenly mad? Sophie didn't know, but it didn't matter (it later occurred to her that it must have been the Hösses' second daughter, Emmi, a blond eleven-year-old with a sullen freckled perfectly circular face, in idle postprandial boredom fiddling with tunes both novel and outlandish); it didn't matter. The ecstatic hosanna moved across her skin like divine hands, touching her with ecstatic ice; chill after chill coursed through her flesh; for long seconds the fog and night of her existence, through which she had stumbled like a sleepwalker, evaporated as if melted by the burning sun. She stepped to the window. In the angled windowpane she saw the reflection of her pale face beneath the checkered scarf, below this the blue and white stripes of her coarse prisoner's smock; blinking, weeping, gazing straight through her own diaphanous image, she glimpsed the magical white horse again, grazing now, the meadow, the sheep beyond, and further still, as if at the very edge of the world, the rim of the drab gray autumnal woods, transmuted by the music's incandescence into a towering frieze of withering but majestic foliage, implausibly beautiful, aglow with some immanent grace. "Our Father . . ." she began in German. Half drowned, borne utterly away by the anthem, she closed her eyes while the archangelic trio chanted its mysterious praise to the whirling earth:

Dem kommenden Tage sagt es der
Tag.
Die Nacht, die verschwand
der folgenden Nacht . . .

"It stopped then, the music," Sophie said to me. "No, not just then but right afterwards. It stopped in the middle of that last passage—do you know it maybe?—that in English have, I think, the words that go 'In all the lands resounds the Word—' It just stopped suddenly, this music, and I felt a complete emptiness. I never finished the paternoster, the prayer I begun. I don't know any more, I think maybe it was that moment that I begun to lose my faith. But I don't know any more, about *when* God leave me. Or I left Him. Anyway, I felt this emptiness. It was like finding something precious in a dream where it is all so real—something or *someone,* I mean, unbelievably precious—only to wake up and realize the precious person is gone. Forever! I have done that so many times in my life, waking up with that loss! And when this music stopped, it was like that, and suddenly I knew—I had this premonition—that I would never hear such music again.

The door was still open and I could hear Höss and Scheffler talking downstairs. And then far down below Emmi—I'm sure it must have been Emmi—put guess what on the phonograph. 'The Beer Barrel Polka.' I felt such rage then. That fat little bitch with this face like a white moon, made of oleo-mar-ga-rine. I could have killed her. She was playing 'The Beer Barrel Polka,' loud; they must have been able to hear it in the garden, in the barracks, in the town. In Warsaw. The singing was in English, that stupid piece.

"But I knew I had to control myself, forget about music, think of other things. Also, you see, I knew that I must use every bit of *intelligence* that I had, every bit of *wit,* I think you would say, in order to get what I wanted out of Höss. I knew he hated Poles, but that was no matter. I have made this—*comment dit-on, fêlure* . . . crack!—crack in the mask already and now I must move further on because time was of *l'essence*. Bronek, that was this handyman, had whispered to us women in the cellar that he heard this rumor that Höss was going soon to be transferred to Berlin. I must move quickly if I was to—yes, I will say it, *seduce* Höss, even if it make me sick sometime when I think of it, hoping that somehow I could seduce him with my mind rather than my body. Hoping I would not have to use my body if I could prove to him these other things. Okay, Stingo, prove to him that Zofia Maria Biegańska Zawistowska okay might be *eine schmutzige Polin,* you know, *tierisch,* animal, just a slave, *Dreckpolack,* et cetera, but still was as strong and fine a National Socialist as Höss was, and I should be made free from this cruel, unfair imprisonment. *Voilà!*

"Finally, well then, Höss come back up the stairs. I could hear his boots on the steps and 'The Beer Barrel Polka.' I make this decision, that in some way I might appear attractive to him, standing there by the window. Sexy, you know. Excuse me, Stingo, but you know what I mean—looking as if I wanted to fuck. Looking as if I wanted to be asked to fuck. But oh, my eyes! Jesus Christ, my eyes! They were all pink, I knew, from weeping, and I was still weeping, and I was afraid this might upset my plan. But I was able to stop and I wiped my eyes with the back of my hand. And I looked again to see the beauty of those woods when I heard this moment of Haydn. But the wind have made this sudden change, you know, and I could see the smoke from the ovens at Birkenau coming down over the fields and the woods. Then Höss came in."

Lucky Sophie. It is remarkable to contemplate, but at this point in her career at the camp, six months after her arrival, she was not only in fairly good health but had been spared most of the worst pangs of starvation. This hardly meant any abundance, however. Whenever she reminisced about that period (and she rarely dwelt on it in any great detail, so I never got from her the sense of the immediacy of living in hell which one obtains from written accounts; yet she obviously had seen hell, felt it, breathed it), she implied she was decently enough fed, but only by comparison with the stark famine which the rank-and-file prisoners endured daily, and thus she fed upon short rations. During the ten days or so she spent in Höss's basement, for instance, she ate kitchen leftovers and the leavings from the Höss table, mostly vegetable scraps and meat gristle—for which she remained grateful. She was managing to survive slightly above the subsistence level, but only because she was lucky. In all slave worlds there soon develops a hierarchic design, a pecking order, patterns of influence and privilege; because of her great good fortune Sophie found herself among a small elite.

This elite, composed of perhaps only several hundred out of the many thousands of prisoners who populated Auschwitz at any single moment, were those who through maneuvering or, again, by luck had begun to fulfill some function that the SS deemed indispensable or at least of vital importance. ("Indispensable" as strictly applied to captive human beings at Auschwitz would be a *non sequitur.*) Such duties implied temporary or even prolonged survival, certainly when compared with roles played by the great multitude of the camp inmates who because of their very superfluity and replaceability had only one purpose: to labor to the point of exhaustion, then to die. Like any group of skilled artisans, the elite of which Sophie was a member (they included such craftsmen as highly accomplished tailors from France and Belgium who were employed in making fine clothes out of the fancy goods snatched on the station ramp from condemned Jews, expert cobblers and workers in high-quality leather, gardeners with green thumbs, technicians and engineers possessing certain specialist capabilities, and a handful like Sophie with combined linguistic and secretarial gifts) were spared extermination for the raw pragmatic reason that their talents came as close to being invaluable as that word had any such meaning in the camp. Thus, until some savage quirk of fate shattered them too—a likely and daily threat—these of the elite at least did not suffer the swift plunge into disintegration which was the portion of nearly all the rest.

It may help clarify what went on between Sophie and Rudolf Höss if we try for a moment to examine the nature and function of Auschwitz in general, but especially during the six months after her arrival in early April of that year 1943. I emphasize the time because it is important. Much can be explained in terms of the metamorphosis which the camp underwent as the result of an order (unquestionably originating with the Führer) which went down to Höss from Himmler sometime during the first week of April. The order was one of the most monumental and sweeping to be promulgated since the "final solution" itself was hatched in the fecund brains of the Nazi thaumaturges: that is, the recently built gas chambers and crematoriums of Birkenau would be employed *solely* for the extermination of Jews. This edict superseded previous rules of procedure which allowed for the gassing of non-Jews (mostly Poles, Russians and other Slavs) on the same "selective" basis of health and age as the Jews. There was a technological and a logistical necessity embedded in the new directive, the impetus of which derived not from any sudden preservative concern on the part of the Germans for the Slavs and other "Aryan" non-Jewish deportees, but from an overriding obsession—springing from Hitler and amounting now to mania in the minds of Himmler, Eichmann and their cousin overlords in the SS chain of command—to finally get on with the Jewish slaughter until every Jew in Europe had perished. The new order was in effect a clearing of the decks for action: the Birkenau facilities, gargantuan as they were, had certain ultimate limitations both spatial and thermal; with their absolute and uncontested priority in the lists of *der Massenmord* now, the Jews were tendered a sudden unaccustomed exclusivity. With few exceptions (Gypsies for one), Birkenau was theirs alone. Just the prospect of their sheer numbers "made my teeth ache at night," wrote Höss, who meant that he ground his teeth, and who, despite the vacuum of his imagination, could turn a crudely descriptive phrase or two.

At this juncture, then, Auschwitz stands revealed in its dual function: as a depot for mass murder but also a vast enclave dedicated to the practice of slavery. Yet of a new form of slavery—of human beings continuously replenished and expendable. This duality is often overlooked. "Most of the literature on the camps has tended to stress the role of the camps as places of execution," Richard L. Rubenstein has written in his masterful little book *The Cunning of History*. "Regrettably, few ethical theorists or religious thinkers have paid attention to the highly significant political fact that the camps were in reality a new form of human society." His book—the work of an American professor of religion—is brief in length but wise and far-seeing in its final dimensions (the subtitle "Mass Death and the American Future" may give an idea of its ambitious—and chilling—attempt both at prophecy and at historical synthesis), and there is no room here to do justice to its full power and complexity, or to the moral and religious resonances it manages to convey; it will surely remain one of the essential handbooks of the Nazi era, a terrifyingly accurate necropsy and an urgent consideration of our own uncertain tomorrows. That new form of human society developed by the Nazis of which Rubenstein writes (extending Arendt's thesis) is a "society of total domination," evolving directly from the institution of chattel slavery as it was practiced by the great nations of the West, yet urged on to its despotic apotheosis at Auschwitz through an innovative concept which by contrast casts a benign light on old-fashioned plantation slavery even at its most barbaric: this blood-fresh concept was based on the simple but absolute *expendability* of human life.

It was a theory splintering all previous hesitancies about persecution. Bedeviled as they may have been at times by the dilemma of surplus population, the traditional slaveholders of the Western world were under Christian constraint to avoid anything resembling a "final solution" to solve the problem of excess labor; one could not shoot an expensively unproductive slave; one suffered with Old Sam when he grew superannuated and feeble, and let him die in peace. (This was not entirely the case. There is much evidence, for instance, that in the West Indies in the mid-1700s the European masters for a time felt no compunction about working slaves to death. In general, however, what I have said is applicable.) With National Socialism there came a sweeping away of leftover pieties. The Nazis, as Rubenstein points out, were the first slaveholders to fully abrogate any lingering humane sentiments regarding the essence of life itself; they were the first who "were able to turn human beings into instruments wholly responsive to their will even when told to lie down in their own graves and be shot."

Those who arrived at Auschwitz were, through discriminating methods of cost accounting and other advanced formulations of input and output, expected to struggle through their existence for only a fixed segment of time: three months. Sophie became aware of this a day or two after her arrival when, herded together with several hundred of her fellow newcomers—Polish women of all ages for the most part, looking like a barnyard full of plucked and blowzy poultry in their castoff rags and their shining scalps freshly shorn of hair—there filtered through her traumatized consciousness the words of an SS functionary, one Hauptsturmführer Fritzch, as he articulated the design of this City of Woe and bade those who had just entered it to abandon all hope. "I remember his exact words," Sophie told me. "He said, 'You have come to a concentration camp, not to a sanatorium, and there is only one way out—up the chimney.' He said, 'Anyone who don't like this can try hanging himself on the wires. If there are Jews in this group, you have no right to live more than two weeks.' Then he said, 'Any nuns here? Like the priests, you have one month. All the rest, three months.' "

So then ultimately the Nazis had with consummate craft

fashioned a death-in-life more terrible than death, and more calculatingly cruel because few of those doomed in the beginning—on that first day—could know that this bondage of torture, disease and starvation was only an evil simulacrum of life through which they would be voyaging irresistibly deathward. As Rubenstein concludes: "The camps were thus far more of a permanent threat to the human future than they would have been had they functioned solely as an exercise in mass killing. An extermination center can only manufacture corpses; a society of total domination creates a world of the living dead . . ."

Or as Sophie said, "Most of them when they first come there, if they had only known, they would have prayed for the gas."

The stripping and searching of prisoners that invariably took place as soon as they arrived at Auschwitz seldom allowed inmates to retain any of their former possessions. Due to the chaotic and often slipshod nature of the process, however, there were occasions when a newcomer was lucky enough to hold on to some small personal treasure or article of clothing. Through a combination of her own ingenuity, for instance, and oversight on the part of one of the SS guards, Sophie managed to keep a much worn but still serviceable pair of leather boots which she had owned since her last days in Cracow. Inside one of the boots, built into the lining, was a small slitlike compartment, and on the day she stood waiting for the Commandant at the window of his attic the compartment contained a thumbed, smudged, badly wrinkled but legible pamphlet of some twelve pages and four thousand words upon the title page of which was written this legend: *Die polnische Judenfrage: Hat der Nationalsozialismus die Antwort?* That is, *Poland's Jewish Problem: Does National Socialism Have the Answer?* It was probably Sophie's most flagrant evasion (and one incorporating her strangest lie) that earlier she kept harping to me about the extraordinary liberality and tolerance of her upbringing, not only deceiving me, just as I'm sure she deceived Nathan, but concealing from me until the last possible moment a truth which, in order to justify her dealings with the Commandant, she could hide no longer: that the pamphlet had been written by her father, Professor Zbigniew Biegański, Distinguished Professor of Jurisprudence at the Jagiellonian University of Cracow; Doctor of Law *honoris causa,* Universities of Karlova, Bucharest, Heidelberg and Leipzig.

It was not easy for her to tell all this, she confessed to me, biting her lips and nervously fingering her drawn and ashen cheek; it was especially difficult to reveal one's lies after having so artfully created a perfect little cameo of paternal rectitude and decency: the fine socialist paterfamilias fretting over the coming terror, a man haloed with goodness in her portrait of a brave libertarian who had risked his life to save Jews in the ferocious Russian pogroms. When she told me this her voice had a touch of the distraught. Her lies! She realized how it undermined her credibility in other matters when she now was forced out of conscience to admit that all that stuff about her father was a simple fabrication. But there it was—a fabrication, a wretched lie, another fantasy served up to provide a frail barrier, a hopeless and crumbly line of defense between those she cared for, like myself, and her smothering guilt. Would I not forgive her, she said, now that I saw both the truth and her necessity for telling the lie? I stroked the back of her hand and, naturally, said of course I would.

For I would not be able to understand this thing with Rudolf Höss, she went on, unless I knew the truth about her father. She had not *completely* lied to me earlier, she insisted, when she described the idyllic years of her childhood. The house she had lived in, there in peaceful Cracow, had been in most ways a place of surpassing warmth and security in those years between the wars. There was a sweet domestic serenity, largely supplied by her mother, a bosomy, expansive, loving woman whose memory Sophie would cherish if only for the passion for music she had passed on to her only daughter. Try to imagine the leisurely paced life of almost any academic family in the Western world during those years of the twenties and the thirties—with ritual teas and evening musicales and summer outings to the rolling drowsy countryside, dinners with students and mid-year trips to Italy, sabbatical years in Berlin and Salzburg—and one will have an idea of the nature of Sophie's life in those days, and its civilized odor, its equable, even jovial cast. Over this scene, however, lay an abidingly somber cloud, a presence oppressive and stifling which polluted the very wellsprings of her childhood and youth. This was the constant, overwhelming reality of her father, a man who had exercised over his household, and especially Sophie, a tyrannical domination so inflexible yet so cunningly subtle that she was a grown woman, fully come of age, before she realized that she loathed him past all telling.

There are rare moments in life when the intensity of a buried emotion one has felt toward another person—a repressed animus or a wild love—comes heaving to the surface of consciousness with immediate clarity; sometimes it is like a bodily cataclysm, ever unforgettable. Sophie said she would never forget the exact moment when the revelation of the hatred she felt for her father enveloped her in a horrible hot radiance, and she could find no voice, and thought she might faint dead away . . .

He was a tall robust-looking man, usually garbed in a frock coat and a shirt with wing collar and a broad foulard tie. Old-fashioned dress, but not at all grotesque in Poland for that time. His face was classically Polish: high wide cheekbones, blue eyes, rather full lips, the broad nose tilting up, large elfin ears. He wore sideburns and his light fine hair was swept back evenly, always nicely coiffed. A couple of artificial teeth made of silver slightly marred his good looks, but only when he opened his mouth wide. Among his colleagues he was considered something of a dandy, though not absurdly so; his considerable academic reputation was a safeguard against ridicule. He was respected despite his extreme views—a superconservative in a faculty of right-wingers. Not only a teacher of law but a practicing lawyer from time to time, he had established himself as an authority on the international use of patents—mainly concerning interchange between Germany and the countries of Eastern Europe—and the fees he had gained by this sideline, all in a perfectly ethical manner, had enabled him to live on a somewhat more substantial level than many of his fellow faculty members, in a subdued, modestly proportioned elegance. He was a connoisseur of Moselle wines and Upmann cigars. The Professor was also a practicing Catholic, though hardly a zealot.

What Sophie had told me earlier about his youth and education was apparently true: his early years in Vienna during the time of Franz Josef had fed the fires of his pro-Teutonic passion and inflamed him everlastingly with a vision of Europe saved by pan-Germanism and the spirit of Richard Wagner. It was a love as pure and as abiding as his detestation of Bolshevism. How could poor backward Poland (Sophie often heard him say), losing its identity with clockwork regularity to oppressor after oppressor—especially the barbarous Russians, who were now also in the grip of the Communist antichrist—find salvation and cultural grace except through the intercession of Germany, which had so magnificently fused a historic tradition of mythic radiance and the supertechnology of the twentieth century, creating a prophetic synthesis for lesser nations to turn to? What better nationalism for a diffuse, unstructured nation like Poland than the practical yet aesthetically thrilling nationalism of National Socialism, in which *Die Meistersinger* was no more or no less a civilizing influence than the great new autobahns?

The Professor—besides being neither liberal nor remotely a socialist, as Sophie had first told me—was a charter adherent of a blazingly reactionary political faction known as the National Democratic party, nicknamed ENDEK, one of whose guiding precepts was a militant anti-Semitism. Fanatic in its identification of Jews with international Communism, and vice versa, the movement was especially influential in the universities, where in the early 1920s physical violence against Jewish students became endemic. A member of the moderate wing of the party, Professor Biegański, then a rising young faculty star in his thirties, wrote an article in a leading Warsaw political journal deploring these assaults, which caused Sophie a number of years later to wonder—when she happened upon the essay—whether he hadn't suffered a spasm of radical-utopian humanism. She was of course absurdly mistaken—just as she was mistaken or perhaps devious (and guilty of another lie to me) when she claimed that her father hated the despotic hand of Marshal Pilsudski, that quondam radical, because he brought a virtually totalitarian regime to Poland in the late twenties. Her father did indeed hate the Marshal, she was later to learn, hated him with a fury, but mainly because in the paradoxical way of dictators he had handed down edict after edict protective of the Jews. The Professor was therefore straining at the bit, so to speak, when after the death of Pilsudski in 1935 the laws guaranteeing Jewish rights were relaxed, exposing Polish Jews once more to the terror. Again, at least at first, Professor Biegański cautioned moderation. Joining a rejuvenated Fascist group known as the National Radical party, which began to exert commanding sway among the students of the Polish universities, the Professor—now a dominant voice—advised temperance, once more cautioning against the wave of clubbings and muggings which had begun to beset the Jews, not only in the universities but in the streets. However, his disapproval of violence was based less on ideology than on a perverse delicacy; with all this apparent hand-wringing, he clung staunchly to the obsession that had for so long dominated and suffused his being: he began methodically to philosophize about the necessity of eliminating Jews from all walks of life, commencing with Academe.

He wrote furiously about the problem, in Polish and German, sending countless articles to distinguished political and legal journals in Poland and in such centers of culture as Bonn, Mannheim, Munich and Dresden. One of his major themes was "superfluous Jews," and he scribbled away at length about the matter of "population transfer" and "expatriation." He was a member of a government mission sent to Madagascar to explore the possibility of Jewish settlements. (He brought Sophie an African mask—she recalled his sunburn.) Though still abstaining from suggestions of violence, he began to waver and his insistence upon the necessity of an immediate *practical* answer to the problem was more and more resolute. A certain franticness entered the Professor's life. He became a leading activist in the movement toward segregation, and was one of the fathers of the idea of separate "ghetto benches" for Jewish students. He was a piercing analyst of the economic crisis. He gave rabble-rousing speeches in Warsaw. In a depressed economy, he raged, what right had alien ghetto Jews to compete for jobs with honest Poles flooding into the city from everywhere? Toward the end of 1938, in the full flood of his passion, he began working on his magnum opus, the aforementioned pamphlet, in which for the first time he broached the idea—very cautiously, backing and filling with a circumspection bordering on the ambiguous—of "total abolishment." Ambiguous, tentative—but there. Abolishment. *Not brutality.* Total abolishment. By this time, indeed for several years, Sophie had been transcribing some of her father's dictation, and humble and subservient as any peonness, had taken on every secretarial chore he demanded. Her submissive labor, which she had executed patiently, like practically all dutiful Polish daughters trapped in a tradition of absolute obeisance to Daddyhood, culminated one week in the winter of 1938 with the typing and editing of the manuscript of *Poland's Jewish Problem: Does National Socialism Have the Answer?* At that moment she understood or, I should say, began to understand just what it was her father was up to.

Despite my badgering inquisitiveness as Sophie related these things, it was difficult for me to gain a thorough picture of her childhood and youth, though some things became very clear. Her subservience to her father, for example, was complete, as complete as in any neopaleolithic pigmy culture of the rain forest, demanding utter fealty from the helpless offspring. She never questioned this fealty, she told me; it was part of her bloodstream, so much so that as a little girl growing up she rarely even resented it. It was all bound up in her Polish Catholicism, in which veneration of a father seemed appropriate and necessary anyway. In fact, she admitted that she may have even rather relished her virtually menial submission, the "Yes, Papa's" and "No, thank you, Papa's" she was compelled to say daily, the favors and attentions she had to pay, the ritual respect, the enforced obsequiousness that she shared with her mother. She may have been, she admitted, truly masochistic. After all, even in her most miserable recollections, she had to concede that he was not actually cruel to either of them; he had a playful if crude sense of humor and was, despite all his aloofness and majesty, not above bestowing, on rare occasions, small rewards. In order to remain happy, a household tyrant cannot be totally unbenign.

Perhaps it was such mitigating qualities (permitting Sophie to perfect her French, which he considered a decadent language; allowing her mother to indulge her love for composers other than Wagner, triflers like Fauré and Debussy and Scarlatti) that caused Sophie to accept without any conscious resentment his complete domination of her life even after she was married. Beyond this, as the daughter of a distinguished though colorfully controversial member of the faculty (many but by no means all of his colleagues shared the Professor's extreme ethnic views), Sophie was only vaguely aware of her father's political beliefs, of his governing rage. He kept that apart from his family, though obviously through the early years of her adolescence she could not remain completely oblivious of his animosity toward Jews. But it could scarcely have been an unprecedented thing in Poland to have an anti-Semitic parent. As for herself—bound up in her studies, in the church, in friends and the modest social events of the time, in books, in movies (dozens of movies, mostly American), in piano practice with her mother, and even one or two innocent flirtations—her attitude in regard to Jews, the greater part of whom were in the Cracow ghetto, wraiths barely visible, was at most one of indifference. Sophie insisted on this; I still believe her. They simply did not concern her—at least until as his dragooned secretary she began to divine the depth and extent of her father's fiery enthusiasm.

The Professor had compelled her to learn typing and shorthand when she was only sixteen. He may already have schemed at using her. Perhaps he was anticipating the time when he would need her skilled services; the fact that she was his daughter would doubtless provide added measures of convenience and confidentiality. At any rate, although for several years she had labored on various weekends typing out much of his bilingual correspondence having to do with patents (sometimes using a British-made Dictaphone which she hated for the spookily faraway and tinnily sinister sound it gave to his voice), she had never, until the Christmas season of 1938, been called upon to deal with any of his many essays; these had been handled until then by his assistants at the university. Thus she was in the position of having drawn upon her like flooding sunrise itself the whole culminating design of his hate-drenched philosophy when he made her take down in Gabelsberger shorthand, then transcribe on the typewriter in Polish and German, the entire text of his chef d'oeuvre: *Poland's Jewish Problem,* etc. She recalled the hectic excitement which from time to time stole into his voice as, champing on a cigar, he paced the damp and smoky study in the house, and she obediently scratched on her shorthand pad the skeletal symbols of his logically formulated, precise but flowing German.

He had a spacious yet discriminative style, flecked with sparks of irony. It could be at the same time caustic and seductively convivial. The language was, in fact, superbly articulated German, which in itself had helped gain Professor Biegański his ample measure of renown in such Olympian centers for the propagation of anti-Semitism as Welt-Dienst in Erfurt. His writing had an idiosyncratic charm. (Once that summer in Brooklyn, I pressed upon Sophie a volume of H. L. Mencken, who was then, as now, one of my infatuations, and I observe for what it is worth that she remarked that Mencken's scathing style reminded her of her father's.) She took his dictation with care, but because of his runaway fervor, in some haste, so it was not until she got down to the job of typing it out for the printer that she began to glimpse seething in that cauldron of historical allusions and dialectical hypotheses and religious imperatives and legal precedents and anthropological propositions the smoky, ominous presence of a single word—repeated several times—which quite baffled and confounded and frightened her, appearing as it did in this otherwise persuasively practical text, this clever polemic which voiced with breezily scurrilous mockery the sly propaganda she had half heard more than once over the Biegański dinner table. But this word that so alarmed her was a new departure. For those several times he had made her change "total abolishment" (*vollständige Abschaffung*) to *Vernichtung*.

Extermination. In the end it was as simple and as unequivocal as that. Even so, subtly introduced as it was, steeped in the pleasantly spiced broth of the Professor's discursive, entertainingly acrid animadversions, the word and its full force and meaning—and thus its full meaning as it informed the entire substance of the essay—was so horrible that she had to shove it into the back of her mind throughout the entire bone-chilling winter weekend during which she labored over her father's impassioned screed. She found herself preoccupied about his rage should she misplace an accent, omit an umlaut. And she was still repressing the very meaning of *Vernichtung* until that moment in the drizzling dusk of Sunday when, hurrying with the bundle of typescript to meet her father and her husband, Casimir, in a café on the Market Square, she was smitten with horror at what he had said and written and what she, in her complicity, had done. *"Vernichtung,"* she said aloud. He means, she thought with stupid belatedness, they should all be murdered.

As Sophie herself implied, it would perhaps add gloss to her image if one could say that her realization of the hatred she bore toward her father not only coincided with but was motivated by her realization that he was an aspiring Jew-killer. But although the two awarenesses did merge together at almost the same moment, Sophie told me (and here I believed her, as I often did, for intuitive reasons) that she must have been emotionally ripe for the blinding revulsion she suddenly felt for her father, and that she very well may have reacted in the way she did had the Professor made no mention whatever of the approaching and wished-for slaughter. She told me she could never be sure. We are speaking here of central truths about Sophie, and I think it is testimony enough to the nature of her sensibilities that exposed for so many years to the rancorous, misshapen, discordant strains of her father's obsession, and now immersed like a drowning creature in the very midst of the poisonous wellspring of his theology, she should have retained the human instinct to respond with the shock and horror that she did, clutching the atrocious bundle to her breast and hurrying through the misty crooked twilight streets of Cracow toward her revelation.

"That evening my father was waiting for me at one of the cafés on the Market Square. I remember it was very cold and damp, bits of sleet in the air, feeling like snow might come, you know. My husband, Kazik, was at the table with my father, waiting too. I was quite late because I worked all afternoon typing the manuscripts and it take much longer than I thought it would. I was terribly afraid that my father would be angry at my lateness. The whole thing have been done in such a hurry, you see. It was what I think you call a rush job, and the printer—the man who would print the pamphlet in German and Polish—was to meet my father at the café at a certain hour and pick up the manuscripts. Before this, my father had planned to spend time at his table there correcting the manuscripts. He was to correct the German typescript while Kazik checked over the one in Polish. That was the way it was supposed to be, but I was very late, and when I arrived there the printer had already come and was sitting with my father and Kazik. My father was very angry, and although I made my apologies, I could tell he was just furious, and he quickly take the manuscripts from me and order me to sit down. I sat down and I could feel something painful happen in my stomach I was so afraid of his rage. Strange, Stingo, how you remember certain details. I mean, just this: that my father was drinking tea and Kazik was drinking slivovitz brandy and the printer—this man that I had met before, named Roman Sienkiewicz; yes, just like the name of the famous writer—was drinking vodka. I'm sure I remember such a detail so clearly because of my father's tea. I mean, you see, after working all afternoon I was just completely exhausted and all I wanted then was a cup of tea, like my father. But I would never order it myself, never! I remember looking at his teapot and his cup and just longing for hot tea like that. And if I had not been so late my father would have offered me tea but now he was furious with me and said nothing about tea, so I just sat there looking down at my fingernails while my father and Kazik began reading the manuscripts.

"It seemed to take hours. The printer Sienkiewicz—he was a fat man with a mustache, I remember he chuckled a lot—I spoke some things to him about the weather, nothing things, but mainly I just sat there at this cold table, keeping my mouth shut, wanting tea like I was dying of thirst. Finally my father looked up from the manuscript and stared at me and said, '*Who* is this Neville Chamberlain who so loves the works of Richard Wagner?' And he was looking at me hard, and I didn't exactly understood what he meant, only that he was terribly displeased. Displeased at me. And I didn't understood and I said, 'What do you mean, Papa?' And he said the question again, this time *avec l'accent* on *Neville,* and I suddenly realized I have make a bad mistake. Because, you see, there was this English writer Chamberlain that my father was using in the essay everywhere to support his own philosophy, I don't know if you have heard of him, he wrote a book called *Die Grundlagen des—* Oh well, in English I think it have the name *Foundation of the Nineteenth Century,* and it is filled with love of Germany and worship of Richard Wagner and this very bitter hatred of Jews, saying they contaminate the culture of Europe and such as that. My father had for this Chamberlain such great admiration, only now I realized that when he dictate this name to me I put down unconsciously Neville over and over, because then he was so much in the news because of Munich, instead of putting down *Houston* Chamberlain, which was the name of the Chamberlain that hates the Jews. And now I am filled with fear because I have repeated this mistake over and over in the footnotes and the bibliography and everywhere else.

"And oh, Stingo, the shame! Because my father, he is so crazy for perfection that this mistake he can't *fermer les yeux* . . . overlook, but he have to make a big thing out of it then and there, and I heard him say in front of Kazik and Sienkiewicz *this,* I'll never forget it, it was so filled with contempt, 'Your intelligence is *pulp,* like your mother's. I don't know where you got your body, but you did not get your brains from me.' And I hear Sienkiewicz make a chuckle, more in embarrassment than anything, I guess, and I look up at Kazik and he is giving this little smile, only I was not surprised that this look on his face seemed to share my father's contempt. You may as well know now, Stingo, about another lie I told you weeks ago. I really had no love for Kazik either at that time, I had no more love for my husband than for a stone-faced stranger I had never seen before in my life. Such an abundance of lies I have given you, Stingo! I am the avatar of *menteuses* . . .

"On and on my father go about my intelligence, or failure of it, and I felt my face burning, but I shut up my ears, turned my hearing off. Papa, Papa, I remember saying to myself, *please,* all I want is a cup of tea! Then my father stopped attacking me and went back to reading the manuscript. And I was suddenly very frightened sitting there, looking down at my hands. It was cold. This café, it was like a premonition of hell. I heard people murmuring on all sides of me, and it all seemed to be in this hurtful key of a profound minor, like one of Beethoven's final quarters, you know, like grief, and there was this . . . this *clammy* wind sighing outside on the streets, and I suddenly realized that around me everyone was whispering about the coming war. I thought I could almost hear guns somewhere far-off, on the horizon past the city. I felt a deep fright and I wanted to get up and run away, but all I could do was sit there. Finally I heard my father ask Sienkiewicz how long it would be for the printing, rush job, and Sienkiewicz said the day after tomorrow. Then I realized that my father was talking to Kazik about the distribution of the pamphlets to the faculty of the university. Most of the pamphlets he was planning to send to places in Poland and in Germany and Austria, but he wanted a few hundred of the pamphlets which was in Polish to be passed around among the faculty—passed around by hand. And I realized that he was telling Kazik—*telling* I say, because he have him under the thumb just like me—that he wanted him to distribute the pamphlets personally at the university as soon as they were printed. Only he would of course need help. And I heard my father say, 'Sophie will help you pass them out.'

"And then I realized that almost the one single thing on earth that I did not want to be forced to do was to be *impliquée* any more with that pamphlet. And it make me revolted to think that I must go around the university with a stack of these things, giving them to the professors. But just as my father said this—'Sophie will help you pass them out'—I knew that I *would* be there with Kazik, passing out these sheets just like I done everything he told me to do since I was a little girl, running these errands, bringing him things, learning to use the typewriter and knowing shorthand just so he could use me whenever he wanted. And this terrible emptiness come over me when I realize just then there was nothing I could do about it, no way of saying no, no way possible to say, 'Papa, I'm not going to help you spread this thing.' But you see, Stingo, there is a truth I must tell you that even now I can't understood or truly make clear. Because maybe it look much better if I said I would not help pass out this thing of my father's just because I finally see he is saying in it: Murder Jews. That was bad I knew, terrible, and even then I couldn't hardly believe this was actually what he'd written.

"But to be truthful, it was something else. It was at last coming clear to me that this man, this father, this man which give me breath and flesh have no more feeling for me than a servant, some peasant or slave, and now with not a word of thanks for all my work was going to make me . . . grovel?—yes, grovel through the halls of the university like some newspaper vendor, once more doing what he said just because he said I must do it. And I was a grown woman and I wanted to play Bach, and at that moment I just thought I must die—I mean, to die not so much for what he was making me do but because I had no way of saying no. No way of saying—oh, you know, Stingo—'Fuck you, Papa.' Just then he said, 'Zosia,' and I looked up and he was smiling at me a little, I could see his two false teeth shining, and the smile was pleasant and he said, 'Zosia, wouldn't you like a cup of tea?' And I said, 'No, thank you, Papa.' Then he said, 'Come, Zosia, you must have some tea, you look pale and cold.' I wanted to fly away on wings. I said, 'No, thank you, Papa, I really don't want any tea.' And at that time to keep control I was biting the inside of my lip so hard that the blood came, and I could taste it like seawater on my tongue. He turned to talk to Kazik then. And it happened, this sharp stab of hatred. It went through me with this surprising quick pain and I got dizzy and I thought I might fall to the floor. I was hot all over, in a blaze. I said to myself: *I hate him*—with a kind of terrible wonder at the hatred which entered into me. It was incredible, the surprise of this hatred, only with awful pain—like a butcher knife in my heart."

Poland is a beautiful, heart-wrenching, soul-split country which in many ways (I came to see through Sophie's eyes and memory that summer, and through my own eyes in later years) resembles or conjures up images of the American South—or at least the South of other, not-so-distant times. It is not alone that forlornly lovely, nostalgic landscape which creates the frequent likeness—the quagmiry but haunting monochrome of the Narew River swampland, for example, with its look and feel of a murky savanna on the Carolina coast, or the Sunday hush on a muddy back street in a village of Galicia, where by only the smallest eyewink of the imagination one might see whisked to a lonesome crossroads hamlet in Arkansas these ramshackle, weather-bleached little houses, crookedly carpentered, set upon shrubless plots of clay where scrawny chickens fuss and peck—but in the spirit of the nation, her indwellingly ravaged and melancholy heart, tormented into its shape like that of the Old South out of adversity, penury and defeat.

Imagine, if you will, a land in which carpetbaggers swarmed not for a decade or so but for millennia and you will come to understand just one aspect of a Poland stomped upon with metronomic tedium and regularity by the French, the Swedes, the Austrians, Prussians, Russians, and possessed by even such greedy incubuses as the Turks. Despoiled and exploited like the South, and like it, a poverty-ridden, agrarian, feudal society, Poland has shared with the Old South one bulwark against its immemorial humiliation, and that is pride. Pride and the recollection of vanished glories. Pride in ancestry and family name, and also, one must remember, in a largely factitious aristocracy, or nobility. The names Radziwill and Ravenel are pronounced with the same intense albeit slightly hollow hauteur. In defeat both Poland and the American South bred a frenzied nationalism. Yet, indeed, even leaving aside these most powerful resemblances, which are very real and which find their origin in similar historical fountains (there should be added: an entrenched religious hegemony, authoritarian and puritanical in spirit), one discovers more superficial yet sparkling cultural correspondences: the passion for horseflesh and military titles, domination over women (along with a sulky-sly lechery), a tradition of storytelling, addiction to the blessings of firewater. And being the butt of mean jokes.

Finally there is a sinister zone of likeness between Poland and the American South which, although anything but superficial, causes the two cultures to blend so perfectly together as to seem almost one in their shared extravagance—and that has to do with the matter of race, which in both worlds has produced centuries-long, all-encompassing nightmare spells of schizophrenia. In Poland and the South the abiding presence of race has created at the same instant cruelty and compassion, bigotry and understanding, enmity and fellowship, exploitation and sacrifice, searing hatred and hopeless love. While it may be said that the darker and uglier of these opposing conditions has usually carried the day, there must also be recorded in the name of truth a long chronicle in which decency and honor were at moments able to controvert the absolute dominion of the reigning evil, more often than not against rather large odds, whether in Poznan or Yazoo City.

Thus when Sophie originally spun out her fairy tale regarding her father's hazardous mission to protect some Jews of Lublin, she surely must have known that she was not asking me to believe the impossible; that Poles on numberless occasions in the near and distant past risked their lives to save Jews from whatever oppressor is a simple matter of fact beyond argument, and even though at that time I had small information about such things, I was not inclined to doubt Sophie, who, struggling with the demon of her own schizoid conscience, chose to throw upon the Professor a falsely beneficent, even heroic light. But if Poles by the thousands have sheltered Jews, hidden Jews, laid down their lives for Jews, they have also at times, in the agony of their conjugate discord, persecuted them with undeviating savagery; it was within this continuum of the Polish spirit that Professor Biegański properly belonged, and it was there that Sophie had eventually to reinstate him for my benefit, in order to interpret the happenings at Auschwitz . . .

The subsequent history of the Professor's pamphlet is well worth recording. Obeying her father to the end, Sophie together with Kazik did spread the pamphlet around in the university hallways, but it turned out to be a decisive flop. In the first place, the members of the faculty, like everyone else in Cracow, were too preoccupied with their apprehension over the coming war—then only months away—to be much concerned with the Biegański message. Hell was beginning to erupt. The Germans were demanding the annexation of Gdansk, agitating for a "corridor"; while Neville Chamberlain still dithered, the Huns were clamoring in the west, shaking the flimsy Polish gates. The cobbled, ancient streets of Cracow became filled daily with the hum of a subdued panic. Under the circumstances, how could even the most committed racists among the faculty be diverted by the Professor's cunning dialectics? There was too much in the air of a sense of onrushing doom for anyone to be diverted by such a shopworn crotchet as the oppression of Jews.

At the moment all Poland felt potentially oppressed. Moreover, the Professor had made some basic miscalculations, so grossly off kilter as to call into question his guiding judgment. It was not only his sordid insertion of the issue of *Vernichtung*—even the most hidebound of the teachers had no stomach for such a notion, presented in whatever Swiftian mode of corrosive ridicule—but it was that Third Reich worship and pan-Germanic rapture of his which at this late date would make him blind and deaf to his colleagues' own throbbing, heartfelt patriotism. Sophie eventually saw that only a few years before, during Poland's Fascist resurgence, her father might have gained some converts; now with the Wehrmacht edging ponderously eastward, these Teutonic screams for Gdansk, the Germans provoking incidents along all the borders, how could it be other than a sublime foolishness to ask whether National Socialism had the answer to anything except Polish destruction? The upshot of the matter was that while the Professor and his pamphlet were generally ignored in the accelerating chaos, he also received a couple of unexpected nasty licks. Two young graduate students, members of the Polish army reserve, roughed him up badly in a university vestibule, breaking a finger, and one night Sophie recalled something shattering the dining-room window—a large paving block painted with a spidery black swastika.

But as a patriot he hardly deserved that, and at least one

small thing might be said on the Professor's behalf. He did not (and of this Sophie said she was certain) create his sermon with the idea in mind specifically to curry favor with the Nazis. The piece had been written from the particular viewpoint of Polish culture, and besides, the Professor was by his own lights too principled a thinker, a man too committed to the broader philosophical truths for it to have entered his mind that he might eventually try to make the pamphlet serve as an instrument of his personal advancement, not to speak of his corporeal salvation. (As a matter of fact, the exigencies of the approaching conflict prevented the essay from appearing in Germany in any form.) Nor was Professor Biegański a true quisling, a collaborator in the now accepted sense of the word, since when the country was invaded that September and Cracow, virtually unharmed, became the seat of government for all Poland, it was not with the intent to betray his fatherland that he sought to offer his services to the Governor General, Hitler's friend Hans Frank (and a distinguished lawyer like the Professor himself), but only as an advisor and expert in a field where Poles and Germans had a mutual adversary and a profound common interest —*die Judenfrage*. There was doubtless even a certain idealism in his effort.

Loathing her father now, loathing his lackey—her husband—almost as much, Sophie would slip by their murmuring shapes in the house hallway as the Professor, suavely tailored in his frock coat, his glamorous graying locks beautifully barbered and fragrant of *Kölnischwasser*, prepared to sally forth on his morning supplicatory rounds. But he must not have washed his scalp. She recalled the dandruff on his splendid shoulders. His murmurings combined fretfulness and hope. His voice had an odd hiss. Surely today, even though the Governor General had refused to see him the day before—surely today (especially with his exquisite command of German) he would be greeted cordially by the head of the *Einsatzgruppe der Sicherheitspolizei,* with whom he had an entrée in the form of a letter from a mutual friend in Erfurt (a sociologist, a leading Nazi theoretician on the Jewish problem), and who could not fail to be further impressed by these credentials, these honorary degrees (on authentic parchment) from Heidelberg and Leipzig, this bound volume of collected essays published in Mainz, *Die polnische Judenfrage,* et cetera and so on. Surely today . . .

Alas for the Professor, although he petitioned and canvassed and hustled, presenting himself to a dozen offices in as many days, his increasingly frenzied efforts came to naught. It must have been a wicked blow to him to get not a moment's attention, to gain no bureaucratic ear. But the Professor had grievously miscalculated in still another way. Emotionally and intellectually he was the romantic inheritor of the Germanic culture of another century, of a time irreparably gone and fallen away, and thus he had no inkling of how impossible it would be to try to ingratiate himself in his antiquated costumery within the corridors of this stainless-steel, jackbooted, mammoth modern power, the first technocratic state, with its *Regulierungen und Gesetzverordnungen,* its electrified filing-card systems and classification procedures, its faceless chains of command and mechanical methods of data processing, decoding devices, telephonic scrambling, hot line to Berlin—all working with blinding speed and with no accommodation whatever for an obscure Polish teacher of law and his sheaf of documents, his snowfall of dandruff, flashing bicuspids, dopey-looking spats and a carnation in his lapel. The Professor was one of the first victims of the Nazi war machine to become a victim simply because he was not "programmed"—it was almost as uncomplicated as that. Almost, one might say, yet not quite, for the other important reason for his rejection was the fact that he was a *Polack,* a German word which has the same sneeringly contemptuous meaning in German as it has in English. Since he was a Polack and at the same time an academic, his overly anxious, beaming, avidly suppliant face was hardly more welcome around Gestapo headquarters than that of a typhoid carrier, but the Professor clearly did not know how far he was behind the times.

And although he could not have realized it as he scuttled about during those days of early fall, the clock was ticking remorselessly away toward his end. Under the indifferent eye of the Nazi Moloch he was another doomed cipher. So on the wet gray morning in November when Sophie, kneeling alone in St. Mary's church, had that premonition she earlier described and leaped up and rushed back to the university—there to discover the glorious medieval courtyard cordoned off by German troops who held one hundred and eighty faculty members captive beneath their rifles and machine guns—the Professor and Kazik were among the unlucky ones shivering in the cold, hands clawing at the heavens. But she never laid eyes on them again. In the later, emended (and, I am convinced, truthful) version of her story she told me she felt no real bereavement over the seizure of her father and husband—she was by this time too alienated from both of them for it to affect her deeply—but she was forced to feel on another level shock that hammered at her bones, glacial fear and a devastating sense of loss. Her entire sense of self—of her identity—was unfastened. For if the Germans could commit this obscene assault on score upon score of defenseless and unsuspecting teachers, it was the forerunner of God only knew what horrors awaiting Poland in the coming years. And it was for that reason alone if for nothing else that she hurled herself sobbing into her mother's arms. Her mother was genuinely shattered. A sweet, unthinking, submissive woman, she had retained a faithful love for her husband to the very end; through the dumbshow of the sorrow Sophie simulated for her benefit she could not help but grieve for her mother's grief.

As for the Professor—sucked like a mere larva into the burial mound of KL Sachsenhausen, dismal clone of the insensate leviathan of human affliction spawned years before at KL Dachau—his efforts to extricate himself were in vain. And it becomes all the more ironic since it is plain that the Germans had unwittingly imprisoned and doomed a man whom later they might have considered a major prophet—the eccentric Slavic philosopher whose vision of the "final solution" antedated that of Eichmann and his confederates (even perhaps of Adolf Hitler, the dreamer and conceiver of it all), and who had the message tangibly in his possession. *"Ich habe meine Flugschrift,"* he wrote piteously to Sophie's mother in a smuggled note, the only communication they ever received, "I have my pamphlet. *Ich verstehe nicht, warum* . . . I cannot understand why I am unable to get through to the authorities here and make them see . . ."

The hold of mortal flesh, and of mortal love, is bewilderingly strong, never so fierce as when love is lodged in childhood memory: strolling along beside her, running his fingers through the tangles of her yellow hair, he had once taken her for a ride in a pony cart amid the summery morning fragrance and birdsong of the gardens below Wawel Castle. Sophie remembered this and could not smother a moment of scalding anguish when the news of his death came and she saw him falling, falling—protesting to the last that they had the wrong man—in a fusillade of hot bullets against a wall in Sachsenhausen.

Ten

Deep in the ground and surrounded by thick stone walls, the basement of Höss's house where Sophie slept was one of the very few places in the camp into which there never penetrated the smell of burning human flesh. This was one of the reasons that she sought its shelter as often as she could, despite the fact that the part of the basement reserved for her straw pallet was damp and ill-lit and stank of rot and mold. Somewhere behind the walls there was an incessant trickle of water in the pipes from the drains and toilets upstairs, and occasionally she was disturbed at night by the furry, shadowy visit of a rat. But all in all this dim purgatory was a far better place to be than any of the barracks—even the one where for the previous six months she had lived with several dozen other relatively privileged female prisoners who worked in the camp offices. Although spared in those confines most of the brutality and destitution which was the lot of the common inmate throughout the rest of the camp, there had been constant noise and no privacy, and she had suffered most from an almost continual lack of sleep. In addition, she had never been able to keep herself clean. Here, however, she shared her quarters with only a handful of prisoners. And of the several seraphic luxuries afforded by the basement, one was its proximity to a laundry room. Sophie made grateful use of these facilities; indeed, she would have been required to use them, since the mistress of the mansion, Hedwig Höss, possessed a Westphalian hausfrau's phobia about dirt and made certain that any of the prisoners lodged beneath her roof keep clothing and person not merely clean but hygienic: potent antiseptics were prescribed for the laundry water and the prisoners domiciled in Haus Höss went around smelling of germicide. There was still another reason for this: Frau Kommandant was deathly afraid of the camp's contagions.

Another precious amenity which Sophie found and embraced in the cellar was sleep, or at least its possibility. Next to food and privacy, the lack of sleep was one of the camp's leading and universal deficiencies; sought by all with a greed that approached lust, sleep allowed the only sure escape from ever-abiding torment, and strangely enough (or perhaps not so strangely) usually brought pleasant dreams, for as Sophie observed to me once, people so close to madness would be driven utterly mad if, escaping a nightmare, they confronted still another in their slumber. So because of the quiet and isolation in the Höss basement Sophie had been able for the first time in months to sleep and to immerse herself in the tidal ebb and flow of dreams.

The basement had been partitioned into two parts roughly down the center. Seven or eight male prisoners were quartered on the other side of the wooden wall; mostly Polish, they worked upstairs as handymen or as dishwashers in the kitchen, and a couple were gardeners. Except in passing, the men and women rarely mingled. Besides herself, there were three female prisoners on Sophie's side of the partition. Two of these were Jewish dressmakers, middle-aged sisters from Liège. Living testimony of the easy expediency in which the Germans often indulged, the sisters had been spared the gas solely because of their energetic yet delicate artistry with needle and thread. They were the special favorites of Frau Höss, who together with her three daughters was the beneficiary of their talents; all day long they stitched and hemmed and refurbished much of the fancier clothing taken from Jews who had gone to the gas chambers. They had been in the house for many months and had grown complacent and plump, their sedentary labor allowing them to acquire a suetlike avoirdupois bizarre-looking amid this fellowship of emaciated flesh. Under Hedwig's patronage they seemed to have lost all fear of the future, and appeared to Sophie perfectly good-humored and composed as they stitched away in a second-floor sunroom, peeling off labels and markers stamped Cohen and Lowenstein and Adamowitz from expensive furs and fabric freshly cleaned and only hours removed from the boxcars. They spoke little, and in a Belgian cadence Sophie found harsh and odd to the ear.

The other occupant of Sophie's dungeon was an asthmatic woman named Lotte, also of middle years, a Jehovah's Witness from Koblenz. Like the Jewish seamstresses, she was another of fortune's darlings and had been saved from death by injection or some slow torture in the "hospital" in order to serve as governess to the Hösses' two youngest children. A gaunt, slab-shaped creature with a prognathous jaw and enormous hands, she resembled outwardly some of the brutish female guards who had been sent to the camp from KL Ravensbrück, one of whom assaulted Sophie savagely early after her arrival. But Lotte had an amiable, generous disposition that refuted the look of menace. She had acted as a big sister, offering Sophie important advice as to how to behave in the mansion, along with several valuable observations concerning the Commandant and his ménage. She said in particular watch yourself around the housekeeper, Wilhelmine. A mean sort, Wilhelmine was a prisoner herself, a German who had served time for forgery. She lived in two rooms upstairs. Kiss her ass, Lotte advised Sophie, lick her ass good and you won't have no trouble. As for Höss himself, he, too, liked to be flattered, but you had to be less obvious about it; he wasn't anybody's fool.

A simple soul, utterly devout, practically illiterate, Lotte seemed to weather the unholy winds of Auschwitz like a crude, sturdy ship, serene in her terrible faith. She did not try to proselytize, only intimating to Sophie that for the suffering of her own imprisonment she would find ample reward in Jehovah's Kingdom. The rest, including Sophie, would certainly go to hell. But there was no vindictiveness in this pronouncement, any more than there was in the remarks Lotte made when—short of breath one morning, panting and pausing with Sophie on the first-floor landing as they ascended to their labors—she sniffed that ambient odor of the Birkenau funeral pyre and murmured that those Jews deserved it. They had earned the mess they were in. After all, wasn't it the Jews who were Jehovah's first betrayers? "Root of all evil, *die Hebräer,*" she wheezed.

On the brink of waking that morning of the day I have already begun to describe, the tenth day she had worked for the Commandant in his attic and the one upon which she had made up her mind to try to seduce him—or if not precisely to seduce him (ambiguous thought), then otherwise to bend him to her will and scheme—just before her eyes fluttered open in the cobwebbed gloom of the cellar, she was conscious of the harsh labor of Lotte's asthmatic breathing from her pallet against the opposite wall. Then Sophie came awake with a jolt, through heavy eyelids perceiving the great heap of a body three feet away, recumbent beneath a moth-eaten woolen blanket. Sophie would have reached out to poke Lotte in the ribs as she had more than once before, but although the scrape of shuffling feet on the floor of the kitchen above told her it was morning, nearly time for all of them to be up and about, she thought: Let her sleep. Then like a swimmer plunging toward benevolent, amniotic depths, Sophie tried to fall back into that dream she had had just before she awakened.

She had been a little girl climbing, a dozen years before, in the Dolomites with her cousin Krystyna; chattering in French, they had been searching for edelweiss. Dark and misty peaks soared up around them. Baffling, like all dreams, touched with shadowy peril, the vision had also been almost unbearably sweet. Above them the milky-white flower had beckoned from the rocks and Krystyna, preceding her up a dizzying path, had called back, "Zosia, I'll bring it down!" Then Krystyna seemed to slip and, in a shower of pebbles, to be on the edge of falling: the dream became murky with terror. Sophie prayed for Krystyna as she would for herself: Angel of God, guardian angel, stay by her side . . . She uttered the prayer over and over again. Angel, don't let her fall! Suddenly the dream was flooded with alpine sunlight and Sophie looked up. Serene and triumphant, framed in a golden aureole of light, the child smiled down at Sophie, securely perched on a mossy promontory, clutching the sprig of edelweiss. *"Zosia, je l'ai trouvé!"* Krystyna cried. And in the dream her feeling of averted evil, of safety, of answered prayer and jubilant resurrection was so piercingly hurtful that when she came awake, hearing Lotte's noise, her eyes stung with salty tears. Then her eyelids had closed again and her head had fallen back in a futile attempt to recapture her phantasmal joy when she felt Bronek roughly shaking her shoulder.

"I've got good grub for you ladies this morning," Bronek said. Cued to the Germanic punctiliousness of the manse, he had arrived exactly on schedule. In a battered copper pan he carried the food, almost invariably leftovers from the Höss dinner table of the night before. It was always cold, this morning provender (as if to feed pets, the female cook left it in the pan each night by the kitchen door, from whence Bronek fetched it at daybreak), and usually consisted of a greasy potpourri of bones with bits of meat and gristle attached, crusts of bread (on propitious days smeared with a little margarine), vegetable remnants and sometimes a half-eaten apple or pear. By comparison with the food fed to the prisoners in the camp at large, this was a sumptuous meal; indeed, it was a banquet in terms of mere quantity, and since this breakfast was occasionally augmented, inexplicably, by such tidbits as canned sardines or a hunk of Polish sausage, it simply was assumed that the Commandant had seen to it that his household staff would not starve. Furthermore, although Sophie had to share her pan with Lotte, and the two Jewish sisters ate in the same way, face to face as over a kennel pail, they were each supplied with an aluminum spoon—an almost unheard-of daintiness for inmates anywhere else behind the wires.

Sophie heard Lotte wake with a groan, muttering disconnected syllabics, perhaps some matutinal invocation to Jehovah, in a sepulchral Rhenish accent. Bronek, thrusting the pan down between them, said, "Look there—what's left of a pig's shank, with meat on it still. Plenty of bread. Also some fine bits of cabbage. I knew you girls would get fed good the minute I heard yesterday that Schmauser was coming to dinner." The handyman, pale and bald in the silvery filtering light, all angular limbs and joints like a mantis, switched from Polish to his crippled clownish German—this for Lotte's benefit as he goosed her with his elbow. *"Aufwecken, Lotte!"* he whispered hoarsely. *"Auf-*

wecken, mein schöne Blume, mein kleine Engel!" Were Sophie ever disposed to laughter, this running by-play between Bronek and the elephantine governess, who plainly enjoyed his attentions, would have come as close as anything to providing her with comic relief.

"Come awake, my little Bible-worm," Bronek persisted, and at this moment Lotte roused herself and sat up. Bleared with sleep, her slab of a face looked monstrous yet ethereally placid and benign, like one of those Easter Island effigies. Then without a moment's hesitation she began to slurp up the food.

Sophie held back for a moment. She knew that Lotte, a godly soul, would take only her share, and so luxuriated in the space of time before she would eat her own portion. She salivated with pleasure at the sight of the slimy mess in the pan and blessed the name Schmauser. He was an SS Obergruppenführer, the equivalent of a lieutenant general and Höss's superior from Wroclaw; his visit had been bruited about the house for days. And thus Bronek's theory had proved to be accurate: get a real bigwig in the house, he had kept saying, and Höss will lay on such a fine feed that there will be enough left over so even the cockroaches will get sick.

"What's it like out, Bronek?" said Lotte between mouthfuls of food. Like Sophie, she knew that he had a farmer's nose for weather.

"Cool. Wind from the west. Sunny now and then. But lots of low clouds. They keep the air down. The air stinks now but it might get better. A lot of Jews going up the chimney. My darling Sophie, please eat." He spoke the last in Polish, grinning, revealing pink gums in which the stubs of three or four teeth protruded like raw white slivers.

Bronek's career at Auschwitz coincided with the history of the camp itself. By happenstance, he was one of its early novitiates, and had begun working in Haus Höss shortly after his incarceration. He was an ex-farmer from the vicinity of Miastko, in the far north. Most of his teeth had fallen out as a result of his involvement in a vitamin-deficiency experiment; like a rat or guinea pig, he had been systematically deprived of ascorbic acid and other essentials until the expected ruination in his mouth: it may have also made him a little daft. Whatever, he had been struck by the preternatural luck that came down on certain prisoners for no good reason at all, like a lightning bolt. Ordinarily, he would have been put away after such a trial, a useless husk sped into the night by a quick injection in the heart. But he possessed a farmer's resilience and a really extraordinary vigor. Save for his destroyed teeth, he displayed almost none of the symptoms of scurvy—lassitude, weakness, weight loss, and so on—which were predicted under the circumstances. He remained as hardy as a billygoat, which brought him under the bemused scrutiny of the SS doctors and, in a roundabout way, to the attention of Höss. Asked to take a look at this phenomenon, Höss did so, and in their fleeting encounter something about Bronek—perhaps only the language he spoke, the droll garbled German of an uneducated Pole from Pomerania—caught the Commandant's fancy. He moved Bronek into the protection of his house, where he had worked ever since, enjoying certain small privileges, leeway to wander through the premises picking up gossip, and that general exemption from constant surveillance that is granted a pet or favorite—and there are such favorites in all slave societies. He was an expert scrounger, and from time to time came up with the most remarkable surprises in the way of food, usually from mysterious sources. More important, Sophie learned, Bronek, despite his outward simple-mindedness, was in day-to-day touch with the camp itself, and was a trusted informant of one of the strongest Polish Resistance groups.

The two dressmakers stirred in the shadows across the floor. *"Bonjour, mesdames,"* Bronek called cheerily. "Your breakfast is coming." He turned back to Sophie. "I also got you some figs," he said, "real figs, imagine that!"

"Where did you get *figs?"* Sophie said. She felt startled delight as Bronek handed her this indescribable treasure; although dried and wrapped in cellophane, they had a marvelous warm heft in her palm, and lifting the package to her face, she saw the streaks of delectable juice congealed on the grayish-green skin, inhaled the distant voluptuous aroma, faded but still sweet, phantom fragrance of the mellow fruit. She had once tasted real figs years before in Italy. Her stomach responded with a joyous noise. She had never had the remotest prospect of any such luxury in months—no, years. *Figs!* "Bronek, I don't believe it!" she exclaimed.

"Save them for later," he said, giving another package to Lotte, "don't eat them all at once. Eat this shit from up above first. It's swill, but it's the best swill you'll have for a long time. Fit for the pigs I used to raise in Pomorze."

Bronek was a non-stop talker. Sophie listened to the stream of chitchat while she greedily gnawed at the chill and stringy stump of pork. It was scorched, cartilaginous and vile. But her taste buds responded, as if slaked with ambrosia, to the small bursting pods and pockets of fat which her body clamored for. She could have gorged herself on any grease. Fancifully, her mind's eye re-created the feast at which Bronek last night had scurried about as busboy: the lordly suckling pig, the dumplings, the steaming potatoes, cabbage with chestnuts, the jams and jellies and gravies, a rich custard for dessert, all sluiced down the SS gullets with the help of portly bottles of Bull's Blood wine from Hungary, and served (when a dignitary as lofty as an Obergruppenführer was present) upon a superb Czarist silver service shipped back from some museum ransacked on the eastern front. Apropos of which, Sophie realized, Bronek was now speaking in the tones of one proud to be privy to portentous tidings. "They keep trying to look happy," he said, "and for a while they seem to be. But then they get on the war, and it's all misery. Like last night Schmauser said the Russians were getting ready to recapture Kiev. Lots of other bad news from the Russian front. Then it's rotten news in Italy too, so said Schmauser. The British and the Americans are moving up there, everyone dying like lice." Bronek rose from his crouch, moving with his other pan toward the two sisters. "But the real big news, ladies, is something you may not hardly believe, but it's the truth—*Rudi* is *leaving!* Rudi is being transferred back to Berlin!"

In mid-swallow, gulping down the gristly meat, Sophie nearly choked on these words. *Leaving?* Höss leaving the camp! It couldn't be true! She rose to a sitting position and clutched at Bronek's sleeve. "Are you sure?" she demanded. "Bronek, are you sure of that?"

"All I'm telling you is what I heard Schmauser say to Rudi after the other officers had left. Said he'd done a fine job but that he was needed at Berlin Central Office. So he could get himself ready for immediate transfer."

"What do you mean—*immediate?*" she persisted. "Today, next month, what?"

"I don't know," Bronek replied, "he just plainly meant soon." His voice became tinged with foreboding. "Me, I'm not happy about it, I'll tell you." He paused somberly. "I mean, who knows who'll take his place? Some *sadist* maybe, you know. Some *gorilla!* Then maybe Bronek too . . . ?" He rolled his eyes and drew his forefinger across his throat. "He could have had me put away, he could have given me a little gas, like the Jews—they were doing that then, you know—but he brought me here and treated me like a human being. Don't think I won't be sorry to see Rudi go."

But Sophie, preoccupied, paid no more attention to Bronek. She was panicked by this news of Höss's departure. It made her realize that she must act with urgency and dispatch if she was to persuade him to take notice of her and thus try to accomplish through him what she had set out to do. For the following hour or so, toiling alongside Lotte over the Höss household laundry (the prisoners in the house were spared the lethally grueling and interminable roll calls of the rest of the camp; luckily, Sophie was compelled only to wash the vast heaps of soiled clothing from upstairs—abnormally plenteous because of Frau Höss's fixation about germs and filth), she fantasized all manner of little skits and playlets in which she and the Commandant had finally been drawn into some intimate connection whereby she was able to pour out the story that would lead to her redemption. But time had begun to work against her. Unless she moved immediately and perhaps even a little recklessly, he might be gone and all she planned to accomplish would come to nothing. Her anxiety was excruciating, and it was somehow irrationally mixed up with hunger.

She had secreted the package of figs in the loose inside hem of her striped smock. At a little before eight o'clock, nearly the time when she had to make her way up the four flights of stairs to the office in the attic, she could resist no longer the urge to eat some of the figs. She stole away to a large cubbyhole underneath the stairs where she would be out of sight of the other prisoners. And there she frantically broke open the cellophane. A film of tears misted her eyes as the tender small globes of fruit (slightly moist and deliciously textured in their chewy sweetness that mingled with archipelagos of minute seeds) slid richly down her throat, one by one; wild with delight, unashamed at her piggishness and the sugary saliva drooling over fingers and chin, she devoured them all. Her eyes were still misted over and she heard herself panting with pleasure. Then after standing there for a moment in the shadows to let the figs settle on her stomach and to compose her expression, she began to ascend slowly to the upper levels of the house. It was a climb of no more than a few minutes' duration but one which was interrupted by two singularly memorable occurrences that seemed to fit with ghastly appropriateness into the hallucinatory fabric of her mornings, afternoons and nights at Haus Höss . . .

On separate landings—one on the floor above the basement and the other just below the attic—there were dormer windows that gave off on a western exposure, from which Sophie usually tried to avert her eyes, though not always successfully. This view contained some nondescript subjects—in the foreground a brown grassless drill field, a small wooden barracks, the electrified wires hemming in an incongruous stand of graceful poplars—but it also presented a glimpse of the railroad platform where the selections were made. Invariably, lines of boxcars stood waiting there, dun-colored backdrop to blurred, confounding tableaux of cruelty, mayhem and madness. The platform dwelt in the middle distance, too near to be ignored, too far away to be seen with clarity. It may have been, she later recounted, her own arrival there on that concrete *quai*, and its associations for her, that caused her to shun the scene, to turn her eyes away, to blot out of her sight the fragmentary and flickering apparitions which from this vantage point registered only imperfectly, like the grainy shadow-shapes in an antique silent newsreel: a rifle butt raised skyward, dead bodies being yanked from boxcar doors, a papier-mâché human being bullied to the earth.

Sometimes she sensed that there was no violence at all, and got only a terrible impression of order, throngs of people moving in shambling docile parade out of sight.

The platform was too distant for sound; the music of the loony-bin prisoner band which greeted each arriving train, the shouts of the guards, the barking of the dogs—all these were mute, though upon occasion it was impossible not to hear the crack of a pistol shot. Thus the drama seemed to be enacted in a charitable vacuum, from which were excluded the wails of grief, cries of terror and other noises of that infernal initiation. It was for this reason perhaps, Sophie thought as she climbed the steps, that she succumbed from time to time to an occasional irresistible peek—doing so now, seeing only the string of boxcars newly arrived, as yet unloaded. SS guards in swirls of steam surrounded the train. She knew from manifests which had been received by Höss the day before that this was the second of two trainloads containing 2,100 Jews from Greece.

Then, her curiosity satisfied, she turned away and opened the door to the salon through which she had to pass to reach the upper stairway. From the Stromberg Carlson phonograph a contralto voice enveloped the room in a lover's hectic grievance, while Wilhelmine, the housekeeper, stood listening to it, audibly humming as she pawed through a stack of silken female underwear. She was alone. The room was flooded with sunlight.

Wilhelmine (Sophie noticed, trying to hurry through) was wearing one of her mistress's hand-me-down robes, pink slippers with huge pink pompons, and her henna-dyed hair was in curlers. The face seemed aflame with rouge. The humming was extravagantly off-key. She turned as Sophie edged past, fixing her with a look that seemed not at all unpleasant, which was a difficult trick, since the face itself was the most unpleasant she had ever beheld. (Intrusive as it may appear now, and possibly lacking in graphic persuasion, I cannot resist repeating Sophie's Manichean reflection of that summer and let it go at that: "If you ever write about this, Stingo, just say that this Wilhelmine was the only beautiful woman I ever saw—no, she was not beautiful really, but good-looking with these hard good looks that some streetwalkers have—the only good-looking woman that the evil inside her had caused this absolute ugliness. I can't describe her any more than that. It was some kind of total ugliness. I look at her and the blood turn to ice inside me.") *"Guten Morgen,"* Sophie whispered, pressing on. But Wilhelmine suddenly arrested her with a sharp "Wait!" German is a loud language anyway, the voice was like a shout.

Sophie turned to confront the housekeeper; oddly, although they had often seen each other, it was the first time they had ever spoken. Despite her unthreatening countenance now, the woman inspired apprehension; Sophie felt the pulse racing in both wrists, her mouth dried up instantly. *"Nur nicht aus Liebe weinen,"* mourned the querulous, lachrymal voice, the scratches on the shellac amplified, echoing from wall to wall. A sparkling galaxy of dust motes swam through the slanting early light, shimmering up and down across the lofty room crowded with its armoires and desks, its gilt sofas and cabinets and chairs. It's not even a museum, thought Sophie, it's a monstrous warehouse. Suddenly Sophie realized that the salon reeked heavily of disinfectant, like her own smock. The housekeeper was weirdly abrupt. "I want to give you something," she cooed, smiling, fingering the stack of underwear. The filmy mound of silken underpants, looking freshly cleaned, rested on the surface of a marble-top commode inlaid with colored wood and ornamented in strips and scrolls of bronze; a huge and hulking thing, it would have grossly obtruded at Versailles, where in fact it may have been stolen from. "Bronek brought them last night straight from the cleaning unit," she continued in her strident singsong. "Frau Höss likes to give a lot of them to the prisoners. I know you're not issued underwear, and Lotte's been complaining that those uniforms scratch so around the bottom." Sophie let out her breath. With no chagrin, no shock, not even with revelation, the thought flew through her mind like a sparrow: They're all from dead Jews. "They're very, very clean. Some of these are made of marvelous sheer silk, I've seen nothing like them since the war began. What size do you wear? I'll bet you don't even know." The eyes flashed indecently.

It had all happened too fast, this sudden gratuitous charity, for Sophie to make immediate sense of it, but soon she had an inkling and she was truly alarmed—alarmed as much by the way Wilhelmine had all but pounced upon her (for now she realized this is what she had done), lurking like a tarantula while she waited for her to emerge from the cellar, as by the precipitate offering of the rather ridiculous largess itself. "Doesn't that fabric chafe around your bottom?" she heard Wilhelmine ask her now, mezza voce and with a slight quaver that made everything more insinuating and flirtatious than her suggestive eyes, or the words that had caused her at first to take warning: *I'll bet you don't even know.*

"Yes . . ." said Sophie, fiercely uneasy. "*No!* I don't know."

"Come," she murmured, beckoning toward an alcove. It was a shadowy space sheltered behind a Pleyel concert grand piano. "Come, let's try a pair on." Sophie moved unresistingly forward, and felt the light touch of Wilhelmine's fingers on the edge of her smock. "I've been so interested in you. I've heard you speaking to the Commandant. You speak marvelous German, just like a native. The Commandant says you are Polish, but I don't really believe him, ha! You're too beautiful to be Polish." The words, vaguely feverish, spilled over one another as she maneuvered Sophie toward the nook in the wall, ominously filled with darkness. "All the Polish women here are so ordinary and plain, so *lumpig,* so trashy-looking. But you—you must be Swedish, aren't you? Of Swedish blood? You look more Swedish than anything, and I hear there are many people of Swedish blood in the north of Poland. Here we are now, where no one can see us and we can try on a pair of these undies. So your nice bottom will stay all white and soft."

Until this instant, hoping against hope, Sophie had said to herself that the woman's advances just *might* be innocuous, but now, so close, the signs of her voracious letch—first her rapid breathing and then the ripe rosiness spreading like a rash over the bestially handsome face, half Valkyrie, half gutter trull—left no doubt about her intentions. They were clumsy bait, those silk panties. And in a spasm of strange mirth it flashed across Sophie's mind that in this psychotically ordered and scheduled household the wretched woman could only have sex on the fly, so to speak, vertically in an alcove behind a mammoth grand piano during these fleetingly few, precious and unprogrammed minutes after breakfast when the children were just off to the garrison school and before the beginning of daily routine. All other hours of the day, down to the last clock-tick, were accounted for: *voilà!* for the desperate challenges, beneath a regulated SS roof, of a taste of Sapphic amour. *"Schnell, schnell, meine Süsse!"* Wilhelmine whispered, more insistently now. "Lift up your skirt a bit, darling . . . no, higher!"

The ogress lunged forward then and Sophie felt herself engulfed in pink flannel, rouged cheeks, henna hair—a reddish miasma stinking of French perfume. The housekeeper worked with the frenzy of a madwoman. She was busy with her hard sticky lupine tongue for only a second or two around Sophie's ear, fondled her breasts urgently, manhandled her buttocks, drew back with an expression of lust so intense that it was like some terminal anguish, then set about her serious labors, slumping earthward in genuflection and squeezing Sophie's hips roundabout with her arms. *Nur nicht aus Liebe weinen* . . . "Swedish kittycat . . . beautiful thing," she mumbled. "Ah, *bitte* . . . higher!" Having made her decision moments before, Sophie was not about to resist or protest—in a kind of headlong autohypnosis she had placed herself beyond revulsion, realizing in any case that she was as helpless as a crippled moth—and let her thighs, submissively, be spread apart as the brutish muzzle and the bullethead of a tongue probed into what, with some dull distant satisfaction, she realized was her obdurate dryness, as parched and without juice as desert sand. She rocked on her heels and raised her arms lazily and resistlessly akimbo, mainly aware now of the woman frantically fingering herself, the flaming becurlered mop of hair bobbing beneath like a huge shredded poppy. Then there was a booming noise from the other end of the huge room, a door was flung open and Höss's voice called, "Wilhelmine! Where are you? Frau Höss wants you in the bedroom."

The Commandant, who should have been in his attic office, had become briefly unpinned from his schedule, and the fear which his unexpected presence caused down below was transmitted instantly to Sophie, who thought that Wilhelmine's sudden spasmodic and agonizing clutch around her thighs might cause the two of them to topple and fall. Tongue and head slipped away. For moments her stricken adorer remained motionless as if paralyzed, the face rigid with fright. Then came blessed relief. Höss called again once, paused, cursed under his breath and quickly departed, stamping across the floor to the attic stairway. And the housekeeper fell apart from her, limp, flopped down in the shadows like a rag doll.

It was not until Sophie was on the stairs to the attic, moments later, that the reaction smote her, and she felt her legs go elastic and weak and she was forced to sit down. The mere fact of the assault was not what left her unstrung—it was nothing new, she had been nearly raped by a woman guard months before, shortly after her arrival—nor was it Wilhelmine's response in her mad scramble for safety after Höss had gone upstairs ("You must not tell the Commandant," she had said with a snarl, then repeated the same words as if imploring Sophie in abject fear, before scuttling out of the room. "He would kill us both!"). For a moment Sophie felt this compromising situation had in an obscure way given her an advantage over the housekeeper. Unless—unless (and the second thought caught her up short and made her sit tremblingly on the stairs) this convicted forger, who wielded so much power in the house, should seize upon that moment of thwarted venery as a way to get back at Sophie, work out her frustration by turning love into vengeance, run to the Commandant with some tale of wrongdoing (specifically, that it was the other prisoner who had initiated the seduction), and in this way shatter to bits the framework of Sophie's all-too-unsubstantial future. She knew, in the light of Höss's detestation of homosexuality, what would happen to her if such a scandal were fabricated, and suddenly felt—as had all her fellow trusty prisoners smothering in their fear-drenched limbo—the phantom needle squirting death into the center of her heart.

Squatting on the stairs, she bent forward and thrust her head into her hands. The confusion of thoughts roiling about in her mind caused her an anxiety she felt she could hardly bear. Was she better off now, after the episode with Wilhelmine, or was she in greater peril? She didn't know. The clarion camp whistle—reedy, harmonic, more or less in B minor and reminding her always of some partly recaptured, sorrow-sick, blowzy chord from *Tannhäuser*—

shattered the morning, signaling eight o'clock. She had never been late before to the attic but now she was going to be, and the thought of her tardiness and of the waiting Höss—who measured his days in milliseconds—filled her with terror. She rose to her feet and continued the climb upward, feeling feverish and unstrung. Too many things crushing down upon her all at once. Too many thoughts to sort out, too many swift shocks and apprehensions. If she didn't take hold of herself, make every effort to keep her composure, she knew she might simply collapse today like a puppet that has performed its jerky dance on strings, then, abandoned by its master, falls into a lifeless heap. A small nagging soreness across her pubic bone reminded her of the housekeeper's rummaging head.

Winded by the climb, she reached the landing on the floor beneath the Commandant's attic, where a partly opened window gave out once more upon the westward view with its barren drill field sloping toward the melancholy stand of poplars, beyond which stood the countless boxcars in drab file, smeared with the dust of Serbia and the Hungarian plains. Since her encounter with Wilhelmine the boxcar doors had been thrown open by the guards, and now hundreds more of the condemned voyagers from Greece milled about on the platform. Despite her haste, Sophie was compelled to halt and watch for an instant, drawn by morbidity and dread in equal measure. The poplar trees and the horde of SS guards obscured most of the scene. She could not clearly see the faces of the Greek Jews. Nor could she tell what they wore: mostly she saw a dull gray. But the platform did give off glints and flickers of multicolored garments, greens and blues and reds, a swirl and flourish here and there of bright Mediterranean hue, piercing her with vivid longing for that land she had never seen except in books and in her fancy and summoning up instantly the child's verse she remembered from the convent school—skinny Sister Barbara chanting in her comic pebbly Slavic French:

Ô que les îles de la Grèce sont belles!
Ô contempler la mer à l'ombre d'un haut figuier
et écouter tout autour les cris des hirondelles
voltigeant dans l'azur parmi les oliviers!

She thought she had long ago become used to the smell, at least resigned to it. But for the first time that day the sweet, pestilential stench of flesh consumed by fire assailed her nostrils with the ripe bluntness of an abattoir, so violently taking command of her senses that her eyes went out of focus and the throng on the distant platform—seeming for one last moment like some country festival viewed from afar—swam away from her vision. And involuntarily, with creeping horror and disgust, she raised her fingertips to her lips.

. . . la mer à l'ombre d'un haut figuier . . .

Thus, simultaneously with her awareness of where Bronek had obtained the fruit, the liquefied figs themselves came flooding up sourly in her throat, pouring out and spattering onto the floor between her feet. With a groan she thrust her head against the wall. She stood heaving and retching for long moments by the window. Then upon limp weak legs she sidled away from the mess she had made and fell to her hands and knees on the tiles, writhing in misery and riven by a feeling of strangeness and loss such as she had never known.

I'll never forget what she told me about this: she realized that she could not remember her own name. "Oh God, *help me!*" she called aloud. *"I don't know what I am!"* She remained for a while in that crouch, trembling as if in arctic cold.

Insanely, a cuckoo clock from the moon-faced daughter Emmi's bedroom scant steps away sounded the hour in eight cuckoo cries. They were at least five minutes late, Sophie observed with grave interest, and odd satisfaction. And slowly she rose erect and proceeded to climb the last steps upward, into the lower vestibule where the framed photographs of Goebbels and Himmler were the only adornments on the wall, and upward further to the attic door, ajar, with the brotherhood's holy motto engraved on the lintel: *My Honor Is My Loyalty*—beyond which Höss in his eyrie waited beneath the image of his lord and savior, waited in that celibate retreat of a calcimine purity so immaculate that even as Sophie approached, unsteadily, the very walls, it seemed, in the resplendent autumn morning were washed by a blindingly incandescent, almost sacramental light.

"Guten Morgen, Herr Kommandant," she said.

Later during that day Sophie could not shake from her mind Bronek's distressing news that Höss was to be transferred back to Berlin. It really meant that she would have to move with haste if she was to accomplish what she had set out to do. And so in the afternoon she resolved to make her advance and prayed silently for the poise—the necessary sang-froid—to carry it off. At one point—waiting for Höss to return to the attic, feeling her emotions subside to something like normal after the tumult provoked in her breast by that brief passage from Haydn's *Creation*—she had been encouraged by some interesting new changes in the Commandant. His relaxed manner, for one thing, then his rather awkward but real attempt at conversation, followed by the insinuating touch of his hand on her shoulder (or was she reading too much into this?) when they had both gazed at the Arabian stallion: these seemed to her to signal cracks in that impregnable mask.

Then, too, there was the letter to Himmler he had dictated to her, regarding the condition of the Greek Jews. Never before had she transcribed any correspondence which was not somehow connected with Polish affairs and Polish language—those official letters to Berlin usually being the province of a poker-faced clerk Scharführer on the floor below who clumped upstairs at regular intervals to hammer out Höss's messages to the various SS chief engineers and proconsuls. Now she reflected on the Himmler letter with mild belated wonder. Wouldn't the mere fact that he had made her privy to such a sensitive matter indicate . . . what? Certainly, at least, that he had allowed her, for whatever reason, a confidentiality that few prisoners—even prisoners of her undoubted privileged status—could ever dream of, and her assurance of reaching through to him before the day was over grew stronger and stronger. She felt she might not even have to avail herself of the pamphlet (*like father, like daughter*) tucked away in one of her boots ever since the day she left Warsaw.

He ignored what she feared might be a distraction—her eyes, raw with weeping—as he stormed through the door. She heard "The Beer Barrel Polka" pounding rhythmically below. He was holding a letter, apparently delivered to his aide downstairs. The Commandant's face was flushed with anger, a wormlike vein pulsed just below his cropped pate. "They know it's compulsory that they write in German, these blasted people. But they constantly break the rules! Damn them to hell these Polish half-wits!" He handed her the letter. "What does it say?"

" 'Honored Commandant . . .' " she began. In rapid translation Sophie told him that the message (characteristically sycophantic) was from a local subcontractor, a supplier of gravel to the German operators of the camp concrete factory, who said that he would be unable to transport the required amount of gravel in the required time, begging the Commandant's indulgence, due to the extremely soggy condition of the ground around his quarry that had not only caused several cave-ins but also hampered and slowed down the operation of his equipment. Therefore, if the honored Commandant would have the forbearance (Sophie continued to read), the schedule of delivery would necessarily be altered in the following manner— But Höss broke in suddenly, fiercely impatient, lighting a cigarette from another in his fingers, coughing his croupy cough as he blurted out a hoarse "Enough!" The letter had plainly unstrung the Commandant. He pursed his lips in a caricature of a mouth drawn and puckered with tension, muttered *"Verwünscht!"*—then quickly ordered Sophie to make a translation of the letter for SS Hauptsturmführer Weitzmann, head of the camp building section, with this typed comment attached: "Builder Weitzmann: Build a fire under this piddler and get him moving."

And at that exact instant—as he said the last words—Sophie saw the fearful headache attack Höss with prodigious speed, like a stroke of lightning that had found a conduit through the gravel merchant's letter down to that crypt or labyrinth where migraine sets its fiery toxins loose beneath the cranium. The sweat poured forth, he pushed his hand to the side of his brow in a helpless fluttering little ballet of white-knuckled fingers, and his lips curled outward to reveal a phalanx of teeth grinding together in a fugue of pain. Sophie had observed this a few days before, a much milder attack; now it was his migraine again and a full-scale siege. In his pain Höss gave a thin whistle. "My pills," he said, "for God's sake, where are my pills!" Sophie went swiftly to the chair next to Höss's cot upon which he kept the bottle of ergotamine he used to alleviate these attacks. She poured out a glass of water from a carafe and handed it and two tablets of ergotamine to the Commandant, who, gulping the medicine down, rolled his eyes at her with a queer half-wild gaze as if he were trying to express with those eyes alone the dimensions of his anguish. Then with a groan and with his hand clapped to his brow he sank down on the cot and lay sprawled out gazing at the white ceiling.

"Shall I call the doctor?" Sophie said. "The last time I remember he said to you—"

"Just be quiet," he retorted. "I can't bear anything now." The voice was edged with a cowed, whimpering tone, rather like that of a hurt puppy.

During his last attack, five or six days before, he had ordered her quickly away to the cellar, as if he wanted no one, not even a prisoner, to be witness to his affliction. Now, however, he rolled over on his flank and lay there rigid and motionless except for the rise and fall of his chest beneath his shirt. Since he made no further sign to her, she went to work: she commenced typing a free translation from the contractor's letter on her German machine, once more aware without shock or even much interest that the gravel dealer's complaint (could a single such annoyance, she wondered idly, have triggered in itself the Commandant's cataclysmic migraine?) meant another critical pause in the construction of the new crematorium at Birkenau. The work stoppage, or slowdown—that is, Höss's apparent inability to orchestrate to his own satisfaction all the elements of supply and design and labor concerning this new oven-and-gas-chamber complex, the completion of which was two months overdue—remained the chief thorn in his side, and now was the obvious cause for all the nervousness and anxiety she had observed in him these past days. And if it was the reason, as she suspected, for his headache, could it be possible too that his failure to get the crematorium built on schedule was in some way linked to his sudden transfer back to Germany? She was typing the last line of the letter and at the same time puzzling over these questions when his voice broke in abruptly, startling her. And when she turned her eyes in his direction she realized with a curious mixture of hope and apprehension that he must have been eying her for many minutes from the cot where he lay. He beckoned to her and she rose and went to his side, but since he made no motion for her to sit down, she remained standing.

"It's better," he said in a subdued voice. "That ergotamine is a miracle. It not only reduces the pain but it subdues the nausea."

"I'm glad, *mein Kommandant,*" Sophie replied. She felt her knees trembling and for some reason dared not look down into his face. Instead, she fixed her eyes on the most obvious and immediate object within view: the heroic Führer in scintillant steel armor, his gaze confident and serene beneath his falling forelock as he looked toward Valhalla and a thousand years' questionless futurity. He seemed irreproachably benign. Suddenly remembering the figs she had thrown up hours before on the stairs, Sophie felt a stab of hunger in her stomach, and the weakness and trembling in her legs increased. For long moments Höss did not speak. She could not look at him. Was he now, in his silence, measuring her, appraising her? *We'll have a barrel of funfunfun,* the voices clamorously chorused from below, the dreadful ersatz polka stuck now in its groove, repeating over and over a faint fat chord from an accordion.

"How did you come here?" Höss said finally.

She blurted the words out. "It was because of a *lapanka,* or as we German-speaking people say, *ein Zusammentreiben*—a roundup in Warsaw. It was early spring. I was on a railroad car in Warsaw when the Gestapo staged a roundup. They found me with some illegal meat, part of a ham—"

"No, no," he interrupted, "not how you came to the camp. But how you got out of the women's barracks. I mean, how you were placed in the stenographic pool. So many of the typists are civilians. Polish civilians. Not many prisoners are so fortunate as to find a stenographic billet. You may sit down."

"Yes, I was most fortunate," she said, seating herself. She sensed the relaxation in her own voice and she gazed at him. She noticed that he was still sweating desperately. Supine now, eyes half closed, he lay rigid and wet in a pool of sunlight. There was something oddly helpless-looking about the Commandant awash in ooze. His khaki shirt was drenched in sweat, a multitude of tiny sweat blisters adorned his face. But in truth he seemed no longer to be suffering such pain, although the initial torment had saturated him everywhere—even the damp blond spirals of belly-hair curling upward through a space between his shirt buttons—his neck, the blond hairs of his wrists. "I was really most fortunate. I think it must have been a stroke of fate."

After a silence Höss said, "How do you mean, a stroke of fate?"

She decided instantly to risk it, to exploit the opening he had given her no matter how absurdly insinuating and reckless the words might sound. After these months and the momentary advantage she had been given, it would be more self-defeating to continue to play the torpid tongue-tied slave than to appear presumptuous, even if it involved the serious additional hazard of being thought actually insolent. So: Out with it, she thought. She said it then, although she tried to avoid any intensity, keeping the plaintive edge in her voice of one who has been unjustly abused. "Fate brought me to you," she went on, not unaware of the melodrama of the utterance, "because I knew only *you* would understand."

Again he said nothing. Below, "The Beer Barrel Polka" was replaced by a *Liederkranz* of Tyrolean yodelers. His silence disturbed her, and suddenly she felt that she was the subject of his most suspicious scrutiny. Maybe she was making a horrible mistake. The queasiness grew within her. Through Bronek (and her own observation) she knew that he hated Poles. What on earth made her think she might be an exception? Insulated by the closed windows from Birkenau's smoldering stench, the warm room had a musty attic's odor of plaster, brickdust and waterlogged timber. It was the first time she had really noticed the smell, and it was like a fungus in the nostrils. Amid the awkward silence between the two of them she heard the stitch and buzz of the imprisoned bluebottle flies, the soft popping sound as they bumped the ceiling. The noise of the shunting boxcars was dull, dim, almost inaudible.

"Understand what?" he said finally in a distant tone, giving her yet another small aperture through which she might try to implant a hook.

"That you would understand that a mistake has been made. That I am guilty of nothing. That is, I mean, that I am guilty of nothing truly serious. And that I should be set immediately free."

There, she had done it, said it, swiftly and smoothly; with fiery fervor surprising even to her she had uttered the words which for days upon end she had rehearsed incessantly, wondering if she could muster the courage to get them past her lips. Now her heartbeat was so violent and wild that it pained her breastbone, but she took bright pride in the way in which she had managed to govern her voice. She also felt secure in the easy mellifluousness of her accent, attractively Viennese. The small triumph impelled her to go on. "I know you might think this foolish of me, *mein Kommandant*. I must admit that on the surface it sounds implausible. But I think that you will concede that in a place like this—so vast, involving such great numbers of people—there can be certain errors, certain grave mistakes." She paused, listening to her heartbeat, wondering if he could hear it, yet conscious that her voice still had not broken. "Sir," she continued, pressing a little on the note of entreaty, "I do hope you will believe me when I say that my imprisonment here is a terrible miscarriage of justice. As you see, I am Polish and indeed I was guilty of the crime I was charged with in Warsaw—smuggling food. But it was a small crime, don't you see, I was trying only to feed my mother, who was very sick. I urge you to try to understand that this was *nothing* when measured against the nature of my background, my upbringing." She hesitated, tumultuously agitated. Was she pushing too hard? Should she halt now and let him make the next move, or should she go on? She instantly decided: Get to the point, be brief but go on. "You see, sir, it is like this. I am originally from Cracow, where my family were passionate German partisans, for many years in the vanguard of those countless lovers of the Third Reich who admire National Socialism and the principles of the Führer. My father was to the depths of his soul *Judenfeindlich*—"

Höss stopped her with a small groan. "*Judenfeindlich,*" he whispered in a drowsy voice. "*Judenfeindlich.* When will I cease hearing that word 'anti-Semitic'? My God, I'm tired of that!" He let out a hoarse sigh. "Jews. *Jews!* Will I ever be done with Jews!"

Sophie retreated before his impatience, aware that her tactical maneuvering had rather misfired: she *had* gotten ahead of herself. Höss's thought process, far from inept, was also as exhaustive and as unimaginatively single-minded as the snout of an anteater and brooked few deviations. When only a moment before he had asked "How did you come here?" and then specified that she explain just how, he meant precisely that, and now wanted no talk about fate, miscarriages of justice and matters *Judenfeindlich*. As if his words had blown down upon her like a north wind, she shifted her tack, thinking: Do as he says, then, tell him the absolute truth. Be brief, but tell the truth. He could find out easily enough anyway, if he wanted to.

"Then, sir, I will explain how I was put into the stenographic pool. It was because of an altercation I had with a *Vertreterin* in the women's barracks when I first arrived last April. She was the assistant to the block leader. Quite honestly, I was terrified of her because . . ." She hesitated, a little wary of elaborating upon a sexual possibility which the shading of her voice, she knew, had already suggested. But Höss, eyes wide open now and level upon hers, anticipated what she was trying to say.

"Doubtless she was a lesbian," he put in. His tone was tired, but acid and exasperated. "One of those whores—one of those scummy pigs from the Hamburg slums they stuck in Ravensbrück and that Headquarters got hold of and sent here in the mistaken idea that they would exercise *discipline* over you—over the female inmates. What a farce!" He paused. "She was a lesbian, wasn't she? And she made advances toward you, am I right? It would be expected. You are a very beautiful young woman." Again he paused while she absorbed this last observation. (Did it mean anything?) "I despise homosexuals," he went on. "Imagining people performing those acts—animalistic practices—makes me sick. I could never stand even to look at one, male or female. But it is something which must be faced when people are in confinement." Sophie blinked. Like a strip of film run at antic jerky speed through the projector, she saw that morning's mad charade, saw Wilhelmine's mop of flaming hair draw back from her groin, the famished damp lips parted in a petrified perfect O, eyes sparkling with terror; looking at the revulsion on Höss's face, thinking of the housekeeper, she felt herself begin to suppress either a scream or a peal of laughter. "Unspeakable!" the Commandant added, curling his lips as if on some loathsome mouthful.

"They were not just advances, sir." She felt herself flush. "She tried to rape me." She could not recall ever having said the word "rape" in front of a man, and the flush grew warmer, then began to fade. "It was most unpleasant. I had not realized that a woman's"—she hesitated—"a woman's desire for another woman could be so—so violent. But I learned."

"In confinement people behave differently, strangely. Tell me about it." But before she could reply he had reached into the pocket of his jacket, draped over the other chair at the side of the cot, and took from it a tinfoil-wrapped chocolate bar. "It's curious," he said, the voice clinical, abstract, "these headaches. At first they fill me with terrible nausea. Then as soon as the medicine begins to take effect I find myself very hungry." Stripping the foil from the chocolate, he extended the bar toward her. Hesitant at the outset, surprised—for it was the first such gesture on his part—she nervously broke off a piece and popped it into her mouth, knowing that she betrayed a greedy eagerness in the midst of her effort to be casual. No matter.

She proceeded with the account, talking rapidly as she watched Höss devour the rest of the chocolate, conscious that the so very recent assault on her cunt by the trusted housekeeper of the man to whom she was speaking allowed her a certain freshness of tone, even vivacity. "Yes, the woman was a prostitute and a lesbian. I don't know where she was from in Germany—I think from the north, she spoke in Plattdeutsch—but she was a huge woman and she tried to rape me. She had had her eyes on me for days. One night in the latrine she approached me. She was not violent at first. She promised me food, soap, clothing, money, anything." Sophie halted for a moment, her gaze fixed now on Höss's violet-blue eyes, which were watchful, fascinated. "I was terribly hungry but—like you too, sir, I am repelled by homosexuals—I did not find it difficult to resist, to say no. I tried to push her away. Then this *Vertreterin* grew enraged and attacked me. I shouted at her loudly and began to plead with her—she had me against the wall and was doing things to me with her hands—and then the block leader came in.

"The block leader put a stop to this," Sophie went on. "She sent the *Vertreterin* away and then told me to come to her room at the end of the barracks. She was not a bad sort—another prostitute, like you say, sir, but not a bad sort. Indeed, she was kindly for such . . . for such a person. She had overheard me shouting at the *Vertreterin,* she said, and she was surprised because all of us newcomers in the barracks were Polish and she wanted to know where I learned such excellent German. We talked for a while and I could tell that she liked me. I don't think she was a lesbian. She was from Dortmund. She was charmed by my German. She hinted that she might be able to help me. She gave me a cup of coffee and then sent me away. I saw her several times after that and could tell that she had taken a liking to me. A couple of days later she told me to come to her room again, and one of your noncommissioned officers, sir, was there, Hauptscharführer Günther of the camp administration office. He interrogated me for some time, asking me about my various qualifications, and when I told him I could type and take expert shorthand in Polish and German, he informed me that perhaps I could be of some use at the typing pool. He had heard that there was a shortage of qualified help—certain language specialists. After a few days he came back and told me that I would be transferred. And so that is how I came to the . . ." Höss had finished eating the chocolate bar and now, stirring, rose up on his elbow, preparing to light one of his cigarettes. "I mean," she concluded, "I worked in the stenographic section until about ten days ago, when I was told that I was needed for special work here. And here—"

"And here," he interrupted, "here you are." He gave a sigh. "You have had good luck." And what he did then caused her electric amazement. He reached up with his free hand, and using the utmost delicacy, plucked a little something from the edge of her upper lip; it was, she realized, a crumb of the chocolate she had eaten, now held between his thumb and forefinger, and she watched with grave wonder as he moved his tar-stained fingers slowly toward his lips and deposited the tiny chestnut-brown flake into his mouth. She shut her eyes, so disturbed by the peculiar and grotesque communion of the gesture that her heart commenced pounding again and her brain was rocked with vertigo.

"What's the matter?" she heard him say. "You're white."

"Nothing, *mein Kommandant,*" she replied. "I'm just a bit faint. It will go away." She kept her eyes closed.

"What have I done wrong!" The voice was a cry, so loud that it frightened her, and she had barely opened her eyes when she saw him roll himself off the cot, stand abruptly erect and walk the few paces to the window. The sweat plastered the back of his shirt and she thought she saw his whole body tremble as he stood there. Sophie was utterly confounded, watching him, having thought that the by-play with the chocolate might have been the prelude to something more intimate. But perhaps it had been; he was now voicing his complaint as if he had known her for years. He struck his hand into his fist. "I can't think what they imagine I've done wrong. Those people in Berlin, they're impossible. They ask the superhuman from a mere human who has only done the best he has known how for three years. They're unreasonable! They don't know what it's like to put up with contractors who can't fulfill their schedules, lazy middlemen, suppliers who fall behind or simply never deliver. They've never dealt with idiot Poles! I've done my faithful best and this is the thanks I get. This *pretense*—that it's a promotion! I get kicked upstairs to Oranienburg and I have to endure the intolerable embarrassment of seeing them put Liebehenschel in my place—Liebehenschel, that insufferable egotist with his bloated

reputation for efficiency. The whole thing, it's *sickening*. There's not the slightest bit of gratitude left." It was strange: there was more petulance in his voice than true anger or resentment.

Sophie rose from her chair and drew near him. She sensed another aperture chinking open ever so slightly. "Excuse me, sir," she said, "and forgive me for suggesting this if I am mistaken. But it may be a *tribute* to you instead. It may be that they fully understand your difficulties, your hardships, and how exhausted you have been made by your work. Forgive me again, but during these few days here in the office I could not help but notice the extraordinary strain you are constantly under, the amazing pressure . . ." How careful was her obsequious solicitude. She heard her voice trail off but meanwhile kept her eyes fixed on the back of his neck. "It may be that this is really in the nature of a reward for all your . . . your devotion."

She fell silent and followed Höss's gaze to the field below. On the capriciously changing wind the smoke from Birkenau had blown off and away, at least momentarily, and in the clear sunlight the great glorious white stallion romped again around the fenced rim of the paddock, tossing tail and mane in a small windstorm of dust. Even through the window they could hear the thudding collision of his galloping hoofs. From the Commandant's throat came an aspirated whistle of air; he fumbled at his pocket for another cigarette.

"I wish you were right," he said, "but I doubt it. If they just understood the *magnitude*, the *complexity!* They seem to have no knowledge of the incredible *numbers* involved in these Special Actions. The endless multitudes! These Jews, they come on and on from all the countries of Europe, countless thousands, millions, like the herring in the spring that swarm into Mecklenburg Bay. I never dreamed the earth contained so many of *das Erwählte Volk.*"

The Chosen People. His use of the phrase allowed her to press her initiative a little further, enlarging the opening where she was confident now she had secured a fragile but real hold. *"Das Erwählte Volk—"* her voice was edged with scorn as she echoed the Commandant—"the Chosen

People, if you'll permit me to say so, sir, may only at last be paying the just price for having arrogantly set themselves apart from the rest of the human race—for having posed as the only people worthy of salvation. I honestly do not see how they could expect to escape retribution when they have commited such a blasphemy for so many years in the sight of Christians." (Suddenly the image of her father loomed, monstrous.) With anxiety she hesitated, then resumed, spinning out another of her lies, impelled forward like a splinter bobbingly afloat upon a rushing stream of fabrication and falsehood. "I am no longer Christian. Like you, sir, I have abandoned that pathetic faith with its pretexts and evasions. Yet it is easy to see why the Jews have inspired such hatred in Christians as well as in people like yourself—*Gottgläubiger,* as you said to me just this morning—righteous and idealistic people who are only striving for a new order in a new world. Jews have threatened this order, and it is only just now that they finally suffer for it. Good riddance, I say."

He still remained standing with his back to her when he replied evenly, "You speak with a great deal of feeling in this matter. For a woman, you talk like one who has a certain amount of knowledge of the crimes of which Jews are capable. I'm curious about this. So few women have any informed knowledge or understanding about anything."

"Yes, but *I* do, sir!" she said, watching him swivel his shoulders ever so slightly and look at her—now for the first time—with truly attentive concern. "I have had personal knowledge, also personal experience—"

"Such as what?"

Impetuously then—she knew it was a risk, a gamble—she bent down and fumblingly plucked the worn and faded pamphlet from the little crevice in her boot. "There!" she said, flourishing it in front of him, spreading out the title page. "I've kept this against the rules, I know I've taken a chance. But I want you to know that these few pages represent everything I stand for. I know from working with you that the 'final solution' has been a secret. But this is one of the earliest Polish documents suggesting a 'final solution' to the Jewish problem. I collaborated with my father—whom I mentioned to you before—in writing it.

Naturally, I don't expect you to read it in detail, filled with so many new worries and concerns as you are. But I do earnestly beg you at least to consider it... I know my difficulties are of no importance to you... but if you could only give it a glance... perhaps you could begin to see the entire injustice of my imprisonment here... I could also tell you more about my work in Warsaw on behalf of the Reich, when I revealed the hiding place of a number of Jews, intellectual Jews who had long been sought..."

She had begun to babble a bit; there was a disconnected quality in her speech which warned her to stop, and she did. She prayed that she would not become unstrung. Sweltering beneath her prisoner's smock with the sweat of mingled hope and trepidation, she was aware that she had made a breach in his consciousness at last, implanted herself as fleshed reality within the scope of his perception. However imperfectly and momentarily, she had made contact; this she could tell by the look of absolute concentrated penetration he gave her when he took the pamphlet from between her fingers. Self-conscious, coquettish, she averted her eyes. And in fatuous recollection a Galician peasants' saying came back to her: *I am crawling into his ear.*

"You maintain, then," he said, "that you are innocent." There was a distant amiability in his tone that filled her with encouragement.

"Sir, to repeat," she answered quickly, "I freely admit my guilt of the minor charge which caused me to be sent here—the business about the little piece of meat. I am only asking that this misdemeanor be weighed against my record not only as a Polish sympathizer with National Socialism but as an active and involved campaigner in the sacred war against Jews and Jewry. That pamphlet in your hand, *mein Kommandant*, can easily be authenticated and will prove my point. I implore you—you who have the power to give clemency and freedom—to reconsider my imprisonment in the light of my past good works, and to return me to my life in Warsaw. It is such a little thing to ask of you, a fine and just man who possesses the power of mercy."

Lotte had told Sophie that Höss was vulnerable to

flattery, but she wondered now if she hadn't overdone it—especially when she saw his eyes narrowing slightly and heard him say, "I'm curious about your passion. Your rage. Just what is it that causes you to hate the Jews with such . . . such intensity?"

This story, too, she had squirreled away for such a moment, relying on the theory that while a pragmatic mind like that of Höss might appreciate the venom of her *Antisemitismus* in the abstract, that same mind's more primitive side would likely relish a touch of melodrama. "That document there, sir, contains my philosophical reasons—the ones I developed with my father at the university in Cracow. I want to emphasize that we would have expressed our enmity toward Jews even if our family had not suffered a terrible calamity."

Impassively Höss smoked and waited for her to continue.

"The sexual profligacy of Jews is well known, one of their ugliest traits. My father, before he met an unfortunate accident . . . my father was a great admirer of Julius Streicher for this reason—he applauded the way in which Herr Streicher has satirized so instructively this degenerate trait in the Jewish character. And our family had a cruel reason to be able to accept the truth of Herr Streicher's insights." She stopped and glanced as if in wretched remembrance toward the floor. "I had a younger sister who went to the convent school in Cracow, she was just a grade behind my own. One evening about ten winters ago she was walking near the ghetto and was sexually assaulted by a Jew—it turned out that he was a butcher—who dragged her into an alley and ravished her repeatedly. Physically, my sister survived the attack by this Jew, but mentally she was destroyed. Two years later she committed suicide by drowning, the tragic child. Certainly this terrible deed validated once and for all the profundity of Julius Streicher's understanding of what atrocities Jews are capable of."

"Kompletter Unsinn!" Höss spat out the words. "That sounds to me like so much *hogwash! Rot!"*

Sophie had the sensation of one who, walking along a serene woodland path, feels herself suddenly without underpinnings, plunged into a murky hole. What had she said wrong? Inadvertently she gave a small wail. "I mean—" she began.

"Hogwash!" Höss repeated. "Streicher's theories are the sheerest rot. I loathe his pornographic garbage. More than any single person he has done a disservice to the Party and the Reich, and to world opinion, with his rantings about Jews and their sexual proclivities. He knows nothing about such matters. Anyone who is acquainted with Jews will attest that, if anything, in the sexual area they are meek and inhibited, unaggressive, even pathologically repressed. What happened to your sister was doubtless an aberration."

"It *happened!*" she lied, dismayed at her unforeseen little predicament. "I swear—"

He cut her off. "I don't doubt that it took place, but it was a freak, an aberration. Jews are perpetrators of many forms of gross evil but they are not rapists. What Streicher has done in his newspaper all these years has brought only the greatest ridicule. Had he told the truth in a persistent way, portraying Jews as they *really are*—bent upon monopolizing and dominating the world economy, poisoning morality and culture, attempting through Bolshevism and other means to bring down civilized governments—he might have performed a necessary function. But this portrayal of the Yid as a diabolical debaucher with an enormous prick"—he used the colloquial *Schwanz,* which rather startled her, as did the gesture he made with his hands, measuring a meter-long organ in air—"is an unwarranted compliment to Jewish masculinity. Most Jewish males I have observed are contemptibly neuter. Sexless. Soft. *Weichlich.* And more disgusting for all of that."

She had made a dumb tactical error in regard to Streicher (she knew she was dumb about National Socialism, but how could she have been expected to be able to gauge the extent of the jealousies and resentments, the squabbles and in-fighting and disaccord which reigned among the Party members of all ranks and categories?), yet actually, now it did not seem to matter: Höss, shrouded in the lavender fumes of his fortieth Ibar cigarette of that day, suddenly broke off his tirade against the Gauleiter of Nuremberg, gave the pamphlet a flat little tap with his fingertips and said something which made her heart feel like a hot ball of lead. "This document means *nothing* to me. Even if you were able to demonstrate in a convincing way your collaboration in the writing, it would prove very little. Only that you despise Jews. That does not impress me, inasmuch as it seems to me a very widespread sentiment." His eyes became frosty and faraway, as if he were gazing at a point yards beyond the back of her bescarfed and frizzled skull. "Also, you seem to forget that you are a Pole, and therefore an enemy of the Reich who would remain an enemy even if you were not also judged guilty of a criminal act. Indeed, there are some in highest authority—the Reichsführer, for one—who consider you and your kind and your nation on a par with the Jews, *Menschentiere,* equally worthless, equally polluted in the racial sense, equally justifying righteous hatred. Poles living in the Fatherland are beginning to be marked with a *P*—an ominous sign for you people." He hesitated for an instant. "I myself do not wholeheartedly share this specific view; however, to be honest, some of my dealings with your countrymen have caused me such bitterness and frustration that I have often felt that there is real cause for this absolute loathing. In the men especially. There is in them an ingrained loutishness. Most of the women are merely ugly."

Sophie burst into tears, although it had nothing to do with his denunciations. She had not planned to weep—it was the last thing from her mind, a display of mawkish weakness—but she could not help it. The tears spilled forth and she thrust her face into her hands. All—all!—had failed; her precarious handhold had crumbled, and she felt as if she had been hurled down the mountainside. She had made no advance, no inroads at all. She was finished. Sobbing uncontrollably, she stood there with the sticky tears leaking through her fingers, sensing the approach of doom. She gazed into the darkness of her wet cupped hands and heard the strident Tyrolean minnesingers from the salon far below, a cackling barnyard of voices propelled upward on a choir of thumping tubas, trombones, harmonicas in soggy syncopation.

Und der Adam hat Liebe erfunden,
Und der Noah den Wein, ja!

Almost never shut, the attic door was closed then upon a squeak of hinges, slowly, gradually, as if by some reluctant force. She knew it could only have been Höss who closed the door and she was conscious of the sound of his boots as he returned toward her, then his fingers grasping her shoulder firmly even before she allowed herself to draw her hands away from her eyes and to look up. She forced herself to stop crying. The clamor beyond the intervening door was muffled.

Und der David hat Zither erschall . . .

"You've been flirting shamelessly with me," she heard him say in an unsteady voice. She opened her eyes. His own eyes were distraught and the way in which they goggled about—seemingly out of control, at least for that brief moment—filled her with terror, especially since they gave her the impression somehow that he was about to raise his fist and strike her. But then with a great visceral heave he seemed to regain possession of himself, his gaze became normal or nearly so, and when next he spoke, his words were uttered with their ordinary soldierly steadiness. Even so, the manner of his breathing—rapid but deep—and a certain tremor about the lips betrayed to Sophie his inner distress, which still, with more terror, she could not help but identify as an extension of his rage at her. Rage at her for what in particular she could not fathom: for her foolish pamphlet, for being a flirt, for praising Streicher, for being born a dirty Pole, perhaps all of these. Then suddenly, to her astonishment, she realized that although his distress clearly partook of some vague and inchoate rage, it was not rage at her at all but at someone or something else. His clutch on her shoulder was hurting her. He made a nervous choking sound.

Then, relaxing his grasp, he blurted out something which, in its overlay of ethnic anxiety, she perceived to be a ludicrous replica of Wilhelmine's own squeamish concern that morning. "It's hard to believe you're Polish, with your superb German and the way you look—the fair complexion of your skin and the lines of your face, so typically Aryan. It's a finer face than that of most Slavic women. And yet you are what you say you are—a Pole."

Sophie now detected a tone both discontinuous and rambling enter his speech, as if his mind were prowling in evasive circles around the threatful core of whatever it was he was trying to express. "I don't like flirts, you see, it is only a way of trying to insinuate yourself into my favor, to try and seek out a few rewards. I have always detested this quality in women, this crude use of sex—so dishonest, so transparent. You have made it very difficult for me, making me think foolish thoughts, distracting me from my proper duties. This flirtatiousness has been damnably annoying, and yet—and yet it can't be all your fault, you're an extremely attractive woman.

"A number of years ago when I would go from my farm up to Lübeck—I was quite young at the time—I saw a silent film version of *Faust* in which the woman who played Gretchen was unbelievably beautiful and made a deep impression on me. So fair, such a perfect fair face and lovely figure—I thought about her for days, weeks afterwards. She visited me in my dreams, obsessing me. Her name was Margarete Something, this actress, her last name escapes me now. I always thought of her simply as Margarete. Her voice too: I could only believe that if I could hear her speak, there would be such a purity in her German. Very much like yours. I saw the film a dozen times. I learned later that she died very young—of tuberculosis, I believe—and it saddened me terribly. Time passed and eventually I forgot about her—or at least she no longer obsessed me. I could never completely forget her." Höss paused and squeezed her shoulder once more, hard, hurting her, and she thought with shock: Strange, with that pain he is really trying to express some tenderness . . . The yodelers below had fallen silent. Involuntarily she closed her eyes tightly, trying not to flinch from the pain and aware now—in the dark hollow of her consciousness—of the camp's symphonic death sounds: of metal clangor, of the boxcars' remote colliding booms and the faint keening of a locomotive whistle, mournful and shrill.

"I am very much conscious that in many ways I am not like most men of my calling—of men brought up in a military environment. I was never one of the fellows. I have always been aloof. Solitary. I never consorted with prostitutes. I went to a brothel only once in my life, when I was very young, in Constantinople. It was an experience that left me disgusted; I am made sick by the lewdness of whores. There is something about the pure and radiant beauty of a certain kind of woman—fair of skin and of hair, although if truly Aryan she can of course also be somewhat darker—that inspires me to idolize that beauty, to idolize it almost to the point of worship. That actress Margarete was one of these—then also a woman I knew in Munich for some years, a splendid person with whom I had a passionate relationship and a child out of wedlock. Basically I believe in monogamy. I've been unfaithful to my wife on very few occasions. But this woman, she . . . she was the most glorious example of this beauty—exquisite of feature and of pure Nordic blood. My attraction to her was of an intensity beyond anything so crude as mere sex, and its so-called pleasures. It had to do with a grander scheme of procreation. It was an exalted thing to deposit my seed within such a beautiful vessel. You inspire in me much the same desire."

Sophie kept her eyes shut as the flow of his weird Nazi grammar, with its outlandishly overheated images and clumps of succulent Teutonic wordbloat, moved its way up through the tributaries of her mind, nearly drowning her reason. Then suddenly the mist from his sweaty torso reeked in her nostrils like rancid meat and she heard herself give a gasp at the very instant that he yanked her body up against his own. She had a sense of elbows, knees and a scratchy cheese-grater of stubble. As insistent in his ardor as his housekeeper, he was incomparably more awkward and his arms around her seemed multitudinous, like those of a huge mechanical fly. She held her breath while his hands at her back tried out some sort of massage. And his *heart*—his rampaging galloping heart! Never had she conceived that a single heart was capable of the riotous romantic thumping which moved against her like a drumbeat through the Commandant's damp shirt. Trembling like a very sick man, he essayed nothing so bold as a kiss, although she was certain she sensed some protuberance—his tongue or nose—mooning restlessly around her bekerchiefed ear. Then an abrupt knock at the door caused him to break apart from her swiftly and he uttered a soft, miserable *"Scheiss!"*

It was his adjutant Scheffler again. Begging the Commandant's pardon, Scheffler said, standing in the doorway, but Frau Höss—now on the landing below—had come upstairs with a question for the Commandant. She was going to the movies at the garrison recreation center and she wanted to know if she might take Iphigenie with her. Iphigenie, the older daughter, was recovering from a week-long case of *die Grippe* and Madame wished to find out whether, in the Commandant's judgment, the girl was well enough to accompany her to the matinee. Or should she consult Dr. Schmidt? Höss snarled something in return which Sophie could not hear. But it was during this brief exchange that she had a desperate flash of intuition, sensing that the interruption with its jejune domestic flavor could only blot out forever the magic moment into which the Commandant, like some soul-eaten Tristan, had had the infirmity to allow himself to be lured. And when he turned again to face her she knew immediately that her presentiment was an accurate one, and that her cause was in its deepest peril yet.

"When he come back toward me," Sophie said, "his face was even more twisted up and tormented than before. Again I have this strange feeling that he was going to hit me. But he didn't. Instead, he come very close to me and said, 'I long to have intercourse with you'—he used the word *Verkehr,* which have in German the same stupid formal sound as 'intercourse'; he said, 'Having intercourse with you would allow me to lose myself, I might find forgetfulness.' But then suddenly his face changed. It was as if Frau Höss had changed everything around in a moment. His face became very calm and sort of impersonal, you know, and he said, 'But I cannot and I will not, it is too much of a risk. It would be doomed to disaster.' He turned away from me then, turned his back to me and walked to the window. I heard him say, 'Also, pregnancy here would be out of the question.' Stingo, I thought I might faint. I felt very weak from all my emotion and this tension; also, I guess, from hunger, from not eating anything since those figs I had vomited up that morning, and only the little piece of chocolate he had given me. He turned around again and spoke to me. He said, 'If I were not leaving here, I would take the risk. Whatever your background is, I feel that in a spiritual way we could meet on common ground. I would risk a great deal to have relations with you.' I thought he was going to touch or grab me again, but he didn't. 'But they have got rid of me,' he said, 'and I must go. And so you must go too. I am sending you back to Block Two where you came from. You will go tomorrow.' Then he turned away again.

"I was terrified," Sophie went on. "You see, I had tried to get close to him and I had failed, and now he was sending me away and all my hopes were destroyed. I tried to speak to him, but all I could feel was this choking in my throat and the words wouldn't come. It was like he was going to cast me back into darkness and there was nothing I could do—nothing at all. I kept looking at him and I was trying to speak. That beautiful Arabian horse was still in the field down below and Höss was leaning against the window, gazing down at it. The smoke from Birkenau had lifted up. I heard him whisper something about his transfer to Berlin again. He spoke very bitterly. I remember he used words like 'failure' and 'ingratitude,' and once he said very clearly, '*I* know how well I have performed my duty.' He didn't say anything for a long while then, only kept looking at that horse, and finally I heard him say this, I am almost sure they were his exact words, 'To escape the body of a man yet still dwell in Nature. To *be* that horse, to live within that beast. That would be freedom.' " She paused for an instant. "I have always remembered those words. They were just so . . ." And Sophie stopped speaking, her eyes glazed with memory, staring toward the phantasmagoric past as if in wonderment.

("They were just so . . .") *What?*

After Sophie told me all this, she broke off talking for a long time. She hid her eyes behind her fingers and bent her head downward toward the table, buried in somber reflection. She had throughout the long telling kept a firm grip on herself, but now the glistening wetness between her fingers told me how bitterly she had begun to weep. I let her cry in silence. We had been sitting for hours together that rainy August afternoon, our elbows propped against one of the Formica tables at the Maple Court. It was three days after the cataclysmic breakup between Sophie and Nathan that I described many pages ago. It may be recalled that when the two of them vanished I had been on my way for a visit with my father in Manhattan. (It was an important visit for me—and in fact I had decided to return to Virginia with him—and I want to describe it in some detail later.) From this get-together I had come back unhappily to the Pink Palace, expecting to find the same abandonment and ruination I remembered from that evening—certainly not anticipating the presence of Sophie, whom I discovered, miraculously, in the shambles of her room, stuffing her last odds and ends into a dilapidated suitcase. Meanwhile Nathan was nowhere in sight—I considered this a blessing—and after our rueful and sweet reunion Sophie and I hurried in the midst of an explosive summer downpour to the Maple Court. Needless to say, I was overjoyed to note that Sophie seemed as genuinely happy to see me as I was to be simply breathing her face and body once more. To the best of my knowledge, I had been, aside from Nathan and perhaps Blackstock, the only person in the world who could claim any real closeness to Sophie, and I sensed her clutching at my presence as if it were something actually life-giving.

She was still in what appeared to be a raw condition of shock over Nathan's desertion of her (she said, not without a touch of grisly humor, that she had contemplated several times hurling herself from the window of the ratty Upper West Side hotel where she had languished those three days), but if grief over his parting had obviously eroded her spirit, it was this same grief, I sensed, that allowed her to open even wider the gates of her memory in a mighty cathartic cataract. But one small impression nags. Should I have become alarmed at something about Sophie which I had never once observed before? She had begun to drink, not heavily—what she drank did not even hesitantly slur her speech—but the three or four mild glasses of whiskey and water she downed during that gray wet afternoon comprised a surprising departure for one who, like Nathan, had been relatively abstemious. Perhaps I should have been more bothered or concerned by those shot glasses of Schenley's at her elbow. At any rate, I stuck to my customary beer and only casually noted Sophie's new inclination. I would doubtless have overlooked her drinking anyway, since when Sophie resumed talking (wiping her eyes and—in as straightforward and as emotionless a voice as anyone could manage under the circumstances—starting to wind up the chronicle of that day with Rudolf Franz Höss) she spoke of something which so rocked me with astonishment that I felt the entire outer surface of my face become enveloped by a tingling frost. I drew in my breath and my limbs grew as weak as reeds. And, dear reader, at least then I knew she was not lying . . .

"Stingo, my child was there at Auschwitz. Yes, I had a child. It was my little boy, Jan, that they have taken away from me on the day I came there. They have put him in this place called the Children's Camp, he was only ten years old. I know it must be strange to you that all this time you've known me I have never told you about my child, but this is something I have never been able to tell to anyone. It is too difficult—too much for me to ever think about. Yes, I did tell Nathan about this once, many months ago. I told him very quickly and then after that I said that we must never once talk about this again. Or tell anyone else. So now I'm telling you only because you will not be able to understand about me and Höss unless you understood about Jan. And after this I will not talk any more about him, and you must never ask me questions. No, never again . . .

"Anyway, that afternoon when Höss was looking down from the window I spoke to him. I knew that I had to play my last card, reveal to him what *au jour le jour* I had buried even from myself—in my fear of dying of grief of it—do anything, beg, shout, scream for mercy, hoping only that I can somehow touch this man enough so that he would just show a bit of mercy—if not for me, then the only thing I had left on earth to live for. So I put my voice under control and said, '*Herr Kommandant,* I know I can't ask much for myself and you must act according to the rules. But I beg of you to do one thing for me before you send me back. I have a young son in Camp D, where all the other boys are prisoners. His name is Jan Zawistowski, age ten. I have learned his number, I will give it to you. He was with me when I arrived but I have not seen him since six months. I yearn to see him. I am afraid for his health, with winter coming. I beg of you to consider some way in which he might be released. His health is frail and he is so very young.' Höss didn't reply to me, just looked straight at me without blinking. I had begun to break down a little and I felt myself going out of control. I reached out and touched his shirt, then clutched at it and said, 'Please, if you have been impressed only the slightest bit by my presence, by my being, I beg of you to do this for me. Not to release *me,* just to release my little boy. There is a certain way you could do this, which I will tell you about . . . Please do this for me. Please. *Please!*'

"I knew then that I was once more only a worm in his life, a piece of Polish *Dreck.* He grabbed my wrist and pulled my hand away from his shirt and said, 'That's enough!' I'll never forget the *frenzy* in his voice when he said, *'Ich kann es unmöglich tun!'* Which means 'It's out of the question for me to do that.' He said, 'It would be *unlawful* for me to release *any* prisoner without proper authority.' Suddenly I realized I have touched some terrible nerve in him by even mentioning what I done. He said, 'It's outrageous, your suggestion! What do you take me for, some *Dümmling* you hope to be able to manipulate? Only because I expressed a special feeling for you? You think you could get me to contravene proper authority because I expressed some little affection?' Then he said, 'I find this disgusting!'

"Would it make sense to you, Stingo, if I said that I couldn't help myself and I threw myself against him, threw my arms around his waist and begged him again, saying 'Please' over and over? But I could tell from the way his muscles become stiff and this trembling that ran through him that he was finished with me. Even so I couldn't stop. I said, 'Then at least let me *see* my little boy, let me visit him, let me see him just once, please do that one thing for me. Can't you understand this? You have children of your own. Just allow me to see him, to hold him once in my arms before I go back into the camp.' And when I said this, Stingo, I couldn't help myself and I fell on my knees in front of him. I fell on my knees in front of him and pressed my face against his boots."

Sophie halted, gazing again for long moments into that

past which seemed now so totally, so irresistibly to have captured her; she took several sips of whiskey and swallowed once or twice abstractedly in a daze of recollection. And I realized that, as if seeking whatever semblance of present reality I was able to offer, she had taken hold of my hand in a numbing grip. "There have been so much talk about people in a place like Auschwitz and the way they acted there. In Sweden when I was in this refugee center, often a group of us who was there—at Auschwitz or at Birkenau, where I later was sent—would talk about how these various people acted. Why this man would allow himself to become a vicious Kapo, who would be cruel to his fellow prisoners and cause many of them to die. Or why this other man or woman would do this or that brave thing, sometime lose their lives that another could live. Or give their bread or a little potato or thin nothing soup to someone starving, even though they were themselves starving. Or there would be people—men, women—who would kill or betray another prisoner just for a little food. People acted very different in the camp, some in a cowardly and selfish way, some bravely and beautifully—there was no rule. No. But such a terrible place was this Auschwitz, Stingo, terrible beyond all belief, that you really could not say that this person *should* have done a certain thing in a fine or noble fashion, as in the other world. If he or she done a noble thing, then you could admire them like any place else, but the Nazis were murderers and when they were not murdering they turned people into sick animals, so if what the people done was not so noble, or even was like animals, then you have to understand it, hating it maybe but pitying it at the same time, because you knew how easy it was for you to act like an animal too."

Sophie paused for a few moments and locked her eyelids shut as if in savage meditation, then gazed once more out onto the baffling distances. "So there is one thing that is still a mystery to me. And that is why, since I know all this and I know the Nazis turned me into a sick animal like all the rest, I should feel so much guilt over all the things I done there. And over just being alive. This guilt is something I cannot get rid of and I think I never will." She paused again, and then said, "I suppose it's because . . ." But she hesitated, failing to round out her thought, and I heard a quaver in her voice—perhaps more because of exhaustion now than anything else—when she said, "I know I will never get rid of it. Never. And because I never get rid of it, maybe that's the worst thing the Germans left me with."

Finally she relaxed her grip on my hand and turned to me, looking me full in the face as she said, "I surrounded Höss's boots with my arms. I pressed my cheek up against those cold leather boots as if they was made of fur or something warm and comforting. And do you know? I think maybe I even licked them with my tongue, licked those Nazi boots. And do you know something else? If Höss had give me a knife or a gun and told me to go kill somebody, a Jew, a Pole, it don't matter, I would have done it without thinking, with joy even, if it mean seeing my little boy for only a single minute and holding him in my arms.

"Then I heard Höss say, 'Get to your feet! Demonstrations like this offend me. Get up!' But when I began to get up his voice got softer and he said, 'Certainly you may see your son, Sophie.' I realized that it was the first time he ever spoke my name. Then—oh Jesus Christ, Stingo, he actually *embraced* me again and I heard him say, 'Sophie, Sophie, certainly you may see your little boy.' He said, 'Do you think I could deny you that? *Glaubst du, dass ich ein Ungeheuer bin?* Do you think I am some kind of monster?' "

Eleven

"Son, the North believes it has a veritable *patent* on virtue," my father said, gingerly stroking with a forefinger his shiny new black eye. "But of course, the North is wrong. Do you think the slums of Harlem truly represent an advance for the Negro over a peanut patch in Southampton County? Do you think the Negro is going to remain content in that insufferable squalor? Son, someday the North is going to sadly rue these hypocritical attempts at magnanimity, these clever and transparent gestures that go by the name of *tolerance*. Someday—mark my word—it will be clearly demonstrated that the North is every bit as steeped in prejudice as the South, if not more so. At least in the South the prejudice is out in the open. But up here . . ." He paused to touch his sore eye again. "I really *shudder* to think of the violence and hatred building up in these slums." An almost lifelong Southern liberal, conscious of the South's injustices, my father had never been given to shifting unreasonably the various racial evils of the South onto the shoulders of the North; with some surprise, therefore, I listened to him attentively, unaware—during that summer of 1947—of just how prophetic his words were to prove.

At some time long past midnight we were sitting in the dim, murmurously convivial bar of the Hotel McAlpin, where I had taken him after the disastrous altercation he had had with a cabdriver named Thomas McGuire, Hack License 8608, only an hour or so after his arrival in New York. The old man (I use the phrase merely in the paternal-vernacular sense; at age fifty-nine he looked strappingly fit and youthful) had not been badly damaged but there had been a considerable uproar and a crimson outpouring of alarming, albeit harmlessly let, blood from a superficial cut on the brow. This had necessitated a small bandage. After order had been restored, and as we sat drinking (he bourbon, I that steadfast spirit of my nonage—Rheingold) and talking, largely about the gulf which separated this devil's spawn of an urban blight north of the Chesapeake and the South's Elysian meadows (in this realm my father could scarcely have been *less* prophetic, not having foreseen Atlanta), I was able more than once to reflect somberly on how my old man's imbroglio with Thomas McGuire had at least allowed me momentary diversion from my newly acquired despair.

For, it may be recalled, all this would necessarily have taken place only brief hours after that moment in Brooklyn when I had assumed that Sophie and Nathan had disappeared from my life forever. Certainly I was convinced—since I had no reason to think otherwise—that I would never lay eyes on her again. And so the melancholy which had taken hold of me when I left Yetta Zimmerman's and journeyed by subway to stay with my father in Manhattan had been as close to creating an excruciating physical malaise as any I had ever known—most surely since my mother's death. It was now a thing of mingled bereavement and anxiety, inextricable and bewilderingly intense. The feelings alternated. Gazing out dully at the stroboscopic dazzle-and-dark of the subway tunnel lights streaking past, I felt the combined pain like an immense and oppressive weight thrusting down directly on my shoulders, so heavy that it somehow actually compressed my lungs and made my breath come in harsh erratic gasps. I did not—or could not—weep, but I halfway knew several times that I was on the verge of getting sick. It was as if I had been privy to sudden senseless death, as if Sophie (and Nathan too, for despite the rage, the resentful chagrin and confusion he had made me suffer, he was too intricately bound up in our triadic relationship for me to suddenly abandon the love and loyalty I felt for him) had been wiped out in one of those catastrophic traffic accidents which occur in an eyewink, leaving the survivors too stunned even to curse heaven. All I knew, as the train rumbled up through the dripping catacombs beneath Eighth Avenue, was that with an instantaneousness I still could barely believe, I had been cut off from the two people in life I cared the most about, and that the primitive sensation of loss it produced was causing me anguish similar to that of being buried alive under a ton of cinders.

"I admire your spunk tremendously," my father had said while we ate a late dinner at a Schrafft's. "The seventy-two hours I plan to spend in this burg is about all most mortal men from civilized parts can stand. I don't know how you do it. Your youth, I suppose, that wonderful flexibility of your age that allows you to be beguiled by, rather than devoured by, this octopus of a city. I've never been there, but really, is it *possibly* true that, as you wrote me, there are parts of Brooklyn that remind one of *Richmond?*"

Despite the long train ride up from the depths of the Tidewater my father was in a splendid mood, which helped me take my mind off my spiritual disarray, at least fitfully. He mentioned that he had not been to New York since the late 1930s and that, if anything, the city appeared more Babylonian in its dissolute wealth than ever. "It's a product of the war, son," said this engineer who had helped fabricate such naval behemoths as the aircraft carriers *Yorktown* and *Enterprise,* "everything in this country has become richer and richer. It took that war to bail us out of the Depression and in the process to turn us into the most powerful nation on earth. If there's one single thing that's going to keep us ahead of the Communists for many years, it's just that: money, and we've got lots of it." (It should not be assumed from this allusion that my father was even remotely a Red-baiter. As I say, he was notably left-leaning for a Southerner: six or seven years later, at the height of the McCarthy hysteria, he furiously resigned as president-elect of the Virginia chapter of the Sons of the American Revolution, to which for largely genealogical reasons he had belonged for a quarter of a century, when that mossback organization issued a manifesto in support of the Senator from Wisconsin.)

Yet no matter how sophisticated they may be in matters

of economics, sojourners from the South (or anywhere else in the hinterland) rarely fail to be dumfounded by New York's tariffs and prices, and my father was no exception, grumbling darkly over the dinner check for two: I think it was around four dollars—imagine!—which was hardly exorbitant by metropolitan standards in that deflated time, and even for Schrafft's profoundly ordinary fare. "For four dollars at home," he complained, "you could feast all weekend." He regained his composure quickly, though, as we strolled through the balmy night up Broadway, north through Times Square—a place which caused the old man to adopt an expression of dazed and pious speculation, although he was never a pious person and his reaction came, I think, less from real disapproval than from the shock, like a slap in the face, of the area's raunchy weirdness.

It occurs to me that compared to the reptilian Sodom into which it later evolved, Times Square that summer offered scarcely more in the way of carnal corruption than some dull beige plaza in a Christly town like Omaha or Salt Lake City; nonetheless, it had its share of sleazy hustlers and garish freaks strutting through the rainbows and whirlpools of neon, even then, and it helped a little in the way of distracting me from my deep gloom to hear his whispered expletives—he could still utter "Jeru-*salem!*" with the rustic openness of a character out of Sherwood Anderson—and to watch his gaze, following the iridescent rayon undulations of some chichi mulatto whore, reflect in quick sequence glassy incredulity and a certain ineluctable itch. Did he ever get laid? I wondered. A widower for nine years, he surely deserved to, but like most Southerners (or Americans, for that matter) of his vintage he was reticent, even secretive, about sex, and his life in that sphere was to me a mystery. In truth, I hoped that in his mature state he had not allowed himself to be sacrificed on the altar of Onan, like his hapless offspring; or could it simply be that just now I had misinterpreted his glance and that he was mercifully free of that fever at last?

At Columbus Circle we hailed a taxi and headed back to the McAlpin. I must have fallen into my despondent mood again, for I heard him say, "What's wrong, son?" I muttered something about a stomach ache—the victuals at

Schrafft's—and let it go at that. As much as I felt the need to unburden myself to someone, I found it impossible to divulge anything about this recent upheaval in my life. How could I ever adequately outline the dimensions of my loss, much less go into the complexities of the situation which led up to that loss: my passion for Sophie, the wonderful comradeship with Nathan, Nathan's crazy fugue of a few hours ago, and the final, sudden, agonizing abandonment? Not being a reader of Russian novels (which that scenario seemed in certain melodramatic respects to resemble), my father would have found the story totally beyond comprehension. "You're not having too much money trouble, are you?" he inquired, adding that he well knew that the proceeds from the sale of the young slave Artiste which he had sent me weeks before could hardly be expected to last forever. Then in what I sensed was a gentle, roundabout way he began to broach the possibility of my coming South to live again. He had just barely edged up on the subject, so briefly and tentatively that I had not had time even to reply, when the taxi slid to a stop in front of the McAlpin. "I wouldn't think it would be too healthy," he was saying, "living in a place with people like the ones we just saw."

It was then that I witnessed an episode which illustrated the sad, schismatic division of North and South more starkly than any conceivable work of art or sociology. And it involved two grievous, mutually unpardonable mistakes, each embedded in a cultural overview which was separated from the other as Saskatoon is from Patagonia. The initial mistake surely was my father's. Although gratuities in the South—at least up until that time—had been in general eschewed or never taken seriously, he should have known better than to tip Thomas McGuire a nickel—wiser to give no tip at all. McGuire's mistake was to react by snarling at my father, descriptively: "fucking asshole." This is not to say that a *Southern* cabdriver, unaccustomed to tips or at any rate accustomed to receiving few tips and those erratically, might not have felt a little stung; yet however violently he might have bristled inwardly, he would have kept his peace. Nor does it mean that the ears of a New Yorker might not have burned at McGuire's epithet; but such words are the common coin of the streets and of taxi drivers, and most New York denizens would have swallowed their gall and likewise kept their mouths shut.

Partway out of the cab, my father poked his nose back into the front window and said, in a nearly incredulous voice, "What did I hear you say?" The phrasing is important—not "What did you say?" or "What's that you said?" but with the emphasis on "hear," a sense that the auditory apparatus itself had never before experienced such vile obscenities, not even separately, much less uttered in tandem. McGuire was a blur of thick neck and reddish hair in the shadows. I did not get a good look at his face, but the voice was fairly young. If he had sped off into the night, then all might have been well, but although I sensed a slight hesitancy, I also felt an intransigence, a feisty Hibernian umbrage at my father's nickel that matched the old man's rage at this indefensible language. When McGuire answered he even supplied a considerably more grammatical shape to his thought: *"I said you must be some fucking asshole."*

My father's voice became a restrained cry—not really loud but throbbing with fury—as he sought retribution. "And I think *you* must be part of the bottomless dregs of this loathsome city that spawned you and all your foul-mouthed breed!" he declaimed, shifting like lightning into the timeless rhetorical mode of his ancestors. "Detestable scum that you are, you are no more civilized than a sewer rat! In any decent place in the United States a person like you disgorging your disgusting filth would be taken out in a public square and horsewhipped!" His voice rose a bit; pedestrians halted beneath the McAlpin's blazing marquee. "But this is neither a decent nor a civilized place, and you are free to spew your putrid language upon fellow citizens—" He was cut off then in mid-torrent by McGuire's hasty escape as he rammed the cab forward, barreling off up the avenue. Clutching at air, my father wheeled about toward the sidewalk, and I was aware in a flash that it was nothing but sheer whirling momentum which then propelled him like a blind man into the upright hard steel shaft of a No Parking stanchion; the sound of his head making contact, as in an animated cartoon, produced a vibrating *boinnng!* But it was not at all amusing. I thought there was going to be a denouement of tragic scope.

Yet there he was, half an hour later, sipping straight bourbon and railing against the North's "patent on virtue." He had bled a lot, but by the sheerest chance the "house doctor" of the McAlpin had been roaming through the lobby just at the moment that I shepherded the victim in. The house doctor appeared to be a seedy alcoholic, but he knew how to take care of a shiner. Cold water and a bandage had finally stanched the blood, though not the old man's outrage. Nursing his wound in the shadows of the McAlpin bar, with his swollen eye looking more and more the simulacrum of his own father divested of half his sight eighty-odd years before at Chancellorsville, he continued to curse Thomas McGuire's guts in a litany of hopeless spleen. It got to be a little tiresome, picturesque as the language was, and I realized that the old man's ire was founded upon neither snobbishness nor prudery—as a shipyard worker and, before that, as a merchant mariner, his ears had surely overflowed with such billingsgate—but upon something as uncomplicated as an abiding belief in good manners and public decency. *"Fellow citizens!"* It actually was a kind of frustrated egalitarianism out of which, I began to understand, he derived much of his sense of alienation. Simply put, people abrogated their equality when they were unable to speak to each other in human terms. Calming down, he abandoned McGuire finally and let his animus spread out and embrace in a general way all the multifarious sins and failings of the North: its arrogance, its hypocritical claim to moral superiority. Suddenly I saw how much of an unreconstructed Southerner he really was, and was struck by the fact that this seemed in no way to contradict his basic liberalism.

At last the diatribe—perhaps combined with the shock of his injury, relatively slight as it was—appeared to exhaust him; he turned pale and I urged him to go upstairs to bed. This he reluctantly did, stretching himself out on one of the twin beds of the room he had reserved for the two of us five floors above the noisy avenue. I was to spend two restlessly insomniac and (largely because of my continuing despair over Sophie and Nathan) demoralized nights there, awash with sweat beneath a humming black spider of an electric fan that dispensed air in puny puffs. In spite of his fatigue, my father kept harping on the

South. (I realized later that at least part of his visit was in effect a subtle mission to rescue me from the clutches of the North; although he never let on in direct terms, the old slyboots had surely dedicated much of his trip to an attempt to preserve me from going over to the Yankees.) That first night his last thoughts before he went off to sleep had to do with his hope that I would leave this confusing city and come back down to the country where I belonged. His voice was faraway as it mumbled something about "human dimensions."

The several days were spent just as one might imagine a twenty-two-year-old youth would while away the hours with a generally discontented Southern daddy during a New York summer. We visited a couple of tourist attractions which both of us confessed to never having visited before: the Statue of Liberty and the roof of the Empire State Building. We took a sightseeing boat trip around Manhattan. We went to the Radio City Music Hall, drowsing there through a comedy with Robert Stack and Evelyn Keyes. (I recall how, during this ordeal, my mourning over Sophie and Nathan enveloped me like a shroud.) We looked in at the Museum of Modern Art, a place which, rather condescendingly, I thought might offend the old man, who instead seemed thoroughly exhilarated—the clean bright orthogonal Mondrians bringing special delight to his technician's eye. We ate at Horn and Hardart's amazing automat, at Nedick's and Stouffer's and—in a fling at what in those days I deemed *haute cuisine*—at a midtown Longchamps. We went to one or two bars (including, accidentally, a gay joint on Forty-second Street, where I watched my father's face, as it confronted the smirking apparitions, turn gray like oatmeal, then become actually disfigured with unbelief), but each night retired early, after more talk about that farm nestled amid the Tidewater peanut fields. My father snored. Oh God, how he snored! The first night I was somehow able to drowse off once or twice through those mighty snorts and gulps. But now I recollect how these prodigious snores (product of a deviated septum, they had been his lifelong bane, and their cannonade through open windows on summer evenings had been known to arouse neighbors) became during the last night part of the very fabric of my insomnia and formed a turbulent counterpoint to the hectic drift of my thought: to a fleeting but bitter seizure of guilt, to a spasm of erotic mania that swooped down on me like some all-devouring succubus, and finally to a wrenching, sweet, nearly intolerable memory of the South which kept me awake through the whitening hours of dawn.

Guilt. Lying there, I realized that as a boy my father had never punished me severely except once—and then only because of a crime for which I sublimely deserved reprisal. It had to do with my mother. In the year before she died, when I was twelve, the cancer which had been devouring my mother began to filter into her bones. One day her weakened leg gave way; she fell and broke the lower bone, the tibia, which never mended. Thereafter she had to wear a brace and walked haltingly with a cane. She disliked lying in bed and preferred to sit when she could. Whenever she sat it was with her leg outstretched in its brace, propped on a stool or an ottoman. She was then only fifty, and I was aware that she knew she was going to die; I sometimes saw the fear. My mother read books incessantly—books were her narcotic until that time when the intolerable pain began and real narcotics replaced Pearl Buck—and my strongest memory of her during that last period of her life is of the gray head above the gentle, bespectacled, wasting face bent over *You Can't Go Home Again* (she had been a devoted fan long before I had read a word of Wolfe, but she also read best sellers with ornate titles—*Dust Be My Destiny, The Sun Is My Undoing*), a portrait of absorbed and placid contemplation and as domestically commonplace in her way as a study by Vermeer, save for the wicked metal brace propped on its footstool. I also remember a certain venerable frayed and patterned afghan which in cold weather she used to cover her lap and the imprisoned leg. Truly low temperatures almost never beset that part of the Virginia Tidewater but it could become briefly, achingly cold in the nasty months, and because it came rarely, the cold always surprised. In our tiny house we had a weak coal-burning furnace in the kitchen, supplemented in the living room by a toy fireplace.

It was on a sofa in front of this fireplace that my mother lay reading on winter afternoons. As an only child, I was classically though not immoderately spoiled; one of the few chores demanded of me, on afternoons after school during the winter months, was that I hurry home and see to it that the fireplace was well fueled, since although my mother was not yet totally incapacitated, it was far beyond her strength to throw wood on a fire. There was a telephone, but in an adjoining room, down steps she could not negotiate. Already it must be easy to guess the nature of the outrage I committed: one afternoon I abandoned her. I was lured away by the promise of a ride with a schoolmate and his grown-up brother in a new Packard Clipper, one of the swank cars of the day. I was mad for that car. I was drunk with its vulgar elegance. We streaked with idiot vainglory through the frosty countryside, and as the afternoon faded and evening fell, so did the mercury; at about five o'clock the Clipper halted somewhere far from home out in the pinewoods and I became aware of the sudden descent of windy, vicious cold. And for the first time I thought of the hearth, and my deserted mother, and became sick with alarm. Jesus Christ, *guilt* . . .

Ten years later, lying in bed on the fifth floor of the McAlpin and listening to my father snore, I reflected with a stab of anguish upon my guilt (ineffaceable to that very moment), but it was anguish mingled with a queer tender gratitude for the grace with which the old man had confronted and dealt with my dereliction. Ultimately (and I don't think I have alluded to this) he was a Christian, of the charitable variety. That gray late afternoon—I remember the pinpricks of snow which began to dance in the wind as the Packard rushed homeward—my father returned from work and was at my mother's side half an hour before I got there. When I arrived he was muttering to himself and massaging her hands. The stucco walls of the modest little house had let winter enter like a foul marauder. The fire had hours before died out and he found her shivering helplessly beneath her afghan, her lips bitter and livid, her face chalky-dry with cold but also fright. The room bloomed with smoke from a smoldering log she had tried futilely to shove onto the fire with her cane. God knows what Eskimo ice-floe visions had engulfed her when she sank back amid her best sellers, all those bloated books of the month with which she had tried to barricade herself against death, propped her leg up on the stool with the onerous two-handed hitching motion I remembered, and felt the rods of the metal brace slowly grow as chill as stalactites against that wretched, useless, carcinoma-riddled limb. When I burst through the doorway, I recollect, one impression captured my soul so completely as to seem to envelop the room: her eyes. Those hazel bespectacled eyes and the way that her ravaged, still terrified gaze caught my own, then darted swiftly away. It was the *swiftness* of that turning away which would thereafter define my guilt; it was as swift as a machete dismembering a hand. And I realized with horror how much I resented her burdensome affliction. She wept then, and I wept, but separately, and we listened to each other's weeping as if across a wide and desolate lake.

I am certain that my father—so ordinarily mild and forbearing—said something harsh, scathing. But it was not his words that I ever remembered, only the cold—the blood-congealing cold and darkness of the woodshed where he marched me and where he made me stay until long after darkness fell over the village and frigid moonlight seeped in through the cracks of my cell. How long I shivered and wept there I cannot recall. I was only aware that I was suffering exactly in the same way that my mother had and that my deserts could scarcely be more fitting; no malefactor ever endured his punishment with less rancor. I suppose I was incarcerated for no more than two hours, but I would willingly have stayed there until dawn or, indeed, until I had frozen to death—so long as I was able to expiate my crime. Could it have been that my father's sense of justice had instinctively responded to this need in me for such a fitting atonement? Whatever—and in his calm unflustered way he had done his best—my crime was ultimately beyond expiation, for in my mind it would inescapably and always be entangled in the sordid animal fact of my mother's death.

She died a disgusting death, in a transport of pain. Amid the heat of July, seven months later, she faded away in a stupor of morphine, while all the night before, I pondered over and over those feeble embers in the cold smoky room and speculated with dread on the notion that my abandonment that day had sent her into the long decline from which she never recovered. Guilt. Hateful guilt. Guilt, corrosive as brine. Like typhoid, one can harbor for a lifetime the toxin of guilt. Even as I writhed on the McAlpin's damp and lumpy mattress, grief drove like a spear of ice through my chest when I recaptured the fright in my mother's eyes, wondered once again if that ordeal had not somehow hastened her dying, wondered if she ever forgave me. Fuck it, I thought. Prompted by a commotion next door, I began to think of sex.

The wind rushing through my father's deviated septum had become a wild jungle rhapsody—monkey cries, parrot yawps, pachydermous trumpetings. Through the interstices, so to speak, of this tapestry of noise I heard two people in the next room making whoopee—the old man's archaic term for fornication. Soft sighs, the noise of a thumping bed, a cry of slippery unclothed pleasure. My God, I thought, thrashing about, would I forever be a mere solitary listener of lovemaking—never, never a partaker? Racked with misery, I recalled how my first knowledge of Sophie and Nathan had come like this: Stingo, the hapless eavesdropper. As if he had become an accomplice to the suffering provided me by the couple beyond the wall, my father rolled over with a sudden grunt and fell momentarily quiet, allowing my ears access to each nuance of that bliss. It was sculpted sound, incredibly close, almost tactile —oh, honeyhoneyhoney, the woman breathed—and a rhythmic liquid slurping (which my imagination amplified like a loudspeaker) drove me to glue one ear against the wall. I marveled at the grave colloquy: he asked if he was big enough, then if she had "climaxed." She said she didn't know. Worries, worries. Then there was a sudden silence (a shift, I imagined, of formation) and the peeping prism of my mind tried out Evelyn Keyes and Robert Stack in a breathless *soixante-neuf,* though I soon gave up the fantasy as logic forced me to repopulate my *mise en scène* with characters far more likely to be clients of the McAlpin— two horny dance instructors, Mr. and Mrs. Universe, a pair of insatiable honeymooners from Chattanooga, and the like; the pornographic pageant which I let unfold in my mind became alternately a cauldron and an immolation. (Impossible for me to imagine then—nor would I have believed it had the millennium been foretold to me—that in a matter of scant decades the steamy cinema bazaars on the avenue below would allow me, for five dollars, freely and without anxiety to view sex like the conquistadores beheld the New World: glistening coral-pink vulvas as lofty as the portals of the Carlsbad Caverns; pubic hair like luxuriant groves of Spanish moss; ejaculating priapic engines the size of sequoias; jumbo-sized dreamy-faced wet-lipped young Pocahontases in all conceivable and meticulously detailed attitudes of suck and fuck.)

I dreamed of darling dirty-mouthed Leslie Lapidus. The humiliation of my barren time with her had forced me these last weeks to blot out her memory. But now, conjuring her up in the "female superior" perch recommended by those two famous family love consultants (Drs. Van de Velde and Marie Stopes) I had clandestinely studied at home a few years before, I let Leslie romp astride me until I was smothered by her breasts, half drowned in the dark torrent of her hair. Her words in my ear—words importunate, unfake now—were exaltingly obscene and satisfying. Ever since puberty my sessions of autoerotism, although fairly inventive, had in general been conducted with the firm hand of Protestant moderation; this night, though, my longing was like a stampede and I was virtually trampled beneath it. Oh Lord, how my balls hurt as I synthesized stormy lovemaking not only with Leslie but with the two other enchantresses who had claimed my passion. These were, of course, Maria Hunt and Sophie. Thinking of all three, I realized that one was a Southern WASP, one a Sarah Lawrence Jewess, and the last a Polack—a gathering distinguished not only by its diversity but for the sense that all three were dead. No, not truly dead (only one, luscious Maria Hunt, had gone to her Maker), but in effect extinguished, defunct, kaput, so far as each of them concerned my life.

Could it be, I wondered in my nutty fantasia, that this craving was so intolerably inflamed by the knowledge that all three of these lost china dolls had slipped through my fingers out of some tragic failing or deficiency of my own? Or that indeed their very final inaccessibility—the realization that they were all gone forever—was an actual *cause* of this inferno of lust? My wrist ached. I was stunned by my own promiscuity, and its recklessness. I envisioned a quick switch of partners. So somehow Leslie was transformed into Maria Hunt, with whom I lay tangled on a sandy beach of the Chesapeake Bay at high noon in summertime; in my fancy her frantic eyes rolled up beneath the lids and she chewed through the lobe of my ear. Imagine, I thought, *imagine*—I was possessing the heroine of my own novel! I was able to extend the ecstasy a long time with Maria; we were still going at it like minks when my father with a primitive strangled sound aborted a snore, sprang up in his bed, then padded off to the bathroom. I waited with a blank brain until finally he returned to bed and began to snore again. And then with desire that was hopeless and tumultuous like ocean breakers of grief I found myself making ravenous love to Sophie. And of course it was she I had wanted all along. It was astounding. For so boyishly idealized and ruinously romantic had been my longing for Sophie all summer that, in truth, I had never really allowed a fully contoured, many-dimensioned, vividly tinted fantasy of sex with her invade or bother, much less take command of, my mind. Now while despair over her loss encircled my throat like hands, I understood for the first time how hopeless was my love for her, and also how immeasurably huge was my lust. With a groan that was loud enough to jar my father from his tormented sleep—a groan that I'm sure sounded inconsolable—I embraced my phantom Sophie, came in an unstoppered deluge, and while coming called out her beloved name. In the shadows, then, my father stirred. I felt his hand reach out to touch me. "You all right, son?" he said in a troubled voice.

Feigning drowsiness, I murmured something intentionally unintelligible. But both of us were awake.

The concern in his voice turned to amusement. "You hollered 'soapy,'" he said. "Crazy nightmare. You must have been caught in a bath."

"I don't know what I was doing," I lied.

He was silent for a while. The electric fan droned on, penetrated intermittently by the city's restless night sounds. Finally he said, "Something's bothering you. I can tell that. Do you want to let me know what it is? Maybe I can help some. Is it a girl—a woman, that is?"

"Yes," I said after a bit, "a *woman*."

"Do you want to tell me about it? I've had my troubles in that sphere."

It helped some to tell him, even though my account was vague and sketchy: a nameless Polish refugee, a few years older, beautiful in a way I could not express, a victim of the war. I alluded dimly to Auschwitz but said nothing about Nathan. I had loved her briefly, I went on, but for various reasons the situation had been impossible. I skimmed over the details: her Polish childhood, her coming to Brooklyn, her job, her lingering disability. She had simply disappeared one day, I told him, and I had no expectation of her returning. I said nothing for a moment, then added in a stoical voice, "I guess I'll manage to get over it after a while." I made it clear that I wanted to change the subject. Talking of Sophie had begun to twist my gut into spasms of pain again, waves of fearful cramps.

My father muttered a few conventionally sympathetic words, then fell silent. "How's your work coming along?" he said at last. I had side-stepped the subject before. "How's that book doing?"

I felt my stomach begin to relax. "It's been going really well," I said, "I've been able to work well out there in Brooklyn. At least until this business with this woman came up, I mean this breakup. It's brought everything pretty much to a dead stop, pretty much to a standstill." This, of course, was an understatement. It was with sickening dread that I faced the possibility of returning to Yetta Zimmerman's, there to try to resume work in a suffocating vacuum without Sophie or Nathan, scribbling away in a place that was a grim echo chamber of memories of shared good times, all vanished now. "I guess I'll get started again pretty soon," I added halfheartedly. I felt our conversation beginning to wind down.

My father yawned. "Well, if you really want to get started," he murmured in a sleep-thick voice, "that old farm down in Southampton is waiting for you. I know it would be just a fine place to work. I hope you think it over, son." He began to snore again, achieving this time no zoolike medley but an all-out bombardment, as of a newsreel soundtrack of the siege of Stalingrad. I plunged my head into my pillow in despair.

Yet I drowsed off and on, even managed to sleep in a fitful way. I dreamed of my ghostly benefactor, the slave boy Artiste, and the dream became somehow fused with the dream of another slave I had known about years before—Nat Turner. I awoke with a wild sigh. It was dawn. I gazed at the ceiling in the opalescent light, listening to the ululation of a police siren on the street below; it grew louder, uglier, demented. I listened to it with the faint anxiety which that shrill alarm always provoked; the sound faded away, a dim demonic warble, at last disappeared up into the warrens of Hell's Kitchen. My God, my God, I thought, how could it be possible that the South and that urban shriek co-existed in this century? It was beyond comprehension.

That morning my father prepared himself for his return to Virginia. Perhaps it was Nat Turner who spawned the flood of memories, the almost feverish nostalgia for the South that overwhelmed me as I lay there in the blossoming morning light. Or perhaps it was only that the Tidewater farm where my father had offered me free lodging now seemed far more of an attractive proposition since I had lost my loved ones in Brooklyn. At any rate, as we ate foam-rubber pancakes in the McAlpin coffee shop, I caused the old man to gape at me with astonishment when I told him to buy another ticket and meet me at Pennsylvania Station. I was coming South with him and would go to the farm, I announced in a chatter of sudden relief and happiness. All he had to do was to give me the rest of the morning to pack up my things and to check out for good from Yetta Zimmerman's.

Yet as I have already mentioned, it did not work out that way—for the time being at least. I called my father from Brooklyn, forced to tell him that I had decided to remain in the city, after all. For that morning I had encountered Sophie upstairs at the Pink Palace, standing alone amid the disarray of that room I thought she had abandoned forever. I realize now that I arrived at a mysteriously decisive moment. Only ten minutes later she would already have collected her odds and ends and departed, and I surely would never have laid eyes on her again. It is foolish to try to second-guess the past. But even today I can't help wondering whether it would not have been better for Sophie had she been spared my accidental intervention. Who knows but whether she might not have made it, might not have actually survived elsewhere—perhaps beyond Brooklyn or even beyond America. Or almost any place.

One of the lesser-known but more sinister operations contained within the Nazi master plan was the program called Lebensborn. A product of the Nazis' phylogenetic delirium, Lebensborn (literally, spring of life) was designed to augment the ranks of the New Order, initially through a systematized breeding program, then by the organized kidnapping in the occupied lands of racially "suitable" children, who were shipped into the interior of the Fatherland, placed in homes faithful to the Führer and thus reared in an aseptic National Socialist environment. Theoretically the children were to be of pure German stock. But that many of these young victims were Polish is another measure of the Nazis' frequent and cynical expediency in racial matters, since although Poles were regarded as subhuman, and along with other Slavic peoples, worthy successors to the Jews of the policy of extermination, they did in many cases satisfy certain crude physical requirements—familiar enough in facial feature to resemble those of Nordic blood and often of a luminiferous blondness that pleased the Nazi aesthetic sense almost more than anything else.

Lebensborn never achieved the vast scope which the Nazis had intended for it but it did meet with some success. The children snatched from their parents in Warsaw alone numbered in the tens of thousands, and the overwhelming majority of these—renamed Karl or Liesel or Heinrich or Trudi and swallowed up in the embrace of the Reich—never saw their real families again. Also, countless children who passed initial screenings but who later failed to meet more rigorous racial tests were exterminated—some at Auschwitz. The program, of course, was meant to be secret, like most of Hitler's squalid schemes, but such iniquity could scarcely be kept completely in the dark. In late 1942 the fair-haired handsome five-year-old son of a woman friend of Sophie's, living in an adjoining apartment in her bomb-blasted building in Warsaw, was spirited away and never again seen. Although the Nazis had taken some pains to throw a smoke screen around the crime, it was clear to everyone, including Sophie, who the culprits were. What bemused Sophie at a later date was how this concept of Lebensborn—which in Warsaw so horrified her and sickened her with fear that she often hid her son, Jan, in a closet at the sound of heavy footfalls on the stairway—became at Auschwitz something she dreamed about and most feverishly desired. It was urged upon her by a friend and fellow prisoner—about whom more later—and it came to mean to her the only way in which to save Jan's life.

That afternoon with Rudolf Höss, she told me, she had had every intention of broaching the notion of the Lebensborn program to the Commandant. She would have had to make her try in a clever, roundabout manner, but it was possible. In the days before their confrontation she had reasoned with considerable logic that Lebensborn might be the only way to free Jan from the Children's Camp. It made special sense, since Jan had been reared bilingual in Polish and German, like herself. She then told me something she had kept from me before. Gaining the Commandant's confidence, she planned to suggest to him that he could use his immense authority to have a lovely blond German-speaking Polish boy with Caucasian freckles and cornflower-blue eyes and the chiseled profile of a fledgling Luftwaffe pilot painlessly transferred from the Children's Camp to some nearby bureaucratic unit in Cracow or Katowice or Wroclaw or wherever, which would then arrange for his transport to shelter and safety in Germany. She would not have to know the child's destination; she would even forswear any need for knowledge of his whereabouts or his future so long as she could be sure that he was secure somewhere in the heart of the Reich, where he would probably survive, rather than remaining at Auschwitz, where he would certainly perish. But of course, that afternoon everything had gone haywire. In her confusion and panic she had made a direct plea to Höss for Jan's freedom, and because of his unpredicted reaction to this plea—his rage—she found herself completely off balance, unable to speak to him of Lebensborn even if she had had the wits to remember it. Yet all was not quite lost. In order to be given the opportunity to propose to Höss this nearly unspeakable means for her son's salvation, she had to wait—and that in itself involved a strange, harrowing scene the next day.

But she was not able to tell me all this at once. That afternoon in the Maple Court, after describing to me how she fell on her knees in front of the Commandant, she suddenly broke off, and turning her eyes directly away from me toward the window, remained silent for a long time. Then she abruptly excused herself and disappeared for some minutes into the ladies' room. The jukebox suddenly: the Andrews Sisters again. I looked up at the flyspecked plastic clock celebrating Carstairs whiskey: it was almost five-thirty, and I realized with a small shock that Sophie had been talking to me nearly the whole afternoon. I had never heard of Rudolf Höss before that day, but through her understated, simple eloquence she had caused him to exist as vividly as any apparition that had stalked my most neurotic dreams. But it was plain that she could not go on talking about such a man and such a past indefinitely, hence this firmly defined interruption. And certainly, despite the sense of mystery and unfulfillment she had left me with, I was not about to be so crude as to urge her to tell more. I wanted to shut it all off, even though I was still rocking with the revelation that she had had a child. What she had poured forth already had plainly cost her much; it was spelled out in a quick glimpse I had of her ghostly eyes, aching and fathomless in a trance of blacker memory than her mind perhaps could bear. So I said to myself that the subject, for the time being at least, was closed.

I ordered a beer from the slovenly Irish waiter and waited for Sophie to return. The Maple Court regulars, the off-duty cops and elevator operators and building supers and random barflies, had begun to filter in, exuding a faint mist of steam from the summer downpour which had lasted hours. Thunder still grumbled over the far Brooklyn ramparts, but the rain's fragile pattering now, like the intermittent sound of a single tap dancer, told me that most of the deluge had ceased. I listened with one ear to talk of the Dodgers, a preoccupation which that summer verged near lunacy. I swilled at the beer with a sudden raging desire to get plastered. Part of this sprang from all of Sophie's Auschwitz images, which left an actual stink in my nostrils as of the rotted cerements and dank crumbling bonepiles I once beheld amid the brambles of New York's potter's field—an island-secluded place I had become acquainted with in the recent past, a domain, like Auschwitz, of burning dead flesh, and like it, the habitat of prisoners. I had been stationed on the island briefly at the end of my military career. I actually smelled that charnel-house odor again, and to banish it I gulped beer. But another part of my funk had to do with Sophie, and I gazed at the ladies'-room door in a sudden prickle of anxiety—what if she had ducked out on me? what if she had disappeared? —unable to figure out how to cope either with the new crisis she had injected into my life or with that craze for her which was like some stupid pathological hunger and which had all but paralyzed my will. My Presbyterian rearing had surely not anticipated such a derangement.

For the terrible thing was that now, just as I had rediscovered her—just as her presence had begun to spill over me like a blessing—she appeared once more to be on the verge of vanishing from my life. That very morning, when I ran into her at the Pink Palace, one of the first things she told me was that she was still leaving. She had come back only to pack up some things she had left. Dr. Blackstock, ever solicitous, concerned about her breakup with Nathan, had found her a tiny but adequate apartment much nearer his office in downtown Brooklyn and she was moving there. My heart had plummeted. It was wordlessly evident that although Nathan had abandoned her for good, she was still mad for him; the vaguest allusion to him on my part caused her eyes to shadow over in grief. Even putting this aside, I utterly lacked the courage to express my longing for her; without appearing foolish, I could not follow her to her new dwelling miles away—could not anyway, even if I had the means to do so. I felt crippled, hamstrung by the situation, but she was obviously on her way out of the orbit of my own existence with its absurdly unrequited love. There was something so ominous in this realization of my approaching loss that I began to feel a dull nausea. Also a leaden, reasonless anxiety. That is why, when Sophie failed to return from the rest room after what seemed an interminable time (it could only have been a few minutes), I rose with the intention of invading those intimate precincts in search of her—*ah!*—when she reappeared. To my delight and surprise she was smiling. Even today I so often remember Sophie glimpsed across Maple Court vistas. Anyway, whether by accident or celestial design a shaft of dusty sunlight, bursting through the last clouds of the departing storm outside, caught her head and hair for an instant and surrounded it with an immaculate quattrocento halo. Given my unabashed hots for her, I hardly needed her to appear angelic, but she did. Then the halo evaporated, she strode toward me with the silk of her skirt flowing in innocent, voluptuous play against her ripely outlined crotch, and I heard some slave or donkey down in the salt mines of my spirit give a faint heartsick moan. How long, Stingo, how long, old brother-self?

"I'm sorry I took so long, Stingo," she said as she sat down beside me. After the chronicle of the afternoon it was hard to believe she was so cheerful. "In the bathroom I met an old Russian *bohémienne*—a, you know, *diseuse de bonne aventure*."

"What?" I said. "Oh, you mean a fortuneteller." I had seen the old hag in the bar several times before, one of Brooklyn's myriad Gypsy hustlers.

"Yes, she read my palm," she said brightly. "She spoke to me in Russian. And do you know what? She said this. She said, 'You have had recent bad fortune. It concerns a man. An unhappy love. But do not fear. Everything will turn out well.' Isn't that wonderful, Stingo? Isn't that just great?"

It was my feeling then, as it is now, and forgive the sexism, that the most rational-seeming females are push-overs for such harmlessly occult *frissons*, but I let it slide and said nothing; the augury seemed to give Sophie great joy and I could not help but start to share her sunny mood. (But what could it mean? I worried. Nathan was *gone*.) However, the Maple Court began to vibrate with unhealthy shadows, I yearned for the sun, and when I suggested that we take a stroll in the late-afternoon air she quickly agreed.

The storm had washed Flatbush sparkling clean. Lightning had struck somewhere nearby; there was a smell in the street of ozone, eclipsing even the fragrance of sauerkraut and bagels. My eyelids felt gritty. I blinked painfully in the blinding glare; after Sophie's dark memories and the Maple Court's crepuscular murk, the bourgeois blocks rimming Prospect Park seemed dazzling, ethereal, almost Mediterranean, like a flat leafy Athens. We walked to the corner of the Parade Grounds and watched the kids playing baseball in the sandlots. Overhead the droning airplane with its trailing banner, ubiquitous that Brooklyn summer against cloud-streaked ultramarine, advertised more nightly thrills at the hippodrome of Aqueduct. For a long while we squatted in a patch of weedy, rain-damp, rank-smelling grass while I explained to Sophie the mechanics of baseball; she was a serious student, sweetly engaged, her eyes attentive. I found myself so caught up in my own didactic spell that at last all the doubts and wonderments about Sophie's past that had lingered there since her recent long recital scattered from my mind, even the most dreadful and mysterious uncertainty: what had finally happened to her little boy?

The question came back to trouble me as we walked the short block to Yetta's house. I wondered if the story of Jan was something she could ever reveal. But this perplexity soon went away. I was dogged by another concern: I had begun to fret powerfully inside over Sophie herself. And the pain intensified when she mentioned again that she would be leaving tonight for her new apartment. Tonight! It was all too clear that "tonight" meant right now.

"I'm going to miss you, Sophie," I blurted as we clumped up the Pink Palace's front steps. I was conscious of the loutish vibrato in my voice, pitched just this side of desperation. "I'm really going to miss you!"

"Oh, we'll be seeing each other, don't worry, Stingo. We really will! After all, I'm not going too far away. I'm still going to be in Broooklyn." The shading of her words brought some reassurance, but of a fragile and anemic sort; it bespoke loyalty and a *kind* of lovingness and a desire—even a resolute desire—to maintain old ties. But it fell short of that emotion that brings cries and whispers. Affection for me she had—of that I was sure—but passion, no. About which I could say that I had harbored hope but no wild illusions.

"We'll have dinner together a lot," she said while I trailed her upstairs to the second floor. "Don't forget, Stingo, I'm going to miss you too. After all, you're about the best friend I have, you and Dr. Blackstock." We went into her room. It looked already close to being vacated. I was struck by the fact that the radio-phonograph was still there; somehow I recalled from Morris Fink that Nathan had intended to come back and carry it away with him, but he obviously had not. Sophie turned the radio on and from WQXR the sound of the overture to *Russlan and Ludmilla* blared forth. It was the sort of romantic fustian we both barely tolerated, but she let it play; the hoofbeats of the Tartar kettledrums began thudding through the room. "I'll write down my address for you," she said, fumbling through her pocketbook. It was an expensive bag—Moroccan, I believe—made of handsome tooled leather, an item that caught my eye only because I remembered the day a few weeks before when Nathan, with extravagant loving pride, had given it to her. "You'll come to see me often and we'll go out to dinner. There are a lot of restaurants there that are good but cheap. Funny, where's that slip of paper with the address on it? I don't even remember the number myself yet. Someplace on a street called Cumberland, it is supposed to be close to Fort Greene Park. We can still take walks together, Stingo."

"Oh, but I'm going to be very lonesome, Sophie," I said.

She looked up from the radio and cocked her eye at me in an expression which I suppose might have been regarded as impish, plainly oblivious of my undisguised Sophiemania, and now uttering words which made up the last type of half-assed sentiment I wanted to hear. "You'll find some beautiful girl, Stingo, very soon—I'm sure of that. Someone very sexy. Someone like that good-looking Leslie Lapidus, only less of the coquette, more *complaisante*—"

"Oh God, Sophie," I groaned, "deliver me from the Leslies of the world."

Then suddenly something about the entire situation—Sophie's imminent departure, but also the handbag and the near-empty room with its associations of Nathan and the days of the recent past, the music and the high hilarity and all the glorious times we had had together—filled me with such ruinously enervating gloom that I let out another groan, loud enough that I saw a startled light like a flash of beads come to Sophie's eyes. And quite violently disturbed now, I found myself gripping her firmly by the arms.

"Nathan!" I cried. "Nathan! Nathan! What in God's name has happened? What has *happened,* Sophie? *Tell me!"* I was close to her, nose to nose, and I was aware of one or two flecks of my spittle landing on her cheek. "Here is this incredible guy who's madly in love with you, the Prince Charming of all time, a man who *adores* you—I've seen it on his face, Sophie, like a form of *worship*—and all of a sudden you're *out of his life*. What in God's name happened to him, Sophie? He puts you out of his life! You can't tell me it's just because of some simple-minded suspicion that you've been *unfaithful* to him, like he said the other night at the Maple Court. It's got to have some deeper meaning, some deeper cause than that. Or what about me? Me? *Me!"* I began to smite my chest to emphasize my own involvement in the tragedy. "What about the way he treated *me,* this guy? I mean, Sophie, Jesus Christ, I don't have to explain to you, do I, that Nathan came to be like a brother to me, a fucking *brother*. I never knew anyone like him in all my life, anyone more intelligent, more generous, more funny and fun to be with, more—oh Jesus, simply no one as *great*. I have *loved* that guy! I mean, practically single-handed it was Nathan who when he read my first stuff gave me the faith to go on and be a writer. I felt he did it out of *love*. And then out of nowhere—out of the fucking *blue,* Sophie—he turns on me like a snarling dog with rabies. Turns on me, tells me my writing is shit, treats me as if I were the most contemptible asshole he had ever known. And then cuts me out of his life as firmly and finally as he cut you." My voice had risen its usual uncontrolled octaves, becoming an epicene mezzo-soprano. "I can't *stand* this, Sophie! *What are we going to do?"*

The tears pouring down Sophie's face in watery bright freshets told me that I should not have unloaded myself in this way. I should have had more control. I now saw that I could not have caused her worse pain had she possessed a hot inflamed cicatrix from which I had savagely yanked the stitches in a horrible ball of fresh sutures and outraged flesh. But I could not help myself; indeed, I felt her grief meet mine in some huge gushing confluence and flow onward with it even as I continued to rage. "He can't take people's love for him and piss on it like that. It's unfair! It's . . . it's . . ." I began to stammer. "It's, by God, fucking *inhuman!*"

She turned away from me then, sobbing. There was something a little somnambulistic about the way in which she walked with arms rigid at her side across the room to the edge of the bed. Then abruptly she flopped face down on the apricot bedspread and smothered her face in her hands. She was silent but her shoulders were heaving. I went to the side of the bed and stood above her, looking down. I began to master my voice. "Sophie," I said, "forgive me for all this. But I just don't understand anything. I don't understand anything about Nathan, and maybe I don't understand anything about you, either. Though I think I'm able to figure out a lot more about you than I ever will about him." I paused. It was, I knew, like creating another wound to mention that matter which she herself had obviously felt was so hateful to talk about—and hadn't she with her own lips warned me away from it?—but I was compelled to say what I had to say. I reached down and laid my hand lightly on her bare arm. The skin was very warm and seemed to throb beneath my fingers like the throat of a frightened bird. "Sophie, the other night . . . the other night at the Maple Court when he . . . when he *cast us out*. That awful night. Surely he knew you had a son in that place—just a while ago you told me that you let him know that. Then how could he have been so cruel to you, taunting you like that, asking you how you lived through it all while so many of the others were"—the word nearly choked me, a clot in my throat, but I managed to get it out—"were *gassed*. How could anybody do that to you? How could anyone love you and be so unbelievably cruel?"

She said nothing for a while, merely lay there with her face buried in her hands. I sat on the edge of the bed beside her and stroked the pleasantly warm, almost febrile surface of her arm, delicately skirting the vaccination scar. From that angle I could plainly see the grim blue-black tattoo, the row of numbers remarkably neat, a little barb-wire fence of orderly ciphers in which one "seven" was bisected with the meticulous European slash. I smelled that herbal perfume she so often wore. Could it be possible, Stingo, I asked myself, that she would ever love you? I suddenly wondered if I dared now make a pass at her. No, definitely not. Lying there, she seemed terribly vulnerable, but my outburst had tired me, leaving me somehow shaken and empty of desire. Moving my fingers upward, I touched the loose strands of her butter-bright hair. Finally I sensed that she had stopped weeping. Then I heard her say, "It was never his fault. He always had this demon, this demon which appeared when he was in his *tempêtes*. It was the demon in control, Stingo."

I do not know which image at this moment, each appearing almost simultaneously at the rim of my consciousness, gave me the chill that traversed the length of my spinal column: that of black monstrous Caliban or of Morris Fink's fearful golem. But I felt myself shiver, and in the midst of the spasm said, "What do you mean, Sophie—a demon?"

She made no immediate reply. Instead, after a long silence, she raised her head up and said something in a soft matter-of-fact voice that truly flabbergasted me, it was so totally out of character, so much a part of some other Sophie I had not witnessed until this very day.

"Stingo," she said, "I can't leave here so quickly. Too many memories. Do me a big favor. Please. Go over to Church Avenue and buy a bottle of whiskey. I want very much to get drunk."

I got her the whiskey—a fifth of rye—which helped enable her to tell me about some bad moments during the turbulent year she spent with Nathan, before I came on the scene. All of which might be considered unnecessary to recount were it not for the fact that he would return to possess our lives again.

In Connecticut, somewhere on the beautiful winding arboreal highway that stretches north and south along the riverbank between New Milford and Canaan, there had been an old country inn with slanted oak floors, a sunny white bedroom with samplers on the wall, two damp panting Irish setters downstairs and the smell of applewood burning in the fireplace—and it was there, Sophie told me that night, that Nathan tried to take her life and then end his own in what has come to be known in the vernacular as a suicide pact. This happened in the fall of the year when the leaves were fiercely incandescent, a few months after their first meeting in the Brooklyn College library. Sophie said she would have remembered the terrible episode for many reasons (for example, it was simply the first time he had really even *raised his voice* at her since they met) but she would never be able to obliterate the *chief* reason: his raging insistence (again for the first time since they had been together) that she justify to his satisfaction the way in which she survived Auschwitz while "the others" (as he put it) perished.

When Sophie described this browbeating and then told the wretched tale of the ensuing events, I was of course immediately reminded of Nathan's wild behavior on that recent night in the Maple Court when he bade both of us his adamantly final, unfond farewell. I was about to point out to Sophie the similarity and question her about it, but by this time—devouring a huge steaming mound of spaghetti in a little Italian restaurant she and Nathan used to frequent on Coney Island Avenue—she had become so totally absorbed in her chronicle of their life together that I hesitated, faltered helplessly, then lumpishly kept silent. I considered the whiskey. It was baffling about Sophie and her whiskey—baffling and a little overpowering. For one thing, she had the capacity of a Polish hussar; it was astounding to see this poised, lovely and usually painfully correct creature put away the booze; fully a quarter of the fifth of Seagram's I had bought her had vanished by the time we took a taxi to the restaurant. (She also insisted on transporting the bottle, upon which, it is important to add, I committed no incursions, sticking, as always, to beer.) I attributed this new indulgence to grief over Nathan's abandonment.

Even so, I was more struck by the manner of Sophie's drinking than the amount. For the fact is that these powerful eighty-six-proof spirits diluted with only a little water had no apparent disorganizing effect on Sophie's tongue or thought processes at all. At least this was true when I first witnessed her new-found diversion. Utterly composed, each yellow lock in place, she could slosh it down with the toothy glee of a barmaid out of Hogarth. I wondered if she was not protected by some genetic or cultural adaptation to alcohol which Slavic people seem to share with the Celts. Save for a tender rosiness, there were only two ways in which Seagram's 7 seemed to alter her expression or her manner. It did turn her into a runaway talker. It made her pour it all out. Not that she had ever held back with me when speaking about Nathan or Poland or the past. But the whiskey transformed her speech into a spillway notable for its precise, unhurried cadences. It was a kind of lubricated diction in which many of the more briery Polish-accented consonants became magically smoothed over. The other thing whiskey did to her was quite fetching. Fetching, that is, in a maddeningly frustrating way: it let loose practically all of her dammed-up reticences about sex. I squirmed with mixed discomfort and delight as she spoke of her past love life with Nathan. The words came out in a charmingly open, unabashed, tickled voice, like that of a child who has discovered pig Latin. "He said I was a wonderful piece of ass," she announced nostalgically, and shortly after this, told me, "We used to love to fuck in front of mirrors." God, if she only knew what manner of sugarplums danced in my head when she gave tongue to such delicious conceits.

But for the most part her mood was funereal when she spoke of Nathan, reminiscing with a persistent use of the past tense; it was as if she were speaking of someone long ago dead and buried. And when she related the story of their "suicide pact" on that weekend in the frosty Connecticut countryside, I was saddened and astonished. Even so, I do not think that my astonishment over that mournful little incident could have been exceeded by *any* form of surprise when, shortly before telling me about that aborted appointment with death, she revealed still another piece of dismal news.

"You know, Stingo," she said a little hesitantly, "you know that Nathan was always taking drugs. I didn't know if you could see this or not. Anyway, for some reason I have not been quite honest with you. I have not been able to mention it."

Drugs, I thought, *merciful God.* I really found it almost impossible to believe. The up-to-date reader of this narrative has most likely assumed such a fact about Nathan already, but certainly I had not. In 1947 I was as innocent about drugs as I was about sex. (Oh, those lamblike forties and fifties!) Our present-day drug culture had not seen, that year, even the glimmerings of dawn, and my notion of addiction (if I had ever really thought of such a thing) was connected with the idea of "dope fiends"—goggle-eyed madmen in strait jackets immured in backwater asylums, slavering molesters of children, zombies stalking the back streets of Chicago, comatose Chinese in their smoky dens, and so on. There was the taint about drugs of the irredeemably depraved, almost as evil as certain images of sexual intercourse—which until I was at least thirteen I visualized as a brutish act committed in secrecy upon dyed blondes by huge drunken unshaven ex-convicts with their shoes on. As for drugs, certainly I knew nothing about the types and subtle gradations of these substances. Save for opium, I do not think that I could name a single drug, and what Sophie disclosed about Nathan produced the immediate effect on me of having heard about something criminal. (That it *was* criminal was incidental to my moral shock.) I told her I didn't believe it, but she assured me it was true, and when directly after this my shock merged into curiosity and I asked her what he had used, I heard for the first time the word amphetamine. "He took this stuff called Benzedrine," she said, "also cocaine. But huge doses. Enough sometimes to make him crazy. It was easy enough for him to get this at Pfizer, at the laboratory where he was doing his work. Although, of course, it was not legal." So that was it, I thought in wonder, *that* was behind those seizures of rage, of seething violence, of paranoia. How blind I had been!

Yet she was aware now, she said, that most of the time he had his habit under control. Nathan had always been high-strung, vivacious, talkative, agitated; since throughout the first five months they were together (and they were together constantly) she rarely saw him in the act of taking "the stuff," she made only the most belated connection between drugs and what she simply thought was his somewhat frenetic but ordinary behavior. And she went on to say that during those months of the previous year his behavior—drug-induced or not—his presence in her life, his entire being, brought her the happiest days she had ever known. She realized how helpless and adrift she had been during that time when she first came to Brooklyn and to Yetta's rooming house; trying to hold on to her reason, trying to thrust away the past from the rim of her memory, she *thought* she was in control of herself (after all, had not Dr. Blackstock told her that she was the most efficient secretary-receptionist he had ever known?), but in reality she was on the verge of becoming emotionally unhelmed, no more in command of her destiny than a puppy that has been hurled floundering into a turbulent pool. "Whoever it was that finger-fucked me that day in the subway made me see that," she said. Even though she had been momentarily restored from that trauma, she knew she was on a downward slide—hurtling fatally and rapidly down—and she could hardly bear to think what might have happened to her had not Nathan (blundering like herself into the library on that momentous day, searching for an out-of-print copy of a book of short stories by Ambrose Bierce; bless Bierce! praise Bierce!) appeared like a redemptive knight from the void and restored her to life.

Life. That is what it was. He had actually given her life. He had (helped by the good offices of his brother Larry) restored her to health, causing her bloodsucking anemia to be corrected at Columbia Presbyterian, where the gifted Dr. Hatfield found a few other nutritional defects that needed straightening out. For one thing, he discovered that even after all these months she had the residual effects of scurvy. So he prescribed huge pills. Soon the ugly little skin hemorrhages, which had plagued her all over, disappeared, but even more remarkable was the change that came over her hair. Her golden hair had always been her most reassuring physical vanity, but having passed through Hades like the rest of her body, it had grown out scruffy, dull and fatigued-looking. Dr. Hatfield's ministrations changed all that too, and it was not very long—six weeks or so—before Nathan was purring like a hungry tomcat into its luxuriance, stroking it compulsively and insisting that she should start modeling for shampoo ads.

Indeed, supervised by Nathan, the splendid apparatus of American medicine brought Sophie as close to a state of smiling fitness as could be wrought upon a person who had suffered such dreadful damage—and this included her marvelous new teeth. Her choppers, as Nathan referred to them, replaced the temporary false teeth which had been installed by the Red Cross in Sweden, and were the handiwork of still another friend and colleague of Larry's—one of New York's classiest practitioners of prosthodontia. Those teeth were hard to forget. They had to be the dental equivalent of Benvenuto Cellini. They were fabulous teeth, with a kind of icy, mother-of-pearl sparkle; every time she opened her mouth really wide I was reminded of Jean Harlow in smoochy close-ups, and on one or two memorably sunny days when Sophie burst into laughter those teeth lit up an entire room like a flashbulb.

So, brought back to the land of the living, she could only treasure the wonderful time she had with Nathan all through that summer and early fall. His generosity was exhaustless, and although a greed for luxury was not a component of her nature, she liked the good life and she accepted his bounty with pleasure—as much of her pleasure deriving from the delight which pure giving plainly gave to him as from the things themselves which he gave. And he gave her and shared in everything she could possibly have wanted: record albums of beautiful music, tickets to concerts, Polish books and French books and American books, divine meals in restaurants of every ethnic description all over Brooklyn and Manhattan. As with his nose for wine, Nathan had an informed palate (a reaction, he said, to a childhood surfeit of soggy kreplach and gefilte fish) and he took obvious joy in making her acquainted with New York's incredible and manifold banquet.

Money itself never seemed to be of any object; his job at Pfizer obviously paid well. He bought her fine clothes (including the droll and beguiling matching "costumes" I first saw them dressed in), rings, earrings, bracelets, bangles, beads. Then there were the movies. During the war she had missed them with almost the same longing as she had missed music. In Cracow before the war there had been a period when she had drenched herself in American movies—the bland innocent romances of the thirties, with stars like Errol Flynn and Merle Oberon and Gable and Lombard. She had also adored Disney, especially Mickey Mouse and *Snow White.* And—oh God!—Fred Astaire and Ginger Rogers in *Top Hat!* And so in New York's paradise of theatres she and Nathan sometimes went on weekend binges—staring themselves red-eyed through five, six, seven films between Friday night and the last show on Sunday. Nearly everything she possessed flowed from Nathan's munificence, including even (she said with a giggle) her diaphragm. Having her fitted for a diaphragm by one more of Larry's associates was a final and perhaps artfully symbolic touch in Nathan's program of restorative medicine; she had never used a diaphragm before and accepted it with a rush of liberating satisfaction, feeling that it was the ultimate token of her leave-taking from the church. But it liberated her in more than one way. "Stingo," she said, "never did I think two people could fuck so much. Or love it so much either."

The only thorn in this bower of roses, Sophie told me, was her employment. That is, the fact that she continued to work for Dr. Hyman Blackstock, who, after all, was a chiropractor. To Nathan, brother of a first-rate doctor, a young man who considered himself a dedicated scientist (and for whom the canons of medical ethics were as sacred as if he himself had taken the Hippocratic oath), the idea of her laboring in the employ of a quack was nearly intolerable. He told her point-blank that in his view it was tantamount to whoring and he implored her to quit. To be sure, for a long time he made an extended joke out of it all, concocting all sorts of gags and stories about chiropractors and their shoddy craft that caused her to laugh despite herself; the general facetiousness of his attitude allowed her to decide that his objections were not to be taken too seriously. Even so, when his complaints grew louder and his animadversions more serious and cutting, she steadfastly refused to entertain any idea of leaving her job, as uncomfortable as the whole situation seemed to make Nathan feel. It was one of the few tangents in their relationship where she felt unable to adopt a subservient point of view. And she was firm about the matter. After all, she was not *married* to Nathan. She had to feel a certain independence. She had to remain employed in that year when employment was devilishly difficult to come by, especially for a young woman who (as she kept pointing out to Nathan) had "no talents." Furthermore, she felt very secure in this job where she could speak in her native tongue to the boss, and she had frankly grown quite fond of Blackstock. He was like a godfather or beloved uncle to her and she made no bones about the fact. Alas, she came to realize that it was this perfectly innocuous fondness, containing no romantic overtone whatever, that Nathan misconstrued, adding fuel to his seething animosity. It would perhaps have been faintly comic had not his misplaced jealousy contained seeds of the violent, and worse . . .

Earlier there was a bizarre, peripheral tragedy affecting Sophie which should be recounted here if only because of the way in which it elaborates all the foregoing. It has to do with Blackstock's wife, Sylvia, and the fact that she was a "problem drinker"; the horrible event itself occurred about four months after Sophie and Nathan began keeping company, in the early fall . . .

"I knew knee-deep she was a problem drinker," Blackstock later told Sophie in his desperate lament, "but I had no idea how great was her problem." He confessed with wrenching guilt to a certain willful blindness: coming home night after night to St. Albans from his office he would try to ignore her slurred speech after the single cocktail, usually a Manhattan, which he served both of them, attributing her addled tongue and unsteady gait to a simple intolerance of alcohol. But even so, he knew he was fooling himself, in his desperate love for her shrinking from the truth that was revealed in graphic figuration a few days after her death. Stuffed into a closet in her private dressing room—a sanctum never penetrated by Blackstock—were over seventy empty quart bottles of Southern Comfort, which the poor woman apparently dreaded to risk disposing of, although she plainly had no trouble acquiring the powerful sweet elixir and stowing it away by the case. Blackstock realized—or allowed himself to realize—only when it was too late that this had been going on for months, maybe years. "If only I hadn't pampered her so," he grieved to Sophie. "If only I had faced up to the fact that she was a—" he hesitated at the word—"a *lush*. I could have put her into *psychoanalytical therapy,* had her cured." His recriminations were terrible to hear. "It's my fault, all mine!" he wept. And chief among his assemblage of griefs was this: that basically aware of her awful plight, he had still permitted her to drive an automobile.

Sylvia was his precious pet, and that is what he called her. My pet. He had no one else to really squander his money on, and so, instead of voicing the standard husband's complaint, he actually encouraged her frequent buying sprees to Manhattan. There with some female friend—flush, plump and idle like herself—she would sweep through Altman and Bergdorf and Bonwit and half a dozen other fancy shops and return to Queens with the back seat stacked high with boxes of ladies' merchandise, most of which languished in pristine condition in her bureau drawers or got stuffed into the recesses of her many closets, where Blackstock later found score upon score of unused gowns and dresses faintly smudged with mildew. What Blackstock did not know until the sad fact was past undoing was that after her orgy of shopping she usually got drunk with her companion of the day; she favored the lounge of the Westbury Hotel on Madison Avenue where the bartender was friendly, indulgent and discreet. But her ability to cope with the Southern Comfort—which even at the Westbury remained her steady tipple—was being swiftly undermined, and the disaster when it struck was sudden, terrifying and, as I say, almost indecently bizarre.

Returning to St. Albans one afternoon by way of the Triborough Bridge, she lost control of the car while driving at ferocious speed (the police said that the speedometer was frozen at eighty-five miles an hour), smashed into the rear end of a truck and spun out against the guardrail of the bridge, where the Chrysler was instantly transmuted into steel splinters and plastic shards. Sylvia's friend, a Mrs. Braunstein, died three hours later in a hospital. Sylvia herself was decapitated, which in itself was ghastly enough; it was intolerable that to Blackstock's nearly insane grief was added the knowledge that the head itself vanished, catapulted by the immense impact into the East River. (There are in the lives of all of us odd instances where one later crosses the path of someone associated with what one regarded as an abstract public event; that spring I had with a small shudder read the *Daily Mirror* headline RIVER SEARCH CONTINUES FOR WOMAN'S HEAD, scarcely realizing that I would soon have at least a distant connection with the victim's spouse.)

Blackstock was virtually a suicide. His grief was an inundation—*Amazonian.* He suspended his end of the practice indefinitely, leaving his patients to the ministrations of his assistant, Seymour Katz. He announced piteously that he might never resume practice, but retire to Miami Beach. The doctor had no near relatives, and in his wild bereavement—so deep and burningly felt that she could not help but be moved by it—Sophie found herself acting as a kind of surrogate kin, a younger sister or daughter. During the several days while the search for Sylvia's head went on, Sophie was at his side in the St. Albans house almost constantly, fetching him sedatives, brewing him tea, patiently listening to his dirge for his wife. Dozens of people moved in and out, but she was his mainstay. There was the matter of the funeral—he refused to have her buried headless; steeling herself, Sophie had to absorb much gruesome theoretical talk about this problem. (What would happen if nothing was ever found?) But mercifully the head soon showed up, washed ashore on Riker's Island. It was Sophie who took the telephone call from the city morgue, and it was she who on the urgent advice of the medical examiner managed (though with great difficulty) to persuade Blackstock to forgo a final look at the remnant. At last reassembled, Sylvia's body was laid to rest in a Hebrew cemetery on Long Island. Sophie was amazed at the vast numbers of the doctor's friends and patients who attended the funeral. Among the mourners was a personal representative from the mayor of New

York, a high-ranking police inspector, and Eddie Cantor, the famous radio comedian whose spine Blackstock had treated.

Riding back to Brooklyn in the mortuary limousine, Blackstock slumped against Sophie and wept hopelessly, telling her in Polish once again how much she meant to him, as if she were the daughter whom he and Sylvia never had. There was no approximation of a Jewish wake. Blackstock preferred solitude. Sophie went with him to the St. Albans house and helped him straighten out a few things. It was early evening when—over her protests that she should take the subway—he drove her to Brooklyn in his bargelike Fleetwood, depositing her at the door of the Pink Palace just as a hazy autumnal dusk fell over Prospect Park. He seemed much more composed now and had even allowed himself a mild joke or two. He had also downed one or two weak Scotches, although he was not much of a drinking man. But standing with her outside the house he broke into pieces again, and there in the shadowy twilight he embraced her convulsively, nuzzling her neck, muttering distraught words in Yiddish and giving forth the loneliest sobbing sounds she had ever heard. So involved and stricken was this embrace, so *total,* that Sophie did begin to wonder whether in his desolation he was not groping for something more than comfort and daughterly assurance; she felt a midriff pressure and an urgency that was almost sexual. But she thrust the idea from her mind. He was such a puritan. And if during the long time of her job with him he had never made a pass at her, it seemed unlikely that he would do so now, drowned as he was in his misery. This assumption would later prove to be correct, although she would have reason to regret that lengthy, moist and rather uncomfortable enfoldment. For by the sheerest chance Nathan had been watching from above.

She was bone-tired from the ordeal of serving as handmaiden to the doctor's grief, and looked forward to an early bedtime. Another reason to go to bed early, she reflected with rising excitement, was that the next morning, a Saturday, she and Nathan had to get a fresh start for their trip to Connecticut. Sophie had looked forward to their excursion for days. Although even as a child in Poland she had heard of the blazing marvel of the New England foliage in October, Nathan had fueled her expectation, describing the landscape she was about to see in his delicious, extravagant way and telling her that this singularly American spectacle, this amok flambeau unique in all Nature, was simply an aesthetic encounter that must not be missed. He had managed once again to borrow Larry's car for the weekend, and he had reserved a room in a well-known country inn. All this alone would have been enough to whet Sophie's appetite for the adventure, but in addition, except for the funeral and a single summer afternoon at Montauk with Nathan, she had never been outside the confines of New York City. And so this fresh American experience with its hint of bucolic beguilements gave her a thrill of joy and anticipation keener than any of its kind since those childhood summers when the train chuffed out from the Cracow station toward Vienna and the Alto Adige and the swirling mists of the Dolomites.

Climbing to the second floor, she began to wonder what she would wear; the weather had become brisk and she contemplated which item among their elaborate "costumery" might be appropriate for the October woodlands, then suddenly she remembered a lightweight tweed suit Nathan had bought her at Abraham & Straus only two weeks before. Just as she reached the landing she heard Brahms' *Alto Rhapsody* on the phonograph, Marian Anderson's flowering dark exultancy, triumph wrested from eons of despair. Perhaps it was her tiredness or the aftereffects of the funeral, but the music brought a sweet choking sensation to her throat and her eyes blurred with tears. She quickened her step and her heart stirred because she knew the music meant that Nathan was there. But when she opened the door—"I'm home, darling!" she called to him—she was surprised to find no one in the room. She had expected him. He had said he would be there from six o'clock on, but he was gone.

She lay down for what she thought would be a nap, but in her exhaustion slept for a long time, although restlessly. Waking up in the dark, she saw by the alarm clock's dim green eyes that it was past ten o'clock and she was seized by grave, immediate alarm. Nathan! It was so unlike him not to be there at the appointed hour, or at least to fail to leave a note. She felt a frantic sense of desertion. She leaped up from bed and turned on the light and began aimlessly to pace the room. Her only thought was that he had come home from work, then gone out for something and had met with a terrible accident on the street. Each recollected sound of a police siren, screeching just now through her dreams, betokened certain catastrophe. Part of her mind told her that this panic was foolish, but it was something she could not help or avoid. Her love for Nathan was so totally consuming, yet at the same time was defined by such childlike dependence in a hundred ways, that the terror that surrounded her in his unexplained absence was utterly demoralizing, like being caught in that strangling fear—the fear that she might be abandoned by her parents—which she had often felt as a little girl. And she knew that this, too, was irrational but beyond remedy. Turning the radio on, she sought a news announcer's empty distraction. She continued to pace the room, visualizing the most ghastly mishaps, and she was on the verge of dissolving into tears when he suddenly and noisily burst through the door. At that instant she felt an immediate blessing like showering light—resurrection from the dead. She remembered thinking: I cannot believe such love.

He smothered her in his arms. "Let's fuck," he breathed into her ear. Then he said, "No, let's wait. I've got a surprise for you." She trembled in his irresistible bear hug, as pliantly feeble with relief as the stalk of a flower. "Dinner—" she began fatuously.

"Don't talk about dinner," he said loudly, releasing her. "We've got better things to do." As he moved around her in a happy little jig she looked into his eyes; the flashing eccentric glitter there, together with his overflowing, overpowering voice—near-frenzy, manic—told her at once that he was high on his "stuff." Yet although she had never seen him quite this extravagantly agitated, she was not alarmed. Amused, vastly relieved, but not alarmed. She had seen him high before. "We're going to a jam session at Morty Haber's," he announced, rubbing his nose like a lovesick moose across her cheek. "Get your coat on. We're going to a jam session and *celebrate!*"

"Celebrate what, darling?" she asked. Her love for him and her sense of salvation were at that moment so lunatic that she would have tried to swim the Atlantic with him had he commanded her to do so. Nonetheless, she was perplexed and all but engulfed by his electric fever (an intense feeling of famishment stabbed her too) and she reached out her hands in a vain, fluttering effort to quiet him down. "Celebrate what?" she said again. She couldn't restrain herself from chortling at his loud runaway enthusiasm. She kissed his *schnoz.*

"Remember the experiment I was telling you about?" he said. "That blood-classification thing that had us stumped all last week. The problem I was telling you about having to do with serum enzymes?"

Sophie nodded. She had never understood the vaguest thing about his laboratory research but had listened faithfully and remained an attentive one-woman gallery for his complex disquisitions on physiology and the chemical enigmas of the human body. Had he been a poet, he would have read her his gorgeous verse. But he was a biologist and he made her captive to macrocytes and hemoglobin electrophoresis and ion exchange resins. She understood nothing of this. But she loved it all because she loved Nathan, and now in reply to his question, which was largely rhetorical, she said, "Oh yes."

"We crashed through on that this afternoon. We got the whole problem licked. I mean *licked,* Sophie! It was our biggest barrier by far. Now all we have to do is to run the whole experiment one more time for the Standards and Control Department—a formality, that's all—and we'll be in like a bunch of burglars. We'll have a clear road to the most important medical breakthrough in history!"

"Hooray!" said Sophie.

"Give me a kiss." He *shmoozed* and whispered around the edge of her lips with his own lips and stuck his tongue in her mouth, insinuating it there with droll titillating little forays and retreats, making movements gently copulatory. Then abruptly he drew away. "So we're going to celebrate at Morty's. Let's go!"

"I'm hungry!" she exclaimed. It was not a very firm objection, but she felt compelled to say it, feeling honest stomach pangs.

"We'll *eat* at Morty's," he replied cheerfully, "don't worry. There'll be plenty for *noshing*—let's go!"

"A special bulletin." It arrested them both at the same instant—that radio announcer's voice with its coached and modulated rhythms. Sophie saw Nathan's face lose all mobility for a split second, as if frozen, and then she herself glimpsed in the mirror her jaw cocked awkwardly sideways in a rigid attitude of dislocation, a pained look in her eyes, as if she had broken a tooth. The announcer was saying that in the prison at Nuremberg ex-Field Marshal Hermann Göring had been discovered dead in his cell, a suicide. The means of death was apparently cyanide poisoning, accomplished orally by a capsule or pill which had been secreted somewhere on his body. Contemptuous to the last (the voice droned on), the condemned Nazi leader thus avoided retribution at the hands of his enemies in the same way as had such of his predecessors in death as Joseph Goebbels, Heinrich Himmler and the master planner Adolf Hitler . . . Sophie felt a shiver run through her body and saw Nathan's face unfreeze, regaining its vivacious shape just as he said with a soft gasp, "Jesus! He beat the man. He beat the man with the rope. That clever, fat son of a bitch!"

He leaped at the radio, hovering over it while he played with the dial. Sophie stirred about restlessly. She had with methodical determination tried to banish from her mind practically everything to do with the past war, and she had completely ignored the Nuremberg trials, which had captured the headlines all during the year. Indeed, her aversion to reading about Nuremberg had provided one of her rationalizations for not applying herself to American journalism and thus improving—or at least enlarging—an important compartment of her English. She had thrust it all from her head, as with nearly everything else of the immediate past. As a matter of fact, so oblivious had she been in recent weeks of the final scene of Götterdämmerung being performed on the stage at Nuremberg that she was quite unaware even that Göring had been sentenced to the gallows, and she was left strangely unmoved by this news that he had thwarted the hangman only hours before his scheduled execution.

Someone named H.V. Kaltenborn was uttering one of those prolonged and portentous obituaries—the voice mentioned among other things that Göring had been a drug addict—and Sophie began to giggle. She giggled at Nathan, carrying on a zany monologue in counterpoint to the depressing biography. "Where in the *fuck* did he hide that capsule of cyanide? Up his ass? Surely they looked up his ass. A dozen times! But in those mountainous cheeks of lard—maybe they missed it. Where else? In his belly button? In a tooth? Didn't the Army morons look into his navel? Maybe in one of those folds of flab. Under his chin! I'll bet you Fatso had that capsule tucked away there all the time. Even as he was grinning at Shawcross, at Telford Taylor, grinning at the madness of the whole proceedings, he had that pill tucked up under his fat chin . . ." A squawk of static. Sophie heard the commentator say, "Many informed observers are of the opinion that it was Göring more than any other single German leader who was responsible for instituting the concept of the concentration camps. Although roly-poly and jolly in appearance, reminding many people of a comic-opera buffoon, Göring, it is believed, in his evil genius was the real father of such places which shall be ever known in infamy as Dachau, Buchenwald, Auschwitz . . ."

Sophie suddenly wandered away behind the Chinese screen and busied herself at the washbasin. She felt a hovering and ominous discomfort at the bubbling-over of all the things on earth she wanted to forget. Why hadn't she left that damned radio turned off? Through the screen she listened to the flow of Nathan's soliloquy. It no longer seemed so funny to her because she knew how wound up Nathan could get, how upset and jangled he could become when in certain moods he tried to reckon with the recently bygone unspeakables. It could at times turn into a preoccupying rage that scared her, so quickly was he transformed from his exuberant, rollicking, outgoing self to a desperate soul riddled with anguish. "Nathan," she called. "Nathan darling, turn off the radio and let's go to Morty's. I'm really so hungy. Please!"

But she could tell he didn't hear her, or didn't care to,

and she wondered if—just possibly—the foundation of his obsession about the Nazi handiwork, the whole intolerable history which she yearned to reject as passionately as he seemingly desired to embrace, had not been laid that afternoon only weeks before when they had seen a certain newsreel. For at the RKO Albee theatre, where they had gone to a film staring Danny Kaye (still her favorite clown in all the world), the glorious mood of tomfoolery had been abruptly shattered by a brief sequence in a newsreel showing the Warsaw ghetto. Sophie had been washed in a flood of recognition. Even in its rubble, like an exploded volcano, the configuration of the ghetto was familiar to her (she had lived on its perimeter), but as with all movie scenes of war-blasted Europe she tended to narrow her eyes to slits, as if to filter out the wasteland and render it even more a smudge, a neutral blur. But she was conscious of some religious ceremony as an assemblage of Jews unveiled a monument commemorating their massacre and their martyrdom and the sound of a tenor voice keened its Hebrew requiem over the desolate gray scene like an angel with a dagger through its heart. In the darkness of the theatre Sophie heard Nathan murmur the unfamiliar word *Kaddish,* and when they emerged into the sunlight he passed his fingers in a distraught motion across his eyes and she saw the tears pouring down his cheeks. She was shocked, for it was the very first time she had ever seen Nathan—her own Danny Kaye, her own adorable clown—show that kind of emotion.

She moved from behind the Chinese screen. "Come on, darling," she called in a lightly begging tone, but she could tell that he was not about to budge from the radio. She heard him cackle with high sardonic glee. "The boneheads—they let Fatso get away with it like all the others!" As she put on lipstick she reflected with wonder on how Nuremberg and its revelations had so powerfully taken possession of Nathan's thoughts during the past couple of months. It had not always been that way; during their first days together he had scarcely seemed aware of the raw actuality of the experience she had gone through, even though the by-products of that experience—her malnutrition, her anemia, her vanished teeth—had been his constant and devoted concern. Certainly he had not been entirely unaware of the camps; perhaps, Sophie thought, the enormity of their existence had been for Nathan, as for so many Americans, part of a drama too far away, too abstract, too *foreign* (and thus too hard to comprehend) to register fully on the mind. But then almost overnight there had come this change in him, this swift turnabout; the newsreel scene of the Warsaw ghetto had smitten him terribly, for one thing, and this was followed almost immediately by a *Herald Tribune* series which caught his eye: an investigative analysis "in depth" of one of the more satanic exposés coughed up by the Nuremberg tribunal, in which the full scope of the extermination of the Jews at Treblinka—almost unimaginable simply in its spilling forth of sheer statistical evidence—was revealed.

Full revelation had been slow yet certain. The first news of the camp atrocities had been made public, of course, in the spring of 1945, just as the European war ended; it was now a year and half later, but the rainshower of poisonous detail, the agglomeration of facts, piling up at Nuremberg and at trials elsewhere like mountainous unmentionable dungheaps, began to tell more than the consciousness of many could bear, even more than those numbing early newsclips of bulldozed cordwood cadavers suggested. As she watched Nathan, Sophie felt she was regarding a person in the grip of a delayed realization, as in one of the later phases of shock. Until now he simply had not allowed himself to believe. But now he believed, all right. He had made up for lost time by absorbing everything available on the camps, on Nuremberg, on the war, on anti-Semitism and the slaughter of the European Jews (many recent nights that were supposed to be movie or concert evenings for Sophie and Nathan had been sacrificed to Nathan's restless prowls through the main Brooklyn branch of the New York Public Library, where in the periodical room he scratched notes by the dozen on Nuremberg revelations he had missed and where he borrowed volumes with titles like *The Jew and Human Sacrifice, The New Poland and the Jews* and *The Promise Hitler Kept*), and with his astonishing retentiveness, made himself an expert on the Nazi saga and the Jew, as he had in so many other areas of knowledge. Wasn't it possible, he asked Sophie once—and, he added, speaking as a cellular biologist—that on the level of human behavior the Nazi phenomenon was analogous to a huge and crucial colony of cells going morally berserk, creating the same kind of danger to the body of humanity as does a virulently malignant tumor in a single human body? He asked her such questions at odd times all during that late summer and fall, and behaved like a soul quite troubled and possessed.

"Like many of his fellow Nazi leaders, Hermann Göring affected a love of art," said H.V. Kaltenborn in his elderly, cricket's voice, "but it was a love that went on a rampage in typical Nazi fashion. It was Göring who was responsible more than anyone in the German high command for the looting of art museums and private collections in countries like Holland, Belgium, France, Austria, Poland . . ." Sophie wanted to stop up her ears. Couldn't that war, those years, be stuffed into some black closet of the mind and be forgotten? Thinking to divert Nathan again, she called, "It's wonderful about your experiment, darling. Don't you want to start to celebrate?"

No answer. The crickety voice still poured out its dry, bleak epitaph. Well, at least, thought Sophie, reflecting on Nathan's obsession, she had no worry about her being drawn into that nasty web. As with so many other things having to do with her feelings, he had been decent and considerate about that. It was one point upon which she was obdurately firm: she had made it clear to him that she would not and could not speak of her experiences in the camp. Almost everything she had ever told him had crept out in meager detail on that single sweetly remembered evening, in this very room, on the day they had met. Just those few words from her made up the extent of his knowledge. Thereafter she did not have to tell him about her unwillingness to mention this part of her life; he was wonderfully responsive, and she was certain that he simply sensed her resolve not to dredge it all up. And so, except for those moments after he chauffeured her for medical tests or checkups at Columbia and it became absolutely necessary, for diagnostic reasons, to pin down some specific form of mistreatment or deprivation, they never discussed anything at all about Auschwitz. Even then she spoke in cryptic terms, but he clearly understood. And his understanding was another thing she had blessed him for.

She heard the radio snap off, and Nathan hustled around behind the screen and took her in his arms. She was used to such precipitate cowboy assaults. His eyes were glittery bright; she could feel how *high* he was from the vibrations that pulsed through him as from some mysterious new source of captured energy. He kissed her again and once more his tongue probed and explored her mouth. Whenever he was on one of these pill jags he became like a stud bull, feverishly and unapologetically sexual, treating her with an enveloping hot epidermal directness which usually had the power to cause her own blood to stampede and make her immediately ready to receive him. And at this moment she felt start her own warm wetness. He guided her hand down to his prick; she stroked it, feeling it as stiff and rigid and as clearly defined beneath the dampish flannel as the thick end of a broomstick. She weakened in the legs, heard herself moan, and plucked at the tab of his zipper. There had evolved—at such moments—between her animated hand and his receptive prick a familiar, symbiotically loving connection that was exquisitely natural; whenever she began to grope for him she was reminded of the way a tiny baby's hand goes out to clutch an outstretched finger.

But suddenly he broke away from her. "Let's go now," she heard him say. Then: "We'll have so much fun later. A ball!" And she knew what he meant. Sex with Nathan in his amphetamine thrall was no mere fun—it was unharnessed, oceanic, otherworldly. And it went on forever . . .

"I didn't think anything terrible was going to happen until late in the party," Sophie told me. "This jam session at Morty Haber's. It was a fear I never felt before with Nathan. Morty Haber had a big loft in a building not far from Brooklyn College and that's where the party was. Morty—you met him on the beach that day—was an instructor in biology at the college and was one of Nathan's good friends. I liked Morty, but to be very honest, Stingo, I wasn't terribly fond of most of Nathan's friends, male or female. Some of this was my fault, I know. I was very shy, for one thing, and my English wasn't all that good then. I really mean it when I say I could speak English better than I could understand it, and I would get so lost when they all begun to talking so fast. And they were always talking about things I have no knowledge of or interest in—Freud and psychoanalysis and penis envy and things such as that which maybe I would have cared for a little bit more if they hadn't been *solemn* and *serious* about it all the time. Oh, I got along with them all right, you must understand. I would just turn my mind off and think of other things when they begun talking about the theory of the orgasm and orgones and such. *Quel ennui!* And I think they liked me okay too, though they had always been a little suspicious of me, and curious, because I would never tell much of my past life and remained a little aloof. Also, I was the only *shiksa* in the crowd and a Polack also. That made me kind of strange and mysterious, I think.

"Anyway, it was late when we come to the party. You see, I tried to persuade him not to, but before we left Yetta's he take another Benzedrine pill—a Benny he called it—and by the time we got into his brother's car to drive to the party he was high, unbelievably high, like a bird, high like an eagle. *Don Giovanni* was playing on the car radio—Nathan knew the libretto by heart, he sang very good opera Italian—and he joined in and sung at the top of his voice and got so wound up in the whole opera that he missed the turn to Brooklyn College and goes all the way down Flatbush Avenue practically to the ocean. He was driving very fast too, and I was beginning to feel a little worried. So all this singing and driving make us late to Morty's, it must have been after eleven. It was a huge party, there were at least a hundred people there. There was a very famous jazz group there—I've forgotten the name of the man who played the clarinet—and I heard the music coming in the door. It was awfully loud, I thought. I am not so very fond of jazz, really, although a little of it I was beginning to like just before . . . before Nathan went away.

"Most of the people were from B.C., graduate students, teachers, et cetera, but a lot of other people too, from all over, a very mixed group. Some quite beautiful girls from Manhattan who were models, many musicians, quite a few

Negroes. I had never seen so many Negroes so close before, they were very exotic to me and I loved to hear them laugh. Everyone was drinking and having a good time. Also, there was this strange-smelling smoke I could smell, the first time I ever have such a smell in my nose, and Nathan told me it was marijuana; he called it tea. Most of the people seemed so happy and at first the party was not so bad, it was good, I didn't feel the terrible thing coming yet. We saw Morty at the door when we come in. The very first thing Nathan told him about was his experiment, he was practically shouting the news. I heard him say, 'Morty, Morty, we broke through! We busted that serum enzyme problem wide open!' Morty had heard all about this—as I say, he teached biology—and he patted Nathan hard on the back and they had a few toasts with beer and a group of other people come up and congratulated him. I remember how wonderfully happy I felt, being so close, I mean being so much loved by this wonderful man who was going to live forever in the history of medical research. And then, Stingo, I could have fainted dead on the spot. Because just then he put his arm around me and squeezed me tight and he said to everyone, 'It is all due to the devotion and companionship of this lovely lady, the finest woman Poland has produced since Marie Sklodowska Curie, who is going to honor me forever by becoming my bride.'

"Stingo, I wish I could describe how I felt. Imagine! To be *married!* I was in a *daze*. It was nothing I could really believe, yet it was happening. Nathan kissing me and the people all coming up with smiles to congratulate us. I thought I was dreaming this. Because, you see, it was so completely *sudden*. Oh, he had talked about us getting married before but always in this light way, sort of joking, and although it always excited me, this idea, I had never taken it seriously. So now I am in this daze, this dream which I couldn't believe."

Sophie paused. When in the process of anatomizing the past or her relationship with Nathan, and the mystery of Nathan himself, she often had the habit of thrusting her face into her hands, as if to seek for an answer or a clue in the encompassing darkness of her cupped palms. She did this now, and only after many seconds raised her head and resumed, saying, "Now it is so easy to see that this . . . this announcement was only a part of his being on the pills, this stuff, this *high* that was taking him farther and farther out into space like some eagle. But at that time I just couldn't make such a connection. I thought it was real, all this about our being married sometime, and I couldn't remember being so happy. I begun to drink a little wine and the party got all wonderfully jumbled. Nathan finally walked off somewhere and I talked to some of his friends. They were still congratulating me. There was one Negro friend of Nathan's I had always liked, a painter named Ronnie Something. I went out on the roof with Ronnie and a very sexy Oriental girl, I've forgotten her name, and Ronnie asked me if I wanted some tea. I didn't quite realize what at first. Naturally, at the moment I thought he meant, you know, the drink you put sugar and lemon in, but he make this big smile and then I know that he was talking of marijuana. I was a little afraid to take it—I have always been frightened to lose control—but oh, anyway, my mood was so happy that I feel that I could take anything without fear. So Ronnie give me the little cigarette and I smoked it deeply and very soon I could understood why people used it for pleasure—it was wonderful!

"The marijuana filled me with this sweet glow. It was chilly on the roof but all of a sudden I was feeling warm and the whole earth and the night and the future seemed more beautiful than ever, if that could be possible. *Une merveille, la nuit!* Brooklyn down below, with a million lights. I stayed out on the roof for a long time talking with Ronnie and his Chinese girl and listening to the jazz music, looking up at the stars and feeling better than I could ever remember. I guess I haven't realize how much time had passed because when I went back inside I see it was late, nearly four o'clock. The party was still going very much, you know, strong, lots of music still, but some of the people were gone and for a short time I hunted for Nathan but couldn't find him. I asked several guests and they pointed out a certain room near one end of the loft. So I went to it and there Nathan was with six or seven other people. There was no fun at all there any more. It was kind of quiet. It was as if someone have just suffered a terrible accident and they were discussing what to do. It was deeply somber there and when I went in I think it was then that I begun to get a little upset, uncomfortable. Begun to realize that something very serious, very bad was going to happen with Nathan. It was an awful feeling, as if I have been hit by a freezing seawave. Bad, very bad, what I felt.

"You see, they were all listening to the radio about the hangings in Nuremberg. It was some special shortwave broadcast, but actual—you know, direct—and I could hear this CBS reporter in the static sounding very far-off describing everything at Nuremberg just as they were doing the hangings. He said that Von Ribbentrop had already gone, and I think Jodl, and then I think he said Julius Streicher was next. Streicher! I couldn't stand this! I suddenly felt clammy all over, sick, awful. It is difficult to describe, this sick feeling, because of course you could only be, I mean, insane with gladness that these men were being hanged—I wasn't sick at that—but because it just reminded me again of so much I wanted to forget. I had this same feeling last spring, like I told you, Stingo, when I saw that picture in the magazine of Rudolf Höss with a rope tied around his neck. And so in that room with these people listening about the hangings at Nuremberg, I just wanted suddenly to escape, you know, and I kept saying to myself: Won't I ever be free of the past? I watched Nathan. He was still on his incredible high, I could tell from his eyes, but he was listening like everyone else to the hangings and his face was very dark and aching. There was something frightening and wrong about his face. And the rest. Everything that was fun, that was truly gay about the party had disappeared, at least in that room. It was like being at a Mass for the dead. Finally the news stopped or maybe the radio become turned off or something and the people all began talking very seriously and with this sudden passion.

"I knew all of them a little, they were friends of Nathan. There was one friend especially I remember. I have talked to him before. His name was Harold Schoenthal, Nathan's age I guess, and he taught I think it was philosophy at the college. He was very intense and serious but he was one of the ones I liked a little more than the others. I thought he was really a very *feeling* person. He always seemed to me very tortured and unhappy, very conscious of being Jewish, and he talked a lot, and this night I remember he was even more in this high key and excited, though I'm sure he wasn't high on anything like Nathan, even beer or wine. He was quite, well, *arresting*-looking, with a bald head and a droopy mustache like—I don't know the animal in English—a *morse* on the iceberg, and a big belly. Yes, walrus. He kept walking up and down the room with his pipe—people always listened when he spoke—and he begun to say things such as 'Nuremberg is a *farce,* these hangings are a *farce*. This is only a token vengeance, a sideshow!' He said, 'Nuremberg is an obscene diversion to give the appearance of justice while murderous hatred of the Jews still poisons the German people. It is the German people who should be themselves exterminated—they who allowed these men to rule them and kill Jews. Not these'—and he used these words—'not these handful of carnival villains.' And he said, 'What about Germany of the future? Are we going to allow those people to grow rich and slaughter Jews again?' It was like listening to a very powerful speaker, this man. I had heard he was supposed to keep his students hypnotized and I remember being fascinated as I watched and listened. He had this terrible *angoisse* in his voice, talking about the Jews. He asked where on earth are the Jews safe today? And then answered himself, saying nowhere. *Alors,* he asked, where on earth have the Jews *ever* been safe? And he said nowhere.

"Then suddenly I realized he was talking about Poland. He was speaking how at one of the trials, Nuremberg or somewhere, there have been this testimony about how during the war some Jews escaped from one of the camps in Poland and tried to find safety among the local people but the Poles turned against the Jews and did not help them. They did horribly worse. In fact, they murdered them all. These Polish people just killed all the Jews. This was a horrible fact, Schoenthal said, and it proves that Jews can never be safe anywhere. He almost shouted that word *anywhere*. Even in America! *Mon dieu,* I remember his rage. When he spoke of Poland I felt even sicker and my heart begun to beat fast, although I don't think he was giving me any special thought. He said Poland might be the worst example, perhaps even worse than Germany or at least as bad, for wasn't it in Poland where after the death of Pilsudski, who protected the Jews, the people leaped to persecute the Jews as soon as they had a chance? He said wasn't it in Poland that young, harmless Jewish students were segregated, made to sit on separate seats at school and treated worse than Negroes in Mississippi? What make people think this couldn't happen in America, things like these 'ghetto benches' for the students? And when Schoenthal speak like this, of course I couldn't stop thinking of my father. My father, who helped create that idea himself. It was suddenly like the presence, *l'esprit* of my father have come into the room very near me, and I wanted to drop through the floor. I couldn't stand no more of this. I had put such things away from myself for so long, buried them, sweeped them under the rug—a coward, I suppose, but I felt this way—and now it was all pouring out of this Schoenthal and I couldn't stand it. *Merde,* I couldn't stand it!

"So when Schoenthal was still talking I went tiptoe around to Nathan's side and make a whisper to him that we must go home, remember the trip to Connecticut tomorrow. But Nathan didn't move. He was like—well, he was like someone who was hypnotized, like one of Schoenthal's students I had heard about, just staring at him, listening to each word. But finally he whispered back to me that he was staying, that I should now go home by myself. He had this wild-eyed look, I was frightened. He said, 'I won't be able to sleep until Christmas.' He said with this crazy look, 'Go home now and sleep and I'll come and get you early in the morning.' So I left in a very big hurry, stopping up my ears to Schoenthal, whose words were half killing me. I took a taxi home, feeling terrible. I completely forgot that Nathan said we were going to be married, I felt that awful. I felt every minute like I must begin to scream."

Connecticut.

The capsule in which reposed the sodium cyanide (tiny granulated crystals as characterless as Bromo-Seltzer, said Nathan, and similarly water soluble, melting almost immediately, though not effervescent) was really quite small, a bit smaller than any medicinal capsule she had ever seen, and was also metallically reflective, so that as he held it inches above her face where she lay against the pillow—wiggling it between thumb and forefinger and causing the pinkish oblong to do a little midair pirouette—she could see shimmering along its surface the miniature conflagration which was only a captured image of the autumnal leaves outside, set afire by the sunset. Drowsily Sophie inhaled the odor of cooking from the kitchen two floors below—a mingled fragrance of bread and, she thought, cabbage—and watched the capsule dance slowly in his hand. Sleep moved up like a tide through her brain; she was aware of steady lulling vibrations that partook of both sound and light, erasing apprehension—blue trance of Nembutal. She mustn't suck it. She would have to bite down hard, he told her, but don't worry: there would be a swift bittersweet taste like that of almonds, an odor a bit like that of peaches, then nothing. Profound black *nothing—rienada fucking nothing!*—accomplished with an instantaneousness so complete as to preclude even the onset of pain. Possibly, he said, just possibly a split second's distress—discomfort rather—but as brief and as inconsequential as a hiccup. *Rien nada niente fucking nothing!*

"Then, Irma my love, then—" A hiccup.

Without looking at him, staring past him at the amber photograph of some faded bekerchiefed grandmother immobilized in the shadows on the wall, she murmured, "You said you wouldn't. So long ago today you said you wouldn't—"

"Wouldn't what?"

"Wouldn't call me that. Wouldn't say Irma again."

"Sophie," he said without emotion. "Sophie love. Not Irma. Of course. Of course. Sophie. Love. Sophielove."

He seemed to be much calmer now, the frenzy of the morning, the raging lunacy of the afternoon stilled or at least momentarily calmed by the same Nembutal he had given her—the blessed barbiturate which in their common terror they thought he would never find but, only two hours ago, found. He was calmer but, she knew, still deranged; curious, she thought, how in this present pacified form of his derangement he seemed no longer so frightening and menacing, despite the unequivocal menace of the cyanide capsule six inches from her eyes. The minuscule Pfizer trademark was clearly imprinted on the gelatine; the capsule was tiny. It was, he explained, a special veterinary capsule, meant to contain antibiotics for small cats and puppy dogs, which he had obtained as a receptacle for the dose; and because of office technicalities, the capsules themselves had been more difficult to get hold of yesterday than the ten grains of sodium cyanide—five grains for her and five for himself. It was no joke, she knew; at some other time and place she would have regarded the whole display as one of his morbid tricks: the shiny pink pod at the last minute popping open between his fingers to reveal a wee flower, a garnet, a chocolate kiss. But not after this day and its unending delirium. She knew quite beyond doubt that the little casket held death. Odd, though. She felt nothing but a spreading lassitude now, watching him as he raised the capsule to his lips and inserted it between his teeth, biting down just hard enough to lightly bend the surface but not to break it. Was her lack of terror due to the Nembutal or to some intuition that he was still faking? He had done this before. He withdrew the capsule from his mouth and smiled. *"Rienada fucking nothing."* She recalled the other moment when he flirted thus, less than two hours before in this very room, although it seemed a week ago, a month. And she wondered now through what miraculous alchemy (the Nembutal?) had he been made to cease his daylong uninterrupted rant. Talktalktalktalktalk . . . The talk had only a few times stopped since that morning at about nine o'clock when he stormed up the steps at the Pink Palace and awakened her . . .

. . . Eyes still shut, her head still woolly from sleep, she hears Nathan make a cackling noise. "Up and at 'em!"

She hears him say, "Schoenthal is right. If it can happen there, won't it happen here? The Cossacks are coming! Here's one Jew-boy who's going to make tracks for the countryside!"

She comes awake. She had anticipated his immediate embrace, wonders if she had put her diaphragm in before going to bed, remembers that she had done so and now lazily rolls over, smiling sleepily, to greet him. She recalls his incredible gluttonous passion when on such a high. Recalls it with voluptuary delight—everything—not alone the beginning hungry tenderness, his fingers on her nipples and their gentle yet insistent search between her legs but all else and one thing specifically, again anticipated with hungry, at last liberated (*adieu, Cracow!*), uninhibited, self-absorbed bliss: his extravagant ability to make her *come*—to come not once or twice but over and over again until an almost sinister final losingness of herself has been achieved, a sucking death like descent into caverns during which she cannot tell whether she is lost in herself or in him, a sense of black whirling downward into an inseparability of flesh. (It is almost the only time she thinks in or speaks Polish any longer, whispering loudly against his ear, "*Weź mnie, weź mnie,*" which spills out mysteriously, spontaneously and means "Take me, take me," although once when Nathan asked her the meaning she was gaily forced to lie, saying, "It means *fuck me, fuck me!*") It is, as Nathan sometimes exhaustedly proclaims afterward, the twentieth-century Superfuck—think how bland human fucking was throughout the ages before the discovery of benzedrine sulphate. Now she is wildly aroused. Stirring, stretching like a cat, she reaches out an arm toward him, inviting him to bed. He says nothing. And then, puzzled, she hears him say again, "Come on! Up and at 'em! This Jew-boy's going to take you for a trip to the country!" She begins, "But, Nathan—" His voice, interrupting, is at once insistent and jazzed-up. "Come on! Come on! We've got to hit the road!" She feels quick frustration while just then a memory of bygone decorums (*bonjour, Cracow!*) gives her a twinge of shame at her urgent and unbuttoned lust. "Come on!" he commands. Naked, she moves out of bed, glances up, sees Nathan gazing into the dappled morning sunlight as he sniffs deeply—from a dollar bill—at what she instantly knows is cocaine . . .

. . . In the New England twilight, past his hand and its poison, she could see the inferno of leaves, one tree awash in vermilion, merging with another crafted of the most violent gold. Outside, the evening woods stood in quietude and the vast patches like maps of color were captured motionless, no leaf astir, in the light of the setting sun. Distantly, cars passed on the highway. She felt drowsy but did not seek sleep. She saw now that there were two capsules between his fingers, pink identical twins. "His and hers is one of the cutest contemporary concepts," she heard him say. "His and hers all over the bathroom, all over the house, why not his and hers cyanide, his and hers fucking nothing? Why not, Sophielove?"

There was a knock at the door and Nathan's hand twitched slightly in response. "Yes?" he said in a flat soft tone. "Mr. and Mrs. Landau," said the voice, "this is Mrs. Rylander. I *hate* to disturb you!" The voice was overly ingratiating, sedulously sweet. "In the off-season the kitchen closes at seven o'clock. Just wanted to tell you, I hate to interrupt your nap. You're the only guests here, so there's no hurry yet, just wanted to tell you. My husband's making his specialty tonight, corned beef and cabbage!" Silence. "Thank you very much," Nathan said, "we'll be down soon."

Footsteps thumped down the ancient carpeted staircase; the timbers squealed like a hurt animal. Talktalktalktalktalk. He had talked himself hoarse. "Consider, Sophielove," he was saying now, caressing the two capsules, "consider how intimately life and death are intertwined in Nature, which contains everywhere the seeds of our beatitude and our dissolution. This, for instance, HCN, is spread throughout Mother Nature in smothering abundance in the form of glycosides, which is to say, combined with sugars. Sweet, sweet sugar. In bitter almonds, in peach pits, in certain species of these autumn leaves, in the common pear, the arbutus. Imagine, then, when those perfect white porcelain teeth of yours bite down upon the delectable macaroon the taste you experience is only a molecule's organic distance removed from that of this . . ."

She blanked out his voice, gazing again at the astonishing leaves, a fire-lake. She smelled the cabbage from below, blooming, dank. And remembered another voice, Morty Haber's, filled with his nervous solicitude: "Don't look so guilty. There's nothing you could have done, since he's been hooked for a long time before you ever laid eyes on him. Can it be controlled? Yes. No. Maybe. I don't *know*, Sophie! I wish to God I knew! Nobody knows much about amphetamines. Up to a point they're relatively harmless. But they obviously can be dangerous, *addictive*, especially when mixed up with something else, like cocaine. Nathan likes to snort cocaine on *top* of the Bennies, and I think that's goddamned dangerous. Then he can get out of control and go into some, I don't know, area of psychosis where no one can reach him. I've checked out all the data, and yes, it's dangerous, *very* dangerous— Oh, fuck it, Sophie, I don't want to talk about it any more, but if he flips out, make sure you get in touch with me right away, me or Larry . . ." She gazed past Nathan at the leaves, and sensed that her lips were tingling. The Nembutal? For the first time in minutes she stirred slightly against the mattress. Instantly she felt a sharp ache in her ribs where he had kicked her . . .

. . . "Fidelity would become you more," he is saying in the midst of his runaway rant. She hears his voice over the roaring slipstream of wind rushing past the convertible's windshield. Although it is chilly, Nathan has put the top down. Sitting next to him, she has covered herself with a blanket. She does not fully understand what he has said to her, half shouts to him, "What did you say, darling?" He turns to face her, she catches a glimpse of his eyes, distraught now, the pupils all but vanished, swallowed up in the violent brown ellipses. "I said *fidelity* would become you more, to use an elegant variation." She is seized with puzzlement and a vague clammy fear. She looks away, heart pounding. Never in their months together has he displayed real anger toward her. Cold dismay begins to wash over her like rain on naked flesh. What does he mean? She fixes her gaze on the landscape wheeling by, the tended evergreen shrubbery at the margin of the manicured parkway, the forest beyond with its explosive turning leaves, blue sky, bright sun, telephone poles. WELCOME TO CONNECTICUT/DRIVE SAFELY. She is aware that he is driving very fast. They overtake car after car, passing with a whooshing noise and a vibration of air. She hears him say, "Or to *not* use an elegant variation, you'd better not *fuck around*, especially where I can see it!" She gasps aloud, she cannot believe he is saying this. As if he had slapped her she feels her head jerk sideways, then she turns. "Darling, what do you—" But "Shut up!" he roars, and now again the words flow forth as upon a spillway, undammed, a babbling continuation of the jumbled semicoherence he has assailed her with since they left the Pink Palace well over an hour before. "It would appear that that luscious Polish ass of yours is irresistible to your employer the adorable quack from Forest Hills, which is quite all right, quite all right, mind you, it is a darling piece of equipment if I do say so myself, having not only fattened it up but availed myself of its uncommon pleasures, this I can understand Dr. Flimflam yearning for with all his heart and aching prick . . ." She hears him give a *heh-heh-heh* brainless giggle. "But for you to cooperate in his enterprise, to actually lay it down and *hump* this despicable cheat, then, *then* to flaunt it all right before my eyes as you did last night, letting him stand there and get one last wet feel, poking that revolting chiropractic tongue down your throat—oh, my little Polish tart, it is more than I can bear." Unable to speak, she fixes her gaze on the speedometer: 70, 75, 80 . . . It is not so bad, she thinks, thinking in kilometers, then in swift adjustment says to herself: *Miles!* We are going to go out of control! Thinks: It is beyond madness, this jealousy, that I am sleeping with *Blackstock*. Far behind them there is the dim sound of a siren, she is somehow aware of a flashing red light, its reflection like a tiny raspberry winking on and off against the windshield. She opens her mouth, poises her tongue for speech ("Darling!" she is trying to say), cannot utter the word. Talktalktalktalktalktalk . . . It is like the sound track of a movie pieced together by a chimpanzee, in part coherent but creating no design, making no final sense; its paranoia causes her to feel weak and ill. "Schoenthal is one hundred percent right, it is pure sentimental rubbish embedded in the Judeo-Christian ethos that makes suicide morally wrong, after the Third Reich suicide should become the legitimate option of any sane human being on earth, isn't that right, Irma?" (Why was he suddenly calling her Irma?) "But I shouldn't be surprised at your hankering to spread your legs for any joint that comes your way, to be quite honest and I haven't said this before, much of you has been a mystery since first we met, I might have suspected you were a fucking *goy kurveh,* but what else—

what else?—ohmyohmy, did some weird self-inflicted *Schadenfreude* cause me to be attracted to such a perfect replica of Irma Griese? She was some looker, according to the people at the trial in Lunenberg, even the prosecutors tipped their hats to that, oh shit, my beloved mama always said I was fatally attracted to blond *shiksas,* why can't you be a decent Jewish boy, Nathan, and marry a nice girl like Shirley Mirmelstein who's so beautiful and has got a father that's made a killing in foundation garments with a summer place in Lake Placid yet." (The siren still trails them, faintly screaming. "Nathan," she says, "there's a policeman.") "The Brahmans *revere* suicide, many Orientals, like what's so big about death anyway, *rienada fucking nothing,* so upon reconsideration not too long ago I said to myself okay, beautiful Irma Griese got the rope for personally killing x-thousands of Jews at Auschwitz but didn't logic dictate a lot of little Irma Grieses getting away, I mean what about this funny little Polish *nafka* I'm shacked up with, that is, could she truly be one hundred percent true-blue Polack, she looks Polack in many ways but also *echt*-Nordic like some Kraut movie star masquerading as the murderous Countess of Cracow, also I might add that absolutely flawless Deutsch I have heard emerge with such precision from your lovely Rhine maiden's lips. A Polack! Ah me! *Das machst du andern weismachen!* Why don't you admit it, Irma! You played footsie with the SS, didn't you? Isn't that how you got out of Auschwitz, Irma? Admit it!" (She has stopped up her ears with both hands, sobbing "No! No!" She feels the car decelerate abruptly. The siren's scream becomes a dragon's growl, diminuendo. The police car pulls abreast.) "*Admit* it, you Fascist cunt!" . . .

. . . As she lay in the dusk watching the leaves dim and fade, she heard the sound of his urine in steady noisy collision with the water in the toilet. She remembered. Amid the fantastic leaves earlier, in the deep woods, standing above her, he had tried to piss into her mouth, had failed; it had been the commencement of his downward slide. She stirred on the bed, smelling the steamy rising fumes of cabbage, her eyes lighting drowsily on the two capsules he had deposited gently in the ashtray.

BOAR'S HEAD INN, read the Old English letters around the china rim, AN AMERICAN LANDMARK. She yawned, thinking how strange it was. How strange it was that she should not fear death, if he was truly going to force death upon her, but that she should fear simply death taking him and him alone, leaving her behind. That through some unforeseen fuck-up, as he would put it, the lethal dose would do its work only on him and she would be once again the hapless survivor. I cannot live without him, she heard herself whisper aloud in Polish, aware of the triteness of the thought but also of its absolute truth. His death would be *my* final agony. From afar a train whistle cried across the valley with its strange name, Housatonic, the long cry a richer and more melodic sound than that of the shrill European horns yet no different in the sudden way that railroad lament wrenched the heart.

She thought of Poland. Her mother's hands. She had so seldom thought of her mother, that sweet dim self-effacing soul, and now for a moment she could only think of her mother's elegant expressive pianist's hands, strong-fingered, at once supple and gentle, like one of the Chopin nocturnes she played, the ivory skin reminding her of the muted white of lilacs. So remarkably white indeed that Sophie only in retrospect ever connected the lovely blanched bloodlessness with the consumption that was devouring her mother even then, and which finally stilled those hands. Mama, Mama, she thought. So often those hands had stroked her brow when as a little girl she spoke the bedtime prayer that every Polish child knows by heart, embedded in the soul more firmly than any nursery rhyme: *Angel of God, my guardian angel, stay always by my side; in the morning, during the day, and in the night, come always to my aid. Amen.* On one of her mother's fingers was a slender golden band in the entwined form of a cobra, the eye of the serpent made of a tiny ruby. Professor Biegański had bought the ring in Aden on his voyage back from Madagascar, where he had gone to reconnoiter the geography of his earliest dream: the relocation of the Polish Jews. His utter vulgarity. Had he shopped long for such a monstrosity? Sophie knew her mother detested the ring but wore it out of her constant deference to Papa. Nathan stopped pissing. She thought of her father and his luxuriant blond hair, beaded with sweat in the bazaars of Arabia . . .

. . . "They got Daytona Beach for car races," says the cop, "this here's the Merritt Parkway, for what we call motorists, now what's the big hurry?" He is fair-haired, youngish, freckle-faced, not unpleasant-looking. He wears a Texas sheriff's hat. Nathan says nothing, staring straight ahead, but Sophie senses him muttering rapidly beneath his breath. Still talktalktalktalktalk but sotto voce. "You want to make you and that nice girl into a statistic?" The cop wears a nameplate: S. GRZEMKOWSKI. Sophie says *"Przepraszam . . ."* ("If you please . . .") Grzemkowski beams, answers, *"Czy jesteś Polakiem?"* "Yes, I'm Polish," Sophie returns, encouraged, continuing her native spiel, but the cop interrupts, "I just understand a few words. My people are Polish, up in New Britain. Listen, what's wrong here?" Sophie says, "This is my husband. He is very upset. His mother's dying in . . ." She frantically tries to think of a Connecticut place, is able to blurt, "In Boston. That's why we were speeding." Sophie stares at the cop's face, eyes innocent violets, the slablike plane faintly bucolic, the countenance of a peasant. She thinks: He could be tending cows in some Carpathian valley. "Please," she cajoles, leaning forward over Nathan, pouting her prettiest, "please, sir, do understand about his mother. We promise to go slow now." The Grzemkowski presence reverts to stolid business, the voice becomes police-gruff. "I'm givin' you a warning this time. Now slow down." Nathan says, *"Merci beaucoup, mon chef."* He gazes directly ahead into infinity. His lips work wordlessly, without cease, as if speaking to some helpless auditor lodged within his breast. He has begun to sweat in glycerine streams. The cop is suddenly gone. Sophie hears Nathan whispering to himself as the car moves once more. It is almost noon. They drive north (more sedately) through bowers and overhanging clouds and raging storms of multichrome leaves in aerial frenzy—here belching color like blazing lava, there like exploding stars, all like nothing Sophie has ever seen or imagined—the pent-up muttering which she cannot comprehend becomes vocal, unleashed in a new spasm of paranoia. And in its encompassing fury it terrifies her as completely as if he had set loose in the car a cage full of savage rats. Poland. Anti-Semitism. And what did *you* do, baby, when they burned the ghettos down? Did you hear the line about what one Polish bishop said to the other Polish bishop? "If I knew you were coming I'd have baked a kike!" *Harharhar!* Nathan, *don't,* she thinks, don't make me suffer so! *Don't make me remember!* The tears are rolling down her face when she plucks at his sleeve. "I've never told you! I've never told you!" she cries. "In 1939 my father risked his life to save Jews! He hided Jews under the floor of his office at the university when the Gestapo came, he was a good man, he died because he saved these . . " On the sticky bolus of her own distress, rising in her gorge like the lie she has just uttered, she strangles, then hears her voice crack. "Nathan! Nathan! Believe me, darling, believe me!" DANBURY CITY LIMITS. "Baked a kike!" *Harharhar!* "I mean not hided, darling, *hid* . . ." Talktalktalk— She half listens now, thinking: If I could get him to stop and eat somewhere, I could steal away and make a phone call to Morty or Larry, get them to come . . . And she hears herself say, "Darling, I'm so hungry, could we stop . . ." Only to hear amid the talktalktalk: "Irma my pet, Irma *Liebchen,* I couldn't eat a single Saltine cracker if you paid me a thousand dollars, oh shit Irma I'm flying, oh Christ I'm in the sky, never so high never so high and gotta big itch for youu-u-u, you little *goy* Fascist *nafka,* hey feel this . . ." He reaches over and places her hand on the outside of his trousers, presses her fingers against the stiff bulge of his prick; she feels it throb then contract then throb again. "A blowjob, that's what I need, one of your five hundred gold zloty Polack blowjobs, hey Irma how many SS pricks did you suck to get out of there, how much master race come swallowed for *Freiheit?* Listen, all kidding aside Irma I've gotta get sucked, oh I've never flown this high, Jesus to get those sweet little gobbling lips to work *right now,* I mean somewhere under the blue sky and the burning maple leaves of autumn, fair autumn, and you'll suck my seed, suck my seed as thick as autumnal leaves that strow the brooks in Vallombrosa, that's John Milton . . ."

Naked, he padded back to the bed and lightly, carefully lay down beside her. The two capsules still glistened in the ashtray, and she wondered drowsily if he had forgotten them, wondered if he again would flirt and tantalize her with their pink menace. The Nembutal, washing her downward toward sleep, pulled at her legs like the warm undertow of a gentle sea. "Sophielove," he said, his voice drowsy too, "Sophielove, I regret only two things." She said, "What, darling?" When he failed to answer, she said again, "What?" "Just this," he said finally, "that all that hard work at the lab, all the research, that I'll never see the fruits of it." Strange, she thought as he spoke, his voice almost for the first time that day had lost its hysteric threat, its mania, its cruelty, had become edged instead with the tenderness, familiar, soothing, which was so naturally a part of him and which all day long she had been certain was past recapture. Had he, too, been rescued at the last instant, was he being borne backward serenely into his salvaging barbiturate harbor? Would he in fact simply forget death and drift off to sleep?

There was a creak on the stairway outside, again the unctuous female voice. "Mr. and Mrs. Landau, excuse me, please. But my husband wants to know if you would care for a drink before dinner. We have everything. But my husband does make a wonderful hot rum punch." After a moment Nathan said, "Yeah, thanks, a rum punch. Two." And she thought: It sounds like the other Nathan. But then she heard him murmur softly, "The other thing, the other thing is that you and I never had any children." She gazed into the glimmering dusk, beneath the coverlet felt her fingernails slice like blades into the flesh of her palm, thought: Why does he have to say that now? I know, as he said sometime today, I was a masochistic cunt and he was only giving me what I wanted. But why can't he at least spare me that agony? "I meant that last night about getting married," she heard him say. She made no reply. She half dreamed of Cracow and time long ago and the clipclop-clipclop of horses' hoofs on the timeworn cobblestones; for no reason at all she saw in some theatre's darkness the bright pastel image of Donald Duck as he bristled about, sailor's hat askew, spluttering in Polish, then heard her mother's gentle laughter. She thought: If I could unlock the past even a little, maybe I could tell him. But the past or guilt, or something, stops up my mouth in silence. Why can't I tell him what I, too, have suffered? And lost . . .

. . . Even with his crazy whispered rhyme repeated again and again—"Don't be a teaser, Irma Griese"—even with his hand remorselessly twisting her hair as if from its roots, even with his other hand at her shoulder clamped down with sickening pain and force, even with the pervasive sense he transmits, lying there, shuddering, of a man far over the brink and prowling his own demented underworld—even with the feverish fright engulfing her she cannot help but feel the old delectable pleasure as she sucks him. And sucks and sucks and sucks. And endlessly loving sucks. Her fingers claw the loamy earth of the wooded hillside upon which he lies underneath her, she feels the dirt impacting itself beneath her fingernails. The ground is damp and chill, she smells woodsmoke, and through her eyelids' translucency is filtered the incredible radiance of the foliage afire. And she sucks and sucks. Beneath her knees fragments of shale gouge and hurt, but she makes no move to ease the pain. "Oh Jesus Christ, oh fuck, suck me Irma, suck the Jew-boy." She cups his firm balls in her palm, strokes the delicate spiderweb hair. As always she envisions within the hollow of her mouth the slippery surface of a marble palmtree, the soft spongy head, its fronds swelling and blossoming in the darkness of her brain. "This relationship, this unique thing we have, this ecstatic symbiosis," she remembers, "could only result from the meeting of a large stiff lonely Semitic *schlong*, which has been successfully circumvented by an army of terrified Jewish princesses, and a set of beautiful Slavic mandibles starved for fellatio." And she thinks even now in her discomfort, in her fear: Yes, yes, he even gave me that, laughing, he took away that guilt anyway when he said how absurd it was for me to feel shame about longing so madly to suck a cock, it wasn't my fault that my husband was frigid and didn't want me to and my lover in Warsaw wouldn't suggest it and I couldn't begin the thing—I was merely, he said, the victim of two thousand years of anti-sucking Judeo-Christian conditioning. That lousy myth, he said, that only faggots love sucking. Suck *me,* he always said, enjoy, enjoy! So even now with the cloud of fear around her, while he taunts her and abuses her—even now her pleasure is not mere mild enjoyment but the perennially re-created bliss, and chill waves shiver down her back as she sucks and sucks and sucks. She is not even surprised that the more he torments her scalp, the more he goads her with the detested "Irma," the more gluttonous becomes her lust to swallow up his prick, and when she ceases, just for an instant, and panting raises her head and gasps "Oh God, I love sucking you," the words are uttered with the same uncomplicated and spontaneous ardor as before. She opens her eyes, glimpses his tortured face, resumes blindly, realizing now that his voice has become a shout which begins to echo from the flanks of the rock-strewn hill. "Suck me, you Fascist pig, Irma Griese Jew-burning cunt!" The delicious marble palm-tree, the slippery trunk swelling and expanding, tells her that he is on the edge of coming, tells her to relax so as to accept the pulsing flood, the seawater gush of palmtree milk, and in that instant of hovering expectancy, as always, she feels her eyes brim over with stinging inexplicable tears . . .

. . . "I'm floating down easy," she heard him murmur in the bedroom after a long silence. "I thought I was going to really crash. I thought I was going to crash hard. But I've been coming down easy. Thank God, I found the barbies." He paused. "We had trouble finding them, didn't we, the barbies?"

"Yes," she replied. She was very sleepy now. Outside, it was nearly dark and the blazing leaves had become lusterless, fading into the smoky gun-metal autumnal sky. The light in the bedroom was flickering out. Sophie stirred next to Nathan, gazed at the wall where the New England grandmother from another century, trapped in an amber ectoplasmic halo, gazed back beneath her kerchief with an expression both benign and perplexed. Sophie thought drowsily: The photographer has just said keep still for a whole minute. She yawned, drowsed for a moment, yawned again.

"Where did we finally find them?" Nathan said.

"In the glove compartment of the car," she said. "You

put them there this morning, then forgot you put them there. The little bottle of Nembutals."

"Christ, how awful. I was really out of it. I was in space. Outer space. Gone!" With a sudden rustle of bedclothes he heaved himself about and groped for her. "Oh, Sophie—Jesus Christ, I love you!" He wrapped an arm around her and with a heavy squeeze drew her toward him; simultaneously, on an outpouring of breath, she screamed. It was not a loud scream she heard herself give, but the pain was stabbingly severe, real, and it was a small, real scream. *"Nathan!"* . . .

. . . But not screaming when the point of the polished leather shoe strikes hard between two of her ribs, draws back, strikes again in the same place, driving the breath from her lungs and causing a white blossom of pain to swell beneath her breast.) *"Nathan!"* It is a desperate groan but not a scream, the hoarse flow of her breath merging in her ears with his voice coming in brutish methodical grunts: *"Und die . . . SS Mädchen . . . spracht* . . . dot vill teach you . . . dirty *Jüdinschwein!"* She does not really flinch from the pain but rather absorbs it, collecting it into some cellar or dustbin deep within her being where she has stored up all his savagery: his threats, his taunts, his imprecations. Nor does she weep, yet, as she lies once again in the deepest woods, a kind of brambly and bethicketed promontory high on the hillside where he has half pulled, half dragged her and from where she can see through the trees, far below, the car, its convertible top down as it stands minute and solitary in the wind-swept parking lot swirling with leaves and debris. The afternoon, partly overcast now, is waning. They have been in the woods for what seems hours. Three times he kicks her. The foot draws back once more and she waits, trembling now less with fear or pain than with the permeating soggy autumnal chill in her legs, her arms, her bones. But the foot does not strike this time, falls to rest in the leaves. "Piss on you!" she hears him say, then, *"Wunderbar*, vot an idea!" Now he uses his polished shod foot as an instrument to pry her face from its sideways posture against the earth to confront him, looking upward; the leather is cold and slippery on her cheek. And even as she watches him unzip his fly and, at his command, opens her mouth she falls into a moment's trance and remembers his words: My darling, I think you have absolutely no ego at all. This spoken to her with enormous tenderness after an episode: calling from the laboratory one summer evening, he had idly expressed a hunger for *Nusshörnchen,* pastries they had eaten together in Yorkville, whereupon without his knowledge she had immediately traveled the miles and miles by subway from Flatbush to Eighty-sixth Street, and following a crazy search had found the goodies, brought them back after many hours, presented them to him with a radiant *"Voilà, monsieur, die Nusshörnchen!"* But you *mustn't* do that, he had said ever so lovingly, that's crazy to indulge my little whim like that, darling Sophie, sweet Sophie, I think you must have no ego at all! (And she thinking then as now: I would do anything for you, anything, *anything!*) But now somehow his attempt to piss down on her begins to unloose his first panic of the day. "Open your mouth wide," he orders her. She waits, watches, mouth agape, receptive, lips quivering. But he fails. One, two, three drops, soft and warm, spatter her brow, and that is all. She shuts her eyes, waiting. There is only the sense of him hovering above her, and the damp and the cold beneath, a far-off thrashing pandemonium of wind, tree branches, leaves. Then she hears him begin to moan, the moan quavering with terror. "Oh Christ, I'm going to crash!" She opens her eyes, stares at him. Suddenly greenish white, his face reminds her of the underbelly of a fish. And she has never (and in this cold) seen a face perspire so; the sweat seems plastered there like oil. "I'm going to crash!" he wails. *"I'm going to crash!"* He sinks down beside her in a crouched position, thrusts his head into his hands, covers his eyes, moans, trembles. "Oh Jesus, I'm going to crash, Irma, you've got to help me!" And then in precipitate dreamlike flight they are hurtling down the mountainside path, she leading him over the hard-pebbled slope like a nurse fleeing with a wounded man, gazing back from time to time to guide his progress beneath the trees as he stumbles, self-blinded by the hand worn like a pale bandage across his eyes. Down and down they go alongside a rushing stream, across a plank bridge, through more woods ablaze with pink, orange, vermilion, slashed by the slender upright white pilasters of birch trees. She hears him, whispering this time, "I'm going to crash!" Finally, then, in the level clearing, the abandoned car lot of the state park where the convertible waits near an upset trash can, the scene a cyclonic cloud of grimy milk cartons, whirling paper plates, candy wrappers. Finally! He leaps toward the rear seat where the luggage is perched, grabs his suitcase and throws it on the ground, begins to rummage through it like some berserk ragpicker in search of an indescribable treasure. Sophie stands aside, helpless, saying nothing while the innards of the suitcase shower the air, festoon the frame of the car: socks, shirts, underwear, ties, a madman's haberdashery thrown to the winds. "That fucking Nembutal!" he roars. "Where did I put it! Oh shit! Oh Jesus, I've got to . . ." But he does not finish his words, instead straightens up and whirls around, hurling himself into the front seat, where he sprawls out beneath the steering wheel and frantically fiddles with the latch of the glove compartment. *Found!* "Water!" he gasps. "Water!" But she, in her own pain and confusion able somehow to anticipate this moment, has plucked over the edge of the back seat a carton of gingerale from the picnic basket they had never touched and now, wrestling with the fiendish opener, flips off the cap of a bottle in a shower of foam and thrusts it into his hand. He gulps the pills, and watching him, she thinks the oddest thought. Poor devil, she thinks, which are the words he—yes, he—had whispered only weeks before while watching *The Lost Weekend* and a crazed Ray Milland in quest of the salvation of his whiskey bottle. "Poor devil," Nathan had murmured. Now, with the green gingerale upended and the muscles of his throat working in rapid convulsions, she is reminded of that movie scene and thinks: Poor devil. Which in itself would not be odd at all, she reflects, were it not for the fact that it is the very first time she has experienced an emotion having to do with Nathan that resembles anything so degrading as pity. She cannot stand pitying him. And the shock of this realization makes her face go numb. Slowly she lowers herself to a sitting position on the ground and leans against the car. The trash in the parking lot eddies about her in gritty slow whirlpools of wind and dust. The pain in her side beneath her breast stabs her, scintillant, glowing sharply like the sudden return of an ugly recollection. She strokes her ribs with her fingertips, lightly, tracing the feverish outline of the ache itself. She wonders whether he might not have broken something. Feeling dazed now, and in the hurtful slow delay of the daze, she is aware that she has lost all track of time. She barely hears him when from the front seat where he lies sprawled with one leg twitching (the twitching mud-spattered trouser cuff is all she can see) he murmurs something which though muffled and obscure sounds like "the necessity of death." And the laugh comes, not loud: *Harharharhar* . . . For a long time there is no sound. Then, "Darling," she says quietly, "you mustn't call me Irma."

"Irma was something I just couldn't bear," Sophie told me. "I could take anything from Nathan but that . . . that he should turn me into Irma Griese. I saw that woman once or twice at the camp—that monster woman, she would have made Wilhelmine appear to be an angel. It hurt me more than all his kicking that he called me Irma Griese. But before we got to the inn that night I tried to make him stop calling me that, and when he begun to call me Sophielove I knew he was not so high—so crazy—any more. Even though he was still playing with those little capsules of poison. This scared me now. I didn't know how far he was going to go. I was out of my mind with the idea of our life with each other and I didn't want us to die—separate or together. No. Anyway, the Nembutal begun to work on him, I could tell that, he came slowly down off his high and when he squeezed me it hurt so bad I thought I would faint and I gave this scream and then he realized what he had done to me. He was so full of guilt then, kept whispering in bed, 'Sophie. Sophie, what have I done to you, how could I have hurt you?' And such as that. But the other pills—what he called the barbies—were beginning to make this effect on him and he couldn't keep his eyes open and pretty soon he was asleep.

"I remember the woman who owned the inn walked upstairs again and asked me through the door when were we coming down, it was getting late, when were we coming down for the rum punch and the dinner. And when I told her we were tired, we were just going to sleep, she got very upset and angry and said it was the most thoughtless thing, et cetera, but I didn't care, I was so very tired and sleepy myself. So I went back and lie down next to Nathan and begun to go to sleep. But then, oh my God, I thought of the capsules of poison that were still in the ashtray. I was filled with this panic. I was just terrified because I didn't know what to do with them. They were so terribly dangerous, you know. I couldn't throw them out the window or even in the trash basket because I was afraid they would crack open and the fumes would kill someone. And I thought of the toilet, and that still worried me, make me afraid about the fumes or poisoning the water or even the earth, and I didn't know what to do. I knew I had to get them away from Nathan. So anyway, I decided to take a chance on the toilet. The bathroom. There was some light in there. I very carefully picked up the capsules from the ashtray and walked through the dark into the bathroom and threw them into the toilet. They didn't float like I had imagined but sank like two little pebbles and I quickly flushed the toilet and they were gone.

"I went back to the bed and slept then. I have never slept in such a dark, dreamless profound way. I don't know how long I slept. But sometime in the night Nathan woke up screaming. It must have been some reaction to all the drugs, I don't know, but it was so frightening to hear him next to me in the middle of the night, shouting like a mad demon. I still don't know how he didn't wake up everybody for miles. But I jumped awake at his screams, he begun to shout about death and destruction and hanging and gas and Jews burning in ovens and I don't know what else. I had been scared all day but this was somehow worse than anything. He had been in and out of craziness for so many hours but this was like someone gone crazy forever. 'We must die!' he begun to rave in the dark. I heard him say in a kind of long groan, 'Death is a necessity,' and then he kept groping across me toward the table as if he was hunting for the poison. But strange, you know, all this lasted only a few moments. He was very weak, it seemed to me, I was able to hold him back with my arms and I pressed him down and said over and over again, 'Darling, darling, go to sleep, everything's all right, you've had a nightmare.' Foolish things like that. But somehow what I said and done have this effect on him because quite soon he was asleep again. It was so dark in that room. I kissed him on the cheek. His skin was cool now.

"We slept for hours and hours and hours. When I finally woke up I could tell from the way the sun shined in the window that it was early in the afternoon. The leaves were bright outside the window, as if the whole woods was on fire. Nathan was still asleep and I just lay there beside him for a long time, thinking. I knew that I couldn't keep buried any longer the thing that was the last thing on earth that I wanted to remember. But I couldn't hide it any longer from myself, and I couldn't hide it from Nathan either. We couldn't live together unless I told him. I knew that there were certain things I could never tell him—*never!*—but there was at least one thing he had to know, otherwise we couldn't continue on, never get married surely, never. And without Nathan I would be . . . nothing. So I make up my mind to tell him this thing which was not a secret really, but just something I had never mentioned because the pain of it was still more than I could bear. Nathan was still sleeping. His face was very pale but all that craziness had gone away from it and he looked peaceful. I had the feeling that maybe all the drugs had left him, the demon had gone and all the black winds, you know, of the *tempête,* and he had returned to being the Nathan I loved.

"I got up and walked to the window and looked at the woods—they were bright and flaming, so beautiful. I almost forgot the pain in my side and all that had happened, and the poison and the mad things Nathan have done. When I was a little girl in Cracow and very religious I would play a game with myself which I called 'the shape of God.' And I would see something so beautiful—a cloud or a flame or the green side of a mountain or the way light filled the sky—and I would try to discover God's shape in it, as if God actually took the form of what I was watching and lived in it and I was able to see Him there. And that day when I looked out the window at those incredible woods that sweeped down to the river and the sky so clear above, why, I forgot myself and for a moment I felt like a little girl again and begun to try to see God's shape in these things. There was a wonderful smell of smoke in the air and I saw smoke rising far off in the woods and I saw God's shape in that. But then—but then it came to my mind what I really knew, what was really the truth: that God have left me again, left me forever. I felt I could actually see Him go, turning His back on me like some great beast and go crashing away through the leaves. God! Stingo, I could see this huge *back* of Him, going away in the trees. The light faded then and I felt such an emptiness —the memory coming back and knowing what I would have to say.

"When Nathan finally waked up I was beside him on the bed. He smiled and said a few words and I felt he hardly knew what had happened all these last hours. We said one or two ordinary things to each other, you know, sleepy waking-up things, and then I bent down close to him and said, 'Darling, I have something I must say to you.' And he begun to come back with a laugh. 'Don't look so—' Stopping like that, and then he said, 'What?' And I said, 'You thought I have been some kind of unattached woman from Poland who was never married and so on, with no family or anything in the past.' I said, 'It has been easier for me to make it look like that, for I've not wanted to dig up the past. I know it has been easier for you, maybe, too.' He looked painful and then I said, 'But I must tell you. It is just this. I was married a number of years ago and I had a child, a little boy named Jan who was with me at Auschwitz.' I stopped speaking then, looking away, and he was silent for a long, long time, and then I heard him say, 'Oh good God, oh good God.' He kept saying this over and over. Then he was quiet again, and finally he said, 'What happened to him? What happened to your little boy?' And I said to him, 'I don't know. He was lost.' And he said, 'You mean dead?' And I said, 'I don't know. Yes. Maybe. It don't matter. Just lost. Lost.'

"And that's all I could say, except for one thing. I said, 'Now that I've told you I must make you promise this. I must make you promise never to ask about my child ever again. Or speak of him. Nor will I ever speak of him either.' And he promised with one word—'Yes,' he said—but the look on his face was filled with such sorrow that I had to turn away.

"Don't ask me, Stingo, don't ask me why—after all this—I was still ready for Nathan to piss on me, rape me, stab me, beat me, blind me, do anything with me that he desired. Anyway, a long time passed before he spoke to me again. Then he said, "Sophielove, I'm insane, you know. I want to apologize for my insanity.' And after a bit he said, 'Want to fuck?' And I said right away without even thinking twice, 'Yes. Oh yes.' And we made love all afternoon, which made me forget the pain but forget God too, and Jan, and all the other things I had lost. And I knew Nathan and me would live for a while more together."

Twelve

In the small hours of that morning, after her long soliloquy, I had to put Sophie into bed—*pour* her into bed, as we used to say in those days. I was amazed that after all the booze she had guzzled she could remain so coherent throughout the evening; but by the time the bar closed at four o'cock I saw that she was pretty well smashed. I splurged and we took a taxi the mile or so back to the Pink Palace; on the way she dozed heavily against my shoulder. I maneuvered her up the stairs, pushing at her waist from behind, and her legs wobbled dangerously. She uttered only the smallest of sighs when I eased her down into her bed, fully clothed, and watched her pass instantly away into a pale coma. I was drunk and exhausted myself. I threw a coverlet over Sophie. Then I went downstairs to my own room and after undressing slithered between the sheets, falling into the blank slumber of a cretin.

I woke up with the late-morning sunlight ablaze in my face, and the sound in my ears of birds squabbling among the maples and sycamores, and the distant froggy noise of boys' adolescent voices—all refracted through an aching skull and the pulsating consciousness of the worst hang-over I had experienced in a year or two. Needless to say, beer too can undermine body and soul, if downed in enough quantity. I succumbed to an abrupt and terrible magnification of all sensations: the nap of the sheet beneath my naked back felt like cornfield stubble, the chitter of a sparrow outside seemed the squawk of a pterodactyl, a truck's wheel striking a pothole on the street made a clamor like the slamming of the gates of hell. All my ganglia were quivering. Another thing: I sweltered with lust, helpless in the throes of an alcohol-induced concupiscence known, at least in that day, by the name of "the hangover hots." Normally the prey of an ever-unfulfilled randiness—as the reader by now must be aware—I became, during these mercifully infrequent seizures of morning-after engorgement, a godforsaken organism in absolute thrall to the genital urge, capable of defiling a five-year-old of either sex, ready for coition with almost any vertebrate having a pulse and warm blood. Nor could loutish self-gratification quell this imperious, feverish desire. Desire like this was too overwhelming, sprang from sources too demandingly procreative to be satisfied by some handy makeshift. I do not think it hyperbolic to describe this derangement (for such it really was) as *primordial:* "I would have fucked mud" was the Marine Corps description for such a mania. But suddenly with a manful zeal that pleased me I bestirred myself and leaped out of bed, thinking of Jones Beach and Sophie in the room above me.

I stuck my head out into the hallway and called upstairs. I heard the faint strains of something of Bach. Sophie's response from behind her door, while indistinct, sounded chipper enough, and I retreated and splashed about in my morning purification. It was a Saturday. The night before, in what seemed a rush of (perhaps inebriate) affection toward me, Sophie had promised to spend the entire weekend at the house before moving off to her new place near Fort Green Park. She also agreed enthusiastically to an outing with me to Jones Beach. I had never been there but I knew it to be an oceanside strand far less congested than Coney Island. Now while I soaped myself beneath the tepid trickle in the pink mildewed upright metal coffin which served as my shower stall, I began to scheme in earnest about Sophie and the immediate future. I was more than ever aware of the tragicomic nature of my passion for Sophie. On the one hand I possessed enough of a sense of humor to be aware of the ludicrousness of the contortions and writhings her very existence inflicted upon me. I had read romantic literature in sufficient bulk to know that my wretched frustrated moonings could in their collective despair almost laughably exemplify the word "lovelorn."

Yet it was only half a joke, really. Because the anxiety and pain which this one-way love caused me was as cruel as the discovery that I had acquired some terminal disease. The only cure for this disease was her love in return—and such a genuine love seemed as remote as a cure for cancer. At times (and this moment was one) I was able actually to curse her out loud—"Bitch, Sophie!"—for I almost would have preferred her scorn and hatred to this proximate love which could be called affection or fondness but never love itself. My mind still echoed with her outpouring of the past night, with its awful vision of Nathan and its brutality and despairing tenderness and perverse eroticism and its stink of death. "God damn you, Sophie!" I said half aloud, slowly enunciating the words while I lathered my crotch. "Nathan's out of your life now, gone for good. That death-force is gone, finished, kaput! So now love me, Sophie. Love me. Love *me!* Love life!"

Drying myself off, I considered in a businesslike way the possible practical objections Sophie might have to me as a suitor, provided of course that I could speak my way through those emotional walls and somehow gain her love. They were rather troublesome, her potential complaints. I was, of course, years younger (and a postpubescent pimple blossoming next to my nose, glimpsed in the mirror just then, underscored the fact), but this was a trifling matter with many historical precedents to make it right, or at least acceptable. Then, too, I was not nearly so solvent financially as Nathan had been. Although she could scarcely be called avaricious, Sophie loved the fat American life; self-denial was not among her most obvious qualities, and I wondered with a soft but audible groan how on earth I'd be able to provide for the two of us. And at that moment, as if in some odd reflexive response to the thought, I reached in and took my Johnson & Johnson bank down out of its hiding place in the medicine chest. And to my absolute horror I saw that every last dollar had vanished from the little box. I was wiped out!

Of the tumult of black emotions that sweeps through one after a robbery—chagrin, despair, rage, hatred of the human race—the one that usually comes last is also one of the most poisonous: suspicion. I could not help pointing an inner finger of accusation at Morris Fink, who prowled around the premises and had access to my room, and the sleaziness I felt at my unproved suspicion was somehow compounded by the fact that I had begun to feel a remote liking for the molelike janitor. Fink had done me one or two small favors, which only complicated the mistrust I felt for him now. And of course I could not voice my suspicion even to Sophie, who received the news of the depredation done me with affecting sympathy.

"Oh, Stingo, no! Poor Stingo! Why?" She clambered out of bed, where, propped against the pillows, she had been reading a French translation of *The Sun Also Rises*. "Stingo! Who could have done such a thing to you?" In a flowered silk robe she threw herself impulsively around me. My turmoil was so intense that I could make no response even to the enjoyable pressure of her breasts. "Stingo! *Robbed?* How awful!"

I felt my lips quiver, I was despicably close to real tears. "Gone!" I said. "All gone! Three hundred and some dollars, all I had between myself and the poorhouse! How in God's name will I ever get my book written now? Every penny I had on earth, except—" As an afterthought I grabbed my wallet and opened it. "Except for forty dollars—*forty dollars* that I was lucky enough to take with me when we went out last night. Oh, Sophie, this is complete disaster!" Half consciously I heard myself imitating Nathan: *"Oy,* have I got *tsuris!"*

Sophie had that mysterious knack of being able to calm wild passions, even those of Nathan when he was not uncontrollably out of his mind. A strange sorcery which I could never quite pin down, it had to do both with her Europeanness and something that was obscurely, seductively maternal. "Shush!" she would say in a certain tone of sham reproof, and a man would simply wilt and end up grinning. While my desolation at this point precluded any such thing as a grin, Sophie did quite easily manage to cool my frenzy. "Stingo," she said, playing with the shoulders of my shirt, "such a thing is terrible! But you mustn't act like the atomic bomb has fallen on you. Such a big baby, you look like you're going to cry. What's three hundred dollars? Soon when you're a great writer you'll be making three hundred dollars a week! Now it is bad, this loss, *mais, chéri, ce n'est pas tragique,* there is nothing you can do about it, so you must forget it all for this moment and come on let us go to Jones Beach like we said! *Allons-y!*"

Her words helped considerably and I quickly settled down. As devastating as my loss was, I realized, as she did, that there was almost nothing I could do to change things, so I resolved to relax and at least try to enjoy the rest of the weekend with Sophie. There would be time enough to confront the monstrous future come Monday. I began to look forward to our outing at the beach with the escapist euphoria of a tax dodger seeking to lose his past in Rio de Janeiro.

Rather surprised at my own priggish objections, I tried to forbid Sophie from stuffing the half-full bottle of whiskey into her beach bag. But she gaily insisted, saying "hair of the dog," which was something I was sure she had picked up from Nathan. "You're not the only one with a hangover, Stingo," she added. Was it at that moment that I first became seriously concerned about her drinking? I think that previously I had regarded this thirst of Sophie's as a temporary aberration, a retreat into momentary solace which was due more to Nathan's abandonment of her than anything else. Now I was by no means so certain; doubt and worry plucked at me as we swayed together in the car of a rackety subway train. We got off soon. The bus itself left for Jones Beach from a dingy terminal on Nostrand Avenue, a place swarming with unruly Brooklynites jostling for position to get to the sun. On our bus Sophie and I were the last to climb aboard; standing in a sepulchral tunnel, the vehicle was malodorous, nearly pitch-black and utterly silent although packed with a dim and shifting mass of human bodies. The effect of silence was sinister, baffling—surely, I thought while we edged our way toward the rear, such a throng should give up a vagrant mumble, a sigh, some evidence of life—until the moment we found our tattered and rumpsprung seats.

Just then the bus lurched forward into sunlight, and I was able to discern our fellow passengers. They were all children, little Jews in their late childhood and early teens, and all of them were deaf-mutes. Or at least I assumed they were Jews, since one of the kids held a big hand-lettered placard which read: BETH ISRAEL SCHOOL FOR THE DEAF. Two motherly, bosomy women roamed the aisle with cheery smiles, flicking their fingers in sign language as if conducting a voiceless choir. Here and there a child, beaming, would flick back winglike fluttering hands. I felt myself shudder within the bottomless drain-pipe of my hangover. I had an awful sensation of doom. My jangled nerves together with the sight of these incapacitated angels and the smell of faulty combustion leaking up from the engine—all merged into a phantasm of aching anxiety. Nor was my panic alleviated by Sophie's voice at my side and the bitter flavor of what she had to say. She had begun to take little nips from the bottle and had become incredibly garrulous. But I was really astounded at the words she spoke about Nathan, the blunt rancor in her voice. I could scarcely believe this new tone, and blamed it on the whiskey. Over the roar of the engine and in a bluish haze of hydrocarbons I listened to her in numb discomfort, praying for the purity of the beach.

"Last night," she said, "last night, Stingo, after I told you about what happened in Connecticut, I realized something for the first time. I realized I was *glad* that Nathan left me like he done. Really and truly glad, I mean. I was so completely dependent on him, you see, and that was not a healthy thing. I couldn't *move* without him. I couldn't make a simple little *décision* without thinking of Nathan first. Oh, I know I had this debt to him, he done so much for me—I know that—but it was sick of me to be just this little kitten for him to fondle. To fuck and fondle—"

"But you said he was on drugs," I interrupted. I felt an odd need to say something in his defense. "I mean, isn't it true that he was so awful to you only when he was high on these drugs—"

"Drugs!" she said sharply, cutting me off. "Yes, he was on drugs, but does that have to be an *excuse,* for God's sake? Always an excuse? I'm so tired of people that always says that we must pity a man, he is under the influence of drugs and so that excuses his behavior. Fuck that noise, Stingo!" she exclaimed in a perfect Nathanism. "He almost killed me. He beat me! He hurt me! Why should I continue to love a man like that? Do you realize that he done something to me that I didn't tell you about last night? He *broke* one of my ribs when he kicked me. One of my *ribs!* He had to take me to a doctor—not Larry, thank God—he had to take me to a doctor and I had x-rays and I had to wear all this *tape* for six weeks. And we had to invent a story for this doctor—that I slipped up and fell and crack my rib on the pavement. Oh, Stingo, I'm glad I'm rid of such a man! Such a cruel person, so . . . so *malhonnête.* I'm happy to leave him," she proclaimed, wiping a tiny smear of moisture from her lip, "I'm really *ecstatic,* if you wish to know the truth. I don't need Nathan no more. I'm still young. I have a nice job, I'm sexy, I can find another man easy. Ha! Maybe I'll marry Seymour Katz! Wouldn't Nathan be surprised if I married this chiropractor he was falsely accusing me of having a relationship? And his friends! Nathan's friends!"

I turned to look at her. There was a glint of fury in her eyes; her voice rose shrilly and I wanted to hush her up, until I realized that there was no one but myself to listen. "I really couldn't stand his friends. Oh, I was very fond of his brother. Larry. I will miss Larry and I liked very much Morty Haber. But all these other friends. These *Jews* with their psychoanalysis, always picking their little sores, worrying about their little brilliant brains and their analysts and everything. You heard them, Stingo. You know what I mean. Did you ever hear anything so ridiculous? 'My analyst this, my analyst that . . .' It is so disgusting, you would think they had *suffered* something, these comfortable American Jewish people with their Doctor So-and-So they pay many dollars an hour to examine their miserable little Jewish souls! *Aaa-h!*" A tremor ran through her body and she turned away.

Something about Sophie's fury and bitterness, combined with her drinking—all of these so new to me—aggravated my jitters until the feeling became almost insupportable. While she babbled on I realized dimly that I had undergone unfortunate bodily changes: I had severe heartburn, I was sweating like a coal stoker, a wayward neurasthenic tumescence had caused my beloved waif of a cock to stiffen bone-rigid against my pants leg. And our conveyance had been rented by the devil. Heaving and rocking its way through the bungalow barrens of Queens and Nassau, clashing gears, exuding fumes, the decrepit bus seemed likely to imprison us forever. As in a trance, I listened to Sophie's voice soar like an aria over the children's speechless, antic mummery. And I wish I had been better prepared emotionally to accept the burden of her message. "Jews!" she exclaimed. "It's really true, in the end they are all exactly alike *sous la peau,* under the skin, you understand. My father was really right when he said that he had never known a Jew who could give something in a free way, without asking for something in return. A *quid pro quo,* as he would say. And oh, Nathan—what an example Nathan was of that! Okay, so he helped me a lot, make me well, but so what? Do you think he done that out of love, out of kindness? No, Stingo, he done such a thing only so he could use me, have me, fuck me, beat me, have some object to possess! That's all, some *object.* Oh, it was so very Jewish of Nathan to do that—he wasn't giving me his love, he was *buying* me with it, like all Jews. No wonder the Jews were so hated in Europe, thinking they could get anything they wished just by paying a little money, a little *Gelt.* Even *love* they think they can buy!" She clutched me by the sleeve and the odor of rye whiskey reached me through the gasoline fumes. "Jews! God, how I hate them! Oh, the lies I have told you, Stingo. Everything I told you about Cracow was a lie. All my childhood, all my life I really hated Jews. They deserved it, this hate. I *hate* them, dirty Jewish *cochons!*"

"Oh, please, Sophie, *please,*" I retorted. I knew she was distraught, knew she couldn't really mean any of this, knew also that with Nathan she found his Jewishness simply an easier target than Nathan himself, for whom obviously she was still daft with love. This nasty discharge vexed me, even though I thought I understood its source. Nonetheless, the power of suggestion is mighty, her savage bile touched in me some atavistic susceptibility, and as the bus rocked its way out onto the asphalt parking lot at Jones Beach, I found myself brooding blackly on my recent robbery. And Morris Fink. *Fink!* That fucking little hebe, I thought, trying vainly to belch.

The little deaf-mutes debark as we did, clambering down around us, stepping on our toes, hemming us in as they filled the air with their butterfly gesticulations. We could not seem to dislodge them; they formed an eerie, soundless retinue in our march across the beach. The sky that had been so bright in Brooklyn had become overcast; the horizon was leaden, the surf swelled with sluggish oily waves. Only a few bathers dotted the beach; the air was muggy and breathless. I felt almost unbearably anxious and depressed, yet my nerves were quiveringly aflame. My ears echoed with a delirious, inconsolable passage from the *St. Matthew Passion* which had wept out of Sophie's radio earlier that morning, and for no special reason yet in fitting antiphony I recalled some seventeenth-century lines I had read not long before: ". . . since Death must be the *Lucina* of life, and even Pagans could doubt, whether thus to live were to die . . ." I perspired in the humid cocoon of my angst, worrying about my theft and my present near-destitution, worrying about my novel and how I would ever get it finished, worrying whether or not I should press charges against Morris Fink. As if responding to some soundless signal, the deaf-mute children suddenly dispersed and scattered like little shore birds, were gone. Sophie and I trudged along the water's edge beneath a sky as gray as moleskin, the two of us alone.

"Nathan had everything that is bad in Jews," Sophie said, "nothing of the little bit that's good."

"What's good about Jews at *all?*" I heard myself say loudly, querulously. "It was that Jew Morris Fink that stole the money from my medicine cabinet. I'm *certain!* Money-mad, money-greedy Jewish bastard!"

Two anti-Semites, on a summer outing.

An hour later I calculated that Sophie had sloshed down perhaps one or two ounces less than half a pint of whiskey. She was putting it away like some female riveter at a Polish bar in Gary, Indiana. Yet there was no discernible lapse in coordination or locomotion. Only her tongue had slipped its tether (making her speech not slurred but simply runaway, sometimes breakneck) and as on the previous night, I listened and watched in wonder while the powerful solvent of those grain neutral spirits set loose her inhibitions. Among other things, the loss of Nathan seemed to have an effect on her that was perversely erotic, causing her to brood on bygone amour.

"Before I was sent to the camp," she said, "I had a lover in Warsaw. He was younger than me by a few years. He wasn't even twenty. His name was Jozef. I never spoke of him to Nathan, I don't know why." She paused, biting her lip, then said, "Yes, I do. Because I knew that Nathan was so jealous, so crazy jealous that he would hate me and punish me for having a lover even in the *past*. That's how jealous Nathan could be, so I didn't ever say a word to him about Jozef. Imagine, hating somebody in the past who had been a lover! And was dead."

"Dead?" I said. "How did he die?"

But she seemed not to hear. She rolled over on our blanket. In her canvas beach bag she had—to my great surprise and greater delight—transported four cans of beer. I was not even annoyed that she had forgotten to give them to me sooner. They were, of course, by now quite warm but I could not have cared less (I, too, badly needed that dog's hair), and she opened the third of these, dripping foam, and handed it to me. She had brought along some nondescript-looking sandwiches too, but these lay uneaten. Deliciously isolated, we lay in a kind of hidden cul-de-sac between two high dunes lightly strewn with coarse grass. From here the sea—listlessly washing against the sand and a curious unsightly gray-green, like engine oil—was plainly visible, but we ourselves could not be seen except by the gulls that wavered overhead on the windless air. The humidity hovered around us in an almost palpable mist, the sun's pale disc hung behind gray clouds that shifted and churned in slow motion. In a certain way it was very melancholy, this seascape, and I should not have wanted for us to stay there long, but the blessed Schlitz had stilled at least momentarily my earlier seizure of dread. Only my horniness remained, aggravated by Sophie next to me in her white Lastex bathing suit and the total seclusion of our sandy nook, the clandestine nature of which made me a little feverish. I was still also so maddeningly and helplessly priapic—my first such fit since the doomed night with Leslie Lapidus—that the image I entertained of self-castration was, for a fleeting moment, not absolutely frivolous. For the sake of modesty I lay determinedly belly-downward in my dumb-looking puke-green Marine Corps-issue swim trunks, playing as usual my patient confessor's role. And again as my antennae went out, they relayed back the information that there was no evasion, nothing equivocal in what she was trying to say.

"But there was another reason I would not have told Nathan about Jozef," she went on. "I wouldn't have told him even if he was not going to be jealous."

"What do you mean?" I said.

"I mean he would not have believed anything about Jozef—anything at all. It had to do with Jews again."

"Sophie, I don't understand."

"Oh, it's so complicated."

"Try to explain."

"Also, it had to do with the lies I had already told Nathan about my father," she said. "I was getting in—what is the expression?—over my head."

I took a deep breath. "Look, Sophie, you're confusing me. Straighten me out. Please."

"Okay. Look, Stingo. Nathan would not believe anything good about Polish people when it come to the Jews. I couldn't convince him that there were decent Polish people who had risked their lives to save Jews. My father—" She broke off for an instant; there was a catch in the back of her throat, then a long hesitation before she said, "My father. Oh, goddamnit, I've already told you—I lied to Nathan about him just like I lied to you. But I finally told *you* the truth, you see, I just *couldn't* have told Nathan because . . . I couldn't have told him because . . . because I was a coward. I had come to see that my father was so big a monster that I had to hide the truth about him, even though what he was and what he done was not my fault. Was not anything I should feel any blame about." Again she hesitated. "It was so frustrating. I lied about my father and Nathan refused to believe it. After that I knew I would never be able to tell him about Jozef. Who was good and brave. And that would have been the truth. I remember this quotation that Nathan had which always sounded so American. 'You win one and you lose one.' But I couldn't win anything."

"What *about* Jozef?" I persisted, a little impatiently.

"We lived in this building in Warsaw that was bombed but fixed up. You could live in it. But only barely. It was a terrible place. You can't imagine how terrible Warsaw was then during the occupation. So little food, often just a little water, and in the winter it was so cold. I worked in a factory that made tar paper. I worked ten, eleven hours a day. The tar paper made my hands bleed. They bled all the time. I didn't work for money, really, but to keep a work card. A work card would keep me from being sent off to Germany to a camp for slave labor. I lived in a tiny little place on the fourth floor of the building and Jozef lived with his half sister downstairs. His half sister was named Wanda, she was a little over my age. They were both involved with the underground, the Home Army it would be called in English. I wish I could describe Jozef good but I can't, don't have the words. I was fond of him so very much. But there was no true romance, really. He was small, muscular, very intense and nervous. He was pretty dark for a Pole. Strange, we didn't make love together very often. Though we slept in the same bed. He said he have to preserve his energies for the fight going on. He wasn't very educated, you know, in a formal way. He was like me—the war destroyed our education chances. But he had read a lot, he was very bright. He wasn't even a Communist, he was an anarchist. He worshipped the memory of Bakunin and was a complete atheist, which was a little strange too, because at that time I was still a very devout Catholic girl and I sometimes wondered how I could fall in love with this young man who don't believe in God. But we made this agreement not ever to talk about religion, and so we didn't.

"Jozef was a murder—" She paused, then reconstructed the thought and said, "Killer. He was a killer. That was what he done for the underground. He killed Polish people that was betraying Jews, betraying where Jews were hiding. There were Jews hiding out all over Warsaw, not ghetto Jews, *naturellement,* but better-class Jews—*assimilés,* many intellectuals. There were many Polish people who would betray the Jews to the Nazis, sometimes for a price, sometimes for nothing. Jozef was one of those which the underground had to kill those who were betraying. He would strangle them with the wire from a piano. He would try to get to know them in some way and then strangle them. Each time he killed someone he would vomit. He killed over six or seven people. Jozef and Wanda and I had a friend in the next building that we were all very fond of—a beautiful girl named Irena, about thirty-five, so beautiful. She had been a teacher before the war. Strange, she taught American literature and I remember she had this expertise in a poet named Hart Crane. Do you know of him, Stingo? She worked for the underground too; I mean, so we thought—because after a while we learned secretly that she was a double agent and was also betraying many Jews. So Jozef had to kill her. Even though he had liked her so much. He strangled her with the piano wire one night late and all the next day he just stayed in my room looking out of the window into space, not saying a word."

Sophie fell silent. I eased my face down against the sand, and thinking of Hart Crane, felt myself shiver to a gull's cry, the rhythmic wash and heave of sullen waves. *And you beside me, blessèd now while sirens sing to us, stealthily weave us into day . . .*

"How did he die?" I said again.

"After he killed Irena the Nazis found out about him. This was about a week later. The Nazis had these huge Ukrainians who done their killing. They came one afternoon when I was out and cut Jozef's throat. When I arrived Wanda had already found him. He was bleeding to death on the stairs . . ."

Minutes passed before either of us spoke. Every word she said had been, I knew, absolutely true, and I was swept with desolation. It was a feeling deeply involved in a bad conscience, and although a logical part of my mind reasoned that I must not blame myself for cosmic events which had dealt with me in one way and with Jozef in another, I could not help but view my own recent career with repugnance. What had old Stingo been up to while Joszef (and Sophie and Wanda) had been writhing in Warsaw's unspeakable Gehenna? Listening to Glen Miller, swilling beer, horsing around in bars, whacking off. God, what an iniquitous world! Suddenly, after the nearly interminable silence, with my face still downward in the sand, I felt Sophie's fingers reach up into my trunks and lightly stroke that spectacularly sensitive epidermal zone down deep where thigh and buttock intersect, a scant centimeter from my balls. It was a sensation at once surprising and unabashedly erotic; I heard an involuntary gurgle rise up from the back of my throat. The fingers went away.

"Stingo, let's take our clothes off," I thought I heard her say.

"What did you say?" I replied dully.

"Let's take our things off. Let's be naked."

Reader, imagine something for a moment. Imagine that you have lived for an indeterminate but longish time with the well-founded suspicion that you are suffering from some fatal disease. One morning the telephone rings and it is the doctor saying this: "You have nothing to worry about, it was all a false alarm." Or imagine this. There have been inflicted upon you severe financial reverses, bringing you so close to penury and ruin that you have considered a way out in self-destruction. Again it's the blessed telephone, with the message that you have won half a million dollars in the state lottery. I am not exaggerating (it may be recalled that I mentioned once that I had never yet really witnessed a female in the nude) when I say that these tidings could not have created the mingled astonishment and sheer brute happiness of Sophie's gentle suggestion. Combined with the touch of her fingers, forthrightly lewd, it caused me to gulp air with incredible rapidity. I think I went into that state known medically as hyperventilation and I thought for a moment that I might black out completely.

And even as I looked up she was wriggling out of her Cole of California special, so that I beheld inches away that which I thought I would see only after reaching early middle age: a young female body all creamy bare, with plump breasts that had perky brown nipples, a smooth slightly rounded belly with a frank eyewink of a belly-button, and (be still, my heart, I remember thinking) a nicely symmetrical triangle of honey-hued pubic hair. My cultural conditioning—ten years of airbrushed Petty girls and a universal blackout of the human form—had caused me to nearly forget that women possessed this last item, and I was still staring at it, wonderstruck, when Sophie turned and began to scamper toward the beach. "Come on, Stingo," she cried, "take off your clothes and let's go in the water!" I got up then and watched her go, transfixed; I mean it when I say that no chaste and famished grail-tormented Christian knight could have gazed with more slack-jawed admiration at the object of his quest than I did at my first glimpse of Sophie's bouncing behind—a delectable upside-down valentine. Then I saw her splash into the murky ocean.

I think it must have been pure consternation that prevented my following her into the water. So much had happened so quickly that my senses were spinning and I stood rooted to the sand. The shift in mood—the grisly chronicle of Warsaw, followed in a flash by this wanton playfulness. What in hell did it mean? I was wildly excited but hopelessly confused, with no precedent to guide me in this turn of events. In an excess of furtiveness—despite the total seclusion of the place—I slid out of my trunks and stood there beneath the strange churning gray summer sky, helplessly flaunting my manly state to the seraphim. I gulped at the last beer, woozy with mingled apprehension and joy. I watched Sophie swim. She swam well and with what seemed relaxed pleasure; I hoped she was not too relaxed, and for an instant I worried about her mixing swimming with all that whiskey. The air was sweltering, close, but I felt myself in the clutch of malarial trembling and chills.

"Oh, Stingo," she said with a giggle when she returned, "*tu bandes.*"

"*Tu* . . . what?"

"You have a hard-on."

She had seen it immediately. Not knowing what to do with it, but trying to avoid the extremes of gaucherie, I had arranged it and me on the blanket in a nonchalant posture—or as nonchalant as possible in my fit of ague—with my distended part concealed beneath my forearm; the attempt was unsuccessful, it flopped into view just before she flopped down beside me, and we rolled like dolphins into each other's arms. I have since then utterly despaired of trying to capture the tortured excitement of that embrace. I heard myself making little ponylike whinnies as I kissed her, but kissing was *all* I could manage; I clutched her around the waist with a maniac's armhold, terrified of stroking her anywhere out of fear that she would disintegrate under my crude fingers. There was a fragile feel to her rib cage. I thought of Nathan's kick but also of past starvation. My shivering and shaking continued; I was conscious now only of the whiskied sweetness of her mouth and my tongue and hers warmly mingled. "Stingo, you're shaking so," she whispered once, drawing back from my canine tongue play. "Just relax!" But I realized I was salivating stupidly—a further humiliation which preyed on my mind as our lips stayed wetly plastered together. I could not figure out why my mouth was leaking so, and this worry itself prevented me even more firmly from exploring breasts, bottom or, God help me, that innermost recess which had figured so thrillingly in my dreams. I was in the grip of a nameless and diabolical paralysis. It was as if ten thousand Presbyterian Sunday School teachers had massed above Long Island in a minatory cloud, their presence resolutely disabling my fingers. The seconds passed like minutes, the minutes like hours, and still I could make no serious move. But then, as if to put a stop to my suffering, or perhaps in an effort simply to get things going, Sophie herself made a move.

"You have a nice *schlong,* Stingo," she said, grasping me delicately but with a subtle, knowing firmness.

"Thank you," I heard myself mumble. A wave of disbelief swept over me (She is actually grabbing me there, I thought) but I tried to affect a saving savoir-faire. "Why do you call it *schlong?* Down South we call it something else." My voice had a bad quaver.

"It's what Nathan calls it," she replied. "What do you call it in the South?"

"Sometimes we call it a pecker," I whispered. "In parts of the upper South they call it a dong or a tool. Or a peter."

"I've heard Nathan call it his dork. Also, his *putz.*"

"Do you like mine?" I could barely hear myself.

"It's sweet."

I no longer recall what—if any one thing precisely—brought this ghastly dialogue to its termination. She was of course supposed to compliment me more floridly—"gigantic," "*une merveille,*" even "big" would do, almost anything but "sweet"—and perhaps it was only my glum silence after this which impelled her to begin to stroke and pump me with a zest that mingled the adroitness of a courtesan and a milkmaid. It was exquisite; I listened to her sigh in rapid breaths, I sighed too, and when she whispered, "Turn over on your back, Stingo darling," there flashed through my mind the scenes of insatiable oral love with Nathan she had so frankly described. But it was too much, too much to bear—all this divine, accomplished friction and (My God, I thought, she called me "darling") the sudden command to join her in paradise: with a bleat of dismay like that of a ram being slaughtered I felt my eyelids slam shut and I let loose the floodgates in a pulsing torrent. Then I died. Certainly in the grief of that moment she was not supposed to giggle, but she did.

Minutes later, however, sensing my despair, she said, "Don't let it make you sad. Stingo. That happens sometimes, I know." I lay crumpled like a wet paper bag, my eyes tightly shut, quite unable to contemplate the depths of my failure. *Ejaculatio praecox* (Psychology 4B at Duke University). A squad of evil imps yammered the phrase derisively in the black pit of my despair. I felt I would never again open my eyes to the world—a mud-imprisoned mollusk, lowliest creature in the sea.

I heard her giggle again, peered upward. "Look, Stingo," she was saying in front of my disbelieving gaze, "it's good for the complexion." And I watched while the crazy Polack took a gulp of whiskey straight from the bottle and with her other hand—the one which had wrought upon me such mixed mortification and pleasure—gently massaged into the skin of her face my hapless exudate.

"Nathan always said that come is filled with these very wonderful vitamins," she said. For some reason my eyes fixed themselves on her tattoo; it seemed profoundly incongruous at this moment. "Don't look so *tragique,* Stingo. It's not the end of the world, it happens to all men sometimes, especially when they are young. *Par example,* in Warsaw when Jozef and me first try to make love he done the same thing, exactly the same thing. He was a virgin too."

"How did you know I was a virgin?" I said with a wretched sigh.

"Oh, I can tell, Stingo. I knew that you had no success with that Leslie girl, you were just making up stories when you said you have gone to bed with her. Poor Stingo— Oh, to be honest, Stingo, I did not really know. I just guessed. But I was right, no?"

"Yes," I groaned. "Pure as the driven snow."

"Jozef was so much like you in many ways—honest, direct, with this quality that make him like a little boy in a certain fashion. It is hard to describe. Maybe that's why I like you so much, Stingo, because you remind me quite a bit of Jozef. I maybe would have married him if he had not been killed by the Nazis. You know, none of us could ever find out who it was who betrayed him after he killed Irena. It was a total mystery, but somebody must have told. We used to go on picnics like this together. It was very difficult during the war—so little food—but once or twice we went out into the country in the summer and spread a blanket this way . . ."

This was astounding. After the steamy sexuality of only moments before, after this encounter—despite fumbling and failure, the single most cataclysmic and soul-stirring event of its kind that I had ever experienced—she was rattling on in reminiscence like someone plunged into a daydream, seemingly no more touched by our prodigious intimacy than if we had done a two-step together innocently on a dance floor. Was part of this due to some perverse effect of the booze? She had gotten a little glassy-eyed by now and was running off at the mouth like a tobacco auctioneer. Whatever the cause, her sudden insouciance gave me acute distress. Here she was, unconcernedly smearing my frenzied spermatozoa across her cheeks as if she were using Pond's cold cream, talking not about me (whom she had called "darling"!)—talking not about *us* but about a lover dead and buried years before. Had she forgotten that only minutes ago she had been on the brink of initiating me into the mysteries of the blow-job, a sacrament I had awaited with anxious joy since the age of fourteen? Could women, then, so instantaneously turn off their lust like a light switch? And *Jozef!* Her preoccupation with her sweetheart was maddening, and I could hardly bear the thought—thrust it into the back of my mind—that this precipitate passion she had for a few hot moments lavished on me was the result of a transfer of identity; that I was merely an instant surrogate Jozef, flesh to occupy space in an ephemeral fantasy. In any case, I also noticed that she was becoming a little incoherent; her voice had an intonation that was both stilted and thick, and her lips moved in an odd artificial way as if they had been numbed by Novocaine. It was more than a little alarming, this mesmerized appearance. I removed the bottle with its few remaining ounces from her hand.

"It make me sick, Stingo, so *sick* to think how things might have been. If Jozef hadn't died. I cared for him very much. So much more than Nathan, really. Jozef never mistreated me like Nathan done. Who knows? Maybe we would have been married, and if we were married, life would have been so different. Just one thing, *par example* —his half sister, Wanda. I would have removed him from her evil influence and that would have been such a good thing. Where's that bottle, Stingo?" Even as she spoke I was pouring—behind my back and out of sight—what was left of the liquor into the sand. "The bottle. Anyway, that *kvetch* Wanda, such a *kvetch* she was!" (I loved *kvetch.* Nathan, Nathan again!) "It was her who was responsible for Jozef being killed. All right, I'll admit it—*il fallait que* . . . I mean it was necessary for *someone* to retaliate for betraying the Jews, but why every time to make Jozef the killer? Why? That was Wanda's power, this *kvetch.* Okay, she was an underground leader, but was it fair to make your brother the only killer in our part of the city? Was it *fair,* I ask you? He vomited every time he kill, Stingo. Vomited! It turn him *half crazy.*"

I held my breath as her face faded into an ashy white, and with a desperate clawing motion she groped about for the bottle, mumbling. "Sophie," I said, "Sophie, the whiskey's all gone."

Abstracted, stranded in her memory, she seemed not to hear, and also was plainly close to tears. Suddenly and for the first time I was aware of the meaning of the phrase "Slavic melancholy": sorrow had flooded across her face like black shadows sweeping over a snowy field. "Goddamned *cunt,* Wanda! She was the cause of everything.

Everything! Jozef dying and me going to Auschwitz and *everything!"* She began to sob, and the tears made disfiguring trails down her cheeks. I stirred miserably, not knowing really what to do. And although Eros had fled, I reached up and took her in my arms, bringing her down next to me. Her face lay against my chest. "Oh, goddamn, Stingo, I'm so awful unhappy!" she wailed. "Where's Nathan? Where's Jozef? Where's *everybody?* Oh, Stingo, I want to die!"

"Hush, Sophie," I said softly, stroking her bare shoulder, "everything's going to be all right." (Fat chance!)

"Hold me, Stingo," she whispered despairingly, "hold me. I feel so lost. Oh Christ, I feel so lost! What am I going to do? What am I going to do? I'm so alone!"

Booze, exhaustion, grief, the limpid soggy heat—it was doubtless all of these which put her to sleep in my arms. Beered-up and depleted, I too fell asleep, tightly hanging on to her body as to a security blanket. I dreamed aimless, convoluted dreams of the sort which all my life have seemed to be a recurrent specialty—dreams within dreams of ludicrous pursuit, of a quest for some unnameable prize taking me to unknown destinations: up steep angular stairways, by rowboat down sluggish canals, through cockeyed bowling alleys and labyrinthine railroad yards (where I saw my adored English professor at Duke, fully clad in his tweeds, standing at the controls of a rapidly moving switch engine), across yawning acres of garishly lit basements, subbasements and tunnels. Also a weird and terrible sewer. My goal as always was an enigma, although it seemed to have something vaguely to do with a lost dog. Then when I awoke, with a start, the first thing I realized was that Sophie had somehow loosened herself from my grasp and was gone. I heard myself utter a cry, which, however, got lodged in the back of my mouth and became a strangled moan. I felt my heart begin a pounding commotion. Struggling back into my trunks, I climbed to the side of the dune where I could look up and down the beach—saw nothing on that gloomy dull expanse of sand, nothing at all. She had vanished from sight.

I looked behind the dunes—a sere wasteland of marsh grass. No one. And no one on the nearby beach, except for an indistinct human shape, squat, thickly set, moving in my direction. I ran toward the figure, which gradually defined itself as a large swarthy male bather munching on a hot dog. His black hair was plastered down and parted in the middle; he grinned with amiable fatuity.

"Have you seen someone . . . a blond girl, I mean a real *dish,* very blond . . ." I stammered.

He gave an affirmative nod, smiling.

"Where?" I said in relief.

"No hablo inglés" was the reply.

It is graven on my memory still, that interchange—perhaps all the more vividly because at the precise instant I heard his answer I caught a glimpse of Sophie over his hairy shoulder, her head no bigger than a golden dot far out on the green petroleum waves. I did not think half a second before plunging in after her. I am a fairly good swimmer, but on that day I possessed truly Olympic bravura, aware even as I thrashed my way through the sluggish brine that sheer fright and desperation were animating the muscles of my legs and arms, propelling me outward and outward with a ferocity of strength I did not know was within me. I made brisk progress through the gently slopping sea; even so, I was amazed at how far out she had managed to get, and when I stopped briefly to tread water and find my bearings and locate her, I saw to my awful distress that she was still slicing her way through the ocean, bound for Venezuela. I shouted once, twice, but she kept on swimming. "Sophie, come back!" I cried, but I may as well have been beseeching the air.

I filled my lungs, prayed a small regressive prayer to the Christian deity—my first in years—and resumed my heroic crawl southward toward that receding wet mop of yellow hair. Then all of a sudden I could tell that I was gaining with dramatic speed; through the salty blur of my eyes I saw Sophie's head grow larger, nearer. I realized that she had stopped swimming and within seconds I was on top of her. Submerged nearly to her eyes, she was not yet quite on the verge of drowning; but her gaze looked as wild as a cornered cat's, she was gulping water and was plainly at the edge of exhaustion. "Don't! Don't!" she gasped, warding me off with feeble little thrusts of her hand. But I lunged for her, grabbed her firmly around the waist from behind and roared "Shut up!" with hysteric necessity. I could have wept with relief at the immediate discovery that once in my embrace, she did not put up the struggle that I had foreseen but relaxed against me and let me swim with her slowly shoreward, uttering little desolate sobs that bubbled against my cheek and into my ear.

As soon as I dragged her up onto the beach she fell on all fours and regurgitated half a gallon of seawater onto the sand. Then, choking and spluttering, she sprawled out face down at the water's edge and like someone in a fit of epilepsy began to shudder uncontrollably, smitten by a convulsion of ragged grief such as I had never before witnessed in a human being. "Oh God," she moaned, "why didn't you let me die? Why didn't you let me drown? I've been so *bad*—I've been so awful bad! Why didn't you let me drown?"

I stood above her naked form, helpless. The solitary beach walker whom I had accosted stood idly by watching us. I noted a smear of ketchup on his lips; he was offering gloomy, barely audible advice in Spanish. Suddenly I slumped down next to Sophie, aware of how utterly pooped I was, and I ran a limp hand down her bare back. A tactile impression still registers from that moment: the skeletal outline of her spine, each vertebra discrete, the whole serpentine length moving up and down with her tortured breathing. It had begun to drizzle a warm misty rain, which collected in droplets against my face. I put my head against her shoulder. Then I heard her say, "You should have let me drown, Stingo. No one is filled with such badness. No one! No one has such badness."

But at last I got her dressed and we took a bus back to Brooklyn and the Pink Palace. With the help of coffee she sobered up finally and slept through the late afternoon and early evening. When she awoke she was still very much on edge—the memory of that lonely swim to nowhere had plainly unnerved her—but even so, she seemed relatively composed for one who had gone so far out toward the brink. As for any physical damage, she appeared to have suffered little, although her engorgement with salt water gave her the hiccups and caused her for hours afterward to erupt in sizable, unladylike belches.

And then—well, God knows she had already taken me with her to some of the nethermost reaches of her past.

But she had also left me with unanswered questions. Perhaps she felt that there was really no returning to the present unless she could come clean, as they say, and shed light on what she had still concealed from me as well as (who knows?) from herself. And so during the remainder of that rain-soaked weekend she told me much more about her season in hell. (Much more, but not everything. There was one matter that remained entombed in her, in the realm of the unspeakable.) And I came at last to discern the outlines of that "badness" which had tracked her down remorselessly from Warsaw to Auschwitz and thence to these pleasant bourgeois streets of Brooklyn, pursuing her like a demon.

Sophie was taken prisoner sometime during the middle of March, 1943. This was several days after Jozef had been killed by the Ukrainian guards. A gray day with wind in gusts and lowering clouds still touched with the raw look of winter. She remembered that it was late in the afternoon. When the speedy little three-car electric train in which she was riding screeched to a halt somewhere in the outskirts of Warsaw she had something more powerful than a mere premonition. It was a certainty—certainty that she would be sent to one of the camps. This deranging flash came to her even before the Gestapo agents—half a dozen or more—clambered onto the car and ordered everyone down to the street. She knew it was the *lapanka*—a roundup—which she had dreaded and anticipated even as the tramway-style car came to its shuddering halt; something in that suddenness and quick deceleration spelled doom. There was doom, too, in the acrid, metallic stench of the wheels braking against the rails and the way in which, simultaneously, the seated and standing passengers in the jammed train all lurched forward, clutching wildly and aimlessly for support. This is no accident, she thought, it's the German police. And then she heard the bellowed command: *"Raus!"*

They found the twelve-kilo cut of ham almost immediately. Her stratagem—fastening the newspaper-wrapped package to her body beneath her dress in a way that would make her appear corpulently pregnant—was shopworn enough by now almost to call attention to itself rather than work as a ruse; she had tried it anyway, urged on by the farm woman who had sold her the precious meat. "You can at least give it a try," the woman had said. "They'll surely catch you if they see you carrying it in the open. Also, you look and dress like an intellectual, not one of our country *babas*. That will help." But Sophie had not foreseen either the *lapanka* or its thoroughness. And so the Gestapo goon, pressing Sophie up against a damp brick wall, made no effort to conceal his contempt for her doltish Polack dodge, extracting a penknife from the pocket of his jacket and inserting the blade with relaxed, almost informal delicacy into that bulgingly bogus placenta, leering as he did so. Sophie recalled the smell of cheese on the Nazi's breath and his remark as the knife sank into the haunch of what had been, until recently, contented pig. "Can't you say ouch, *Liebchen?*" She was unable, in her terror, to utter anything more than some desperate commonplace, but for her small pains, received a compliment on the felicity of her German.

She felt sure that she was going to be tortured, but she somehow escaped this. The Germans seemed to be caught up in an enormous hullaballoo that particular day; all over the streets hundreds of Poles were being corralled and taken into custody, and thus the crime she had committed (a grave one, smuggling meat), which at another time would certainly have caused her to be subjected to the most detailed scrutiny, got overlooked or forgotten in the general confusion. But by no means did she go unnoticed, nor did her ham. At the infamous Gestapo headquarters—that terrible Warsaw simulacrum of Satan's antechamber—the ham lay unwrapped and pinkly glistening on the desk between herself, handcuffed, and a hyperactive, monocled zealot who almost exactly resembled Otto Kruger and who demanded to know where she had obtained this contraband. His interpreter, a Polish girl, had a coughing fit. "You be a smuggler!" he said loudly in clumsy Polish, and when Sophie replied in German she received her second compliment of the day. A big molar-filled greasy Nazi smile, right out of a 1938 Hollywood movie. But it was barely even a pleasantry. Did she not know the seriousness of her act, did she not know that meat of any kind but especially of this quality was designated for the Reich? With a long fingernail he pried loose a fat sliver of the ham and conveyed it to his mouth. He nibbled. *Hochqualitätsfleisch.* His voice suddenly became tough, a snarl. Where did she get such meat? Who supplied her with this? Sophie thought of the poor farm woman, knew of the vengeance awaiting her too, and temporizing now, replied, "It was not for me, sir, this meat. It was for my mother who lives on the other side of the city. She is seriously ill from tuberculosis." As if such an altruistic sentiment could have the vaguest effect on this caricature of a Nazi, who was already being besieged by knocks at the door and an irruptive jangle of the telephone. What a wild day for the Germans and their *lapanka.* "I don't give a damn for your mother!" he roared. "I want to know where you got this meat! Tell me now or I'll have it beaten out of you!" But the hammering at the door continued, another telephone began ringing; the little office became the cell of a madman. The Gestapo officer shrieked to a subordinate to have this Polish bitch taken away—and that was the last Sophie ever saw of him, or the ham.

On another day she might not even have been caught. The irony of this smote her over and over while she waited in an almost totally dark detention cell with a dozen other Warsovians of both sexes, all strangers. Most of these—although not all—were young, in their twenties and thirties. Something about their manner—perhaps it was only the stolid, stony communion of their silence—told her that they were members of the Resistance. The AK—Armia Krajowa. Home Army. Here it suddenly occurred to her that had she waited only another day (as she had planned) to journey out toward Nowy Dwór to procure the meat, she would not have been on the railroad car, which she now realized may have been ambushed in order to trap certain members of the AK who had been passengers. By casting a wide net for as many exceptional fish as possible, as they sometimes did, the Nazis came up with all sorts of minor but interesting minnows, and this day Sophie was one of them. Sitting there on the stone floor (it was midnight now), she was smothered by despair, thinking of Jan and Eva at home with no one to look after them. In the corridors outside the cell there was a constant jabber and hubbub, a shuffling of feet and a jostling of bodies as the jail continued to fill up with the victims of the day's roundup. Once through the grilled aperture of the door above her she caught a quick glimpse of a familiar face, and her heart turned to lead. The face was streaming with blood. It belonged to a young man whom she had known only by his first name, Wladyslaw; the editor of an underground newspaper, he had spoken to her several times briefly at Wanda and Jozef's apartment on the floor beneath her own. She did not know why, but she was at that moment certain that this meant that Wanda had been arrested too. Then something else occurred to her. *Mother of God,* she breathed in an instinctive prayer, and felt herself go limp as a wet leaf with this realization: that the ham (quite aside from the fact of its having been devoured by the Gestapo) had doubtless been forgotten, and that her own fate—whatever it might be—was tied up with the fate of these members of the Resistance. And such a fate swooped down on her with a black foreboding overwhelming enough to make stale the word "terror."

Sophie spent the night without sleep. It was cold and tomb-dark in the cell and she could only distinguish the fact that the human form—hurled in next to her during the early hours of the morning—was female. And as dawn seeped in through the grating she was shocked though not really surprised to see that the dozing woman beside her was Wanda. In the pale light she could slowly make out the huge bruise on Wanda's cheek; it was repulsive, reminding Sophie of mashed purple grapes. She started to wake her, thought better of it, hesitated, withdrew her hand; just then Wanda awoke and groaned, blinked, staring Sophie in the eye. She would never forget the look of astonishment on Wanda's battered face. "Zosia!" she exclaimed, embracing her. "Zosia! What in God's name are *you* doing here?"

Sophie burst into tears, weeping with such desperation and wretchedness against Wanda's shoulder that it was long minutes before she could even begin to mumble a word. Wanda's patient strength was consoling, as usual; her soothing whispers and pats between the shoulder blades were at once sisterly, maternal and like the attentions of a nurse; Sophie could have fallen fast asleep in her arms. But she was tortured with too much anxiety, and after taking hold of herself she blurted out the tale of her arrest on the train. It took her only seconds. She heard her words spilling over one another in a rush, conscious of the haste and abbreviation and her consuming need to arrive at the answer to the question which had been literally twisting her intestines for twelve hours: "The children, Wanda! Jan and Eva. Are they safe?"

"Yes, they're safe. They're here somewhere, in this place. The Nazis didn't hurt them. They arrested everyone in our building—everyone, including your kids. They made a clean sweep of it." A tormented look passed over her wide strong features, ravaged now by the appalling bruise. "Oh God, they picked up so many people in the movement today. I knew we wouldn't have long after they killed Jozef. It's a catastrophe!"

At least the children had not been harmed. She blessed Wanda, feeling exquisite relief. Then she could not restrain the impulse; she let her fingers hover over the disfigured cheek, the empurpled spongy outraged flesh, but did not touch it, finally drew her hand away. As she did so she found herself weeping again. "What did they do to you, Wanda darling?" she whispered.

"A Gestapo ape threw me down the stairs, then stomped on me. Oh, these . . ." She raised her eyes upward, but the imprecation she was plainly about to utter faded on her lips. The Germans had been cursed without cessation and for so long that the dirtiest anathema, no matter how novel, sounded vapid; better to let the tongue fall dumb. "It's not so bad, I don't think he broke anything. I'll bet it looks worse than it feels." She put her arms around Sophie again, making little tut-tut sounds. "Poor Zosia. Imagine *you* falling into their filthy trap."

Wanda! How could Sophie ever fathom or define her ultimate feeling about Wanda—composed as that emotion was of love, envy, distrust, dependence, hostility and admiration? They were so much alike in certain ways, yet so different. In the beginning it had been their mutual bewitchment with music that had drawn them together. Wanda had come to Warsaw to study voice at the Conservatory, but the war had blasted those aspirations, as it had Sophie's. When by chance Sophie came to live in the same building as Wanda and Jozef, it had been Bach and Buxtehude, Mozart and Rameau who had glued together their friendship. Wanda was a tall, athletically built young woman with boyish, graceful arms and legs and flaming red hair. Her eyes were of the most arrestingly clear sapphire-blue that Sophie had ever seen. Her face was a cloud of tiny amber freckles. A somewhat too prominent chin marred the suggestion of real beauty, but she had a vivacity, a luminous intensity which sometimes transformed her in a spectacular way; she glowed, she became all sparks and fire (Sophie often thought of the word *fougueuse*) like her hair.

There was at least one strong similarity about Sophie's and Wanda's background: they had both been brought up in an ambience of rapturous Germanism. Indeed, Wanda had a transcendentally German surname, Muck-Horch von Kretschmann—this being the result of her birth to a German father and a Polish mother in Lodz, where the influence of Germany upon commerce and industry, mainly textiles, had been pervasive if not almost complete. Her father, a manufacturer of cheap woolens, had made her learn German early; like Sophie, she spoke the language with accentless fluency, but her heart and soul were Polish. Sophie never believed that such violent patriotism could dwell within a human breast, even in a land of throbbing patriots. Wanda was the reincarnation of the young Rosa Luxemburg, whom she worshipped. She seldom mentioned her father, nor did she ever try to explain why she had rejected so completely the German part of her heritage; Sophie only knew that Wanda breathed, drank and dreamed the idea of a free Poland—most radiantly, a liberated Polish proletariat after the war—and such a passion had turned her into one of the most unbudgingly committed members of the Resistance. She was sleepless, fearless, clever—a firebrand. Her perfection in the language of the conquering hordes made her, of course, exceedingly valuable to the underground movement, quite aside from her zeal and her other capabilities. And it was her knowledge that Sophie, too, had an inbred command of German but refused to place this gift at the service of the Resistance that at first caused Wanda to lose patience with her and then later brought the two friends to the edge of ruinous discord. For Sophie was deeply, agonizingly, mortally afraid of getting herself involved in the underground fight against the Nazis, and such disengagement seemed to Wanda not only unpatriotic but an act of moral cowardice.

A few weeks before Jozef's murder and the roundup, some members of the Home Army had made off with a Gestapo van in the town of Pruszków, not far from Warsaw. The van contained a treasure trove of documents and plans, and Wanda was able to tell at a glance that the thick, voluminous files contained items of the highest level of secrecy. But there were many of them and it was urgent that they be translated. When Wanda approached Sophie, asking her to help with these papers, Sophie once again was unable to say yes, and they resumed their old, painful argument.

"I am a socialist," Wanda had said, "and *you* have no politics at all. Furthermore, you are something of a Christer. That is all right with me. In the old days I would have had nothing but contempt for you, Zosia, contempt and dislike. There are still friends of mine who will have nothing to do with a person like you. But I suppose I've outgrown such a point of view. I hate the stupid rigidity of some of my comrades. Also, I'm simply so fond of you, as you certainly realize. So I'm not trying to appeal to you on political grounds or even ideological grounds. You wouldn't want to get mixed up with a lot of them anyway. I'm not typical, but *they* are not your type at *all*—something you already know. Anyway, not everyone in the movement is political. I am appealing to you in the *name of humanity*. I am trying to appeal to your sense of *decency*, to a sense of yourself as a *human being* and a *Pole*."

At this point Sophie had, as usual after one of Wanda's fervent come-ons, turned away, saying nothing. She had gazed out the window at the wintry Warsaw desolation, bomb-shattered buildings and rubble heaps shrouded (there was no other word) by the sulphurous soot-blackened snow—a landscape which had once brought tears of sorrow but now only evoked sickish apathy, so much a dingy part did it seem of the day-to-day dreariness and misery of a city ransacked, fearful, hungry, dying. If hell had suburbs, they would look like this wasteland. She sucked at the ends of her ragged fingers. She could not keep herself in even cheap gloves. Gloveless toil at the tar-paper factory had wrecked her hands; one thumb had become badly infected and it hurt. She replied to Wanda, "I've told you and I'll tell you again, my dear, I can't. I won't. That's that."

"And for the same reason, I suppose?"

"Yes." Why couldn't Wanda accept her decision as final, lay off, leave her alone? Her persistence was maddening. "Wanda," she said softly, "I don't want to press the point any more than I have to. It's embarrassing for me to repeat what should be evident to you, because I know you're basically a sensitive person. But in my position—I say it again—I *can't* risk it, with children—"

"Other women in the Home Army have children," Wanda put in abruptly. "Why can't you get that through your head?"

"I told you before. I'm not *'other women'* and I'm not in the Home Army," Sophie retorted, this time with exasperation. "I'm *myself!* I have to act according to my conscience. *You* don't have children. It's easy for you to talk like this. I cannot jeopardize the lives of my children. They're having a hard enough time as it is."

"I'm afraid I find it very offensive of you, Zosia, placing yourself on a level different from the others. Unable to sacrifice—"

"I've *sacrificed,*" Sophie said bitterly. "I've lost a husband and a father already, and my mother is dying of tuberculosis. How *much* do I have to sacrifice, in the name of God?" Wanda could scarcely be expected to know of the antipathy—call it indifference—which Sophie harbored toward husband and father, dead in their graves these past three years at Sachsenhausen; nonetheless, what she had said comprised a telling point of sorts, and Sophie detected in Wanda a consequent moderation of tone. A quality that was almost wheedling entered her voice.

"You wouldn't necessarily be in a very vulnerable position, you understand, Zosia. You wouldn't be required to do anything truly risky—nothing remotely like what some of the comrades have been doing, even myself. It's a matter of your brain, your head. There are so many things that you can do that would be invaluable, with your knowledge of the language. Monitoring their shortwave broadcasts, translating. Those documents that were stolen yesterday from that Gestapo van in Pruszków. Let's get to the point about this right now. They're worth their weight in gold, I'm certain! It's something I could help do, certainly, but there are so many of them and I have a thousand other things on my mind. Don't you see, Zosia, how incredibly useful you could be if we could just have some of those documents delivered to you here, quite safely—no one would suspect." She paused, then said in an insistent voice, "You must reconsider, Zosia. This is becoming *indecent* of you. Consider what you can do for all of us. Consider your country! Consider Poland!"

Dusk was coming on. From the ceiling a tiny lightbulb pulsed spiritlessly—lucky tonight, often there was no light. Since dawn Sophie had been shifting piles of tar paper, and she was aware now that her back was hurting her more even than her swollen and infected thumb. As usual she felt unclean, begrimed. With tired, gritty eyes she brooded out across the desolate cityscape, over which the sun never seemed to cast a glimmer. She yawned an exhausted yawn, no longer listening to Wanda's voice, or rather, no longer hearing the actual words, which had become strident, singsong, hectoring, inspirational. She wondered where Jozef was, wondered if he was safe. She knew only that he was stalking someone in another part of the city, his piano wire in a lethal coil beneath his jacket—a boy of nineteen bent upon his mission of death and retribution. She was not in love with him but she, well—*cared* for him intensely; she liked the warmth of him in bed beside her, and she would be anxious until he returned. Mary Mother of God, she thought, what an existence! On the ugly street below—gray and grainy and featureless like the worn sole of a shoe—a platoon of German soldiers tramped into the gusty wind, the collars of their tunics blowing, rifles slung at the shoulder; listlessly she watched them pass the corner, turn, disappear up a street where but for an intervening bombed-out building she knew she could have seen the steel-and-iron curbside public gallows: it was as functional as a rack upon which secondhand dealers displayed used clothes, and from its horizontal bar citizens of Warsaw beyond counting had twisted and hung. And still hung and twisted. *Christ, would it never end?*

She was too weary to attempt even a bad joke, but it did occur to her, *almost*, to break in on Wanda, to reply to her by saying something that was outrageously lodged in her heart: The one and only thing which might lure me into your world would be that radio. Would be to listen to London. But not to war news. Not to news of Allied victories, nor word of the Polish army fighting, nor to orders from the government of Poland in exile. Not to any of these. No, quite simply I think I would risk my life as you do and also give an arm or a hand to listen just once again to Sir Thomas Beecham conducting *Così fan tutte.* What a shocking, selfish idea it was—she was aware of its infinite ignobility even as the thought crossed her mind—but she could not help it, it was what she felt.

For a moment shame washed over her for thinking the thought, shame at entertaining the notion in the same habitation where she shared room with Wanda and Jozef, these two selfless, courageous people whose allegiance to humanity and their fellow Poles and concern for the hunted Jews were a repudiation of all that her father had stood for. Despite her own actual blamelessness, she had felt dirtied, defiled by her association with her father in his last obsessed year, and with his atrocious pamphlet, and so her brief relationship with this consecrated sister and her brother had brought her moments of cleansing grace. She gave a small shudder and the fever of shame worsened, became hotter. What would they think if they knew about Professor Biegański, or knew that for three years she had carried on her person a copy of that pamphlet? And for what reason? *For what unspeakable reason?* To use it as a small wedge, an instrument of possible negotiation with the Nazis, should the loathsome occasion ever arise? Yes, she replied to herself, *yes*—there was no way out of that vile and disgraceful fact. And now as Wanda rambled on about duty and sacrifice she became so troubled by her secret that simply to save her composure she thrust it from her mind like some foul leaving. She listened again.

"There comes a point in life where every human being must stand up and be counted," Wanda was saying. "You know what a beautiful person I think you are. And Jozef would die for you!" Her voice rose, now began to scrape her raw. "But you can no longer treat us this way. You have to assume responsibility, Zosia. You've come to the place where you can no longer fool around like this, you have to make a choice!"

Just then on the street below she caught sight of her children. They moved slowly up the sidewalk, talking earnestly, dallying as little children do. A few pedestrians straggled past them, homeward bound in the dusk; one, an elderly man bundled up against the wind, clumsily bumped Jan, who made an impudent gesture with his hand, then strolled on with his sister, deep in his chat, explaining . . . explaining. He had gone to fetch Eva from her flute lesson—a haphazard, sometimes quite sudden and impromptu affair (depending on daily pressures) held in a gutted basement a dozen blocks away. The teacher, a man named Stefan Zaorski, had been a flutist with the Warsaw Symphony, and Sophie had had to cajole and flatter and plead in order to get him to take Eva as a student; aside from the money that Sophie could pay, a pitiful amount, there was little incentive for a dispossessed musician to give lessons in that stark and cheerless city—there were better (although mainly illegal) ways to earn one's bread. He was seriously crippled with arthritis in both knees, which didn't help things. But Zaorski, a man still youngish and a bachelor, had a crush on Sophie (as did so many men who saw her and became instantly moonstruck), and doubtless agreed in order to be able to delight in her fair beauty from time to time. Also, Sophie had been energetically, quietly insistent, ultimately persuasive, convincing Zaorski that she could not consider raising Eva without giving her a knowledge of music. One might as well just say no to life itself.

The flute. The enchanted flute. In a city of destroyed or tuneless pianos it would seem a fine instrument for a child's first leap into music. Eva was mad for the flute, and after four months or so Zaorski had begun to dote on the little girl, amazed at her natural gift, fussed over her as if she were a prodigy (which she might have been), another Landowska, another Paderewski, another Polish offering to music's pantheon—and finally even refused the trifling amount that Sophie was able to pay. Zaorski popped up now down on the street, appearing as if from nowhere, astonishingly, like a blond genie—a half-starved-looking, limping, florid-faced, broomstraw-haired man with jittery concern in his pale eyes. The woolen sweater he wore, a sooty green, was a mosaic of moth holes. Sophie, startled, leaned forward against the window. The generous, neurotic man had obviously followed Eva, or rather, chased as well as he could after the children, hurrying these many blocks out of some preoccupation or reason which Sophie could not possibly divine. Then all of a sudden his mission became clear. Ever the passionate pedagogue, he had hobbled after Eva in order to correct, or explain, or elaborate on something he had taught her in her most recent lesson—a matter of fingering or phrasing—what? Sophie didn't know, but she was both touched and amused.

She pushed the window open slightly in order to call down to the group, now huddled near the entrance of the building next door. Eva wore her yellow hair in pigtails. She had lost her front teeth. How, Sophie wondered, could she play a flute? Zaorski had made Eva open her leather case and remove the flute; he flourished it aloft in front of the child, not blowing on it but merely demonstrating some soundless arpeggio with his fingers. Then he put his lips to the instrument and blew several notes. For a long moment Sophie was unable to hear. Huge shadows swept across the wintry heavens. Overhead a squadron of Luftwaffe bombers droned deafeningly eastward toward Russia, flying very low—five, ten, then twenty monster machines spreading their vulturous shapes against the sky. They came late every afternoon as if on schedule, shaking the house with clattering vibrations. Wanda's voice was drowned out in their roar.

When the planes had passed, Sophie looked down and was able to hear Eva play, but only for the barest instant. The music was familiar but unnameable—Handel, Pergolesi, Gluck?—an intricate sweet trill of piercing nostalgia and miraculous symmetry. A dozen notes in all, no more, they struck antiphonal bells deep within Sophie's soul. They spoke of all she had been, of all she longed to be—and all she wished for her children, in whatever future God willed. Her heart swooned in those depths; she grew faint, unsteady, and she felt herself in the grip of an aching, devouring love. And at the same time joy—joy that was inexplicably both delicious and despairing—swept across her skin in a cool blaze.

But the small, perfect piping—almost as soon as it had begun—had evaporated on the air. "Wonderful, Eva!" she heard Zaorski's voice. "Just right!" And she saw the teacher give first Eva then Jan a tender pat on the head before turning and moving jerkily up the street toward his basement. Jan tugged at one of Eva's pigtails and she gave a yell. "*Stop* it, Jan!" Then the children rushed into the hallway downstairs.

"You *must* come to a decision!" she heard Wanda say insistently.

For a time Sophie was silent. At last, with the sound of the children's tumbling, ascending footsteps in her ears, she replied softly, "I have already made my choice, as I told you. *I will not get involved.* I mean this! *Schluss!*" Her voice rose on this word and she found herself wondering why she had spoken it in German. "*Schluss—aus!* That's final!"

During the five months or so before Sophie was taken prisoner the Nazis had made a vigorous effort to ensure that the north of Poland would become *Judenrein*—cleansed of Jews. Beginning in November, 1942, and extending through the following January, a program of deportation was instituted whereby the many thousands of Jews living in the northeastern district of Bialystok were jammed onto trains and shipped to concentration camps throughout the country. Funneled down into the railway complex in Warsaw, the majority of these Jews from the north eventually found themselves at Auschwitz. Meanwhile, in Warsaw itself there had come a lull in the action against the Jews—at least in terms of gross deportations. That the deportations from Warsaw had already been extensive may be seen from some twilight statistics. Before the German invasion of Poland in 1939 Warsaw's Jewish population was in the neighborhood of 450,000—next to New York, the largest concentration of Jews to be found in any city on earth. Only three years later the Jews living in Warsaw numbered 70,000; most of the others perished not only at Auschwitz but at Sobibór, Belzec, Chelmno, Maidanek and, above all, Treblinka. This last camp was located in wild country at an advantageously short distance from Warsaw, and unlike Auschwitz, which to a large extent was involved in slave labor, became a place totally consecrated to extermination. It was plainly not chance that the huge "resettlements" from the Warsaw ghetto which occurred in July and August of 1942, and which left that quarter a ghostly shell, were coincident with the establishment of the bucolic hideaway of Treblinka and its gas chambers.

In any case, of the 70,000 Jews who stayed in the city, approximately half were living "legally" in the ravaged ghetto (even as Sophie languished in the Gestapo jail many of these were preparing for martyrs' deaths in the April uprising only a few weeks away). Most of the remaining 35,000—clandestine denizens of the so-called interghetto—dwelt in despair amid the ruins like hunted animals. It was not enough that they were pursued by the Nazis: they endured unending fear of betrayal by hoodlum "Jew-catchers"—Jozef's prey—and other venal Poles like his lady American Lit. prof; it even happened (and more than once) that their exposure came about through the contortionate artifices of fellow Jews. Ghastly, as Wanda said to Sophie over and over, that Jozef's own betrayal and murder somehow marked the breakthrough which the Nazis were anticipating. This shattered segment of the Home Army—God, how sad! But after all, she had added, it could hardly have been unexpected. So it was really because of the Jews that they all ended up simmering in the same big kettle. It is a significant fact that the membership included some consecrated Jews. And there is this: although the Home Army, like members of the Resistance elsewhere in Europe, had other concerns besides the succor and safekeeping of the Jews (as indeed there were one or two partisan factions in Poland that remained malignantly anti-Semitic), such help, generally speaking, was still high on their list of priorities; thus it is safe to say that it was at least partly because of their efforts in behalf of some of these incessantly stalked, mortally endangered Jews that dozens upon dozens of members of the underground were rapidly corralled, and that Sophie too—

Sophie the stainless, the inaccessible, the uninvolved—was adventitiously ensnared.

During most of the month of March, including the two-week period in which Sophie was lodged in the Gestapo jail, the transports of Jews from the Bialystok district to Auschwitz by way of Warsaw had temporarily ceased. This would probably explain why Sophie and the members of the Resistance—now numbering nearly 250 prisoners—were not themselves sent off immediately to the camp; the Germans, always efficiency-minded, were waiting to engraft their new captives to a more massive shipment of human flesh, and since no Jews were being deported from Warsaw, a delay must have seemed expedient. Another key matter—the interruption in the deportation of the Jews from the northeast—requires comment; this was most likely connected with the building of the Birkenau crematoriums. Since the camp's inception the original crematorium at Auschwitz together with its gas chamber had served as the chief utility of mass death for the entire camp. Its earliest victims were Russian prisoners of war. It was a Polish structure: the barracks and buildings of Auschwitz made up the homely nucleus of a former cavalry installation when it was appropriated by the Germans. At one time this low rambling edifice with its slanted slate roof had been a storage warehouse for vegetables, and the Germans obviously found its architecture congenial to their purpose; the large underground grotto where turnips and potatoes had been piled high was perfectly suited to the asphyxiation of people en masse, just as the adjoining anterooms were so naturally fit for the installation of cremation ovens as to appear almost custom-made. All that was needed was the addition of a chimney, and the butchers were in business.

But the place was too limited for the hordes of the doomed which had begun to pour into the camp. Although several smallish temporary bunkers for extermination were thrown up in 1942, there was a crisis that arose in terms of facilities for killing and disposal which could only be remedied by the completion of the immense new crematoriums at Birkenau. The Germans—or rather, their Jewish and Gentile slaves—had been hard at work that winter. The first of these four gigantic incinerators was placed in operation a week after Sophie's capture by the Gestapo, the second only eight days later—mere hours before her arrival at Auschwitz on the first of April. She left Warsaw on the thirtieth of March. On that day she and Jan and Eva and the nearly 250 members of the Resistance, including Wanda, were herded aboard a train containing 1,800 Jews sent down finally from Malkinia, a transit camp northeast of Warsaw where the remainder of the Jewish population from the Bialystok district had been held. Besides the Jews and the Home Army fighters on the train, there was a contingent of Poles—Warsaw citizens of both sexes, numbering around two hundred—who had been picked up by the Gestapo in one of their spasmodic but ruthless *lapankas,* the victims in this case being guilty of nothing more than the calamitous luck to be caught on the wrong street at the wrong hour. Or at most, the nature of the guilt of all of these was technical if not illusory.

Among the unfortunates was Stefan Zaorski, who lacked a work permit and had already confided to Sophie his premonition that he would get into serious trouble. Sophie was stunned when she learned that he, too, had been caught. She saw him from a distance at the jail and once caught a glimpse of him on the train, but she was never able to speak to him amid the steam and the press of bodies and the pandemonium. It was one of the most populous transports to reach Auschwitz in some time. The very size of the shipment is perhaps an indication of how eager the Germans were to employ their new facilities at Birkenau. No selections were made among these Jews in order to winnow out those who would be assigned to labor, and while it was not particularly rare for an entire transport to be exterminated, the slaughter should in this case be remarked upon as perhaps representing the Germans' zeal to exploit and show off to themselves their latest, largest and most refined instrument in the technology of murder: all 1,800 Jews went to their deaths in the inaugural action of Crematorium II. Not a single soul among them escaped immediate gassing.

Although Sophie was extremely open with me about her life in Warsaw and her capture and her stay in the jail, she became curiously reticent about her actual deportation to Auschwitz and her arrival there. I thought at first it had to do with too much horror, and I was right, but I would only later learn the real reason for this silence, this evasiveness—certainly I thought little enough about it at the time. If the foregoing paragraphs with their accumulation of statistics seem, then, to have an abstract or static quality, it is for the reason that I have had to try to re-create, these many years afterward, a larger background to the events in which Sophie and the others were helpless participants, using data which could scarcely have been available to anyone except the professionally concerned in that long-ago year just following the war's end.

I have brooded a lot since then. I have often wondered what might have dwelt in Professor Biegański's thoughts had he lived to know that the fate of his daughter but especially his grandchildren was ancillary to, yet inextricably bound up with, the accomplishment of the dream he shared with his National Socialist idols: the liquidation of the Jews. Despite his worship of the Reich, he was a proud Pole. He also must have been exceptionally astute about matters pertaining to power. It is hard to understand how he could have been blind to the fact that the great death-happening wrought upon the European Jews by the Nazis would descend like a smothering fog around his compatriots—a people loathed with such ferocity that only the precedence of an even more urgent loathing accorded the Jews was a rampart against their own eventual obliteration. It was that detestation of Poles, of course, which doomed the Professor himself. But his obsession must have blinded him to many things, and it is an irony that—even if the Poles and other Slavs were not next on the list of people to be annihilated—he should have failed to foresee how such sublime hatred could only gather into its destroying core, like metal splinters sucked toward some almighty magnet, countless thousands of victims who did not wear the yellow badge. Sophie told me once—as she went on to reveal certain bits of her life in Cracow which she had previously withheld—that whatever the Professor's grim authoritarian disdain for her, his adoration of his two little grandchildren had been melting, genuine, complete. It is impossible to speculate on the reaction of this tormented man had he survived to see Jan and Eva fall into the black pit which his imagination had fashioned for the Jews.

I will always remember Sophie's tattoo. That nasty little excrescence, attached like a ridge of minute bruised tooth-bites to her forearm, was the single detail of her appearance which—on the night when I first saw her at the Pink Palace—instantly conveyed to my mind the mistaken idea that she was a Jew. In the vague and uninformed mythology of the day, Jewish survivors and this pathetic marking were indissolubly tied together. But if I had known then of the metamorphosis which the camp underwent during the terrible fortnight I have dwelt upon, I would have understood that the tattoo had an important and direct connection with Sophie's being branded like a Jew though she herself was not Jewish. It was this . . . She and her fellow Gentiles acquired a classification which paradoxically removed them from the immediately death-bound. A revealing bureaucratic matter is involved here. The tattooing of "Aryan" prisoners was introduced only in the latter part of March, and Sophie must have been among the first of the non-Jewish arrivals to receive the marking. If initially it would seem puzzling, the redefined policy is easy to explain: it had to do with the cranking up of the dynamo of death. With the "final solution" now accomplished and Jews consigned in satisfying multitudes to the new gas chambers, there would be no longer any need for their numeration. It was Himmler's order that all Jews would die without exception. Taking their place in the camp, now *Judenrein,* would be the Aryans, tattooed for identification —slaves dying by stagnant slow degrees their other kind of death. Thus Sophie's tattoo. (Or such were the outlines of the original plan. But as so often happened, the plan changed yet again; the orders were countermanded. There was a conflict between the lust for murder and the need for work. Upon the arrival at the camp of the German Jews late that winter, it was decreed that all able-bodied prisoners—men and women—would be assigned to slave labor. So in the society of the walking dead of which Sophie became a part, Jews and non-Jews were mingled.)

And then there was April Fools' Day. Fishy jokes.

Poisson d'avril. In Polish, like the Latin: *Prima Aprilis.* Each time that day has rolled around, ticking off the years during these recent domestic decades, it has been my association of the date with Sophie which has given me a twinge of real anguish when I have been exposed to those small, sweet, silly tricks perpetrated by my children ("April fool, Daddy!"); the gentle paterfamilias, usually so forbearing, has turned cross as a skunk. I hate April Fools' Day as I hate the Judeo-Christian God. That is the day which marked the end of Sophie's journey, and for me somehow the bad joke has been less attached to that rather pedestrian concidence than to the fact that only four days later an order to Rudolf Höss from Berlin directed that no more captives who were not Jewish would be sent to the gas.

For a long time Sophie refused to supply me with any details about her arrival, or perhaps her equilibrium simply could not let her do so—and perhaps that is just as well. But even before I learned the full truth concerning what happened to her, I was able to re-create a smudged view of the events of that day—a day which the records describe as being prematurely warm and greenly burgeoning with spring, ferns unfolding, the forsythia in early bud, the air sunshiny and clear. The 1,800 Jews were expeditiously loaded into vans and driven to Birkenau, an operation which occupied the two hours just past noon. There were, as I say, no selections; fit and healthy men, women, children—all died. Shortly after that, as if seized by the same desire to make a clean sweep of whatever victims were at hand, the SS officers on the ramp consigned a carload (that is, two hundred) of the Resistance members to the gas chambers. They, too, departed in vans, leaving behind them perhaps fifty of their comrades, including Wanda.

There now came a curious interruption in the proceedings, and a wait which lasted well through the afternoon. On the two still-occupied cars, besides the leftovers from the Resistance group there remained Sophie and Jan and Eva and the bedraggled mob of Poles who had been captured in the last Warsaw roundup. The delay stretched out through several more hours, until nearly dusk. On the ramp the SS men—the officers, the learned physicians, the guards—seemed to be milling about in an anxious sweat of indecision. Orders from Berlin? Counterorders? One can only speculate upon their nervousness. It doesn't matter. Finally it became clear that the SS had decided to continue their work, but this time on terms of selection. The officiating noncommissioned officers ordered everybody out, down, made them form lines. Then the doctors took over. The selection process lasted somewhat over an hour. Sophie, Jan and Wanda were sent to the camp. About half of the prisoners were elected to this status. Among those ordered to their deaths in Crematorium II at Birkenau were the music teacher Stefan Zaorski and his pupil, the flutist Eva Maria Zawistowska, who in a little more than a week would have been eight years old.

Thirteen

I must now set down a brief vignette, which I have tried to refashion from the outpouring of Sophie's memories as she talked to me that summer weekend. I suspect that the indulgent reader will not be able to perceive immediately how this little recollecton adumbrates Auschwitz but—as will be seen—it does, and of all of Sophie's attempts to gain a hold on the confusion of her past, it remains, as a sketch, a fragment, among the most odd and unsettling.

The place is Cracow again. The time: early June in the year 1937. The characters are Sophie and her father and a personage new to this narrative: Dr. Walter Dürrfeld of Leuna, near Leipzig, a director of IG Farbenindustrie, that *Interessengemeinschaft*, or conglomerate—inconceivably huge even for its day—whose prestige and size are alone enough to set Professor Biegański's mind abubble with giddy euphoria. Not to mention Dr. Dürrfeld himself, who because of the Professor's academic specialty—the international legal aspects of industrial patents—is well known to him by reputation as one of the captains of German industry. It would demean the Professor needlessly, would place too much emphasis on the sycophancy he had occasionally displayed in the face of manifestations of German might and potency, to portray him as buffoonishly servile in Dürrfeld's presence; he possesses, after all, his own illustrious repute as a scholar and an expert in his field. He is also a man of considerable social facility. Nonetheless, Sophie can tell that he is flattered beyond measure to be near the flesh of this titan, and his eagerness to please falls a hair short of the outright embarrassing.

There is no professional connection to this meeting; the encounter is purely social, recreative. Dürrfeld with his wife is making a vacation trip through Eastern Europe, and a mutual acquaintance in Düsseldorf—a patent authority, like the Professor—has arranged the get-together through the mail and by a flurry of last-minute telegrams. Because of Dürrfeld's pressing schedule the little occasion must not take much time, cannot even include a meal together: a brief sightseeing fling at the university with its resplendent Collegium Maius; then Wawel Castle, the tapestries, a pause for a cup of tea, perhaps a tiny side trip elsewhere, but that is all. An afternoon's pleasant companionship, then off on the wagons-lits to Wroclaw. The Professor plainly pines for more contact. Four hours will have to do.

Frau Dürrfeld is indisposed—a touch of *der Durchfall* has confined her to their room at the Hotel Francuski. As the trio sits sipping midafternoon tea after their descent from the Wawel parapets, the Professor apologizes with perhaps a touch too much acerbity on the poorness of Cracow water, intones with perhaps a shade too much feeling his regret at having had only the most fleeting glimpse of the charming Frau Dürrfeld before she hastened upstairs to her chambers. Dürrfeld nods pleasantly, Sophie squirms. She knows that the Professor will later require her to help re-create their conversation for his diary. She also knows that she has been dragooned into this outing for two purposes of display—because she is a knockout, as they say in the American movies that year, but also because by her presence, poise and language she can demonstrate to this distinguished guest, this dynamic helmsman of commerce, how fidelity to the principles of German culture and German breeding is capable of producing (and in such a quaint Slavic outback) the bewitching replica of a fräulein of whom not even the most committed racial purist in the Reich could disapprove. At least she looks the part. Sophie continues to squirm, praying that the conversation—once it becomes serious, if it does—will skirt Nazi politics; she is just beginning to be sickened by the extreme turn taken in the evolution of the Professor's racial views, and she cannot bear listening to or being forced to echo, out of duty, those dangerous imbecilities.

But she need not worry. It is culture and business—not politics—which are on the Professor's mind as he tactfully leads the conversation. Dürrfeld listens, wearing a thin smile. Polite, attentive, he is a sparely fleshed and handsome man in his mid-forties, with pink healthy skin and (she is struck by this detail) incredibly clean fingernails. They seem almost lacquered, painted on, the terminal edges crescent moons of ivory. His grooming is immaculate and his suit of tailored charcoal flannel, obviously English, makes her father's broad bright pin-stripe look hopelessly dowdy and old-fashioned. His cigarettes, she notices, are also British—Craven A's. As he listens to the Professor his eyes have a pleasant, amused, quizzical look. She feels attracted to him, vaguely—no, quite strongly. She finds herself blushing, knows that her cheeks are flushed. Her father is casting gemlike slivers of history around the table now, emphasizing the effect of German-speaking culture and tradition on the city of Cracow and indeed upon all of southern Poland. What a long-lasting and indelible tradition this has been! Of course, and it goes without saying (although the Professor is saying it), Cracow not so long ago was for three-quarters of a century under beneficent Austrian rule—*natürlich,* this Dr. Dürrfeld knew; but did he also know that the city was almost unique in Eastern Europe in possessing its own constitution, called even now "the Magdeburg rights" and based upon medieval laws formulated in the city of Magdeburg? Was it any wonder, then, that the community was richly steeped in German lore and law, in the very spirit of Germany, so that even now there was among Cracovian citizens the perpetual impulse to nurture a passionate devotion for the language which, as Von Hofmannsthal said (or was it Gerhart Hauptmann?), is the most gloriously expressive since the ancient Greek? Suddenly Sophie realizes that he has focused his attention on her. Even his daughter here, he continues, little Zosia, whose education had perhaps not been of the broadest, speaks with such fluency that she not only has perfect mastery of *Hochsprache,* the standard German of the schools, but of the colloquial *Umgangs-*

sprache, and furthermore, can duplicate for the Doctor's enjoyment almost any accent which lies in between.

There follows a distressing (to Sophie) several minutes in which, egged on pointedly by her father, she must utter a random phrase in various local German accents. It is a trick of mimicry which she picked up easily as a child and which the Professor has relished exploiting ever since. It is one of the misdemeanors he commits upon her from time to time. Sophie, who is shy enough anyway, detests being forced to perform for Dürrfeld, but, smiling a twisted embarrassed smile, complies, speaking at her father's command in Swabian, then in the indolent cadences of Bavaria, now in the tones of a native of Dresden, of Frankfurt, quickly followed by the Low German sound of a Saxon from Hannover and at last—aware that the desperation shows in her own eyes—blurting out an imitation of some quaint denizen of the Schwarzwald. *"Entzückend!"* she hears Dürrfeld's voice, along with a delighted laugh. "Charming! Just charming!" And she can tell that Dürrfeld, fetched by the little act but at the same time sensing her discomfort, has brought her demonstration adroitly to an end. Is Dürrfeld offended by her father? She doesn't know. She hopes so. Papa, Papa. *Du bist ein . . . Oh merde . . .*

Sophie is barely able to conquer her boredom but manages to remain attentive. The Professor has now turned subtly (without appearing to be inquisitive) to the subject second most dear to his heart—industry and commerce, especially German industry and commerce, and the power excitingly attending those activities, now so energetically on the upswing. It is easy to gain Dürrfeld's confidence; the Professor's knowledge of the architecture of world trade is comprehensive, encyclopedic. He knows when to open up a subject, when to shy away from it, when to be direct, when to be discreet. He does not once mention the Führer. Accepting with perhaps a little too much gratitude the fine hand-rolled Cuban cigar offered him by Dürrfeld, he expresses his profuse admiration for a recent German achievement. He has only recently read about it in the Zürich financial newspaper to which he subscribes. It is the sale to the United States of large quantities of synthetic rubber newly perfected by IG Farbenindustrie. What a glorious coup for the Reich! exclaims the Professor—at which point Sophie notices that Dürrfeld, who appears to be a man not easily flattered, nonetheless smiles in a responsive way and begins to speak with some animation. He seems pleased with the Professor's technical grasp of the subject, to which now he himself warms, leaning forward and for the first time employing his beautifully manicured hands to make one point, then another and another. Sophie loses track of much of the arcane detail, meanwhile regarding Dürrfeld once more from a point of view that is singularly female: he *is* attractive, she thinks, then in a dampness of mild shame banishes the thought. (Married, the mother of two little children; how could she!)

Now, while plainly exercising control over himself, Dürrfeld is seized by some churning interior anger; the knuckles of one hand grow white as he clenches his fist, the area around his mouth also becomes blanched, tense. With barely stoppered rage he is speaking of imperialism, of *die Engländer* and *die Holländer*, of the conspiracy on the part of two rich powers to so rig and control prices in natural rubber as to drive all others out of the market. And they accuse IG Farben of monopolistic practices! What else could we do? he says in a caustic, cutting voice which surprises Sophie, so at variance does it seem with his previous milky equanimity. No wonder that the world is amazed at our coup! With the British and the Dutch sole owners of Malaya and the East Indies, criminally fixing astronomical rates on the world market, what else could Germany do but employ its technological ingenuity to create a synthetic substitute that would not only be economical, durable, resilient, but—*"Oil-resistant!"* There! The Professor has taken the words right out of Dürrfeld's mouth. Oil-resistant! He has mastered his homework, the shrewd Professor, in whose memory has lodged the salient fact that it is the *oil-resistance* of the new synthetic product which is so revolutionary and which is the key to its value and attractiveness. Another touch of flattery that almost works: Dürrfeld smiles pleasantly at the Professor's expertise. But as often happens, her father does not know when to stop. Preening slightly beneath his bedandruffed pin-striped shoulders, he begins to show off, murmuring chemical terms like "nitrile," "Buna-N," "polymerization of hydrocarbons." His German is mellifluous—but now Dürrfeld, sidetracked from his righteous rage at the British and the Dutch, subsides into his previous detached self, gazing at the turgid Professor beneath arched eyebrows, looking remotely irritated and bored.

Yet oddly enough, the Professor at his best can be a charmer. Sometimes he is able to redeem himself. And so on the ride to the great salt mine of Wieliczka south of the city, the three of them sitting abreast in the rear seat of the hotel limousine, an ancient but pampered Daimler smelling of wood polish, his well-practiced disquisition on the Polish salt industry and its millennial history is captivating, bright, anything but tedious. He is exercising that talent which has made him an alluring lecturer and a public speaker of vibrant flair. No longer is he so pompous and self-conscious. The name of the king who was the founder of the Wieliczka mine, Boleslaw the Bashful, provides a moment of amusement; one or two low-keyed jokes, nicely timed, again put Dürrfeld at his ease. As he sinks back Sophie feels her liking for Dürrfeld increase; how little like a powerful German industrialist he seems, she thinks. She gives him a sidelong glance, and is affected by the lack of any arrogance in him, touched by something obscurely warm, vulnerable—is it only a kind of loneliness? The countryside is green with spreading, trembling foliage, lush fields ablaze with wildflowers—the Polish spring in its voluptuous prime. Dürrfeld remarks on the scene with genuine delight. Sophie senses the pressure of his arm against her own, and realizes that her bare skin there is chill with goose flesh. She tries—without success on the cramped seat—to draw away. She shivers slightly, then relaxes.

Dürrfeld has unbent so naturally that he even feels constrained to utter a vague apology: he should not allow the British and the Dutch to agitate him so, he says to the Professor in a mild voice, forgive the outburst, but surely their monopolistic practices and manipulations of the supply of a natural product like rubber, which all the world should receive equitably, was an abomination. Surely a native of Poland, which like Germany has no rich overseas possessions, could appreciate this. Surely it is not militarism or blind desire for conquest (which have been libelously imputed to certain nations—Germany, yes, damnit, *Germany*) that makes some ghastly war probable, but this *greed.* What must a nation like Germany do when—deprived of the colonies which might have served as its own Straits Settlements, divested of the equivalent of its own Sumatra, its own Borneo—it faces a hostile world rimmed about at the edge by international pirates and profiteers? The legacy of Versailles! Yes, *what!* It must go creatively *wild.* It must manufacture its *own* substance—everything!—out of chaos and by its own genius, and then stand with its back against the wall, confronting a host of enemies. The little speech ends. The Professor beams and actually applauds with his hands.

Dürrfeld falls silent then. Despite his passion he is very calm. He has spoken not angrily or with alarm but with gentle, easy, brief eloquence, and Sophie finds herself affected by the words and the utter conviction they convey. She is a naïf in politics and world affairs, but she has the wit to know it. She cannot tell if she is stirred more by Dürrfeld's ideas or by his physical presence—perhaps it is a mingling of both—but she feels an honest, heartfelt reasonableness in what he has said, and certainly he does not in the least resemble the paradigmatic Nazi who has been the object of so much savage lampooning rage at the hands of the tiny liberal and radical elements around the university. Maybe he is *not* a Nazi, she thinks optimistically—but then, surely a man so highly placed must be a member of the Party. Yes? No? Well, no matter. Two things she now knows well: she is beset by a pleasant, wayward, tickling eroticism, and the eroticism itself fills her with the same sweetly queasy sense of danger she once felt in Vienna years ago as a child at the very peak of the terrifying Prater Ferris wheel—danger both delicious and nearly unendurable. (Yet even as the emotion sweeps over her she cannot help but writhe in the memory of the cataclysmic domestic happening which she knows gives her the liberty, the warrant to possess such electrifying desire: the silhouette of her husband, in his robe, standing in the doorway of their dark bedroom only a month before. And Kazik's words, as excruciatingly hurtful as the sudden slice across her face of a kitchen knife: You must get this under your thick skull, which may be thicker even than your father says it is. If I am no longer able to function with you, it is, you understand, due to no lack of virility but because almost everything about you, especially your body, leaves me totally without sensation . . . I cannot stand even the smell of your bed.)

Moments later, outside the entrance to the mine, where the two of them are gazing down across a sun-flooded field swaying and rippling with green barley, Dürrfeld asks her about herself. She replies that she is—well, a housewife, a faculty wife, but she is studying the piano, she hopes to be able to continue in Vienna in a year or two. (They are alone for a moment, standing close to each other. Never has Sophie wished so keenly to be alone with a man. What has permitted this moment is a small crisis—a sign announcing no visitors, the mine closed for repairs, the Professor storming off with a cascade of apologies pouring from his lips, telling them to wait, declaring that his personal acquaintanceship with the superintendent will resolve this impasse.) He says she looks so youthful. A girl! He says that it is hard to believe that she has two children. She replies that she was married very young. He says that he has two children, too. "I am a family man." The remark seems roguish, ambiguous. For the first time their eyes encounter each other's, his gaze mingles with hers; it is unabashedly admiring, that look, and she turns away feeling a spasm of adulterous guilt. She moves a few paces off from him, shielding her eyes, wondering aloud where Papa is. She hears the tremor in her throat, another voice deep within her tells her that tomorrow she must go to early Mass. Over her shoulder his voice now asks her if she has ever been to Germany. She replies that yes, one summer years ago she stayed in Berlin. Her father's vacation. She was just a child.

She says that she would love to go to Germany again, to see Bach's grave in Leipzig—and she halts, embarrassed, wondering why on earth she has said this, although indeed to place flowers on Bach's grave has long been a secret wish. Yet in his gentle laugh there is understanding. Leipzig, my home! He says why of course we could do that if you came. We could go to all the great musical shrines. She gasps inwardly—the "we," the "if you came." Is she to construe this is an invitation? Delicate, even devious—but an invitation? She feels the pulse twitch at her brow and flees the subject, or warily moves away. We have much good music in Cracow, she says, Poland is filled with wonderful music. Yes, he says, but not like Germany. If she were to come, he would take her to Bayreuth—does she like Wagner?—or to the great Bach festivals, or to hear Lotte Lehmann, Kleiber, Gieseking, Furtwängler, Backhaus, Fischer, Kempff . . . His voice seems to be an amorous melodic murmur, cajoling, politely but outrageously flirtatious, irresistible and (to her utter distress now) wickedly exciting. If she loves Bach, then she must love Telemann. *We* shall toast *his* memory in Hamburg! And Beethoven's in Bonn! Just at this moment a splashing of feet through gravel announces the return of the Professor. He babbles delightedly, saying "Open Sesame." Sophie can almost hear the sound her heart makes as it deflates, sickly pounding. My father, she thinks, is everything that music cannot be . . .

And that (as it evolved in her recollection) is nearly all. The prodigious subterranean castle of salt which she has visited often and which may or may not be, as the Professor claims, one of Europe's seven man-made wonders, is less an anticlimax in itself than a spectacle which simply fails to register on her awareness, so agitated has she been made by this indefinable whatever-it-is—this infatuation—which has struck her with the random heat of a lightning bolt, making her weak and a little ill. She dares not let her eyes meet Dürrfeld's again, although once more she glances at his hands: why do they fascinate her so? And now as they descend in the elevator and then embark on a stroll through this glittering white kingdom of vaulted caverns and labyrinthine passageways and soaring transepts—an upended anti-cathedral, buried memorial to ages of human toil, plunging giddily toward the underworld—Sophie blots out both Dürrfeld's presence and her father's perambulating lecture, which anyway she has heard a dozen times before. She wonders despondently how she can truly be the victim of an emotion at once so silly and so devastating. She will just have to put this man firmly out of her mind. Yes, put him out of her mind... *Allez!*

And this she did. She recounted later how she so firmly obliterated Dürrfeld from her thoughts that after he and his wife left Cracow—only an hour or so following their visit to the Wieliczka mine—he never troubled her memory again, did not dwell on the farthest margin of her consciousness even as a romantic figment. Perhaps this was the result of some unconscious force of will, perhaps it was only because of the futility she felt at entertaining the hope of seeing him again. Like a rock falling into one of those bottomless Wieliczka grottoes, he plummeted from her remembrance—another innocuous flirtation consigned to the dusty unopened scrapbook. Yet six years later she did see him again, when the creature of Dürrfeld's passion and desire—synthetic rubber—and its place in the matrix of history had caused this corporate prince to become master of Farben's huge industrial complex known as IG-Auschwitz. When they met each other there at the camp the encounter was even briefer and less personal than their meeting in Cracow. Yet from the separate encounters, Sophie carried away two significantly linked and powerful impressions. And they were these: During that spring afternoon's jaunt in the company of one of Poland's most influential anti-Semites, her admirer Walter Dürrfeld, like his host, uttered not a word about Jews. Six years later almost all that she heard from Dürrfeld's lips concerned Jews and their consignment to oblivion.

During that long weekend in Flatbush, Sophie did not speak to me about Eva except to tell me in a few words what I have already set down: that the child was killed at Birkenau on the day of their arrival. "Eva was taken away," she said, "and I never saw her again." She offered no embroidery on this and I plainly could not and did not press the point; it was—in a word—terrible, and this information, which she imparted to me in such a listless, offhand way, left me beyond speech. I still marvel at Sophie's composure. She returned quickly to speak of Jan, who had survived the selection and who, she learned through the grapevine after a number of days, had been thrown into that desperate enclave known as the Children's Camp. I could only surmise from what she said about her first six months at Auschwitz that the shock and grief caused by Eva's death created a bereavement which might have destroyed her, too, had it not been for Jan and *his* survival; the very fact that the little boy still lived, even though beyond her reach, and that she might somehow eventually get to see him was enough to sustain her through the initial phases of the nightmare. Almost every thought she had concerned the child, and the few grains of information she collected about him from time to time—that he was healthy enough, that he still *lived*—brought her the kind of mild, numb solace which enabled her to get through the infernal existence she woke to every morning.

But Sophie, as I pointed out before and as she elaborated to Höss on that strange day of their aborted intimacy, was one of the chosen elite and therefore had been "lucky" by comparison with most of the others newly arrived at the camp. She had first been assigned to a barracks, where in the ordinary course of events she would doubtless have endured that precisely calculated, abbreviated death-in-life which was the lot of nearly all her fellow sufferers. (It was at this point that Sophie told me about the welcoming statement of SS Hauptsturmführer Fritzch, and it might be well to repeat what they both said, verbatim. "I remember his exact words. He said, 'You have come to a concentration camp, not to a sanatorium, and there is only one way out—up the chimney.' He said, 'Anyone who don't like this can try hanging himself on the wires. If there are Jews in this group, you have no right to live more than two weeks.' Then he said, 'Any nuns here? Like the priests, you have one month. All the rest, three months.' " Sophie had been aware of her death sentence within twenty-four hours of her arrival, it only took Fritzch to validate the fact in SS language.) But as she later explained to Höss in an episode I have earlier narrated, an odd cluster of little events—the attack on her in the barracks by a lesbian, a fight, intercession by a friendly block leader—had led her to a translator-stenographer's job and lodging in another barracks, where she was sheltered for the time being from the camp's mortal attrition. And of course at the end of six months another stroke of good fortune brought her the protective comforts and advantages of Haus Höss itself. Yet first came a critical meeting. It was only a few days before she was to take up residence under the Commandant's roof that Wanda—who had been immured in one of the unspeakable kennels at Birkenau this entire time and whom Sophie had not seen since that April day of their arrival—made her way to Sophie's side and through a tumultuous outpouring filled her with hope about Jan and the possibility of his salvation, but also terrified her with demands upon her courage which she felt certain she could not meet.

"You will have to be working for us every moment you're in that insect's nest," Wanda had whispered to her in a corner of the barracks. "You can't imagine what kind of an opportunity this is. It's what the underground has been waiting for, praying for, to have somebody like you in a situation like this! You'll have to use your eyes and ears every minute. Listen, darling, it's so important for you to get word out about what's going on. Shifts of personnel, changes of policy, transfers of the top SS pigs—anything is priceless information. It's the lifeblood of the camp. War news! Anything to counter their filthy propaganda. Don't you see, our morale is the only thing we have left in this hellhole. A radio, for instance—that would be priceless! Your chances of getting one would be practically nil, but if you could smuggle out a radio just so we could listen to London, it would be nearly the same as saving thousands and thousands of lives."

Wanda was sick. The dreadful bruise inflicted on her face in Warsaw had never really gone away. Conditions in the women's compound at Birkenau were hideous and a chronic bronchial ailment to which she had always been prone had flared up, bringing to her cheeks a hectic and alarming flush so bright that it almost matched her brick-red hair, or the grotesque frizzles that were left of it. With mingled horror, grief and guilt Sophie had a swift intuition that the present moment would be the last time she would ever lay eyes on this brave, resolute, luminous flame of a girl. "I can only stay a few more minutes," Wanda said. She suddenly switched from Polish to a rapid, breezy colloquial German, murmuring to Sophie that the nasty-faced assistant block leader lingering nearby, a Warsaw whore, looked like a stool pigeon and a traitorous rat, which she was. Quickly then she outlined to Sophie her scheme about Lebensborn, trying to make her see that the plan—however quixotic it might appear—was perhaps the only way of assuring Jan's deliverance from the camp.

It would require a lot of conniving, she said, would require a lot of things which she knew Sophie would instinctively shrink from. She paused, coughed in painful racking spasms, then resumed. "I knew I had to see you when I heard about you through the grapevine. We hear everything. I've so wanted to see you anyway all these months, but this new job of yours made it absolutely necessary. I've risked everything to get here to see you—if I'm caught I'm done for! But nothing risked, nothing gained in this snakepit. Yes, I'll tell you again and believe me: Jan is well, he's as well as can be expected. Yes, not once—three times I saw him through the fence. I won't fool you, he's skinny, skinny as I am. It's lousy in the Children's Camp—everything's lousy at Birkenau—but I'll tell you another thing. They're not starving the children as badly as some of the rest. Why, I don't know, it can't be their conscience. Once I managed to take him some apples. He's doing well. He can make it. Go ahead and cry, darling, I know it's awful but you mustn't give up hope. And you've got to try to get him out of here before winter comes. Now, this Lebensborn idea may sound bizarre but the thing really exists—we saw it happening in Warsaw, remember the Rydzón child?—and I'm telling you that you simply must make a stab at using it to get Jan shipped out of here. All right, I know there's a good chance that he might get lost if he's sent to Germany, but at least he'll be alive and well, don't you see? There's a good chance that you'll be able to keep track of him, this war can't last forever.

"Listen! It all depends on what kind of relationship you strike up with Höss. So much depends on that, Zosia darling, not only what happens to Jan and yourself but to all of us. You've got to *use* that man, work on him—you're going to be living under the same roof. Use him! For once you've got to forget that priggish Christer's morality of yours and use your sex for all it's worth. Pardon me, Zosia, but give him a good fucking and he'll be eating out of your hand. Listen, underground intelligence knows all about that man, just as we've learned about Lebensborn. Höss is just another susceptible bureaucrat with a blocked-up itch for a female body. Use it! And use him! It won't be any skin off his nose to take one Polish kid and have him committed to that program—after all, it'll be another bonus for the Reich. And sleeping with Höss won't be collaboration, it'll be espionage—a fifth column! So you've got to work this ape over to every possible limit. For God's sake, Zosia, this is your chance! What you do in that house can mean everything for the rest of us, for every Pole and Jew and misbegotten bundle of misery in this camp—*everything.* I beg of you—don't let us down!"

Time was running out. Wanda had to go. Before she went, she left Sophie with a few last instructive words. There was the matter of Bronek, for instance. At the Commandant's house she would encounter a handyman named Bronek. He would be a crucial link between the mansion and the camp underground. Ostensibly a stooge for the SS, he was not quite the bootlicker and Höss's lackey that a necessity for accommodation would make him appear. Höss trusted him, he was the Commandant's pet Polack; but within this simple being, superficially servile and obliging, there beat the heart of a patriot who had shown that he could be counted upon for certain missions, provided they were not too mentally taxing or complex. The truth was, he was harebrained but clever—made into such a reliable turnip by the medical experiments which had addled his thought processes. He could initiate nothing on his own but was a willing instrument. Poland forever! In fact, said Wanda, Sophie would soon discover that Bronek was so secure in his role as the submissive, harmless drudge that from Höss's viewpoint he could only be beyond suspicion—and therein lay both the beauty and the crucial nature of his function as an underground operative and go-between. Trust Bronek, Wanda said, and use him if she could. Now Wanda had to go, and after a long and tearful embrace she was gone—leaving Sophie weak and hopeless, with a sense of inadequacy . . .

Thus Sophie came to spend her ten days under the

Commandant's roof—a period culminating in that hectic, anxiety-drenched day which she remembered in such detail and which I have already described: a day when her feckless and flat-footed attempt at seducing Höss yielded not the possibility of freedom for Jan but only the bitterly wounding yet sweetly desirable promise of seeing her child in the flesh. (And this might be too brief to bear.) A day on which she had miserably failed, through a combination of panic and forgetfulness, to broach the idea of Lebensborn to the Commandant, thereby losing the richest chance she had of offering him the legitimate means to oversee Jan's removal from the camp. (*Unless,* she thought, as she descended toward the cellar that evening, unless she collected her wits and was able to outline to him her plan the next morning, when Höss had promised to bring the little boy to his office for the reunion.) It was also the day on which to her other frights and miseries had been added the almost intolerable burden of a challenge and a responsibility. And four years later, in a bar in Brooklyn, she spoke of the desperate shame that still engulfed her at the memory of how such a challenge and a responsibility had frightened her and finally defeated her. This was ultimately one of the darkest parts of her confession to me and the focus of what she called, again and again, her "badness." And I began to see how this "badness" went far beyond what—it seemed to me—was misplaced guilt over her clumsy effort to seduce Höss or even her equally clumsy attempt to manipulate him through her father's pamphlet. I began to see how, among its other attributes, absolute evil paralyzes absolutely. In the end, Sophie recalled with anguish, her failure was reduced to such a cheaply trivial yet overwhelmingly important agglomeration of metal, glass and plastic as the radio that Wanda thought Sophie would never have the incredible chance to steal. And she blew her chance to pieces . . .

On the floor just underneath the landing which served as the antechamber to Höss's attic was the small room occupied by Emmi, age eleven, middle member of the Commandant's five offspring. Sophie had passed the room many times on her way up to and down from the office, and had noted that the door was often left open—not a remarkable fact really, she had reflected, when one realized that petty theft in this despotically well-regulated stronghold was nearly as unthinkable as murder. Sophie had paused for a glimpse more than once and had seen the orderly, dustless child's bedchamber which would have been unexceptional in Augsburg or Münster: a sturdy single bed with a flowered coverlet, stuffed animals heaped on a chair, some silver trophies, a cuckoo clock, a wall with gingerbread picture frames enclosing photographs (an alpine scene, marching Hitler Youth, a seascape, the child herself in a swimsuit, ponies at play, portraits of the Führer, "Onkel Heini" Himmler, smiling Mummy, smiling Daddy in civvies), a dresser with a cluster of boxes for jewelry and trinkets, and next to these a portable radio. It was the radio that always captured her attention. Only rarely had Sophie seen or heard the radio in operation, no doubt because its charms had been superseded by the huge phonograph downstairs which blared forth night and day.

Once when passing by the room she had noticed the radio on—dreamy, modern ersatz-Strauss waltzes strained through a voice which identified the source as a Wehrmacht station, possibly Vienna, perhaps Prague. The limpid, muted strings were stunningly clear. But the radio itself bewitched her not by its music but by its very being—ravished her by its size, its shape, its adorable shrunken self, its cuteness, its miniatureness, its incredible portability. Never had it occurred to Sophie that technology could achieve such marvelous compactness, but then, she had overlooked what the Third Reich and its newborn science of electronics had been up to all these exploding years. The radio was no bigger than a medium-sized book. The name Siemens was written across a side panel in intaglio script. Deep maroon in color, its plastic front cover sprang up on hinges to form the antenna, standing sentinel over the little tube-and-battery-filled chassis small enough to be balanced easily in the palm of a man's hand. The radio afflicted Sophie with terror and desire. And at dusk on that October day after her confrontation with Höss, when she descended to her dank quarters in the basement, she caught sight of the radio through the open door and felt her bowels give way with fear at the very idea that at last, with no more hesitations or delays, she must manage somehow to steal it.

She stood in the shadows of the hallway, only a few feet from the bottom of the attic stairs. The radio was playing soft murmurous schmaltz. Above, there was a sound of the booted feet of Höss's adjutant, thumping about on the landing. Höss himself had left the house on an inspection tour. She stood still for a moment, feeling strengthless, hungry, chill-swept and on the edge of illness or collapse. No day in her life had been longer than this one, wherein all that she had hoped to achieve had come to an ugly, gaping naught. No, not absolutely nothing: Höss's promise to at least let her see Jan was something salvaged out of the wreckage. But to have mismanaged things so utterly, to have returned virtually to where she had started, faced with the oncoming night of the camp's perdition—all this was beyond her acceptance or comprehension. She closed her eyes and leaned against the wall in a dizzy siege of nausea, brought on by hunger. That morning on this very spot she had puked up those figs: the mess had long since been scrubbed away by some Polish or SS minion, but in her fancy there lingered a ghostly sour-sweet fragrance, and hunger suddenly clamped down upon her stomach in a spasm of aching colic. Unseeing, she reached up with wandering fingers, suddenly touched fur. It felt like the hairy balls of the devil. She uttered a foreshortened scream, a squeaky gasp, realizing as her eyes popped open that her hand had grazed the chin of an antlered stag, shot in 1938—as Höss had told an SS visitor within her hearing—squarely behind the brain at three hundred meters, "open sight," on the slopes above the Königssee so deep within the very shadow of Berchtesgaden that the Führer, had he been in residence (and who knows, perhaps he had been!), might have heard the fatal *crack!* . . .

Now the protuberant glass eyeballs of the deer, artfully detailed even to its minute bloodshot flecks, gave back twin images of herself; frail, wasted, her face bisected by cadaverous planes, she gazed deeply at her duplicate self, contemplating how, in her exhaustion and in the tension and indecision of the moment, she could possibly hold on to her sanity. During the days Sophie had plodded up and down the stairs past Emmi's room she had pondered her strategy with increasing dread and anxiety. She was hag-ridden by the need not to betray Wanda's trust, but—oh God, the difficulties! The key factor lay in one word: suspicion. The disappearance of such a scarce and valued instrument as a radio would be a matter of appalling gravity, inviting the possibility of reprisal, punishment, torture, even random killing. The prisoners in the house would automatically fall under suspicion; they would be the first to be searched, interrogated, beaten. Even the fat Jewish dressmakers! But there was a saving element upon which Sophie realized she had to depend—this was the fact of the members of the SS themselves. If a few prisoners like Sophie alone had access to the upper regions of the house, any such contrived theft would be completely out of the question. It would be suicide. But SS members by the dozens beat a path up to Höss's office door day after day—messengers, bearers of orders and memorandums and manifests and transfers, all sorts of enlisted Sturmanns and Rottenführers and Unterscharführers on various missions from every corner of the camp. They, too, would have laid covetous eyes on Emmi's little radio; there were a few at least who were not beyond larceny and they, too, would scarcely be immune to suspicion. Indeed, because far more SS troops than prisoners had cause to frequent Höss's roost under the eaves, it seemed logical to Sophie to assume that trusted inmates like herself might escape the burden of the most immediate suspicion—allowing an even better opportunity to get rid of the goods.

It became, then, a question of precision, as she had whispered to Bronek the day before: secreting the radio beneath her smock, she would hurry downstairs and pass it along to him in the darkness of the cellar. Bronek in turn would hustle the little set quickly to his contact on the other side of the mansion gate. Meanwhile there would be an outcry. The cellar would be ransacked. Joining in the search, Bronek would limp about with gobbets of advice, exhibiting the collaborator's odious zeal. The fury and commotion would yield nothing. The frightened prisoners would gradually relax. Somewhere in the garrison a pimply-faced Unterscharführer, frozen with terror, would hear himself accused of this reckless felony. A minor triumph in itself for the underground. And here in the depths of the camp, huddled dangerously in the dark around the precious little box, men and women would listen to the far faint sound of a Chopin polonaise, and to voices of exhortation and good tidings and support, and would feel the closest thing to a restoration of life.

She knew she had to move swiftly now and take it, or be forever damned. And so she moved, heart rampaging, not shedding her fear—it clung to her like an evil companion—and sidled her way into the room. She had to walk only a few paces, but even as she did so, swaying, she sensed something wrong, sensed a ghastly error in tactics and timing: the moment she placed her hand on the cool plastic surface of the radio she had a premonition of disaster which filled the space of the room like a soundless scream. And she recalled later more than once how at that exact instant of contact with that longed-for little object, knowing her mistake (why was it instantly jumbled with a game of croquet?), she heard her father's voice in some remote summer garden of her mind, almost exultant in its contempt: *You do everything wrong.* But she had the merest instant to reflect on this before hearing the other voice behind her, so unsurprising in its inevitability that even the cool, didactic, Germanic sense of *Ordnung* in the words themselves were no surprise: "Your business may take you up and down the hallway but you have no business in this room." Sophie whirled about then and beheld Emmi.

The girl was standing at the closet door. Sophie had never seen her so close at hand. She was clad in pale blue rayon panties; her precocious eleven-year-old breasts bulged in a bra of the same washed-out shade. Her face was very white and astonishingly round, like an underdone biscuit, crowned by a fringe of frizzy yellow hair; her features were both handsome and degenerate; trapped within that spherical frame the puffed prettiness of nose, mouth and eyes appeared to be painted on—at first, Sophie thought, on a doll, then as if on a balloon. On second thought she looked less depraved than . . . *pre-innocent*? Unborn? Speechless, Sophie gazed at her, thinking: Papa was right about my wrongdoing, I mess up everything; here all I had to do was to investigate things first. She stammered, then found speech. "I'm sorry, *gnädiges Fräulein,* I was only—" But Emmi interrupted. "Don't try to explain. You came in here to steal that radio. I saw you. I saw you almost pick it up." Emmi's face wore, or perhaps was incapable of, very little expression. With an aplomb that belied the fact of her near-nudity she slowly reached into her closet and drew on a robe of white terry cloth. Then she turned and said with bland matter-of-factness, "I'm going to report you to my father. He will have you punished."

"I was only going to look at it!" Sophie improvised. "I swear it! I've passed by here so many times. I've never seen a radio so . . . so small. So . . . so *cunning!* I couldn't believe it really worked. I just wanted to see—"

"You're a liar," said Emmi, "you were going to steal it. I could tell by the look on your face. You had an expression as if you were going to steal it, not just pick it up and look at it."

"You must believe me," Sophie said, aware of the sob in the back of her throat, and feeling a hopeless infirm lassitude, legs heavy and cold. "I wouldn't want to take your . . ." But she halted, struck by the idea that it didn't matter. Now that she had so preposterously bungled the job, nothing seemed to matter. It only mattered, still, that on the next day she would see her little boy, and how could Emmi interfere with that?

"You *would* want to take it," the girl persisted, "it cost seventy Deutschmarks. You could listen to music on it, down in the cellar. You're a dirty Polack and Polacks are thieves. My mother says that Polacks are worse thieves than Gypsies and dirtier too." The nose puckered in the circular face. "You smell!"

Sophie sensed darkness surging at the back of her eyes. She heard herself groan. Because of incalculable stress or hunger or grief or terror, or God knew what, her period had been delayed for at least a week (this had happened to her in the camp twice before), but now at her loins the wet warm downward-pulling sensation came in a rush; she felt the huge abnormal flood and at the same time was aware in her eyes of the spreading, irrepressible darkness. Emmi's face, a lunar blur, became caught up in this web of darkness, and Sophie found herself falling, falling... Lulled as if amid sluggish waves of time she drowsed in a blessed stupor, awoke listlessly to the sound of a distant gathering ululation that blossomed in her ears, grew louder, becoming a savage roar. For the barest instant she dreamed that the roar was the roar of a polar bear and that she was floating on an iceberg, swept by frigid winds. Her nostrils burned.

"Wake up," said Emmi. The face, white as wax, hovered so close that she felt the child's breath on her cheek. Sophie then knew that she was lying flat and supine on the floor while the girl crouched next to her, flourishing a phial of ammonia beneath her nose. The casement window had been flung open, letting the frosty wind fill the room. The shriek in her ears had been the camp whistle; she heard its distant voice now, decrescendo. At eye-level, next to Emmi's bare knee, was a small plastic medical kit embellished with a green cross. "You fainted," she said. "Don't move. Keep your head horizontal for a minute so it will get the flow of blood. Sniff deeply. That cold air will help revive you. Meanwhile, remain still." Recollection came sweeping back, and as it did Sophie had the feeling that she was the performer in a play from which the central act was missing: wasn't it only a minute or so ago (it could not have been much longer) that the child had been raging at her like an urchin storm trooper, and could this really be the same creature who was now attending to her with what might pass for humane efficiency, if hardly angelic compassion? Had her collapse brought out in this frightening *Mädel* with her face like that of a swollen fetus the stifled impulses of a nurse? The question was answered just then, when Sophie groaned and stirred. "You must keep still!" Emmi commanded her. "I have a certificate in first aid—junior grade, first class. Do as I say, do you understand?"

Sophie lay still. She wore no underwear and she wondered how extensively she had stained herself. The back of her smock felt soaked. Surprised at her own delicacy, under the circumstances, she also wondered if she had not at the same time soiled Emmi's spotless floor. Something in the child's manner enlarged her sense of helplessness, the feeling of being simultaneously ministered to and victimized. Sophie began to realize that Emmi had her father's voice, utterly gelid and remote. And in her officious busy bossiness, so lacking in any quality of the tender as she prattled away (now she was smartly smacking Sophie's cheeks, saying that the first-aid manual stated that smart smacks might help in reviving a victim of *die Synkope*, as she persisted, with medical precision, in calling a fainting spell), she seemed an Obersturmbannführer in microdimension, the SS spirit and essence—its true hypostasis—embedded in her very genes.

But at last the barrage of slaps on Sophie's cheeks created, apparently, a satisfactory rosiness, and the child ordered her patient to sit erect and lean against the bed. This Sophie did, slowly, suddenly grateful that she had fainted at the moment and in the way she had. For as she gazed toward the ceiling now through pupils gradually shrinking back to their normal focus, she was aware that Emmi had stood up and was regarding her with an expression resembling benignness, or at least a certain tolerant curiosity, as if there had been expelled from her mind her fury at Sophie for being both a Polack and a thief; the nursing seizure appeared to have been cathartic, allowing her enough in the way of an exercise of authority to satisfy the most frustrated SS dwarfling, after which she now assumed once again the plump round outlines of a little girl. "I will say one thing," Emmi murmured, "you're very pretty. Wilhelmine said you must be Swedish."

"Tell me," Sophie said in a gentle solicitous voice, aimlessly exploiting the lull, "tell me, what's that design sewn onto your robe? It's so attractive."

"It's the insignia of my swimming championship. I was the champion in my class. The beginners. I was only eight. I wish we had swimming competition here, but we don't. It's the war. I have had to swim in the Sola, which I don't like. The river's filled with muck. I was a very fast swimmer in the beginners' competition."

"Where was that, Emmi?"

"At Dachau. We had a wonderful pool for the garrison children. It was even heated. But that was before we were transferred. Dachau was ever so much nicer than Auschwitz. But then, it was in the Reich. See my trophies there. The one in the middle, the big one. That was presented to me by the Reich Youth Leader himself, Baldur von Schirach. Let me show you my scrapbook."

Into her dresser drawer she pounced and filled the crook of one arm with a huge album that spilled out photographs and clippings. She lugged it to Sophie's side, pausing only to switch on the radio. Cracklings and peeps disturbed the air. She made an adjustment and the static vanished, replaced by a far faint chorus of horns and trumpets, exultant, victorious, Handelian: a shiver flowed down Sophie's backbone like a benediction of ice. *"Das bin ich,"* the girl began to say over and over again, pointing to herself in endlessly repeated postures of bathing costume encasing juvenile adipose flesh, mushroom-pale. Had the sun never shone in Dachau? Sophie wondered in somnolent sickish despair. *"Das bin ich . . . und das bin ich,"* Emmi continued in her childish drone, stabbing at the photographs with her button thumb, the rapt *"me me me"* uttered again and again in a half-whisper like an incantation. "I also began to learn diving," she said. "Look here, this is me."

Sophie ceased looking at the pictures—all became a blur—and her eyes sought instead the window flung open against the October sky where the evening star hung, astonishingly, as bright as a blob of crystal. An agitation in the air, a sudden thickening of the light around the planet, heralded the onset of smoke, borne earthward by the circulation of cool night wind. For the first time since the morning Sophie smelled, ineluctable as a smotherer's hand, the odor of burning human beings. Birkenau was consuming the last of the voyagers from Greece. Trumpets! The brazen triumphant hymnody poured out of the ether, hosannas, bleats of rams, angelic annunciations—making Sophie think of all the unborn mornings of her life. She began to weep and said, half aloud, "At least tomorrow I will see Jan. At least that."

"Why are you crying?" Emmi demanded.

"I don't know," Sophie replied. And then she was about to say this: "Because I have a little boy in Camp D. And because your father, tomorrow, is going to let me see him.

He is almost your age." But instead she was brought up short by an abrupt voice on the radio, interrupting the choir of brass: *"Ici Londres!"* She listened to the voice, remote, spoken as if through tinfoil but for the moment clear, a transmission meant for the French but vaulting the Carpathians to make itself heard here on the twilit rim of this *anus mundi.* She blessed the unknown announcer as she would a cherished sweetheart, smitten with wonder at the tumbling rush of words: *"L'Italie a déclaré qu'un état de guerre existe contre l'Allemagne . . ."* Though exactly how, or why, Sophie could not fathom, her instinct combined with a certain subtle jubilation in the voice from London (which, gazing straight at Emmi now, she knew the child could not understand) told her that this news spelled for the Reich real and lasting woe. It mattered not that Italy itself lay wasted. It was as if she had heard tidings of the Nazis' sure, eventual ruin. And as she strained to hear the voice, fading out now into a fogbank of static, she continued to weep, aware that she wept for Jan, yes, but also for other things, mainly herself: for her failure to steal the radio and her certain knowledge that she could never retrieve the courage to try to steal it again. That preservative and maternal passion of hers which in Warsaw, only months before, Wanda had deemed so selfish, so indecent, was something that, brought to its cruelest trial, Sophie could not overcome—and she wept now, helplessly, in the shame of her dereliction. She placed quivering fingers in front of her eyes. "I'm crying because I'm so hungry," she said to Emmi in a murmur, and this was at least in part the truth. She thought she might faint again.

The stench became more powerful. A dim fire-glow was reflected from the night's horizon. Emmi went to the window to close out either the cold or the pestilential air, or both. Following her with her eyes, Sophie caught sight of a sampler on the wall (the embroidery as florid as the German words), framed in shellacked and curlicued pine.

> Just as the Heavenly Father saved people
>   from sin and from Hell,
> Hitler saves the German Volk
>   from destruction.

The window slammed shut. "That stink is of Jews burning," Emmi said, turning back to her. "But I guess you know that. It's forbidden to ever speak of it in this house, but you—you're just a prisoner. The Jews are the chief enemy of our people. My sister Iphigenie and I have a jingle we made up about the Yids. It begins *'Der Itzig—'* "

Sophie stifled a cry and blinded her sight with her hands. "Emmi, Emmi . . ." she whispered. In her blindness she was overtaken, again, with the mad vision of the child as a fetus, yet fully grown, gigantic, a leviathan brainless and serene, silently stroking its way through the black, incomprehensible waters of Dachau and Auschwitz.

"Emmi, Emmi!" she managed to say. "Why is the name of the Heavenly Father in this room?"

It was, she said a long time after, one of the last religious thoughts she ever had.

After that night—her final night as a prisoner-resident in the Commandant's house—Sophie spent nearly fifteen more months at Auschwitz. As I have said before, because of her silence this long period of her incarceration remained (and still remains) largely a blank to me. But there are one or two things I can say for a certainty. When she left Haus Höss she was lucky enough to regain her status as a translator and typist in the general stenographic pool, and so remained among the small group of the relatively privileged; thus, while her life was wretched and her privations were often severe, she was for a long time spared the slow and inevitable sentence of death which was the lot of the multitude of prisoners. It was only during the last five months of her imprisonment, when the Russian forces approached from the east and the camp underwent a gradual dissolution, that Sophie endured the worst of her physical sufferings. It was then that she was transferred to the women's camp at Birkenau and it was there that she experienced the starvation and diseases that brought her very close to death.

During those long months she was almost completely untroubled or untouched by sexual desire. Illness and debilitation would account for this state, of course—

especially during the unspeakable months at Birkenau—but she was certain it was also psychological: the pervasive smell and presence of death caused any generative urge to seem literally obscene, a travesty, and thus—as in the depths of illness—to remain at so low an ebb as to be virtually snuffed out. At least that was Sophie's personal reaction, and she told me that she had sometimes wondered whether it might not have been this total absence of amorous feeling which threw into even sharper focus the dream she had that last night while sleeping in the basement of the Commandant's house. Or perhaps, she thought, it was the dream that helped dampen all further desire. Like most people, Sophie rarely remembered dreams for long in vivid or significant detail, but this dream was so violently, unequivocally and pleasurably erotic, so blasphemous and frightening, and so altogether memorable, that much later she was able to believe (with a touch of facetiousness which only the passage of time could permit) that it might have scared her away from thoughts of sex all by itself, quite aside from bad health and mortal despair . . .

After leaving Emmi's room she had made her way downstairs and then fallen into a heap on her pallet. She had sunk into almost instantaneous sleep, with only a moment's anticipation of the coming day when she would finally see her son. And she was soon walking alone along a beach—a beach, in the manner of dreams, both familiar and strange. It was a sandy shore of the Baltic Sea, and something told her that it was the coast of Schleswig-Holstein. To the right of her was the shallow wind-swept Kiel Bay, dotted with sailing craft; on her left as she strolled north toward the distant coastal barrens of Denmark were sand dunes, and behind these a forest of pinetrees and evergreen shimmered in the noonday sun. Although she was clothed she sensed a nakedness, as if she were enveloped in a fabric of seductive transparency. She felt unashamedly provocative, conscious of her backside swaying amid the folds of her transparent skirt, attracting the eyes of the bathers umbrella-shrouded along the beach. Immediately the bathers were left behind. A path through the marsh grass made a junction with the beach; she continued past this place, aware now that a man was following her, and that his eyes were fastened on her hips and the extravagant swaying motion she felt compelled to make. The man came abreast of her, looked at her, and she returned his gaze. She could not possibly recognize the face, which was middle-aged, jovial, fair, very German, attractive—no, it was more than attractive, it made her melt with desire. But the man himself! Who was he? She struggled for an instant's recognition (the voice, so familiar, purred "*Guten Tag*") and in a flash she thought him to be a famous singer, a *Heldentenor* from the Berlin Opera. He smiled at her with clean white teeth, stroked her on the buttocks, uttered a few words that were at once barely comprehensible and flagrantly lewd, then disappeared. She smelled the warm sea breeze.

She was at the doorway of a chapel which itself was situated on a dune overlooking the sea. She could not see him but she felt the presence of the man somewhere. It was a sunny, simple chapel with plain wooden pews on either side of a single aisle; over the altar hung a cross of unpainted pine, almost primitive in its stripped, unadorned angularity, and somehow loomingly central to Sophie's apprehension of the place, into which she now wandered, feverish with lust. She heard herself giggle. Why? Why should she giggle when the little chapel was suddenly suffused by the grief of a single contralto voice and the strains of that tragic cantata *Schlage doch, gewünschte Stunde?* She stood before the altar, unclothed now; the music, pouring forth softly from some source both distant and near, enveloped her body like a benison. She giggled again. The man from the beach reappeared. He was naked, but again she could not name him. He was no longer smiling; a murderous scowl clouded his face and the threat embedded in his countenance excited her, inflaming her lust. He told her sternly to look down. His penis was thick and erect. He commanded her to get down on her knees and suck him. She did so in a frenzy of craving, pulling back the foreskin to expose a spade-shaped glans of a deep blue-black hue and so huge that she knew that she could not surround it with her lips. Yet she was able to do this, with a choking sensation that wilted her with pleasure, while at the same time the Bach chimes, freighted with the noise of death and time, shivered down her spine. *Schlage doch, gewünschte Stunde!* He pushed her away from his belly, told her to turn around, commanded her to kneel at the altar beneath the skeletal cruciform emblem of God's suffering, glowing like naked bone. She turned at his order, knelt on hands and knees, heard a clattering of hoofs on the floor, smelled smoke, cried out with delight as the hairy belly and groin swarmed around her naked buttocks in a tight cloaklike embrace, the rampaging cylinder deep within her cunt, thrusting from behind again and again . . .

The dream still hung in her mind hours later when Bronek awakened her, bearing his pail of slops. "I waited for you last night but you didn't come," he said. "I waited as long as I could but it got too late. My man at the gate had to leave. What happened to the radio?" He spoke in low tones. The others were still asleep.

That dream! She could not dislodge it from her mind after these many hours. Groggily, she shook her head. Bronek repeated the question.

"Help me, Bronek," she said listlessly, gazing up at the little man.

"What do you mean?"

"I've seen someone . . . *awful*." Even as she spoke, she knew she was making no sense. "I mean, Christ, I'm so hungry."

"Eat this, then," said Bronek. "It's what's left over from their rabbit stew. Lots of meat in it."

The mess was slippery, greasy and cold but she slurped it up ravenously, watching the rise and fall of Lotte's breast as she slept on the pallet nearby. Between gulps she informed the handyman that she was leaving. "God, I've been so hungry since yesterday," she murmured. "Bronek, thank you."

"I waited," he said. "What happened?"

"The little girl's door was locked," she lied. "I tried to get in but the door was locked."

"And today you're going back to the barracks. Sophie, I'm going to miss you."

"I'll miss you too, Bronek."

"Maybe you could still get the radio. That is, if you go up to the attic again. I can still pass it on this afternoon, get it through the gate."

Why didn't the imbecile shut up? She was finished with

that radio—finished! She might easily have escaped suspicion before, but certainly not now. Surely if the radio were to disappear today, that terrible child would blab all about last night's visit. Anything further having to do with the radio was out of the question, especially on a day like this with its electric certainty of Jan's appearance—this reunion which she had looked forward to with a suspenseful greed beyond imagining. And so she repeated her lie. "We'll have to forget that radio, Bronek. There's no way to get at it. The little monster always keeps her door locked."

"All right, Sophie," said Bronek, "but if something happens . . . if you can get it, just give it to me quickly. Here in the cellar." He made an empty chuckle. "Rudi would never suspect me. He thinks he's got me in his pocket. He thinks I'm mentally deficient." And in the morning shadows, from an orifice filled with cracked teeth, he shed upon Sophie a luminous, enigmatic smile.

Sophie had a confused and unformed belief in precognition, even of clairvoyance (on several occasions she had sensed or predicted coming events), although she did not connect it with the supernatural. I admit that she inclined toward this explanation until I argued her out of it. Some inner logic persuaded us both that such moments of supreme intuition followed from perfectly natural "keys" —circumstances which had been buried in memory or had lain dormant in the subconscious. Her dream, for example. Anything but a metaphysical explanation seemed utterly impossible for the fact that the love partner in her dream should have been a man whom she finally recognized as Walter Dürrfeld and that she should have dreamed of him only the night before setting eyes on him for the first time in six years. It was quite beyond the bounds of plausibility that that suave and seductive visitor who had so captivated her in Cracow should appear in the flesh only hours after such a dream (duplicating the very face and voice of the dream figure)—when she had not thought of the man or even heard his name spoken in all that time.

But had she not? Later, as she sorted out her recollections, she understood that she *had* heard the name spoken, and more than once. How often had she heard Rudolf Höss order his aide Scheffler to put in a telephone call to Herr Dürrfeld at the Buna factory without realizing (except in her subconscious) that the recipient of the call was her romantic fixation of long ago? Certainly a dozen times. Höss had been on the phone to someone named Dürrfeld day in and day out. Moreover, the same name had figured prominently on some of those papers and memoranda of Höss's she had glanced at from time to time. Thus in the end, upon analysis of these keys, it was not at all difficult to explain Walter Dürrfeld's role as protagonist in Sophie's terrifying yet exquisite *Liebestraum.* Nor was it really difficult, either, to see why her dream lover became so easily metamorphosed into the devil.

That morning the voice she heard from the anteroom outside Höss's office in the attic was identical to that of the man in the dream. She had not entered the office immediately, as she had each morning for the past ten days, although she burned to rush through the door and smother her child in her arms. Höss's adjutant, perhaps aware of her new status, had brusquely ordered her to stand outside and wait. She then felt sudden, unspeakable doubt. Could it really be that since Höss had promised to let her see Jan, the little boy was inside the office, listening to the strange loud colloquy between Höss and the person with the voice of the man in her dream? She stirred nervously under Scheffler's gaze, aware from his icy manner of her loss of privilege; she was only a common prisoner again, among the lowliest of the low. She sensed his hostility, it was like a graven sneer. She fixed her eyes on the framed photograph of Goebbels adorning the wall and as she did so an odd picture leaped to mind: that of Jan standing between Höss and the other man, the child peering upward first at the Commandant and then at the stranger with the voice that was so perplexingly familiar. Suddenly, like a chord drawn forth from the bass pipes of an organ, she heard words from the past: *We could go to all the great musical shrines.* She gasped, sensed the adjutant's startled response to the choked noise she made. As if she had been struck a blow in the face, she rocked backward with a recognition of the voice, whispered to herself the name of its owner—and for the swiftest instant this October day and that afternoon years ago in Cracow melted together almost indistinguishably.

"Rudi, it's true that you are answerable to authority,"

Walter Dürrfeld was saying, "and how I respect your problem! But I'm answerable too, and so there seems to be no way to resolve this issue. You have upper echelons watching you; ultimately I have stockholders. I am answerable to a corporate authority which is now simply insisting on one thing: that I be supplied with more Jews in order to maintain a predetermined rate of production. Not only at Buna but at my mines. We must have that coal! So far so good, we have not yet substantially fallen behind. But all the formulations, the statistical predictions which I have available are . . . are ominous, to say the least. I must have more Jews!"

Höss's voice at first seemed muffled, but then the reply was clear: "I cannot *force* the Reichsführer to make up his mind about this. You know that. I can only ask for a certain guidance, also suggest things. But he seems—for whatever good reason—to be unable to come to a decision about these Jews."

"And your personal feeling is, of course . . ."

"My personal feeling is that only really strong and healthy Jews should be selected for employment in a place like Buna and in the Farben mines. The sick ones simply become an expensive drain on medical facilities. But my personal feeling counts for nothing here. We must wait for a decision."

"Can't you *worry* Himmler into a decision?" There was an edge of querulousness in Dürrfeld's voice. "As a friend of yours he might . . ." A pause.

"I tell you I can only make suggestions," Höss replied. "And I think you know what my suggestions have been. I understand your point of view, Walter, and I certainly don't take offense that you don't see eye to eye with me. You want bodies at all cost. Even an aged person with advanced consumption is capable of a certain number of thermal units of energy—"

"Precisely!" Dürrfeld broke in. "And this is all I'm asking at first. A trial period of, let us say, no more than six weeks, to see what utilization might be made of those Jews who are presently being submitted to . . ." He seemed to falter.

"Special Action," Höss said. "But here is the very crux of the matter, don't you see? The Reichsführer is pressed on one side by Eichmann and by Pohl and Maurer on the other. It is a matter of security versus labor. For security reasons Eichmann wishes to see every Jew undergo Special Action, no matter what the age or the physical condition of the individual Jew. He would not save a Jewish wrestler in perfect physical condition, if there were such a thing. Plainly, the Birkenau installations were promulgated to advance that policy. But see for yourself what's happened! The Reichsführer had to modify his original order regarding Special Action for all Jews—this obviously at the behest of Pohl and Maurer—to satisfy the need for labor, not only at your Buna plant but at the mines and all the armament plants supplied by this command. The result is a split—completely down the middle. A split— You know . . . what is the word that I mean? That strange word, that psychological expression meaning—"

"Die Schizophrenie."

"Yes, that's the word," Höss replied. "That mind doctor in Vienna, his name escapes—"

"Sigmund Freud."

There was a space of silence. During this small hiatus Sophie, almost breathless, continued to focus upon the image of Jan, his mouth slightly parted beneath snub nose and blue eyes as his gaze shifted from the Commandant (pacing the office, as was so often his restless habit) to the possessor of this disembodied baritone voice—no longer the diabolical marauder of her dream, but simply the remembered stranger who had enchanted her with promises of trips of Leipzig, Hamburg, Bayreuth, Bonn. *You're so youthful!* that same voice had murmured. *A girl!* And this: *I am a family man.* She was so intent upon laying her eyes on Jan, so smothered with anticipation over their reunion (she recalled later her difficulty in breathing), that her curiosity over what Walter Dürrfeld might look like now registered in her mind fleetingly, then faded into indifference. However, something in that voice—something hurried, peremptory—told her that she would be seeing him almost instantly, and the last words he spoke to the Commandant—every nuance of tone and meaning—were implanted in her memory with archival finality, as if within the grooves of a phonograph record which can never be erased.

There was a trace of laughter in the voice. He uttered a word heretofore unspoken. "You and I know that, either way, they will be *dead*. All right, let's leave it there for the moment. The Jews are giving us all schizophrenia, especially me. But when it comes to a failure of production, do you think I can plead sickness—I mean schizophrenia—to my board of directors? Really!" Höss said something in an offhand, obscure voice, and Dürrfeld replied pleasantly that he hoped they would confer again tomorrow. Seconds later, when he brushed past her in the little anteroom, Dürrfeld clearly did not recognize Sophie—this pallid Polish woman in her stained prisoner's smock—but as he inadvertently touched her he did say *"Bitte!"* with instinctive politeness and in the same polished gentleman's tones she recalled from Cracow. However, he looked a caricature of the romantic figure gone to seed. He had grown swollen around the face and porkishly rotund in the midriff, and she noticed that those perfect fingers which, describing their gentle arabesques, had so mysteriously aroused her six years before seemed like rubbery little wurstlike stubs as he adjusted upon his head the gray Homburg that Scheffler obsequiously handed him.

"Then, what finally happened to Jan?" I asked Sophie. Once again I felt I had to know. Of all the many things she had told me, the unresolved question of Jan's fate was the one which nagged at me the most. (I think I must have absorbed, then pushed to the back of my mind, her odd, offhand mention of Eva's death.) I began also to see that she shied away from this part of her story with the greatest persistence, seeming to circle about it hesitantly, as if it were a matter too painful to touch upon. I was a little ashamed of my impatience and was certainly loath to intrude upon this obviously cobweb-fragile region of her memory, but in some intuitive way I also knew she was on the verge of giving up this secret, and so I pressed her to go on in as delicate a voice as I could manage. It was late on Sunday night—many hours after our near-disastrous bathing episode—and we were sitting at the bar of the Maple Court. Since the hour was close to midnight and since it was the tag end of an exhaustingly humid Sabbath, the two of us were nearly alone in the cavernous place. Sophie was sober; both of us had stuck to 7-Up. During this long session she had talked almost ceaselessly, but now she paused to look at her watch and to mention that it might be time to go back to the Pink Palace and call it a night. "I've got to move my things out to my new place, Stingo," she said. "I've got to do that tomorrow morning, and then I've got to go back to Dr. Blackstock. *Mon Dieu,* I keep forgetting that I'm a working girl." She looked drawn and tired, now musing down upon the scintillant little treasure which was the wristwatch Nathan had given her. It was a gold Omega with tiny diamonds at the four quarter points of the dial. I hesitated to consider what it might have cost. As if reading my thoughts, Sophie said, "I really shouldn't keep these expensive things that Nathan gave me." A new sorrow had entered her voice, of a different, perhaps more urgent tone than the one which had infused her reminiscences of the camp. "I guess I should give them away or something, since I'll never see him again."

"Why *shouldn't* you keep them?" I said. "He gave them to you, for heaven's sake. Keep them!"

"It would make me think of him all the time," she replied wearily. "I still love him."

"Then *sell* them," I said, a little irritably, "he deserves it. Take them to a pawnshop."

"Don't say that, Stingo," she said without resentment. Then she added, "Someday you will know what it is to be in love." A sullen Slavic pronouncement, infinitely boring.

We were both silent for a while, and I pondered the profound failure of sensibility embedded in this last statement, which—aside from its boringness—expressed such oblivious unconcern for the lovelorn fool to whom it was addressed. In silence I cursed her with all the force of my preposterous love. Suddenly I felt the presence of the real world again, I was no longer in Poland but in Brooklyn. And even aside from my heartache over Sophie, I stirred inside with a fretful, unhappy malaise. Self-lacerating worries began to dog me. I had been so caught up in Sophie's story that I had utterly lost sight of the unshakable fact that I was nearly destitute as a result of yesterday's robbery. This, combined with the knowledge of Sophie's imminent departure from the Pink Palace—and my consequent solitude there, floundering pennilessly around Flatbush with the fragments of an uncompleted novel—gave me a real wrench of despair. I dreaded the loneliness I faced without Sophie and Nathan; it was far worse than my lack of money.

I continued to writhe inwardly, gazing at Sophie's pensive and downcast face. She had assumed that reflective pose I had become so accustomed to, hands cupped lightly over her eyes in an attitude that contained an inexpressible combination of emotions (What would she be thinking about now? I wondered): perplexity, amazement, recollected terror, recaptured grief, rage, hatred, loss, love, resignation—all these dwelt there for an instant in a dark tangle even as I watched. Then they went away. As they did I realized that she as well as I knew that the dangling threads of the chronicle she had told me, and which had obviously neared its conclusion, still remained to be tied. I also realized that the momentum which had been building up in her memory all evening had not really diminished, and that despite her weariness she was under a compulsion to scrape out the rest of her appalling and inconceivable past to its bottommost dregs.

Even so, a curious evasiveness seemed to prevent her from closing in directly on the matter of what happened to her little boy, and when I persisted once more—saying "And Jan?"—she let herself fall into a moment's reverie. "I'm so ashamed about what I done, Stingo—when I swam out into the ocean. Making you risk yourself like that—that was so bad of me, so bad. You must forgive me. But I will be truthful with you when I say that there have been many times since those days in the war when I have thought to kill myself. It seems to come and go in this rhythm. In Sweden right after the war was over and I was in this center for displaced persons I tried to kill myself there. And like in that dream I told you about, the chapel—I had this obsession with *le blasphème*. Outside the center there was a little church, I do not believe it was Catholic, I think it must have been Lutheran, but it don't matter—I had this idea that if I killed myself in this church, it would be the greatest sacrilege I could ever commit, *le plus grand blasphème,* because you see, Stingo, I didn't care no more; after Auschwitz, I didn't believe in God or if He existed. I would say to myself: He has turned His back on me. And if He has turned His back on me, then I hate Him so that to show and prove my hatred I would commit the greatest sacrilege I could think of. Which is, I would commit my suicide in His church, on sacred ground. I was feeling so bad, I was so weak and sick still, but after a while I got some of my strength back and one night I decide to do this thing.

"So I come out of the gate of the center with a piece of very sharp glass I found in the hospital where I was kept. It was easy enough to do. The church was quite near. There weren't any guards or anything at this place and I arrived at the church in the late evening. There was some light in the church and I sat in the back row for a long time, alone with my piece of glass. It was summertime. In Sweden there is always light in the summer night, cool and pale. This place was in the countryside and I could hear the frogs outside and smell the fir and the pines. It was a lovely smell, it remind me of the Dolomites when I was a child. For a while I imagined having this conversation with God. One of the things I imagined that He said was 'Why are you going to kill yourself, Sophie, here in My holy place?' And I remember saying out loud, 'If You don't know in all Your wisdom, God, then I can't tell You.' Then He said, 'So it's your secret.' And I answered, 'Yes, it's my secret from You. My last and only secret.' So then I started to cut my wrist. And do you know something, Stingo? I did cut my wrist a little and it hurt and bled some, but then I stopped. And do you know what make me stop? I'll swear to you, it was one thing. One thing! It was not the hurt or the fear. I had no fear. It was Rudolf Höss. It was thinking of Höss very suddenly and knowing he was alive in Poland or Germany. I saw his face in front of me just as the piece of glass cut my wrist. And I stopped cutting and—I know it sounds like *folie,* Stingo—well, I have this understanding which comes in a flash that I cannot die as long as Rudolf Höss is alive. It would be his final triumph."

There was a long pause, then: "I never saw my little boy again. You see, on that morning Jan was not in Höss's office when I went in. He was not there. I was so certain that he was there that I thought he might be hiding under the desk—you know, for fun. I looked around but there was no Jan. I thought it must be some joke, I *knew* he had to be there. I called out for him. Höss had closed the door and was standing there, watching me. I asked him where was my little boy. He said, 'Last night after you were gone I realized that I couldn't bring your child here. I apologize for an unfortunate decision. To bring him here would be dangerous—it would compromise my position.' I couldn't believe this, couldn't believe he was saying this, I really couldn't believe it. Then all of a sudden I *did* believe it, I believed it completely. And then I went crazy. I went insane. Insane!

"I don't remember anything I done—everything was black for a time—except I must have done two things. I *attacked* him, I attacked him with my hands. I know this because after the blackness went away and I was sitting in a chair where he had pushed me I looked up and I saw the place on his cheek where I had scraped him with my fingernails. He was wiping a little blood away from the place with his handkerchief. He was looking down at me, but there was no anger in his eyes, he seemed very calm. The other thing I remember is this echo in my ears, the sound of my own voice when I screamed at him just a minute before. 'Gas me, then!' I remember shouting at him. 'Gas me like you gassed my little girl!' I shouted at him over and over. 'Gas me, then, you . . .' Et cetera. And I must have screamed a lot of dirty names in German because I remember them like an echo in my ear. But now I just put my head in my hands and wept. I didn't hear him say anything and then finally I felt his hand on my shoulder. I heard his voice. 'I repeat, I'm sorry,' he said, 'I should not have made that decision. I will try to make it up to you somehow, in some other way. What is there that I can do?' Stingo, it was so strange, hearing this man talk like this—asking me such a question in such a voice, apologetic, you know, asking *me* what *he* might do.

"And then, of course, I thought about Lebensborn, and what Wanda had said I must try to do—the thing I should have mentioned to Höss the day before but was somehow unable to. And so I made myself calm and stopped crying and finally I looked up at him and said, 'You can do this for me.' I used the word 'Lebensborn' and I knew right away from the look in his eyes that he had a knowledge of what I was speaking about. I said something like this, I said, 'You could have my child moved away from the Children's Camp and into the program of Lebensborn which the SS has and which you know about. You could have him sent to the Reich, where he would become a good German. Already he is blond and looks German and speaks perfect German like I do. There are not many Polish children like that. Don't you see how my little boy Jan would be excellent for Lebensborn?' For a long time I remember Höss didn't say anything, just stood there lightly touching the place on his cheek where I had cut him. Then he said something like this: 'I think that what you say might be a possible solution. I will look into the matter.' But that was not enough for me. I knew I was groping for straws, desperate, he could have simply shut me up right there—but I had to say it, had to say, 'No, you've got to give me a more definite answer than that, I cannot bear it living with any more uncertainty.' After a moment he said, 'All right, I will see that he is removed from the camp.' But even this was not good enough for me. I said, 'How will I know? How will I know for certain that he has been taken away from here? Also, you must promise me this,' I went on, 'you must promise to let me know where he has been taken in Germany so that someday when the war is over I will be able to see him again.'

"This last thing, Stingo, I could hardly believe I was saying, making these demands on such a man. But in truth, you see, I was relying on his feeling for me, depending on that emotion he had shown for me the day before, you know, when he had embraced me, when he had said, 'Do you think I am some kind of monster?' I was depending on some small remaining piece of humanity in him to help me. So after I said this he kept quiet again for a time and then he answered me by saying, 'All right, I promise. I promise that the child will be removed from the camp and you will hear of his whereabouts from time to time.' Then I said—I knew I was maybe risking his anger, but I couldn't help it, 'How can I be sure of this? My little girl is already dead, and without Jan I will have nothing. You said to me yesterday that you would let me see Jan today, but you didn't. You went back on your word.' This must have—well, *hit* him in some way, because he said then, 'You can be sure. You will have a message from me from time to time. You have my assurance and word as a German officer, my word of honor.'"

Sophie paused and gazed into the murky evening light of the Maple Court, invaded by a fluttering crowd of vagrant moths, the place deserted now except for ourselves and the bartender, a weary Irishman making a muffled clacking sound at the cash register. Then she said, "But this man did not keep his word, Stingo. And I never saw my little boy any more. Why should I think this SS man might have a thing called honor? Maybe it was because of my father, who was always talking about the German army, and officers and their high sense of honor and principles and such. I don't know. But Höss did not keep his word, and so I don't know what happened. Höss left Auschwitz for Berlin soon after this and I went back to the barracks, where I was an ordinary stenographer. I never got any kind of message from Höss, ever. Even when he came back the next year he did not contact me. For a long time I figure, well, Jan has been taken out of the camp and sent to Germany and soon I will get a message saying where he is and how his health is, and so on. But I never heard nothing at all. Then sometime later I got this terrible message on a piece of paper from Wanda, which said this—just this and nothing more: 'I have seen Jan again. He is doing as well as can be expected.' Stingo, I almost died at this because, you see, it meant that Jan had *not* been taken out of the camp, after all—Höss had not arranged for him to be put in Lebensborn.

"Then a few weeks after this I got another message from Wanda at Birkenau, through this prisoner—a French Resistance woman who came to the barracks. The woman said that Wanda had told her to say to me that Jan was gone from the Children's Camp. And this for a short time filled me with joy until I realized that it really meant nothing—that it might mean only that Jan was dead. Not sent to Lebensborn, but dead of disease or something—or of just the winter, it had become so cold. And there was no way for me to find out what was truly the case about Jan, whether he had died there at Birkenau or was in Germany somewhere." Sophie paused. "Auschwitz was so vast, so hard to get news of anyone. Anyway, Höss never sent me any message like he said he would. *Mon Dieu,* it was *imbécile* for me to think that such a man would have this thing he called *meine Ehre.* My honor! What a filthy liar! He was nothing but what Nathan calls a crumbum. And I was just a piece of Polish *Dreck* for him to the end." After another pause she peered up at me from her cupped hands. "You know, Stingo, I never knew what happened to Jan. It would almost be better that . . ." And her voice trailed off into silence.

Quietude. Enervation. A sense of the summer's wind-down, of the bitter bottom of things. I had no voice to answer Sophie after all this; certainly I had nothing to say when her own voice now rose slightly to make a quick blunt statement which, ghastly and heartbreaking as it was to me as a revelation, seemed in light of all the foregoing to be merely another agonizing passage embedded in an aria of unending bereavement. "I thought I might find out something. But soon after I got this last message from Wanda, I learned that she had been caught for her Resistance activity. They took her to this well-known prison block. They tortured her, then they hung her up on a hook and made her slowly strangle to death . . . Yesterday I called Wanda a *kvetch.* It's my last lie to you. She was the bravest person I ever knew."

Sitting there in the wan light, both Sophie and I had, I think, a feeling that our nerve endings had been pulled out nearly to the snapping point by the slow accumulation of too much that was virtually unbearable. With a feeling of decisive, final negation that was almost like panic within me, I wanted to hear no more about Auschwitz, not another word. Yet a trace of the momentum of which I have spoken was still at work upon Sophie (though I realized that her spirits were bedraggled and frayed) and she kept going long enough to tell me, in one brief insistent burst, of her last leave-taking from the Commandant of Auschwitz.

"He said to me, 'Go now.' And I turned and started to go and I said to him, '*Danke, mein Kommandant,* for helping me.' Then he said—you must believe me, Stingo—

he said this. He said, 'Hear that music? Do you like Franz Lehár? He is my favorite composer.' I was so startled by this strange question, I could barely answer. Franz Lehár, I thought, and then I found myself saying, 'No, not really. Why?' He looked disappointed for a moment, and then he said again, 'Go now.' And so I went. I walked downstairs past Emmi's room and there was the little radio playing again. This time I could have taken it easily because I looked around very carefully and there was no Emmi anywhere. But as I say, I didn't have the courage to do what I should have done, with my hope for Jan and everything. And I knew that this time they would suspect me *first*. So I left the radio there, and was suddenly filled with a terrible hatred for myself. But I left it there and it was still playing. Can you imagine what it was that the radio was playing? Guess what, Stingo."

There comes a point in a narrative like this one when a certain injection of irony seems inappropriate, perhaps even "counterindicated"—despite the underlying impulse toward it—because of the manner in which irony tends so easily toward leadenness, thus taxing the reader's patience along with his or her credulity. But since Sophie was my faithful witness, supplying the irony herself as a kind of coda to testimony I had no reason to doubt, I must set her final observation down, adding only the comment that these words of hers were delivered in that wobbly tone of blurred, burned-out, exhausted emotional pandemonium—part hilarity, part profoundest grief—which I had never heard before in Sophie, and only rarely before in anyone, and which plainly signaled the onset of hysteria.

"What was it playing?" I said.

"It was the overture to this operetta of Franz Lehár," she gasped, *"Das Land des Lächelns—The Land of Smiles."*

It was well past midnight when we strolled the short blocks home to the Pink Palace. Sophie was calm now. No one was abroad in the balmy darkness, and along the maple-lined summer streets the houses of the good burghers of Flatbush were lightless and hushed with slumber. Walking next to me, Sophie wound her arm around my waist and her perfume momentarily stung my senses, but I understood the gesture by now to be merely sisterly or friendly, and besides, her long recital had left me far beyond any stirrings of desire. Gloom and despondency hung over me like the August darkness itself and I wondered idly if I would be able to sleep.

Approaching Mrs. Zimmerman's stronghold, where a night light glowed dimly in the pink hallway, we stumbled slightly on the rough sidewalk and Sophie spoke for the first time since we had left the bar. "Have you got an alarm clock, Stingo? I've got to get up so early tomorrow, to move my things into my new place and then get to work on time. Dr. Blackstock has been very patient with me during these past few days, but I really must get back to work. Why don't you call me during the middle of the week?" I heard her stifle a yawn.

I was about to make a reply about the alarm clock when a shadow, dark gray, detached itself from the blacker shadows surrounding the front porch of the house. My heart made a bad beat and I said, "Oh my God." It was Nathan. I uttered his name in a whisper just as Sophie recognized him too and gave a soft moan. For an instant I had the, I suppose, reasonable idea that he was going to attack us. But then I heard Nathan call out gently, "Sophie," and she disengaged her arm from my waist with such haste that my shirttail was pulled out of my trousers' waistband. I halted and stood quite still as they plunged toward each other through the chiaroscuro of dimly trembling, leafy light, and I heard the sobbing sounds that Sophie made just before they collided and embraced. For long moments they clung together, merged into each other amid the late-summer darkness. Then at last I saw Nathan slowly sink to his knees on the hard pavement, where, surrounding Sophie's legs with his arms, he remained motionless for what seemed an interminable time, frozen in an attitude of devotion, or fealty, or penance, or supplication—or all of these.

Fourteen

Nathan recaptured us easily, not a minute too soon.

After our remarkably sweet and easy reconciliation—Sophie and Nathan and Stingo—one of the first things that I remember happening was this: Nathan gave me two hundred dollars. Two days after their happy reunion, after Nathan had reestablished himself with Sophie on the floor above and I had ensconced myself once more in my primrose-hued quarters, Nathan learned from Sophie the fact that I had been robbed. (Morris Fink, incidentally, had not been the culprit. Nathan noticed that my bathroom window had been forced—something Morris would not have had to do. I was ashamed of my nasty suspicion.) The next afternoon, returning from lunch at a delicatessen on Ocean Avenue, I found on my desk his check made out to me for that sum which in 1947, to a person in my state of virtual destitution, can only be described as, well, imperial. Clipped to the check was the handwritten note: *To the greater glory of Southern Literature*. I was flabbergasted. Naturally, the money was a godsend, bailing me out at a moment when I was frantic with worry over the immediate future. It was next to impossible to turn it down. But my various religious and ancestral scruples forbade my accepting it as a gift.

So after a great deal of palaver and good-natured argument, we reached what might be called a compromise. The two hundred dollars would remain a gift so long as I remained an unpublished writer. But when and if my novel found a publisher and made enough money to relieve me from financial pressure—*then* and only then would Nathan accept any repayment I might wish to make (without interest). A still, small, mean-spirited voice at the back of my mind told me that this largesse was Nathan's way of atoning for the horrid attack he had made on my book a few nights before, when he had so dramatically and cruelly banished Sophie and me from his existence. But I dismissed the thought as unworthy, especially in the light of my newly acquired knowledge, through Sophie, of that drug-induced derangement which had doubtless caused him to say hatefully irresponsible things—words it was now clear he no longer remembered. Words which I was certain were as lost to his recollection as his own loony, destructive behavior. Besides, I was quite simply devoted to Nathan, at least to that beguiling, generous, life-enhancing Nathan who had shed his entourage of demons—and since it was *this* Nathan who had returned to us, a Nathan rather drawn and pale but seemingly purged of whatever horrors had possessed him on that recent evening, the reborn warmth and brotherly affection I felt was wonderful; my delight could only have been surpassed by the response of Sophie, whose joy was a form of barely controlled delirium, very moving to witness. Her continuing, unflagging passion for Nathan struck me with awe. His abuse of her was plainly either forgotten or completely pardoned. I'm certain she would have gathered him into her bosom with as much hungry and heedless forgiveness had he been a convicted child molester or ax murderer.

I did not know where Nathan had spent the several days and nights since that awful performance he had put on at the Maple Court, although something Sophie said in an offhand way made me think that he had sought refuge with his brother in Forest Hills. But his absence and his whereabouts did not seem to matter; in the same way, his devastating attractiveness made it seem of small importance that he had recently reviled Sophie and me in such an outpouring of animosity and spite that it made us both physically ill. In a sense, the in-and-out addiction which Sophie had so vividly and scarily described to me had the effect of drawing me closer to Nathan, now that he was back; romantic as my reaction doubtless was, his demonic side—that Mr. Hyde persona who possessed him and devoured his entrails from time to time—seemed now an integral and compelling part of his strange genius, and I accepted it with only the vaguest misgivings about some frenzied recurrence in the future. Sophie and I were—to put it obviously—pushovers. It was enough that he had reentered our lives, bringing to us the same high spirits, generosity, energy, fun, magic and *love* we had thought were gone for good. As a matter of fact, his return to the Pink Palace and his establishment once again of the cozy love nest upstairs seemed so natural that to this day I cannot remember when or how he transported back all the furniture and clothing and paraphernalia he had decamped with that night, replacing them so that it appeared that he had never stormed off with them at all.

It was like old times again. The daily routine began anew as if nothing had ever happened—as if Nathan's violent furor had not come close to wrecking once and for all our tripartite camaraderie and happiness. It was September now, with the heat of summer still hovering over the sizzling streets of the borough in a fine, lambent haze. Each morning Nathan and Sophie took their separate subway trains at the BMT station on Church Avenue—he to go to his laboratory at Pfizer, she to Dr. Blackstock's office in downtown Brooklyn. And I returned happily to my homely little oaken writing desk. I refused to let Sophie obsess me as a love object, yielding her up willingly again to the older man to whom she so naturally and rightfully belonged, and acquiescing once more in the realization that my claims to her heart had all along been modest and amateurish at best. Thus, with no Sophie to cause me futile woolgathering, I got back to my interrupted novel with brisk eagerness and a lively sense of purpose. Naturally, it was impossible not to remain haunted and, to some extent, intermittently depressed over what Sophie had told me about her past. But generally speaking, I was able to put her story out of my mind. Life does indeed go on. Also, I was caught up in an exhilaratingly creative floodtide and was intensely aware that I had my own tragic chronicle to tell and to occupy my working hours. Possibly inspired by Nathan's financial donation—always the most bracing form of encouragement a creative artist can receive—I began to work at what for me has to be described as runaway speed, correcting and polishing as I went, dulling one after another of my Venus Velvet pencils as five, six, seven, even eight or nine yellow sheets became piled on my desk after a long morning's work.

And (totally aside from the money) Nathan returned once more to that role of supportive brother-figure, mentor, constructive critic and all-purpose cherished older friend whom I had so looked up to from the very beginning. Again he began to absorb my exhaustively worked-over prose, taking the manuscript upstairs with him to read after several days' work, when I had acquired twenty-five or thirty pages, and returning a few hours later, usually smiling, almost always ready to bestow upon me the single thing I needed most—praise—though hardly ever praise that was not modified or honestly spiced by a dollop of tough criticism; his eye for the sentence hobbled by an awkward rhythm, for the attitudinized reflection, the onanistic dalliance, the less than felicitous metaphor, was unsparingly sharp. But for the most part I could tell that he was in a straightforward way captivated by my dark Tidewater fable, by the landscape and the weather which I had tried to render with all the passion, precision and affection that it was within my young unfolding talent to command, by the distraught little group of characters taking flesh on the page as I led them on their anxiety-sick, funereal journey across the Virginia lowlands, and, I think, finally and most genuinely by some fresh vision of the South that (despite the influence of Faulkner which he detected and to which I readily admitted) was uniquely and, as he said, "electrifyingly" my own. And I was secretly delighted by the knowledge that subtly, through the alchemy of my art, I seemed gradually to be converting Nathan's prejudice against the South into something resembling acceptance or understanding. I found that he no longer directed at me his jibes about harelips and ringworm and lynchings and rednecks. My work had begun to affect him strongly, and because I so admired and respected him I was infinitely touched by his response.

"That party scene at the country club is terrific," he said to me as we sat in my room early one Saturday afternoon. "Just that little scrap of dialogue between the mother and the colored maid—I don't know, it just seems to me right on target. That sense of summer in the South, I don't know how you do it."

I preened inwardly, murmuring my thanks, and swallowed part of a can of beer. "It's coming along fairly well," I said, conscious of my strained modesty. "I'm glad you like it, really glad."

"Maybe I should go down South," he said, "see what it's like. This stuff of yours whets my appetite. You could be the guide. How would that suit you, old buddy? A trip through the old Confederacy."

I found myself positively leaping at the idea. "God, yes!" I said. "That would be just tremendous! We could start in Washington and head on down. I have an old school pal in Fredericksburg who's a great Civil War buff. We could stay with him and visit all the northern Virginia battlefields. Manassas, Fredericksburg, the Wilderness, Spotsylvania—the whole works. Then we'd get a car and go down to Richmond, see Petersburg, head toward my father's farm down in Southampton County. Pretty soon they'll be harvesting peanuts . . ."

I could tell that Nathan had warmed immediately to this proposal, or endorsement, nodding vigorously while in my own wound-up zeal I continued to embellish the outlines of the travelogue. I saw the trip as educative, serious, comprehensive—but fun. After Virginia: the coastal region of North Carolina where my dear old daddy grew up, then Charleston, Savannah, Atlanta, and a slow journey through the heart of Dixieland, the sweet bowels of the South—Alabama, Mississippi—finally ending up in New Orleans, where the oysters were plump and juicy and two cents apiece, the gumbo was glorious and the crawfish grew on trees. "What a trip!" I crowed, cutting open another can of beer. "Southern cooking. Fried chicken. Hush puppies. Field peas with bacon. Grits. Collard greens. Country ham with redeye gravy. Nathan, you gourmet, you'll go crazy with happiness!"

I was wonderfully high from the beer. The day itself lay nearly prostrate with heat, but a light breeze was blowing from the park and through the fluttering which the breeze made against my windowshade I heard the sound of Beethoven from above. This, of course, was the handiwork of Sophie, home from her half-day's work on Saturday, who always turned on her phonograph full blast while she took a shower. I realized even as I spun out my Southland fantasy that I was laying it on thick, sounding every bit like the professional Southerner whose attitudes I abhorred nearly as much as those of the snotty New Yorker gripped by that reflexive liberalism and animosity toward the South which had given me such a pain in the ass, but it didn't matter; I was exhilarated after a morning of especially fruitful work, and the spell of the South (whose sights and sounds I had so painfully set down, spilling quarts of my heart's blood) was upon me like a minor ecstasy, or a major heartache. I had, of course, experienced this surge of bittersweet time-sorrow often before—most recently when in a seizure considerably less sincere my cornpone blandishments had so notably failed to work their sorcery on Leslie Lapidus—but today the mood seemed especially fragile, quivering, poignant, translucent; I felt that at any moment I might dissolve into unseemly albeit magnificently genuine tears. The lovely adagio from the Fourth Symphony floated down, merging like the serene, steadfast throb of a human pulse with my exalted mood.

"I'm with you, old pal," I heard Nathan say from his chair behind me. "You know, it's *time* I saw the South. Something you said early this summer—it seems so long ago—something you said about the South has stuck with me. Or I guess I should say it has more to do with the North *and* the South. We were having one of the arguments we used to have, and I remember you said something to the effect that at least Southerners have ventured North, have come to see what the North is like, while very few Northerners have really ever troubled themselves to travel to the South, to look at the lay of the land down there. I remember your saying how *smug* Northerners appeared to be in their willful and self-righteous ignorance. You said it was intellectual arrogance. Those were the words you used—they seemed awfully strong at the time—but I later began to think about it, began to see that you may be right." He paused for a moment, then with real passion said, "I'll confess to that ignorance. How can I really have hated a place I have never seen or known? I'm with you. We'll take that trip!"

"Bless you, Nathan," I replied, glowing with affection and Rheingold.

Beer in hand, I had edged into the bathroom to take a leak. I was a little drunker than I had realized. I peed all over the seat. Over the plashing stream I heard Nathan's voice: "I'm due a vacation from the lab in mid-October and by that time the way you're going you should have a big hunk of your book done. You'll probably need a little breathing spell. Why don't we plan for then? Sophie hasn't had a vacation from that quack during the entire time she's worked for him, so she's due a couple of weeks too. I can borrow my brother's car, the convertible. He won't need it, he's bought a new Oldsmobile. We'll drive down to Washington . . ." Even as he spoke my gaze rested upon the medicine chest—that depository which had seemed so secure until my recent robbery. Who had been the perpetrator, I wondered, now that Morris Fink was absolved of the crime? Some Flatbush prowler, thieves were always around. It no longer really mattered and I sensed that my earlier rage and chagrin were now supplanted by an odd, complex unrest about the purloined cash, which, after all, had been the proceeds of the sale of a human being. Artiste! My grandmother's chattel, source of my own salvation. It was the slave boy Artiste who had provided me with the wherewithal for much of this summer's sojourn in Brooklyn; by the posthumous sacrifice of his flesh and hide he had done a great deal to keep me afloat during the early stages of my book, so perhaps it was divine justice that Artiste would support me no longer. My survival would no more be assured through funds tainted with guilt across the span of a century. I was glad in a way to get shut of such blood money, to get rid of slavery.

Yet how could I *ever* get rid of slavery? A lump rose in my gorge, I whispered the word aloud, "Slavery!" There was dwelling somewhere in the inward part of my mind a compulsion to write about slavery, to make slavery give up its most deeply buried and tormented secrets, which was every bit as necessary as the compulsion that drove me to write, as I had been writing today, about the inheritors of that institution who now in the 1940s floundered amid the insane apartheid of Tidewater Virginia—my beloved and bedeviled bourgeois New South family whose every move and gesture, I had begun to realize, were played out in the presence of a vast, brooding company of black witnesses, all sprung from the loins of bondage. And were not all of us, white and Negro, still enslaved? I knew that in the fever of my mind and in the most unquiet regions of my heart I would be shackled by slavery as long as I remained a writer. Then suddenly, through a pleasant, lazy, slightly intoxicated mental ramble which led from Artiste to my father to the vision of a white-robed Negro baptism in the muddy river James to my father again, snoring in the Hotel McAlpin—suddenly I thought of Nat Turner, and was riven by a pain of nostalgia so intense that it was like being impaled upon a spear. I removed myself from the bathroom with a lurch and with a sound on my lips that, a little too loudly, startled Nathan with its incoherent urgency.

"Nat Turner!" I said.

"Nat Turner?" Nathan replied with a puzzled look. "Who in hell is Nat Turner?"

"Nat Turner," I said, "was a Negro slave who in the year 1831 killed about sixty white people—none of them, I might add, Jewish boys. He lived not far from my hometown on the James River. My father's farm is right in the middle of the country where he led this bloody revolt of his." And then I began to tell Nathan of the little I knew about this prodigious black figure, whose life and deeds were shrouded in such mystery that his very existence was scarcely remembered by the people of that backwater region, much less the rest of the world. As I spoke, Sophie entered the room, looking scrubbed and fresh and pink and utterly beautiful, and seated herself on the arm of Nathan's chair. She began to listen too, her face sweet and absorbed as she negligently stroked his shoulder. But I was soon finished, for I realized that there was very little I could tell about this man; he had appeared out of the mists of history to commit his gigantic deed in one blinding cataclysmic explosion, then faded as enigmatically as he had come, leaving no explanation for himself, no identity, no after-image, nothing but his name. He had to be discovered anew, and that afternoon, trying to explain him to Nathan and Sophie in my half-drunken excitement and enthusiasm, I realized for the first time that I would have to write about him and make him mine, and re-create him for the world.

"Fantastic!" I heard myself cry in beery joy. "You know something, Nathan, I just began to see. I'm going to make a *book* out of that slave. And the timing is absolutely perfect for our trip. I'll be at a point in this novel where I can feel free to break off—I'll have a whole solid chunk of it down. And so when we get down to Southampton we can ride all over Nat Turner country, talk to people, look at all the old houses. I'll be able to soak up a lot of the atmosphere and also make a lot of notes, collect information. It'll be my next book, a novel about old Nat. Meanwhile, you and Sophie will be adding something very valuable to your education. It'll be one of the most fascinating parts of our trip . . ."

Nathan put his arm around Sophie and gave her an enormous squeeze. "Stingo," he said, "I can't wait. We'll be heading in October for Dixieland." Then he glanced up into Sophie's face. The look of love they exchanged—the merest instant of eyes meeting then melting together, but marvelously intense—was so embarrassingly intimate that I turned briefly away. "Shall I tell him?" he said to Sophie.

"Why not?" she replied. "Stingo's our best friend, isn't he?"

"And also our best man, I hope. We're going to get *married* in October!" he said gaily. "So this trip will also be our honeymoon."

"God Almighty!" I yelled. "Congratulations!" And I strode over to the chair and kissed them both—Sophie next to her ear, where I was stung by a fragrance of gardenia, and Nathan on his noble blade of a nose. "That's perfectly wonderful," I murmured, and I meant it, having totally forgotten how in the recent past such ecstatic moments with their premonitions of even greater delight had almost always been a brightness that blinded the eyes to onrushing disaster.

It must have been ten days or so after this, during the last week of September, that I received a telephone call from Nathan's brother, Larry. I was surprised when one morning Morris Fink summoned me to the greasy pay phone in the hallway—surprised to get any call at all, but especially from a person whom I had so often heard about but never met. The voice was warm and likable—it sounded almost the same as Nathan's with its distinctly Brooklyn resonance—and was casual enough at first but then took on a slight edge of insistence when Larry inquired whether it was possible for us to arrange a meeting, the sooner the better. He said he would prefer not to come to Mrs. Zimmerman's, and therefore would I mind paying him a visit at his home in Forest Hills. He added that I must be aware that all this had to do with Nathan—it was urgent. Without hesitation I said that I would be glad to see him, and we arranged to meet at his place late in the afternoon.

I got hopelessly lost in the labyrinth of subway tunnels that connects the counties of Kings and Queens, took a wrong bus and found myself in the desolate sprawl of Jamaica, and thus was well over an hour late; but Larry greeted me with enormous courtesy and friendliness. He met me at the door of a large and comfortable apartment in what I took to be a rather fashionable neighborhood. I had almost never encountered anyone for whom I felt such an immediate and positive attraction. He was a bit shorter and distinctly more stocky and fleshed out than Nathan, and of course he was older, resembling his brother in an arresting way; yet the difference between the two was quickly apparent, for where Nathan was all nervous energy, volatile, unpredictable, Larry was calm and soft-spoken, almost phlegmatic, with a reassuring manner which may have been part of his doctor's make-up but which I really think was due to some essential solidity or decency of character. He put me quickly at ease when I tried to apologize for my lateness, and offered me a bottle of Molson's Canadian ale in the most ingratiating manner by saying, "Nathan tells me that you are a connoisseur of malt beverages." And as we sat down on chairs by a spacious open window overlooking a complex of pleasant ivy-covered Tudor buildings, his words helped make me feel that we were already well-acquainted.

"I need not tell you that Nathan regards you highly," Larry said, "and really, that's partly why I've asked you to come here. As a matter of fact, in the short time I think he's known you I'm certain that you've become maybe his best friend. He's told me all about your work, what a hell of a good writer he thinks you are. You're tops in his book. There was a time, you know—I guess he must have told you—when he considered writing himself. He could have been almost anything, under the proper circumstances. Anyway, as I'm sure you've been able to tell, he's got very keen literary judgments, and I think it might give you a charge to know that he not only thinks you're writing a swell novel but thinks the world of you as a—well, as a *mensh*."

I nodded, coughing up something noncommittal, and felt a flush of pleasure. God, how eagerly I lapped up such praise! But I still remained puzzled about the purpose of my visit. What I then said, I realize now, inadvertently brought us to focus upon Nathan much more quickly than we might have done had the talk continued in respect to my talent and my sterling personal virtues. "You're right about Nathan. It's really remarkable, you know, to find a scientist who gives a damn about literature, much less has this enormous comprehension of literary values. I mean, here he is—a first-rate research biologist in a huge company like Pfizer—"

Larry interrupted me gently, with a smile that could not quite mask the pain behind the expression. "Excuse me, Stingo—I hope I can call you that—excuse me, but I want to tell you this right away, along with the other things you must know. But Nathan is *not* a research biologist. He is *not* a bona-fide scientist, and he has no degree of any kind. All that is a simple fabrication. I'm sorry, but you'd better know this."

God in heaven! Was I fated to go through life a gullible and simple-minded waif, with those whom I cared for the most forever pulling the wool over my eyes? It was bad enough that Sophie had lied to me so often, now Nathan— "But I don't understand," I began, "do you mean—"

"I mean this," Larry put in gently. "I mean that this biologist business is my brother's masquerade—a cover, nothing more than that. Oh, he does report in to Pfizer each day. He does have a job in the company library, an undemanding sinecure where he can do a lot of reading without bothering anyone, and occasionally he does a little research for one of the legitimate biologists on the staff. It keeps him out of harm's way. No one knows about it, least of all that sweet girl of his, Sophie."

I was as close to being speechless as I had ever been. "But how . . ." I struggled for words.

"One of the chief officials of the company is a close friend of our father's. Just a very nice favor. It was easy enough to arrange, and when Nathan's in control of himself he apparently does a good job at the little he is required to do. After all, as you well know, Nathan is boundlessly bright, maybe a genius. It's just that most of his life he's been haywire, off the track. I have no doubt that he could have been fantastically brilliant at anything he might have tried out. Writing. Biology. Mathematics. Medicine. Astronomy. Philology. Whatever. But he never got his mind in order." Larry gave again his wan, pained smile and pressed the palms of his hands silently together. "The truth is that my brother's quite mad."

"Oh Christ," I murmured.

"Paranoid schizophrenic, or so the diagnosis goes, although I'm not at all sure if those brain specialists really know what they're up to. At any rate, it's one of those conditions where weeks, months, even years will go by without a manifestation and then—pow!—he's off. What's aggravated the situation horribly in these recent months is these drugs he's been getting. That's one of the things I wanted to talk to you about."

"Oh Christ," I said again.

Sitting there, listening to Larry tell me these wretched things with such straightforward resignation and equanimity, I tried to still the turmoil in my brain. I felt stricken by an emotion that was very nearly grief, and I could not have been victim of more shock and chagrin had he told me that Nathan was dying of some incurably degenerative physical disease. I began to stammer, grasping at scraps, straws. "But it's so hard to believe. When he told me about Harvard—"

"Oh, Nathan never went to Harvard. He never went to any college. Not that he wasn't more than capable mentally, of course. On his own he's read more books already than I ever will in my lifetime. But when one is as sick as Nathan has been one simply cannot find the continuity to get a formal education. His real schools have been Sheppard Pratt, McLean's, Payne Whitney, and so on. You name the expensive funny farm and he has been a student there."

"Oh, it's so goddamned sad and awful," I heard myself whisper. "I knew he was . . ." I hesitated.

"You mean you have known that he was not exactly stable. Not . . . normal."

"Yes," I replied, "I guess any fool could tell that. But I just didn't know how—well, how *serious* it was."

"Once there was a time—a period of about two years when he was in his late teens—when it looked as if he were going to be completely well. It was an illusion, of course. Our parents were living in a fine house in Brooklyn Heights then, it was a year or so before the war. One night after a furious argument Nathan took it into his head to try to burn the house down, and he almost did. That was when we had to put him away for a long period. It was the first time . . . but not the last."

Larry's mention of the war reminded me of a puzzling matter which had nagged at me ever since I had known Nathan but which for one reason or another I had ignored, filing it away in some idle and dusty compartment of my mind. Nathan was, of course, of an age which logically would have required him to spend time in the armed forces, but since he had never volunteered any information about his service, I had left the subject alone, assuming that it was his business. But now I could not resist asking, "What did Nathan do during the war?"

"Oh God, he was strictly 4-F. During one of his lucid periods he did try to join up with the paratroopers, but we nipped that one in the bud. He couldn't have served anywhere. He stayed home and read Proust and Newton's *Principia*. And from time to time paid his visits to Bedlam."

I was silent for a long moment, trying to absorb as best I could all this information which validated so conclusively the misgivings I had had about Nathan—misgivings and suspicions which up until now I had successfully repressed. I sat there brooding, silent, and then a lovely dark-haired woman of about thirty entered the room, walked to Larry's side and, touching his shoulder, said, "I'm going out for a minute, darling." When I rose Larry introduced her to me as his wife, Mimi.

"I'm so glad to meet you," she said, taking my hand, "I think maybe you can help us with Nathan. You know, we care so much for him. He's talked about you so often that somehow I feel you're a younger brother."

I said something mild and accommodating, but before I could add anything else she announced, "I'm going to leave you two alone to talk. I hope I'll see you again." She was stunningly pretty and meltingly pleasant, and as I watched her depart, moving with easy undulant grace across the thick carpet of the room—which for the first time I perceived in all of its paneled, hospitably warm, book-lined, unostentatious luxury—my heart gave a heave: Why, instead of the floundering, broke, unpublished writer that I was, couldn't I be an attractive, intelligent, well-paid Jewish urologist with a sexy wife?

"I don't know how much Nathan ever told you about himself. Or about our family." Larry poured me another ale.

"Not much," I said, momentarily surprised that this indeed was so.

"I won't bore you with a great deal of detail, but our father made—well, quite a few bucks. In, of all things, canning kosher soups. When he arrived here from Latvia he spoke not a word of English, and in thirty years he made, well, a bundle. Poor old man, he's in a nursing home now—a very expensive nursing home. I don't mean to sound vulgar. I'm only bringing this up to emphasize the kind of medical care the family has been able to afford for Nathan. He's had the very best treatment that money can buy, but nothing has really worked on a permanent basis."

Larry paused, and with the pause came a drawn-out sigh, touched with hurt and melancholy. "So for all these last years it's been in and out of Payne Whitney or Riggs or Menninger or wherever, with these long periods of relative tranquillity when he acts as normally as you or I. When we got him this little job at the Pfizer library we thought it might be a time when he had undergone a permanent remission. Such remissions or cures are not unheard of. In fact, there's a reasonably high rate of cure. He seemed so content there, and although it did get back to us that he was boasting to people and magnifying his job all out of proportion, that was harmless enough. Even his grandiose delusions about creating some new medical marvel haven't harmed anyone. It looked as if he had settled down, was on his way to—well, normality. Or as normal as a nut can ever become. But now there's this sweet, sad, beautiful, fouled-up Polish girl of his. Poor kid. He's told me they're going to get married—and what do you, Stingo, think of that?"

"He can't get married, can he, when he's like this?" I said.

"Hardly." Larry halted. "But how can one prevent him, either? If he were out-and-out uncontrollably insane, we would have to put him away forever. That would solve everything. But the terrible difficulty, you see, lies in the fact that there are these lengthy periods when he appears to be normal. And who is to say that one of these long remissions doesn't really represent what amounts to a complete cure? There are many such cases on record. How can you penalize a man and prevent him from living a life like everyone else by simply assuming the worst, assuming that he will go completely berserk again, when such might not be the case? And yet suppose he marries that nice girl and suppose they have a baby. Then suppose he really goes off his rocker again. How unfair that would be to—well, to everyone!" After a moment's silence he gazed at me with a penetrating look and said, "I don't have any answer. Do you have an answer?" He sighed again, then said, "Sometimes I think life is a hideous trap."

I stirred restlessly in my chair, suddenly so unutterably depressed that I felt I was bearing on my back the weight of all the universe. How could I tell Larry that I had just seen his brother, my beloved friend, as close to the brink as he had ever been? Throughout my life I had heard about madness, and considering it an unspeakable condition possessed by poor devils raving in remote padded cells, had thought it safely beyond my concern. Now madness was squatting in my lap. "What is it that you think I can do?" I asked. "I mean, why did you—"

"Why did I ask you here?" he interrupted gently. "I'm not quite sure that I know myself. I think it's because I have an idea that you could be useful in helping him stay off the drugs. That's the most treacherous problem for Nathan now. If he stays away from that Benzedrine, he *might* have a fair chance to straighten himself out. I can't do much. We're very close in many ways—whether I like it or not, I am a kind of model for Nathan—but I also realize that I am an authority figure that he's apt to resent. Besides, I don't see him that frequently. But you—you're really close to him and he respects you, too. I'm just wondering if there isn't some way in which you might be able to persuade him—no, that's too strong a word—to *influence* him so that he lays off that stuff that might kill him. Also—and I wouldn't ask you to be a spy if Nathan weren't in such a perilous condition—also, you could simply keep tabs on him and report back to me by phone from time to time, letting me know how he's getting on. I've felt completely out of touch so often, and rather helpless, but if I could just hear from you now and then, you'd be doing all of us a great service. Does any of this seem unreasonable?"

"No," I said, "of course not. I'd be glad to help. Help Nathan. And Sophie too. They're very close to me." Somehow I felt it was time to go, and I rose to shake Larry's hand. "I think things might get better," I murmured with what could only seem, in the innermost part of my conscience, despairing optimism.

"I certainly hope so," said Larry, but the look on his face, forlorn despite his twisted effort at a smile, made me feel that his optimism was as bleak and troubled as my own.

I'm afraid that soon after my meeting with Larry, I was guilty of a grave dereliction. Larry's brief conference with me had been in the nature of an appeal on his part, an appeal to me to keep an eye on Nathan and to act as liaison between the Pink Palace and himself—to serve both as sentinel and as a kind of benign watchdog who might be able to gently nip at Nathan's heels and keep him under control. Plainly, Larry thought that during this delicate hiatus in Nathan's period of drug addiction I might be able to calm him, settle him down, and perhaps even work some lasting, worthwhile effect. After all, wasn't this what good friends were for? But I copped out (a phrase not then in use, but perfectly descriptive of my negligence, or, to be more exact, my abandonment). I have sometimes wondered whether if I had stayed on the scene during those crucial days I might not have been able to exercise some control over Nathan, preventing him from going on his last slide toward ruin, and too often the answer to myself has been a desolating "yes" or "probably." And shouldn't I have tried to tell Sophie of the grim matters I had learned from Larry? But since, of course, I cannot ever be perfectly certain of what would have happened, I have tended always to reassure myself through the flimsy excuse that Nathan was in the process of a furious, unalterable and predetermined plunge toward disaster—a plunge in which Sophie's destiny was welded indissolubly to his own.

One of the odd things about this was that I was gone for a short time—less than ten days. Except for my Saturday jaunt with Sophie to Jones Beach, it was my only journey outside the confines of New York City since my arrival in the metropolis many months before. And the trip was barely beyond the city limits at that—to a peaceful rustic house in Rockland County barely half an hour by car north of the George Washington Bridge. This was all the result of another unexpected voice on the telephone. The caller was an old Marine Corps friend who had the notably unexceptional name of Jack Brown. The call had been a total surprise, and when I asked Jack how in God's name he had tracked me down, he said that it had been simple: he had telephoned down to Virginia and had obtained my number from my father. I was delighted to hear the voice: the Southern cadence, as rich and broad as the muddy rivers that flowed through the low-country South Carolina of Jack Brown's birth, tickled my ear like beloved banjo music long unheard. I asked Jack how he was doing. "Fine, boy, just fine," he replied, "livin' up here among the Yankees. Want you to come up here to pay me a visit."

I adored Jack Brown. There are friends one makes at a youthful age in whom one simply rejoices, for whom one possesses a love and loyalty mysteriously lacking in the friendships made in afteryears, no matter how genuine; Jack was one of these friends. He was bright, compassionate, well-read, with a remarkably inventive comic gift and a wonderful nose for frauds and four-flushers. His wit, which was often scathing and which relied on a subtle use of Southern courthouse rhetoric (doubtless derived in part from his father, a distinguished judge), had kept me laughing during the enervating wartime months at Duke, where the Marine Corps, in its resolve to transform us from green cannon fodder into prime cannon fodder, tried to stuff us with two years' education in less than a year, thereby creating a generation of truly half-baked college graduates. Jack was a bit older than I—a critical nine months or so—and thus became chronologically scheduled to see combat, whereas I was lucky and escaped with my hide intact. The letters he wrote to me from the Pacific—after military exigencies had separated us and he was preparing for the assault on Iwo Jima while I was still studying platoon tactics in the swamps of North Carolina—were wondrous long documents, drolly obscene and touched with a raging yet resigned hilarity which I assumed was Jack's exclusive property until I saw it miraculously resurrected years later in *Catch-22*. Even when he was horribly wounded—he lost most of one of his legs on Iwo Jima—he maintained a cheerfulness I could only describe as exalted, writing me letters from his hospital bed that bubbled with a mixture of *joie de vivre* and Swiftian corrosiveness and energy. I am sure it was only his mad and sovereign stoicism that prevented him from falling into suicidal despair. He was completely unperturbed by his artificial limb, which, he said, gave him a kind of seductive limp, like Herbert Marshall.

I remark upon all this only to give an idea of Jack's exceptional allure as a person, and to explain why I jumped at his invitation at the cost of neglecting my obligations in regard to Nathan and Sophie. At Duke, Jack had wanted to become a sculptor, and now after postwar study at the Art Students' League, he had removed himself to the serene little hills behind Nyack to fashion huge objects in cast iron and sheet metal—aided (he allowed to me without reticence) by what might be construed as a fine dowry, since his bride was the daughter of one of the biggest cotton-mill owners in South Carolina. When at first I made some faint-hearted objections, saying that my novel which was rolling along so well might suffer from the abrupt interruption, he put an end to my worries by insisting that his house had a small wing where I could work all by myself. "Also, Dolores," he added, referring to his wife, "has her sister up here visiting. Her name is Mary Alice. She's a very filled-out twenty-one and, son, believe me, she's pretty as a picture. By Renoir, that is. She's also *very* eager." I happily pondered that word *eager*. It may be easily assumed, given my perennially renewed, pathetic hope for sexual fulfillment as already set down in this chronicle, that I needed no further enticement.

Mary Alice. Good Christ, Mary Alice. I will deal with Mary Alice almost immediately. She is important to this story for the perverse psychic effect she had on me—an effect which for a time, though mercifully brief, malignantly colored my final relationship with Sophie.

As for Sophie herself, and Nathan, I must briefly mention the little party we had at the Maple Court on the evening of my departure. It should have been a gay event—and to an outsider it would have appeared so—but there were two things about it which filled me with discomfort and foreboding. First, there was the matter of Sophie's drinking. During the short space of time since Nathan's return Sophie had, I noticed, abstained from the booze, possibly only because of Nathan's cautionary presence; in the "old days" I had rarely seen either of them indulge much more in alcohol than their ritual bottle of Chablis. Now, however, Sophie had reverted to the drinking pattern she had adopted with me during Nathan's absence, slugging down shot after shot of Schenley's, though as usual holding it all rather well despite an eventual clumsiness of the tongue. I had no idea why she had gone back to the hard stuff. I said nothing, of course—Nathan being the ostensible master of the situation—but it troubled me painfully, troubled me that Sophie appeared to be so rapidly turning into a lush; and I was further disconcerted over the fact that Nathan did not seem to notice, or if he did, failed to take the protective measures that such heavy, distracted and potentially dangerous drinking called for.

That evening Nathan was his usual engaging, garrulous self, ordering for me schooners of beer until I was woozy and ready to float away. He captivated Sophie and me with a series of howlingly funny show-biz stories, profoundly Jewish, which he had picked up somewhere. I thought him to be in the healthiest shape I had seen him since the first day months before when he had laid siege to my consciousness and heart; I felt myself actually shivering with delight in the presence of such a funny, rambunctiously appealing human being, and then in one swift short statement he caused my good cheer to flow away like water gurgling down a drain. Just as we had risen to go back to the Pink Palace his tone turned serious, and gazing at me from that smoky region behind the pupil of the eye where I knew dementia lurked, he said, "I didn't want to tell you this until now, so you'll have something to think about tomorrow morning on your way to the country. But when you come back we'll have something really incredible to celebrate. And that's this: my research team is on the verge of announcing a vaccine against"—and here he paused and ceremoniously spelled out the word, so touched with fear in those days, in all of its involute syllables—"pol-i-o-my-e-li-tis." *Finis* to infantile paralysis. No more March of Dimes. Nathan Landau, mankind's deliverer. I wanted to cry. Doubtless I should have said something, but remembering all that Larry had told me, simply could not speak, and so I walked slowly back in the dark to Mrs. Zimmerman's, listening to Nathan's loony embroidery on tissue and cell cultivation, pausing once to whack Sophie on the back to exorcise her tipsy hiccups, but all the while remaining utterly without words as my heart filled up with pity and dread . . .

Even these many years later it would be pleasant to report that my stay in Rockland County brought me some sort of compensating release from my worries over Nathan and Sophie. A week or ten days of hard productive work and the jolly fornication which Jack Brown's innuendoes had caused me to anticipate—such activities might have been sufficient reward for the anxiety I had suffered and, God help me, would suffer again soon to a degree I had not thought possible. But I recall the visit, or much of it, as a fiasco, and I have retained convincing evidence of this within the covers of the same notebook where earlier in this narrative I memorialized my affair with Leslie Lapidus. My sojourn in the country logically should have been the heady, halcyon happening I so warmly looked forward to. After all, the ingredients were there: an appealingly weathered and rambling old Dutch Colonial homestead set back deep in the woods, a charming young host and his vivacious wife, a comfortable bed, plenty of good Southern cooking, lots of booze and beer, and bright hope for consummation at last in the embrace of Mary Alice Grimball, who had a shiny flawless triangular face with saucy dimples, lovely moist lips parted *eagerly,* overflowing honey-hued hair, a degree in English from Converse College, and the most gorgeous sweetheart of an ass that ever sashayed its way north from Spartanburg.

What could be more inviting and freighted with promise than such a setup? Here is the horny young bachelor hard at his writing all day, aware only of the pleasant *chink-chink* of the tools of his peglegged sculptor friend and the smell of chicken and hush puppies frying in the kitchen, his work impelled to even greater flights of exquisite nuance and power by the knowledge, pleasurably roosting at the mind's edge, that the evening will bring friendly relaxation, good food, talk murmurous with down-home Southern nostalgia—all this fragrantly buoyed by the presence of two delightful young women, one of whom in the darkness of the coming night he will make whisper, moan and squeal with joy amid tangled sheets in the hotter tangle of love. Indeed, the purely domestic aspects of this fantasy were well realized. I did work a great deal during those days with Jack Brown and his wife and Mary Alice. The four of us swam often in the pool in the woods (the weather remained quite warm), the mealtime get-togethers were festive and good-natured, and the talk was filled with rich reminiscence. But there was suffering too, and it was in the early hours of those mornings when, time after time, I would steal away with Mary Alice that I found myself exposed, literally, to a form of sexual eccentricity I had never dreamed existed and have never experienced since. For Mary Alice was—as I grimly and comparatively anatomized her in my notes (set down in the same frantic unbelieving scrawl which I had used to record my other disastrous liaison several months before)—

—something worse than a Cock Tease, a Whack-off artist. I sit here in the hours just before dawn listening to the crickets and contemplating her dismal artistry for the third morning running, wondering at the calamity that has happened to me. Again I have inspected myself in the bathroom mirror, seen nothing amiss in my physiognomy, indeed I must say modestly that all is well: my strong nose and brown intelligent eyes, good complexion, excellent bone structure (not so fine, thank God, as to appear "aristocratic," but possessing enough angularities to prevent my looking coarsely plebeian) and rather humorous mouth and chin all merge into a face that could reasonably be called handsome, though it is certainly far from the stereotype handsomeness of a

Vitalis ad. So she could not be repelled by my looks. Mary Alice is sensitive, literate, which is to say, widely read in one or two of the same books in which I have an interest, has a decent sense of humor (hardly a barrel of laughs, but then, who could be in the shadow of Jack Brown's wit), seems relatively advanced and liberated in "worldly" matters for a girl of her background, which is intensely Southern. Rather atavistically, she does seem to mention church-going a little too often. Neither of us has done anything so rash or heedless as to utter protestations of love, but it is evident that she is, at least mildly, aroused sexually. In this regard, however, she is a reverse image of Leslie, since despite her (I think, partly counterfeit) passion in our hottest embrace, she is utterly prudish (like so many Southern girls) in the realm of language. When, for instance, an hour or so into our first "lovemaking" session night before last I was carried away enough to softly remark upon the marvelous ass I thought she had and, in my excitement, made a vain attempt to reach around and lay a hand on it, she drew away with a savage whisper ("I hate that word!" she said. "Can't you say 'hips'?") and I realized then that any further indecencies might prove fatal.

Pleasant enough little round knockers like plump cantaloupes, but nothing about her approaches the perfection of that ass which, save perhaps for Sophie's, is the paragon of world behinds, two lunar globes of such heartless symmetry that even in the rather drab Peck & Peck-type flannel skirts she sometimes wears, I feel an ache shoot through my gonads as though they'd been kicked by a mule. Osculatory ability: so-so, she is a piker compared to Leslie, whose gymnastic tongue-work will haunt me forever. But even though Mary Alice, like Leslie, will permit me to lay not a finger on any of the more interesting crannies or recesses of her incredibly desirable body, why is it that I am discomfited by the bizarre fact that the one thing she will do, though in a pleasureless and rather perfunctory way, is to whack me off hour after hour until I am a lifeless and juiceless stalk, ex-

hausted and even humiliated by this dumb pursuit? At first it was wildly exciting, almost the first contact of its kind in my life, the feel of that little Baptist hand on my prodigiously straining shaft, and I capitulated immediately, drenching us both, which to my surprise (given her general squeamishness) she didn't seem to mind, blandly swabbing herself off with my proffered handkerchief. But after three nights and nine separate orgasms (three each night, counted methodically) I have become very close to being desensitized, and I realize that there is something nearly insane about this activity. My unspoken hint (a very gentle downward urging of her head with my hand) that she might wish to commit upon me what the Italians call the act of fellatio was met with such an abrupt show of revulsion—as if she were about to eat raw kangaroo meat—that I abandoned that avenue once and for all.

And so the nights wear on in sweaty silence. Her sweet young breasts remain firmly imprisoned, rigid in their iron Maidenform behind the chaste cotton blouse. There is no welcome or access to that longed-for treasure which she keeps between her thighs: it is as safe as Fort Knox. But lo! every hour on the hour out pops my rigid rod again and Mary Alice grabs it with stoical indifference, pumping wearily away like some marathon bellringer while I pant and groan ludicrously and hear myself whimpering such asininities as "Oh God, that's good, Mary Alice!" and catch a glimpse of her lovely and totally unconcerned face even as there rises in me lust and despair in almost equal measure—with despair, however, ascendant regarding this loutish business. It is full dawn now and the serene Ramapo hills are filled with mist and the chatter of birds. Poor old John Thomas is as limp and as moribund as a flayed worm. I wonder why it has taken me these several nights to realize that my nearly suicidal despondency arises at least in part from the pathetic knowledge that the act which Mary Alice performs upon me with such sangfroid is something I could do much better myself, certainly with more affection.

It was toward the end of my stay with Jack Brown—one gray rainy morning with the first chilly breath of autumn in it—that I made the following entry in my notebook. The spidery, uncertain handwriting, which of course I am unable to reproduce here, is testimony to my emotional distress.

A sleepless night, or nearly so. I cannot blame Jack Brown, whom I like so much, either for my discomfiture or for his own misconception. It's not his fault that Mary Alice is such a thorn to me. Plainly, he thinks that for the past week or so Mary Alice and I have been fucking like polecats, for some remarks he has made to me in private (accompanied by meaningful nudges) clearly indicate that he believes that I have had my pleasure with his beautiful sister-in-law. Coward that I am, I cannot force myself to disabuse him of this belief. Tonight after a fine dinner which included the best Virginia ham I have ever tasted, the four of us go to a cretinous movie in Nyack. Afterwards, at a little past midnight, Jack and Dolores retire to their bedchamber while Mary Alice and I, ensconced in our love nest on the downstairs sunporch, resume our doomed ritual. I drink a great deal of beer, to make myself magisterial. The "smooching" begins, quite pleasurable at first, and after interminable minutes of this foreplay, there starts the repetitious and inevitable build-up toward what for me has now become a boring, nearly unbearable messiness. No longer needing me to initiate the move, Mary Alice gropes for my zipper, her mean little hand ready to perform its spiritless operation on my equally jaded appendage. This time, however, I halt her midway, prepared for the showdown I have anticipated all day. "Mary Alice," I say, "why don't we level with each other? For some reason we haven't really talked about this problem. I like you so much, but quite frankly I can't take any more of this frustrating activity. Is it fear of . . ." (I hesitate to be explicit, largely because she is so sensitive about language.) "Is it fear of . . . you know what? If it is, I just wanted to say that I have the means to prevent any . . . accident. I promise I'll be very careful." After a silence she leans her head with its fine luxuriant hair smelling so hurtfully of gardenia against my shoulder, sighs, then says, "No, it's not that, Stingo." She falls silent. "What is it, then?" I say. "I mean, don't you understand that except for kissing I literally haven't touched you—anywhere! It just doesn't seem right, Mary Alice. In fact, there's something downright perverse about what we're doing." After a pause, she says, "Oh, Stingo, I don't know. I like you very much too, but you know we're not in love. Sex and love for me are inseparable. I want everything to be right for the man I love. For both of us. I was burnt so badly once." I reply, "How do you mean burnt? Were you in love with someone?" She says, "Yes, I thought so. He burnt me so badly. I don't want to get burnt again."

And as she talks to me, telling me about her late lamented amour, a ghastly Cosmopolitan short story emerges, explaining simultaneously the sexual morality of these 1940s and the psychopathology which permits her to torment me in the way she has been doing. She had a fiancé, one Walter, she tells me, a naval aviator who courted her for four months. During this time before their engagement (she explains to me in circumlocutory language to which Mrs. Grundy would not have taken exception) they did not participate in formal sexual relations, although at his behest she did learn, presumably with the same lackluster and rhythmic skill she has practiced on me, to flog his dick ("stimulate him"), and indulged in this pastime night after night as much to give him some "release" (she actually uses the odious word) as to protect the velvet strongbox he was perishing to get into. (Four months! Think of Walt's Navy-blue trousers and those oceans of come!) Only when the wretched flyboy formally declared his intentions to marry and then produced the ring (Mary Alice continues to tell me in vapid innocence) did she yield up her darling honey pot, for in the Baptist faith of her upbringing, woe as certain as death would alight upon those who would engage in carnal congress without at least the prospect of matrimony. Indeed, as she goes on to say, she felt it wicked enough to do what she did before the actual hitching of the knot. At this point Mary Alice pauses and, backtracking, says something to me which causes me to grind my teeth in rage. "It's not that I don't desire you, Stingo. I have strong desires. Walter taught me to make love." And while she continues to talk, murmurously spinning out her banalities about "consideration," "tenderness," "fidelity," "understanding," "sympathy" and other Christian garbage, I have an unusual and overpowering longing to perpetrate a rape. Anyway, to conclude her tale, Walter left her before the wedding day—the shock of her life. "That was how I got burnt so badly, Stingo, and I just don't want to get burnt that way again."

I am silent for a while. "I'm sorry," I say. "It's a sad story," I add, trying to still the sarcasm striving to be expressed. "Very sad. I guess it happens to a lot of people. But I think I know why Walter left you. And tell me something, Mary Alice, do you really think that two healthy young people who are attracted to each other have to go through this masquerade about marriage before they fuck each other? Do you really?" I feel her turn rigid and hear her gasp at the horrid verb; she pulls away from me, and something about her prissy chagrin enrages me more. She is suddenly (and I now see justifiably) astounded at my unplugged fury spilling forth and as I too pull away and stand up shaking, quite out of control now, I see her lips, all smeared with the red goo of our kissing, form a little oval of fright. "Walter didn't teach you to make love, you lying creepy little idiot!" I say loudly. "I'll bet you've never had a good fuck in your life! All Walter taught you was how to jerk off the poor slobs who want to get into your pants! You need something to make that beautiful ass of yours gyrate with joy, a big stiff prick rammed into that cunt you've got locked up, oh shit—" I break off in a strangled cry, smothered with shame at my outburst but near loony laughter too, for Mary Alice has stuck her fingers in her ears like a six-year-old and the tears are rolling down her cheeks. I give a beery belch. I am repulsive. Yet I still cannot restrain myself from howling at her, "You cock teasers have turned millions of brave young men, many of whom died for your precious asses on the battlefields of the world, into a generation of sexual basket cases!" Then I storm off the porch and stomp upstairs to bed. And after hours of sleeplessness I drowse off and have what because of its Freudian obviousness I would be loath to put into a novel but what, Dear Diary, I must not shrink from telling You: my First Homosexual Dream!

Sometime late that morning, not long after finishing the foregoing entry in my journal and writing a few letters, I was sitting at the table where I had worked so well those past days, brooding glumly over the dumfounding homoerotic apparition which had passed like a thick black cloud across my consciousness (festering in my heart and making me fear for the basic well-being of my soul), when I heard Jack Brown's limping footsteps on the stairs, followed by the sound of his voice calling me. I did not really hear or respond right away, so deeply had I fallen into my funk over the appalling and very real possibility that I had turned queer. The nexus between Mary Alice's rejection of me and my sudden metamorphosis into sexual deviation seemed a little too pat; nonetheless, I could not deny the possibility.

I had read quite a bit about sexual problems while studying at that noted athenaeum of psychology, Duke University, and had come away with some fairly well established facts: that male primates in captivity, for instance, when denied female companionship, will try to bugger each other, often with gleeful success, and that many prisoners after long periods of incarceration will turn so readily to homosexual activity that it will almost appear to be the norm. Men who have been many months at sea will take their pleasure with one another; and when I was in the Marine Corps (a branch, of course, of the Navy) I was intrigued to learn the ancient origin of "pogey bait," the slang name for candy: it obviously sprang from the inducement held out by older sailors for the favors of fair-cheeked, smooth-bottomed young cabin boys. Ah well, I thought, if I have become a pederast, so be it; there was ample precedent for my condition, since although I had not been formally confined or caged, I may have just as well been in prison or on a timeless voyage on a brigantine as far as my lifelong efforts at good, wholesome, heterosexual screwing were concerned. Was it not plausible that some psychic valve in me, analogous to whatever controls the libido of a twenty-year convict or a lovelorn ape, had blown its gaskets, leaving me guiltlessly different, victim of the pressures of biological selection but nonetheless a pervert?

I was darkly considering this proposition, and then Jack's commotion at the door brought me up sharp. "Wake up, junior, there's a telephone call!" he shouted. I knew on the way downstairs that the call could only come from the Pink Palace, where I had left Jack's number, and I had a sense of foreboding which was amplified enormously when I heard the familiar voice, dolorosa, of Morris Fink.

"You got to come down here right away," he said, "all hell has broke loose."

My heart faltered, then raced on. "What happened?" I whispered.

"Nathan's went off his trolley again. This time it's real bad. The miserable fucker."

"Sophie!" I said. "How is Sophie?"

"She's all right. He beat her up again, but she's all right. He said he was goin' to kill her. She ran out of the house and I don't know where she is. But she asked me to call you. You'd better come."

"And Nathan?" I said.

"He's gone too, but he said he'd be back. The crazy bastard. You think I should call the police?"

"No, no," I replied quickly. "For Christ's sake, don't call the police!" After a pause I said, "I'll be there. Try and find Sophie."

After I hung up I stewed for a few minutes, and when Jack came downstairs I joined him in a cup of coffee to try to settle my agitation. I had spoken to him before about Sophie and Nathan and their *folie à deux* but only in dim outline. Now I felt compelled to hurriedly fill in some of the more painful details. His immediate suggestion was to do what for some dumb reason it had not occurred to me to do. "You've got to call the brother," he insisted.

"Of course," I said. I jumped to the phone again, only to be met with that impasse which more often than not throughout life seems to stymie people at moments of extreme crisis. A secretary told me that Larry was in Toronto, where he was attending a professional convention. His wife was with him. In those antediluvian pre-jet days Toronto was as far away as Tokyo, and I gave a moan of despair. Then just as I had hung up, again the phone rang. Once more it was the steadfast Fink, whose troglodyte manners I had cursed so often but whom I now blessed.

"I just heard from Sophie," he said.

"Where is she?" I shouted.

"She was at the office of that Polish doctor she works for. But she's not there now. She went out to the hospital to get an x-ray of her arm. She said Nathan might of broke it, the fuckin' bum. But she wants you to come down. She'll stay at that doctor's office this afternoon until you get there." And so I went.

For many young people in the throes of late-adolescent growth, the twenty-second year is the most anxiety-filled of all. I realize now how intensely discontented, rebellious and troubled I was at that age, but also how my writing had kept serious emotional distress safely at bay, in the sense that the novel I was working on served as a cathartic instrument through which I was able to discharge on paper many of my more vexing tensions and miseries. My novel of course was more than this, too, yet it was the vessel I have described, which is why I so cherished it as one cherishes the very tissues of one's being. Still, I was quite vulnerable; fissures would appear in the armor I had wrapped around me, and there were moments when I was assaulted by Kierkegaardian dread. The afternoon I hurried away from Jack Brown's to find Sophie was one of these times—an ordeal of extreme fragility, ineffectualness and self-loathing. On the bus rocking south through New Jersey to Manhattan, I sat cramped and exhausted in a nearly indescribable miasma of fright. I had a hangover, for one thing, and the jangling nervousness heightened my apprehension, causing me to shudder at the coming showdown with Sophie and Nathan. My failure with Mary Alice (I had not even said goodby to her) had unpinned the very moorings of what was left of my virility, and made me all the more despondent over the suspicion that throughout these years I had deluded myself about my faggot propensities. Somewhere near Fort Lee, I caught a reflected glimpse of my ashen, unhappy face superimposed against a panorama of filling stations and drive-ins and tried to close my eyes and mind to the horror of existence.

The hour was getting on toward five in the afternoon by the time I made it to Dr. Blackstock's office in downtown Brooklyn. It was apparently after office hours, for the reception room was empty save for a rather pinched and spinsterish woman who alternated with Sophie as secretary-receptionist; she told me that Sophie, who had been gone since late morning, had not yet returned from having her arm x-rayed but should be back at any moment. She invited me to sit and wait, but I preferred to stand, and then found myself pacing about restlessly in a room painted—drowned would be more exact—in the most gruesome shade of deep purple I had ever seen. How Sophie had worked day after day basking in such a creepy hue baffled me. The walls and ceiling were done in the same mortician's magenta which Sophie had told me adorned the Blackstock home in St. Albans. I wondered if such berserk decorator's witchery might not also have been concocted by the late Sylvia, whose photograph—decked with black bunting, like that of a saint—smiled down from one wall with a kind of engulfing benignancy. Other photographs plastered everywhere attested to Blackstock's familiarity with the demigods and goddesses of pop culture, in one after another frantically *gemütlich* display of palship: Blackstock with a popeyed Eddie Cantor, Blackstock with Grover Whalen, with Sherman Billingsley and Sylvia at the Stork Club, with Major Bowes, with Walter Winchell, even Blackstock with the Andrews Sisters, the three songbirds with their plentiful hair closely surrounding his face like large grinning bouquets, the doctor poutingly proud above the inked scrawl: *Love to Hymie from Patty, Maxene and LaVerne.* In the morbid, nervous mood I was in, the pictures of the merry chiropractor and his friends brought me as far down into bottomless despondency as I had ever been, and I prayed for Sophie to arrive and help relieve my angst. And just then she came through the door.

Oh, my poor Sophie. She was hollow-eyed and disheveled, exhausted-looking, and the skin of her face had the washed-out sickly blue of skim milk—but mainly she looked aged, an old lady of forty. I took her gently in my arms and we said nothing for a while. She did not weep. Finally I looked at her and said, "Your arm. How is it?"

"It's not broken," she replied, "just a bad bruise."

"Thank God," I said, then added, "Where is he?"

"I don't know," she murmured, shaking her head, "I just don't know."

"We've got to do something," I said, "we've got to get him in some kind of custody where he won't harm you." I paused, a sense of futility overpowering me, along with ugly guilt. "I should have been here," I groaned. "I had no business going away. I might have been able to—"

But Sophie halted me, saying, "Hush, Stingo. You mustn't feel that way. Let's go get a drink."

Sitting on a stool at the fake-morocco bar of a hideous mirrored Chinese restaurant on Fulton Street, Sophie told me what had happened during my absence. It was bliss at first, unqualified joy. She had never known Nathan to be in such a serene and sunny mood. Much preoccupied with our coming trip south, and plainly looking forward to the wedding day, he went into a kind of prothalamic fit, taking Sophie through a weekend buying spree (including a special excursion to Manhattan, where they spent two hours at Saks Fifth Avenue) during which she wound up with a huge sapphire engagement ring, a trousseau fit for a Hollywood princess, and a wildly expensive travel wardrobe calculated to knock the eyes out of the natives of such backwater centers as Charleston, Atlanta and New Orleans. He had even thought to drop into Cartier's, where he had bought me a watch as a best man's gift. Subsequent evenings they spent boning up on Southern geography and Southern history, both of them tackling various travel guides and he spending long hours with *Lee's Lieutenants* as preparation for the tours around the Virginia battlefields I had promised to inflict upon them.

It was all done in Nathan's careful, intelligent, methodical way, with as much attention to the arcana of the various regions we would be traveling through (the botany of cotton and peanuts, the origins of certain local dialects such as Gullah and Cajun, even the physiology of alligators) as that of a British colonial empire builder of the Victorian era setting forth toward the sources of the Nile. He infected Sophie with his enthusiasm, imparting to her all sorts of useful and useless information about the South, which he accumulated in gobs and bits like lint; loving Nathan, she loved it all, including such worthless lore as the fact that more peaches are grown in Georgia than in any other state and that the highest point in Mississippi is eight hundred feet. He went so far as to go around to the Brooklyn College library and check out two novels by George Washington Cable. He developed an adorable drawl, which filled her with gaiety.

Why had she not been able to detect the warning signals when they began to glimmer? She had watched him carefully all this time, she was certain he had stopped taking his amphetamines. But then the day before, when they had both gone to work—she to Dr. Blackstock's, he to his "lab"—something must have caused him to slip off the path, just what, she would never know. In any case, she was stupidly off guard and vulnerable when he put out the first signals, as he had before, and she failed to read their portent: the euphoric telephone call from Pfizer, the voice too high-pitched and excited, the announcement of incredible victories in the offing, a grandiose "breakthrough," a majestic scientific discovery. How *could* she have been so dumb? Her description of Nathan's furious eruption and the ensuing damage and debris was for me—in my frazzled state—agreeably laconic, but somehow more searing by its very brevity.

"Morty Haber was giving a party for a friend who was going off for a year to study in France. I worked late to help send out bills at the office and I had told Nathan that I would eat near the office and meet him later at the party. Nathan didn't come until long after I got there, but I could tell when I first saw him how high he was. I almost fainted when I saw him, knowing that he'd probably been that way all day, even when I got that phone call, and that I had been too stupid to even—well, even be alarmed. At the party he behaved all right. I mean, he wasn't . . . *unruly* or anything but I could tell so well he was on Benzedrine. He talked to some people about his new cure for polio, and my heart sort of died. I said to myself then that maybe Nathan would come down off this high and just go to sleep finally. Sometimes he would do that, you know, without getting violent. Finally Nathan and I went home, it was not too late, about twelve-thirty. It was only when we got home that he began screaming at me, building up into this great rage. Doing what he always done, you know, when he was in the middle of his worst *tempête,* which is to accuse me of being unfaithful to him. Of, well, screwing somebody else."

Sophie halted for an instant, and as she raised her left hand to throw back a lock of hair I sensed something slightly unnatural in the gesture, wondered what it was, then realized that she was favoring her right arm, which hung limply at her side. It obviously was causing her pain.

"Who was he after you about this time?" I demanded. "Blackstock? Seymour Katz? Oh Christ, Sophie, if the poor guy wasn't so wacky, I wouldn't be able to stand this without wanting to knock his teeth out. *Jesus,* who does he have you cuckolding him with now?"

She shook her head violently, the bright hair tossing in an uncombed and untidy way above the forlorn, haggard face. "It don't matter, Stingo," she said, "just somebody."

"Well, then what else happened?"

"He screamed and shouted at me. He took more Benzedrine—maybe cocaine too, I don't know what exactly. Then he went out the door with this enormous slam. He shouted that he was never coming back. I lay there in the dark, I couldn't sleep for a long time, I was so worried and scared. I thought of calling you but it was terribly late by then. Finally I couldn't stay awake any more and went to sleep. I don't know how long I slept, but when he come back it was dawn. He come in the room like an explosion. Raving, shouting. He woke up the whole house again. He dragged me out of bed and throwed me on the floor and shouted at me. About me having sex with—well, this man, and how he would kill me and this man and himself. Oh *mon Dieu,* Stingo, never, never was Nathan in such a state, never! He kicked me hard finally—hard, on the arm here, and then he left. And later I left. And that was all." Sophie fell silent.

I put my face down slowly and gently on the mahogany surface of the bar with its damp patina of cigarette ash and water rings, wanting desperately to be overtaken by coma or some other form of beneficent unconsciousness. Then I raised my head and looked at Sophie, saying, "Sophie, I don't want to say this. But Nathan simply *must* be put away. He's dangerous. He has to be *confined.*" I heard gurgle up in my voice a sob, vaguely ludicrous. *"Forever."*

With a trembling hand she signaled to the bartender and asked for a double whiskey on ice. I felt I could not dissuade her, even though her speech already had a glutinous, slurred quality. After the drink came she took a hefty gulp and then, turning to me, said, "There is something else I didn't tell you. About when he come back at dawn."

"What?" I said.

"He had a gun. A pistol."

"Oh shit," I said. "Shit, shit, shit," I heard myself murmur, a cracked record. "Shit, shit, shit, shit . . ."

"He said he was going to use it. He pointed it at my head. But he didn't use it."

I made a whispered, not entirely blasphemous invocation, "Jesus Christ, have mercy."

But we could not just sit there bleeding to death with these gaping wounds. After a long silence I decided on a course of action. I would go with Sophie to the Pink Palace and help her pack up. She would leave the house immediately, taking a room for that night, at least, in the St. George Hotel, which was not far away from her office. Meanwhile, throughout all this, I would somehow find the means to get in touch with Larry in Toronto, telling him of the extreme danger of the situation and urging him to come back at all costs. Then, with Sophie safely in her temporary seclusion, I would do my damnedest to find Nathan and somehow deal with him—though this prospect filled my stomach with dread like a huge, sick football. I was so unstrung that even as I sat there I came close to regurgitating my single beer. "Let's go," I said. "Now."

At Mrs. Zimmerman's I paid that faithful mole Morris Fink fifty cents to help us cope with Sophie's baggage. She was sobbing and, I could see, rather drunk as she tramped about her room stuffing clothes and cosmetics and jewelry into a large suitcase.

"My beautiful suits from Saks," she mumbled. "Oh, what should I do with them?"

"Take them with you, for Christ's sake," I said impatiently, heaving her many pairs of shoes into another bag. "Forget protocol at a time like this. You've got to hurry. Nathan might be coming back."

"And my lovely wedding dress? What shall I do with it?"

"Take it, too! If you can't wear it, maybe you can hock it."

"Hock?" she said.

"Pawn."

I had not meant to be cruel, but my words caused Sophie to drop a silk slip to the floor and then raise her hands to her face, and bawl loudly, and shed helpless, glistening tears. Morris looked on morosely as I held her for a moment and uttered futile soothing sounds. It was dark outside and the roar of a truck horn along a nearby street made me jump, shredding my nerve endings like some evil hacksaw. To the general hubbub was added now the monstrous jangle of the telephone in the hallway, and I think I must have stifled a groan, or perhaps a scream. I became even further unstrung when Morris, having silenced the Gorgon by answering it, bellowed out the news that the call was for me.

It was Nathan. It was Nathan, all right. Plainly, unmistakably, unequivocally it was Nathan. Then why for an instant did my mind play an odd trick on me, so that I thought it was Jack Brown calling up from Rockland County to check on the situation? It was because of the Southern accent, that perfectly modulated mimicry which made me believe that the possessor of such a voice had to be one teethed on fatback and grits. It was as Southern as verbena or foot-washing Baptists or hound dogs or John C. Calhoun, and I think I even smiled when I heard it say, "What's cookin', sugah? How's your hammer hangin'?"

"Nathan!" I exclaimed with contrived heartiness. "How are you? *Where* are you? God, it's good to hear from you!"

"We still gonna take that trip down South? You and me an' ol' Sophie? Gonna do the Dixie tour?"

I knew that I had to humor him in some way, make small talk while trying at the same time to discover his whereabouts—a subtle matter—so I replied instantly, "You're damn right we're going to make that trip, Nathan. Sophie and I were just talking it over. God, those are sensational clothes you bought her! Where are you now, old pal? I'd love to come and see you. I want to tell you about this little side trip I've got planned—"

The voice broke in with its ingratiating molasses pokiness and warmth, still an uncanny replica of the speech of my Carolina forebears, lilting, lulling: "I'm sho' lookin' forward to that trip with you an' Miz Sophie. We gonna have the time of our lives, ain't we, ol' buddy?"

"It's going to be the best trip ever—" I began.

"We'll have a lot of free time, too, won't we?" he said.

"Sure, we'll have a lot of free time," I replied, not knowing quite what he meant. "All the time in the world, to do anything we want. It's still warm in October down there. Swim. Fish. Sail a boat on Mobile Bay."

"That's what I want," he drawled, "lots of free time. What I mean is, three people, they travel around a lot together, well, even when they are the *best* of friends, it might be a little *sticky* bein' together every single minute. So I'd have free time to go off by myself every now an' then, wouldn't I? Just for an hour or two, maybe, down in Birmingham or Baton Rouge or someplace like that." He paused and I heard a rich melodious chuckle. "An' that would give *you* free time too, wouldn't it? You might even have enough free time to get you a little nooky. A growin' Southern boy's got to have his poontang, don't he?"

I began to laugh a trifle nervously, struck by the fact that in this weird conversation with its desperate undertone, at least on my part, we should already have foundered on the shoals of sex. But I willingly rose to Nathan's bait, quite unaware of the savage hook he had fashioned for my precipitate capture. "Well, Nathan," I said, "I do expect that here and there I'll run into some good, ready stuff. Southern girls," I added, thinking grimly of Mary

Alice Grimball, "are tough to penetrate, if you'll excuse the phrase, but once they decide to put out, they're awfully sweet in the sack—"

"No, buddy," he put in suddenly, "I don't mean Southern nooky! What I mean is *Polack* nooky! What I mean is that when ol' Nathan goes off to see Mr. Jeff Davis's White House or the ol' plantation where Scarlett O'Hara whupped all those niggers with her ridin' crop—why, there's ol' Stingo back at the Green Magnolia Motel, and guess what he's doin'? Just guess! Guess what ol' Stingo's up to with his best friend's wife! Why, Stingo and her are in bed and he has actually *mounted* that tender *willing* little Polish piece an' they jus' *fuckin'* their fool heads off! Hee hee!"

As he said these words I was aware that Sophie had drawn near, hovering at my elbow, murmuring something I could not comprehend—the incomprehensibility being partly due to the blood pounding at a hot gallop in my ears and perhaps also to the fact that, distracted and horrified, I could pay little attention to anything save for the incredible jellylike weakness in my knees and my fingers, which had begun to twitch out of control. "Nathan!" I said in a choked voice. "Good God—"

And then his voice, transmuted back into what I had always conceived as Educated High Brooklyn, became a snarl of such ferocity that even the myriad intervening and humming electronic synapses could not filter out the force of its crazed but human rage. "You unspeakable creep! You wretched swine! God damn you to hell forever for betraying me behind my back, you whom I trusted like the best friend I ever had! And that shit-eating grin of yours day after day cool as a cucumber, butter wouldn't melt in your mouth, would it, when you gave me a piece of your manuscript to read—*'ah gee, Nathan, thank you so much—'* when not fifteen minutes earlier you'd been humping away in bed with the woman I was going to marry, I say was *going* to, past tense, because I'd burn in hell before I'd marry a two-timing Polack who'd spread her legs for a sneaky Southern shitass betraying me like . . ."

I removed the receiver from my ear and turned to Sophie, who, with mouth agape, had clearly divined what it was that Nathan had been raging about. "Oh God,

Stingo," I heard her whisper, "I didn't want you to know that he kept saying it was *you* that I was . . ."

I listened again, in impotence and anguish: "I'm coming to get you both." Then there was a moment's silence, resonant, baffling. And I heard a metallic click. But I realized the line was not dead.

"Nathan," I said. *"Please!* Where are you?"

"Not far away, old pal. In fact, I'm right around the corner. And I'm coming to get you treacherous scum. And then you know what I'm going to do? Do you know what I'm going to do to you two deceitful, unspeakable pigs? Listen—"

There was an explosion in my ear. Too diminished by the distance or by whatever in a phone mercifully de-amplifies noise and prevents it from destroying human hearing, the impact of the gunshot stunned rather than hurt me yet nonetheless left a prolonged and desolate buzzing against my eardrum like the swarming of a thousand bees. I will never know whether Nathan fired that shot into the very mouth of the telephone he was holding, or into the air, or against some forlorn, anonymous wall, but it sounded close enough for him to be, as he had said, right around the corner, and I dropped the receiver in panic and, turning, clutched for Sophie's hand. I had not heard a shot fired since the war, and I'm almost certain that I thought I would never hear another shot again. I pity my blind innocence. Now, after the passing of time in this bloody century, whenever there has occurred any of those unimaginable deeds of violence that have plundered our souls, my memory has turned back to Nathan—the poor lunatic whom I loved, high on drugs and with a smoking barrel in some nameless room or phone booth—and his image has always seemed to foreshadow these wretched unending years of madness, illusion, error, dream and strife. But at that moment I felt only unutterable fear. I looked at Sophie, and she looked at me, and we fled.

Fifteen

The next morning the Pennsylvania train that Sophie and I were riding to Washington, D.C., on our way down to Virginia, suffered a power failure and stalled on the trestle opposite the Wheatena factory in Rahway, New Jersey. During this interruption in our trip—a stop which lasted only fifteen minutes or so—I subsided into a remarkable tranquillity and found myself taking hopeful stock of the future. It still amazes me that I was able to maintain this calm, this almost elegant repose, after our headlong escape from Nathan and the fretful, sleepless night Sophie and I spent in the bowels of Penn Station. My eyes were gritty with fatigue and a part of my mind still dwelt achingly on the catastrophe we had barely avoided. As time had worn on that night it seemed more and more probable to both Sophie and me that Nathan had not been in our vicinity when he made that telephone call; nonetheless his merciless threat had sent us running madly from the Pink Palace with only one large suitcase each to get us down to the farm in Southampton County. We agreed that we would worry about the rest of our belongings later. From that moment on we had both been possessed—and in a sense united—by a single-minded and terrible urge: to flee Nathan and get as far away from him as we could.

Even so, the spell of enervated composure which finally came over me on the train would scarcely have been possible had it not been for the first of two telephone calls I was finally able to complete from the station. This was to Larry, who understood immediately the desperate nature of his brother's crisis and told me that he would leave Toronto without delay and come down and cope with

Nathan in the best way he could. We wished each other luck and said we would keep in touch. So at least I felt I had discharged some final responsibility toward Nathan and had not exactly abandoned him in my scramble to get away; after all, I had been running for my life. The other call was to my father; he of course welcomed with joy my announcement that Sophie and I were on our way south. "You've made a splendid decision!" I heard him shout over the distant miles, with obvious emotion. "Leaving that no-good world!"

And so, sitting high above Rahway in the crowded coach with Sophie dozing beside me, munching on a stale Danish pastry bought from the candy butcher along with a lukewarm carton of milk, I began to regard the unfolding years ahead with equanimity and affection. Now that Nathan and Brooklyn were behind me, I was about to turn the page on a new chapter in my life. For one thing, I calculated that my book, which would be a longish one, was nearly one-third completed. By chance the work I had done on it at Jack Brown's house had brought me to a congenial way station in the narrative, a place where I felt it would be easy to pick up the loose ends once I got settled with Sophie down on the farm. After a week or so of adjusting to our new rural surroundings—getting to know the Negro help, stocking the larder, meeting the neighbors, learning to run the old beat-up truck and tractor which my father had told me came with the place—I would be in a fine way to resume advancing the story, and with honest application I might be lucky enough to have the whole thing wrapped up and ready to hawk to a publisher by the end of 1948.

I looked down at Sophie as I thought these buoyant thoughts. She was fast asleep, her tousled blond head lay against my shoulder, and I very gently surrounded her with my arm, lightly touching her hair with my lips as I did so. A vagrant pang of memory stabbed me but I thrust the ache aside; certainly I could not be a homosexual, could I, feeling for this creature such abiding, heartbreaking desire? We would of course have to get married, once established in Virginia; the ethos of the time and place would certainly permit no casual cohabitation. But despite the nagging problems, which included eradicating the memory of Nathan and the difference in our ages, I had the feeling that Sophie would be willing, and I resolved to nibble around the edges of this proposition with her once she woke up. She stirred and murmured something in her slumber, looking even in her haggard exhaustion so lovely that I wanted to weep. My God, I thought, this woman is soon likely to be my wife.

The train gave a lurch, moved forward, faltered, stopped again, and a low concerted groan went through the car. A sailor standing above me in the aisle swilled at a can of beer. A baby began to squall with hellish abandon behind me, and it occurred to me that in public conveyances fate inevitably positioned the single screaming infant in the seat nearest my own. I hugged Sophie softly and thought of my book; a thrill of pride and contentment went through me when I considered the honest workmanship I had so far put into the story, making its predestined way with grace and beauty toward the blazing denouement which remained to be set down but which I had already foretokened in my mind a thousand times: the tormented, alienated girl going to her lonely death on the indifferent summertime streets of the city I had just left behind. I had a moment of gloom: Would I be able to summon the passion, the insight to portray this young suicide? Could I make it all seem *real?* I was sorely bothered by the approaching struggle of *imagining* the girl's ordeal. Nonetheless I felt so serenely secure in the integrity of this novel that I had already fashioned for it an appropriately melancholy title: *Inheritance of Night.* This from the *Requiescat* of Matthew Arnold, an elegy for a woman's spirit, with its concluding line: "Tonight it doth inherit the vasty hall of Death." How could a book like this fail to capture the souls of thousands of readers? Gazing out at the grime-encrusted façade of the Wheatena factory—hulking, homely, its blue industrial windows reflecting the morning light—I shivered with happiness and again with pride at the sheer *quality* of what I had put into my book by dint of so much solitary work and perspiration and, yes, even occasional freshets of grief; and thinking once more of the as yet unwritten climax, I allowed myself to fantasize a line from the review of a dazzled critic of 1949 or 1950: "The most powerful passage of female interior monologue since Molly Bloom's." What folly! I thought. What conceit!

Sophie slept. Tenderly I wondered how many days and nights she would be drowsing next to me in the coming years. I speculated on our matrimonial bed at the farm, thought of its size and shape, wondered if its mattress was constructed with sufficient amplitude, bounce and resilience to accommodate the industrious venery it would certainly receive. I thought of our children, the many young towheads skipping around the farm like little Polish buttercups and thistles, and my merry paternal commands: "Time to milk the cow, Jerzy!" "Wanda, feed the chickens!" "Tadeusz! Stefania! Close up the barn!" I thought of the farm itself, which I had not seen outside of my father's snapshots, tried to visualize it as the abode of a prominent literary figure. Like Faulkner's Mississippi home, "Rowan Oak," it would have to be given a name, one possibly appropriate to the peanut crop that provided its reason for being. "Goober Haven" was far and away too facetious, and I abandoned all other changes on the nut motif, playing instead with names more tony, stately, dignified: "Five Elms" perhaps (I hoped the farm had five elms, or even one) or "Rosewood," or "Great Fields," or "Sophia," in tribute to my beloved dame. In my mind's prism the years like blue hills rolled peacefully away toward the horizon of the far future. *Inheritance of Night* a remarkable success, gaining laurels rarely shed upon the work of a writer so young. A short novel then, also acclaimed, having to do with my wartime experiences—a taut, searing book eviscerating the military in a tragicomedy of the absurd. Meanwhile, Sophie and I living on the modest plantation in dignified seclusion, my reputation growing, the author himself being increasingly importuned by the media but steadfastly refusing all interviews. "I just farm peanuts," says he, going about his work. At age thirty or thereabouts another masterpiece, *These Blazing Leaves,* the chronicle of that tragic Negro firebrand Nat Turner.

The train lurched forward, began to churn with smooth and oily precision as it gained momentum, and my vision evaporated in an effervescent blur against the grimy, receding walls of Rahway.

Sophie awoke abruptly, with a little cry. I glanced down at her. She seemed a bit feverish; her brow and cheeks were flushed, and a fragile, dewy mustache of perspiration hovered above her lip. "Where are we, Stingo?" she said.

"Somewhere in New Jersey," I replied.

"How long does it take, this trip to Washington?" she asked.

"Oh, between three and four hours," I said.

"And then to the farm?"

"I don't know exactly. We'll get a train to Richmond, then a bus down to Southampton. It'll be quite a few more hours. It's practically in North Carolina. That's why I think we've got to spend the night in Washington and then head down to the farm tomorrow morning. We could stop in Richmond for the night, I guess, but this way you'll get to see a little bit of Washington."

"Okay, Stingo," she said, taking my hand. "I'll do whatever you say." After a silence she said, "Stingo, would you go get me some water?"

"Sure." I pressed down the aisle crowded with people, mostly servicemen, and near the vestibule found the fountain, where I trickled warm unsavory-looking water into a paper cup. When I returned, still airily elated by my fanciful pipe dreams, my spirits sank like pig iron at the sight of Sophie clutching a full pint bottle of Four Roses which she had plucked from her suitcase.

"Sophie," I said gently, "for God's sake, it's *morning* still. You haven't even had breakfast. You're going to get cirrhosis of the liver."

"That's all right," she said, sloshing whiskey into the cup. "I had a doughnut at the station. And a Seven-Up."

I groaned softly, aware from past experience that there was no way of dealing with this problem short of complicating matters and creating a scene. The most I could hope for would be to catch her off guard and swipe the bottle, as I had done once or twice before. I sank back in my seat. The train sped across New Jersey's satanic industrial barrens, the clickety-clack momentum hurling us past squalid slums, sheet-metal sheds, goofy drive-ins with whirling signs, warehouses, bowling alleys built like crematoriums, crematoriums built like roller rinks, swamps of green chemical slime, parking lots, barbarous oil refineries with their spindly upright nozzles ejaculating flame and mustard-yellow fumes. What would Thomas Jefferson have thought, viewing this? I mused. Sophie, jittery, restless, alternately gazed out at this landscape and poured whiskey into her cup, finally turning to me to say, "Stingo, does this train stop anywhere between here and Washington?"

"Only for a minute or two to take on passengers or let them off. Why?"

"I want to make a telephone call."

"Who to?"

"I want to call and find out about Nathan. I want to see if he's all right."

Ogreish gloom encompassed me in recapitulation of the agony of the night before. I took Sophie's arm and squeezed it hard, too hard; she winced. "Sophie," I said, "listen. Listen to me. That part is *over*. There is nothing you can do. Can't you realize that he actually was on the point of *killing us both?* Larry will come down from Toronto and locate Nathan and—well, *deal* with him. After all, he's his brother, his closest relative. Nathan is *insane*, Sophie! He's got to be . . . *institutionalized*."

She had begun to weep. The tears spilled down around her fingers, which suddenly looked very thin, pink and emaciated as she clutched her cup. And once again I was conscious of that pitiless blue toothbite of a tattoo on her forearm. "I just don't know how I'm going to face things, I mean, without him." She paused, sobbing. "I could call Larry."

"You couldn't reach him now," I insisted, "he must be on a train somewhere near Buffalo."

"Then I could call Morris Fink. He might be able to tell me if Nathan came back to the house. Sometimes, you know, he would do that when he was on a high. He would come back and take some Nembutal and sleep it off. Then when he woke up he would be all right. Or almost all right. Morris would know if he did that this time." She blew her nose, continuing to make little hiccupy sobs.

"Oh, Sophie, Sophie," I whispered, wanting to say but unable to say, *"It's all over."*

Thundering into the station in Philadelphia, the train screeched and shuddered to a stop amid the sunless cavern, touching me with a pang of nostalgia I could scarcely have foreseen. In the window I caught a glimpse of my reflected face, pale from too much indoor literary endeavor, and behind that face I thought for an instant I saw a younger replica—my little-boy self over ten years before. I laughed out loud at the remembrance, and suddenly invigorated and inspired, resolved both to distract Sophie from her gathering disquiet and to cheer her up, or try to.

"This is Philadelphia," I said.

"Is it a big place?" she asked. Her curiosity, though lachrymal, encouraged me.

"Mmm, medium big. Not a huge metropolis like New York, but big enough. I would think about the size of Warsaw maybe, before the Nazis got to it. It was the first truly big city I ever saw in my life."

"When was that?"

"Back around 1936, when I was eleven. I'd never been to the North before. And I remember the funniest damn story about the day I arrived. I had an aunt and uncle living in Philadelphia, and my mother—this was about two years before she died—decided to send me up here for a week's visit in the summer. She sent me by myself, on a Greyhound bus. Little kids traveled alone a lot in those days, it was perfectly safe. Anyway, it was an all-day trip on the bus—it went the long way around from the Tidewater to Richmond, then up to Washington and through Baltimore. My mother had the colored cook—her name was Florence, I remember—fix me a big paper bag full of fried chicken and I had a thermos of cold milk—very gourmet travel cuisine, you understand, and I gobbled my lunch somewhere between Richmond and Washington, and then along about midafternoon the bus stopped in Havre de Grace—"

"Like the French, you mean?" Sophie said. "Harbor . . ."

"Yes, it's a small town in Maryland. We'll be going through it. Anyway, we all trooped out at a rest stop, a tacky little restaurant where you could take a pee and where they sold soda pop and such, and I saw this horse-racing machine. In Maryland, you see, unlike Virginia, they had a certain amount of legal gambling and you could put a nickel in this machine and bet on one of, oh, say a dozen tiny metal horses running down a track. I remember my mother had given me exactly four dollars spending money—that was a lot of money in the Depression—and I got very excited at the idea of betting on a horse, so I put in my nickel. Well, Sophie, you can't imagine. That goddamned machine hit the jackpot—you know what jackpot means? Everything lit up and out came an absolute *torrent* of nickels—dozens of them, *scores* of them. I couldn't believe it! I must have won fifteen dollars' worth of nickels. They were all over the floor. I was out of my mind with happiness. But the problem was, you see, how to transport all this loot. I remember I was wearing these little white linen short pants and I stuffed all these nickels into the pockets, but even so, there were so many of them that they just kept spilling out all over everywhere. And the worst part was this: there was this mean-looking woman who ran the place, and when I asked her to please exchange my nickels for dollar bills she flew into a terrible rage, screaming at me that you had to be eighteen to play the horse-race machine and that I was obviously still wet behind the ears and that she'd lose her license and if I didn't get the hell out of there, she'd call the police."

"You were eleven," said Sophie, taking my hand. "I can't believe Stingo at eleven. You must have been a cute little boy in your white linen short pants." Sophie was still pink-nosed, but the tears had momentarily stopped and in her eyes I thought I saw a sparkle of something like amusement.

"So I got back on this bus for the rest of the drive to Philadelphia. It was a long way. Every time I made the slightest move a nickel or several of them would slip out of these bulging pockets of mine and roll down the aisle. And when I'd get up to retrieve them it would make it only worse, because more nickels would fall out and roll away. The driver was half crazy by the time we got to Wilmington and all through the trip the passengers were looking down at this trickle of money." I paused, gazing out at the faceless shadow figures on the station platform, which moved away in soundless retrograde as the train pulled out now, gently vibrating. "Anyway," I said, returning the squeeze Sophie gave my hand, "the final tragedy happened at the bus station, which must be not far from here. That evening my aunt and uncle were waiting for me and when I ran toward them I tripped and fell down flat on my little ass, my pockets split, and almost every goddamned one of those nickels poured out off the ramp and underneath the buses into this dark parking bay far down below, and I think when my uncle picked me up and brushed me off, there were about five nickels left in my pockets. The others were gone forever." I halted, tickled at this sweetly absurd fable which I had told Sophie truthfully, with no need for embroidery. "It is a cautionary tale," I added, "about the destructive nature of greed."

Sophie held one hand to her face, obscuring her expression, but since her shoulders were trembling I thought she had succumbed to laughter. I was mistaken. There were tears again, tears of anguish from which she simply could not seem to free herself. Suddenly I realized that I must have inadvertently summoned up memories of her little boy. I let her cry in silence for a while. Then the weeping became less. Finally she turned to me and said, "Down in Virginia where we're going, Stingo, do you think there will be a Berlitz school, a school for language?"

"What on earth would you want that for?" I said. "You already know more languages than anyone I know."

"It would be for English," she replied. "Oh, I know I speak it good now, and even read it, but what I must learn to do is to write it. I'm so poor at writing English. The spelling is so very strange."

"Well, I don't know, Sophie," I said, "there are probably language schools in Richmond or Norfolk. But they are both pretty far away from Southampton. Why do you ask?"

"I want to write about Auschwitz," she said, "I want to write about my experiences there. I suppose I could write in Polish or German or maybe French, but I'd so much rather be able to write in English . . ."

Auschwitz. It was a place which, amid the events of the past few days, I had thrust so far in the back of my mind that I had almost forgotten its existence; now it returned like a blow at the back of my skull, and it hurt. I looked at Sophie as she took a swig from her cup and then gave a small burp. Her speech had taken on the swollen-tongued quality which I had learned was a presentiment of unruly thinking and difficult behavior. I longed to dump that cup on the floor. And I cursed myself for the weakness or indecisiveness or spinelessness, or whatever it was, that still prevented my dealing more firmly with Sophie at such moments. Wait until we're married, I thought.

"There are so many things that people still don't know about that place!" she said fiercely. "There are so many things I haven't even told *you,* Stingo, and I've told you so much. You know, about how the whole place was covered with the smell of burning Jews, day and night. I've told you that. But I never even told you hardly anything about Birkenau, when they begun to starve me to death and I got so sick I almost died. Or about the time I saw a guard take the clothes off a nun and then make his dog attack her and bite her so bad on the body and the face that she died a few hours later. Or . . ." And here she paused, gazed into space, then said, "There are so many terrible things I could tell. But maybe I could write it as a novel, you see, if I learned to write English good, and then I could make people understood how the Nazis made you do things you never believed you could. Like Höss, for instance. I never would have tried to make him fuck me if it hadn't been for Jan. And I never would have pretended that I hated Jews so much, or that I wrote my father's pamphlet. All that was for Jan. And that radio that I didn't take. It still almost kills me that I didn't steal it, but don't you see, Stingo, how that would have ruined everything for my little boy? And at that same time I just couldn't open my mouth, just couldn't report to the Resistance people, couldn't say a word about all the things I'd learned working for Höss, because I was afraid . . ." She faltered. Her hands were trembling. "I was *so* afraid! They made me afraid of everything! Why don't I tell the truth about myself? Why don't I write it down in a book that I was a terrible coward, that I was a filthy *collaboratrice,* that I done everything that was bad just to save myself?" She made a savage moan, so loud above the racket of the train that heads turned nearby and eyes rolled. "Oh, Stingo, I can't stand living with these things!"

"Hush, Sophie!" I commanded. "You *know* you weren't a collaborator. You're contradicting yourself! You know you were just a *victim.* You told me yourself this summer that a place like that camp made you behave in a different way than in the ordinary world. You told me yourself that you just couldn't judge what you did or what anyone else did in terms of accepted conduct. So please, Sophie, please, *please* leave yourself alone! You're just eating your guts out about things that weren't your fault—and it's going to make you *ill!* Please stop it." I lowered my voice, and I used a word of endearment I had never used before, the word itself surprising me. "Please stop this now, darling, for your own sake." It sounded pompous with the "darling"—already I was talking in a husbandly way—but I somehow had to say it.

I was also on the verge of speaking those words which had been on my tongue a hundred times that summer—"I love you, Sophie." The prospect of uttering that plain phrase made my heart pound and skip beats, but before I could open my mouth Sophie announced that she had to go to the bathroom. She finished off the cup before she went. I watched anxiously as she began to shove her way toward the rear of the car, the blond head bobbing, the pretty legs unsteady. Then I turned back to reading *Life* magazine. I must have dozed off then, or rather, slept, sunk as if drowned after the exhaustion of a wide-awake night and its tension and chaos, for when the conductor's nearby voice woke me by bellowing "All aboard!" I jumped straight up out of my seat and then realized that an hour or more had passed. Sophie had not returned to her place next to me, and sudden fear wrapped itself around me like a quilt fashioned of many wet hands. I glanced into the darkness outside, saw the passing sparkle of tunnel lights, and knew that we were leaving Baltimore. It might have been a normal two-minute struggle to the other end of the car, pressing and shoving past the bellies and rumps of fifty standees, but I made it in a few seconds, actually knocking a small child down. In senseless dread I pounded at the door of the women's lavatory—what made me think she was still in there? A fat Negro woman with wild wiglike hair and bright marigold powder on her jowls stuck her face out and shrilled, "Git outa here! You crazy?" I plunged on.

In the swanker regions of the train I was enveloped by moist Muzak. The elderly-auntie strains of Percy Grainger's *Country Gardens* followed me as I frantically peered into roomette after roomette, hoping that Sophie had strayed into one and perhaps gone to sleep. I was now alternately obsessed by the notion that she had gotten off in Baltimore and that— Oh shit, the other was even more unthinkable. I opened the doors of more lavatories, stalked the funereal plush reaches of four or five parlor cars, hopefully scanned the diner where white-aproned colored waiters flapped their way up and down the aisle through fumes fragrant with stale cooking oil. At last: the club car. A little desk, a cash register—its custodian a pleasant gray-haired middle-aged woman who gazed up from her work with mournful eyes.

"Yes, poor dear," she said after I had blurted the queasy question, "she was hunting for a telephone. Imagine, on a train! She wanted to call Brooklyn. Poor dear, she was crying. She seemed, well, a little drunk. She went that way."

I found Sophie at the end of the car, which was a bleak cage of a vestibule, clangingly noisy, that was also the end of the train. A padlocked glass door crisscrossed by wire mesh looked down on the receding rails that glittered in the late-morning sun and converged at a point marking infinity amid the green pinewoods of Maryland. She was sitting on the floor slumped against the wall, her yellow hair adrift in the windy draft, and in one hand she clutched the bottle. As in that swim to oblivion weeks before—when exhaustion had so unmanned her, and guilt, and grief—she had gone as far as she could go. She gazed up and said something to me, but I couldn't hear. I bent down closer, and now—partly reading her lips, partly responding to that infinitely sorrowful voice—heard her say, "I don't think I'm going to make it."

Hotel employees certainly must come face to face with a lot of weird ones. But I still wonder what went through the mind of the grandfatherly desk clerk at the Hotel Congress, not far from our nation's Capitol, when he confronted the young Reverend Wilbur Entwistle, wearing a distinctly unecclesiastical seersucker suit but conspicuously carrying a Bible, and his violently rumpled fair-haired wife, who muttered disconnectedly in a foreign accent during the registration process, her face potty with train soot and tears, and clearly blotto. In the end he doubtless took it in his stride, for I had worked out a camouflage. Despite my informal dress, the masquerade I had contrived seemed as effective as one could imagine. In the 1940s unmarried people were not permitted to check into the same hotel room together; in addition, it was a felonious risk to falsely register as man and wife. The hazard increased if the lady was drunk. Desperate, I knew I was taking a risk, but it was one that seemed minimized if I could cast over it a modest halo of sanctimony. Therefore, there was the black leather Bible which I fished out of my suitcase just before the train pulled into Union Station, and also there was the address I inscribed in a large hand on the register, as if to decisively validate my dulcet-voiced and unguentary ministerial bearing: Union Theological Seminary, Richmond, Virginia. I was relieved to see that my ruse served to distract the clerk's attention from Sophie; the dewlapped old gentleman, being Southern (like so many Washington hirelings), was impressed by my credentials and also had a Southerner's genial garrulousness: "Have a nice stay, Reverend, you and the missus. What denomination you a preacher in?"

I was about to reply "Presbyterian," but he had begun to ramble on like a beagle hound softly barking down the ravines of godly fellowship. "Me, I'm a Baptist, fifteen years I've attended the Second Baptist Church of Washington, mighty fine preacher we've got there now, Reverend Wilcox, maybe you've heard of him. Comes from Fluvanna County, Virginia, where I was born and raised, though of course he's a much younger man." As I began to edge away, with Sophie clinging heavily to my arm, the clerk rang for the single sleepy Negro bellboy and handed me a card. "You like good seafood, Reverend? Try this restaurant down on the waterfront. It's called Herzog's. Best crab cakes in town." And when we approached the aged elevator with its stained pea-green doors, he persisted: "Entwistle. You wouldn't be related to the Entwistles down around Powhatan County, would you, Reverend?" I was back in the South.

The Hotel Congress breathed an air of *troisième classe*. The cubbyhole of a room we took for seven dollars was drab and stifling, and its exposure on a nondescript back street let in feeble light from the midday sun. Sophie, wobbling and desperate for sleep, plunged onto the bed even before the bellboy had deposited our bags on a rickety stand and accepted my twenty-five cents. I opened a window upon a ledge calcimine with pigeon droppings, and a warm October breeze suddenly freshened the room. Far off I could hear the clangor and muffled hoots of the trains at Union Station, while from some nearer source there came ruffles and flourishes, trumpets, cymbals, the piping self-esteem of a military band. A couple of flies made a bloated buzzing in the shadows near the ceiling.

I lay down next to Sophie on the bed, which had become unsprung in the middle, not so much allowing me as forcing me to roll toward her, as in the bosom of some shallow hammock, and on top of threadbare bedclothes that exuded a faint musky chlorinated smell either of laundry bleach or semen, perhaps both. Almost total exhaustion and worry over Sophie's condition had dampened the cruder urgencies of the desire I had continually felt for her, but the fragrance and slope of the bed—seminal, erotic, sagging with ten thousand fornications—and her simple touch and proximity made me stir, squirm, fidget, unable to sleep. I heard a distant bell chime the noon hour. Sophie slept against me with lips apart, her breath faintly odorous of whiskey. The low-cut silk dress she wore had allowed most of one breast to become exposed, causing me such an irresistible hunger to touch it that I did just that, stroking the blue-veined skin at first lightly with my fingertips, then beginning to press and fondle the creamy fullness more elaborately with palm and thumb. The seizure of pure lust which accompanied this tender manipulation was accompanied in turn by a twinge of shame; there was something sneaky, almost necrophiliac in the act, molesting even the epidermal surface of Sophie in the privacy of her drugged slumber—and so I stopped, withdrew my hand.

Still I could not sleep. My brain swam with images, sounds, voices, the past and the future trading places, sometimes commingled: Nathan's howl of rage, so cruel and mad that I had to thrust it from my thoughts; recently written scenes from my novel, the characters babbling their dialogue in my ear like actors on a stage; my father's voice on the telephone, generous, welcoming (was the old man not right? shouldn't I now make the South forever my home?); Sophie on the mossy shore of some imaginary pond or pool deep within the woods beyond "Five Elms' " spring fields, her lithe restored body glorious and long-legged in a Lastex bathing suit, our grinning elf of a first-born perched on her knee; that hideous gunshot swarming in my ear; sunsets, abandoned love-crazed midnights, magnanimous dawns, vanished children, triumph, grief, Mozart, rain, September green, repose, death. Love. The distant band, fading away on the "Colonel Bogey March," made me ache with a hungry nostalgia and I recalled the war years not so long before, when on leave from some camp in Carolina or Virginia, I would lie awake (womanless) in a hotel in this same city—one of the few American cities stalked by the revenants of history —and think of the streets below and how they must have looked only three-quarters of a century ago, in the midst of the most grief-blasted war that ever set brother to murdering brother, when the sidewalks teemed with soldiers in blue and with gamblers and whores, sharp swindlers in stovepipe hats, splashy Zouaves, hustling journalists, businessmen on the make, pretty flirts in flowered hats, shadowy Confederate spies, pickpockets and coffinmakers—these last ever-hurrying to their ceaseless labor, awaiting those tens of thousands of martyrs, mostly boys, who were being slaughtered on the desperate earth south of the Potomac and who lay piled up like cordwood thick in the bloody fields and woods just beyond that sleeping river. It was always strange to me—awesome even—that the cleanly modern capital of Washington, so impersonal and official in its expansive beauty, should be one of the few cities in the nation disturbed by authentic ghosts. The band vanished into the far distance, its brazen diminishing harmony soft, heartbreaking on my hearing like a lullaby. I slept.

When I awoke, Sophie was sitting crouched on the bed on her knees, looking down at me. I had slept like one in a coma, and I could tell from the alteration of light in the room—it had been like twilight even at noon but was now nearly dark—that several hours had passed. How long Sophie had been gazing down I could not tell, of course, but I had the uneasy feeling that it had been for quite a spell; the expression she wore was sweet, speculative, not without humor. There was the same wan haggardness in her face, and beneath her eyes there were dark patches, but she seemed revived and reasonably sober. She appeared to have recovered, at least for the moment, from that awful fit on the train. When I blinked up at her she said, in the exaggerated accent she sometimes affected in fun, "Well, Reverend En-*weestle,* deed you 'ave a good sleep?"

"Christ, Sophie," I said in vague panic, "what time is it? I slept like a corpse."

"I heard the bell ring in the church outside just now. I think it rang three o'clock."

I stirred drowsily, stroking her arm. "We've got to move out, as they used to say in the service. We can't hang around here all afternoon. I want you to see the White House, the Capitol, the Washington Monument. Also Ford's Theatre, you know, where Lincoln was shot. And the Lincoln Memorial. There's so many damned things. And we might think of getting a bite to eat . . ."

"I'm not at all hungry," she replied. "But I do want to see the city. I feel so much better after that sleep."

"You went out like a light," I said.

"So did you. When I woke up, there you were with your mouth open, snoring."

"You're kidding," I said, feeling a touch of real consternation. "I don't snore. I've never snored in my life! No one ever told me that before."

"It's because you haven't ever *slept* with anybody," she retorted in a teasing voice. And then she bent down and glued upon my lips a wonderful moist rubbery kiss, replete with a surprising tongue which made a quick playful foray in my mouth, then vanished. She returned to her propped-up position above me before I could even begin to respond, though my heart had begun a runaway thudding. "God, Sophie," I began, "don't do that unless—" I reached up and wiped my lips.

"Stingo," she interrupted me, "where are we going?"

A little puzzled, I said, "I just told you. We're going out to see the Washington sights. We'll go by the White House, we might even get a look at Harry Truman—"

"No, Stingo," she put in, more seriously now, "I mean, where are we *really* going? Last night after Nathan— Well, last night after he done what he done and we were packing our bags so fast, all you kept saying was 'We've got to get back home, back home!' Over and over you said 'Back home!' And I just followed you like this because I was so scared, and here we are together in this strange city and I really don't know why. Where are we truly going? What home?"

"Well, you know, Sophie, I told you. We're going to that farm I told you about down in southern Virginia. There's nothing much I can add to what I've already described to you about the place. It's a peanut farm mainly. I've never seen it, but my father has said it's very comfortable, with all the modern American conveniences. You know—washing machine, refrigerator, telephone, indoor plumbing, radio and everything. The works. After we get settled I'm sure we'll be able to drive up to Richmond and invest in a fine phonograph and lots of records. All the music we both love. There's a department store there called Miller and Rhoads that has an excellent record department, at least it did when I was going to school down in Middlesex—"

Now again she interrupted, saying gently but probingly, " 'Once we get settled'? What's going to happen then? How do you mean 'get settled,' Stingo dear?"

There was a huge and troubling vacuum created by this question which I could not possibly fill with an immediate answer, so freighted with ponderous meaning did I realize that the answer now had to be, and I gave a sort of foolish gulp and was silent for a long moment, aware of the blood flowing in rapid arrhythmic pulse at my temples, and of the desolate tomblike quietude of that shabby little room. Finally I said slowly, but with more ease and boldness than I thought I could ever muster, "Sophie, I'm in love with you. I want to marry you. I want us to live down on that farm together. I want to write my books there, maybe for the rest of my life, and I want you to be there with me and help me and raise a family." I hesitated for an instant, then said, "I need you very much. So very, very much. Is it too much to hope that you need me too?" Even as I pronounced these words I was aware that they had the exact timbre and quavering resonance of a proposal I had once seen and heard George Brent, of all the solemn assholes, make to Olivia de Havilland on the promenade deck of some preposterous Hollywood ocean liner, but having said what I had to say so decisively, I let the bathos pass, thinking in a flash that perhaps all first protestations of love had to sound like movie crud.

Sophie put her head down next to mine so that I felt her faintly fevered cheek, and she spoke into my ear with a muffled voice while I watched her silk-clad hips swaying lightly above me. "Oh, sweet Stingo, you're such a love. You've taken care of me in so many ways. I don't know what I'd do without you." A pause, her lips brushing my neck. "Do you know something, Stingo, I'm beyond thirty. What would you do with an old lady like me?"

"I'd manage," I said. "I'd manage somehow."

"You would want someone closer to your age to have children with, not someone like me. Besides . . ." She fell silent.

"Besides what?"

"Well, the doctors have said I must be very careful about having children after . . ." There was another silence.

"You mean after what you went through?"

"Yes. But it's not just that. Someday I'll just be old and ugly and you'll still be quite young and I won't blame you if you go chasing after all the young and pretty mademoiselles."

"Oh, Sophie, Sophie," I protested in a whisper, thinking despairingly: She hasn't said "I love you" in return. "Don't talk like that. You'll always be my—well, my . . ." I groped for a phrase that was properly tender, could say only, "Number One." It sounded hopelessly banal.

She sat erect again. "I do want to go with you to this farm. I so much want to see the South after all you've said and after reading Faulkner. Why don't we just go to this place for a little while and I could stay with you without us being married, and we could decide—"

"Sophie, Sophie," I put in, "I'd *love* that. There's nothing I'd like better. I'm not a maniac for marriage. But you don't realize what kind of people live down there. I mean, they're decent, generous, good-hearted Southern folks, but in a little country place like we'd be living in, it would be *impossible* not to be married. Jesus Christ, Sophie, it's full of *Christians!* Once it got around that we were living in sin, as it's called, those good Virginia people would cover us with tar and feathers and tie us to a long two-by-four and dump us over the Carolina line. God's truth, that's what would happen."

Sophie gave a small giggle. "Americans are so funny. I thought Poland was so very puritanical, but imagine . . ."

I realize now that it was the siren, or choir of sirens, and the drumming pandemonium that accompanied their shrieks, that ruptured the fragile membrane of Sophie's mood, which thanks in part to my own attentive ministrations had become peaceful, even luminous around the edges, if hardly sunny. City sirens even at a distance generate a hateful noise, almost always set loose in a soul-damaging, unnecessary frenzy. This one, rising from the narrow street only three floors directly below us, was amplified as if by canyon walls, bouncing from the grimy building opposite and entering the window next to us like an elongated snout, a solidified scream. It maddened the eardrum, pure sadistic torment made aural, and I jumped from the bed to pull the window down. At the end of the dark street a smudge of smoke plumed away from what looked like a warehouse, but the fire trucks just below, stalled by some nameless impediment, kept releasing skyward their unbelievable blasts.

I slammed down the window, which was of some relief, but it appeared not to have helped Sophie at all; she lay sprawled on the bed kicking her heels and with a pillow jammed down over her head. Recent city dwellers, we were both used to this common enough intrusion, but rarely so loud or so close. The pokey town of Washington had produced a racket I had never heard in New York. But slowly now the fire engines moved past their obstruction, the noise diminished, and I turned my attention to Sophie on the bed. She looked up at me. Where the horrible clamor had merely set my nerves ajangle, it had plainly lacerated her like some evil bullwhip. Her face was pink and contorted and she rolled over toward the wall, shuddering and once more in tears. I sat down beside her. I watched in silence for a long minute or so until finally her sobs gradually ceased and I heard her say, "I'm so sorry, Stingo. I don't seem to be able to control myself."

"You're doing fine," I said without much conviction.

For a while she was completely silent where she lay, contemplating the wall. At last she said, "Stingo, did you ever have dreams in your life that came back over and over again? Isn't it called *recurring* dreams?"

"Yes," I replied, recalling the dream I had as a young boy after my mother's death—her open coffin in the garden, her rain-damp ravaged face gazing at me in agony. "Yes," I said again, "I had one that came back constantly after my mother died."

"Do you think they have to do with parents? The one I've had all my life is about my father."

"It's strange," I said. "Maybe. I don't know. Mothers and fathers—they're at the core of one's own life somehow. Or they can be."

"When I was asleep a while ago I had this dream about my father that I've had many times. But I must have forgotten it when I woke up. Then that fire engine just now—that siren. It was awful but it had a strange musical sound. Could that be it—the music? It shocked me and made me think of the dream again."

"What was it about?"

"You see, it has to do with something that happened to me when I was a child."

"What was that, Sophie?"

"Well, first you would have to understand something, before the dream. It was when I was eleven, like you. It was in the summer when we spent vacations in the Dolomites, like I've already told you. You remember I told you my father each summer rented a chalet there above Bolzano—in a little village called Oberbozen, which was German-speaking, of course. There was a small colony of Polish people there, professors from Cracow and Warsaw and some Polish—well, I suppose you would call them Polish aristocrats, at least they had money. I remember one of the professors was the famous anthropologist Bronislaw Malinowski. My father tried to cultivate Malinowski, but Malinowski detested my father. Once, in Cracow, I overheard a grownup say that Professor Malinowski thought my father, Professor Biegański, was a parvenu and hopelessly vulgar. Anyway, there was a rich Polish woman at Oberbozen named Princess Czartoryska, whom my father had come to know well, and he saw quite a bit of her during these summers. She was from a very old, very noble Polish family and my father liked her because she was rich and, well, she shared his feelings about Jews.

"This was the time of Pilsudski, you see, when the Polish Jews were protected and having, I guess you would call, a fairly decent life, and my father and Princess Czartoryska would get together and talk about the Jewish problem and the necessity of getting rid of the Jews someday. It is strange, you know, Stingo, because my father when he was in Cracow was always discreet about talking about Jews and his hatred of them in front of me or my mother or anyone like that. At least when I was a child. But in Italy, you see, at Oberbozen with Princess Czartoryska it was different. She was an eighty-year-old woman who always wore fine long gowns even in the middle of the summer, and wore jewelry—she had an immense emerald brooch, I remember—and she and my father would have tea in her very elegant *Sennhütte*, chalet, that is, and talk about the Jews. They always spoke in German. She had a beautiful Bernese mountain dog and I would play with the dog and overhear their conversation, almost always about the Jews. About sending them off somewhere, all of them, getting rid of them. The Princess even wanted to establish a fund for it. They were always talking about islands—Ceylon and Sumatra and Cuba but mostly Madagascar, where they would send the Jews. I would half listen while I played some game with Princess Czartoryska's little grandson, who was English, or played with the big dog or listened to the music on this phonograph. It was the music, you see, Stingo, that has to do with my dream."

Sophie fell silent again, and she pressed her fingers against her closed eyes. Something quickened in the monotone of her voice. She turned to me, as if she had become diverted from her remembrance. "We *will* have music where we're going, then, Stingo. I wouldn't be able to last long without music."

"Well, I'll be honest, Sophie. Out in the sticks—outside New York, that is—there's nothing on the radio. No WQXR, no WNYC. Only Milton Cross and the Metropolitan Opera on Saturday afternoon. The rest is hillbilly. Some of it's terrific. Maybe I'll make you a Roy Acuff fan. But like I say, the first thing we'll do after we move in is to buy a record player and records—"

"I've been so spoiled," she put in, "after all the music Nathan bought me. But it's my blood, my life's blood, you know, and I can't help it." She paused, once again collecting the strands of her memory. Then she said, "Princess Czartoryska had a phonograph. It was one of those early machines, not very good, but it was the first one I had ever seen or heard. Strange, isn't it, this old Polish Jew-hater with her love of music. She had a lot of records and it almost drove me mad with pleasure when she'd put them on for our benefit—my mother and my father and me and maybe some other guests—and we'd listen to these recordings. Most of them were arias from Italian and French operas—Verdi and Rossini and Gounod—but there was one record that I remember just made me nearly swoon, I loved it so. It must have been a rare and precious record. It's hard to believe now, because it was very old and filled with noise, but I just adored it. It was Madame Schumann-Heink singing Brahms *Lieder*. On one side there was 'Der Schmied,' I remember, and on the other was 'Von ewige Liebe,' and when I first heard it I sat there in a trance listening to that wonderful voice coming through all those scratches, thinking all the while that it was the most gorgeous singing I had ever heard, that it was an angel come down to earth. Strange, I heard those two songs only once during all the times I went with my father to visit the Princess. I longed to hear them again. Oh God, I felt I would do almost anything—do something very naughty, even—to hear them once more, and I was just so hungry to ask that they be played again, but I was too shy, and besides, my father would have punished me if I had ever been so . . . so bold . . .

"So in the dream that has returned to me over and over I see Princess Czartoryska in her handsome gown go to the phonograph and she turns and always says, as if she were talking to me, 'Would you like to hear the Brahms *Lieder?*' And I always try to say yes. But just before I can say anything my father interrupts. He is standing next to the Princess and he is looking directly at me, and he says, 'Please don't play that music for the child. She is much too stupid to understand.' And then I wake up with this pain . . . Only this time it was even worse, Stingo. Because in the dream I had just now he seemed to be talking to the Princess not about the music but about . . ." Sophie hesitated, then murmured, "About my death. He wanted me to die, I think."

I turned away from Sophie. I walked the few steps to the window, filled with a disquietude and unhappiness that was like a deep, twisting, visceral pain. A faint and bitter odor of combustion had seeped into the room, but despite this I opened the window and saw where smoke drifted down the street in fragile bluish veils. In the distance over the burning building a cloud rose in dingy turbulence but I saw no flame. The stench, growing stronger, was of scorched paint or tar or varnish mingled with hot rubber.

More sirens sounded, but this time dimly, from the opposite direction, and I glimpsed a plume of water that gushed skyward toward hidden windows, met some hidden inferno and then evaporated in a nimbus of steam. Along the sidewalks below gawkers in shirt sleeves sidled tentatively toward the fire, and I saw two policemen begin to block the street with wooden barricades. There was no threat to the hotel, or to us, but I found myself shivering with anxiety.

Just as I turned back to Sophie, she looked up at me from the bed and said, "Stingo, I must tell you something now that I've never told anyone before. Never before."

"Tell me, then."

"Without knowing this, you wouldn't understood anything about me at all. And I realize I must tell someone at last."

"Tell me, Sophie."

"You must get me a drink first."

With no hesitation I went to her suitcase and plucked from the slippery jumble of linen and silk the second pint bottle of whiskey which I knew she had hidden there. Sophie, get drunk, I thought, you earned it. Then I walked to the tiny bathroom and half filled a sickly-green plastic glass with water and brought it to the bed. Sophie poured whiskey into the glass until it was full.

"Do you want some?" she said.

I shook my head and returned to the window, inhaling the brown chemical, acrid breaths of the distant blaze.

"On the day I arrived at Auschwitz," I heard her say behind me, "it was beautiful. The forsythia was in bloom."

I was eating bananas in Raleigh, North Carolina, I thought, thinking this not for the first time since I had known Sophie, yet perhaps for the first time in my life aware of the meaning of the Absurd, and its conclusive, unrevocable horror.

"But you see, Stingo, in Warsaw one night that winter Wanda had foretold her own death and also my death and the death of my children."

I don't recall precisely when, during Sophie's description of those happenings, the Reverend Entwistle began to hear himself whisper, "Oh God, oh my God." But I did seem to be aware, during the time of the telling of her story, while the smoke churned up over the nearby roofs and the fire erupted at last toward the sky in fierce incandescence, that those words which had commenced in pious Presbyterian entreaty became finally meaningless. By which I mean that the "Oh God" or "Oh my God" or even "Jesus Christ" that were whispered again and again were as empty as any idiot's dream of God, or the idea that there could be such a Thing.

"I sometimes got to think that everything bad on earth, every evil that was ever invented had to do with my father. That winter in Warsaw, I didn't feel any guilt about my father and what he had written. But I did feel often this terrible *shame,* which is not the same as guilt. Shame is a dirty feeling that is even more hard to take than guilt, and I could barely live with the idea that my father's dreams were coming true right in front of my eyes. I got to know a lot of other things because I was living with Wanda, or very close to her. She got so much information about what was going on everywhere, and I knew already about how they were transporting thousands of Jews to Treblinka and Auschwitz. At first it was thought that they were just being sent for labor, but the Resistance had good intelligence and pretty soon we knew the truth, knew about the gassings and cremations and everything. It was what my father had wanted—and it made me ill.

"When I went to my job at the tar-paper factory I would go on foot or sometimes by streetcar past the ghetto. The Germans had not bled dry the ghetto yet, but they were in the process. Often I could see these lines of Jews with their arms upraised being pushed along like cattle, the Nazis pointing guns at them. The Jews looked so *gray* and helpless; once I had to get off the streetcar and get sick. And all through this my father seemed to . . . *authorize* this horror, not only authorize it but *create* it in some way. I couldn't keep it bottled up any longer and I knew I had to tell someone. No one in Warsaw knew much about my background, I was living under my married name. I decided to tell Wanda about this . . . about this badness.

"And yet . . . and yet, you know, Stingo, I had to admit something else to myself. And this was that I was fascinated by this unbelievable thing that was happening to the

Jews. I couldn't put my finger on it, this feeling. It was not at all pleasure. It was the opposite, if anything—sickening. And yet when I'd walk past the ghetto at a distance I would stop and really be *entranced* by certain sights, by seeing them rounding up the Jews. And I knew then the reason for this fascination, and it stunned me. I could barely breathe with the knowledge. It was just that I suddenly knew that as long as the Germans could use up all this incredible energy destroying the Jews—superhuman energy, really—I was safe. No, not really safe, but *safer*. Bad as things were, we were oh so much safer than these trapped, helpless Jews. And so as long as the Germans were draining off so much power destroying the Jews, I felt safer for myself and for Jan and Eva. And even Wanda and Jozef, with all the dangerous things they were doing. But this just made me feel more ashamed, and so, on this night I am talking about, I decided to tell Wanda.

"We were finishing this very poor meal, I remember—beans and turnip soup and a kind of joke sausage. We had been talking about all the music we'd missed hearing. I had delayed all during the dinner to say what I really wanted, then I finally got the courage, saying, 'Wanda, did you ever hear the name Bigański? Zbigniew Bigański?'

"Wanda's eyes looked vacant for a moment. 'Oh yes, you mean the Fascist professor from Cracow. He was well known for a while before the war. He made hysterical speeches here in the city against the Jews. I had forgotten all about him. I wonder what ever happened to him. He's probably working for the Germans.'

" 'He's dead,' I said. 'He was my father.'

"I could see Wanda shiver. It was so cold outside and inside. There was this spitting sound of sleet against the window. The children were in bed in the next room. I'd put them there because I'd run out of fuel, coal or wood, in my own apartment downstairs, and Wanda had at least a big comforter on the bed to keep them warm. I kept looking at Wanda, but there was no emotion on her face. She said after a bit, 'So he was your father. It must have been strange to have had such a man for a father. What was he like?'

"I was surprised at this reaction, she seemed to take it

so calmly, so naturally. I mean, of all the people in the Resistance in Warsaw, she was the one who maybe done the most to help the Jews—or to *try* to help the Jews, it was so difficult. I suppose you could call it her specialty, trying to get aid to the ghetto. She felt, too, that anyone who betrayed the Jews, or a single Jew, was betraying Poland. It was Wanda who started Jozef on this way of murdering Poles who betrayed Jews. She was so *militant* about this, so dedicated, a socialist. But she didn't seem to be at all shocked or anything that my father had been who he had been, and she obviously didn't feel that I was—well, contaminated. I said, 'I find it very difficult to talk about him.' And she said back to me very gently, 'Well, don't, dear heart. I don't care who your father was. You can't be blamed for his miserable sins.'

"Then I said, 'It's so strange, you know. He was killed by the Germans inside the Reich. At Sachsenhausen.'

"But even this—well, even this *irony* didn't seem to impress her. She just blinked and ran her hand through her hair. Her hair was red and wispy, with no gleam in it at all—so drab and wispy because of the bad food. She just said, 'He must have been one of those faculty members at the Jagiellonian who caught it right after the occupation began.'

"I said, 'Yes, and my husband too. I never told you about that. He was a disciple of my father's. I hated him. I've lied to you. I hope you'll forgive me for once telling you that he died fighting during the invasion.'

"And I started to finish what I was saying—this apology—but Wanda cut me off. She lit a cigarette, I remember she smoked like a fiend whenever she could get cigarettes. And she said, 'Zosia sweetheart, it don't matter. For God's sake, do you think I care what they were? It's *you* that matters. Your husband could have been a gorilla and your father Joseph Goebbels and you'd still be my dearest friend.' She went to the window then and pulled down the blind. She only did this when there was some danger coming. The apartment was five floors up, but it was in this building that stuck up out of some bombed-out lots and anything that went on could perhaps be spotted by the Germans. So Wanda never took any chances. I remember she looked at her watch and said, 'We're going to have visitors in a minute. Two Jewish leaders from the ghetto. They're coming to collect a bundle of pistols.'

"I remember thinking: Christ in heaven! My heart always gave a terrible jump and I'd feel this nausea go through me whenever Wanda mentioned guns, or secret rendezvous, or anything having to do with danger or the possibility of being ambushed by the Germans. To get caught helping Jews meant death, you know. I would get all clammy and weak—oh, I was such a coward! I would hope Wanda had not noticed these symptoms, and whenever I had them I would sometimes wonder if cowardice wasn't another bad thing I inherited from my father. But Wanda was saying, 'I've heard of one of these Jews through the grapevine. He's supposed to be a very brave type, very competent. He's desperate, though. There's some resistance now, but it's disorganized. He sent a message to our group saying that there's bound to be a full-scale revolt in the ghetto soon. We've had some dealings with others, but this man's a powerhouse—a mover. I think his name is Feldshon.'

"We waited for a while for the two Jews, but they didn't come. Wanda told me the guns were hidden in the basement of the building. I went into the bedroom to look at the children. Even in the bedroom the air was so cold it was like a knife, and there was this little cloud of vapor over Jan's and Eva's heads. I could hear the wind whistling through the cracks around the window. But this comforter was a huge old Polish comforter filled with goose down and it protected the children in place of heating. I remember praying, though, that I would be able to get some coal or wood for my own place the next day. Outside the window it was so incredibly black, a whole city in darkness. I was just shuddering with the cold. That evening Eva had had a cold and a very bad earache and she had taken a long time to go to sleep. She had been in such pain. But Wanda had found some aspirin, which was very scarce—Wanda could find almost anything—and Eva was asleep. I gave another prayer that in the morning her infection would be gone, and the pain. Then I heard a knock at the door and I went back to the living room.

"I don't remember the other Jew too well—he didn't say much—but I do remember Feldshon. He was stocky and sandy-haired and in, I guess, his mid-forties and had these piercing, intelligent eyes. They pierced through you even though they came through these thick glasses, and I remember one lens was cracked and had been glued back. I remember how angry he seemed, beneath the politeness. He just seemed to be seething with anger and resentment, even though his manners were okay. He said right away to Wanda, 'I won't be able to pay you now, to reimburse you right away for the weapons.' I couldn't understand his Polish too well, it was rather, you know, groping and difficult. 'Certainly I'll be able to pay you soon,' he said in this clumsy, angry voice, 'but not now.'

"Wanda told him and the other Jew to sit down, and began speaking in German. What she first said was very crude. 'Your accent is German. You may talk German with us, or Yiddish if you'd care to—'

"But he interrupted her in this angry, irritated way, in perfect German, 'I don't need to speak Yiddish! I was speaking German before you were born—'

"Then Wanda very quickly interrupted *him*. 'There's no need for elaborate explanations. Speak German. My friend and I both speak German. You won't be required to pay us for weapons at any time, particularly not now. These were stolen from the SS, and we wouldn't want your money under such circumstances. We can use funds, though. We'll talk about money some other time.' We sat down. She sat next to Feldshon underneath this dim bulb. The light was yellow and pulsing, we never knew how long it would last. She offered Feldshon and the other Jew cigarettes, which they took. She said, 'They're Yugoslav cigarettes, also stolen from the Germans. This light may go out at any minute now, so let's talk business. But first I want to know something. What's your background, Feldshon? I want to know whom I'm dealing with and I have the right to know. So spit it out. We might be doing business for some time.'

"It was remarkable, you know, this way that Wanda had, this absolutely direct way she had of dealing with people—anybody, strangers. It was almost— The word would be *brazen*, I guess, and she was like a tough man that way, but there was enough in her that was young and female, a certain softness too, that allowed her to get by with it. I remember looking at her. She looked very... *haggard,* I guess you would say. She hadn't had any sleep for two nights, always working, moving, always in some danger. She spent much time working on an underground newspaper; this was so dangerous. I think I told you, she was not really beautiful—she had this milky-pale freckled face with a large jaw—but there was such magnetism in her that it transformed her, made her strangely attractive. I kept looking at her—her face was as harsh and impatient as the Jew's—and this intensity was just very remarkable to see. Hypnotic.

"Feldshon said, 'I was born in Bydgoszcz, but my parents took me to Germany when I was a small child.' Then his voice became angry and sarcastic: 'That's the reason for my poor Polish. I confess that some of us speak it as little as possible in the ghetto. It would be pleasant to speak a language other than that of an oppressor. Tibetan? Eskimo?' Then he said more softly, 'Pardon the diversion. I grew up in Hamburg and was educated there. I was one of the first students at the new university. Later I became a teacher in a gymnasium. In Würzburg. I taught French and English literature. I was teaching there when I was arrested. When it was discovered that I was born in Poland, I was deported here, in 1938, with my wife and daughter, along with quite a few other Jews of Polish birth.' He stopped, then said bitterly, 'We escaped the Nazis and now they're hammering down the walls. But whom should I fear more, the Nazis or the Poles—the Poles whom I suppose I should consider my compatriots? At least I know what the Nazis are capable of.'

"Wanda ignored this. She began talking about the guns. She said that at the moment they were in the basement of the building, wrapped in heavy paper. There was also a box of ammunition. She looked at her watch and said that in exactly fifteen minutes two Home Army members would be in the basement ready to transfer the boxes to the hallway. There was a prearranged signal. When she heard it she said she would give a sign to Feldshon and the other Jew. They would leave the apartment immediately and go down the stairs to the hallway, where the parcels would be waiting. Then they would get out of the building as fast as possible. I remember she said she wanted to point one thing out. One of the pistols—they were Lugers, I remember—had a broken firing pin or a broken something or other, but she would try to get a replacement as soon as she was able.

"Feldshon then said, 'There's one thing you haven't told us. How many weapons are there?'

"Wanda looked at him. 'I thought you had been told. Three Luger automatics.'

"This face of Feldshon went white, it actually went white. 'I can't believe it,' he said in a whisper. 'I was told that there would be a dozen pistols, perhaps fifteen. Also some grenades. I can't believe it!' I could see how filled with rage he was, but it was also despair. He shook his head. 'Three Lugers, one with a broken firing pin. My God!'

"Wanda said in this very businesslike way—trying to control her own feelings, I could tell, 'It's the best we could do at the moment. We are going to try to get more. I think we will. There are four hundred rounds of ammunition. You'll need more and we'll try to get that too.'

"Feldshon suddenly said in this softer voice, a little apologetic, 'You'll forgive my reaction, I hope. I had just been led to believe more, and it's a disappointment. Also, earlier today I was trying to deal with another partisan group, trying to see whether we might be confident of help.' And he paused and looked at Wanda with this furious expression. 'It was horrible—it was unbelievable! Drunken bastards! They actually laughed at us, they sneered at us—and they enjoyed laughing and sneering. They called us kikes! These were *Poles*.'

"Wanda asked in this matter-of-fact way, 'Who were these people?'

" 'The O.N.R. they call themselves. But I had the same difficulty yesterday with another Polish Resistance group.' He looked at Wanda, filled with this rage and despair, and said, 'Three pistols I get, and sneers and laughter, to hold off twenty thousand Nazi troops. In the name of God, what is *happening?*'

"Wanda was getting very agitated at Feldshon, I could tell, just enraged at everything—at *life*. 'The O.N.R., that bunch of collaborators. Fanatics, Fascists. As a Jew, you could have received more sympathy from the Ukrainians or Hans Frank. But let me give you a further word of warning. The Communists are just as bad. Worse. If you ever meet the Red partisans under General Korczynski, you risk being shot on sight.'

"'It's unspeakable!' Feldshon said. 'I'm grateful for the three pistols, but can't you see how it makes me want to laugh? There is something beyond belief going on here! Did you ever read *Lord Jim?* About the officer who deserts the sinking ship, taking to a lifeboat while the helpless passengers are left to their fate? Forgive me this reference, but I can't help seeing the same thing here. We are being left to drown by our countrymen!'

"I saw Wanda get up and put her fingertips on the table and lean a little toward Feldshon. Again she was trying to control herself, but I could tell it was hard. She looked so pale and exhausted. And she began to talk in this desperate voice. 'Feldshon, you're either stupid or naïve or both. It seems doubtful that someone who appreciates Conrad is stupid, so you must be naïve. Surely you haven't forgotten the simple fact that Poland is an *anti-Semitic country*. You yourself just used the word "oppressor." Living in a nation which practically invented anti-Semitism, living in a ghetto, which we Poles originated, how could you *expect* any help from your compatriots? How could you expect anything except from a few of us who for whatever reason—idealism, moral conviction, simple human solidarity, whatever—want to do what we can to save some of your lives? My God, Feldshon, your parents probably left Poland with you to get Jew-haters off their backs. Poor creatures, they certainly couldn't have known that that warm, assimilating, Jew-loving, humanistic bosom of Germany would turn to fire and ice and cast you out. They couldn't have known that when you returned to Poland, there would be the same Jew-haters waiting for you and your wife and daughter, ready to grind all of you into the dust. This is a cruel country, Feldshon. It has grown so cruel over the years because it has so many times tasted *defeat*. Despite the *Dreck* that's been written in the Gospels, adversity produces not understanding and compassion, but cruelty. And defeated people like the Poles know how to be supremely cruel to other people who have set themselves apart, like you Jews. I'm surprised you got away from that O.N.R. bunch with just being called a kike!' She stopped for a second, then said, 'Do you find it strange, then, that I still love this country more than I care to say—more than life itself—

and that if I had to I would willingly die for it ten minutes from now?'

"Feldshon glared back at Wanda and said, 'I'm afraid I want to, but of course I can't, being ready to die myself.'

"I was getting worried about Wanda. I had never seen her so tired, I guess you would say *unstrung*. She had been working so hard, eating so little, going without sleep. Her voice would crack every now and then, and I saw her fingers tremble where she had them pressed against the table. She closed her eyes, clenched them shut, and shivered, swaying a little. I thought she might faint. Then she opened her eyes and spoke again. Her voice was hoarse and strained, filled with such grief. 'You were speaking of *Lord Jim,* a book I happen to know. I think your comparison is a good one, but you somehow have forgotten the ending. I think you've forgotten how in the end the hero redeems himself for his betrayal, redeems himself through his own death. His own suffering and death. Is it too much to think that some of us Poles will be able to redeem the betrayal of you Jews by our countrymen? Even if our struggle doesn't save you? No matter. Whether it does or doesn't save you, I for one will be satisfied that we tried—through our suffering, and probably even our own deaths.'

"After a moment Wanda said, 'I haven't wanted to offend you, Feldshon. You're a brave man, that's plain. You've risked your life getting here tonight. I know what your ordeal is. I've known ever since last summer when I saw the first photographs smuggled out of Treblinka. I was one of the first to see them, and like everyone else, I didn't believe them at first. I believe them now. Your ordeal can't be surpassed in horror. Every time I go near the ghetto I am reminded of rats in a barrel being shot at by a madman with a machine gun. That's how I see your helplessness. But we Poles are helpless in our own way. We have more freedom than you Jews have—much more, more freedom of movement, more freedom from immediate danger—but we're still under daily siege. Instead of being like rats in a barrel, we're like rats in a burning building. We can move away from the flame, find cool spots, get down in the basement where it's safe. A tiny few can even escape from the building. Every day many of us are burned alive, but it's a big building and we are also saved by our very numbers. The fire can't get us all, and then someday—maybe—the fire is going to burn out. If it does, there'll be plenty of survivors. But the barrel—almost none of the rats in the barrel will live.' Wanda took a deep breath and looked directly at Feldshon. 'But let me ask you, Feldshon. How much concern can you expect the terrified rats in the building to have for the rats outside in the barrel—the rats whom they've never felt any kinship with, anyway?'

"Feldshon just looked at Wanda. He hadn't taken his eyes off her in minutes. He didn't say anything.

"Wanda looked at her watch then. 'In exactly four minutes we'll hear a whistle. That means the two of you get out of here and downstairs. The parcels will be waiting at the door.' Then, after saying that, she went on, 'Three days ago I was negotiating in the ghetto with one of your compatriots. I won't mention his name, no need for that. I'll just say that he's a leader of one of those factions which violently opposes you and your own group. I think he's a poet or a novelist. I liked him, all right, but I couldn't stand a certain thing he said. It sounded so pretentious, this way he was speaking of Jews. He used the phrase "our precious heritage of suffering." '

"At this point Feldshon broke in and said something that made us all laugh a little. Even Wanda smiled. He said, 'That could only be Lewental. Moses Lewental. Such *Schmalz*.'

"But then Wanda said, 'I despise the idea of suffering being precious. In this war everyone suffers—Jews, Poles, Gypsies, Russians, Czechs, Yugoslavs, all the others. Everyone's a victim. The Jews are also the victims of victims, that's the main difference. But none of the suffering is precious and all die shitty deaths. Before you go I want to show you some photographs. I was carrying them in my pocket when I was speaking to Lewental. I had just gotten hold of them. I wanted to show them to him, but for some reason I didn't. I'll show them to you.'

"Just then the light went out, the little bulb simply flickered out. I felt this stab of fear in the middle of my heart. Sometimes it was just the electricity failing. Other times I knew that when the Germans laid an ambush they would stop the power to a building so they could trap people in their searchlights. We all stayed still for a moment. There was some light in a glow from the little fireplace. Then when Wanda was sure it was just a light failure she got a candle and lit it. I was still shivering, afraid, when Wanda threw several snapshots on the table beneath the candle and said, 'Look at this.'

"We all bent forward to look. At first I couldn't make out what it was, just a jumble of sticks—a great mass of sticks like small tree limbs. Then I saw what it was—this unbearable sight, a boxcar full of dead children, scores of them, maybe a hundred, all of them in these stiff and jumbled positions that could only come from being frozen to death. The other photographs were the same—other boxcars with scores of children, all stiff and frozen.

" 'These are not Jewish children,' Wanda said, 'these are little Polish children, none of them over twelve years old. They're some of the little rats who didn't make it in the burning building. These pictures were taken by Home Army members who broke into these boxcars on a siding somewhere between Zamość and Lublin. There are several hundred in these pictures, from one train alone. There were other trains that were put on sidings where the children either starved or froze to death, or both. This is just a sample. The others who died number in the thousands.'

"No one spoke. I could just hear all of us breathing, but no one spoke. Finally Wanda began to talk, and for the first time her voice was truly choked and unsteady—you could almost feel the exhaustion in it, and the grief. 'We still don't know exactly where these children came from but we think we know who they are. It is believed that they are the rejected ones from the Germanization program, the Lebensborn program. We think they came from the region around Zamość. I've been told that they were among the thousands who were taken from their parents but not considered racially suitable and so consigned for disposal—meaning extermination—at Maidanek or Auschwitz. But they didn't get there. In due time the train, like a lot of others, was diverted onto sidings where the children were allowed to die in the condition you see here. Others starved to death, still more suffocated in hermetically sealed cars. Thirty thousand Polish children have disappeared from the Zamość region alone. Thousands and thousands of these have died. This is mass murder too,

Feldshon.' She ran her hands over her eyes, then said, 'I was going to tell you of the adults, the thousands of innocent men and women slaughtered in Zamość alone. But I won't. I'm very tired, suddenly I feel very dizzy. These children are enough.'

"Wanda was swaying a little. I remember catching her by the elbow and trying to pull her gently down, make her sit down. But she kept talking in the candlelight, in this flat monotonous voice now, as in a trance. 'The Nazis hate you the most, Feldshon, and you will suffer the most by far, but they're not going to stop with the Jews. Do you think when they finish with you Jews they're going to dust off their hands and stop murdering and make their peace with the world? You underestimate their evil if you have such a delusion. Because once they finish you off they're going to come and get me. Even though I'm half German. I imagine they will not let me off easy, before the end. Then they're going to seize my pretty blond friend here and do with her what they've done to you. At the same time they will not spare her children, any more than they spared these little frozen ones you see right here.' "

In the darkening shoebox of a room in Washington, D.C., Sophie and I, almost without our being aware of it, had exchanged places, so that it was I who lay on the bed staring up at the ceiling while she stood by the window where I had first placed myself, brooding over the distant fire. She fell silent for a while and I could see the side of her face, which was deep in remembrance, her gaze resting on the smoky horizon. Amid the silence I heard the clucking and chortling of the pigeons on the ledge outside, a far-off blurred commotion where men struggled with the blaze. The church bell struck again: it was four.

At last Sophie spoke again. "At Auschwitz the next year, as I told you, they seized Wanda and tortured her and they hung her up on a hook and let her strangle to death. After I heard that, I would think about her in so many ways, but mainly I would remember her on that night in Warsaw. I would see her in my mind after Feldshon and the other Jew had left to get the guns, sitting at the table with her face buried in her arms, completely worn-out and weeping. It's strange, I never saw her cry before. I think she always considered it a weakness. But I remember leaning over next to her with my hand on her shoulder, watching her weep. She was so young, only my age. So brave.

"She was a lesbian, Stingo. It don't matter any more what she was, it didn't matter then. But I thought you might want to know, after me telling you so much about everything else. We slept together once or twice—I might as well tell you that too—but it didn't mean much to either of us, I think. She knew deep down that I—well, I didn't really respond to her that way and so she never pressed me to go on. Never got angry or anything. I loved her, though, because she was better than me, and so incredibly brave.

"So as I say, she foretold her own death, and my death, and the death of my children. She went to sleep with her head in her arms at the table. I didn't want to disturb her right then, and I thought of what she had said about the children, and the pictures of those little frozen bodies—I was suddenly haunted and terrified in a way I'd never been before, even in the middle of the gloom that I'd experienced so many times, gloom like the taste of death. I went into the room where my children were sleeping. I was so overcome by what Wanda had said that I did something that I knew I shouldn't do even as I was doing it—waking Jan and Eva and taking them both up in my arms next to me. So heavy they both were, waking and moaning and whispering, yet strangely light, I guess, because of my frantic desire to hold them both in my arms. And being filled with terror and despair over Wanda's words about the future, knowing the truth of her words and not being able to deal with anything so monstrous, so immense.

"Beyond the window it was cold and black, no lights in Warsaw, a city cold and black beyond description, with nothing there except the darkness and freezing sleet in it, and the wind. I remember I opened the window and let in the ice and the wind. I can't tell you how close I came to hurling myself with my children out into that darkness just then—or how many times since then I've cursed myself for not doing it."

The car of the train which conveyed Sophie and her children and Wanda to Auschwitz (together with a mixed bag of Resistance members and other Poles trapped in the most recent roundup) was an unusual one. It was neither a boxcar nor the livestock car which the Germans normally employed in their transports. Amazing to say, it was an ancient but still serviceable wagons-lits carriage complete with carpeted aisle, compartments, lavatories and small lozenge-shaped metallic signs in Polish, French, Russian and German at each window, admonishing the passengers not to lean out. From its fittings—its badly worn but still comfortable seats, the ornate and now tarnished chandeliers—Sophie could tell that the venerable coach had once carried people first-class; save for a singular difference, it might have been one of those cars of her girlhood in which her father—always the stylish voyager—had taken the family to Vienna or Bozen or Berlin.

The difference—so ominous and oppressive as to make her gasp when she saw it—was that all the windows were securely boarded up. Another difference was that into each compartment made for six or eight persons the Germans had jammed as many as fifteen or sixteen bodies, together with whatever luggage had been brought along. Awash in dim light, thus compressed, half a dozen or more prisoners of both sexes stood upright or partly upright in the meager foot space, clinging together for support against the incessantly braking and accelerating movement of the train and constantly plunging into the laps of the seated ones. One or two quick-witted Resistance leaders took command. A scheme was worked out whereby sitters and standees regularly alternated positions; this helped, but nothing could help the effect of the stifling body heat of so many squeezed-together human beings, or the sour and fetid odor that persisted during the trip. Not quite torture, it was a limbo of desolating discomfort. Jan and Eva were the only children in the compartment; they took turns sitting on Sophie's lap and the laps of others. At least one person vomited in the nearly lightless cell, and it was a muscular and desperate struggle to wriggle out of the compartment and down the jammed aisle to one of the toilets. "Better a boxcar," Sophie remembered someone groaning, "at least you could stretch out." But curiously, by the standards of those other hell-destined transports crisscrossing Europe at that time, stalled and sidetracked and delayed at a thousand inert junctures of space and time, her trip was not inordinately long: what should have been a morning's journey, from six o'clock until noon, required not days but a mere thirty hours.

Possibly because (as she had confessed to me over and over again) so much of her behavior had always been governed by wishful thinking, she had drawn a certain amount of comfort from the fact that the Germans had thrust her and her fellow prisoners aboard this novel means of transport. It was by now common knowledge that the Nazis used railroad cars meant for freight and animals to ship people to the camps. Thus, once aboard with Jan and Eva, she swiftly rejected the logical idea which flitted through her head that her captors were using this classy if threadbare car simply because it was expedient and available (the makeshift boarded windows should have been evidence of that). Instead, she hit upon a somewhat more soothing notion that these almost lounge-like facilities, where comfortable Poles and rich tourists had nodded and drowsed in prewar days, now indicated special privilege, now meant that she would be treated rather better than the 1,800 Jews from Malkinia in the forward part of the train, bottled up tight in their black cattle wagons where they had been sealed for several days. As it turned out, this was as foolish and as fanciful (and as ignoble, really) as the idea she had formed about the ghetto: that the mere presence of the Jews, and the preoccupation the Nazis had with their extermination, would somehow benefit her own security. And the safety of Jan and Eva.

The name Oświęcim—Auschwitz—which had at first murmured its way through the compartment made her weak with fear, but she had no doubt whatever that that was where the train was going. A minuscule sliver of light, catching her eye, drew her attention to a tiny crack in the plywood board across the window, and during the first hour of the journey she was able to see enough by the dawn's glow to tell their direction: south. Due south past the country villages that crowd around Warsaw in place of the usual suburban outskirts, due south past greening fields and copses crowded with birch trees, south in the direction of Cracow. Only Auschwitz, of all their plausible destinations, lay south, and she recalled the despair she felt when with her own eyes she verified where they were going. The reputation of Auschwitz was ominous, vile, terrifying.

Although in the Gestapo prison rumors had tended to support Auschwitz as the place where they would eventually be shipped, she had hoped incessantly and prayed for a labor camp in Germany, where so many Poles had been transported and where, according to other rumor, conditions were less brutal, less harsh. But as Auschwitz loomed more and more inevitably and now, on the train, made itself inescapable, Sophie was smothered by the realization that she was victim of punishment by association, retribution through chance concurrence. She kept saying to herself: I don't belong here. If she had not had the misfortune of being taken prisoner at the same time as so many of the Home Army members (a stroke of bad luck further complicated by her connection with Wanda, and their common dwelling place, even though she had not lifted a finger to help the Resistance), she might have been adjudged guilty of the serious crime of meat smuggling but not of the infinitely more grave crime of subversion, and hence might not be headed for a destination so forbiddingly malign. But among other ironies, she realized, was this one: she had not been *judged* guilty of anything, merely interrogated and forgotten. She had then been thrown in haphazardly among these partisans, where she was victim less of any specific retributive justice than of a general rage—a kind of berserk lust for complete domination and oppression which seized the Nazis whenever they scored a win over the Resistance, and which this time had even extended to the several hundred bedraggled Poles ensnared in that last savage roundup.

Certain things about the trip she remembered with utter clarity. The stench, the airlessness, the endless shifting of positions—stand up, sit down, stand up again. At the moment of a sudden stop a box toppling down on her head, not stunning her, not hurting too much, but raising an egg-size bulge at the top of her skull. The view outside the crack, where spring sunlight darkened into drizzling rain: through the film of rain, birch trees still tormented by the past winter's crushing snowfall, bent into shapes of white parabolic arches, strongbows, catapults, beautiful broken skeletons, whips. Lemon dots of forsythia everywhere. Delicate green fields blending into distant forests of spruce and larch and pine. Sunshine again. Jan's books, which he tried to read in the feeble light as he sat on her lap: *The Swiss Family Robinson* in German; Polish editions of *White Fang* and *Penrod and Sam*. Eva's two possessions, which she refused to park in the luggage rack but clutched fiercely as if any moment they might be wrested from her hands: the flute in its leather case and her *mís*—the one-eared, one-eyed teddy bear she had kept since the cradle.

More rain outside, a torrent. Now the odor of vomit, pervasive, unextinguishable, cheesy. Fellow passengers: two frightened convent girls of sixteen or so, sobbing, sleeping, waking to murmur prayers to the Holy Virgin; Wiktor, a black-haired, intense, infuriated young Home Army member already plotting revolt or escape, ceaselessly scribbling messages on slips of paper to be passed to Wanda in another compartment; a fear-maddened shriveled old lady claiming to be the niece of Wieniawski, claiming the bundle of parchment she kept pressed close to her to be the original manuscript of his famous *Polonaise*, claiming some kind of immunity, dissolving into tears like the schoolgirls at Wiktor's snarled remark that the Nazis would wipe their asses on the worthless *Polonaise*. Hunger pangs beginning. Nothing at all to eat. Another old woman —quite dead—laid out in the exterior aisle on the spot where her heart attack had felled her, her hands frozen around a crucifix and her chalk-white face already smudged by the boots and shoes of people treading over and around her. Through her crevice once more: Cracow at night, the familiar station, moonlit railroad yards where they lay stranded hour after hour. In the greenish moonglow an extraordinary sight: a German soldier standing in *feldgrau* uniform and with slung rifle, masturbating with steady beat in the half-light of the deserted yard, grinningly exhibiting himself to such curious or indifferent or bemused prisoners as might be looking through the peepholes. An hour's sleep, then the morning's brightness. Crossing the Vistula, murky and steaming. Two small towns she recognized as the train moved westward through the dusty pollen-gold morning: Skawina, Zator. Eva beginning to cry for the first time, torn by spasms of hunger. Hush, baby. A few more moments' drowse riven by a sun-flooded, splendid, heart-wrenching, manic dream: herself begowned and bediademed, seated at the keyboard before ten thousand onlookers, yet somehow—astoundingly—flying, *flying,* soaring to deliverance on the celestial measures of the Emperor Concerto. Eyelids fluttering apart. A slamming, braking stop. Auschwitz.

They waited in the car during most of the rest of the day. At an early moment the generators ceased working; the bulbs went out in the compartment and what remaining light there was cast a milky pallor, filtering through the cracks in the plywood shutters. The distant sound of band music made its way into the compartment. There was a vibration of panic in the car; it was almost palpable, like the prickling of hair all over one's body, and in the near-darkness there came a surge of anxious whispering—hoarse, rising, but as incomprehensible as the rustle of an army of leaves. The convent girls began to wail in unison, beseeching the Holy Mother. Wiktor loudly told them to shut up, while at the same instant Sophie took courage from Wanda's voice, faint from the other end of the car, begging Resistance members and deportees alike to stay calm, stay quiet.

It must have been early in the afternoon when word came regarding the hundreds upon hundreds of Jews from Malkinia in the forward cars. *All Jews in vans* came a note to Wiktor, a note which he read aloud in the gloom and which Sophie, too numb with fright to even clutch Jan and Eva close against her breast for consolation, immediately translated into: All the Jews have gone to the gas. Sophie joined with the convent girls in prayer. It was while she was praying that Eva began to wail loudly. The children had been brave during the trip, but now the little girl's hunger blossomed into real pain. She squealed in anguish while Sophie tried to rock and soothe her, but nothing seemed to work; the child's screams were for a moment more terrifying to Sophie than the word about the doomed Jews. But soon they stopped. Oddly, it was Jan who came to the rescue. He had a way with his sister and now he took over—at first shushing her in the words of some private language they shared, then pressing next to her with his book. In the pale light he began reading to her from the story of Penrod, about little boys' pranks in the leafy Elysian small-town marrow of America; he was able to laugh and giggle, and his thin soprano singsong cast a gentle spell, combining with Eva's exhaustion to lull her to sleep.

Several hours passed. It was late afternoon. Finally another slip of paper was passed to Wiktor: *AK first car in vans.* This plainly meant one thing—that, like the Jews, the several hundred Home Army members in the car just forward had been transported to Birkenau and the crematoriums. Sophie stared straight ahead, composed her hands in her lap and prepared for death, feeling inexpressible terror but for the first time, too, tasting faintly the blessed bitter relief of acceptance. The old niece of Wieniawski had fallen into a comalike stupor, the *Polonaise* in crumpled disarray, rivulets of drool flowing from the corners of her lips. In trying to reconstruct that moment a long time later, Sophie wondered whether she might not then have become unconscious herself, for the next thing she remembered was her own daylight-dazzled presence outside on the ramp with Jan and Eva, and coming face to face with Hauptsturmführer Fritz Jemand von Niemand, doctor of medicine.

Sophie did not know his name then, nor did she ever see him again. I have christened him Fritz Jemand von Niemand because it seems as good a name as any for an SS doctor—for one who appeared to Sophie as if from nowhere and vanished likewise forever from her sight, yet who left a few interesting traces of himself behind. One trace: the recollected impression of relative youth—thirty-five, forty—and the unwelcome good looks of a delicate and disturbing sort. Indeed, traces of Dr. Jemand von Niemand and his appearance and his voice and his manner and other attributes would remain with Sophie forever. The first words he said to her, for example: "*Ich möchte mit dir schlafen.*" Which means, as bluntly and as unseductively as possible: "I'd like to get you into bed with me." Dreary loutish words, spoken from an intimidating vantage point, no finesse, no class, callow and cruel, an utterance one might expect from a B-grade movie Nazi *Schweinhund.* But these, according to Sophie, were the words he first said. Ugly talk for a doctor and a gentleman (perhaps even an aristocrat), although he was visibly, indisputably drunk, which might help explain such coarseness. Why Sophie, at first glance, thought he might be an aristocrat—Prussian perhaps, or of Prussian origin—was because of his extremely close resemblance to a Junker officer, a friend of her father's, whom she had seen once as a girl of sixteen or so on a summer visit to Berlin. Very "Nordic"-looking, attractive in a thin-lipped, austere, unbending way, the young officer had treated her frostily during their brief meeting, almost to the point of contempt and boorishness; nonetheless, she could not help but be taken by his arresting handsomeness, by—surprisingly—something not really effeminate but rather silkily feminine about his face in repose. He looked a bit like a militarized Leslie Howard, whom she had had a mild crush on ever since *The Petrified Forest*. Despite the dislike he had inspired in her, and her satisfaction in not having to see this German officer again, she remembered thinking about him later rather disturbingly: If he had been a woman, he would have been a person I think I might have felt drawn to. But now here was his counterpart, almost his replica, standing in his slightly askew SS uniform on the dusty concrete platform at five in the afternoon, flushed with wine or brandy or schnapps and mouthing his unpatrician words in an indolently patrician, Berlin-accented voice: "I'd like to get you into bed with me."

Sophie ignored what he was saying, but as he spoke she glimpsed one of those insignificant but ineffaceable details —another spectral trace of the doctor—that would always spring out in vivid trompe l'oeil from the confused surface of the day: a sprinkling of boiled-rice grains on the lapel of the SS tunic. There were only four or five of these; shiny with moisture still, they looked like maggots. She gave them her dazed scrutiny, and while doing so she realized for the first time that the piece of music being played just then by the welcoming prisoners' band—hopelessly off-key and disorganized, yet flaying her nerves with its erotic sorrow and turgid beat as it had even in the darkened car—was the Argentine tango "La Cumparsita." Why had she not been able to name it before? Ba-dum-*ba*-dum!

"Du bist eine Polack," said the doctor. *"Bist du auch eine Kommunistin?"* Sophie placed one arm around Eva's shoulders, the other arm around Jan's waist, saying nothing. The doctor belched, then more sharply elaborated: "I know you're a Polack, but are you also another one of these filthy Communists?" And then in his fog he turned toward the next prisoners, seeming almost to forget Sophie.

Why hadn't she played dumb? *"Nicht sprecht Deutsch."* It could have saved the moment. There was such a press of people. Had she not answered in German he might have let the three of them pass through. But there was the cold fact of her terror, and the terror caused her to behave unwisely. She knew now what blind and merciful ignorance had prevented very few Jews who arrived here from knowing, but which her association with Wanda and the others had caused her to know and to dread with fear beyond utterance: a selection. She and the children were undergoing at this very moment the ordeal she had heard about—rumored in Warsaw a score of times in whispers—but which had seemed at once so unbearable and unlikely to happen to her that she had thrust it out of her mind. But here she was, and here was the doctor. While over there—just beyond the roofs of the boxcars recently vacated by the death-bound Malkinia Jews—was Birkenau, and the doctor could select for its abyssal doors anyone whom he desired. This thought caused her such terror that instead of keeping her mouth shut she said, *"Ich bin polnisch! In Krakow geboren!"* Then she blurted helplessly, "I'm not Jewish! Or my children—they're not Jewish either." And added, "They are racially pure. They speak German." Finally she announced, "I'm a Christian. I'm a devout Catholic."

The doctor turned again. His eyebrows arched and he looked at Sophie with inebriate, wet, fugitive eyes, unsmiling. He was now so close to her that she smelled plainly the alcoholic vapor—a rancid fragrance of barley or rye—and she was not strong enough to return his gaze. It was then that she knew she had said something wrong, perhaps fatally wrong. She averted her face for an instant, glancing at an adjoining line of prisoners shambling through the golgotha of their selection, and saw Eva's flute teacher Zaorski at the precise congealed instant of his doom—dispatched to the left and to Birkenau by an almost imperceptible nod of a doctor's head. Now, turning back, she heard Dr. Jemand von Niemand say, "So you're not a Communist. You're a believer."

"Ja, mein Hauptmann. I believe in Christ." What folly! She sensed from his manner, his gaze—the new look in his eye of luminous intensity—that everything she was saying, far from helping her, from protecting her, was leading

somehow to her swift undoing. She thought: Let me be struck dumb.

The doctor was a little unsteady on his feet. He leaned over for a moment to an enlisted underling with a clipboard and murmured something, meanwhile absorbedly picking his nose. Eva, pressing heavily against Sophie's leg, began to cry. "So you believe in Christ the Redeemer?" the doctor said in a thick-tongued but oddly abstract voice, like that of a lecturer examining the delicately shaded facet of a proposition in logic. Then he said something which for an instant was totally mystifying: "Did He not say, 'Suffer the little children to come unto Me'?" He turned back to her, moving with the twitchy methodicalness of a drunk.

Sophie, with an inanity poised on her tongue and choked with fear, was about to attempt a reply when the doctor said, "You may keep one of your children."

"Bitte?" said Sophie.

"You may keep one of your children," he repeated. "The other one will have to go. Which one will you keep?"

"You mean, I have to choose?"

"You're a Polack, not a Yid. That gives you a privilege —a choice."

Her thought processes dwindled, ceased. Then she felt her legs crumple. "I can't choose! I can't choose!" She began to scream. Oh, how she recalled her own screams! Tormented angels never screeched so loudly above hell's pandemonium. *"Ich kann nicht wählen!"* she screamed.

The doctor was aware of unwanted attention. "Shut up!" he ordered. "Hurry now and choose. Choose, goddamnit, or I'll send them both over there. Quick!"

She could not believe any of this. She could not believe that she was now kneeling on the hurtful, abrading concrete, drawing her children toward her so smotheringly tight that she felt that their flesh might be engrafted to hers even through layers of clothes. Her disbelief was total, deranged. It was disbelief reflected in the eyes of the gaunt, waxy-skinned young Rottenführer, the doctor's aide, to whom she inexplicably found herself looking upward in supplication. He appeared stunned, and he returned her gaze with a wide-eyed baffled expression, as if to say: I can't understand this either.

"Don't make me choose," she heard herself plead in a whisper, "I can't choose."

"Send them both over there, then," the doctor said to the aide, *"nach links."*

"Mama!" She heard Eva's thin but soaring cry at the instant that she thrust the child away from her and rose from the concrete with a clumsy stumbling motion. "Take the baby!" she called out. "Take my little girl!"

At this point the aide—with a careful gentleness that Sophie would try without success to forget—tugged at Eva's hand and led her away into the waiting legion of the damned. She would forever retain a dim impression that the child had continued to look back, beseeching. But because she was now almost completely blinded by salty, thick, copious tears she was spared whatever expression Eva wore, and she was always grateful for that. For in the bleakest honesty of her heart she knew that she would never have been able to tolerate it, driven nearly mad as she was by her last glimpse of that vanishing small form.

"She still had her *mís*—and her flute," Sophie said as she finished talking to me. "All these years I have never been able to bear those words. Or bear to speak them, in any language."

Since Sophie told me this I have brooded often upon the enigma of Dr. Jemand von Niemand. At the very least he was a maverick, a sport; surely what he made Sophie do could not have been in the SS manual of regulations. The young Rottenführer's incredulity attested to that. The doctor must have waited a long time to come face to face with Sophie and her children, hoping to perpetrate his ingenious deed. And what, in the private misery of his heart, I think he most intensely lusted to do was to inflict upon Sophie, or someone like her—some tender and perishable Christian—a totally unpardonable sin. It is precisely because he had yearned with such passion to commit this terrible sin that I believe that the doctor was exceptional, perhaps unique, among his fellow SS automata: if he was not a good man or a bad man, he still retained a potential capacity for goodness, as well as evil, and his strivings were essentially religious.

Why do I say religious? For one thing, perhaps because

he was so attentive to Sophie's profession of fai would risk speculating further on this because gnette which Sophie added to her story a short w She said that during the chaotic days immediately arrival she was in such shock—so torn to frag what happened on the ramp, and by Jan's disa into the Children's Camp—that she was barel hold on to her reason. But in her barracks on could not help paying attention to a conversatio two German Jewish women, new prisoners who aged to live through the selection. It was plain physical description that the doctor of whom speaking—the one who had been responsible for survival—was the one who had sent Eva t gas chamber. What Sophie had remembered most v y was this: one of the women, who was from the Charlottenburg part of Berlin, said that she distinctly remembered the doctor from her youth. He had not recognized her on the ramp. She in turn had not known him well, although he had been a neighbor. The two related things she did recall about him—aside from his striking good looks—the two things she had not been able to forget about him, for some reason, were that he was a steadfast churchgoer and that he had always planned to enter the ministry. A mercenary father forced him into medicine.

Other of Sophie's recollections point to the doctor as a religious person. Or at least as a failed believer seeking redemption, groping for renewed faith. For example, as a hint—his drunkenness. All that we can deduce from the record indicates that in the pursuit of their jobs SS officers, including doctors, were almost monkish in their decorum, sobriety and devotion to the rules. While the demands of butchery at its most primitive level—mainly in the neighborhood of the crematoriums—caused a great deal of alcohol to be consumed, this bloody work was in general the job of enlisted men, who were allowed (and indeed often needed) to numb themselves to their activities. Besides being spared these particular chores, officers in the SS, like officers everywhere, were expected to maintain a dignified comportment, especially when going about their duties. Why, then, did Sophie have the rare experience of meeting a doctor like Jemand von Niemand in his plastered condition, cross-eyed with booze and so unkempt that he still bore on his lapel grains of greasy rice from a probably long and sodden repast? This must have been for the doctor a very dangerous posture.

I have always assumed that when he encountered Sophie, Dr. Jemand von Niemand was undergoing the crisis of his life: cracking apart like bamboo, disintegrating at the very moment that he was reaching out for spiritual salvation. One can only speculate upon Von Niemand's later career, but if he was at all like his chief, Rudolf Höss, and the SS in general, he had styled himself *Gottgläubiger*—which is to say, he had rejected Christianity while still outwardly professing faith in God. But how could one believe in God after practicing one's science for months in such a loathsome environment? Awaiting the arrival of countless trains from every corner of Europe, then winnowing out the fit and the healthy from the pathetic horde of cripples and the toothless and the blind, the feebleminded and the spastic and the unending droves of helpless aged and helpless little children, he surely knew that the slave enterprise he served (itself a mammoth killing machine regurgitating once-human husks) was a mockery and a denial of God. Besides, he was at bottom a vassal of IG Farben. Surely he could not retain belief while passing time in such a place. He had to replace God with a sense of the omnipotence of business. Since the overwhelming number of those upon whom he stood in judgment were Jews, he must have been relieved when once again Himmler's order arrived directing that all Jews without exception would be exterminated. There would no longer be any need for his selective eye. This would take him away from the horrible ramps, allowing him to pursue more normal medical activities. (It may be hard to believe, but the vastness and complexity of Auschwitz permitted some benign medical work as well as the unspeakable experiments which—given the assumption that Dr. von Niemand was a man of some sensibility—he would have shunned.)

But quickly Himmler's orders were countermanded. There was a need for flesh to fill IG Farben's insatiable maw; it was back to the ramps again for the tormented doctor. Selections would begin again. Soon only Jews would go to the gas chambers. But until final orders came, Jews and "Aryans" alike would undergo the selection process. (There would be occasional capricious exceptions, such as the shipment of Jews from Malkinia.) The renewed horror scraped like steel files at the doctor's soul, threatened to shred his reason. He began to drink, to acquire sloppy eating habits, and to miss God. *Wo, wo ist der lebende Gott?* Where is the God of my fathers?

But of course the answer finally dawned on him, and one day I suspect the revelation made him radiant with hope. It had to do with the matter of sin, or rather, it had to do with the absence of sin, and his own realization that the absence of sin and the absence of God were inseparably intertwined. No sin! He had suffered boredom and anxiety, and even revulsion, but no sense of sin from the bestial crimes he had been party to, nor had he felt that in sending thousands of the wretched innocent to oblivion he had transgressed against divine law. All had been unutterable monotony. All of his depravity had been enacted in a vacuum of sinless and businesslike godlessness, while his soul thirsted for beatitude.

Was it not supremely simple, then, to restore his belief in God, and at the same time to affirm his human capacity for evil, by committing the most intolerable sin that he was able to conceive? Goodness could come later. But first a great sin. One whose glory lay in its subtle magnanimity—a choice. After all, he had the power to take both. This is the only way I have been able to explain what Dr. Jemand von Niemand did to Sophie when she appeared with her two little children on April Fools' Day, while the wild tango beat of "La Cumparsita" drummed and rattled insistently off-key in the gathering dusk.

Sixteen

All my life I have retained a streak of uncontrolled didacticism. God knows into what suffocating depths of discomfort I have, over the years, plunged family and friends, who out of love have tolerated my frequent seizures and have more or less successfully concealed yawns, the faint crack of jaw muscles and those telltale drops at the tear ducts signaling a death struggle with tedium. But on rare occasions, when the moment is exactly right and the audience is utterly responsive, my encyclopedic ability to run on and on about a subject has served me in good stead; at a time when the situation demands the blessed release of witless diversion, nothing can be more soothing than useless facts and empty statistics. I employed all my knowledge about—of all things—*peanuts* to try to captivate Sophie that evening in Washington, as we ambled past the floodlight-drenched White House and then made our roundabout way toward Herzog's restaurant and "the best crab cakes in town." After what she had told me, peanuts seemed the appropriate commonplace out of which to refashion new conduits of communication. For during the two hours or so following her story I don't think I had been able to say more than three or four words to her. Nor had she been able to say much to me. But peanuts allowed me at last to breach our silence, to try to break out of the cloud of depression hovering over us.

"The peanut's not a nut," I explained, "but a pea. It's a cousin of the pea and the bean but different in an important way—it develops its pods under the ground. The peanut's an annual, growing low over the soil. There are three major types of peanut grown in the United States—the large-seeded Virginia, the runner and the Spanish. Peanuts have to have a lot of sunshine and a long frost-free growing period. That's why they grow in the South. The major peanut-growing states are, in order, Georgia, North Carolina, Virginia, Alabama and Texas. There was an incredibly gifted Negro scientist named George Washington Carver who developed dozens of uses for peanuts. Aside from just food, they're used in cosmetics, plastics, insulation, explosives, certain medicines, lots of other things. Peanuts are a booming crop, Sophie, and I think that this little farm of ours will grow and grow, and pretty soon we'll not only be self-sufficient but maybe even rich—at least, very well-off. We won't have to depend on Alfred Knopf or Harper and Brothers for our daily bread. The reason I want you to know something about peanuts as a crop is simply because if you're going to be the chatelaine of the manor, there are times when you'll have to have a hand in the running of the operations. Now, as for the actual *growing,* peanuts are planted after the last frost by seeding three to ten inches apart in rows about two feet apart. The pods usually mature about a hundred and twenty to a hundred and forty days after planting . . ."

"You know, Stingo, I just thought of something," Sophie said, breaking in at some point on my soliloquy. "It's something very important."

"What's that?" I said.

"I don't know how to drive. I don't know how to drive a car."

"So?"

"But we'll be living on this farm. From what you say, so far away from things. I'll have to be able to drive a car, won't I? I never learned in Poland—so few people had cars. At least, you never learned to drive until you were so much older. And here— Nathan said he was going to teach me but he never did. Surely I'll have to learn how to drive."

"Easy," I replied. "I'll teach you. There's a pickup truck already there. Anyway, in Virginia they're very lax about driver's licenses. Jesus"—I had a sudden fit of recollection —"I remember I got my license on my *fourteenth* birthday. I mean, it was *legal!*"

"Fourteen?" said Sophie.

"Christ, I weighed about ninety pounds and could barely see over the steering wheel. I remember the state trooper who was giving the test looked at my father and said, 'Is he your son or a midget?' But I got the license. That's the South . . . There's something that's so different about the South even in trivial ways. Take the matter of youth, for instance. In the North you'd never be allowed to get a driver's license so young. It's as if you got older much younger in the South. Something about the lushness, the ripeness maybe. Like that joke about what's the Mississippi definition of a virgin. The answer is: a twelve-year-old girl who can run faster than her daddy." I heard myself giggle self-indulgently, in the first spell of what could even remotely be called good humor I had experienced in hours. And suddenly the hunger in me to get down to Southampton County, to start planting roots, was nearly as intense as the real need I had by this time to consume some of Herzog's celebrated crab cakes. I began jabbering at Sophie with brainless unrestraint, not so much actually forgetful of what she had just finished telling me as, I think, thoughtlessly oblivious of the fragile mood her confessional had created within herself.

"Now then," I said in my best pastor's counseling voice, "I have a feeling from some of the things you mentioned that you think you're going to be out of place down there. But listen, nothing's further from the truth. They might be a little stand-offish at first—and you'll worry about your accent and your foreignness, and so on—but let me tell you something, Sophie darling, Southerners are the warmest and most *accepting* people in America, once they get to know you. They're not like big-city hooligans and shysters. So don't worry. Of course, we'll have to do a little adjusting. As I said before, I think the wedding ceremony will have to come pretty soon—you know, to avoid ugly gossip if nothing else. So after we get the feel of the place and introduce ourselves around—this'll take several days, that's all—we'll make out a big shopping list and take the truck and drive up to Richmond. There'll be thousands of things we'll need. The place is filled with all the basics, but we'll need so many other things. Like I told you, a phonograph and a bunch of records. Then there's the little matter of your wedding clothes. You'll naturally want to be dressed nice for the ceremony, and so we'll shop around in Richmond. You won't find Paris couture there but there are some excellent stores—"

"Stingo!" she cut in sharply. "Please! Please! Don't run on like that, about wedding clothes and such as that. What do you think I have in my suitcase right now? Just what!" Her voice had risen, cross and quavering, touched with an anger she had rarely ever aimed at me.

We stopped walking, and I turned to look at her face in the shadows of the cool evening. Her eyes were clouded with murky unhappiness and I knew then, with a painful catch in my chest, that I had said the wrong thing, or things. "What?" I stupidly asked.

"Wedding clothes," she said somberly, "the wedding clothes from Saks that Nathan bought me. I don't *need* any wedding clothes. Don't you see . . ."

And yes, I did see. To my awful distress, I did see. It was bad. At this instant I sensed for the first time a distance separating us—an intolerable distance which, in my delusory dreams about a Southern love nest, I had not realized had been keeping us apart as effectively as a wide river in flood, preventing any real communion. At least on the loving level I so craved. Nathan. She was still totally absorbed in Nathan, so much so that even the sad nuptial garments she had transported so far had some huge importance to her that was both tactile and symbolic. And I suddenly grasped another truth: how ludicrous it was of me to think of a wedding and sweet uxorious years down on the old plantation when the mistress of my passion—standing before me now with her tired face so twisted with hurt—was lugging around with her wedding clothes meant to please a man she had loved to the point of death. Christ, my stupidity! My tongue had turned to a lump of concrete, I struggled for words but could say nothing. Over Sophie's shoulder George Washington's cenotaph, a blazing stiletto in the night sky, was washed in October mist, and tiny people crawled around its foundation. I felt weak and hopeless, with a central part of me in shambles. Each ticking moment seemed to bear Sophie away from me with the speed of light.

Yet just then she murmured something I didn't understand. She made a sibilant sound, almost inaudible, and right there on Constitution Avenue, moved toward me in a rush and pressed herself into my arms. "Oh, Stingo dear," she whispered, "please forgive me. I didn't mean to raise my voice. I still want to go to Virginia with you. Really I do. And we are going tomorrow together, aren't we? It's just that when you mention getting *married,* I get so . . . so full of trouble. So uncertain. Don't you understand?"

"Yes," I replied. And of course I did, although with thick-witted belatedness. I held her close. "Of course I do, Sophie."

"Oh, we'll go to the farm tomorrow," she said, squeezing me, "we really will. Just don't talk about marriage. Please."

At that moment I also realized that something not quite genuine had attended my little spasm of euphoria. There had been an ingredient of escapism in my trying so doggedly to lay out the attractions of this garden of terrestrial happiness hard by the Dismal Swamp, where no blowflies buzzed, no pumps broke down, no crops failed, no underpaid darkies ever sulked in the cotton patch, no pig shit stank; for all I knew, despite the trust I had in my father's opinion, dear old "Five Elms" might be a squalid demesne and a gone-to-seed wreck, and to booby-trap Sophie, so to speak, by enticing her into some tumbledown Tobacco Road would be an indefensible disgrace. But I dismissed all this from my mind, it was something I could not even consider. And there was a more troubling matter. What now had become hideously apparent was that our brief bubble bath of good spirits was flat, finished, dead. When we resumed strolling along, the gloom hovering around Sophie seemed almost visible, touchable, like a fog from which one, after reaching out to her, would withdraw a hand damp with despair. "Oh, Stingo, I need a drink so bad," she said.

We walked through the evening in total silence. I gave up pointing out the landmarks of the capital, abandoning the tour-guide approach I had used to try to perk up Sophie during the beginning of our meander. It was clear to me that try as she might, she could not shake off the horror which she had felt compelled to spill forth in our little hotel room. Nor indeed could I. Here on Fourteenth Street in the frosty cider air of an early autumn night, with L'Enfant's stylish oblong spaces luminescent all around us, it was plain that Sophie and I could appreciate neither the symmetry of the city nor its air of wholesome and benevolent peace. Washington suddenly appeared paradigmatically American, sterile, geometrical, unreal. I had identified so completely with Sophie that I felt Polish, with Europe's putrid blood rushing through my arteries and veins. Auschwitz still stalked my soul as well as hers. Was there no end to this? No end?

And finally, seated at a table overlooking the sparkling moon-flecked Potomac, I asked Sophie about her little boy. I watched Sophie take a gulp of whiskey before she said, "I'm glad you asked that question, Stingo. I thought you would and I wanted you to, because for some reason I couldn't bring it up myself. Yes, you're right. I've often thought to myself: If I only knew what happened to Jan, if I could only find him, that might truly save me from all this sadness that comes over me. If I found Jan, I might be—oh, *rescued* from all these terrible feelings I still have, this desire I have had and still have to be . . . finished with life. To say *adieu* to this place which is so mysterious and strange and . . . and so wrong. If I could just find my little boy, I think that could save me.

"It might even save me from the guilt I have felt over Eva. In some way I know I should feel no badness over something I done like that. I see that it was—oh, you know—beyond my control, but it is still so terrible to wake up these many mornings with a memory of that, having to live with it. When you add it to all the other bad things I done, it makes everything unbearable. Just unbearable.

"Many, many times I have wondered whether the chances are possible that Jan is still alive somewhere. If Höss done what he said he would do, then maybe he still is alive, somewhere in Germany. But I don't think I could ever find him, after these years. They took away the identities of those children in Lebensborn, changed their names so fast, turned them so quickly into Germans—I wouldn't know where to start to find him. If he's really there, that is. When I was in the refugee center in Sweden it was all I could think about night and day—to get well and healthy so that I could go to Germany and find my little boy. But then I met this Polish woman—she was from Kielce, I remember—and she had the most tragic, haunted face I ever saw on a person. She had been a prisoner at Ravensbrück. She had lost her child, too, to Lebensborn, a little girl, and for months after the war she'd wandered all through Germany, hunting and hunting. But she never found the little girl. She said no one ever found their children. It was bad enough, she told me, not to find her daughter, but the search was even worse, this agony. Don't go, she told me, don't go. Because if you do you'll see your child everywhere, in those ruined cities, on every street corner, in every crowd of schoolchildren, on buses, passing, in cars, waving at you from playgrounds, everywhere—and you'll call out and rush toward the child, only he will not be yours. And so your soul will break apart a hundred times a day, and finally it is almost worse than knowing your child is dead . . .

"But to be quite honest, Stingo, like I told you, I don't think Höss ever done anything for me, and I think Jan stayed in the camp, and if he did, then I am certain he didn't live. When I was so sick myself in Birkenau that winter just before the war ended—I didn't know anything about this, I heard about it later, I was so sick I almost died—the SS wanted to get rid of the children who were left, there were several hundred of them far off, in the Children's Camp. The Russians were coming and the SS wanted the children destroyed. Most of them were Polish; the Jewish children were already dead. They thought of burning them alive in a pit, or shooting them, but they decided to do something that wouldn't show too many marks and evidence. So in the freezing cold they marched the children down to the river and made them take off their clothes and soak them in the water as if they were washing them, and then made them put on these wet clothes again. Then they marched them back to the area in front of the barracks where they had been living and had a roll call. Standing in their wet clothes. The roll call lasted for many, many hours while the children stood wet and freezing and night came. All of the children died of being exposed that day. They died of exposure and pneumonia, very fast. I think Jan must have been among them . . .

"But I don't know," Sophie said at last, gazing at me dry-eyed but sliding into the slurred diction which glass after glass of alcohol lent to her tongue, along with the merciful and grief-deadening anodyne it provided for her battered memory. "Is it best to know about a child's death, even one so horrible, or to know that the child lives but that you will never, never see him again? I don't know either for sure. Suppose I had chosen Jan to go . . . to go to the left instead of Eva. Would that have changed anything?" She paused to look out through the night at the dark shores of the Virginia of our destination, removed by staggering dimensions of time and space from her own benighted, cursed and—to me even at that moment—all but incomprehensible history. "Nothing would have changed anything," she said. Sophie was not given to actresslike gestures, but for the first time in the months I had known her she did this strange thing: she pointed directly to the center of her bosom, then pulled away with her fingers an invisible veil as if to expose to view a heart outraged as desperately as the mind can conceive. "Only this has changed, I think. It has been hurt so much, it has turned to stone."

I knew that it was best that we should get well rested before continuing our trip down to the farm. Through various conversational stratagems, including more agricultural wisdom leavened by all the good Southern jokes I could extract from memory, I was able to infuse Sophie with enough cheer to make it through the rest of the dinner. We drank, ate crab cakes and managed to forget Auschwitz. By ten o'clock she was again quite befuddled and unsteady of gait—as was I, for that matter, with an unconscionable amount of beer stowed away—and so we took a taxi back to the hotel. She was already drowsing against my shoulder by the time we reached the stained marble steps and tobacco-fragrant lobby of the Hotel Congress, and she clung with weary heaviness to my waist as we rode the elevator up to the room. Onto the swayback bed she flung herself wordlessly, without removing her clothes, and was instantaneously asleep. I put a blanket over her, and after stripping to my skivvy drawers, lay down beside her and fell asleep myself like one bludgeoned. At least for a time. Then came dreams. The church bell sounding intermittently through my slumber was not entirely unmusical, but it had a clangorous, hollow, Protestant ring, as if fashioned of low-pitched alloys; demonically, in the midst of my turbulent erotic visions, it tolled with the voice of sin. The Reverend Entwistle, drugged with Budweiser and in bed with a woman not his wife, was basically ill-at-ease in this illicit ambience, even while asleep. *DARK DOOM! DARK DOOM!* pealed the wretched bell.

Indeed, I'm sure it was both my residual Calvinism and my clerical disguise—also that damnable church bell—which helped cause me to falter so badly when Sophie woke me. This must have been around two in the morning. It should have been that moment in my life when literally, as the saying goes, all my dreams came true, for in the half-light I realized both by feel and evidence of my sleep-blurred eyes that Sophie was naked, that she was tenderly licking the recesses of my ear, and that she was groping for my cock. Was I asleep or awake? If all this were not puzzlingly sweet enough—the simulacrum of a dream—the dream melted instantly away at the sound of her whisper: "Oh . . . now, Stingo darling, I want to fuck." Then I felt her tugging off my underpants.

I began to kiss Sophie like a man dying of thirst and she returned my kisses, groaning, but this is all we did (or all I could do, despite her gently expert, tickling manipulation) for many minutes. It would be misleading to emphasize my malfunction, either its duration or its effect on me, although such was its completeness that I recall resolving to commit suicide if it did not soon correct itself. Yet there it remained in her fingers, a limp worm. She slid down over the surface of my belly and began to suck me. I remember once how, in the abandonment of her confession regarding Nathan, she fondly spoke of him calling her "the world's most elegant cocksucker." He may have been right; I will never forget how eagerly and how naturally she moved to demonstrate to me her appetite and her devotion, planting her knees firmly between my legs like the fine craftswoman she was, then bending down and taking into her mouth my no longer quite so shrunken little comrade, bringing it swelling and jumping up by such a joyfully adroit, heedlessly noisy blend of labial and lingual rhythms that I could feel the whole slippery-sweet union of mouth and rigid prick like an electric charge running from my scalp to the tips of my toes. "Oh, Stingo," she gasped, pausing once for breath, "don't come yet, darling." Fat chance. I would lie there and let her suck me until my hair grew thin and gray.

The varieties of sexual experience are, I suppose, so

multifarious that it is an exaggeration to say that Sophie and I did that night everything it is possible to do. But I'll swear we came close, and one thing forever imprinted on my brain was our mutual inexhaustibility. I was inexhaustible because I was twenty-two, and a virgin, and was clasping in my arms at last the goddess of my unending fantasies. Sophie's lust was as boundless as my own, I'm sure, but for more complex reasons; it had to do, of course, with her good raw natural animal passion, but it was also both a plunge into carnal oblivion and a flight from memory and grief. More than that, I now see, it was a frantic and orgiastic attempt to beat back death. But at the time I was unable to perceive this, running as I was the temperature of an overheated Sherman tank, being out of my wits with excitement, and filled all night long with dumb wonder at our combined frenzy. For me it was less an initiation than a complete, well-rounded apprenticeship, or more, and Sophie, my loving instructress, never ceased whispering encouragement into my ear. It was as if through a living tableau, in which I myself was a participant, there were being acted out all the answers to the questions with which I had half maddened myself ever since I began secretly reading marriage manuals and sweated over the pages of Havelock Ellis and other sexual savants. Yes, the female nipples did spring up like little pink semi-hard gumdrops beneath the fingers, and Sophie emboldened me to even sweeter joys by asking me to excite them with my tongue. Yes, the clitoris was really there, darling little bud; Sophie placed my fingers on it. And oh, the cunt was indeed wet and warm, wet with a saliva-slick wetness that astounded me with its heat; the stiff prick slid in and out of that incandescent tunnel more effortlessly than I had ever dreamed, and when for the first time I spurted prodigiously somewhere in her dark bottomlessness, I heard Sophie cry out against my cheek, saying that she could feel the gush. The cunt also tasted good, I discovered later, as the church bell—no longer admonitory—dropped four gongs in the night; the cunt was simultaneously pungent and briny and I heard Sophie sigh, guiding me gently by the ears as if they were handles while I licked her there.

And then there were all those famous positions. Not the twenty-eight outlined in the handbooks, but certainly, in addition to the standard one, three or four or five. At some point Sophie, returning from the bathroom where she kept the liquor, switched on the light, and we fucked in a glow of soft copper; I was delighted to find that the "female superior" posture was every bit as pleasurable as Dr. Ellis had claimed, not so much for its anatomical advantages (though those too were fine, I thought as from below I cupped Sophie's breasts in my hands or, alternately, squeezed and stroked her bottom) as for the view it afforded me of that wide-boned Slavic face brooding over me, her eyes closed and her expression so beautifully tender and drowned and abandoned in her passion that I had to avert my gaze. "I can't stop coming," I heard her murmur, and I knew she meant it. We lay quietly together for a while, side by side, but soon without a word Sophie presented herself in such a way as to fulfill all my past fantasies in utter apotheosis. Taking her from behind while she knelt, thrusting into the cleft between those smooth white globes, I suddenly clenched my eyes shut and, I remember, thought in a weird seizure of cognition of the necessity of redefining "joy," "fulfillment," "ecstasy," even "God." Several times we stopped long enough for Sophie to drink, and for her to pour whiskey and water down my own gullet. The booze, far from numbing me, heightened the images as well as the sensations of what then bloomed into phantasmagoria . . . Her voice in my ear, the incomprehensible words in Polish nonetheless understood, urging me on as if in a race, urging me to some ever-receding finish line. Fucking for some reason on the gritty bone-hard floor, the reason unclear, dim, stupid—*why,* for Christ's sake?—then abruptly dawning: to view, as on a pornographic screen, our pale white entwined bodies splashing back from the lusterless mirror on the bathroom door. A kind of furious obsessed wordlessness finally—no Polish, no English, no language, only breath. *Soixante-neuf* (recommended by the doctor), where after smothering for minute after minute in her moist mossy cunt's undulant swamp, I came at last in Sophie's mouth, came in a spasm of such delayed, prolonged, exquisite intensity that I verged on a scream, or a prayer, and my vision went blank, and I gratefully perished. Sleep then—a sleep that was beyond mere sleep. Cold-cocked. Etherized. Dead.

I woke up with my face afloat in a puddle of sunlight,

and I reached with an instinctive twitch for Sophie's arm, hair, breast, something. The Reverend Entwistle was, to put it with exactitude, ready for another fuck. This matutinal grope, the somnolent reaching out, was a Pavlovian reflex which I would experience often in later years. But Sophie was gone. Gone! Her absence, after the most complete (or perhaps I should say only) propinquity of flesh in my life, was spooky, almost palpable, and I drowsily realized it had partly to do with the smell of her, which remained like a vapor in the air: a musky genital odor, still provocative, still lascivious. In my waking daze I glanced down amid the landscape of tangled bedclothes, unable to believe that after all of its happy, exhausting toil my member still stood valiantly upright, serving as a tentpost to the worn and tacky sheet. Then I was washed by an awful panic, aware from the slant of the mirror that Sophie was not in the bathroom and therefore not in the room at all. Just as I leaped from the bed the headache of a hangover smote my skull like a mallet, and during my struggle with my trousers I was seized by further panic, or I should say, dread: the bell tolled outside and I counted the strokes—it was *noon!* My yells over the decrepit telephone brought no response. Half clothed, murmuring to myself curses, recriminations, filled with auguries of foul tidings, I burst out of the room and galloped down the fire stairs to the lobby with its single Negro bellboy pushing a mop, its potted rubber plants and rump-sprung armchairs and overflowing spittoons. There the old codger who had first greeted me drowsed behind the desk, mooning over the waiting room's midday desuetude. At the sight of me he came alert, and proceeded to unfold what was simply the worst news I had ever heard.

"She came down real early, Reverend," he said, "so early she had to wake me up." He looked at the bellboy. "What time you reckon it was, Jackson?"

"Hit must have been aroun' six."

"Yes, it was about six o'clock. Just dawn. She looked like she was in a real state, Reverend." His pause seemed a little apologetic. "I mean, well, I think she'd had several beers. Her hair was every whichaway. Anyway, she got on the phone here, long-distance to Brooklyn, New York. I couldn't help overhearing. She was talkin' to someone—a man, I guess. She began to cry a lot and told him she was leavin' here right away. Kept callin' to him—she was real upset, Reverend. Mason. Jason. Something like that."

"Nathan," I said, hearing the catch in my voice. "Nathan! Oh, Jesus Christ . . ."

Sympathy and concern—an emotional amalgam which suddenly appeared to me rather Southern and old-fashioned—welled up in the old clerk's eyes. "Yes—Nathan. I didn't know what to do, Reverend," he explained. "She went on upstairs and then she came down with her bag and Jackson here took her over to Union Station. She looked awfully upset and I thought of you, and wondered . . . I thought of calling you on the phone but it was so early. And anyway, I didn't want to butt in. I mean, it wasn't my business."

"Oh, Jesus Christ, Jesus Christ," I kept hearing myself mutter, half aware of the questioning look on the face of the old man, who as a member of the Second Baptist Church of Washington was doubtless unprepared for such impiety from a preacher.

Jackson took me back upstairs in the aged elevator, against whose curlicued cast-iron, unfriendly wall I leaned with my eyes closed in a state of stupefaction, unable to believe any of this or, even more intransigently, to accept it. Surely, I thought, Sophie would be lying in bed when I returned, the golden hair shining in a rectangle of sunshine, the nimble loving hands outstretched, beckoning me to renewed delight . . .

Instead, tucked against the mirror above the lavatory in the bathroom, there was a note. Scrawled in pencil, it was testimony indeed to the imperfect command of written English of which Sophie had so recently lamented to me, but also to the influence of German, which she had learned from her father so many years before in Cracow and which until this moment I had not realized had embedded itself with such obstinacy, like cornices and moldings of Gothic stone, in her mind's architecture.

> My dearest Stingo, your such a beautiful Lover I hate to leave and forgive me for not saying Good-Bye but I must go back to Nathan. Believe me you will find some wunderful Mademoiselle to make you happy on the Farm. I am so fond of you—you must not think bei this I am being cruel. But when I woke I was

feeling so terrible and in Despair about Nathan, bei that I mean so filled with Gilt and thoughts of Death it was like ~~Eis~~ Ice flowing in my Blut. So I must be with Nathan again for whatever that mean. I may not see you again but do believe me how much knowing you have meaned to me. Your a great Lover Stingo. I feel so bad, I must go now. Forgive my poor englisch. I love Nathan but now feel this Hate of Life and God. FUCK God and all his Hände Werk. And Life too. And even what remain of Love.

Sophie

There was never any way of discovering precisely what took place between Sophie and Nathan when she returned that Saturday to Brooklyn. Because she had told me in such detail of the awful weekend in Connecticut the previous autumn, I may have been the only person knowing them both who had an inkling of what went on in their room where they met for the last time. But even I could only guess; they left no last-minute memos to help provide a key. As with most unspeakable events, there were certain troublesome "ifs" involved, making it all the more painful, in retrospect, to ponder the ways in which the whole thing might have been prevented. (Not that I think it really could have been prevented, in the end.) The most important of these suppositions involved Morris Fink, who, given his limited capabilities, had already performed more intelligently than anyone had a right to expect. No one ever determined just when Nathan came back to the house during the thirty-six hours or so after Sophie and I fled and before Sophie herself returned. It seems strange that Fink—who had for so long and so assiduously kept his eye on the goings and comings in the house—had not noticed that Nathan at some point had made his way back and secluded himself in Sophie's room. But he later protested that he had not had a glimpse of Nathan, and I never saw any reason to doubt him, any more than I doubted his claim to having failed to see Sophie when she, too, reached the house. Assuming no mishaps or delays in the railroad and subway timetable, her return to the Pink Palace must have been at around noon on the day she left me in Washington.

The reason I place Fink at such a critical focus in

respect to these movements is simply that Larry—who had gotten back from Toronto and hurried to Flatbush to talk to Morris and Yetta Zimmerman—had entrusted the janitor to telephone him if and when he saw Nathan enter the house. I had given Fink the same instructions, and additionally, Larry had encouraged Morris with a fat tip. But doubtless Nathan (in whatever frame of mind and with what motive it is impossible to say) sneaked in when Morris was not looking or asleep, while Sophie's later arrival simply must have escaped his notice. Also, I suspect that Morris was in bed when Sophie made her call to Nathan. Had Fink got in touch with Larry earlier, the doctor would have been there within minutes; he was the only person on earth who could have dealt with his demented brother, and I am certain that if he had been called, the outcome of this story would have been a different one. Perhaps no less calamitous, but different.

On that Saturday, Indian summer had descended over the eastern seaboard, bringing shirt-sleeve weather, flies, a renascence of Good Humor men, and to most people that absurdly deceptive feeling that the onset of winter is a wicked illusion. I had that feeling the same afternoon in Washington (although my mind was really not on the weather), just as I imagine that Morris Fink had a touch of this sensation at the Pink Palace. He later said that he first realized, with growing astonishment, that Sophie was in her room when he heard the music floating down from above. This was around two o'clock. He knew nothing about the music she and Nathan had played so constantly, merely identifying it as "classic," and confessing to me once that although it was too "deep" for him to understand, he found it more palatable than some of the popular crud that came from the radios and record players of the other tenants.

At any rate, he was surprised—no, really flabbergasted—to find that Sophie had returned; his mind jumped to an instantaneous connection with Nathan, and he alerted himself to the possibility that he might have to make that telephone call to Larry. But he had no evidence that Nathan was on the premises and he hesitated to call Larry when it might be a false alarm. He was by now deathly afraid of Nathan (he had been near enough to me two nights before to see me recoil from Nathan's telephoned gunshot) and he pined hungrily to be able to appeal to the police—for protection, if nothing else. He had sensed a creepy presence in the house ever since Nathan's last rampage, and had begun to feel so nervous about the Nathan–Sophie situation in general, so jittery and insecure, that he was on the verge of giving up the half-price room he received in exchange for his janitorial functions and telling Mrs. Zimmerman that he was going to move in with his sister in Far Rockaway. He had no longer any doubt that Nathan was the most sinister form of golem. A menace. But Larry had said that under no circumstances should he or anyone else get in touch with the police. So Morris waited downstairs by the hallway door, feeling the stickiness of the summery heat and listening to the complicated and fathomless music as it showered down.

Then to his swelling wonder he watched the door upstairs open slowly and saw Sophie emerge partway from her room. There was nothing unusual in her appearance, he later recalled; she looked perhaps, well, a bit fatigued, with shadowy places beneath her eyes, but little in her expression betrayed strain or unhappiness or distress or any other "negative" emotion she might have logically been expected to show after the ordeal of the past few days. To the contrary, while she stood there for a moment with one hand caressing the doorknob, a curious, fleeting glint of mild amusement crossed her face, as if she might give a gentle laugh; her lips parted, her gleaming teeth caught the bright afternoon light, and then he saw her tongue run across her upper lip, interrupting the words she had been poised to say. Morris realized that she had caught sight of him, and his gut made a small lurch. He had had a crush on her for many months; her beauty still continued to pain him, as it had day in and day out, hopelessly, replenishing within him mingled freshets of heartache and horniness. She certainly deserved better than that *meshuggener* Nathan.

But now he was struck by what she was wearing—a costume which even to his unpracticed eye appeared out of vogue, old-fashioned, but nonetheless served to set off her extraordinary loveliness: a white jacket worn over a wine-colored pleated satin skirt, a silk scarf wound around the neck, and tilted over the forehead a red beret. It made her look like a movie star from an earlier time—Clara

Bow, Fay Wray, Gloria Swanson, somebody like that. Hadn't he seen her dressed like this before? With Nathan? He couldn't remember. Morris was intensely puzzled, not simply by her appearance but by the very fact of her being there. Only two nights before, she had left, with her luggage, in such a panic and with . . . That was another puzzlement. "Where's Stingo?" he was about to ask in a friendly voice. But before he could open his mouth she walked the few steps to the banister, and leaning over, said, "Morris, would you mind getting me a bottle of whiskey?" And she let fall a five-dollar bill, which fluttered down and which he caught in midair, between his fingers.

He ambled the five blocks over to Flatbush Avenue and bought a fifth of Carstairs. Returning in the sweltering heat, he loitered for a moment at the edge of the park, watching the playing fields of the Parade Grounds where the young men and boys kicked and passed footballs and tackled each other, and flung happy obscenities in the familiar flat clamorous yawp of Brooklyn; lack of rain for days made the dust rise in conical cyclones and whitened the brittle grass and the foliage at the edge of the park. Morris was easily distracted. He remembered later that for fifteen or twenty minutes he totally forgot that he was on an errand, when "classic" music jarred him from his empty diversion, blasting forth from Sophie's window several hundred yards away. The music was boisterous and filled with what seemed to be trumpets. It reminded him of the task he had set out to perform, and of Sophie waiting, and he hurried back to the Pink Palace at a dogtrot now, nearly getting run down on Caton Avenue (he recalled vividly, as he did so many details of that afternoon) by a yellow Con Edison maintenance truck. The music grew louder as he approached the house, and he thought it might be wise to ask Sophie, as delicately as he could, to turn down the volume, but then reconsidered: it was daytime, after all, a Saturday to boot, and the other boarders were gone. The music washed harmlessly out over the neighborhood. Let the fucker play.

He knocked at Sophie's door, but there was no answer; he hammered again, and still there was no response. He set the bottle of Carstairs on the floor by the doorjamb and then went downstairs to his room, where he brooded for half an hour or so over his albums of matchbook covers.

Morris was a collector; his room was also filled with soft-drink bottle caps. Soon he decided to have his customary nap. When he awoke it was late in the afternoon and the music had stopped. He remembered the clammy ominousness he felt; his apprehension seemed to be a part of the unseasonable and oppressive heat, close as a boiler room, which even in the approaching twilight remained stagnant on the breezeless air, drenching him in sweat. It had suddenly become so *quiet* in the place, he remarked to himself. On the remotest skyline of the park, heat lightning whooshed up, and to the west he thought he heard dull thunder. In the silent, darkening house he tramped back upstairs. The bottle of whiskey still stood at the bottom of the door. Morris knocked once again. The much-used door had a slight give, or play, which made a crack at the juncture with its frame, and while the door fastened shut automatically, there was another bolt that could be secured from inside; through the crack Morris could see that this interior mechanism was firmly latched, and so he knew that Sophie could not have left the room. Twice, three times he called out her name, but there was only silence, and his perplexity grew into worry when he noticed by peeping into the crack that no light shone in the room, even though it was rapidly growing dark. And so then he decided that it might be a good idea to call Larry. The doctor came within an hour, and together they broke down the door . . .

Meanwhile, stewing in another little room in Washington, I came to a decision which effectively prevented *me* from having any influence on the matters at hand. Sophie had gotten a good six hours' head start on me; even so, if I had pursued her without delay, I might have arrived in Brooklyn in time to deflect the blow which was hammering down. As it was, I fretted and agonized, and for reasons I still cannot perfectly understand, decided to go on down to Southampton without her. I think an element of resentment must have entered into my decision: petulant anger at her defection, a stab of real jealousy, and the bitter, despondent conclusion that from now on she could just damn well look after her own ass. Nathan, that *shmuck!* I had done all I could. Let her go back to her crazy Jewish sweetheart, that sheeny bastard. So, checking the dwindling resources of my wallet (ironically, I was still subsisting on Nathan's gift), I decamped from the hotel in a vague sweat of anti-Semitism, trudged the many blocks in jungle heat to the bus station, where I bought a ticket for the long ride to Franklin, Virginia. I made up my mind to forget Sophie.

By then it was one o'clock in the afternoon. I barely realized it but I was in a deep crisis. I actually had ached so intensely over this wicked, this monstrous disappointment—this betrayal!—that a kind of quivering St. Vitus' dance had begun to possess my limbs. In addition, the carnal, raw-nerved discomfort of my hangover had become a crucifixion, my thirst was unquenchable, and by the time the bus nosed its way through the clotted traffic of Arlington, I was suffering from an anxiety attack which each one of my psychic monitors had begun to regard gravely, flashing alerts all through my flesh. Much of this had to do with that whiskey Sophie had sluiced down my throat. Never in my life had I seen my fingers tremble so uncontrollably, nor could I remember ever having trouble lighting a cigarette. There was also an extravagant nightmarishness about the passing moonscape which aggravated my depression and fear. The dreary suburbs, the high-rise penitentiaries, the broad Potomac viscid with sewage. When I was a child, not so long ago, the southern outskirts of the District had drowsed in dusty charm, a chain of bucolic crossroads. My God, look at it now. I had forgotten the illness which my native state had so rapidly undergone; bloated by war profits, the obscenely fecund urban squalor of Fairfax County swept across my vision like an hallucinated recapitulation of Fort Lee, New Jersey, and the sprawling concrete blight which only the day before I thought I was leaving behind forever. Was all this not merely Yankee carcinoma, spreading its growth into my beloved Old Dominion? Surely things would get better further south; nonetheless I felt compelled to lay my tender skull back against the seat, writhing as I did so with a combined fear and exhaustion such as I had never in my life known before.

The driver called out, "Alexandria." And here I knew I had to flee the bus. What, I wondered, would some intern at the local hospital think at the sight of this skinny distraught apparition in rumpled seersucker requesting to be put into a strait jacket? (And was it then that I knew with certainty that I would never again live in the South? I think so, but to this day I cannot be sure.)

Yet I managed at last to put myself under reasonable control, fighting off the goblins of neurasthenia. By a series of interurban conveyances (including a taxi, which left me nearly broke) I got back to Union Station in time to catch the three o'clock train to New York. Until I seated myself in the stuffy coach I had not been able to permit myself images, memories of Sophie. Merciful God, my adored Polack, plunging deathward! I realized, in a stunning rush of clarity, that I had banished her from my thoughts during that aborted foray into Virginia for the simple reason that my subconscious had forbidden me to foresee or to accept what my mind in its all too excruciating awareness now insisted upon: that something terrible was going to happen to her, and to Nathan, and that my desperate journey to Brooklyn could in no way alter the fate they had embraced. I understood this not because I was prescient but because I had been willfully blind or dim-witted, or both. Hadn't her last note spelled it out, so plainly that an innocent six-year-old could have divined its meaning, and hadn't I been negligent, feloniously so, in failing to hurry after her immediately rather than taking that brainless bus ride across the Potomac? I was swept by anguish. To the guilt which was murdering her just as surely as her children were murdered must there now be added my own guilt for committing the sin of blind omission that might help seal her doom as certainly as Nathan's own hands? I said to myself: Good Christ, where is a telephone? I've got to warn Morris Fink or Larry before it's all over. But even as I thought this the train began to shudder forward, and I knew there could be no more communication until . . .

And so I went into a bizarre religious convulsion, brief in duration but intense. The Holy Bible—which I carried in a bundle along with *Time* magazine and the Washington *Post*—had been part of my itinerancy for years. It had also, of course, served as an appendage to my costume as the Reverend Entwistle. I had not been in any sense a godly-minded creature, and the Scriptures were always largely a literary convenience, supplying me with allusions and tag lines for the characters in my novel, one or two of whom had evolved into pious turds. I considered myself an agnostic, emancipated enough from the shackles of belief and also brave enough to resist calling on any such questionable gaseous vertebrate as the Deity, even in times of travail and suffering. But sitting there—desolate, weak beyond description, terrified, utterly lost—I knew that I had let slip all my underpinnings, and *Time* and the *Post* seemed to offer no prescription for my torment. A fudge-colored lady of majestic heft and girth squeezed into the seat beside me, filling the ambient space with the aroma of heliotrope. We were speeding north now, moving out of the District of Columbia. I turned to glance at her, for I was aware of her gaze on me. She was scrutinizing me with round, moist, friendly brown eyes the size of sycamore balls. She smiled, gave a wheeze, and her expression embraced me with all the motherly concern my heart at that hopeless moment longed for. "Sonny," said she, with an incredible amplitude of faith and good cheer, "dey is only *one* Good Book. And you got it right in yo' hand." Credentials established, my fellow pilgrim pulled out of a shopping bag her own Bible and settled back to read with an aspirated sigh of pleasure and a wet smacking of lips. "Believe in His word," she reminded me, "an' ye *shall* be redeemed—dat's de holy Gospel an' de Lawd's truth. Amen."

I replied, "Amen," opening my Bible to the exact middle of its pages where, I remembered from idiot Sunday School lessons, I would discover the Psalms of David. "Amen," I said again. *As the hart panteth after the water brooks so panteth my soul after thee, O God . . . Deep calleth unto deep at the noise of thy waterspouts: all thy waves and thy billows are gone over me.* Suddenly I felt I had to be secreted from all human eyes. Lurching to the washroom, I locked myself in and sat on the can, scrawling in my notebook apocalyptic messages to myself whose content I barely understood even as they streamed out from my scrambled consciousness: last bulletins of a condemned man, or the ravings of one who, perishing on the earth's most remote and rotted strand, floats crazed jottings in bottles out upon the black indifferent bosom of eternity. "Why you cryin', sonny?" said the woman later when I slumped down beside her. "Somebody done hurt you bad?" I could say nothing in reply, but then she made a suggestion, and after a bit I mustered enough possession to read in unison with her, so that our voices rose in a harmonious and urgent threnody above the clatter of the train. "Psalm Eighty-eight," I would suggest. To which she would reply, "Dat is some fine psalm." *O Lord God of my salvation, I have cried day and night before thee: Let my prayer come before thee: incline thine ear unto my cry; For my soul is full of troubles . . .* We read aloud through Wilmington, Chester and past Trenton, turning from time to time to Ecclesiastes and Isaiah. After a while we tried the Sermon on the Mount, but somehow it didn't work for me; the grand old Hebrew woe seemed more cathartic, so we went back to Job. When at last I raised my eyes and looked outside, it had grown dark and lightning in green sheets heaved up over the western horizon. The dark priestess, whom I had grown attached to, if not to love, got off in Newark. "Ev'ything gone be all right," she predicted.

That night the Pink Palace from the outside looked like the set of one of those glossy, brutal detective movies I had seen a hundred times. To this day I remember so plainly my feeling of acceptance when I made my way up the sidewalk—my willingness not to be surprised. All the avatars of death were there as I had prefigured them: ambulances, fire engines, emergency vans, police cars with pulsing red lights—these in gross excess of need, as if the poor ramshackle house had harbored some terrible massacre instead of two people who had willed themselves into an almost decorous ending, going off silently to sleep. A floodlight enveloped all in its acetylene glare, there was one of those grim barricades with its cardboard sign—Do Not Cross—and everywhere stood clots of thuggish policemen chewing gum and negligently swatting their thick behinds. I argued with one of these cops—a choleric ugly Irishman—asserting my right to enter, and I might have remained outside for hours had it not been for Larry. He spied me and spoke brusquely to the meat-faced brute, whereupon I was allowed to go into the downstairs hallway. In my own room, with its door ajar, Yetta Zimmerman half lay, half sat sprawled in a chair, muttering distractedly in Yiddish. Plainly, she had just been informed of the happenings; her wide homely face, usually such an image of fine humor, was bloodless, had the vacant stare of shock. An ambulance attendant hovered near her, ready to administer a syringe. Saying nothing, Larry led me upstairs past a cluster of wormy-looking police reporters and two or three photographers who seemed to respond to any moving object by exploding flashbulbs. Cigarette smoke hung so thickly over the landing that for an instant I thought the place might have earlier been on fire. Near the entrance to Sophie's room Morris Fink, even more drained of color than Yetta and looking genuinely bereft, spoke in trembling tones to a detective. I stopped long enough for a word with Morris. He told me a little about the afternoon, the music. And finally there was the room, glowing in coralline softness beyond the battered-down door.

I blinked in the dim light, then gradually caught sight of Sophie and Nathan where they lay on top of the bright apricot bedspread. They were clad as on that long-ago Sunday when I first saw them together—she in her sporty togs from a bygone time, he in those wide-striped, raffish, anachronistic gray flannels that had made him look like a successful gambler. Dressed thus, but recumbent and entwined in each other's arms, they appeared from where I stood as peaceful as two lovers who had gaily costumed themselves for an afternoon stroll, but on impulse had decided to lie down and nap, or kiss and make love, or merely whisper to each other of fond matters, and were frozen in this grave and tender embrace forever.

"I wouldn't look at their faces, if I were you," said Larry. Then after a pause he added, "But they didn't suffer. It was sodium cyanide. It was over in a few seconds."

To my shame and chagrin I felt my knees buckle and I nearly fell, but Larry grabbed and held me. Then I recovered and stepped through the door.

"Who's this, Doctor?" said a policeman, moving to block my way.

"Member of the family," Larry said, speaking the truth. "Let him in."

There was nothing much in the room to add to, or subtract from, or explain the dead couple on the bed. I couldn't bear to look at them any longer. For some reason I edged toward the phonograph, which had shut itself off, and glanced at the stack of records that Sophie and Nathan had played that afternoon. Purcell's *Trumpet Voluntary*, the Haydn cello concerto, part of the Pastoral Symphony, the lament for Eurydice from Gluck's *Orfeo*—

these were among the dozen or so of the shellac records I removed from the spindle. There were also two compositions whose titles had particular meaning for me, if only because of the meaning I knew they had possessed for Sophie and Nathan. One was the larghetto from the B-flat major piano concerto of Mozart—the last he wrote—and I had been with Sophie many times when she played it, stretched out on the bed with one arm flung over her eyes as the slow, sweet, tragic measures flooded the room. He was so close to the end of his life when he wrote it; was that the reason (I remember her wondering aloud) why the music was filled with a resignation that was almost like joy? If she had ever been fortunate enough to have become a pianist, she went on, this would have been one of the first pieces she would have wished to commit to memory, mastering every shading of what she felt was its sound of "forever." I knew almost nothing of Sophie's history then, nor could I fully appreciate what, after a pause, she said about the piece: that she never heard it without thinking of children playing in the dusk, calling out in far, piping voices while the shadows of nightfall swooped down across some green and tranquil lawn.

Two white-jacketed morgue attendants entered the room with a rustle of plastic bags. The other piece of music was one that both Sophie and Nathan had listened to all summer long. I don't want to give it a larger connotation than it deserves, for Sophie and Nathan had fled faith. But the record had been on the top of the stack, and I could not help making this instinctive conjecture as I replaced it, assuming that in their final anguish—or ecstasy, or whatever engulfing revelation may have united them just before the darkness—the sound they heard was *Jesu, Joy of Man's Desiring.*

These final entries should be called, I suppose, something like "A Study in the Conquest of Grief."

We buried Sophie and Nathan side by side in a cemetery in Nassau County. It was less difficult to get organized than one might have imagined. Because there had been worries. After all, a Jew and a Catholic in a "suicide pact" (as the *Daily News* termed it, in a garishly illustrated story on page three), unmarried lovers dwelling in sin, suggestive beauty and good looks, the instigator of the tragedy a young man with a history of psychotic episodes, and so on—this was the stuff of superscandal in the year 1947. One could envision all sorts of objections to a double burial. But the ceremony was relatively easy to arrange (and Larry arranged it all) because there were no strict religious injunctions to observe. Nathan and Larry's parents had been Orthodox Jews, but the mother was dead and the father, now in his eighties, was in precarious health and quite senile. Furthermore—and why not face it? we said—Sophie had no closer relative than Nathan. These considerations made it all the more reasonable for Larry to settle on the rites that were held that following Monday. Neither Larry nor Nathan had been inside a synagogue for years. And I told Larry, when he asked my advice, that I thought Sophie would not have wanted a priest or any ministrations of her church—perhaps a blasphemous assumption, and one that consigned Sophie to hell, but I was certain (and still am) that I was correct. In the afterlife Sophie would be able to endure any hell.

So at a downtown outpost of Walter B. Cooke we had obsequies that were as civilized and decent as were possible under the circumstances, with their accompanying whiff (to the public that goggled outside, at least) of dirty and fatal passion. We were to have a little trouble regarding the officiating divine; he was a disaster, but I was happily unaware of this as I stood with Larry that afternoon, greeting the mourners. There was only a small group of these. The first to arrive was the older Landau sister, married to a surgeon. She had flown from St. Louis with her teen-age son. The two expensively dressed chiropractors, Blackstock and Katz, came with a couple of youngish women who had worked with Sophie in the office; they were weeping blindly and had drawn faces and pink noses. Yetta Zimmerman, teetering on prostration, arrived with Morris Fink and the fat rabbinical student Moishe Muskatblit, who was helping to support Yetta but who from his drained, wheylike face and uncertain gait looked in need of support himself.

A handful of Nathan and Sophie's friends turned up—six or seven of the young professionals and teachers at Brooklyn College who comprised what I had called the "Morty Haber group," including Morty himself. He was a soft-spoken, gentle scholar. I had come to know him slightly and like him, and I attached myself to him for a while that day. There was a top-heavy, almost overpowering air of solemnity to the occasion, with not even a breath of the fugitive facetiousness that some deaths permit: the hush and the strained, miserable masks bespoke an awareness of real shock, real tragedy. No one had bothered to consult about the music, and this was both an irony and a shame. As the mourners trouped into the vestibule to the popping of flashbulbs I could hear a whiny Hammond organ playing Gounod's "Ave Maria." Reflecting on Sophie's—and for that matter, Nathan's—loving and noble response to music, that peevish, vulgar utterance made my stomach turn over.

My stomach was in poor enough shape anyway, also my general equilibrium. After the train ride up from Washington, I had experienced hardly a moment's sobriety or a moment's sleep. I had been left a pacing, driven, gritty-eyed insomniac by what had happened; and since sleep would not come, I had filled the unholy hours—in which I had skulked about the streets and into the bars of Flatbush, murmuring "Why, why, why?"—with obsessive guzzling, mostly beer, which kept me marginally but not completely drunk. I was half drunk and undergoing the queerest sense of dislocation and exhaustion (prelude to what might have been true alcoholic hallucinosis, I later realized) I had ever felt when I sank into one of Walter B. Cooke's commercial pews and listened to Reverend DeWitt "sermonize" above Nathan's and Sophie's coffins. It was not really Larry's fault about the Reverend DeWitt. He felt that he needed a clergyman of some kind, but a rabbi seemed inappropriate, a priest unacceptable—so a friend of his, or a friend of a friend, suggested Reverend DeWitt. He was a Universalist, a man in his forties, with a synthetically serene face, wavy blond, carefully groomed hair and pinkly mobile, rather girlish lips. He wore a tan business suit with a tan vest tucked around his nascent paunch, upon which glittered the golden key of Omicron Delta Kappa, the college leadership fraternity.

I made then my first half-dotty, audible chuckle, causing a small stir among the people nearest me. I had never seen that key worn by anyone much over my own age, especially beyond the bounds of a campus, and it added a further touch of ludicrousness to a person I already had detested on sight. And how Nathan would have howled at this watery newt of a *goy!* Slouched down next to Morty Haber in the gloom, inhaling the syrupy fragrance of calla lilies, I decided that the Reverend DeWitt, more than any person I had ever encountered, summoned up in me all my homicidal potential. He droned on insultingly, invoking Lincoln, Ralph Waldo Emerson, Dale Carnegie, Spinoza, Thomas Edison, Sigmund Freud. He mentioned Christ once, in rather distant terms—not that I minded. I sank lower and lower in my stall, and began to tune him out as one cancels sound with the dial of a radio, allowing my mind to capture drowsily only the plumpest and moistest platitudes. These lost children. Victims of an age of rampant materialism. Loss of universal values. Failure of the old-fashioned principles of self-reliance. *Inability to intercommunicate!*

"What fucking bullshit!" I thought, then realized that I had spoken the words aloud, for I felt Morty Haber's hand tap my leg and heard his gentle "Shh-h!" which mingled with a half-stifled laugh to make it plain that he agreed with me. I must have nodded off then—not into sleep but into some cataleptic realm where all thoughts scamper away like truants from the brain—because my next sensation was the horrible sight of the two gun-metal coffins being wheeled up the aisle past me on their sparkling trolleys.

"I think I'm going to vomit," I said, too loud.

"Shh-h," said Morty.

Before embarking for the cemetery in the limousine, I slipped into a nearby bar and bought a large cardboard container of beer. One could obtain a quart for thirty-five cents in those days. I was aware of my probable tactlessness, but no one seemed to mind, and I was quite stiff by the time we got to the burial ground just beyond Hempstead. Oddly enough, Sophie and Nathan were among the very first to occupy space in this brand-new necropolis. Under the warm October sun the huge acreage of virgin greensward stretched to the horizon. As our procession wound its way to the distant grave site I feared that my two beloveds were going to be interred in a golf course. For an instant the notion was quite real. I had fallen into a spell of upside-down fantasy or psychic legerdemain that drunks are sometimes seized by: I saw generation after generation of golfers teeing off from Sophie and Nathan's plot, shouting "Fore!" and busying themselves with their midirons and drivers while the departed souls stirred unquietly beneath the vibrating turf.

In one of the Cadillacs, sitting next to Morty, I leafed through the Untermeyer American poetry anthology I had brought along, together with my notebook. I had suggested to Larry that I read something, and he had liked the idea. I was determined that before our last leave-taking Sophie and Nathan would hear my voice; the indecency of the Reverend DeWitt having the final word was more than I could abide, and so I thumbed diligently through the section generously allotted to Emily Dickinson, in search of the loveliest statement I could find. I recalled how, at the Brooklyn College library, it had been Emily who had brought Nathan and Sophie together; I thought it fitting that she should also bid them farewell. Euphoric, inebriate glee welled up in me irresistibly when I found the appropriate, or, should I say, perfect poem; I was softly cackling to myself at the moment that the limousine rolled up to the graveside and I spilled myself out of the car, nearly sprawling on the grass.

The Reverend DeWitt's requiem at the cemetery was a capsulated version of what he had told us at the mortuary. I had the impression that Larry had hinted to him that he might do well to be brief. The minister contributed a tacky liturgical touch in the form of a phial of dust, which at the end of his talk he extracted from his pocket and emptied over the two coffins, half on Sophie's and half on Nathan's, six feet away. But it was not the ordinary humble dust of mortality. He told the mourners that the dust had been gathered from the six continents of the world, plus subglacial Antarctica, and represented our need to remember that death is universal, afflicting people of all creeds, colors and nationalities. Again I had a wrenching remembrance of how in his lucid periods Nathan had so little patience for DeWitt's brand of imbecility. With what joy he would have mocked and skewered, on the genius of his mimicry, this ponderous charlatan. But Larry was nodding in my direction, and I stepped forward. In the stillness of the hot, bright afternoon the only sound was a soft thrumming of bees, lured by the flowers banked at the edge of the two graves. Wobbling and rather numb now, I thought of Emily, and bees, and their immensity in her song, their buzzing metaphor of eternity.

"Ample make this bed.
Make this bed with awe;
In it wait till judgment break
Excellent and fair."

I hesitated for some time before I continued. I had no trouble shaping the words, but hilarity halted me, this time mixed with grief. Wasn't there some inexpressible meaning in the fact that my entire experience of Sophie and Nathan was circumscribed by a bed, from the moment—which now seemed centuries past—when I first heard them above me in the glorious circus of their lovemaking to the final tableau on that same bed, whose image would stay with me until dotage or my own death erased it from my mind? I think it was then that I began to feel myself falter and fail, and break slowly apart.

"Be its mattress straight,
Be its pillow round;
Let no sunrise' yellow noise
Interrupt this ground."

Many pages ago I mentioned the love-hate relationship I maintained toward the journal I kept in those days of my youth. The vivid and valuable passages—the ones which in general I refrained from throwing away—seemed to me later to be the ones having to do with my emasculations, my thwarted manhood and truncated passions. They involved my nights of black despair with Leslie Lapidus and Mary Alice Grimball, and they also had a legitimate place in this narrative. So much of the rest of what I wrote was made up of callow musings, pseudo-gnomic pretentiousness, silly excursions into philosophical seminars where I had no business horning in, that I decisively cut off any chance of their perpetuation, by consigning them, a few years ago, to a spectacular backyard auto-da-fé. A few random pages survived the blaze, but even these I kept less for any intrinsic worth than for what they added to the historical record—the record, that is, of myself. Of the half-dozen or so leaves I've kept from those final days, for instance—beginning with the frenzied scribbling I made in the latrine of the train coming up from Washington and extending to the day after the funeral—there are exactly three short lines I've found worth preserving. And even these have interest not because there is anything about them that is close to imperishable, but because, artless as they now seem, they were at least wrung like vital juices from a being whose very survival was in question for a time.

Someday I will understand Auschwitz. This was a brave statement but innocently absurd. No one will ever understand Auschwitz. What I might have set down with more accuracy would have been: *Someday I will write about Sophie's life and death, and thereby help demonstrate how absolute evil is never extinguished from the world.* Auschwitz itself remains inexplicable. The most profound statement yet made about Auschwitz was not a statement at all, but a response.

The query: "At Auschwitz, tell me, where was God?"

And the answer: "Where was man?"

The second line I have resurrected from the void may be a little too facile, but I have kept it. *Let your love flow out on all living things.* These words at a certain level have the quality of a strapping homily. Nonetheless, they are remarkably beautiful, strung together in their honest lump-like English syllables, and as I see them now on the ledger's page, the page itself the hue of a dried daffodil and oxidized slowly by time into near-transparency, my eyes are arrested by the furious underlining—*scratch scratch scratch,* lacerations—as if the suffering Stingo whom I once inhabited, or who once inhabited me, learning at firsthand and for the first time in his grown-up life about death, and pain, and loss, and the appalling enigma of human existence, was trying physically to excavate from that paper the only remaining—perhaps the only bearable—truth. *Let your love flow out on all living things.*

But there are a couple of problems about this precept of mine. The first is, of course, that it is not mine. It springs from the universe and is the property of God, and the words have been intercepted—on the wing, so to speak—by such mediators as Lao-tzu, Jesus, Gautama Buddha and thousands upon thousands of lesser prophets, including your narrator, who heard the terrible truth of their drumming somewhere between Baltimore and Wilmington and set them down with the fury of a madman sculpting in stone. Thirty years later they are still abroad in the ether; I heard them celebrated exactly as I have written them in a splendid twangy song played on a country-music program while I drove through the New England night. But this brings us to the second problem: the words' truth—or, if not their truth, their impossibility. For did not Auschwitz effectively block the flow of that titanic love, like some fatal embolism in the bloodstream of mankind? Or alter the nature of love entirely, so as to reduce to absurdity the idea of loving an ant, or a salamander, or a viper, or a toad, or a tarantula, or a rabies virus—or even blessed and beautiful things—in a world which permitted the black edifice of Auschwitz to be built? I do not know. Perhaps it is too early to tell. At any rate, I have preserved those words as a reminder of some fragile yet perdurable hope . . .

The last words I've kept from the journal comprise a line of poetry, my own. I hope they are forgivable in terms of the context out of which they arose. For after the funeral I drew a near-blank, as they said in those days about drunkenness in its most amnesic mode. I went down to Coney Island by subway, thinking to somehow destroy my grief. I didn't know at first what had drawn me back to those honky-tonk streets, which had never seemed to me to be among the city's most lovable attractions. But that late afternoon the weather held warm and fair, I was infinitely lonely, and it seemed as good a place as any to lose myself. Steeplechase Park was shut down, as were all the other amusement emporia, and the water was too cold for swimmers, but the balmy day had attracted New Yorkers in droves. In the neon glare at twilight hundreds of sports and idlers jammed the streets. Outside Victor's, the drab little café where my gonads had been so chimerically agitated by Leslie Lapidus and her hollow lewdness, I paused, went on, then returned; with its reminder of defeat it seemed as good a place as any to let myself drown. What causes human beings to inflict upon themselves these stupid little scissor snips of unhappy remembrance? But soon I forgot Leslie. I ordered a pitcher of beer, and then another, and drank myself into a nether world of hallucinations.

Later in the night's starry hours, chill now with the breath of fall and damp with Atlantic wind, I stood on the beach alone. It was silent here, and save for the blazing stars, enfoldingly dark; bizarre spires and minarets, Gothic roofs, baroque towers loomed in spindly silhouette against the city's afterglow. The tallest of those towers, a spider-like gantry with cables flowing from its peak, was the parachute jump, and it was from the highest parapet of that dizzying contraption that I had heard Sophie's peals of laughter as she sank earthward with Nathan—falling in joy at the summer's beginning, which now seemed eons ago.

It was then that the tears finally spilled forth—not maudlin drunken tears, but tears which, beginning on the train ride from Washington, I had tried manfully to resist and could resist no longer, having kept them so bottled up that now, almost alarmingly, they drained out in warm rivulets between my fingers. It was, of course, the memory of Sophie and Nathan's long-ago plunge that set loose this flood, but it was also a letting go of rage and sorrow for the many others who during these past months had battered at my mind and now demanded my mourning: Sophie and Nathan, yes, but also Jan and Eva—Eva with her one-eyed *mís*—and Eddie Farrell, and Bobby Weed, and my young black savior Artiste, and Maria Hunt, and Nat Turner, and Wanda Muck-Horch von Kretschmann, who were but a few of the beaten and butchered and betrayed and martyred children of the earth. I did not weep for the six million Jews or the two million Poles or the one million Serbs or the five million Russians—I was unprepared to weep for all humanity—but I did weep for these others who in one way or another had become dear to me, and my sobs made an unashamed racket across the abandoned beach; then I had no more tears to shed, and I lowered myself to the sand on legs that suddenly seemed strangely frail and rickety for a man of twenty-two.

And slept. I had abominable dreams—which seemed to be a compendium of all the tales of Edgar Allan Poe: myself being split in twain by monstrous mechanisms, drowned in a whirling vortex of mud, being immured in stone and, most fearsomely, buried alive. All night long I had the sensation of helplessness, speechlessness, an inability to move or cry out against the inexorable weight of earth as it was flung in *thud-thud-thud*ing rhythm against my rigidly paralyzed, supine body, a living cadaver being prepared for burial in the sands of Egypt. The desert was bitterly cold.

When I awoke it was early morning. I lay looking straight up at the blue-green sky with its translucent shawl of mist; like a tiny orb of crystal, solitary and serene, Venus shone through the haze above the quiet ocean. I heard children chattering nearby. I stirred. *"Izzy, he's awake!" "G'wan, yah mutha's mustache!" "Fuuu-ck you!"* Blessing my resurrection, I realized that the children had covered me with sand, protectively, and that I lay as safe as a mummy beneath this fine, enveloping overcoat. It was then that in my mind I inscribed the words: *'Neath cold sand I dreamed of death / but woke at dawn to see / in glory, the bright, the morning star.*

This was not judgment day—only morning. Morning: excellent and fair.

ABOUT THE AUTHOR

William Styron was born in Newport News, Virginia, in 1925, and grew up in a nearby town listening to his grandmother's tales of her slave-owning days. His first story appeared in a student collection at Duke University, where he was a marine officer candidate. Summoned to Okinawa, he arrived there, bearing the fresh stripes of a lieutenant, just as WW II was ending. Styron returned to Duke and graduated in 1947. Later that year he moved to New York and enrolled in Hiram Haydn's short story course at the New School. His work there became part of his first novel, LIE DOWN IN DARKNESS (1951), which brought him fame at the age of 26 when he was awarded the Prix de Rome by the American Academy of Arts and Letters. Shortly after, Styron moved to Paris, where he helped found, together with George Plimpton, Peter Matthiessen and Donald Hall, the *Paris Review*. Before travelling on to Rome, Styron wrote—in one intense six-week period during the summer of 1952—THE LONG MARCH. His third novel, SET THIS HOUSE ON FIRE, based partly on Styron's journey to Italy, was published in 1960. Seven years later, he completed THE CONFESSIONS OF NAT TURNER—his brilliant and controversial portrayal of the historical black revolutionist, which won the 1967 Pulitzer Prize. After a long literary silence, Styron emerged with another monumental work: SOPHIE'S CHOICE (1979), his impassioned and emotionally devastating novel of a Holocaust survivor, and one of the great critical and popular successes of recent years.